The Infidel

The Infidel

Georgia Elizabeth Taylor

St. Martin's Press
New York

Library of Congress Cataloging in Publication Data

Taylor, Georgia Elizabeth.
The infidel.

1. Díaz de Vivar, Jimena, 11th cent.—Fiction. 2. D9íaz de Vivar, Rodrigo,
called El Cid, d. 1099?—Fiction. I. Title.
PZ4.T24164In WPS3570.A929E   811O.5O4   78-4002   ISBN 0-312-41598-2

for
Wallace Garcia
". . . O princely Heart! . . ."

✠ *PROLOGUE* ✠

His voice rolled like thunder across the sands of Arabia. A faint light seemed to glow beside him, flickering weakly at first, then bedazzling, as his gentle and persuasive voice quickly enveloped and enlightened a nation. An ignorant, idol-worshiping race of unorganized tent dwellers listened eagerly to the magnificent claims of this holy man and they believed him, vowing to unite for all time under the banner of one God. A new religion had been born, a new Prophet acknowledged. The sons of the desert gathered by the thousands, then by the hundreds of thousands, to propagate the new faith, the voice of Muhammed ever calling them to arms. What once was scattered tribes of wandering natives became suddenly one massive fighting unit. Every man had been reduced to pure muscle by the rigorous demands of desert life. A primitive manhood was at its highest level, in the best fighting condition, comprising the finest light troops and the most formidable menace that civilization had ever seen. Muhammed's inspired prediction rang in their ears: "I have seen before my eyes the East and the West and every one of the regions comprised in them shall be subdued to my people." They feared nothing, for they were the chosen of Allah. With exultant cries of *"Allah il Allah"* — God is God — and *"Allah Achbar"* — God is victorious — they marched toward farflung lands, and the spread of Islam began.

The dust from the hooves of their steeds rose in great clouds behind them, consuming Persia, smothering the now-weary land of Egypt, taking ancient Damascus, moving swiftly across the face of North Africa. Despite their fierceness in battle and their religious zeal, the conquering Muslims were the most merciful invaders the world had yet seen. Plunder was forbidden by Muhammed. They were kind and gentle masters. Only combatants were attacked; women and children were left unharmed in their homes and churches. But the gentleness of the Muslims did not extend to the battlefields, and the stench of blood marked their trail.

Ever onward their victorious leader led them, until the sands of the Atlantic shore churned beneath bloodied hooves. There, linens flapping in the swift breezes, the red-haired, one-eyed commander rode into the waves up to the saddle girth of his stallion and swore that had not the vast waters stopped him, the whole world would have belonged to Islam. Then he glanced across the sea, and his gaze fell upon the shimmering loveliness of the southern coast of Spain. In that instant the destiny of Gothic Spain was sealed.

The horde swarmed across the narrow straits, landing upon the great rock called the Pillars of Hercules, then swept into the land of Rodrigo, king of Spain, who, careless if not entirely ignorant of the deadly blast about to fall upon the beautiful fields of the southern coast, dreamed away the hours amidst his lotus-eating, effeminate court. In one day that Gothic nation, stable and mighty for three hundred years, crumbled before the onrush of Muslims. By the year of the Incarnation 717, six years after the invasion, all of Spain was under Arab rule.

Immediately and in vast numbers Arabians left the tents of their fathers, their migration to colonize Spain far overshadowing in its magnitude their rush to conquer. The land of Muhammed lost prestige and Cordova was proclaimed the center of earthly paradise.

In the North, sheltered by the formidable Pyrenees Mountains, a small band of unconquered Goths sowed the seed of reconquest, a seed that was to take over eight hundred years to reach full maturity. The Arab conquest had only just reached its peak, when these warriors began an attack and withdrawal procedure that was to gain them an ever-widening foothold upon the land of their fathers. Slowly they spread out, disturbing in their persistence, terrifying in their barbaric destruction, until most of the northern tip of the peninsula was back in their possession.

But the Christian horde was no more than a mere flyspeck upon a heap of iced sherbet to the Infidel, whose valleys burst forth with an unbelievable splendor of orchards and gardens; who raised their sons in this new land, and their son's sons, until there was no memory left of another land, for this, their beloved Andalusia, was home.

Three hundred and fifty years had passed since the invasion of Spain by the Infidel. It was the year of the Incarnation, 1052, and the year of Muhammed, 431, and only the northernmost reaches of the peninsula had been reclaimed by the Spaniards, who now called themselves Castilians. Castile was a new nation, created by Don Ferrando Gonzales de Castile twenty-three years past by means of ruthless wars against the neighboring Christian states of Leon and Galicia. The lords of New Spain, before Ferrando's time, were autonomous counts, but Ferrando had demanded that he be crowned king and made ruler over all counts. As the first king of Castile, his rule was fragile; the land-rich counts of the once independent states were constantly attacking one another across stubbornly maintained borders, forcing Don Ferrando to turn his attention away from expulsion of the Infidel, in an effort to hold together that which he had joined. Christians battled Christians, slaughtering one another over a sack of gold, or a petty insult. The passion of their forefathers for total restoration of the land had long since faded into history. Muslim cities flourished border to border with Christian towns; gold, paid at regular intervals, was the small price the Infidel had to pay for peace with the Castilians. Further payments in gold purchased protection for the Infidel from his enemies. Castilian counts and their knights, acting as mercenaries, fought side by side with Muslim warriors against the Infidel's foes, with no mind as to whether the enemy was Christian or Muslim. For Castile this was an era of constant unrest—war, siege, pillage, and duels to the death. What the Infidel had built and planted in Castile before being pushed southward had been pounded into dust. A few surviving orange trees abundantly blossomed and bore fruit, and giant acacia trees exploded into golden bloom in May—lonely reminders of a people who had conquered and then retreated.

Part
ONE

✠

RODRIGO

There was the door to which I found no key
There was the veil through which I could not see:
Some little talk awhile of me and thee
There was—and then no more of thee and me.

Omar Khayyam

Chapter
✠ ONE ✠

Jimena Gomez was nine years old the day her sister Leonora was wed to Don Jaime Martinez de Gormaz. It was spring and the giant acacia tree near the plaza was in full flower. Count Gomez had come home from the wars with his army, and relatives had been arriving from all over Castile for a week. Jimena had awakened that morning very excited; there would be so much to see and to do. She bolted out of bed, hastily dressed, and, without eating a bite, dashed out of her chamber. She ran down the long, dark corridors of Gormaz Castle then sped down the precariously steep staircase in leaps and bounds. Outside in the spring sunshine, she darted about like a golden honeybee skittering from flower to flower, from the stables, to the steps of the church, and to where a group of young knights were playfully wrestling. Then she thought that she could easily see absolutely everything that was happening in the courtyard and the plaza if she climbed into the highest branch of the acacia tree. She whirled about-face and raced to the tree, scampering up into it with the agility of a playful squirrel.

Fixed in her favorite crotch of the tree, amidst branches heavy with cascading yellow blooms, Jimena, her legs swinging back and forth, laughed delightedly at the scope of her view. In places the gigantic tree brushed the walls surrounding the castle grounds. Behind her, she could see a street of the city and the hovels of serfs. Before her the entire courtyard and castle plaza were visible; she could see everybody and what they were doing. Reaching out, she broke off a great spray of blossoms and pushed her face into the bouquet, sniffing deeply. This caused her to sneeze violently again and again but she did not mind; the flowers were softer to the touch and of a more glorious color than anything else she knew.

A sudden flurry of activity below and to her right captured

Jimena's attention. She tilted her head to see around a bloom-thickened branch and saw that the bishop of Gormaz, Don Pedro, was moving hastily in her direction, with a parade of peasants, knights and several ladies trailing behind him. It was a long moment before she noticed the man in the center of the parade, and another few moments before she realized the man was tethered at wrist and ankles. The prisoner was being dragged along by rough hands on his arms, and Pedro, the armorer, had hold of his hair, nearly pulling it out by the roots as he jerked the man's head from side to side.

Jimena frowned, deeply curious. She had heard that an infidel was to be burned today, in honor of Leonora and Jaime, and she had been excited at the prospect of such a spectacle—but this creature in no way looked like a devil. She watched as the group approached, and was startled when it became obvious that they meant to fasten the fiend to the trunk of her tree. She leaned back, so as not to be seen, as the group came close.

She had hidden up here many times, undiscovered until she chose to make herself visible. No one among the group would think to look forty feet up into the yellow tree for a child. Nor would they have cared, particularly, if they had known she was there. Still, she chose to remain secreted. She watched, open-mouthed, as they noisily wrapped leather straps round and round the infidel and the tree's trunk, until he was securely fastened. One knight spit upon him, and another threw dung at him, before the bishop ordered them off to begin the task of building the pyre.

About fifty feet away from the tree, in the open, the men began construction of a mountain of sticks and straw, leaving Jimena to stare curiously at the creature far below her. Because he looked so ordinary she was very disappointed in him. Leonora had told her many stories about how the Infidel had come out of hell to overrun Spain, driving their ancestors into the northern mountains. It had been great fun to sit upon Leonora's ample lap of a winter evening, shivering with a delicious horror as she listened for hours to her tales. Their grandfather's grandfather had been one of the first to lead an army against the monsters and prevail, then his sons, and their sons, drove them back still further. It was God's will that Spain be wrested from the Devil's breed, and it was under the spell of God's angels that their grandfathers had prevailed. The Muslims lived in a Sodom and Gomorrah, lustful, depraved, and God-detested. Their sins had turned their skins black, and their women were sold at fairs, like cattle and goats. The sounds that emerged from the throats of infidels were the gibberish of men possessed, so that not one understood the other; they spoke the language of the Devil. And they built golden temples for the worship of an idol called—here Leonora would stop and look extremely uneasy. "His very name upon the lips of a Christian, Jimena, would cause God to strike that person down with a bolt of lightning, or, if not that, then he could be burned—at the stake!"

But this man's skin was only slightly darker than her own; he looked, in all ways, like any other man. His hair was black and fell curling over his forehead and to his shoulders. For a moment he cast his eyes upward, as if to Heaven, and she noted his eyes were strangely fearless. He did not see her, thank the Lord. If he were indeed a servant of the Devil, as Leonora had said all infidels were, then his mere glance might be her doom.

Hours passed. Jimena was too much in dread of the infidel to climb down. The pyre was completed according to the bishop's explicit instructions. "Ah," he exclaimed, "that is good, excellent. Do you think it is a bit too close to the tree, there? No? Yes, yes, excellent." The heat was not to be too intense at first, he insisted, but was to build very slowly, or the creature would die too quickly and spoil the entertainment. He commented, too, that his brethren to the south and east were privileged to do God's work in this vein; these days one seldom saw an infidel in the north. A rare and splendid occasion, then, the burning of one of the dogs anywhere in Castile.

Thus trapped at the top of her tree, Jimena missed her sister's wedding. Stubbornly she ignored her aunt's calls for her. Men searched for her everywhere, several times directly below her, but under no circumstance was she going to put herself so much as an inch closer to the fiend tied down there, no matter how harmless he might *look*. It wasn't until after the wedding feast that men came, unfastened the brute and dragged him to the pyre, where they tied him to the post at its center.

At last Jimena was free to leave her sanctuary. She scrambled down and ran across the plaza toward the pyre, ducking around individuals and groups of people, to claim a seat on one of the benches closest to the pyre. On her race for a good seat, she grabbed a hunk of cheese and half a loaf of bread off a tray held in a servant's hands. She sat munching on the cheese and bread, engrossed in the actions of the bishop as he read emotionally from the Bible and at the same time touched a torch to the twigs scattered at the lower edge of the pyre. She watched, fascinated, as a young priest tossed into the flickering blaze all the infidel's possessions, crying out that they were touched by Satan and God-detested. Something tiny struck a log and bounced away, falling almost at Jimena's feet. She saw it and glanced around her to see if anyone else had noticed. A crowd had gathered behind and on both sides of her, all laughing and talking at once and apparently unaware of the object that had captured her curiosity. She stared down at it there in the dust. It glittered strangely, and had tiny red, gold, and green stones embedded in it. It was so small that it could be held in the palm of her hand. Her fingers could close around it and completely hide it. It was a thing of the Devil, but it was also very pretty. Impulsively Jimena darted forward, clutched it up, made a fist around it, then within seconds was back on her seat looking perfectly innocent.

The fire grew very slowly. Jimena began to be uneasy about the infidel, who squirmed against his tethers and looked to be greatly in fear; the brave calm of hours ago had vanished. Count Gomez moved through the crowd, speaking cheerfully to this person, then that one, stopping close beside Jimena. He looked down at her, offering her a thin smile.

"Father," Jimena blurted out, "the bishop has said that a commandment is, 'Thou shalt not kill.' Is it not a sin, then, to kill this . . ."

"No!" the count interrupted emphatically. "No, Jimena—it is not a sin to kill an infidel. They are believers in a false God, a false prophet. God has placed the destruction of the unbelievers into the hands of the True Church. They are a bad people, Jimenita. They stole our land from us and defiled it. They live the most corrupt lives . . ." His voice suddenly broke off in mid-sentence. Hatred of the Infidel gleamed so brightly in his eyes that it frightened Jimena, and she backed away from him. "Enough of this! Of course it is not a sin, or we would not be here watching the event! Never ask such a foolish question of me again."

Jimena flinched and turned away from her father's anger. She bit off another mouthful of cheese and chewed vigorously at it, eyes again fixed upon the man in the center of the fast-reddening pyre. The small treasure felt hot in her fist.

Suddenly the cheese did not taste quite right, then an unexpected nausea closed her throat. The infidel, frantic now, clenched his teeth tight together, squeezing his eyes closed as he struggled. Then a burst of flame shot up from a smoldering log at his back—and he screamed, a scream that was endless. Terror-stricken, agonized, he thrashed about in a vain attempt to loose himself. Flame burned the skin of his feet black, then away. The flesh of his arms became crisp, and the fat boiled and burbled under it. His hair caught fire. He wailed and bellowed like a wild animal, a man in hell.

Jimena bolted to her feet, her own screams blending in with those of the infidel. She ran toward the pyre, intent upon saving him; she would stamp out those devouring flames, smother them with her own objecting flesh. "Stop," she wailed. "He is burning to death!"

Jimena was abruptly caught up from behind round the waist, and hauled over the heads of laughing spectators. She was shoved roughly to her feet and told to go to her chambers.

"I will—*not!*" she dared to scream at the giant glowering down at her, horror now more dominant within her than fear of her father. "He is burning to death—make them stop—I hate you. Why do you allow it—why?"

Her father struck her so hard across the face that she stumbled backward and fell to the ground. "Your father has spoken! Remove yourself from this company immediately. Spare us the insult of your ignorance and blasphemy. Go, I say! Get from my sight!"

From her sprawled position at his feet, Jimena glared tearfully up at her father for long moments. Then she set her jaw and dove forward, on hands and knees, right through his legs, which were set wide apart. She was at the pyre in seconds, reaching up to clutch the infidel's roasted, flailing hand. Her skirts caught fire, but she did not notice. "I will save you!" she cried up to the man. His head dropped and his wild eyes focused on her for a brief moment. Jimena was certain she saw his blistered lips turn up into a grateful smile.

Count Gomez and two of his knights dragged Jimena from the pyre and rolled her over and over on the earth to put out the flames that had caught her skirts. Then she was picked up and carried at a run into the castle, up the long staircase and to her chamber. She was then tossed upon her bed, but when she hit the bed she bounced and landed on her two feet. She was so determined that she was out the door before the knight who had carried her knew what she was about. He caught her at the top of the stairs. Enraged, the man grabbed her up and returned her kicking and screaming to the door of her chamber. When he attempted to shove her inside the room, she refused to let go of him, clawing at his face and pulling at his hair; she sent a fist crashing against his mouth and drew blood. At last the knight managed to loose himself from her. He dropped her to the floor of her chamber and quickly slammed the door closed, bolting it from the outside. Jimena leaped to her feet and kicked at the door in a fury. Then she burst into tears, knowing she was defeated. She ran to her bed, shoving her hands tight over her ears to shut out the delirious cries of the infidel that were carried on the wind to torment her.

The cries of the infidel ceased, and Jimena slowly pulled her fists from her ears. She shuddered at the deathly silence. Turning her head, she fixed her gaze upon one grimy hand that opened to reveal the infidel's treasure still in her palm. She stared at it for a long moment, amazed that she had held it fast throughout her struggles with her father and the knight. Impulsively she leaped to a kneeling position on the bed, hiding the treasure in a crevice in the granite wall behind her small statue of the Holy Mother.

Never again did Jimena climb the acacia tree. Each spring the blossoms came and seemed to call out to her, but all she could see when she looked at them were the flames and the black, burned flesh of a man. It was well over a year after the burning before she dared bring out from its hiding place behind her bed that clutched-up treasure that had fallen away from the pyre to her feet. All the time it had been there she had thought of it as some little piece of the man that had not died, a bit of him that she *had* managed to save. If, after more than a year, God had not struck her down for the keeping of such an evil thing, then surely, she prayed, it would not happen now.

It was a miniature book. Jimena turned it over and over in her hands, marveling at the beauty of it. She was able to recognize it as a book because it slightly resembled the bishop's Bible, the only book she had ever seen. The Bible was covered in leather, with straps. This book was of another material, a cloth that was unfamiliar to her. Tiny colored rocks had been fastened to the cloth in intricate designs. She knew the scratchy lines on the pages was writing, because her father was one of the few men in Castile who could read and write and she had on occasion watched over his shoulder as he wrote with the quill—greatly awed by the magic of it. It was a true wonder, that a man could take a quill and make scratch marks that said his thoughts, thoughts that could be sent by horse to another man, who would understand by looking at the scratches what her father had wished to say. Truly wonderful.

Jimena stole into her father's chamber in the dark of night, taking one of his quills, some parchment, and a flask of black, which she carried off to be placed beside the little book in its secret place. Thereafter, for many months, when the castle was asleep, she would take out everything and meticulously copy the scratches that she saw on the pages, making up thoughts of her own for each combination of lines. This said, "I am so lonely." Another pattern of lines meant to her, "My favorite color is yellow." And, one night, in extreme anxiety, she created a new combination to communicate to the imaginary friends to whom she addressed all her words, "Holy Mary! I am bleeding to death, I think. The blood comes from between my legs. I dare not tell the aunt, or she may guess I am in league with Satan in the holding of this book."

Jimena had been unwittingly prophetic. Only days later her guardian was sleepless and walking the corridors, when she thought she heard strange sounds coming from Jimena's chamber, as if the child were speaking to someone. The elderly woman quietly entered, and saw Jimena totally engrossed at her table, a candle burning at her elbow, parchment before her, quill in hand. She was softly speaking the meanings of the "scratches" she was making.

The entire household was awakened by the aunt's shrieks. The bishop, Don Pedro, eyes still dull with sleep, rushed into Jimena's chamber. He hesitantly reached out and picked up the tiny book from her table, his skeletal hands quivering. His eyes bulged with disbelief as the realization of exactly what he held in his two hands overwhelmed him. His glance fell to the parchments covered with Jimena's remarkably accurate imitations, and his horror increased to such a degree that he had to gasp for breath, momentarily speechless.

Jimena had dashed to her bed when her aunt surprised her, and she sat there now, pulling back against the hard oak backboard, heart crashing against her ribs. She did not have to be told that she had sinned. She swallowed hard against hot tears that burned her eyes.

Finding his tongue, the bishop held up the malignancy to all who had entered the room, family members and servants, and screeched, "The Koran! This child has been reading—and copying—the Infidel . . . BIBLE!"

Don Pedro thereupon charged the bed where Jimena crouched. He reached out and caught hold of her, yanking her toward him. He jerked Jimena to her feet before him, nearly breaking her arm in his fury.

"Stretch out your hands, girl!" he shouted at her, as he whipped off the chained cross that hung around his neck.

Defensively Jimena slipped both hands behind her back as

he swung the heavy chain of his cross in a circle, ominously. She glanced to her aunt, hoping to find sympathy there, but saw only eye-popping terror on the old woman's face.

"I said give your hands to me! Depraved—foul—detestable hands!"

"NO!" Jimena cried, realizing that there was no one in this room that would aid her. She was either to protect herself or fall victim. "It was only . . . a . . . a game, Bishop. Only a . . ."

"INFIDEL!" the bishop yowled, at the same time signaling someone with a nod of his head.

Two men were quickly upon Jimena and within seconds her hands were held out to the bishop. She kicked and thrashed, but to no avail. Don Pedro beat her hands with the chain until there was not a shred of flesh left unbroken.

"Now," the bishop said at last, on an outrush of breath, "you will wear gloves upon these hands for thirty days and thirty nights, and all who look upon you will know you to have been in league with Satan. Until you are forgiven, until the sins you have committed have been washed away, you shall be known as—Infidel! It is fortunate you are only twelve years of age, Jimena Gomez. If you were an adult, you would be burned at the stake. No daughter of a count is exempt from God's laws, nor His punishments!"

It was *sixty* days before the bishop allowed that the sin was forgiven. Sixty days of torment, for she was all that time in a state of impurity. If she should die, hellfire was inescapable. She lay awake nights in dread of sleep, counting each breath, each beat of her heart. Hell was no longer a ghastly place into which *others* descended, but was an everlasting torment that now awaited her own soul. For merely touching the dead Arab's treasure she could be burned at the stake? Dear God, she had not realized the vastness of that little book's evil. It had been with relief that she watched the bishop burn it on the stone floor of her chamber. Destroyed, now, it could never tempt her again.

It was as if Don Pedro had put Jimena's childhood beside the miniature book, burning the two at once. She was a woman when the sixty days was over. From that time on she confined herself for the most part to her chamber, spending many hours gazing out one window or another, mysteriously fascinated by the peaks of the Sierra de Guadarramas far in the distance, from beyond which that infidel had come. She was never able to overcome that first impression of the man as ordinary. Never was she able to resign herself to the righteousness of his execution by fire. For several years afterward, Jimena was tormented by nightmares that caused her to lurch up in bed with a scream in her throat, thinking she heard the cries of a man being burned alive. But by the time she was sixteen years old such attacks in the night were rare. There was no doubt in her mind that the Infidel was an enemy to Castile and to God; it would be stupidity to think otherwise. It was an emotional weakness in herself that had caused such an over-reaction; everyone else, without exception, had enjoyed the entertainment immensely.

At sixteen, Jimena was like some remarkably configured butterfly that was unlike any other of its species that had existed before it or ever would again—but a butterfly's spectacular markings are visible to the eye, and Jimena's extraordinary qualities were hidden within her. It was as if she had been caught in a net, placed against the dark mounting of the life she was born to, her wings pinned fast; she fluttered there, captured, her colors fading in the stark light of futility. She had been born profoundly well-suited to her *times*—but not to her *place.*

Jimena was the last born of the three children of Count Gomez of Gormaz. Her father was, indisputably, second in power and wealth only to King Don Ferrando himself, and he was considered second to none in physical strength and prowess in the fight. On the tenth day of May, in the year 1059, Count Gomez returned from the wars after two years' absence. It was of deep concern to Jimena that she had reached the advanced age of sixteen years, without being betrothed. Now that her father had returned, she prayed that he would approach her at last on the subject of a suitable marriage. She hoped that the great wealth he possessed would afford her a dowry so rich as to overcome the fact that she was not comely.

Jimena was completely unaware that she possessed rare gifts of character or that she could ever be considered lovely. Nor did those who looked upon her, in this time and space of her existence, see her as beautiful. But the bone structure of her face was perfect, her nose narrow and neatly curved. Her eyes were remarkably large, deep set, shaded by thick double lashes, and were the color of burnt chestnuts, almost black. She was tall, compared to the average Castilian woman, measuring five feet and four. Her voice was soft and lyrical, suggesting that, if she had thought to attempt it, she might sing better than any of the troubadors who came with the fairs to entertain the castle several times a year. Her eye was quick, catching the forms that light and shadow took upon objects, noticing the perspectives of depth and line, which spoke of a talent for artistic endeavors, but the quill and the brush were the exclusive tools of men, and few men at that.

Jimena's environment and her unique constitution had faded her colors and created an illusion of homeliness. Most of her days were spent within the confines of her father's castle, where the air was stale—in mid-winter, putrid with the stench of unwashed bodies and the droppings of dogs and pigs that were allowed in as scavengers to clean up the floors of dining rooms, cookhouses, and corridors. The castle diet primarily consisted of boiled, salted meats, some fresh pork and fowl, goat's milk and cheese. Since the preservation of vegetables and fruits beyond their seasons had not yet come into practice in Castile, and since vegetables and fruits were not thought to be particularly interesting foods, very few were ever offered at table. Jimena's constitution was somewhat delicate and therefore resistant to the thick, peppery sauces that often drenched the meats, disguising the fact that they had gone bad. She had, early in life, discovered that eggs would not stay in her stomach. Her appetite as a child had been ravenous, but it had decreased as she grew older, so that now she ate very little, subsisting on goat's milk, black bread, honey, and cheese. She was, then, extremely thin. Her finely proportioned long-legged frame that, if filled out, would have constituted a figure for poets to write about, was instead barely covered by flesh, so that the bones of her shoulders, neck, knees, and elbows protruded sharply. She had little energy. Physical exercise was limited to a twice-daily walk from her chamber in the castle to the courtyard, across the yard, then several hundred yards farther to the church for Mass. And the Church had set an inviolable prohibition against bathing, on the premise that to wash one's self was to indulge in a sinful preoccupation with the purity of the body, at the expense of the soul. This Church interdict had left Jimena unwashed since the day of her christening.

It was painfully obvious to Jimena that she was unlike other young women of her station. She would have liked to join in their tittering, meaningless conversations, but she could not; they bored her to distraction. When they whispered and squirmed while a fine singer entertained, they infuriated Jimena. Often they mocked her, suggesting she thought herself something more than a count's daughter, perhaps the daughter of God Himself. Margarita Gonzales, the daughter of her father's standard bearer, had recently remarked at table that the reason

Jimena was not betrothed was because she was so unattractive that not even the dowry of a man as rich as her father could overcome it; no one would have her. Jimena knew that the remark was only a mean striking out in retaliation for her undisguised irritation at the fifteen-year-old's silliness, but she had wept nevertheless.

There were no occupations that could satisfactorily fill Jimena's days. She could not read nor write, though these were skills she had once earnestly attempted to teach herself. Needle-and-thread work was the task of servant women and beneath her station. Most celebrations and tournaments took place within the city and Jimena had never been allowed to enter Gormaz City. She spent endless hours watching the changing seasons from her windows, attending Mass, napping, and occasionally, much less often than when she was a child, dreaming.

Count Gomez loved and admired his daughter, Jimena, but he was a man who found it difficult to demonstrate his affections; from infancy on she had been a source of great pride to him. She had spoken and walked at the astonishingly early age of eight months. At that age an infant was supposedly incapable of speech or taking steps, so there were some in the household, Jimena's guardian aunt first among them, who went so far as to suggest to the count that his last born was possessed of demons. But Count Gomez saw no demons in Jimena, only an exceptional intelligence. From that time on he had protected her from the world, setting severe limits upon her movements. The child was never to be allowed beyond the castle ground's walls; the city was to be kept closed to her.

Intelligent himself, the count was well aware that extreme sensitivity was the close companion of extreme intelligence. Remembering the first time he had seen a rotting corpse dangling from a gallows in the city square and the nightmares that had followed, he refused to allow this child of his to see such cruelties of life while too young to understand them. "Let her play and dream and grow," he had insisted to her guardian, "in a world that is secure and without ugliness and brutality." He had meant well for her, but his personal opinion as to what was ugly and brutal, and what was not, was distorted. The killing of men had become the business of his life. Separating men's heads from their shoulders, slicing his sword or lance into soft bellies, had hardened him more than he realized. He had struck Jimena in a rage on that occasion when she saw a brutality that

had eluded himself. When he was at home he had often neglected her more than he had wanted to, leaving her to her aunt
because he was exhausted, wounded, or deeply troubled.

It was Jimena's spirit that her father had most admired in
her, and it was also the root of his greatest concern for her.
Audacity, bravery, and stubbornness were traits considered dis-
tinctly improper in a woman. But Gomez personally could not
abide the average mute, passive, praying woman of Castile. By
sheer luck, since his wife had been the choice of his father and
none of his, Jimena's mother had remained an unbroken colt of
a woman, unsquelchably cheerful and determined, to the day of
her death. With a great, heaving push, refusing to scream
though she knew the effort might kill her, Maria had thrust
Jimena into this world. Jimena had inherited the spirit of her
mother, but that spirit, combined with her intelligence, which
was far superior to the mother's, caused Jimena's mind all too
often, with logic and keen perception, to overrule her instinct to
throw the heavy weight of life from her back; she was being
broken to the constricting reins and bit of the world she lived
in, as he himself had been. Gomez saw Jimena as in danger of
losing everything within her that was unique and admirable,
and he feared that she would bury her most admirable qualities
deeper and deeper, until her true self was entombed forever in
some dark closet of her soul.

Neither the count nor his daughter were able to foretell the
future. That their fates might be written in the stars was a
pagan belief held by the Infidel; even the word *fate* was meaningless to them. Yesterday and today were indistinguishable, so
there was no reason to suppose that tomorrow would bring any
drastic alterations in their lives. When a courier, who had sped
from the castle of King Don Ferrando three days past, arrived at
Gormaz Castle at sunset, neither suspected the fateful importance of the message he had been called upon to deliver into the
hands of Count Gomez.

> I, Rodrigo Diaz de Bivar, knight of the court of King
> Don Ferrando, do hereby call upon you, Count
> Gomez de Gormaz, to protect your honor, as I intend
> to regain the honor of my beloved father, Don Diego
> Lainez, who fell to your sword six years past. Upon
> the shoulder of the righteous will God sit. The meet-
> ing place, the city of Zamora. The time, the thirteenth
> day of May.
>
> Ruy Diaz

Jimena awoke before sunrise that May morning and called her servants to her. Supervised by her guardian aunt, Galiana, the aging elder sister of her dead mother, she was dressed in her most elegant attire. She was certain her father would call for her this day and she wanted him to be pleased by what he saw. She hoped he would quickly note that she was not the child he had left behind two years ago, but a woman now.

The two maids and her aunt helped Jimena into a fine woolen chemise that descended to her knees, then pulled over her head a brown pelisse, also of wool, that was trimmed with white rabbit fur and fell loosely over the chemise, dropping to her feet. Over this was drawn a white tunic with long trailing sleeves and lacings at the back, which were energetically pulled by the two maids at once, to draw the garment snug against Jimena's frail figure. Then a girdle of woven cords, to hold the ensemble in place. Since she must attend Mass, Jimena slipped her feet into black leather shoes with silver buckles. Usually she wore felt shoes and much preferred them for comfort, but the weather had not yet turned warm enough to wear the felts to church. She leaned over, lifted her skirts, and smoothed the woolen stockings that were part of the undergarment she had slept in, an article of clothing that she removed only once a year—at the turn of summer, when she substituted underwear of a lighter weight—then put on again when the winter came. Her long, ash-blond hair was then twisted into braids, which were pinned in rounds at the nape of her neck. Jimena bent her head low, so that the snug-fitting wimple could be placed carefully over the braids. She drew herself up and with her own hands, which trembled slightly from nervousness, pulled the face opening down under her chin, adjusting the folds of the white cloth upon her shoulders.

Jimena was a woman of wealth and noble birth, so the cloth that she wore was of the finest in Castile, but it nevertheless brutally scratched her delicate flesh and caused her to writhe in constant irritation. She had discovered no way to move that successfully avoided a brush with the wool. It did no good to dig at the itching with her fingers, which only caused red rashes that sometimes blossomed into boils. When the limbs of her body and the folds of the cloth met, the cloth, as always, was the victor. From the table she lifted the cross that hung on a heavy metal chain, reached up and dropped it around her neck.

Aunt Galiana and the servant girls left her. Jimena glanced at the east window of her chamber, noting that the sun was not yet high enough in the sky for her to leave for the church. She stood hesitantly near her bed, her mind filled with a confusion of thoughts. What she wished for conflicted with what she believed she could reasonably expect from life. The future and the past stood glaring at each other within her. She knew that she was still a part of the child she had been, and not yet fully the woman she would be. She wanted very much to marry and to bear children that she could devote herself to, but at the same time the prospect of marriage frightened her. Both her sisters had been given to men old enough to be their fathers. That part of her mind that was still childish sinfully longed to be a Bathsheba, with her very own David; a secret wickedness she had not once spoken of at confession. Realistically, she was a woman of noble birth and would therefore be given to a man of more or less equal station. A knight, then—a man like her father, constantly away from the castle and always in danger of his life. "One must expect widowhood, Jimena, when one is the wife of a soldier,"—that was what Leonora always said, adding forlornly, "and loneliness is a disease we all suffer, for which there is no cure."

Jimena sighed, thinking about the farming serfs, the falconers, blacksmiths, all the common men retained as servants to the castle, who remained at home with their wives and children. Fortune was on the side of the humble women, in this instance, if in no other. Another deep sigh, and Jimena stepped toward the window. She rested her elbows against the high granite sill and let her eyes slide over every detail of the outstretched scene straight ahead and far below. The sky was turning a brilliant orange, tinted with yellow, the ball of the rising sun hidden behind the monolithic donjon tower. The barbicans rose, purple-shadowed, over the distant gates. Due to heavy spring rains, the moats between the successive ten-foot-thick walls that surrounded the city were high and clear, reflecting the glittering sunrise colors and delighting Jimena's eye for long moments. The Sierra de Guadarramas were still deeply snowcapped, but their foothills were verdant with lush new growth. Magical spring had painted the world green. But soon all would be shades of brown and dust clouded, as the heat of summer scorched the plains. "Three months of winter and nine months of hell," the saying went. A few days of spring.

Jimena turned away from the window to move to the door and begin her walk to church, but she hesitated, studying her chamber with new eyes. She had been born in this room, had lived her entire life in this space. Soon she would marry and leave it forever. A small panic wrenched her mid-section and caused her heart to beat a little faster. It was almost like remembering, the way everything appeared to her at this moment—as if she had left long ago and was vividly recalling the place that had filled her childhood. Details, unnoticed for years, captured her attention. The configurations of the carvings on the frame of her oak bed, with the early morning sunlight sparkling off the rounds. Her mattress of straw sagging miserably in the middle, the flat fur covering badly worn in an exact tracing of the lines of her body. The table and its two wooden chairs, deeply gouged by use and age. She saw herself sitting at the table the little book open before her, the quill in her hand. She shivered and forced that iniquity from her mind. A brass-studded chest sat open, spewing out a profusion of wrinkled tunics, mantles and sleepwear. A small figure of the Mother, her face lovely and serene, stood in the niche over the head of her bed. Jimena thought about serenity, wishing she could somehow achieve it and dispel the nervousness that had her in its grip this morning.

The door to Jimena's chamber burst open, startling her out of deep thought. Her Aunt Galiana rushed toward her, a hand against her breast as she puffed and wheezed.

"Those stairs!" the aunt gasped. "So help me God, I shall not make those steps another year! Hurry, child! Your father awaits you in his chamber, on a matter of the greatest urgency."

Jimena had hoped that her father would call for her today, had prayed for this moment, but now she stood transfixed, numb, unable to find a word in reply. Her heart was racing now, and her knees were quaking. Please God, she silently prayed, do not let it be an old man.

"For God!" the aunt raged. "Do not stand there with your mouth agape! I said, your father—"

"I heard you, Aunt," Jimena said with difficulty, around a knot in her throat, "but—you see, I was about to go to Mass. And . . ."

"Mass!" the aunt echoed furiously. "You will forget Mass this once and get yourself straightaway to your father's chamber. This instant! Dallying, for God, while the count waits upon you."

Helpless against feelings that pulled her in two separate directions—an obedient stride to her father's chamber, and a fast run in the opposite direction—Jimena stood her ground and fumbled for words that might stall a decision one way or the other. "Uh . . . do you, do you know the *reason* why he wishes to see me, Aunt? I cannot see what could be so urgent, that I should miss Mass . . ."

Her aunt pushed her hands against her mounded hips and

shouted, "So help me God, Jimena Gomez, old as you are I shall beat you soundly, if you do not start moving toward your father. I have no idea why he wants to see you! But I grant you this; you will find out quickly enough, once you are before him. Now, out! Out, I say!" She waved an arm toward the door for emphasis.

Jimena stared coldly at her nagging aunt, then made her decision. She stepped quickly, passing the old woman without a word, moving through the open doorway into the castle corridor. She could barely see in the dim light. Fighting for breath against the stagnant air and the uncontrollable anxiety that was now a whirlwind in her lungs, she moved forward, carefully making her way down the long, steep staircase. Glancing down over the wooden banister, she could see the entire entrance lobby lit only slightly by torches set into crevices in the walls. A cock crowed from the yard, reminding her it was time for Mass; she had not missed a morning Mass since she was twelve years old and abed with fever.

When she reached the bottom stair, Jimena hesitated, looking first to the door that led out to the courtyard, then to her right down the corridor, to the wing that housed her father's rooms. She straightened her shoulders, lifted her chin, and turned right. Within moments she stood before his door, looking down at the torchlight flickering on the floor through the door crack. She had put her hand out to the latch, when the door was jerked open from the other side.

"Oh! Jaime!" Jimena exclaimed, laughing shakily at the man who lunged out of the chamber in a rage, nearly knocking her over.

Jimena's brother-in-law was several strides down the corridor before he realized Jimena was there and that he had rudely sent her stumbling aside to avoid his hulking frame. He whirled around, his weathered face a tight mask of restrained anger and forced civility. "Sister—pardon me," he said, attempting a smile.

Jimena smiled affectionately at him, nodding as affirmation that she gladly pardoned him. "You look so grim, Jaime," she said, "which makes me wonder if I should take myself to Mass, after all, and wait until a better mood overtakes my father."

Don Jaime made an effort, but he could not control the workings of his face. He felt his expression writhing with the emotions that were gagging him. At last he said roughly, "I would say you should do *exactly* that, my dear sister; take yourself to church, then to your chamber—and wait until his sanity returns. The man has lost his *mind!*" He gazed upon her for long moments, his heart sick with pity for her. She looked so damned unsuspecting and so hellishly vulnerable. He wished he could find words of comfort that would make what she was about to hear easier for her, but anything he said would only strike apprehension in her and do no good.

Don Jaime rushed Jimena, took her shoulders in his two hands and planted a sound kiss on her cheek. "*Vaya con Dios,* Jimenita," he whispered in her ear. Then he turned on his heel and hurried away from her down the long corridor.

Jimena stared after the man, stunned. Jaime was the dearest of men. She had never seen him angry, not once in the seven years he had been married to Leonora. He loved her sister as a good husband should, but more than he loved anyone, or anything on this earth, Jaime loved Jimena's father. It was beyond belief that anything her father had said or done could so enrage this man of smiles, jokes, and infinite thoughtfulness.

"Jimena! Will you stand on my threshold forever?"

Jimena's head jerked around at the sharp sound of her father's voice emerging from the shadows of his chamber. She sucked in a breath and marched into the cavernously large room.

The count was sitting at his table, shoulders slumped, his eyes cast down to a parchment held fast in his hands. Jimena noticed that the gray in his thick blond hair was much more pronounced than it had been when she last saw him. A candle, burned down to its base, flickered a weak light at his elbow. He did not look up or speak as she stepped uneasily toward him and hesitated, waiting, a few steps from the gigantic oak table. She shivered and hugged herself with her arms. Impending doom seemed to permeate the room, she thought, like a nauseating, invisible smoke.

Her father at last raised his eyes to Jimena. For a moment he did not see her clearly, seeing, instead, the little girl of fourteen that he had left behind to wage Ferrando's war against La Coruña at the farthest point of northwestern Castile. Though Jimena had made every effort to look her best for him, the count was not pleased by what he saw: he was shocked. To cover his negative reaction, he quickly said, "I thank you for coming on such short notice, Daughter. Ah, you have grown. A woman now."

Jimena smiled with pleasure. "Thank you, Father," she said shyly.

"I am grieved that I had to be away from Gormaz for so

long a time. The king insisted I hold the siege, in spite of the
fact that—but you are not interested in the affairs of knights.
Come, sit yourself. . . ."

Count Gomez lunged from his chair, knocking the seat
over in his urgency with the heel of his boot. He rushed to pull
a chair in place for Jimena. Reaching out, he took her hands in
his and eased her into the high-backed chair. For long moments
he stood looking solemnly down at her, then said, "I must
speak with you, Jimena—about matters of extreme importance."

Jimena nodded acknowledgment, steeling herself against the
apprehension that increased with each passing moment. She
wondered why Jaime had been so angry, and why he had
looked at her with pity in his eyes. Dear God, the man her
father had chosen for her must not only be old but otherwise
repulsive as well.

"Never have we discussed the matter of a suitable marriage
for you, Jimenita," the count said, striding away from her, one
hand nervously pulling at his beard. "You were not too young
when I left for La Coruña. You will be seventeen within a few
months. I have hesitated in your case because . . . uh, Jimena,
how do you feel about the matter of marriage?"

Jimena frowned. "I have no particular feelings about marriage, Father," she replied. "I have always assumed I would
marry eventually, like Leonora and Sol."

Her father came to a halt near his table, leaning against it
for extra support. He studied her with a frowning intensity,
then said hesitantly, "You . . . would you, perhaps, prefer to
enter a monastery?"

Jimena's eyes widened in surprise. "No! Certainly not!" she
exclaimed.

The count laughed. "Well! Apparently there is no doubt in
your mind on *that* subject. . . . But have you ever given a
monastic life serious consideration?"

"No," she replied, eyes hungrily searching his face for answers to her confusion. She knew very little about the monastic
life, only that nuns did not bear children, and having many
children was the one joy in life that she anticipated; she would
adore having as many as ten. Leonora already had three, two
daughters and a son, and her sister Sol had four sons. A
breathtaking miracle, that an infant could grow inside a woman's body without smothering to death, then push its way out.

"You are certain, then? You do not wish to become a
nun?"

"I am very certain."

"Well, then. As you know, it is my duty as your father to choose the man, settle the marriage contracts. But this would require much time, Jimena—and I do not have that time. This is what I must discuss with you. You need to know what lies ahead, what difficulties you might be faced with in the immediate future."

"Difficulties? But, I cannot see . . ."

"Please," he interrupted, "listen to me, child. An unexpected circumstance has arisen that forces me to leave Gormaz within the hour on a journey to Zamora. There I must fight to the death a knight called Rodrigo Diaz . . ."

He had stopped speaking. He was looking at her, Jimena thought, as if he expected her to recognize the name Rodrigo Diaz and be somehow impressed by it. The name was unfamiliar to her and she saw no connection between this duel and arrangements for her marriage. She waited uncomfortably for him to continue.

"Have you been well, Jimenita?" the count asked gently, moving close to her to lean over and brush back a wisp of hair that had escaped from her wimple.

"Yes, Father."

"But you are so pale, and far too spare. I have spoken with your good aunt and she tells me you spend the hours of your days in your chambers, that often you do not eat at table . . . and consume so little food that you are in danger of starving to death—one of her usual exaggerations, of course— but you do not look *well.*"

A sinking disappointment overcame Jimena. She had so hoped to make a good impression upon him. Mirrors were not allowed by the Church, because they were the tools of vanity, so she had no real vision of herself in her mind. Margarita's comments upon her homeliness rushed into her head, and she suffered an awful suspicion that they were true. Instinctively she brought her hands up to her face, searching for some heretofore missed deformity. "I . . . I feel quite well," she murmured, avoiding her father's eyes. "Truly I do."

"Yes . . . Well, perhaps it is the long confinement of winter that has you so pale, eh? However, you do seem, shall I say, subdued." He laughed softly. "Once you had the high spirits of a purebred colt, and it was all we could do to keep you in rein. I recall a wildcat of a child that gave one of my most powerful knights a battle he came damn close to losing. Nine, I think you were;—yes, nine."

Jimena stiffened. In the back of her mind she heard screams

of agony that made the hair at the back of her neck crawl, and caused her stomach to heave. She covered her mouth tightly with a hand, to hold back an eruption of volcanic emotions. Biting hard at her lower lip, she fought down the black horror that memories of the burning always brought. "I am—a woman—now," she whispered.

"Of course you are, but you must not lose your spirit, Jimena. You cannot survive without it. Contrary to the preachings of Don Pedro, the meek inherit only defeat and dust in the mouth. The earth belongs to the strong. Do you understand what I am trying to say to you, Jimenita? You must find the strength, the spirit, to face what is directly before you. You must *fight* to make something good of your life, and never accept anything that is intolerable to you."

"Yes, Father" she whispered, clearing roughness from her throat, her eyes staring up at him in bewilderment.

"Damnit! Now that is what I am talking about," he shouted at her. "This is not a moment for meek, whispering obedience! Whatever I say to you during this meeting between us, you are free to argue as heatedly as you must to keep the reins of your life in your own hands!" He flung his great arms up in impatience, striding away from her. He paced back and forth before Jimena, then abruptly began a tirade, one word stumbling over the next as his emotions ran out of control.

To Jimena, her father seemed to be talking more to himself, or to God in Heaven, than to her.

"I never minded having only daughters, not really, Jimena. Sons. What would their choices have been, eh? Either the emptiness of a cloister or knighthood; there are no alternatives for a man of noble birth. A hard choice it was for me, I can tell you—I almost took the cloth. But I had a noble ideal, you see; I was going to singlehandedly rescue Spain from the Infidel that pollutes our soil. Ha! Constant war has been my life, but it has ended with a thousand Christian deaths on my conscience and no more infidels to my credit than I can count on my two hands! Christ forgive us! The Infidel lives in peace not a day's journey away!

"No, I have never regretted having only female children. And I have loved you, Jimena, more dearly than the other two. You are so like your mother, God rest her soul. And, in subtle ways, you are like myself, I think. Our natures were wrongly designed for the world into which we were born. I lift the lance and the sword to strike down my brothers in Christ, while in my heart I envy the brutes out there in the fields who plant the seeds and reap the harvest. And you—at the age of twelve you retired to your quarters. Resignation. We each resigned our-selves at a very early age. And I loathe resignation, Jimena Gomez, because it is a death before dying! We kill the truest parts of our selves with resignation, the shell of a human being carrying on until the real death comes, and calls a halt to this—this *mockery!*"

Jimena looked at her father in astonishment. Jaime's cry that he had gone mad whipped into her mind but departed as quickly. No, he was only greatly overwrought; this duel was obviously a severe worry to him. She did not understand what he had meant by the word *resignation.*

"A death before dying." Was he implying, then, that she was only half alive? It was simply that she had grown up. It made no sense to wish for things one could never have. As a child she had longed to be a great bird, with broad wings that could carry her over the castle walls and moats to anywhere and everywhere; this was nonsense well laid to rest, because the only profit in wishing to be somewhere else, or someone other than who you were was tears of regret. She could imagine no occupation other than attending Mass and waiting in her room for the day she would marry. She was not without hopes, how-ever. There were those ten children she looked forward to; God willing, she would survive the birth of the tenth and see them all grown. She would like to grow old, like Aunt Galiana, though she realized that it was unlikely, since few women lived past the age of thirty and five. And there was the hope for a young husband, who would not leave her a widow. She would have him be as powerful as her father, so that he, too, would survive to near fifty years.

As for my nine-year-old spirit, Jimena thought bitterly, my reward from my father was a blow to the face that sent me sprawling. Now he wants me to dig from the grave the spirit that he himself buried? What he now called coltishness, had, at the time, been condemned by the household as "brattish." How her aunt had cursed her father's propensity for "spoiling" and "coddling" and "overprotecting" her.

The count harshly cleared his throat. "Ah, yes," he said, trying to smile, "I seem to have lost track of the reason I brought you here, Jimena. I hope you will pardon me for being sentimental and introspective today. Back to the subject of my responsibility to see you well married. If an event should occur that makes it impossible for me to return to Gormaz to carry out those duties. . . ."

"Not return? Ever . . . ?" Jimena's eyes darted up to meet his. He might not be able to see to marriage agreements?

"Do not interrupt me, please, Jimena. Listen closely. If I am killed by Rodrigo Diaz, you are to go to the king. I have already made arrangements for your journey to Palencia, just in case. Jaime and Don Manuel will accompany you. You must assure the king that you find it in your heart to pardon Rodrigo Diaz with a good will. You will say that since your father left you to the cruel world with no one to care for you, you must beg his mercy—and a favor." Count Gomez halted in the midst of his speech, annoyance creasing his brow. "Damnit, Jimena, are you listening to me? You stare at me as if I am speaking a foreign tongue!"

Jimena was totally confused and could find no words. She nodded vigorously, swallowing hard. Journey to Palencia? Dear God, he was making no sense at all. He spoke of marriage again and again, but had yet to mention the name of the man whom she was to wed and when the betrothal might be announced. All this about not returning and travel with Jaime. She did not want to hear any more of it. A small panic was rising in her, and an instinct to run away before he could finish what he had to say.

"You have understood me so far?" the count asked irritably.

"I think so, yes."

"Good. What you must do, then, is this. You are to beg the king for the hand of Rodrigo Diaz in marriage."

"No!" Jimena exploded to her feet, her face flushing hot, then draining. "No! I could never do such a thing! Never."

Gomez threw his arms up in despair. "At least you do not call me mad, as your good brother-in-law did. I am not insane, Jimena, merely crafty. You take with you a handsome dowry indeed, which includes this city of Gormaz. And Don Ferrando is in debt to me. Jimena, it is with cunning that I seek to force this match. Diaz is all the man your father once was, and more. He will produce worthy grandsons, a proud heritage. I could, though I pondered the night through, think of no other man in Castile so eligible or so worthy of a daughter whom I favor. I have written and signed a letter, which you will present to the king, demanding this favor of him. He owes it to me."

The crumbling expression on Jimena's face moved the count to stride over to her and take her cold hands in his. He eased her back into her chair and then knelt before her, clutching her hands tight in his. "Jimenita," he began emotionally, "do not weep. For God! I am a man staring death in the eye this day. I am deeply concerned for you. If God wills it, I will return to Gormaz by sunset six days hence, and we will follow tradition in seeing you wed. But, if God sees fit to end it for me there—damnit, girl, you are being given the inheritance that by right belongs to Leonora and her husband. Where is your gratitude?"

"I do not *want* Leonora's inheritance!" Jimena exclaimed. "I cannot understand why you would do such a thing to her, leave her destitute."

The count laughed. "Destitute Leonora will *never* be. She did not marry a pauper, I saw to that. And I will leave both your sisters sufficient monies to see them through *two* lifetimes. Jimena, I beg you to obey me in this. Think, when you are wife to the man that slew me: if not he, then another would have been my slayer. A knight is destined for such a death from the day he takes his oath. I admit to fear. I have been forewarned of defeat, but I swear to you, I do not despise this man who so righteously challenges me. You see, I killed his father, so he could not continue to live in honor lest he slay me, or die in the attempt. It is the way of men and not to be thought upon by women. And there is *more* to my choosing of Diaz, more than your best welfare, but it is much too complicated for you to understand. Just take the man, as I bid you, and be grateful to your father for such a husband. The pox, or the sword of Rodrigo Diaz—I see no difference. You need not concern yourself that it was he who snuffed out my life."

Jimena sat with her eyes squeezed closed, shaking her head hard in protest. This had to be a nightmare. Death was on his face, in his voice; it was almost as if he did not want to win this duel. Already defeated, dead on the ground, he was tempting his killer to marry her by heaping upon her an inheritance far richer than she might reasonably have expected at his death. Did he think her so unattractive that an ordinary, respectable dowry would be insufficient inducement? "Father, why?" she whispered. "Why *this* man? If you must bribe my way to a husband, surely many men in Castile would . . ."

"Bribe!" Gomez roared indignantly. "It is no gift to Diaz, Jimena. Gormaz is my gift to *you*, and *he* is for my people!" His voice broke and he leaped to his feet, quickly putting his back to her. "Gormaz," he began huskily, "will continue to be your home, you see. You will not have to take yourself into a strange and perhaps hostile household. You are mistress of Gormaz now—and that you shall remain." He whirled around.

"For Christ's sake, Jimena, he is a magnificent young man. A lion. A champion in the making. I repeat, he is young, just nineteen years of age. Would you prefer that I seek out an ancient one who has worn out one or two wives already, eh? Speak up—is this what you would have of me? I understand you better than you think. You are a dreamer, Jimenita. With this plea to you, I attempt to make at least one of your dreams come true, a man that you can love, admire, and glory in. Trust me, for God's sake!"

Relief and guilt washed over Jimena at once. Nineteen years of age, thank God. But how dare she be happy about the man's youthfulness, when to become his wife she must first see her father dead? The two attitudes seemed at war within her, waging a ferocious battle under her ribs with swords and lances. "This man will not . . ." she began unsteadily, "Rodrigo Diaz will not accept such a plea from me! He would not marry the daughter of a—"

"Jimena," her father interrupted, "the king will not allow Diaz to refuse you. And, I have told you, the boy is extraordinary. Therefore he would never play the fool. His mother's blood runs half peasant. His father was cousin to the king but was not a man of great wealth and property. The boy is master over a village called Bivar, which is a town of mud huts. Jimena, you will be as much an answer to his prayers as he will be to yours."

"He bears no title" Jimena said, desperately searching for an escape from this madness, "so it would seem that he is, I mean, that I am above his station?"

"Yes, you are, at least for the moment. But that situation will be reversed in a very few years. It is my firm conviction that Rodrigo Diaz will dominate Castile one day, if not as king, then just short of it." He cast his dark eyes to the vaulted ceiling and said low, "I see a promising future in this lad, Jimena, and he has challenged me. So it is illogical for me to assume there is any future left for *me*. One of us must die at Zamora. Will you accept this choice of a man, Jimenita? I will leave this world a happier man if you do."

"There is no way for you to avoid this duel?" she asked, tears blinding her.

"No way whatsoever."

"You will prevail over him, I know you will!"

"Perhaps. But if I do not?"

Jimena met his hard, pleading gaze. Her mind frantically searched for an argument, but none came and she resigned herself. "So be it, then" she murmured. "If you do not prevail over this Rodrigo Diaz, I will go the king according to your wish."

"Excellent!" he exclaimed with a pleased smile. "You will not regret this decision, Jimena—I promise you." He moved to her, took her in his arms and hugged her to him. "I will pray for your happiness, Jimenita. Go with God . . .''

Jimena put her hands on his great chest and eased herself away from him. She hesitated, thinking she should find words of comfort, or of goodbye, but none came to her. Their eyes held for long moments, silence upon them both like a shroud. Tears blinding her, she whirled away from him, running from the room into the darkness of the corridor, rushing headlong toward the staircase, then taking the steps up breathlessly, two and three at a time.

She exploded into her chamber, charged her bed and collapsed face down upon it.

"*Madre mia!* Jimena Gomez, have you lost your senses?"

She heard her aunt's voice as from a great distance, a thick cloud of conflicting emotions caught between herself and reality. A new mood replaced fear and despair. She felt suddenly furious. She wished she *was* nine year's old again; she would run back down those stairs and give her father that kick in the shins he deserved for asking such a thing of her.

"I said, have you lost your *senses?*"

"No!" Jimena shouted into her mattress, "I have not. But my *father* has!"

"Is that so? And since when have you become your father's judge? Sit yourself up and stop behaving like a child."

"He is going to be *killed!*" Jimena shrieked into the palms of her hands.

"Absurd. Sit yourself up and look at me." The old woman took hold of Jimena's shoulders and shook her roughly. "Up, I say!"

Jimena rolled over and shoved herself to a sitting position. She swiped tears from her eyes with the back of a hand, sniffed, and made an effort to control herself. "He is!" she insisted. "He said it himself. A man called Rodrigo Diaz is going to kill him in a duel and then I am to go to the king with Jaime. Oh, Leonora is just going to—to *hate* me! And . . ."

"Wait now! Slow down. Make some sense, child."

Jimena threw her head back in exasperation and fixed her teeth tight together in an annoyed grimace. "I have been commanded," she began impatiently between clenched teeth, "to marry the man who is going to kill my father! And Leonora will get only monies, because I—I am to inherit Gormaz. There!"

"*Por Dios!*" the aunt gasped, lurching back from the bed, her watery eyes rounded in disbelief. "But the count must know, he must, that your sister's husband will never accept such a; . . . I cannot believe the husband of my sister would make such a decision. Gormaz belongs to Leonora by right of birth!"

"I know!" Jimena cried. "I told him I did not want Gormaz, but he insisted. It was all such a shock, and I was so confused; I just listened and agreed. What else could I do?"

The aunt shuddered, then shook her head hard. "No. There is no need to concern ourselves. He will not be killed. There is no man alive on this earth who could best your father in a contest. Now get yourself off that bed, take yourself to the church, and say your prayers."

"But, Aunt" Jimena argued, "he told me he was forewarned. And I could see defeat in his—"

"Nonsense! I will hear no more of this kind of talk. Go to the church and pray for him."

Jimena hesitated. "Will you go with me, Aunt?"

"No. Go without me, child. I must speak with your father."

"But he said that he was to leave within the hour."

"Go—curse you, go! Give me a moment's peace. At least *some* good will come of all this, if the worst is to happen: you will be wed and my burden will be lifted from me at long last! Go! And pray to God that your father's life be spared."

The sharpness of her aunt's tone was not in the least unusual, exactly what Jimena would expect from her lifelong guardian, but today the woman's intolerance cut like a knife. As she scrambled off the bed and moved toward the door in obedience, she thought how fortunate Leonora and Sol had been, being so much older than she; they had had a mother for years and years, someone to fondle them, say kind words to them that made them know they were loved. To her aunt she had always been an unwanted responsibility, burden.

Once again in the corridor, Jimena stepped cautiously in the murky light. Her shadow followed her, a grotesque black ghost. A manservant rushed toward her, just as she approached the head of the stairs, then passed her without a word of greeting. She stopped, following him with her eyes as he hurried to her own room, his shoulders bent under the weight of the stones he carried in his basket. Alfredo was probably the only person in the entire castle who never cursed the awful heat of summer, the single person not relieved when the cold nights of winter returned. His task of warming the beds throughout the castle with hot stones, then collecting those stones again in the morning, was an exhausting one. He did not cease his complaining from beginning to end of the cold season. Very soon now he would no longer have to meet this task, since the nights were becoming warmer as the month of June approached. It was a castle joke that Alfredo's wife had had all her children in March and April because her husband was too tired to service her until the month of June.

Jimena took the stairs, then made her way to the courtyard door. She had to pull hard on the latch with both hands to open the massive, iron-faced door. Stepping out into the brilliant sunlight, she squinted, halting her step until she could see clearly. As her eyes adjusted, she glanced around her, solemnly examining the sights and sounds of home. To her left, the stable. She caught the soft whinny of a horse, the sharp clang of a hammer against metal, men's voices muffled by distance, and the whistle of soft breezes humming through cracks in the castle's granite walls. To her right ran the wall that enclosed the castle, shutting it off from the city itself. A wide gate, closed now, was the entrance to a world that was beyond Jimena's experience. The barbicans that towered at each side of the gate were deserted, except for one gateman who leaned his elbows against the balcony shelf as he calmly watched the gate far below him. Her father's voice echoed in her head, once again telling her she must travel to Palencia and present herself to the king, and ask for . . .

Jimena bolted, running across the cobbled courtyard as if she could somehow leave behind, if she moved quickly enough, the reality of that confrontation with her father and somehow convince herself that all was the same as it had been, that life was as predictable and safe as ever. Down the slight grade, past and behind the stables, along the stone path that led to the church.

Jimena sped around a bend in the path, then abruptly came to a halt, breathing in great gasps. Jaime, Manuel Gonzales, and three other of her father's knights stood in a tight group, blocking her way. They were speaking in low tones, their expressions fiercely intent. At the sight of her they broke apart, all turning to stare coldly at her, their words cutting off in midsentence.

"Sister," Jaime said, his expression as tight and angry as it had been earlier, "what news have you for us? What was your decision?"

Jimena flushed, her glance moving from Jaime to Don Manuel, who was her father's standard bearer, and then to each of the other three. Normally she would have cheerfully greeted them, and Jaime would have made some joke for her to laugh at; he might even have lifted her off her feet and given her a great hug. But now he was scowling at her, waiting for her to tell him whether she had agreed to accept his wife's inheritance. It was unfair of him to take this attitude, she thought, since it had been her father's decision and not her own. She had no idea as to how she might have set about refusing an inheritance that her father insisted upon legally giving to her. "I made no decision," she said evasively. "The decision was made for me by my father. He *pleaded* with me, Jaime!"

Don Manuel swore under his breath and turned to meet Jaime's eyes; messages silently passed between them. Jaime returned his gaze to Jimena and said, "You were given an alternative, Jimena Gomez. If you refused to enter a monastery, then the decision was your own!"

Jaime's tone was so viciously accusatory that tears instantly burned behind Jimena's eyes. Furious with herself for being so easily intimidated, she stiffened her shoulders, threw out her chin, and snapped, "My father is the most powerful knight in Castile, Jaime Martinez! You insult him by assuming he will be defeated by—by a nineteen-year-old *boy!*"

With that, she boldly stepped toward the group that stood like a wall against her. They eased apart, allowing her to pass, and she walked stiffly and proudly through the gap they made. Feeling their eyes upon her back, she moved, as quickly as she could without running, away from them down the path. Her hands were shaking and her knees did not want to support her as she pushed her body up the long flight of stone steps that led to the open door of the church. She dared not look back to see if they were still watching her. Darting into the church, she sighed with relief, knowing herself to be out of their sight. She chose a bench close to the altar. Leaning back, breathing heavily, she rested her trembling hands in her lap, sighed, and let her eyes slide up and around the vaulted cathedral.

The building that housed the church of Gormaz had been built by the Romans centuries ago, and now stood as a monument to the strength of the Christian faith. The Infidel had tried to destroy the church but had only managed to burn out its inner trappings, leaving the granite walls scorched, battered, and all the more sacred. Torches lighted the room dimly. Statues of the saints glared down upon Jimena, their eyes alive with reflected firelight. The shadows of several other worshipers, scattered in small groups, rose elongated and weird on the walls.

Don Pedro slipped through the curtains behind the altar. With his graying head bowed, he moved to the lectern and passed quivering fingers lovingly over the pages of his open Bible. His face, scarred and blotchy from a congenital skin disease, shone white and cadaverous in the flickering torchlight.

When she saw the bishop, guilt washed over Jimena; he was well aware that she had missed Mass. She pushed forward, fell to her knees, clutched up the cross that hung around her neck, bowed her head, and began to say her prayers.

At the sound of boots against stone and wood, Jimena turned her head. Her heart hesitated in her breast as she saw Jaime and Don Manuel moving purposefully toward her down the aisle. She whipped her head around, tilting her chin as low as possible, forehead against the knuckles of her folded hands. Dear God, she would never have believed that the mere sight of Jaime could strike such fear in her. Without a word to her, he slid onto the bench beside her. The bishop had begun mumbling to himself up at the lectern, as if practicing for sunset Mass. She wished that she could be alone with the bishop, so she could speak to him of the pain and doubt she suffered, seek his reassurances and blessings. Truly the bishop was more father to her than the man she had confronted at dawn. Don Pedro was with her every day of her life, he had never left Gormaz for battle but was always there when she needed him, guiding, praising, and punishing, as was the duty of a good father.

Jimena's thoughts were interrupted by the bishop's voice, which had raised in volume to almost a shout, so that she could no longer fail to catch his words.

"Woman! You are the gate of hell, the unsealer of that forbidden fruit, the first deserter of the divine law . . ."

Jimena's chin lifted, and she stared open-mouthed at the bishop. She had known, without having to look at him, that he was aiming his remarks directly at her. As the daughter of the count, she often drew his attention at Mass; he did not want any of his more humble parishioners to believe she received any special dispensations. His fiery gaze fixed upon her until she began to squirm in embarrassment.

"You who think to marry, remember! She who too ardently loves her own husband is an adulteress! Such is the nature of sexual love, even within marriage, that during and just after it you are separated from the Holy Spirit, soiled, impure, and can neither pray nor take communion for three days thereafter. Deny your lusts, that you may enjoy the bounty and forgiveness of the Lord. Abstain! Abstain, if you would be loved by Him. But, if you cannot do this, then restrain yourself. Control your vile lusts. Women were created as helpmates for man, yet have brought ruin upon him with their sinful pride and lust. I tell you . . ."

Terrified and revolted, Jimena impulsively lurched to her feet, shoved blindly past Jaime, and ran down the aisle to the door. Out in the sun again, she sucked in deep breaths of the cool spring air, drinking it in as if it were a medicine that could cure the fear and sickness she felt.

"Jimena?"

It was Jaime's voice behind her. She refused to turn and look at him.

"I ask your forgiveness, Sister," he said. "I had no right to question your judgment, nor the judgment of your father. Will you forgive me?"

Jimena slowly turned to study the man's face. Though he was approaching forty and seven, Jaime was still a handsome man. His beard was black as crow's feathers, his head of hair thick and curling, with only wisps of gray at each temple. He wore many scars, like badges of honor, but none upon his face. He seemed genuinely penitent, his dark eyes filled with regret.

"Oh, Jaime!" Jimena exclaimed, "Of *course* I forgive you. My father has upset us all with his predictions of doom. I am certain God will be with him, that he will prevail, as always."

"Yes," Jaime agreed unenthusiastically, "he will prevail. Thank you, Jimenita. I could not have left the city without offering you my apology."

"I would think my father had left by now, Jaime. Will you not stand with him at Zamora?"

"I will be with him, my sister. There was business to conclude. Don Manuel and I will catch up with him by fast horse."

Jaime stood staring at her with that same darkness behind his eyes that had made her so painfully uncomfortable before. To break the silence, she said, "How will we know? I mean— will the news come by courier? And how soon might we expect . . ."

"Within six days you will know the answer, Jimena," he

said in a low voice. "The courier will ride out of the west, carrying a white flag. Or a black one."

Jimena's stomach abruptly went into a spin, as her mind envisioned a courier with a black flag flying. "For God, Jaime," she wailed, "I cannot imagine how I shall survive the suspense of six long days and nights. This—this man he is to fight, do you know him?"

Don Jaime's face lost its peaceful expression, as that strange rage overtook him again. "I know him," he said hotly, "only too *well* do I know him. Farewell, Jimena. May our next meeting be a happier one."

Jaime whirled about and strode away from her, the spurs of his boots clanking a kind of dirge, one scarred hand upon the hilted sword that swung at his side.

Jimena infuriated her guardian by beginning her watch at the south window of her chamber the same day that her father departed for Zamora. The aunt shrieked over and over again that to watch for what could not come was pointless and not a little stupid. But Jimena was drawn to that window as a moth was to flame. She would make every effort to occupy herself, saying her prayer beads one hundred times, forcing herself to leave her chamber to take meals in the dining hall or to walk in the blessedly fresh air. It would seem to her that many hours had passed since she last stepped to the window, but Aunt Galiana would snarl that it had been no more than a few minutes.

At night she was unable to sleep, a million butterflies swarming in her mid-section; they refused to be subdued even by the wine Aunt Galiana forced upon her, insisting she must get some rest. Thinking she heard the thunder of hooves in the distance Jimena would rear up in bed, listening, and then dash to the window. Logic told her that she could not see whether the flag was black or white in the dead of night, all she was likely to see was the courier's torch, but she could not remain on that bed. It was as if some demon had hold of her, propelling her back and forth from bed to window, window to bed, night after night. She was so overwrought that she was uncertain which she dreaded most, the black or the white. If the flag was black, then she would marry a young and valiant knight and return to Gormaz a married lady of means and stature, probably already with child. It would be difficult to mourn a father whom she hardly knew, who had meant little more than scowls and neglect to her. And if the flag was white? A return to neglect, uncertainty as to what kind of man would be chosen for her, or when. A monastery loomed as a terrible threat. Her father had implied that he thought she was unfit for marriage, that she should become a nun; she was certain that had been the meaning behind his words to her. Given further time to think upon it, he might decide to turn her over to an order, which he had every right to do as her father, and she would never see the world beyond those monastery walls again—never. It just did not make sense, the way he had lectured her about the virtues of unbridled spirit, then suggested in almost the same breath that she become a nun. She could not imagine a nun frisking about like a purebred colt.

It did not occur to Jimena that the count was offering her an escape, a refuge, from a temporal life that offered no satisfaction or peace of mind to anyone, man or woman. She did not know that there were nuns who could read the Bible and copy the scriptures in a fine and elegant hand, that some were splendid singers of psalms, and that a few of them were as ruggedly self-determined as the king of Castile himself. She saw the high walls that surrounded nuns as imprisoning rather than as protection against a profoundly hostile world. She had not seen the world yet, did not know its baser side, because she, like the nuns, had been walled in all her days. But the walls around Gormaz Castle were a part of home and therefore acceptable. Jimena had never considered herself imprisoned and had always known she would scale the walls some day. But now, black flag or white, the prospects were nothing short of terrifying.

Late in the afternoon of the fifth day, Jimena was stubbornly at the window, where she had been most of the night and steadily since sunrise. She had refused her meals, had missed morning Mass for the second time in a week. Everything that moved on the landscape struck ice in her and sparked a flurry of nerves that set her head spinning. Margarita Gonzales had come to see her early in the day, saying she hoped to console Jimena in her time of worry. But Jimena had been unable to give the girl her attention, since her eyes were constantly turning to fix upon the distant beginnings of the road from Zamora.

"Our fathers are at battle or fighting against challengers all the time, Jimena," Margarita had said, in that high-pitched, purring little voice of hers, "so why do you worry so about this one?"

"This one is *different*," Jimena had said curtly, not looking at the girl.

"Yes . . ." Margarita had agreed, "I suppose it is. My father said that Rodrigo Diaz has been training himself for six years, just for this fight with your father. And he said he was grateful to God that it was your father Diaz had challenged and not himself; he was not ready to lose his head."

Jimena had whirled on the girl in a rage. "If you do not get out of my chamber this instant, it will be *your* head that will be lost, Margarita! Go, and leave me be!"

Margarita had drawn herself up indignantly to her full height of five feet and with bitter intent snapped "My betrothal to Layn Sanchez will be announced within the month, as soon as my father returns from Zamora. That is what should be preying upon your mind, Jimena Gomez—the fact that you are without a husband!"

"A husband is *exactly* what is on my mind!" Jimena had shouted back at the girl. "Now get out!"

Jimena shivered as a chilll wind swept in from the window. She knew she had been unnecessarily sharp with Margarita but today she was edgy enough to turn a sharp tongue on God Himself. Only five days. It seemed an eternity ago that the aunt had come rushing in to say her father wanted to see her. She yawned, then yawned again. Her eyelids felt as if they had weights upon them. Water filled her eyes from the yawning, so that she could barely see. With her fists, she rubbed the mist from her eyes, straining to see the tiny puff of dust that would mean a rider was approaching.

Soon will power alone was keeping her on her feet. In desperation, she moved unsteadily across the room, took hold of a chair, and dragged it back to the window. She sat down and leaned her elbows on the high sill, propping her chin up with both hands. Her knees were pressed hard against the granite wall under the window. She watched. Her eyelids fluttered, closed, then popped open again. She blinked hard, because she could not see a thing anymore. Then she was asleep, fixed there in a position much like that of prayer. Clouds rolled in on the wind and darkened the sky.

Hours later a scream woke Jimena . . . a shattering wail of despair. It was her aunt, from somewhere below stairs. More moans and shrieks followed, then a cry from the yard—"The count is dead! God save us all: the count is dead!"

Chapter
✠ *TWO* ✠

Jimena stood before a priest who was dark and threatening, his face shadowed. She knew that she was being married, but she was *alone* before the man of God. Panic seized her as a great net, much like a spider's web, appeared over her head and began to descend upon her. Then she saw a tiny light blinking into view over the shoulder of the priest. It was far in the distance, coming toward her out of darkness. She watched the light, entranced as it shimmered in shades of red, gold, and green. Her feet began to move, at first hesitantly, then more surely. The priest was gone. She ran alone, faster and faster, toward the growing brilliance. But the radiance always seemed to be beyond reach, never closer—and she had to get to it, she must; there was joy and beauty in the light, and satisfactions beyond measure.

With a jolt Jimena awakened, all the joy of racing toward that strange light erased by the realization that she was in her own bed, surrounded only by darkness. A cruel dream. And quite silly. She suspected that somewhere inside her the child that she had been still lived and wished to be a falcon, flying to a magic somewhere.

Jimena rolled over, shoving her face deep into her down pillows, squeezing her eyelids tight closed, as if the effort would bring on the return of sleep. But it was to no avail. All the butterflies in the world seemed to be permanent residents in her mid-section. Thrashing over to her side, she tried again.

Her chamber door opened softly. Jimena ignored the sound. Her aunt had made a habit of looking in on her many times every night, since the news of her father's death had come. The old woman seemed acutely anxious about her these days, God knew why; her burden was as good as lifted from her now. Only two more days were left before her departure for Palencia with Jaime.

"Jimena . . . !"

She continued to ingore her aunt, whose voice now hissed over her where she lay. The woman had never tried to discover if she were truly asleep on these nightly checks.

"Jimena, child, wake yourself!"

Jimena groaned and rolled over onto her back, faking a wide yawn. "What is it, Aunt?"

"Get yourself up and dressed. You leave immediately."

"Leave!" Jimena sat up, frowning. "There is no light. It cannot be time for Mass."

"For the love of God, do as I tell you."

Jimena stared at the woman, who shuffled around the room lighting candles, and then began to thrash about with both hands in the trunk for a pelisse, a tunic, and a wimple. And a cloak.

"Aunt . . ." Jimena began impatiently, "will you tell me, please, what is going on? I will not leave this bed until you do."

With a grunt and a hand supporting her back, her aunt pulled herself erect beside the trunk, glaring across the room at Jimena. "Your sister's husband is taking you out of the city immediately. You are no longer safe here. Your departure for Palencia can be delayed no longer. Now, do as I tell you, and cease this bickering. Must I thrash you, for God!"

"Not safe? At *Gormaz*?"

Galiana let out a blast of air from her lungs. "*Stupida!* Where are your brains? The moment that black flag entered this city, all eyes turned to Don Jaime Martinez as the new overlord. But he has not taken the reins. Suspicions are getting too close to the truth. You, brainless one, are in the middle of it. If you would prefer to sit there and have your throat cut, then do so. Otherwise, get yourself up and dressed. Don Jaime will come to fetch you within the hour."

Bewildered and shaken, Jimena threw back the fur coverlet and leaped out of bed. Her aunt rushed her and tugged off her nightdress with an urgency that lent validity to the threats she had mentioned. When the girdle was tightly in place over her tunic, Jimena leaned to reach for a brown wimple, but the aunt jerked it away from her hands.

"First we must hide the letter in your hair. Sit yourself, and I will . . ."

"In my *hair*! What letter? Has my father's death and funeral caused you to lose your mind, Aunt? Has this entire castle gone insane?"

Galiana took Jimena's shoulders in her two hands and with surprising strength shoved her toward a chair, then pushed her soundly down upon it. "Now sit still and keep your mouth shut! While I see to the hiding, I will explain what should be obvious to you. Little fool! Do you see this—do you?" She thrust a small folded and sealed parchment before Jimena's eyes. "Your father put this letter into my hands just minutes before he departed for Zamora. It is either of two things—your inheritance, or your death warrant."

"Death war—"

"*Callarse!* Listen to me. It is his letter to the king that he spoke to you about. There are men in this city who would gladly kill you for it. *Madre mia,* Jimena, you must realize the riches, the power, that you carry with you in this single bit of parchment, which you are to deliver into the hands of the king, and the man who killed your father. Think, for the love of God. Do you imagine that the knights of Gormaz love the man that dropped your father into his grave? Do you think it likely they will stand meekly by and allow you to marry this man, which will bring him to this city as lord over them?"

Jimena arched her head back to watch the workings of her aunt's face as she spoke. But the words were beyond comprehension. "But, how could the city know—I mean, did my father announce his intention from the top of the donjon?"

"Rumors, I told you. Suspicion. Only Don Jaime and Don Manuel are supposed to know the contents of this letter. The council has raised questions Don Jaime has been unable to answer, and all eyes are beginning to focus on you. No, I do not think they know it is Rodrigo Diaz you are to marry. How could they! The idea is too preposterous. But Don Jaime's silence has made them dangerously suspicious. It is better that you slip away, before suspicion becomes certainty."

Jimena flinched and yelped with pain as Galiana jerked on her long hair, twisting it into tight braids. "I cannot see the point of carrying a letter in my hair," she protested, scrunching her neck and letting out grunts of discomfort. "You are hurting me! Must you pull so hard?"

"I trust no one. And *you* must trust no one. Just remember that Don Jaime and Don Manuel have the most to gain by burning this letter. Sit still, for God. Stop pulling away from me like that. The pain of braiding, or a knife at your throat, eh?"

"Jaime would never . . ." Jimena began, then screeched as her aunt pulled the short hairs at the back of her neck in the process of twisting the finished braids over the letter that had been pushed against the top of her head. "If you do not trust Jaime, then why do you allow him to—Aunt! The pins. Must you jab them straight into my brain?"

"It was your father's last request of me. He said Don Jaime was to take you, so he takes you. Trust him if you will, I care not. The idea, agreeing to marry your father's murderer . . ." With that she shoved a last metal pin roughly into place, scratching it brutally across Jimena's scalp. "If the choice had been mine, I would have become a nun ten times over. Ten times over, Jimena Gomez! Do not expect *me* to fall at that brute's feet, when you bring him here to lord it over us all. Sinful, no less than sinful; but it is your conscience and none of mine. There—it is safe. No eye could discern it. Turn your head. Now the other way. *Bien.* You are ready."

The braids had been pulled so tight that Jimena felt like her face had shrunk. Her eyelids were drawn to the side so that it was difficult to blink. She put a hand to her head and brought it back, expecting to see blood from the wounds the pins had made, but there was none. She watched her aunt sourly packing several ensembles and nightdresses into a carrying case, throwing in two pairs of leather shoes and two pairs of felts; then she vigorously yanked on the straps of the case to tie it fast.

"Is that *all* I will be taking, Aunt?"

"All. Your father wished you to seem an orphan, so forlorn that you would be lost without the king's favor. An absurdity! I cannot see how a daughter of the richest knight in Castile could appear destitute. But I shall not question the dead, nor sully his honor by neglecting his last requests of me. I have done all I can for you. May God forgive and protect you, for your father's sake."

The aunt gave her a final, sour inspection, then turned on her heel and moved with a stiff gait to the door. She did not look back, but opened the door, stepped into the corridor, and closed the door behind her, without a parting word.

Overwhelmed by conflicting emotions, Jimena rose from the chair and stepped to the east window. She saw only the flickering lamplight in several barbican windows. There was no moon; the clouds obscured it and all the stars. Doubt suddenly washed over her and she wondered if her aunt and Jaime were right. Should she have chosen the monastery? She felt the letter to the king heavy against her scalp, felt it like an accusation. Everyone at the castle said that Rodrigo Diaz was a monster, a murderer, an enemy who had struck down a man they had deeply loved—the lord who had seemed to them as indestructible and holy as God Himself. Serfs and knights alike had wept, and still did, cursing the name of Rodrigo Diaz, praying that soon a knight of Gormaz would rise against him in retribution and leave him dead. But her father had said the man was noble, a champion in the making, the perfect husband for her. Surely it would be no less wrong for her to go against his last wish, than for her aunt. What she was about to do was what he had begged her to do. Therefore it was a matter of honor that she fully comply and not weaken—his honor and her own. To fly to a monastery now would be an insult to his memory, would it not?

The door of her chamber opened and Jimena turned to face a grim Jaime. He stood there looking at her solemnly.

"I am ready . . ." she said to him, as she moved to fetch her cloak and throw it over her shoulders.

As Jaime stepped into the room to pick up her carrying case, she asked him, "Where is Don Luis? When we talked yesterday about my coming marriage the bishop said Don Luis would not leave my side a moment until. . . ."

"We have no time for waking priests," Jaime said unpleasantly.

"But the bishop was insistent! And I would feel a great deal more at ease."

Jaime stepped toward her, case in hand. "It was your father's command that you be accompanied by only myself and Manuel. The bishop be damned, with his pious insistence that you have God as a chaperone. Bad enough that it is known that Palencia is our destination; we need not confirm a marriage by the presence of a priest. Come, Jimena—there is no time to waste in questioning."

Jimena nodded and said no more. She followed Jaime into the corridor and skipped occasionally to keep up with him as he strode toward the staircase. Poor Jaime, how he had wept at the funeral, beating his fists against his thighs again and again, as if to punish himself. Until now he had not said more than a good morning or a good evening to her, since his return with the body from Zamora. Leonora and Sol had come to Gormaz for the funeral, both of them avoiding her company, often looking at her as if *she* were their father's killer, rather than Rodrigo Diaz. She understood that it had quickly become apparent to Leonora that Gormaz had been removed from her inheritance in favor of her youngest sister, so Jimena did not blame them. But Leonora's cold stares, in particular, had hurt. Eyes that once had looked upon her with warmth, the full mouth from which so many joyous stories had emerged, were all ice now. It was easy for Jimena to accept the fact that she was not loved, because this had been true of her entire life, but she had never before felt *hated*. It was devastating to know that nothing she could say or do would put things back the way they were. Not only had her father passed away ten days past; but with him into the grave had gone the expectations of his first born, and the security of his last.

"No, Jimena," Jaime said to her when they reached the bottom of the stairs and Jimena automatically stepped toward the courtyard door. "This way."

He led her to the wine cellar doorway, which they passed through. In the darkness, lit only by a single torch taken down from the wall by Jaime to guide their way, Jimena held up her skirts and stepped carefully down the damp stone staircase that twisted and turned until it came to an end deep underground. It was cold and wet in the cellars. Jimena shivered behind Jaime as he pressed on with a tense, determined stride. Up another staircase, then out into the air, emerging into a cobblestone alley just beneath one of the gate's barbicans. There Don Manuel waited with two horses and a carriage hitched to a black mare. The wagon driver turned his head to stare accusingly at Jimena.

Jaime quickly tossed Jimena's case into the carriage, then took her arm to help her in. She was just seated on the hard wooden bench when the carriage jerked forward, rattling over the stones in a jarring race with unknown enemies. Jimena sat stiffly on the seat, refusing to think about anything more serious than her bitter regret that her first time outside the walls of Gormaz Castle had to be in absolute darkness. The world she had so longed to see was being passed unseen. All that existed beyond the walls of Gormaz was a mystery, as illusive as Heaven, and equally as awesome.

The sun rose to Jimena's right and she leaned toward the uncovered window of the carriage, craning her neck to get a first close look at what she had gazed at for so many years from the great height and distance of her chamber windows. The clouds were dusted with ravishing shades of pink and gold that seemed to wash down upon the plain across which they were dashing at this continuously mad pace. A new uneasiness disturbed her, but she could not fix it in her mind. The sun to her right. Then they were traveling north? From her chamber windows she knew which was east, west, south, north, but here . . . Palencia was certainly south of Gormaz; couriers from the king always rode in from that direction. She tried to place herself mentally in her chamber, imagining the sun on her right and her left, but she was too nervous and confused to solve the problem, and gave it up.

Jaime rode up alongside the carriage occasionally, glancing in at Jimena, but he had no words for her. Uneasily Jimena reached a hand up to her braids, wondering if her aunt's precautions had been all that ridiculous. She tried to think what Jaime would accomplish by burning the letter. Of course Gormaz would return to Leonora for want of a testament from her father stating otherwise. But surely her father had been wise enough to know that Gormaz was too much to place in her inexperienced hands, that she would be dangerously vulnerable. Would he not have insured the carrying out of his wish by sending another letter by courier to the king? No, that would have been an admission of weakness, suggesting that he had not expected to win against a mere boy, a frailty that he would have had to face if he *had* prevailed. Ah! A message to be carried to the king . . . only if he did not survive; that made sense. The king could be expecting her then.

How would Jaime explain why his wife's sister did not arrive at court? Time; her father had been pressed for time, and quite obviously depressed. It was possible, then, that he had not had the presence of mind or the time to write more than this one letter that now rode hot against her scalp. She shuddered and hugged herself with both arms. She thought that no human being on earth could be more defenseless than she was at this moment. Confused as to north and south, unable to ride a horse, without weapon of any kind, not possessed of any physical strength: If Jaime proved disloyal, there would be nothing for it but to give him the letter and let him burn it. She heard the aunt's voice saying, "There are men in this city who would gladly kill you . . ." Fear was flame and ice at once in her. Not Jaime. Never. Desperately she began to pray for protection, her fingers shakily moving from bead to bead of her rosary.

The sun was to Jimena's left now. She held on to the sides

of the carriage for support, the road so rough here that she was thrown in every direction at once, barely able to keep her seat. Earlier in the day she had called out to Jaime as he rode alongside, begging him for rest. Every muscle in her body ached.

"Not until we reach the river," he had shouted to her, spurring his mount and vanishing up ahead.

When the road was smooth enough, she had occasionally managed to enjoy the passing scenes. A fine castle rising in the distance, perched upon a high ridge and silhouetted against the now cloudless sky. Wildflowers along the road being visited each in turn by bustling yellow bees. Green. The whole world was green. Tall wild grasses bending in the winds, swaying as if to a music only they could hear.

Suddenly the carriage came to a halt. Jimena sat on the bench, staring straight ahead, her body feeling the lurch and sway as if the vehicle were still in motion. Weakness overcame her and her stomach cramped. She had not eaten before their departure, nor had she been given so much as a swallow of water throughout the day.

"We will rest now, Jimena."

Jaime had opened the door of the carriage and stood there offering her a hand. She took his hand and stepped to the ground. Weakness suddenly affected her knees and she stumbled, lurching against him.

"Steady now," he said. "Do not try to walk, yet. Let your legs get the feel of the ground again."

"I sincerely hope you are going to give me something to eat, Jaime," she said, steadying herself by leaning heavily on his arm. "I am famished! Is it so urgent that I get to Palencia quickly—that I must arrive unconscious?"

Jaime laughed. To Jimena's enormous relief, he actually laughed, a real laugh, lighting his whole face. "How does mutton sound . . . and bread and wine?"

"Cold mutton—or hot?"

"Roasted over a fire and so hot you will burn your fingers."

"Marvelous . . ."

Jimena felt enormously relieved as Jaime strode off to help Don Manuel and the wagon driver prepare a fire. They had come to a halt under trees, some distance from the road. She heard the sound of rushing water, but could see only shadows, underbrush, and clusters of wildflowers sticking their elegant heads up over the grasses here and there. Curiously she stepped into the brush, shoving bushes aside, ducking her head under low swinging branches.

Jimena gasped as she broke apart a barrier of growth to find herself upon the sandy bank of a river. She had never seen anything like it in all her days. Water had existed for her in moats, horse troughs, wells, and pitchers and cups. This water was rushing headlong from an unknown somewhere, moving toward someplace else—truly miraculous. It was wider than a moat but not as deep. Awed, she dropped to her knees and flicked her fingers across the swirling surface. She heard the crunch of someone coming through the underbrush toward her and looked back to see Jaime carrying two wooden buckets.

"Jaime!" she exclaimed as he came up beside her. "Wherever does it all *come* from?"

"The water? From the mountaintops. The snow melts and—"

"But where is it *going?*" she interrupted excitedly, leaning forward and craning her neck to see around the curve of the river.

"It empties into an even larger river," he replied, leaning to swing a bucket into the water to fill it.

"And then where does *that* river go?"

Jaime laughed and said, "I have no idea. I would suppose it eventually sinks into the earth, which provides us with our wells. Or perhaps it springs up again and—*qien sabe,* Jimena, only God knows."

"*Que linda!*" she cried, overwhelmed. She dropped to her knees and splashed the water up to her face, relishing the sweetness of it and the relief it offered to her parched throat.

She remained at the riverbank watching the moving waters with the fascination of a child, until Jaime called her to come and eat.

Jaime and Don Manuel sat across the fire from Jimena, eating in silence. They had taken her carrying case from the carriage to serve as a seat for her. The sun was beginning to settle down behind the far mountains, a blue haze enveloping them. The sound of the river was like a song, dozens of birds were chiming in.

"Well, Jimena," Jaime said when she had finished eating and sat back satisfied, "I think it is time we talked."

Jimena's eyes darted over the fire to his face, then to Don Manuel's. They were ominously serious but not particularly threatening. "Talk about what, Jaime?" she asked, forcing innocence into her voice. She sat stiffly prepared for the worst and praying for something less. Don Manuel's homely, lividly scarred face reminded her of a death mask, unreal in its lack of expression. Whatever he was thinking, he was masterfully concealing it from her.

"I want the letter," Jaime said softly, his manner gentle, even apologetic.

Jimena stared at him. She tried to speak, but the muscles of her throat had constricted.

"Please, Jimena," Jaime pleaded with her, "do not look at me like that, as if I am somehow criminal. I am not the greedy man you must think me, hungering after the power and wealth of Gormaz. I do this as much for your sake as my own. You simply have no conception of what would have awaited you in Palencia, if we had chosen to take you there—none."

Jimena found her voice and asked unsteadily, "Where *are* you taking me, Brother?"

Jaime flinched at her use of the word *brother,* his face reddening. "To the monastery at Coimbra, Jimenita."

"No," Jimena whispered, tears filling her eyes.

"In the name of Christ, woman," Don Manuel shouted at her, lunging to his feet. "You cannot have expected us to passively deliver ourselves into the hands of Diaz! If you had been at Zamora . . . if you had seen what that—that *pig* did to your father, then, I think, you would not shudder so at the prospect of Coimbra."

Jaime was now on his feet, too, scowling at her. "Jimena," he said emotionally, "it was not a duel; it was a murder! Diaz ignored all the rules of chivalry. When your father's sword dropped from his hands, Diaz refused to step back and allow him to retrieve it! He lunged in for the kill and sliced your father's head from his shoulders as he might slaughter a goat! Then, as if that were not enough, he grabbed up your father's severed head in a hand and raised the head to the sky, bellowing 'Father! You are avenged!' . . . Blood of your blood oozed through his fingers, running down his sleeve to drip off his elbow. But he still had not had enough. He dropped that blessed head to the earth and kicked it across the field so that it came to rest at my feet. So help me God, Jimena, Diaz is not a man—he is an animal! I cannot allow you to place yourself under him as his wife, nor let the city of Gormaz with all its citizens and knights be made subject to him."

The mutton and wine in Jimena's stomach were threatening to return. She desperately tried to shake the image Jaime had painted of her father's death from her mind, but it remained fixed there, his head in a man's upraised hand . . . his blood. Kicking a man's head aside as if it were trash—Holy Mary Mother of God, what had her father been thinking when he chose such a man for her? It seemed to her at this moment that he had been acting upon a dislike for her rather than extraordinary affection. Jaime and Don Manuel stood waiting for her to say something, their expressions angry but at the same time sympathetic.

"Sister . . ." Jaime said at last, when she continued to stare at him in mortified indecision. "The monastary—it will only be for a short time, until I can settle the unrest at Gormaz. Then I can find you a proper husband. You must understand. As long as you carry your father's letter, the city is yours and none of mine. I cannot risk the continued existence of a testament that denies my right to rule. You are not worldly wise, Jimenita, and could easily fall prey to my enemies. Do you understand?"

"No!" Jimena blurted out, tears sliding down her cheeks. "No, Jaime, I do *not* understand. I think you are being devious with me. You could ask for the letter. I could give it to you. No one would argue your right to rule. So, I question the need to place me in a monastery for so much as an *hour!*"

"Christ, woman," Don Manuel shouted at her, "you are not safe at Gormaz. Your aunt was told to explain that to you. You are not safe, nor your sisters, nor Don Jaime—nor myself!"

"That is ridiculous! Gormaz is my home and . . ."

"Jimena," Jaime interrupted impatiently, "there is always this kind of unrest when a king dies. . . ."

"My father was no king . . ."

"You are *wrong*. Don Ferrando may be king of Castile, but his power, though it technically crosses all borders, is profoundly limited. Distance is a factor, as is wealth. Each of the counts of Castile are kings, who oblige Ferrando, if they choose to, by vowing allegiance to him. But within their domains they are almighty. If they decide to defy Don Ferrando, they do so, and with impunity. So your father was, in effect, king of Gormaz and of all the territory that he controlled by the force of his influence and his army. He is dead. Now a struggle for power is emerging among the lesser nobility and the more powerful knights. If every heir to the seat of power were dead . . ." Jaime lifted his eyebrows and made a face that completed the statement; the rest had to be obvious to her.

Jimena suddenly experienced a strange, unnatural calm. She

heard her father saying to her, "He is all the man your father once was—and more." Gormaz was his gift to her, he had said, and Rodrigo Diaz was for his people. Could he have wanted this man Diaz to take the power in Gormaz because he saw no one else about him qualified to take his seat? Only girl children. Jaime was . . .

Jimena studied her brother-in-law closely, trying to see him through her father's eyes. Charming, jovial, kind, a good husband and father, a devoted knight, strong in battle. But he did not possess that head-high, overpowering dignity that had been her father's most outstanding trait; arrogance was missing. Jaime did not have the makings of a king. Certainly Sol's husband, sixty years old and retired to a sickbed, was not a candidate.

"I will not go to the monastery," Jimena said flatly, clenching her hands together in her lap.

"You have no choice!" Don Manuel roared. "Now give us that letter, damn you, and let us have done with this game."

"Give us the letter, Jimenita," Jaime said worriedly.

Jimena shook her head hard. "I accept your argument against Rodrigo Diaz as my husband—I would not want to be married to such a man—but I refuse to allow myself to be put into a monastery. I know very well that you can legally, and against my will, leave me there until the day I die, Jaime Martinez. I know that. I am at least *that* wise."

Jaime started to reply, but Don Manuel nudged him and said quickly, "Fair enough, Jimena. Give us the letter, and we will return you to Gormaz."

Jimena saw Jaime's quick, startled glance at his companion. "No, Don Manuel," she said stubbornly. "You may not have the letter."

Don Manuel's face contorted with rage. He leaped over the fire and had her by the arm within seconds. Jimena was thrown aside, stumbling. The man tugged at the straps of her case, opened it and threw out her belongings piece by piece, searching for the document. When the case proved unrewarding, he turned his head and said to her, "I will strip you naked if I must!"

"Oh, no," Jaime shouted, now beside the man. "You will not degrade nor abuse my sister!"

Jimena watched, terrified, as the two men stood facing each other like two arch-backed cats, fairly hissing in their fury. Then a distant rumble, as of thunder, distracted her. She whirled around to see what it was.

A cloud of dust rose above the trees just ahead, barely visible in the increasing darkness, and she identified the sound as that of swiftly moving wagons and many horses at full gallop. Quickly the train came into view, heading directly toward their camp. The lead rider had the banner of King Don Ferrando raised on his staff. The second rider carried a banner Jimena did not recognize.

Jaime rushed to Jimena's side and clutched hold of her elbow. "It is the *Infanta*," he said urgently, his handsome face revealing great respect and a certain anxiety.

"Damn!" Don Manuel swore behind her, as the entourage turned in from the road and began surrounding them. Men on horses, at the least thirty and five, footmen bringing up the rear, wagons and their drivers, and an ornate carriage drawn by two white stallions. A company of at least fifty.

Jimena watched entranced as the Infanta's carriage was drawn to a halt next to her own. She waited expectantly for the princess to emerge with a golden crown on her head and wearing a magnificent robe. But not one of the footmen moved to open the carriage door. From off one of the dozens of horses surrounding them leaped a slim young man in the clothes of a stable boy, his face smudged with dust, hands grimy, his shirt no longer white but stained with sweat and road grime. Unsightly he was and in pauper's clothing, but in him Jimena saw the same arrogance that her father had possessed. His head was high, and there was unlimited confidence in his stride and the swing of his arms.

"God be damned, Jaime Martinez!" the young man bellowed animatedly, rushing Jaime and giving him a bear hug. "What in the name of hell are you doing on the road to Coimbra? . . . And Don Manuel. Greetings. Well, have you both lost your tongues?"

"We escort Doña Jimena Gomez," Jaime said in a nervous voice, "to the monastery."

The young man turned and glanced at Jimena, studying her disinterestedly. "I see. The monastery." He returned his attention to the two men. "Good enough. My monasteries can always use another devoted spirit willing to do our work for us—at a wage of one meal a day, eh?" He laughed uproariously. "Come . . . join me in some wine and talk, while my people set up our camp. We left Coimbra at sunrise and made excellent time. You there, Maria! Fetch my mantle; it is getting chilly. Christ, will summer never arrive?"

Jaime fairly dragged Jimena along with him as he followed

the young man to the mammoth fire being built by hurrying servants. The youth dropped to a seat on the ground, wearing a wide grin on his face. Jaime sat down, drawing Jimena to a seat beside him.

"Who *is* he?" Jimena hissed aside to Jaime.

Jaime ignored her but answered the question by addressing the man as *Doña* Urracca. Jimena's eyes widened in shocked disbelief.

"Do you return to Palencia, Doña Urracca? Or are you on a tour of your monasteries?"

"I have just completed a tour of them all," the Infanta replied. "Yes, I return to Palencia. A command appearance. My father ordered me, by courier, to return—oh, that must have been a fortnight ago." She laughed heartily. "Can I help it if couriers are inept and I do not receive their communications? Hmmm? I do believe the old goat thinks that he is on his deathbed again, and wants to reassure himself that I am not eight months gone with an heir to the throne who could one day challenge Sancho's right to rule." Her laughter had a bitter ring to it now. "Let him die worried; he has it coming to him. . . . So how goes it at Gormaz, Don Jaime? I heard about Rodrigo's triumph over Gomez while I was at Santiago."

"There is unrest," Jaime replied respectfully, "which was to be expected."

Doña Urracca studied Jaime's face for long moments, a slight smile turning up the corners of her mouth, but a coldness in her eyes now. "Hmmmm. . . ." she murmured, squinting across the fire at Jaime. "I wonder why Gormaz' heir apparent is playing escort to the count's daughter, when he should be in the city putting the unrest to rest?"

"It was the count's last wish. . . ." Jaime said weakly.

"Oh, I see." Urracca glanced at Jimena, who was obviously distraught and not a little overawed, then turned back to Jaime. "A meager escort, to say the least—two knights and a wagon driver. An unmarried daughter of Gomez would seem to be a natural target for those who are creating the unrest you spoke of. Yet she travels to all intents unguarded. Curious . . ."

Jaime glanced helplessly at Don Manuel, who sat to his left sulking and restless. "It would appear so," Jaime said evasively, turning a charming smile on the Infanta.

"A puzzle," Doña Urracca said, mocking a severe frown. "What fun. I do love a puzzle. You truly have me curious, Don Jaime."

Jimena glanced from one to the other, her heart racing.

This woman was so foreign to her, behaving so strangely, that she seemed unreal. She thought about speaking out, telling the Infanta of Jaime's threat against her, but was afraid the woman would simply laugh at her. Or she might have Jaime's head; there was no predicting what a person who was a woman but at the same time a man would do. Jaime had stood between Don Manuel and herself, placing his life over her own. He truly meant her no real harm. She could not put him in jeopardy with the daughter of the king.

"Not only did I hear of Gomez' death at Santiago," Urracca added teasingly, "but several rumors came to me, as well. It was said that the count had sorely angered the husband of his first born. Sharp words were overheard. Gomez had gone mad, you were heard to say. Assumption—the count has disinherited your wife in favor of his youngest and unmarried daughter." She glanced once again to Jimena, then quickly back to Jaime. "Could this be true? And I have found you spiriting her off to Coimbra to protect your interests, hmmmm?"

"As always," Jaime began with studied humor, "you are astute, Doña Urracca. But, as you said, you always need new devotees at your monasteries."

Urracca accepted a tankard of wine from a servant, gulped the brew down and shoved the cup out to be refilled without taking her eyes off Jaime. "That is true, yes it is. But there is more to this riddle, I think. Gomez would not leave this helpless creature to the world without seeing to it that she was properly betrothed. I smell a marriage in the making, one that does not please you, Jaime."

Jimena's heart leaped. The Infanta knew—she knew, and was not guessing at all. Her father had indeed sent word by courier to the king. Wide-eyed, she waited to see what would happen next. The Holy Mother knew, it would not be a joyous life, whichever way she went, to Coimbra or to Palencia. But if she had to make a choice, it would be Palencia.

"Doña Urracca . . ." Jaime purred, "you give me more credit for ambition and cunning than I deserve."

"Jaime! I have known you most of my life. Stop playing me for the fool. I am intrigued. What do I care what you do with this girl? It's a matter of total indifference to me."

Encouraged, Don Manuel spoke up for the first time, a thin, forced smile on his lips. "Rodrigo Diaz is your good friend, Doña Urracca, but he is no friend of ours. Therefore you ask too much of us, when you demand to know the whole truth behind our presence here."

"He killed the count fairly," she said amiably, "did he not?"

Impulsively, Jimena exclaimed, "No, he did *not!* He slaughtered my father, as if he were a—a—" Her words trailed off and she flushed, miserably dropping her eyes to her lap. She had forgotten the need to protect Jaime.

Don Manuel quickly covered Jimena's audacity with "Women cannot be expected to comprehend the complexities of life. Being a typical female Doña Jimena sees her father's death as a murder, rather than a natural and noble end."

"Indeed." Doña Urracca's voice was suddenly edged with ice. "Is this child truly as empty-headed as any other female? A pity. Naturally, I carry the same cross. I am the first born of a king, but this lack of intelligence you speak of makes it impossible for me to rule after my father. My brother Sancho will take the throne. Unlike Doña Jimena here, I *fully* comprehend my situation. Tell me, Don Manuel, which of the knights of Castile did Count Gomez choose for this girl?" When the man looked away from her, remaining silent, she turned to Jaime. "If you do not tell me, I shall start naming them one by one, and watch your face until it tells me when I have hit upon it."

"The choice would not please you any more than it pleases us," Jaime said angrily.

"No? There is not a name in Castile that would raise me from indifference."

"That is where you are wrong. There is one name that would definitely agitate you, you simply have not considered it."

Doña Urracca stared at Jaime, blinked, then abruptly choked on a swallow of wine as the name came to her. "Not—Rodrigo Diaz!" she fairly shrieked, coughing. Then she doubled over with laughter. "Oh, my dear God . . . no wonder you are so grimly determined to imprison the wench. Incredible! How remarkably cunning of Gomez. If I had been standing in his shoes I would have done the same, or given it a try. Rodrigo Diaz! Good Christ, you were right! I am most definitely raised out of indifference."

Jimena felt the sting of the woman's laughter. Too much that was truly terrible was hilariously amusing to this peculiar woman. Now she was saying, between giggles and gulps of wine, that she had been extraordinarily fortunate to have come upon the saving of Rodrigo Diaz from a fate worse than death—marriage to an empty-headed child; but then, no woman he married would have a brain in her head. God had endowed brains upon men exclusively. And *this* wench, all anger and tears over the "murder" of her father, when in truth he had died nobly. Poor Rodrigo would never have lived it down, chilled all his days by her cold stares of accusation. When Jimena glanced to Jaime, she was surprised to see that he was not amused, but Don Manuel had brightened considerably.

"She is so witless," Don Manuel said sarcastically, "that she thought to keep the *letter* from us. Weak as a newborn pup, she stood there," he said in a high-pitched, mocking voice, "and said 'You may not have the letter.' With my little finger I could have struck her unconscious." He coughed on a gulp of wine that emptied his tankard for the fifth time. "No, she says to me. No-you-great-big-brute-I-will-not-give-you-my-letter. Christ! Out here in the middle of nowhere, and she says *no* to me!"

Doña Urracca laughed appreciatively. "Witless indeed," she agreed, "but what else could you expect from a woman? Mmm?"

"Right . . ." Don Manuel exclaimed happily. "You have it exactly. But you—you, Doña Urracca, are the exception, of course. Diaz is your loving friend, eh? So you would not appreciate his entrance into a marriage—and are clever enough to see that he does not. Am I right, eh? Eh?"

"My dear fellow, you stand as a prime example of the intelligence of the male. How can I argue with an observation so acute?" Her smile upon Don Manuel was radiant. "I enjoyed a visit with Rodrigo and his mother, at Bivar, but a few days ago. He was overjoyed at his triumph over Gomez. We talked at length about his future and he confided in me that he now had to add further glory to his name, through similar victories, before he would be worthy of a lady who in turn was worthy of him. In all humility, he thought to achieve sufficient glory within five years. Of course, it had never occurred to him that such a lady as this . . ." nodding in Jimena's direction, "would be offered to him while he was as yet unglorified, a mere pauper, a mere boy. A pity that the three of us, each for our own reason, have chosen to deny him this unexpected, premature windfall. A pity."

"My heart bleeds for him," Don Manuel snarled.

"Doña Urracca," Jaime said, rising to his feet and pulling Jimena up to stand beside him, "we thank you for your hospitality, but we must be off. We have delayed long . . ."

"But, Don Jaime," she protested, "you cannot mean to travel at night!"

"It is urgent that we return to Gormaz as quickly as possible. We must see Doña Jimena to Coimbra, and . . ."

"I will not hear of it! Why, just look at the child. She is exhausted. Doña Jimena is not a vigorous lady, quite frail in fact—which is obvious to me, and should be to you, who know her better." She turned her head and shouted at a servant. "Pedro! Take this lady to a tent and see to it she has a double mattress and anything else she would like to make her comfortable for the night."

"Forgive me," Jaime began tensely, his hand that held Jimena's trembling slightly, "but we must refuse. Truly, our return is extremely urgent."

"Then return to Gormaz, and I will have several of my men take her on, in the morning." Her smile had not lost any of its radiance. She sat cross-legged, firelight illuminating her delicate face, sparkling in her violet eyes that mockingly fixed themselves upon Jaime.

"No. No, I must see her to Coimbra myself."

"Then there is no more to discuss." She jumped to her feet and began brushing twigs and dust from her trousers. "I need a bath. I think I shall take a swim in the river. Have a good night's rest, sirs—and you, Doña Jimena." With that she turned heel and grabbed a torch from the hand of a footman, then moved surely in the direction of the river, passing quickly into darkness.

Jimena stared after the Infanta, stunned. A *bath*! It suddenly occurred to her that not a single priest was included in the company—extraordinary. A bath . . . ? Her vivid imagination went to work and she saw Doña Urracca as some kind of Lazarus—*Bathsheba* raised from the grave to haunt the plains of Castile. She heard a screech emerge from the direction of the river, and a happy yelping that the water was ice, absolutely ice.

Jaime left Jimena's side and moved to speak to Don Manuel. A manservant came up to Jimena, bowed, and said, "This way, my lady, your bed awaits you."

Jimena hesitated, looking to Jaime, but he was completely occupied, unaware of her. She shrugged and moved to follow the servant, feeling the exhaustion the Infanta had observed in her weakened legs and heavy eyelids. For God, it had been, undoubtedly, the worst day of her life, and the longest. When she entered the tent and saw the fine down mattresses awaiting her, they looked like paradise. And a rabbit fur coverlet. She dropped down upon the bed, brushing off the servant's offer of

some wine, or perhaps a bit of cheese. All she wanted to do
was sleep, God willing, for a week. She would worry about
being consigned to a monastery tomorrow.

Jimena awoke to see the same servant bending over her, and
at first she thought only a few moments had passed. Then she
saw the brightness of day through the tent opening and jerked
up to a sitting position. It was tomorrow already, and now it
had to be faced. Tears welled into her eyes.

"The carriage awaits you, my lady," the servant said to
her, a curious smile on his pocked face.

Jimena threw back the coverlet and swung her feet over to
the earth floor. She stood and made an attempt to straighten her
disheveled clothing. When she stepped out of the enclosure she
was shocked to see that the campsite was almost deserted. The
sun must have risen hours ago. The Infanta's carriage had been
left behind; her own was gone. Three knights stood near the
carriage, casually talking together. One of them noticed her and
they all came to attention, smiling at her.

"Where is Don Jaime Martinez?" she asked the servant,
who stood a humble step or two behind her.

"The carriage, my lady," he replied, making an arm toward the vehicle.

"But—I . . ."

The tallest of the knights strode over to Jimena and made a
slight bow. "The Infanta is pleased to offer to you, Doña
Jimena," he began with exaggerated formality, "the use of her
carriage, on your journey to Palencia. And we are honored to
excort you. I am Don . . ."

"But . . . this is; I do not understand. My brother, he was
to— Where is Don Jaime, sir?"

The two knights by the carriage snickered and put their
heads together, to pass some private joke between them.

"As I was saying, my lady, I am Don Diego Bermudez. As
for your good brother . . . he departed many hours ago for
Coimbra. Our mistress saw him off with all good wishes for a
swift and safe journey."

"This is ridiculous! He would not go to Coimbra without
me!"

"No, my lady, he would not. You were asleep on the
bench of the carriage. The Infanta reminded him of your
exhaustion of the night just past, begging him not to disturb
you."

Completely confused, Jimena threw up her hands and

cried, "For God, man, will you make sense? I cannot be in two places at once . . ."

"You speak the truth," Don Diego said, grinning wide at her. "The Infanta's servant, called Maria, is of the same age as yourself, and looks remarkably like you. Doña Jimena, your brother has been *tricked*. My mistress gave me a message for you, and it is this . . . 'Let this serve as a lesson to you regarding the intelligence of men, as compared to that of a woman.'"

Jimena gaped at the man, as the implications of what had happened slowly penetrated her confusion. "You mean—Jaime went off—; I cannot *believe* it!" A giggle upsurged into her throat. "I just cannot believe it," she exclaimed. The knights by the carriage were laughing uproariously now, Don Diego Bermudez and the servant, too.

"Well," Don Diego said happily, "are you ready to begin your journey to Palencia, my lady?"

Jimena laughed at him and said, "I most certainly am, sir, thank you very much. But I cannot help wondering why your mistress played such a joke upon my brother, and why she would aid me in getting to Palencia."

Don Diego shrugged and said, "*Qien sabe?* A whim, perhaps. Come, the hour is late. If we are lucky, we will arrive at Palencia by sunset."

Still confused and distrustful, Jimena sat on the bench of the carriage as it banged and thrashed over ruts in the road. First she was on her way to Palencia, only to discover that it was not her destination . . . and now it *was* again. Or was it? How could she be sure of anything at this point? Perhaps the Infanta was intent upon playing more than one trick. Apprehensively she watched the sun, to her left now, which *would* indicate a reverse in direction. In truth, she would trust Jaime far more than that bizarre woman, who cursed, bathed, and drank like a peasant. "What you do with this girl is a matter of total indifference to me . . ." Then why this gesture? It made no sense. Jaime had several times referred to the monasteries of Castile as "her" monasteries. Perhaps Jaime had left it to the Infanta to see her safely locked in a cell.

After several hours Jimena noticed a rider coming alongside the carriage. She turned her head to focus on him. It was Jaime! Her heart leaped in her breast, and she thrust her body half out the window to shout at him over the clatter of the wheels and the pounding of the horses' hooves.

"Jaime Martinez—whatever happened? I cannot . . ." Her words broke off as he turned his face to her. Complete humiliation was written all over him. She exploded into laughter. "It is *true*, then," she cried out. "Oh, Jaime—for shame, allowing a woman to make such a fool of you."

"Laugh now, Jimena Gomez," he yelled at her, his face red, "because there will be little laughter in your life when this day is over. We will see which of us is more the fool, you or me, eh?" With that he spurred his mount and raced forward out of her view.

Jaime's jab at her quickly sobered Jimena. She fell back into the carriage, frowning. The king's daughter had decided her fate, it seemed. On a whim. Or as a joke. For whatever reason, it was, apparently, decided. She put a hand up to her mouth, sucking in a breath. She must confront the king of Castile within days, and after that, Rodrigo Diaz.

Chapter

✠ *THREE* ✠

Church bells clanged a monotonous, discordant greeting. The impassioned citizens loudly hailed the regal procession as it moved slowly through the narrow streets of Palencia. William de Montrueil, resplendent in robes of purple and gold, holding high the banner of Alexander, His Holiness, pope of the Catholic Empire, rode at the forefront of the parade. Within the jeweled portfolio held fast by a golden cross to his saddle was a sealed decree to be delivered into the hands of the king of Castile. Bishops, priests, and monks from all over Castile were gathered in Palencia to meet and to kiss the skirts of the pope's standard bearer, mingling with the crowds, shoving eagerly for a glimpse of this monarchical holy man. Outside the walls of the city, the five hundred Italian knights that had followed de Montrueil from Italy to Castile were making camp. A great crusade against the Infidel was in the offing. German troops were joining the five hundred, as were French troops, and the armies of the counts of Castile who were loyal to the king and to their God.

The king's anteroom was a long, narrow, windowless chamber with vaulted ceilings so high that the arches at the very top were obscured by darkness. Torches, set about ten feet apart around the walls, lighted the room. The black smoke from the torches had created a thick, almost unbreathable haze. Jimena sat on a bench, leaning against the cold granite wall behind her, her eyes beginning to burn and water. She coughed softly into a hand.

An unbelievable turmoil was taking place all around her. A dignified-looking old gentleman, whom Jaime had identified for her as the king's counsel, would come bustling out of the king's audience hall, sweep past her, and then go back again, men tagging at his heels, his hands flying about him in gestures of protest or amusement. Men seemed to fill the room one moment and then the next moment the place was suddenly empty and silent—then was abruptly teeming with activity again. She heard de Montrueil's name spoken over and over again; the pope's standard bearer was obviously on everyone's mind. From the window of the guest chamber which she occupied, Jimena had seen His Holiness passing directly below her, a sight she had never expected to see in all her life. If the man had been God Himself, she could not have been more awed; he was, indeed, very close to it.

Don Diego Bermudez had seen Jimena to the guest chamber upon their arrival at Palencia, at midnight two days past. Once again darkness had denied her a view; she had missed seeing the capital city of Spain as they approached. She entered the city the same way she had departed from Gormaz—hidden inside a carriage, surrounded by night, passing through gates with rising barbicans. What she had seen of this castle, so far, was unimpressive, it was almost a duplicate of her father's castle at Gormaz.

Jaime had knocked upon her door only moments after Don Diego left her. She had opened the door to see him standing there looking terribly sad and earnest. After long moments of uncomfortable silence, Jaime said, "If you have overcome your inclination to laugh at me, Jimena, perhaps we could talk." His eyes were red-rimmed with weariness and defeat.

"Yes, Jaime," she had said, stepping back to allow him in, "I am finished laughing. What is it you wish to say to me?"

"First, I wish to ask your permission to remain at your side, until all matters that concern your best welfare are settled. This I promised your dead father. . . ."

He was still standing in the open doorway. Jimena urged him in and closed the door, then leaned back against it, studying him closely. "You were unwilling to keep that promise yesterday," she said bitingly. "Now your conscience . . ."

"Please," he had interrupted wearily. "That is over with. You have come this far, and I am the only person here who is not a stranger to you. I will not ask your forgiveness. I believe that I was right in what I did; it was for your sake more than my own. Now that the decision has been taken from my hands, I wish to stand as your protector until such time as Diaz takes that responsibility from me through marriage."

"It is no longer so urgent that you return to Gormaz?"

"It is. But your protection is more urgent."

"Jaime . . . how can you expect me to believe that," she exclaimed, "after what you have—"

"I know," he interrupted emotionally, "I understand how difficult it will be for you to trust me again. I can only ask."

Jimena thought upon it, then offered him a thin smile. "I accept, because I am indeed alone here, uncomfortably so. I am frightened, Jaime. You drew a terrible picture of Rodrigo Diaz for me, you and Don Manuel—a picture that I find very difficult to live with. I accept—I accept." She waved a hand impatiently at him, then pressed the hand against her aching forehead.

"I must also tell you that I will never accept Rodrigo Diaz as my lord, never, Jimena. The same picture you carry in your mind, I carry in my own. Christ, if only I could erase from my mind the sight of your father's head against the toe of that man's boot, rolling to a stop at my feet, his poor, dead eyes staring up at me!" His voice broke and he whipped around, putting his back to her. "I would rather be dead, than vow my allegiance to Diaz!"

"Then take your allegiance elsewhere," she snapped, annoyed with him and bewildered. "Simply because Gormaz is included in my dowry, does not mean—"

Jaime whirled around angrily. "I am as much a part of Gormaz as the stones of the castle! When you turn the city over to him, you turn Don Jaime Martinez over to him. He will stand before us all and call out, 'Are you with me? Am I your lord?' All those who say 'aye' will bring a smile to his lips. Those who say 'no' will end as your father did, with their heads rolling in the dust. I am telling you that I will say no."

Jimena stared at him, uncomprehending. "But I cannot see why you could not take yourself to another nobleman and give him the love and loyalty you offered my father!"

"Oh, I could, Jimena, I could do that. If Diaz left my head on my shoulders long enough to accomplish the transfer of loyalties, which is doubtful, since I would have insulted him, dishonored him by refusing to accept him as my lord." He flashed the side of a hand across his throat and snapped, "Off with my head!"

"Oh, Jaime!"

"No . . . I do not mean to disturb you with this. I merely inform you, so that you will not be taken unaware when the day comes. You are doing what you feel you must do. I will do what *I* must. . . . Now, tell me, do you have the letter to the king safe?"

"Yes."

"Good. I will see to everything, then. Get an appointment with the king, see that you are given a servant or two. Will you be able to speak to the king, face him forcefully with your plea, do you think?"

Jimena threw up her hands. "I don't know. I can only try."

"I could set the plea before him in your place, while you stand aside. . . ."

She shook her head. "I must try, Jaime. But I *will* feel more at ease, truly, if you are there with me."

"Fine. Rest assured that if your tongue fails you, I will step in. I promise that I will not in any way jeopardize your position. Marriage to Rodrigo Diaz is what you want, so that is what you shall have."

Jimena flinched, trembling on the anteroom bench, as she recalled the way Jaime had shot those words at her. He had rushed out of the room before she could protest. Marriage to Rodrigo Diaz was *not* what she wanted, it was simply what she had to accept, like it or not. She glanced to where Jaime stood across the anteroom from her, leaning a shoulder against the wall and staring down at his boots. They had been waiting for hours, continuously ignored by the king's counsel.

A group of boisterous knights rushed into the hall, and she tremulously examined them, each one. Any one of them could have been Rodrigo Diaz. All were young, with powerful physiques. Not one noticed her where she sat anxious and inconspicuous on the bench.

"Don Jaime Martinez de Gormaz—the king will see you now."

Jimena's heart pounded so that it was thunder in her ears. Jaime quickly stepped to her, offering a hand. She stared helplessly up at him, unable to move.

"Come, Jimena," Jaime said down to her, "it is too late now for regrets and indecision. The fat is in the fire."

She smiled waveringly and pushed herself to her feet, refusing his offered hand. The room was blurred, everything indistinct, as if she walked in a dream. Her mind began to fill with words; she was confused as to exactly how to address the king and how to phrase her plea. Then a terrible vision of royal disdain appeared before her mind's eye, of His Highness contemptuously ordering her back to Gormaz because he had never heard of such nonsense, nor had he met another person who was as grossly unfeeling.

The counsel led them into the king's chamber, which was littered with the debris of daily conferences and nightly brawls, and rank with the combined stench of stale wine, dung, and spoiled food. Two enormous hounds sniffed about the garbage on the floor, one of them, with bored detachment, lifting his leg upon the chair in which the king sat.

King Don Ferrando, taking no notice of the hound's disrespect, sat with one leg crossed over the other, as he leaned to jab at one of his big toes, his small, red-rimmed eyes studying Jaime and Jimena from under heavy eyelids as they approached him. His face was red and blotchy. His thin gray hair fell in limp strands to his shoulders. The ravages of recent illnesses had collapsed his once powerful frame into a mockery of the relentless, unconquerable warrior he had once been. He allowed the two to stand before him and be ignored while he concentrated upon digging at a scabious wart that had infected his toe.

"*Buenas noches . . .*" the king said at last, without looking up. "I am a busy man. Come directly to the point of your visit."

Jaime looked at Jimena. She was staring at the king in disbelief. This mound of limp, wrinkled, flaccid flesh draped in soiled, disheveled attire could not be the king of Castile. She had seen stablemen who looked more royal. He had straightened himself and was now squinting at them, his breath coming in rattles and wheezes.

"May I present to you . . ." Jaime began uneasily, indicating Jimena with a flourish and a bow, "Doña Jimena Gomez, daughter . . ."

"I *know* who she is!" the king spat out. "For Christ, will you get to it. Say it, man—what is it you want of the king, eh?"

"Doña Jimena wishes to set a plea before you. . . ."

"Then let her state it, for Christ's sake!" His myopic eyes fixed upon Jimena, where she stood with her chin dipped so low it touched her collarbone. "Well, girl, have you no tongue?"

Jimena reacted by frantically raising her arms to begin pulling the pins from her hair. "Sir, uh, Your Highness, I . . ." Frustrated by a pin that refused to budge, she jerked hard, then yelped at the pain that resulted. At last her braids tumbled down, the bit of parchment fluttering to the floor behind her. Clumsily she whipped around and retrieved it. "This," she said shakily, holding the letter out to the king in a way that she might offer food to a hunger-crazed lion, "this is a letter from my father, addressed to yourself, my lord—I mean, Your Highness. Sir."

The king took the letter with a palsied hand, roughly unfolding it and breaking the seal. He held the letter so close to his eyes it almost touched his nose, to get a clear focus on the writing. Jimena stepped close to Jaime and slipped an arm through his, leaning against him for support.

"Aw, haw!" the king barked, throwing his head back in a boisterous laugh. "So it is true, then! I thought my daughter had completely lost her mind, or was playing another of her jests. Urracca is much inclined toward practical jokes." He turned his eyes upon Jaime, "—as I understand you well know, sir. Eh?" He exploded into laughter again. Abruptly he sobered, dipped his chin and glared at Jimena. "It is true? You can forgive Rodrigo Diaz with a good will and be a good and faithful wife to him?"

"I can," Jimena murmured. She cleared her throat hard, then said more strongly. "Yes, I would be a good and faithful wife to him, Your Highness."

Giggles overcame the king. "Thank *God* for something about this day that is amusing," he roared. "I find this letter *extremely* amusing, Doña Jimena." Choking on laughter, the king shouted for his chief counsel, who almost immediately rushed into the chamber. "I wish to send a communication. See that it is delivered to Ruy Diaz at Bivar by fast horse." He hesitated, biting at his lower lip and grinning at Jimena. "Say this—I herewith enjoin and command that you should come incontinently to Palencia, uh . . . for I have much to communicate to you upon affairs that are greatly to God's service and your own welfare—and great honor." He thought further upon it, then brushed the man off with, "What you have is sufficient to bring him at a fast clip. I want him here within three days!"

King Ferrando put both hands on the arms of his chair and pushed his body to a stand, grunting at pain that seemed to strike him at all his joints. "Well, then, that is settled. Now, let us take ourselves to table, eh? Rodrigo is a cherished member of our family, Doña Jimena. Since you are, already, as good as wife to him, you will be expected to join us, and will be welcomed."

Jimena jerked her head around to look at Jaime, but he was rigid and impassive beside her. Settled? She had said almost nothing! And Rodrigo Diaz had not been consulted. Bewildered, she allowed Jaime to lead her in a march behind the king, as the

old man walked bent and with difficulty toward one of the
chamber doors. The dogs ran playfully around their legs, sniffing at their feet, following them into the king's private dining
hall.

Male and female servants were rushing madly about, setting platters of food upon the long wooden table. Three young
men and a ravishingly beautiful woman who were seated at the
table rose from their chairs as the king entered.

"Sit yourselves where you can find a chair," the king said
over his shoulder to Jaime, then took his own place at the head
of the table.

The king offhandedly introduced Jimena to the small group
in general, "Doña Jimena Gomez—and her escort, Don Jaime
Martinez, whom you all know." Then, snappishly to a servant,
"Fill the goddamned tankard, man, *fill* it!" as he waved his
brass cup furiously in the servant's face. "Sancho! Have you
spoken yet to de Montrueil? I would enjoy being forewarned, if
possible, as to his full intentions regarding Barbastro."

The young man to the king's right kept his eyes on his
plate, which was being heaped high with roast kid by a servant
girl. "I have not spoken to him, Father, but his intentions
would appear obvious. He will demand an unrestrained attack,
giving no quarter to the Infidel."

"The bastard!" Ferrando yelped, then emptied his tankard
of wine. "He has the insolence, the effrontery, to come and
give me, the king of Castile, orders. I will do this—I will do
that. March on the Muslim, eh? Take his cities from him. Destroy them to the last woman and child. Gather up their gold.
For this, I, king of Castile, will receive the eternal gratitude of
God. Well, God be damned! That is what I say, God be
damned to *hell!*"

Jimena gasped and flinched, instinctively shooting her eyes
heavenward, expecting an instantaneous reaction from God. She
saw only a small flock of doves fluttering in the rafters. The
only punishment the king received for his blasphemy was to
have one of his dogs leap up and grab the meat off his plate.
The king swung an arm, catching the dog sharply across the
head and sent the beast sprawling and yelping. He retrieved the
stolen meat and began chewing on it, talking so fast and furiously as he ate that bits of food dropped from his chin or flew
about his face. He washed it all down with noisy gulps of wine.

Jimena found it impossible to eat, and she could not look at
the king. She tried not to hear what he was saying, fearful that
he would blaspheme God again at any second. She glanced to

her left, studying the woman in black who sat at the opposite head of the table from the king. Something about her was familiar, but she could not have seen her before; any woman that lovely would not be easy to forget. The woman was eating daintily, giving her full attention to her plate. Jimena envied her hair that, black and waving and softer than any hair she had ever seen, fell down her back to her waist. Her own hair had no color, really, neither yellow nor brown, but a shade somewhere in between. The woman's skin was unblemished and sun brightened. Jimena glanced down at her hands, noting their roughness and the faintly gray cast to the flesh. She reminded herself that pride was a sin, but could not suppress a sharp jab of regret that she had not been given the gift of physical beauty.

"Never!" King Ferrando shouted, slamming a fist against the table, "never has Castile paid tribute to any nation, to any pope! This—this puny bag of bones, de Montrueil, belches out protests about our system of tribute, then turns right around and tells us *we* must pay *tribute* to his pope—put the gold we collect from the Muslim into the hands of Alexander. I spit upon him! So long as the Muslim is willing to pay me so dearly, I will leave him in peace, even protect him against his enemies."

"No, Father," the lovely woman interrupted softly, "you will kiss de Montrueil's skirts, just like the rest of us."

The instant the woman spoke, Jimena recognized her. The grime removed by river water. Her hair no longer hidden by a cap. Dressed in properly female attire. Jimena thought that she could as well have not been present in the room, for all the recognition Doña Urracca was giving her.

"Indeed," the king shouted across the table. "Yes, Urracca, I will kiss his skirts—but only because it suits me to do so, suits my own purposes. You will watch your tongue with me, Daughter." He shook the meat bone he held at her in a warning gesture. "I need no comments from the women of my house, regarding matters of war or popes."

"Urracca means no disrespect, Father . . ." The words came from the tallest of the three young men.

The king's features softened, as he turned his eyes to the young man. He smiled and said, "Your mother, is she feeling better today?"

"Yes, Father. The fever has broken. Within the week she will rejoin us, I think."

"Ah, Alphonso, *bien*. You are a good son. You think me needlessly sharp with your sister, eh?"

"We are family here, Father, so I can see no embarrassment in receiving comments from my sister on *any* subject."

"I need no defense, Alphonso," Urracca snapped, "Wait to defend me, until I have committed an act that deserves it!" She turned her blazing eyes back to her father. "Puny de Montrueil may be," she stubbornly argued, "but his power is almost limitless. You will bring the armies of Europe upon Spain like a tidal wave, if you do not watch your tongue, ease your temper, and reduce your daily intake of wine. With your brain swimming in alchohol, you can hardly summon any cunning, or . . ."

"Damn you!" the king shrieked, lurching to his feet. "Why did God curse me with a daughter, when I—"

"It is not *your* curse, Father, that I am a woman. It is *mine!* I will tell you again, whether you want to hear it or not, step carefully with de Montrueil. Spain stands alone in Christendom in its refusal to pay tribute to the pope. Indefensible. Give the bastard whatever he wants, promise him anything, send him back to Rome so heavy-laden with loot that he will kiss *your* skirts when he departs. Good advise, so take it!"

With that the Infanta kicked her chair away from her and swept from the room, chin high. She brushed past Jimena on her way out without a sign of recognition.

"So help me God!" the king screamed after his daughter, "I shall disinherit you completely, remove the monasteries from your dominion, see you . . ." His words broke off as Doña Urracca slammed the door of the dining room closed behind her.

"Damned witch!" the Infante Sancho exclaimed.

The king whirled upon his son and shouted, "Watch your mouth! Urracca is my daughter and I will not have you insult her in my presence. In any case, if she is witch, then you, my son, are warlock. Determining which of you is the meanest has been a puzzle to me for almost thirty years! Your mother's seed had sweetened considerably, by the time your brother Alphonso, here, was conceived."

"And gone completely rancid, by the time it was *my* turn." The remark had come from the impish, chubby boy sitting to the king's left.

Don Ferrando turned his head and coldly eyed the boy. "Not rancid, Garcia, but completely putrid! You are not clever enough for meanness. The blood runs water in your veins, therefore you are without wisdom, or courage, or goodness. You are nothing! Worthless!"

Garcia laughed delightedly. "Thank you, Father. When I

am king—when Sancho is dead for all the enemies he has made by virtue of his meanness, and Alphonso is in his grave because of his goodness—I will remember your words, and find myself the cleverest people in Castile to advise me."

The king snorted and refused to reply. He fixed his gaze upon Don Jaime and said, "I do not like the news that comes out of Gormaz these days, sir. It has come to my attention that Don Nuño Garces de Estramadura has gained sufficient support in Gormaz to take the overlordship from you. And this displeases me greatly. Don Nuño cannot be trusted to abide by his oaths, to me or to God. I do not like it, Don Jaime!"

"Rumor," Jaime said matter-of-factly, "nothing more. The power is in delicate balance, I admit, but in no danger of slipping from my hands, my lord."

The king grinned at him. "Unless this young lady, who is to inherit the lot, marries a man strong enough and clever enough to—"

"Of course," Jaime interrupted, a hint of anger in his voice, "that was understood."

"Understood . . ." the king echoed sarcastically. "Rodrigo Diaz is very loyal to me. I could trust him with my life, and have, in fact, several times. Tell me where the knights of Gormaz are at this moment, will you, Don Jaime? Considering that the crusade against Barbastro is but weeks away, I wonder why Gormaz is not represented in the army?"

"Considering the unrest that prevails, my lord, we cannot spare our forces at this moment. But rest assured, we will join you in this crusade with full vigor. We but delay our departure as long as possible; you understand."

"Indeed, sir. I understand that Gomez failed to leave a son to carry on after him, one who was close to his equal; in truth, few men on this earth were his equal, or ever will be. I know of only one. One, eh? And as loyal to me as Gomez always was, God rest his soul."

Jimena felt eyes hot upon her and glanced across the table. She met the hard gaze of the king's son Sancho. His eyes were black, so dark the pupils did not show, and cold. He was studying her with severe curiosity and an icy kind of amusement. She guessed that he had been told the news by his sister and suspected he did not approve. But, then, who on this earth did approve?

"Doña Jimena," Sancho said politely, "you honor us by your visit. Is it one of mere pleasure, or do I detect from my father's words an importance in your presence here that is being left unspoken?"

Before Jimena could think how to reply, Don Garcia happily suggested, "She has come to ask our father for your hand in marriage, my brother. You heard our father. Gormaz needs an equal to Gomez—and who *else*? Eh? What you lack in physical stature, you make up for in meanness." He laughed heartily at his gibe, then sobered quickly when Sancho turned a murderous eye upon him.

"I brought a letter," Jimena said, pulling her quaking hands into her lap and clenching them tightly together, "addressed to the king . . . written by my father the night before he departed for Zamora. It was his wish that I deliver it personally."

Jaime reached over under the table and patted her hands, to speak of his approval. Her lips fluttered into a relieved smile that quickly collapsed.

"He had a premonition of death, did he?" Don Sancho asked, a frigid smile turned on Jimena.

"Yes, yes, I believe he did, sir."

Sancho laughed. "That happens to all but the most foolhardy who are faced with a challenge from Rodrigo Diaz. He is my ward, you know. I trained him personally. Took him directly after Count Gomez cut off his father's head in a duel. He was there and saw it—only twelve at the time. What a scrawny, lack-muscled wretch he was, with his head filled with dreams of revenge. Now—well, now he is a giant, in every sense of the word, and scares the hell out of men like Don Jaime, here—even men as noble as your departed father, God rest his soul."

Jimena stiffened in her chair. "My father was *not* afraid of Rodrigo Diaz," she snapped, indignantly holding Sancho's gaze. "He was in fear, yes, but of the death, not of the man! He spoke admiringly of Rodrigo Diaz, telling me that Diaz was forced to challenge him, in order to maintain his honor."

"How very admirable of him," Sancho smirked.

Don Jaime rose to his feet, placing a hand gently upon Jimena's shoulder. "Sire, Doña Jimena is a frail lady, as you can see, and quite exhausted by a long day. She begs your permission to retire."

The king waved an arm in Jaime's direction, impatiently. "Go! Leave. Take her to her quarters." Then he angrily turned his attention to Sancho. "That runt from Rome prances through the streets of my city at this very moment, the populace kissing his feet! Within the hour I will be expected to do the same. The devil take him! I shall plead an inability to bend myself, play crippled before him, rather than . . .''

Jimena heard no more of the king's ravings as the door of the dining hall closed behind her. "Thank you, Jaime," she exclaimed, "I doubt I could have survived another minute."

Jaime held her elbow firmly, leading her swiftly toward her chamber along the gloomy, often crowded corridors of Palencia Castle.

"It will not serve your purpose," Jaime said to her, as they approached her chamber door, "to alienate the Infante Sancho. As he told you, he is Diaz' guardian. They are also the closest of friends. If you are to win the willingness of Diaz, you must also win over Don Sancho."

"He was pompous and unpleasant," she argued, "and disrespectful of the dead. I dislike him intensely."

"Wait until you meet his ward and friend, my dear sister. You have yet to learn the extent to which pomposity and unpleasantness can be carried."

With that, Don Jaime gave Jimena a light kiss on the cheek and said goodnight. She stood in the open doorway of her chamber, watching him disappear down the corridor, fighting a compulsion to call him back, to plead with him not to leave her alone. A drunken group of knights and their ladies came yowling down the passageway, almost knocking Jaime over as they staggered and cavorted. Jimena stepped backward into her room and quickly closed the door and threw the latch. She leaned her forehead against the cold wood, hearing their shouts on the other side, wincing at the crudeness of their remarks to one another. Turning around, she put her back against the door, gazing sadly about the room that suddenly seemed like a prison cell. She had thrown the latch herself, no one had locked her in, still she could not shake off a sense of being caged. The king and his children went at each other like dogs at bones. She could not contend with hardened people like Doña Urracca and the Infante Sancho. "You are not worldly wise," Jaime had said to her on the plain. Dear God, no truer words had ever been spoken. How, if she could not contend with the king and his children, could she conceivably deal with Rodrigo Diaz? Three days. The king had commanded him to appear within three days.

That night Jimena once again dreamed about the priest and the brilliant light. The joys and satisfactions were again beyond reach, in colors of gold, red, and green and she ran toward them with even more desperation than before. She awoke with a sense of loss that was almost unbearable.

For the next five days Jimena refused to leave her chamber. She would not suffer the company of the king and his family again as long as it was in her power to avoid it. The hours of the days she spent pacing the room, or gazing out one of the windows. It was apparent to her that nothing had really changed. Another granite-walled room in another castle, the same stretching out of time, and a suffocatingly familiar boredom. Waiting again.

Rodrigo Diaz arrived at Palencia Castle two days after receiving the king's communication. He notified the chief counsel of his presence, then waited impatiently to be called into audience with Don Ferrando. To his extreme aggravation, the summons did not come for three days. Sancho had set off on a falconing expedition the day before his arrival. Urracca was peculiarly aloof, avoiding him as if he had suddenly grown a gigantic wart on the end of his nose. The king was too busy with de Montrueil and the plans for the crusade to sit with his family at table, so he had not even seen the king socially. Rodrigo's mind was so heavily upon those matters "greatly to God's service and your own welfare and great honor," that his normal appetite for drink, harlots and brawling lay dead in him. He was bored to distraction. His father avenged, he was now fully prepared for the future, and the king was the best means toward the end he envisioned. He would not merely survive— he would ascend to the crest; he would outwit, outfight, outflank, and outmaneuver, until he was undisputed champion, master over Castile. Rodrigo Diaz de Bivar, the conqueror, the greatest knight the world had ever seen. Inconceivable that he could end as his father had, with his head rolling in the dust. He would die in his sleep, or as the result of an illness, not by the hand of any man who thought himself powerful enough to steal from him even one moment of his precious existence.

After three days' wait, Rodrigo was summoned to meet with the king at ten of the clock. At noon he had not been called in yet and was sulkily pacing the anteroom, counting the times he trekked the length. When Don Jaime Martinez entered the hall with a wench on his arm, Rodrigo's muscles tensed and he came to a halt in the center of the room, legs set wide apart, a hand on the scabbard of the knife that hung from a chain belt around the waist of his tunic. He watched Gomez' son-in-law closely for any sign of attack. When the man refused to acknowledge his presence with so much as a glance or a nod, he laughed softly and continued his pacing. Don Jaime had bravely cursed him when the head of Gomez was at his feet and he was surrounded by ten knights of Gormaz, but here, man to man, he was not so courageous.

The chief counsel emerged from Ferrando's chamber and Rodrigo stopped dead at the far end of the hall, waiting for the man to call his name. "Damn," he swore, when the counsel ignored him and called in an Italian captain of de Montrueil's guard, who had entered the anteroom only minutes before. He stepped to the wall and threw his body backward, pushing his shoulders against the cold stone, his eyes casting upward into the rafters. He folded his arms across his massive chest and let out a sigh of annoyance. Dropping his gaze, he looked directly at Don Jaime, who stood beside a bench on which sat the young woman with her hands folded demurely in her lap. Don Jaime was staring at him, seeing him now and making no effort to conceal the fact. Rodrigo smiled broadly and offered the man a jaunty salute. Don Jaime ignored the gesture, turning his head to say something to the girl.

Rodrigo curiously examined the female, guessing her to be the youngest daughter of Gomez. Rumor had it that Don Jaime had been disinherited by Gomez in favor of the unmarried daughter, and that he was now involved in some kind of plot to see her wed to a man of sufficient power, in men and influence, to put down the unrest at Gormaz and settle the seat of over-lordship firmly into family control. He wondered which unmarried lord of Castile Don Jaime had in mind. Don Nuño de Estramadura was an unlikely prospect, since he was practically at war with Don Jaime over the city; if he expected to marry her he would not be making such a passionate effort to take Gormaz by force of influence. Don Nuño's power was strictly limited to influence and money—he avoided challengers at any cost to his honor and was therefore still alive at the age of thirty.

"Hoh! *Tigrito* . . . !"

Rodrigo was jolted out of thought as Sancho exploded into the anteroom, rushing toward him with open arms. They met in the center of the room and swung their arms around each other, affectionately pounding each other on the back with the flat of their hands. Sancho was followed by five of his comrades, who crowded around Rodrigo, all talking at once, asking how long he had been at Palencia, why he had come, and what the hell was he doing in here waiting upon the king? Each addressed him with Sancho's nickname for him, *Tigrito,* bestowed upon him at his first lesson with a sword, when he had dropped it onto his toes through lack of muscle and over-zealousness. When his new guardian laughed at him, he had grabbed up the sword, holding it with both hands, and attacked, thereby acquiring the title of "Little Tiger." It was a nickname no longer to his liking, and he meant to soon have done with it, earning a better title through deeds of valor; something like *"Compeador"* would suit him well.

"I have been in the city three and one half days," Rodrigo laughed, "and I have no idea why I am here. Hopefully I shall find out sometime before midnight. I have been kept waiting half a day already."

Don Sancho turned slightly and for the first time noticed Jimena Gomez sitting on the bench, her brother-in-law standing guard over her with a sullen expression on his face. Pointedly he said, "A bravo to you, Tigrito, on your latest victory in the field. Not a feather in your cap, but a *plume,* eh?"

Rodrigo grinned and said, "I wear it nicely, do I not?" He strutted around Sancho, running his fingers up and down an imaginary plume on top of an invisible helmet. "Not five minutes, I swear to you—it took no more time than that to . . ." His entire body snapped to rigid alertness, as from the corner of his eye he saw Don Jaime make a quick move. It took no more than a second for him to determine that the man had merely whipped around in anger. Martinez stalked away from the woman and put himself as far from Rodrigo and his cluster of friends as he could. He stood there glaring at Rodrigo, arms crossed over his chest, his features drawn into a tight mask that spoke of the effort it took to control his rage and hatred. "As I was saying," Rodrigo said, returning his attention to his friends, "I took him in less than five minutes."

The group cheered and applauded him. Laughing with them, Rodrigo glanced again to Don Jaime to make certain he had not changed location. Then he turned his head to inspect the woman. She was dressed entirely in black, of course, having attended her father's funeral less than two weeks past. She looked like a nun, sitting there with her hands folded in her lap, her chin dipped as if in prayer. Curious, he thought, how a man of the heroic proportions of Count Gomez could produce an offspring so delicate in stature, and how a man like his own father, shorter than the average man, could produce himself, an equal to Gomez.

Rodrigo turned around at a light touch against his arm from behind. The king's counsel stood there smiling up at him and said, almost in a whisper, "The king will see you now, Tigrito."

"Christ!" Sancho exclaimed, "Why do you sneak about like that, man, tiptoeing up behind us? No shout from the door? Something has gone wrong with your voice, has it?"

The counsel, still whispering, said respectfully to Sancho, "Your father did not wish me to call Tigrito's name, Infante, for reasons of his own . . ."

Rodrigo and Sancho looked at each other, making faces that expressed a mocking bewilderment and curiosity. Rodrigo shrugged and turned to stride across the hall. The skirt of his pelisse whipped about his ankles and was stretched almost to the limit by the briskness and length of his step; his felt shoes made no sound upon the floor. Sancho shouted "good luck" at Rodrigo just as the door was being closed behind him by the chief counsel.

Sancho arrogantly strode over to Jimena Gomez. "*Buenas tardes,* Doña Jimena," he said to her with exaggerated politeness.

Don Jaime rushed to put himself beside Jimena. Placing a hand firmly on her shoulder, he eyed Sancho coldy and warningly.

Sancho laughed and said, "You are most honorably protective of this lady, sir, but there is no need. I merely stepped over to wish her a good afternoon."

"And now that you have, you will be on your way, correct?"

"You are not only overly protective, Don Jaime, but excessively rude, as well."

"If I have offended you," Jaime replied icily, "you have my sincerest apology."

Sancho smirked at Jaime and said, "Will *you* lead your army at Barbastro, sir, or will you leave that honor to Gonzales, eh?"

It was a deliberate questioning of Jaime's courage, but he controlled his indignation and merely stared frigidly at Don Sancho, without giving him the satisfaction of a reply. Don Ferrando was not a well man. In a very short time this young man now goading him would be king of Castile. It was no more to his profit to alienate Sancho than to Jimena's.

"Thank you for your good wishes," Jimena said to Don Sancho, successfully managing a smile. If she remained close-mouthed, simply because she absolutely loathed the man, the two men would be at each other's throats. Don Sancho turned a radiant smile upon her, one that reminded her of Doña Urraca's smiles upon Don Manuel that night at the campsite. At the king's table she had not noticed the strong resemblance between them; the same coal black, waving hair and rather delicate bone structure. Don Sancho was not a tall man or broad in the chest, but there was no doubt in her mind that he was physically very strong.

"What did you think of my ward, eh?" Sancho said to Jimena, with intent to rub the wound of her father's death. "A giant among men, eh? As I said?"

Jimena stared up at him, frowning. "I have never seen your ward, sir," she said uneasily.

Sancho's mouth dropped open in amazement and disbelief. The woman was an idiot, if she could not pick Rodrigo out of that gaggle of nonentities. Rodrigo was so extraordinary in all ways, it was inconceivable that anyone could see him as just another young knight of the court. Her obvious sincerity threw him into confusion. "For Christ, woman, before he was called in to my father, he stood not ten steps from you! What do you mean, you have yet to lay eyes upon him?"

Jimena's head shot around and her eyes met Jaime's questioningly. He had not told her Rodrigo Diaz was in this room! Jaime looked apologetic and shrugged. Her heart was in her throat and her mind was racing over the past few minutes; she tried desperately to recall a man who stood out as strikingly as the Infante apparently thought Rodrigo Diaz did. She had been sitting here only half seeing, half hearing, completely involved in memorizing the words she would say to Rodrigo Diaz when they met. Terrified and deep in thought, how could she have noticed the man?

"You actually did not recognize him?" Sancho asked incredulously.

Jimena threw up her hands and murmured, "I am sorry. No, I did not, sir."

Sancho gaped at her a few seconds, swore under his breath, then turned and strode away from her, disgusted.

"Jaime!" Jimena cried, leaping to her feet to accusingly face him. "You should have told me—given me some warning."

He shrugged again and said, "I was curious to see if you *would* pick him out. It satisfies me considerably that you did not, which neatly put him into the category of 'ordinary.' "

"Which one?" she insisted.

"Did you see any one of them clearly . . . ?"

"No."

"Then how can I tell you which one, eh?"

She stamped a foot on the floor in frustration. Turning, she frantically searched the room, examining all the faces to see if she could call to mind a figure that was now gone from the room. "Why didn't I hear his name being called?" she exclaimed.

"The counsel brought the call to him in a whisper. I suspect the king hoped you would not know him or be told who he was, so he could play out a game with the two of you. Diaz walked in there with no idea as to what will befall him." He laughed bitterly. "Wait, and listen, Jimena. When you hear a roar, one that shakes the rafters over your head, then you will know he has been told he is to marry you."

"Holy Mary," she wailed, slapping her hands over her face in exasperation, "I have changed my mind. I think I will become a nun, after all!"

"Too late," Jaime muttered. "The king is overjoyed at the prospect of his foster son as lord over Gormaz—so much so I believe he would drag you from a monastery and throw you into Diaz' bed before you had time to say a single prayer."

Ferrando sat slumped in his chair, slyly watching Rodrigo as he approached him. He grinned at the boy when he came to a respectful halt before him. "I see no scars upon you, Tigrito. You handled yourself well against Gomez. I congratulate you. But, please, do not slay any more of my most valued knights."

Rodrigo beamed. "My father avenged, sire, leaves me your humble servant. Your enemies will be my enemies. I will slay only those knights who dishonor your name or your house."

"Of course," Ferrando responded, unconvinced. "Your good mother is well?"

"She is, sire, very well indeed."

"Bien. As I informed you in my communication, I have much to say to you. First, I ask that you make me a pledge, and it is this. Swear to me that you will fight for Sancho, die for him if need be, that you will, until the day he dies, remain loyal to him . . . and that you will counsel him well."

"Sire, Sancho is like a brother to me. I gladly make the pledge."

Rodrigo's mind soared, ais future outstretched before him. He saw himself as ensign to Sancho, next in line of power to the king of Castile. Coldly he eyed Ferrando, noting with satisfaction the scars left upon him by his last illness. The king would die before many more winters passed.

Ferrando's eyes had turned cold. He said roughly, "I will speak, now, of a matter that all will know about by tomorrow. I have drawn my will. It will never be altered. I have gone directly against all who advise me, making a decision both difficult and seemingly foolhardy—but it was the only one possible for me. I fought mercilessly to unite Leon, Galicia and Castile. Now," he hesitated, sighing heavily, "now I divide it once more into three kingdoms." At Rodrigo's stunned jerk to attention, Ferrando held up a hand impatiently. "Allow me to finish. Sancho is to receive only the state of Castile, the boundaries of which are to be the same as my father left to me. Alphonso succeeds to Leon. My son, Garcia, is to reign over Galicia. Now—did you have a comment, lad?"

"No, sire—except that it does seem foolhardy to divide that for which so much blood was spilled to unite."

"You too, eh? Like all the rest, thinking me a fool, that the blood of my sons will run red on the plains until one of them possesses it all. Well, could there be a better way to discover which of my sons is the fittest, which the stronger, the more clever? In my heart I believe Alphonso to be that man born to be king after me, but I cannot overlook the fact that Sancho, as the eldest, is rightful heir. I will not view the result, but you will, Rodrigo—you will see it. Guard Sancho well, according to your vow, for he is likely to be the first to strike out against his brothers, and well might be the first to die. He will be the angriest, the most resentful, naturally; the others never expected to rule. Watch over him . . ."

Rodrigo flushed. Damn the man to hell! He had tricked him into pledging himself to Sancho's cause against the two brothers. If Sancho was indeed the first to die, he, as his ensign, would end either dead or exiled. Impossible. Alphonso and Garcia would have to be destroyed. But there was the law that a man could not reign if he had slain his rival for the throne. There were endless methods of circumventing the laws. Blast Ferrando and his effeminate love for Alphonso. It was this ignoble passion that had designed the will—a father nursing a mother's love for a son. The old fool! Alphonso would never be king of a reunited Castile; never.

". . . Now for . . ."

"Uh? Ah, forgive me, sire—I was not listening."

"I have said nothing for you to listen to. You are that disturbed by my announcement, hmmm?"

"Oh, no, I was only thinking how Sancho will receive the news."

Ferrando threw his head back and roared with laughter. "Oh, he will be enraged; rest assured." The king shifted in his chair, sobering. "Enough of my death, and to a matter I am certain will be more to your liking. You, Rodrigo, will be second in command of the Castilian forces at Barbastro. Ah ha, I see I have pleased you this time."

"Indeed," Rodrigo exclaimed breathlessly. He swallowed hard against a surge of elation. "I am a knight of almost no following, nor do I possess a title, so I never expected to receive such a command! But—I cannot help wondering if the lords will accept my—"

"Do not worry on *that* count," the king interrupted, a secretive smile spreading over his face. "It is amazing how our fortunes can alter, sometimes overnight."

Rodrigo frowned, bewildered by the seemingly irrelevant remark. "Am I correct in supposing this is a crusade to impress His Holiness, de Montrueil, sire?"

"Impress him, hell! I pretend obedience, to guarantee that his five hundred knights and the Germans and the French aid me in the battle. I need them to take such a stronghold. Here is what I would have you and Sancho do. Follow de Montrueil to Barbastro with all humility and obedience; fight beside him. But when the city is taken, repair immediately with our Castilian forces to the castle of the Muslim king of Barbastro. Set a guard around that palace and hold this Muslim prince in my name. When de Montrueil objects, you say to him thus, 'Go to hell!' Let him boil and scream at his loss, but pay no mind. What can he say, eh? Our Holy mission is to crush the Infidel. He will be crushed. How, then, can he complain, lest he tell the world it is gold, after all, that he hungers for, rather than extinction of the unbelievers?"

"I do not understand what we have to gain, sire, by taking the Muslim prince hostage.

"Ransom, Rodrigo—ransom! Maktadir of Zaragossa is the richest Muslim prince of the north, and he is brother to the king of Barbastro. Now what vast price might he be willing to pay, hmmm, for his brother's life?"

Rodrigo made no reply, merely grinning his appreciation of Ferrando's wit. His earlier disappointment temporarily forgotten, he let his mind slide over all the possibilities and excitements this adventure would bring with it. He was not sufficiently honored to be qualified for such a command, but if Ferrando wished to give it to him, he was not going to refuse it. Sancho and himself in full command of the Castilian troops after the initial attack! It had begun—his glorious future was so close now he could taste the sweetness of it upon his tongue.

"Ach, damn me! I almost forgot." Ferrando's lips twisted into a wicked smile.

"And what is that, sire?" Rodrigo asked, uncomfortable before the old man's leering scrutiny.

"I want to discuss the matter of a marriage for you, Tigrito."

"Marriage! *Me*, sire? You cannot be serious. I am only nineteen and had not planned to wed for quite some time."

Ferrando laughed, nodding his head agreeably. "Someone of noble birth, I should think. A woman of higher lineage than yourself would be advantageous. Certainly not a peasant wench like the one your maternal grandfather took as wife . . ."

Rodrigo stiffened at the jab at his ancestry. "But I must *earn* the right to marry such a lady, which will take some years, sire."

"Not necessarily. True, you possess no following to speak of, nor title, but a woman whose dowry offers a walled city and more monies than you could steal from the Muslim in a lifetime . . . well, that would alter the condition of your material worth considerably, and broaden your influence profoundly. Would it not?"

"Certainly. But . . ."

"You cannot expect that she be beautiful as well as rich in money and blood. You would not object if she was not fair, would you, lad?"

Rodrigo had tired of the game and refused to reply, glaring at Ferrando, waiting for him to get to the point.

Ferrando threw up his hands and laughed heartily. "Allow your king his little jest, Tigrito. To it, then. The fact is, I have found just such a wife for you. She is not a hag. A bit scrawny, but not a hag . . ."

"Damn!" Rodrigo swore. "Sire! I will find a wife for myself, when the time is right, when I am worthy of such a woman. I am your vassal, but you do not own me. You will not choose a wife for me as if I am your slave!"

Ferrando doubled over. Holding his paunch in his arms he rolled back and forth in his chair, tears of laughter running down his cheeks. "Come, Rodrigo," he giggled, "marriage is not as tragic as all that. You become angrier with me by the minute, but I have yet to mention her name. Oh, wait—wait until you hear her name!"

Rodrigo sucked in a breath and held it. In another instant

he would smash in the man's ugly face with a fist. Shaking with fury he turned heel and sped to the door, meaning to leave the king alone with his amusement.

"Ho there!" The laughter was gone. The tone of the king's voice was deadly serious. Rodrigo halted abruptly, one hand resting upon the door latch, his back remaining to the king.

"I am serious in this, my hotheaded young friend. You will marry this lady before you depart for Barbastro. Is that quite clear?"

"Yes indeed, sire," Rodrigo snarled. He waited, immobile. When the king said no more, he said, "May I leave now?"

"For Christ's sake, lad! Come back here and sit down."

"I do *not* intend to marry at this stage of my life," Rodrigo said between clenched teeth, stubbornly refusing to move.

"And I intend otherwise! If you would be something more than a foot soldier at Barbastro, I would strongly suggest that you turn yourself around and do as you are told!"

Rodrigo whipped about-face, scowling ferociously at the king, then marched forward and threw himself into a chair across from Ferrando. "You should have told me there were conditions to my being named second in command!"

Exasperated, Ferrando shouted for his chief counsel. When the man stuck his head in the door, he said, "Bring her in, Don Ramon, bring the wench in, for god's sake!"

The two sat glum and silent across from one another. Rodrigo had his back to the door. When he heard the chief counsel enter and felt the presence of the man and the wench behind him, he refused to turn and look at them. He heard the counsel return to the door, open it, and depart.

Jimena stood behind Rodrigo's chair, facing the king. She did not dare so much as glance at the youth slumped in the chair an arm's length from her. Jaime had refused to come in with her, saying when it came to her introduction to Diaz there was no place for him. Dear God, she thought, I am going to faint for certain. But with concentrated effort she held herself on her two feet.

"*Buenas tardes,* señorita," the king said politely. His eyes danced from one to the other; he was enjoying himself again. "Rodrigo, get to your feet, turn yourself, and greet the lady." When Rodrigo sourly slumped deeper in his chair, Ferrando said in his most royal manner, "Rodrigo Diaz de Bivar—I introduce you to Doña Jimena Gomez de Gormaz."

"*Gomez!*"

It was precisely the kind of roar Jaime had suggested would

emerge from his throat. Diaz was out of his chair in a second and facing her, his hands clenching into fists at his sides. Jimena lurched backward several steps, terrified. She had never seen such rage in a man in all her life.

Rodrigo's breath was coming in gasps. He was so shocked and enraged that the woman was blurred before his eyes; all he saw clearly was the blackness of her mourning attire. All the while he had paced that anteroom, she and Don Jaime had been watching him slyly, fully aware of the plan. "What kind of joke *is* this?" he yowled. "I apologize to you both, but I am totally unable to see the humor. I find you not in the least amusing, sire. And you! How dare you presume to play such a game with me? How dare you!"

Jimena held herself steady by force of will, refusing to give the man the satisfaction of seeing the fear in her. She managed a rigidly erect stance. With false bravado, she met his blazing eyes, putting as much heat as she could into her own. She said, in a hoarse whisper, "My father commanded this of me. It was no choice of mine, sir."

Ferrando was delighted. "*Bravo,* señorita!" he exclaimed. "*That* should put him in his place."

"You would have me believe," Rodrigo shouted at her, "that Count Gomez would command his daughter to seek the hand of his slayer!"

Ferrando broke in with, "I have a letter from Gomez that attests to the fact, Tigrito."

Rodrigo's head snapped around, and he turned a murderous eye upon the king. "Do you actually think that I will accept— accept this . . . this absurdity?"

"No! I do not *think* so—I *know* so! It is my command. When you marry Doña Jimena, you marry the city of Gormaz and the stature that comes with the overlordship of such a stronghold. I want you at Gormaz, need you there. I have accepted Doña Jimena's proposal for you, on the assumption that I am the last man on this earth you would want to vex."

Rodrigo threw up his arms in aggravation. He said to Jimena, "I am also to believe, I suppose, that you seek no revenge for your father's death, hmmm?"

"None," Jimena replied quickly, feeling more composed, her voice now reasonably steady. "There is nothing to forgive. My father killed your father, so you were forced to kill mine. Finding me still unmarried when he received your challenge, he disposed of me as best he could in the short time allowed him. If you refuse me, I do not know where or to whom I will turn.

If you accept me, then I will be wife to you in all ways subject to your will as my lord." She had said it all, exactly as she had memorized it, and she felt a brief surge of pride and renewed confidence.

Rodrigo gaped at her in disbelief, then shook his head hard. He whirled about and began to pace the chamber.

Jimena studied him as he marched like a trapped beast back and forth before her. He was quite handsome, in a rough-carved way. His features seemed to be chiseled from granite, merely blocked in and uneven. His short-clipped beard was incongruous in its fine texture, but it would match his features in a year or so, when it would be as coarse and rugged as the rest of him. His hair and beard were so light in color as to be considered white; his eyes were an ice blue.

"Christ!" Rodrigo yelped, coming to a halt before the king. "What can I say other than so be it. I accept. No, I certainly would not vex my king. And what man would refuse a dowry as rich as Gomez decided to bestow upon me?" He turned to Jimena. "But tread cautiously with me, my lady, tread very softly with me . . . I warn you. You might be honest, but you could as well be an opportunist with a cold, unfeeling heart for your departed father. Perhaps his letter is a forgery. Or you might be a pawn of some unknown enemy. I do not *trust* you!" He stepped angrily to her and roughly lifted her chin with a forefinger. "I say it firmly. Give me reason to believe you are less than honorable in this proposal, and your fate will be the same as your father's."

Standing that close to him, his touch upon her face, Jimena fully realized the proportions of the man. The Infante Sancho had been right, he was a giant, almost two heads taller than herself, and so massively muscled as to make her feel like a fawn being overwhelmed by a lion. She heard her father's voice saying again, "You will not regret this decision, I promise you." Dear God, regret was not a strong enough word for what she felt at this moment. If Doña Urracca had not come along when she did, she would, at this moment, be at peace in the monastery at Coimbra.

"The ceremony will of necessity have to be soon," Jimena heard the king say, "and I suggest it be private, considering the somewhat bizarre relationship between the two of you. But we will have a proper celebration, that I promise you . . . a great feast in honor of the event." Then he said something about their having little time together, since the march to Barbastro would follow the ceremony within a week or two. Her head was swimming. She had to escape before she collapsed and humiliated herself before these men.

Jimena begged the king's permission to leave, not knowing exactly what she was saying, uncertain if she was putting the words together in coherent sentences. Somehow she managed to move to the door. She escaped into the anteroom. Jaime was quickly beside her and enclosed her in his arms. The next thing she knew, she was awakening on her bed, not sure whether she had fainted or had simply fallen asleep. An elderly servant woman was moving about the room straightening things, and Jaime stood at a window, gazing forlornly out over the city of Palencia.

Chapter
✠ *FOUR* ✠

Palencia Castle was a bedlam of activity. Servants rushed madly about, responding to a hundred separate orders and counterorders, dragging weary feet, tempers near to exploding. But when the one hundred guests descended upon them, they were fully prepared. A sixty-foot banquet table was ponderously spread. Wooden platters were heaped with steaming mutton slices. Whole roasted goats, placed back in their skins after cooking, lay sagging upon beds of boiled rice. Barrels of wine and sacks of bread—everything was waiting as if no effort whatsoever had been expended.

Late into the evening the sounds of jubilant celebration echoed along the corridors and floated out of the castle windows to be carried on soft winds to the city streets. William de Montrueil, with his favored Italian knights, German and French commanders, and all those most-trusted noblemen that were vassal to King Ferrando, were gathered in feasting to wish the just married couple long life and good fortune. So short a time had passed between the announcement of their betrothal and the execution of the ceremony, that gossip had not had a chance to brew; the Castilians present were still in a state of surprise and confusion. The foreigners, pleased at having an excuse for revelry, were enjoying a meal at table after so many weeks of encampment. The sisters of Jimena Gomez had been invited, but had refused to make an appearance. The mother of Rodrigo Diaz was given an honored seat to the right of the queen of Castile, who had been well enough to attend. Doña Urracca put in an appearance early but slipped away within an hour, a satisfied smile on her lips. Don Manuel had been right, she was indeed a loving friend to Rodrigo Diaz and had been most pleased to see him receive this reward. Don Jaime Martinez had stood beside Jimena during the private ceremony. Afterward he kissed her, wished her well, and immediately departed for Gormaz. His responsibility to her was finished.

Jimena sat at the banquet table beside Rodrigo, her head bowed in seeming modesty. The noise pressed against her ears with unbearable persistence, causing a throbbing ache across her forehead. She pushed her damp plams against her temples as if the effort could squeeze out the pain and tension she suffered. Suddenly, above the thunderous boom of voices and clatter, there was a piercing scream. Jimena whipped her head around in the direction of the cry. A girl, not more than a child, leaped up onto the table and raced down its length in Jimena's direction, a hee-hawing, very drunk young knight in close pursuit. The girl was completely naked. Dishes and food splattered in every direction under her feet. The knight carried the tattered remains of her clothing in a wine- and food-stained hand. They had reached a spot directly in front of Jimena when the lad's grappling hands found their prey. He whirled the child around to face him, his open mouth seeking and finding hers. Without taking his mouth from that kiss, he lifted her in his arms and vaulted down from the table, nearly knocking Jimena from her seat. Almost immediately they were lost in the crowd and Jimena was left to contend with a flagon of wine that had spilled into her lap.

"Ho—" Rodrigo shouted after them, "do not leave. Let us watch!" Then, grinning, he turned back to Don Sancho, who sat to his left, and became deeply engrossed in conversation.

Jimena mopped at the spilled wine with the hem of her pelisse, feeling its coldness against her flesh. Her tunic clung stickily to her pelisse and it to her chemise, and the more she rubbed at the wetness, the worse. That poor, poor girl, she thought, treated with such disrespect and Godless lust. Abruptly her heart flopped over, and she felt the hair at the back of her neck crawl. Holy Mary, that was what this night held for herself. If not *this* night, certainly one in the very near future. In spite of her efforts to control tears, they came, running down her cheeks and dropping upon her bosom. She uttered not a sound, praying no one would notice, particularly her new husband.

"Good Christ, de Montrueil, we cannot slaughter them all, all of them! They are not locusts but men—and they fight back!" King Ferrando leaned upon the table on one very unsteady elbow, his usually red face like fire now, his facial muscles loose and uncontrolled from wine. He shoved a grimy finger inside his cheek, gouged out a hunk of mutton caught there and spat it out in a great spray of saliva.

William de Montrueil's expression was one of studied distaste. He gulped at his wine, then passed a palsied hand over his shining bald head, a nervous habit that made him appear to be constantly petting himself. "Ah, but the Indifel *can* be destroyed, Don Ferrando. You have simply never attempted it. Do you keep their cities once you have besieged them, won them? No. You withdraw, leaving them to their sinful orgies. You place gold before your God, Ferrando."

Ferrando giggled. "I place gold before anything, sir, except perhaps the neat backside of a wench. How about wenches, de Montrueil, eh? Do you, for God, forsake that most suh—succulent of pleasures on this earth? Eh?"

"Father—" Don Sancho said warningly to the king.

Ferrando's head wobbled in the approximate direction of his son's voice. "What's the matter, eh, Sancho? You do not like the way your father speaks to the pope's right hand?"

Sancho glanced apprehensively to Rodrigo, then turned to answer his father in murmuring tones, "I think only that you will regret in the morning what you say while drunk tonight."

"You cannot conceal your sins from God, Ferrando," de Montrueil shouted. "Your son warns you to keep secrets from me. That you may do, perhaps, but there are no secrets from the Almighty, no secrets from Him!"

Ferrando shook his head in exaggerated disgust, mumbling under his breath, "sanctimonious bastard." Then he pounded his fists on the table and raised his voice to a bellow. "What would you have of me, pope's standard bearer? Ah! I recall. Slay them all. Send my own people to dwell in their cities. Jesus! The cities of Castile are poor. Poor! From the Muslims I receive gold, barrels—wagons full—of gold! And from the Castilian cities, what? Practically nothing." Ferrando waved his arms excitedly, one of them striking a flagon of wine, sending it slamming over. A red wetness washed across the table, spilling over the edges and into retreating laps. Once again Jimena found herself sopping up wine from her tunic, but barely noticing what she was doing now, her eyes fixed upon the king in revolted fascination.

"You!" Ferrando yowled, lurching to his feet and clutching at the table edge for support, "the pack of you! You think me the fool—admit it." Tears came to his eyes. "But I love him, my Alphonso. First born or not, he should be a *king*. Take this bastard, here . . ." he waved a flopping hand in front of Sancho's reddening face. "Ah, forgive me, I withdraw that remark, humbly, not a bastard, but take him regardless. Mean. Weak. God-be-damned and to hell with the *lot* of you! Wretches. It is my kingdom and I have a *right* to divide it—a right!" His words ebbed, and he fell limp upon the table, his mouth open and drooling.

Jimena's face flushed and her eyes pulled away from that ugly, red mass that was a man's face. She glanced to de Montrueil, whose eyes gleamed with an agony of self-restraint. The poor soul, she thought, forced to tolerate such men as King Ferrando on his missions for God. She was overwhelmed with pity for the pope's standard bearer.

Don Ferrando was carried from the hall like a limp sack of flour by four staggering knights. The festivities were over for him, but continued throughout the night for all the rest.

Jimena sighed and stretched out her aching legs, pushing her tired shoulders back. She wiggled her bottom from side to side, feeling a tingling numbness; she had been sitting on it so long it had gone to sleep. She smiled wanly, glad to find something amusing about this day.

"Hey, Rodrigo," a drunk young knight shouted, "a kiss for the bride, eh? A neat wench she is, man."

Jimena's eyes widened. Her head whipped around, but before her eyes could focus on the knight who was talking she was lifted bodily from her chair and thrown up high over Rodrigo's head, then plopped down with her feet upon the tabletop. Stunned, she felt the eyes of an hundred people on her, as she stared in shock down into her husband's laughing face. He was drunk. His white hair was damp and fell in oily strings about his face. He laughed only with his mouth, his eyes frigid. "Oh!" she gasped, lurching away from the hot hand that slipped under her skirt, pressing against her thigh.

"I want to view the merchandise, wife," he smirked up at her. "Come, Jimena, show me your legs—that's a good girl."

"No, please," she hissed, pushing his hand away clumsily.

Rodrigo shrugged, then leaped up beside her, his hands forming a tight belt around her waist. "Then—if I cannot view what is at the bottom, I shall see what is at the *top*!" A resounding roar of approval from the crowd encouraged him. He made a quick move with a hand, pulling out the bodice of her tunic to take a fast look inside. He gasped exaggeratedly and whirled away from her to face his audience. Pushing his fists against his hips, his legs set wide apart, he stood there openmouthed in pretended dismay. The crowd waited eagerly for his report. He threw his arms in the air and shouted indignantly, "Flat! Jesus

Christ, I have been cheated! 'Tis not a wench at all, but a *boy!*"

The audience collapsed into hysterical laughter, then applause. Jimena struggled helplessly to free herself from his grasp; his hand now held on to one of her wrists so tightly she was certian the bone would snap at any moment. A sea of leering faces was below her. She exploded into tears, fighting to turn her face away to hide her shame, but she was surrounded.

"For Christ—" Rodrigo spat out, "I cannot abide a weeping woman." He gave her arm a wrenching twist and a push that sent her stumbling away from him. "Get out of my sight! Out, I say—damn you."

Shaking so that her legs barely held her, Jimena fumbled to get down, but a dense wall of insolent faces and bodies blocked her way. Then someone was pushing his way to her, holding up a hand for her to take for support. It was the Infante Alphonso, his violet eyes moist with pity for her. He roughly shoved an opening for her in the mob. With his help, she jumped down from the table and lunged forward, her head down, losing Don Alphonso in the crowd. She shoved and pressed through the vomiting, lovemaking, drunken mass of humanity, sobbing all the while, blinded by tears. "Mmm . . ." someone mumbled hot into her ear, "fresh ripe fruit, and never been plucked." Her bottom was pinched and slapped. A rough hand clutched at her, moving and relentless. "Diaz!" the man yowled across the room, "your eyesight fails you. 'Tis not flat. Use your hand next time and not those weak eyes!"

"Keep those vile hands of yours off my woman, worthless bastard, or I shall leave you only two bloody stubs!"

Jimena flinched at the sound of Rodrigo's voice behind her. He was not angry, but amused. Stumbling and catching herself up, she made a headlong dash for a door. A blast of fresh, cold air struck her and she gulped in great breaths until her lungs hurt from the effort. Staggering to the low railing, she leaned weakly upon it with her elbows and was violently sick.

Drained, Jimena lifted her head to look around her. She was confused, having stepped out upon an unfamiliar balcony that overlooked a barbican tower; a faint light flickered at one of the tower windows. Leaning over the railing, she saw that a narrow flight of stone steps led down from the balcony to a side entrance of the castle. She breathed a sigh of relief; she would not have to return to the bedlam, to find her way back to her chambers. She looked up to the sky. It was close to dawn; the sun was already rising over the walls and towers of the city. The clouds glowed with all the shades from pink to deep red and here and there a splash of yellow completed the dramatic effect. No need to hurry to her chamber, she thought. The priest had explained to her that wedding celebrations at this palace often lasted two or three days, and that her husband would not come to her until he felt so inclined, be it one hour after the ceremony, or one year. She would be informed as to when she was expected to await him in her chamber.

"Holy Mary Mother of God," she whispered to the brightening sky, "what have I come to?"

If there had been somewhere to run to, Jimena would have bolted then and there, running until she dropped face down and exhausted on some unknown island of safety. To her, the world was narrow and unvaried. Gormaz and this capital city of Palencia were different only in size, and across all the miles in between she had seen nothing to indicate that millions of human beings sharing this earth and time with her lived vastly different lives, in an environment so dissimilar that no mere telling of it would have sufficed. She would have had to see, to touch and taste this other world, to consider it real, to fully believe in its existence. Jimena could not know that this remarkable "somewhere" was almost within range of her vision from this balcony, because it was hidden from her by a curtain of ignorance. She could have walked at an easy pace and entered it within twenty-four hours. She had resigned herself to the will of her father, agreeing to that which she need not have accepted, and thus became the victim of her own meager expectations. She believed that there was no alternative for her but to bear this iniquity, this marriage to Rodrigo Diaz, to endure it this day and forever after. The light, in shades of gold, red and green, continued to hover beyond her reach, visible to her only in her dreams.

Rodrigo Diaz quickly became the butt of endless jokes and the subject of gossip and rumor following his marriage to the daughter of Count Gomez. It was said that there had, obviously, been more than revenge in his challenge of Count Gomez—he had had the man's title in mind, half his wealth and all his power. Speculations as to exactly *how* Diaz had managed to kill the count and marry the daughter went to the wildest extremes, including a persistent rumor that Gomez had actually made a bargain with Rodrigo beforehand, that his death was a suicide. Never before had the count allowed his sword to be thrown from his hand like that. Straight from the mouth of the Infanta Urracca's carriage driver had come the story of Don Jaime Martinez' attempt to thwart the plot between Diaz and Gomez, by spiriting Doña Jimena off to the monastery at Coimbra. Others insisted it was a plot between Gomez and the daughter, to give muscle to the overlordship of Gormaz and to catch for the uncomely wench a young, handsome and promising husband; the count had been weakened by consumption and fully aware that he did not have the strength to subdue Diaz. There was a large group of gossipers, mostly women, who saw Jimena Gomez as entirely heartless; she had forged a letter to the king, shamelessly plotting to marry the man every young noble woman in Castile would have given her soul to call husband. Doña Jimena was not at all concerned that her father was dead and that her husband had killed him. She had sat there at the wedding feast, looking for all the world as innocent as a babe, while inside she was gloating triumphantly.

Rodrigo's honor and his pride were sorely wounded. He was not the kind of man who had to marry into wealth and power, he could well earn it for himself, which had been his intention, until Ferrando stole his pride with a command. He suffered the situation several days, then proclaimed before the king and his counsel, and before God, that he would not consummate his marriage to Jimena Gomez until he had won five battles in the field, thereby earning the right to be named lord over Gormaz and husband to Gomez' daughter. His vow satisfied some, but not others. Those who hated and feared him said he had devised a poor excuse indeed for avoiding his wife's bed—he certainly had not given up beds altogether; ask any harlot under the castle roof. Don Jaime Martinez, at Gormaz, received the news with enormous relief. Jimena would not be forced to suffer the man, and he would not be interfered with in the settling of affairs at Gormaz. Don Jaime received an official communication from Ruy Diaz, stating that Diaz did not intend taking the overlordship of Gormaz until such time as his vow was fulfilled—meanwhile, Don Jaime was to consider himself lord of Gormaz with full authority. When Rodrigo felt himself worthy, he would communicate with Don Jaime and they would discuss and settle the matter between them. Don Nuño Garces de Estramadura also received a communiqué, but from Don Ferrando, informing him that to contend with Don Jaime Martinez for the overlordship of Gormaz was to contend with Rodrigo Diaz de Bivar, and no substitute would be accepted in his place if he were challenged by Diaz; he would meet Diaz man to man on the field. Don Nuño immediately withdrew from Gormaz and returned to Estramadura to ready his forces that were to join in the crusade against Barbastro.

The army would begin the march to Barbastro in three days. Rodrigo was encamped five miles from Palencia, falconing with the Infante Sancho. A messenger rode into camp with a summons from Don Ferrando, who wished to speak with Rodrigo immediately.

"Can it be that I am to have another rich wife chosen for me?" Rodrigo sarcastically said to Sancho, as he dropped the message to his feet and set his heel grinding it to dust. "I have yet to *earn* the one already vowed to me!"

Sancho laughed and said, "I think that highly unlikely, Tigrito. You are far too sensitive about all this, my friend. Pride cometh before a fall, eh? Take the woman, the dowry, and enjoy them. What the hell do you care what people are saying or thinking?"

"For God's sake, Sancho," Rodrigo exclaimed, "honor exists only in the minds of others. What honor can there be for me that is *not* a matter of what people are saying and thinking?"

Sancho shrugged. "Honor is not the only profit in this life. I consider power a far more important asset—and money."

"That is because you are a king's son and heir to the throne! You can afford to place honor last, but I cannot."

"Heir to one *third* of a throne," Sancho argued, all humor vanishing from his eyes.

"Yes, but we will correct that situation quickly enough, when the time is right."

Sancho cast his eyes down to his boots, then kicked at the earth to send up a small cloud of dust. "Easy to say, Rodrigo. I wonder just how easy it will be when it is you and me against Garcia and Alphonso. We cannot overlook Urracca. With the power the monasteries afford her, and her unqualified preference for Alphonso . . ." He twisted his mouth into an expression of concern and frustration, leaving the thought unfinished.

Rodrigo grinned, then leaned and slapped Sancho on the back. "But the three of them do not equal one Rodrigo Diaz, eh? You have not only my muscle, Brother, you also have my brain. We will subdue them easily, I promise you."

Sancho slapped Rodrigo on the buttocks. "Get away from me, you conceited wretch. Take yourself to my father, before his guard descends upon you and drags you to him."

Rodrigo gave his guardian a smart salute, turned heel, broke into a run and with a powerful leap landed neatly into the saddle of his palfrey. He yanked on the reins, dug in his heels, and raced to Palencia, spurring his mount all the way.

On this occasion he was not forced to wait upon the king's favor, but was quickly ushered into Don Ferrando's chamber. The king was in a somber mood, with not so much as a hint of humor or cantankerousness in his swollen, watery eyes.

Don Ferrando leaned back deeply into his chair, studying Rodrigo. At last he sighed and said in a rasping voice, "Would that just *one* of my sons was such a man as you are, Tigrito. I love you well. You have pleased me in your obedience to my command that you marry the Gomez woman."

Rodrigo's mouth dropped open in amazement and no little satisfaction. "I thank you, sire, and sit before you most eager to accept whatever further commands you would place upon me."

"Ah," Ferrando sighed, nodding his head to indicate his approval. He sat with his eyes closed for a long moment, then said softly, "It is not a command, Tigrito, but a request. Before you depart for Barbastro, I would have you go to Jimena Gomez and husband her, according to your vow before the priest and the eyes of God." At Rodrigo's instantaneous bristling, he raised a hand. "Wait—please, lad—hear me out. Your failure to consummate this marriage is the cause of great humilation to the girl. I have this from Urracca, who is, apparently, quite taken with the girl. Your wife is the subject of whispers, vicious gossip, and mockery. As the daughter of Count Gomez, she deserves much better of you. If not for her sake, then in respect for her father, who was a beloved and loyal friend to me for thirty years."

If it had been put to him any other way, Rodrigo would have vehemently resisted. But the king's tone had been gentle, almost pleading. "Sire," he began carefully, "you understand the situation I am in. I am as much a subject of ridicule as she."

"Yes, yes, of course I understand. I would not have had Leon and Galicia given to me, when I was your age—no, I fought for them, and I won them. I understand, I assure you, but I ask you to forsake that half of your vow that excludes Jimena Gomez from your bed. Only half your vow, Rodrigo. And I *ask,* I do not order you to do this."

Rodrigo squirmed in his chair. That it was asked of him made the decision very difficult. To outright refuse would be an insult to Ferrando, a slight he might never live down. To obey would jeopardize his honor.

"Rodrigo," the king said, pushing his weary body forward so that he could lay a hand upon the lad's knee, "she will be left behind when you depart for Barbastro and will dwell in this castle for perhaps a year, facing the disrespect of every person in this house. Your honor will be glorified superbly at Barbastro, while hers darkens by the day. You see?"

"My bedding her will not stop all gossip and vicious talk, sire."

"No—but it will call a halt to speculation that she is unpleasing to you, that you have no interest in her other than her dowry."

Rodrigo sighed. He said with difficulty. "You speak truly, sire. Gomez was indeed valorous, loyal, and much worthy of the respect of all men, including myself. I will not further sully his name by dishonoring his daughter; you have my word on it."

The king fell back in his chair. "I am very pleased. Very pleased, Rodrigo." Frowning as if in great pain, he let his head fall to rest against the high back of his chair. "*Vaya con Dios,*" he whispered. "I have discharged my soul, before God, and with my signature upon the will. As my tasks end, Castile awaits the deeds of Rodrigo Diaz de Bivar, to further glorify its name. Farewell, Tigrito."

Stunned by the king's outspoken compliments, Rodrigo sat speechless, awaiting anything further his king might have to say. But Don Ferrando remained silent, head back, eyes closed, breathing deeply as if in sleep. Rodrigo eased himself out of his chair and quietly walked away, softly closing the door of the king's chamber behind him.

When Jimena heard the news of Rodrigo's vow not to consummate the marriage, the tension in her gave way so suddenly that every muscle in her body seemed to turn to water; she almost fainted with relief. For two days and a night after the feast she had anxiously kept watch in a chair that faced the door of her chamber, listening for the knock that would bring word that she was to prepare herself for her husband. She did not dare fall asleep, for fear she would awaken to see Rodrigo Diaz standing over her, his face all loose with drink and fired with lust, like the knight who had chased that poor naked girl down the length of the banquet table.

Five battles in the field. She had no idea how much time it would take to achieve this, but chose to move through the days with the idea that he *never* would. The king was abed with an illness, and Rodrigo Diaz was away from the city with the Infante Sancho, so she had begun taking her evening meals at the family table. The Infanta Urracca had finally acknowledged her existence by polite conversation, and she had begun to enjoy the company of the younger brothers, Garcia and Alphonso, who were charming, very gracious to her, and amusing. The queen, Doña Sancha, was a soft-spoken, delicate lady who smiled easily and treated Jimena as she might one of her own children, scolding when she did not eat enough, and insisting that, now that she was a married woman, her black mourning clothes were unsuitable. The queen sent seamstresses, who efficiently measured Jimena and produced a fine wardrobe of pelisses and tunics, girdles of gold cord, and shoes of artfully patterned leather. When Jimena mentioned to the queen her preference for felt shoes, six pairs were delivered to her chamber the next morning.

When she walked the corridors on her way to the dining room, or to Mass at the small family chapel, Jimena frigidly kept her eyes straight ahead of her, trying not to notice the whispers and titterings of the men and women she passed. She allowed no stranger to halt her stride, brushing off every attempt to address her with a cool disdain. "Jezebel!", a matron had snarled at her on one occasion, to her total mortification and disbelief. She could not *imagine* why the woman would make such an accusation, nor how she could have fostered such a general dislike at this castle. She ached to return to Gormaz, to those familiar spaces and people, even Aunt Galiana's nagging meanness would be preferable to this daily humiliation of disrespectful eyes upon her, hateful thoughts pressing all around her.

Sitting at ease at a window of her chamber, Jimena watched the sunset sky, thinking that she would retire early for the night; she felt unusually tired this evening. She had just returned from evening Mass, and a servant had laid out her nightclothes on the bed while she was absent. She lifted the chained cross, pulled it over her head, and put it down on the window sill. She stared at the cross for long moment. Into her mind leaped images from the past; she saw flames, and a man struggling, screaming in their midst. She heard the bishop cry out, "INFIDEL!" She shivered and sped away from the window.

A knock on the chamber door startled Jimena. She whipped around and rushed to the door, then cautiously opened it. She expected a servant, or perhaps a message from Jaime sent with one of the many knights of Gormaz that had arrived just yesterday to join the army. Instead, Doña Urracca stood there smiling at her, which threw Jimena into a state of speechless confusion. She had not decided what she thought of this woman, whether she hated her, or was grateful to her, whether she should trust her or not.

"*Buenas noches,* Doña Jimena," the Infanta said politely, her limpid eyes scanning Jimena as rudely as she herself was being scrutinized, her smile unfaltering.

Jimena fidgeted, rocking from foot to foot, her hands firmly on the door, her body blocking the woman's entry. "A—a good evening to *you*, Doña Urracca." Then, for the first time, Jimena noticed a young girl hovering behind the Infanta, almost lost in the darkness of the corridor.

Urracca's expression wavered between amusement and annoyance. She stepped aside and made a hand toward the girl. "This is my servant girl, Maria—Doña Jimena. I bring her to you as a gift, for the duration of your stay at this castle. It is my understanding that you have been given no personal attendant, only the service of the general staff."

Jimena glanced to the girl, immediately taken with her; she was quite pretty and very shy. "I thank you, Doña Urracca. That was most thoughtful of you."

Urracca smiled and said, "May we come in . . . ?"

Flushing, Jimena stepped aside. Urracca brushed elegantly past her, her black skirts rustling strangely as she stepped. Her clothing was not made of wool, but out of a material that was unfamiliar to Jimena. It was very soft and had a sheen to it. The light cast shadows on it like sunlight on a river's surface. It suddenly occurred to Jimena that while the queen had insisted she remove herself from black garments, she obviously had no influence over her own daughter, who had worn black every time Jimena had seen her dressed as a woman. The Infanta was, as usual, iniquitously clean. Her long hair was piled high on her head this evening, in thick, twisted braids.

Doña Urracca seated herself comfortably in a chair, waving the servant girl to her side. A playful smile twisted her lips as she gazed up at Jimena and said matter-of-factly, "I brought Maria to you *tonight,* thinking you would appreciate her assistance in your preparations for the deflowering?"

Jimena disappointed the Infanta, because she did not understand the word *deflowering.* She merely stood several feet from the Infanta's chair, smiling uneasily. "I thank you, Doña Urracca. I could indeed use some help in dressing, and the girl could fetch my meals."

"Doña Jimena," the Infanta interrupted, "I do believe I did not make myself entirely clear. Rodrigo Diaz, your husband, has sent me to you, to inform you that he will come to you tonight to fulfill his duty to you, according to the marriage vows. Do you understand?"

"Oh my dear God!" Jimena blurted out. Her hands flew up to cover her mouth, and she blushed. She had shamefully revealed her emotions, but she had been so taken off guard that reaction had come before thought.

Urracca got to her feet and moved to take Jimena's cold, trembling hands in hers. "Child, do not be afraid. Maria and I will remain with you throughout the evening and aid you in preparing yourself. And comfort you, if comfort is what you require. It is a *good* thing, Jimena, that which happens between a man and a woman, not a thing to be so feared, but joyfully anticipated."

Jimena had barely understood the woman's words, her mind was in such turmoil. She felt nauseous, and her head had begun to swim. Numbly she watched as the Infanta stepped away from her to rummage about her chamber in search of something.

"For God!" Urracca exclaimed, "you do not have a single decent nightdress. One would think your father had been a pauper. The richest knight in Castile, yet his daughter comes to us with no wardrobe. Something in Muslim silk would be good, I think."

The Infanta rushed out of the room, leaving Jimena and the servant, Maria, staring shyly at each other and wondering what Doña Urracca was up to. After several minutes Urracca returned, a load of nightdresses over one arm. She threw the armload onto a chair, then rummaged through them with both hands, tossing gowns aside impatiently. She finally chose a black dress and insisted that Jimena put it on.

Jimena held the dress in her two hands, staring at it. It had no weight to it, almost none at all. And no *scratch*. She had never seen cloth so lovely, as delicate as the wings of butterflies. She glanced to Doña Urracca uncertainly.

Urracca smiled at her encouragingly. "It is made of silk, Jimena. Made from bolts of cloth found amidst the loot from a raid on a Muslim town. The clothes I am wearing are made of velvet, also Muslim. In the privacy of our chambers, where the priests cannot see us, we can indulge ourselves, mmh?" Jimena dropped the dress from her hands in alarm and the Infanta laughed delightedly. Urracca bent over and retrieved the dress, holding it out to Jimena. "Go, put it on, child. It is absolutely marvelous against the flesh in its softness, light as air."

In a daze, Jimena took the dress and moved to her dressing screen. Maria followed at her heels and quickly got behind her to loosen the laces of her tunic. When her tunic, pelisse and chemise had been removed, Jimena reached for the silk dress, but Maria stayed her hand, saying, "Your underwear, my lady." Jimena stared at the girl in disbelief.

"Do as she says," the Infanta said from the other side of the screen. "Right down to the skin, Doña Jimena."

"No," Jimena retorted, pulling herself away from Maria's hands, which were attempting to unfasten the back of her undergarment.

An exasperated sigh emerged from behind the screen. "Do you know how ridiculous that dress will look on you, Jimena, with woolen underwear showing through? The dress has flared sleeves. The snug sleeves of your underwear will look ghastly—like great sore thumbs sticking out of the sublime drape of the silk! Come now, be cooperative. We came to help, not to punish you."

Defeated, Jimena grabbed up the gown and pulled it over her head, indicating to Maria, with a murderous look, that she would manage by herself. Bringing her hands up underneath the dress, she removed the wool garment, ripping the fastenings loose in her impatience. The black transparent material clung to her body, revealing every detail. Jimena was overwhelmed by dual emotions: sensuous pleasure at the whispering touch of the cloth against her body, and shame at the extent of her nakedness. Blushing, she folded her arms over her bosom, and stepped out from behind the screen.

"*Que bien!*" Urracca exclaimed, throwing up her hands to express her pleasure. "Now, Maria, take down her hair and brush it out."

Jimena sat on a stool while Maria unfastened her braids, loosening them by running her fingers through again and again. Then she took a stiff brush from the pocket of her apron and began vigorously attacking the knots and snags. Never had Jimena had her hair so thoroughly brushed. The girl kept at it for at least half of an hour, occasionally sprinkling water upon it, to smooth it down, she explained, and take out the kinks the braids had made. "Lovely," Doña Urracca said once, as the girl was brushing. "You have quite lovely hair, Jimena. You should take better care of it, brush it every day."

Jimena sat with her chin against her chest, pulling down against the drawing-back of the brush upon her hair. She thought the Infanta was probably thinking she should also *wash* it, and was relieved Urracca had not said so. That would have put an end to this nonsense, and quickly. As far as she knew, Muslim cloth was not considered a mortal sin, but bathing *was*.

At last Jimena was as prepared as she would ever be. Maria left the chamber to fetch food and drink, which the Infanta firmly insisted upon. "Diaz is drowning his reluctance in wine," she scolded, "and may not appear before dawn. You cannot starve yourself, my dear child. You will need your strength."

Jimena sat stiffly in a chair, arms folded over her bosom. She gazed upon the Infanta with a growing curiosity and approval. Her smiles seemed genuine, her concern quite sincere. "Excuse me, Doña Urracca," she began shyly.

"Just Urracca," the Infanta interrupted softly. "The title isn't necessary between us."

"Urracca," Jimena echoed, smiling uneasily. "I was wondering. Why did you turn me away from the monastery, at that encampment?"

"A simple question. Because you said no to them."

Jimena stared at her, uncomprehending. "But that was such a *stupid* thing for me to do!" she exlaimed.

"It was not stupid to say no, Jimena—it was very brave, and I respect bravery, particularly in a woman."

Jimena laughed and said, "Oh, but they could have killed me where I stood, so—"

"That is exactly what made it brave," Urracca interrupted. "I saw a glint of myself in you . . . the eternal rebel in me; or *infernal,* depending upon the viewpoint." She laughed half-heartedly. "I am sure you have noticed my tendency to defy tradition, to do as I please, rather than what is expected of me. As the daughter of the king and mistress of the monasteries, I can defy the Church and tradition with some impunity, as long as I do not carry it to extremes."

Jimena thought that bathing was decidedly extreme, but said nothing. She recalled her father's lecture about resignation, saying she must fight to make something good of her life, never accepting what was intolerable to her. Was it possible that Urracca was, in spirit, what he had wished *her* to be? Never. She would never dare such independence of action and thought. As the Infanta had said, she was the daughter of a king, which gave her certain privileges beyond the ordinary. A mere daughter of a count would find herself fastened to a stake with fire licking at her toes. But Urracca had apparently seen such independence in her. How very odd—it simply wasn't there. Jimena Gomez a rebel? Never!

"Are you happy that I diverted you to Palencia?" Urracca asked, studying Jimena closely.

Jimena shrugged. "I am not sure. Sometimes, yes, but at this moment. . . ."

Urracca threw her head back, delighted, as if Jimena had told her a hilarious joke. "Excellent! You have humor as well, Jimena. I like that."

"Why did Rodrigo Diaz send *you* to me?" Jimena asked, embarrassed because she had no idea what was funny about her comment. "I had expected it would be a priest. And, how did he *ever* manage to win five battles in so short a time?"

Again Urracca was convulsed by laughter. "He forsook that part of the vow, dear," she said forcing down giggles. "And it was not exactly at his request that I came to you. We have known each other since childhood. I was raised at a monastery very near his town of Bivar and his father and mine are related, so we became friends. He *is* a good deal younger than myself—seven years." She paused, a strange glint in her eye. She added, "At least for the *moment* we are friends. At any rate, he told me that he would bed you tonight, but he would not speak of it openly, because he did not choose to put up with the traditional audience and priestly checking of the sheets for virginal blood. Therefore, you would have been taken by surprise. I spoke harshly to him, saying that this was to say the least an ungenerous approach, disrespectful of the sensitivities of his bride. I rather strongly suggested he send an understanding woman to warn you and give you aid in preparation. Then he said, with equal vehemence, that if I felt so strongly about the tender feelings of his wife, I could come to you myself. If I refused, then it would be a surprise. So there you have it. Here I am." She threw up her pretty hands and smiled broadly.

"For God!" Jimena exclaimed, "the man is cruel beyond belief. I cannot imagine how I shall bear his touch."

"No," Urracca protested earnestly. "No, Jimena, do not think of Rodrigo as brutish. He is a noble, truly brilliant, physically and politically powerful young man. You are indeed well married, and for this you should be deeply grateful. He is no more cruel than any other man; I would say Rodrigo is less brutal than most." Noting Jimena's severely skeptical expression, Urracca persisted with, "Truly, Jimena. If I knew you better, then I could explain why I am able to say this to you with such assurance. Believe me, if you can. He would not intentionally cause you physical harm, honestly."

Maria returned with two male servants carrying trays

heaped with steaming mutton and rice and loaves of bread. Urracca ate with enthusiasm, talking animatedly about such things as the weather and a peculiar wildflower she had discovered near a riverbank a week past while on a fishing expedition with her brother Alphonso. Jimena could not get a bite down her throat, past the knot of apprehension there.

After the meal, Urracca got to her feet, offered Jimena a sympathetic smile and said, "He means you no harm, Jimena. He forsook half his vow for your sake, in respect for your reputation. His coming is an act of generosity, remember that, hmmm?" Then she took Maria by the hand and left the room, leaving Jimena to wait. It was three hours after sunset.

Jimena remained in the chair, arms folded tightly over her chest, so tense every muscle in her body ached. Many hours passed. The moon now cast its light through one of the windows, illuminating her where she sat in otherwise total darkness; the candles Maria had lighted soon after she and Urracca arrived had burned down to their bases and flickered out. A cock crowed from somewhere far off. The longer she waited for her husband to appear, the more ghastly and terrifying Jimena's imaginings became. Over and over again she told herself that when a woman was wed, it could no longer be considered rape, but she remained unconsoled. He would clutch her, force himself upon her, look at her nakedness and do that vague thing that men did to women which gave them babies. Would it be painful? She felt sick again and tried to chase the hateful visions from her mind by looking down at the black dress, which she could not help but admire. It did feel so exceedingly soft against her flesh, like the breath of a kiss upon the cheek.

The door burst open and crashed back against the wall. Jimena gasped and sank into her chair. Rodrigo Diaz stood swaying in the opening, dressed in a white tunic, a candle in his hand casting grotesque shadows on his wine-limp features. Not only he, drunk and ferocious, but a crowd of staggering knights and their ladies who had riotously followed him, suspecting his intention.

Jimena forced herself out of the chair, pushing herself to her feet. She would not face him cowering, like some kind of cornered beast; she was not his prey, she was his wife!

In the dim light Rodrigo could barely see his bride, but what he did see surprised him a little. The transparent black gown revealed a form that, though spare, was reasonably well proportioned. Her small breasts were rising and falling in tantalizing rhythm with her frightened breathing. Her hair had

been combed and fell loose over her shoulders in strands of dull
gold. Adequate. He blew out the candle he carried, then slammed the door closed in the faces of the smirking spectators, ignoring the muffled howls of protest that came from the other
side. Blinking, adjusting his eyes to the darkness, he started toward Jimena on unsteady feet, stumbling over a chest and cursing under his breath. Hah—he thought, delighted—see her backing away like a frightened fawn, those brown eyes all round
and full of dread. Excellent, forcing her, fighting her for it
would lend some additional pleasure to the business. But, once
it began, she would not struggle long. All women wished to be
forced, playing the game of reluctant virgin all their lives. Soon
she would tire of the pretense and submit to him tearfully. Virtuous wretch! Slowly he stalked her, until he had her cornered
against the solid oak of her bed.

Jimena cried out, terrified, when her thighs struck the impassable barrier of the bed. "Do not touch me!" she hissed at
him. Desperation had closed her mind to thought, and all she
could do now was blindly react.

Rodrigo came to a halt with his body touching hers. He
laughed heartily and reached out a hand to touch her cheek.

Jimena jerked her head away from his touch. "I said—do
not touch me, sir! I mean what I say. You are not welcome
here."

Rodrigo swore and threw his weight against her, so hard
that she fell back across the mattress; his body dropped upon
her and held her there.

He was so heavy that Jimena could only thrash her arms
wildly and wail out pitiful protests. He reached for the neck of
her dress, then pulled it with all his strength, tearing it from her
breasts. With shaking, weak fists Jimena frantically beat upon
the man's back. His mouth came down onto the flesh of her
neck, then slid up to her mouth, crushing, forcing her lips
apart, his own lips open, moving, wet, his tongue pushing
against her teeth. A sudden eruption of emotion within her, a
scream, unreleased, squeezed her throat closed until the pain
was almost more than she could bear. His mouth was moving
away from hers, down to her chin . . . to her neck. When his
open mouth fastened to one of her breasts, it was as if Jimena
had been struck in the chest with an arrow. "Aaaaaahch!" she
screeched, and with a sudden, maniacal explosion of uncontrollable rage, she reached down and grabbed his hot face between
her two hands, tearing his mouth from her body with fury-
increased strength. She dug her fingernails into his flesh, claw-

ing, slicing, until his blood was warm on her hands. The scream in her found full release. Blind hatred blackened everything from her mind except this rape, this ghastly defilement. Her breath came in short, painful gasps, her eyes glazed. She was lost in a dark nightmare, battling for her life against the invisible Devil, against an all-too-real attacker.

At the first stab of her nails, Rodrigo had lunged backward from her, his face torn open in thin lines, blood dripping into his beard and onto his tunic. But she came charging at him, screaming like a mad woman, tearing at his clothing, clawing at his face like a crazed wildcat. Though he used all his agility and strength, he could not keep hold of her. She slipped from his grasp again and again. "For the love of Christ, woman!" he shouted at her, an arm flashing out as he made a grab for her hair, which he at last caught tight in his fist. Jerking hard, he jarred her head around to him and slapped her hard across the face, once, then again.

Jimena ceased screaming abruptly, the only sound now the harsh gasps of her breathing, and his. She hung there, held up by the hair, limp, semiconscious, still floundering in a black pit of rage. Rodrigo scowled down at her contemptuously, then, with a brutal thrust, let loose of her, throwing her across the room and against the wall. He stalked out of the room, slamming the door so hard behind him that the floor shook beneath Jimena's naked buttocks. Her head was throbbing, an awful pain stabbing at her behind the eyes.

"Dear God," she wept, "what have I done—what have I *done!*"

Chapter
✠ *FIVE* ✠

The crowd pressed close to the marching men, who walked
four abreast through the streets of Palencia, carrying their pikes
and axes awkwardly on their shoulders. Wives called out to departing husbands, sadness in their eyes as they contemplated the
long months of loneliness before them. William de Montrueil
led the parade astride an immense, rearing war-horse, looking
comically small though he sat as tall in the silver saddle as he
could. Behind the pope's standard bearer rode the priests and
monks, then the Italian knights, their banners colorfully waving in the hot summer winds, and following them, the knights
of Castile, the Germans and the French. Oxen labored patiently
against the unwieldy weight of wagons that carried seemingly
endless supplies and war machines. The clattering noise of
horses' hooves against cobblestones gave way to the shuffling,
scratching sound the boots of the foot soldiers made and the din
of voices calling out goodbyes and last-minute messages. The
soldiers were a moving, mindless mass of duplications, all ragged and poor, all obediently following the will of their
superiors. It mattered little to these conscripted men whether
the Infidel was destroyed, or not: their individual lots would
remain unaltered in any case. When not at war, they labored
endlessly in the fields, slaves to their masters. For centuries
many of their kind had been deserting the fields to seek and find
a better life among the Muslims, where the ordinary man could
make a more significant place for himself—at least he ate better
and his clothing was of better stuff. But the men who went
forth against Barbastro were the kind of men who lacked the
courage to leave behind everything that was familiar and predictable, for the vague promise of a sweeter existence elsewhere.
Trudging dismally ahead, they were willing to destroy that

which, if they had only known, might have been their salvation.

Jimena had watched the parade from a balcony, half hoping to catch sight of Rodrigo Diaz. He had steadfastly avoided her the entire week since that hideous night. Then, there he was, an awesome sight in full armor; he looked like an enormous apparition from some unknown world, clasping the staff of his orange and yellow banner tight in a gloved hand, his coat of mail reflecting sunlight in graceful, flickering lights. He did not look in her direction, though he passed just below her and could not help but notice her presence. She had never felt more despairing. Rodrigo would probably never forgive her, and, if he did not, years of emptiness would loom ahead. She must manage some manner of understanding with him. She watched him until he disappeared round a curve in the narrow street.

Jimena remained at the balcony until the army was indicated by only the faintest wisp of dust on the horizon far beyond the city walls. Then she turned and with grim determination went straight out upon the streets, unescorted, making her way to the Cathedral of Palencia and confession.

"Father, forgive me, for I have sinned. I accepted the Holy Sacrament of marriage and refused my husband my—I, uh, I fought him, lashed out against him. I denied him my body. Doubly have I sinned, for I have withheld confession of it these seven days. My soul is black with guilt. I sincerely repent and humbly beg forgiveness . . ."

A deep, dread silence lay heavy upon Jimena, after the last whispered word left her lips. The closet was dark, the heavy curtain still and threatening. Not the slightest hint of a breath told her the priest was still there and had heard. She suffered a vague hope that he had indeed not heard the words that were so difficult for her to say.

The voice came, deep and clear, the words melting together in an almost melodic, memorized chant. "Know in your heart, my child, that you are but the victim of a lustful man, that you are more blessed than he, for having fought so against his vile passions. Preserve thy virginity, good woman, if you can, for continent marriage is nearest in all manner to that of sacred celibacy. If your husband persists, you must comply. But flames need not spark. Speak to him of the bliss of virtue, and soon, perhaps, he will be freed of his desires and become uplifted in spirit through your divine graces, holding your hand throughout eternity in the sweetest love that exists. Go with God, my child, knowing there has been no sin on your part. Your husband is the one to seek absolvement, for his intent to despoil your blessed virginity."

Jimena left the confessional and moved wearily down the aisle of the church to the statue of the Blessed Mother. She knelt before it, eyes closed, hands folded before her face, her mind wandering and unable to pray. She should feel comforted, but she did not; her heart was still heavy with guilt and regret.

Blessed Mary Mother of God, she silently prayed, *forgive me, for I am not as pious as the Father supposed. It was the rape, his brutal approach. I live in dread that one day the fires of lust that smolder within me will burst forth, fanned by the winds of a lover's touch and tender words. I yearn for the things of this life on earth, Mother, yet I would be as virtuous as you. Pray to God for me, to help me in my struggle.*

She knelt before the cold figure of the Virgin until her knees were stabbed with knifelike jabs of pain and her shoulders ached from the stooping position. Often she glanced up into the eyes of the figure, searching for some sign of life and truth, a mere hint of a divine smile, but the eyes remained dead bulges of carved stone, lifeless. There was no smile, only a grim slice of cold granite.

Jimena remained in the church for the evening Mass, then filed out with the noisy, jostling congregation. As she reached the top of the long flight of steps that wound down to the courtyard, someone gave her shoulder a severe jolt. She stumbled. Futilely reaching out with her hands for something to support her, she felt herself falling helplessly, over and over, rolling down the hard, stone steps as people leaped out of her path. Badly bruised but otherwise unhurt, she came to an abrupt stop against the wall where the stairs curved.

"Oh! Damn me—" she cursed, thoroughly humiliated. She could hear laughter and witty remarks being made about her, which sorely damaged her pride. She vowed to remain exactly where she was for as long as it took to collect her dignity. Then a pair of leather boots appeared before her eyes. She looked up slowly and saw that it was the Infante Alphonso. Jimena flushed and offered him a sheepish smile.

"Here now, allow me to assist you, señora. Have you injured yourself?"

"Oh, no, no, I am perfectly all right, thank you." Jimena jumped to her feet and busily brushed at her clothing, avoiding the man's eyes. Don Alphonso was a pleasant man, and under ordinary circumstances quite easy to be relaxed with, but now she felt utterly foolish.

Doña Urracca stepped up beside Alphonso. "Is something wrong?"

Alphonso said, "She took a fall, but she is fine now—are you not?" He winked at Jimena, then grinned at her as if they shared a secret.

"It is that cursed second step," Urracca said indignantly. "I fell from it myself not two weeks past." She took Jimena's arm. "You might best carry her to her chamber, Alphonso. Are you *certain* nothing is broken, my dear?"

"Truly," Jimena said, laughing. "I am just fine."

Walking toward the castle with Jimena, Alphonso and Urracca were in the best of spirits, laughing and talking together about the indignities one suffered at such moments, taking a clumsy fall just when one would hope to appear supremely regal. Jimena had never had a friend and began to enjoy their company immensely. It made her feel warm inside to laugh with them; she had never felt as at ease with Urracca as she did today. Alphonso was apparently unconcerned that he was not with the army; his father had demanded that he remain at the castle, and he had obeyed cheerfully—he was a man not overly anxious to add badges of glory to his name. Once he had said at dinner that he would have enough of battles when he was king of Leon. For now, the fewer the better, since he was only twenty and two. This statement had produced a snarl of disgust from his brother Sancho, and a cheer from Garcia.

"Jimena," Urracca said, "would you care to join us on Saint's Day? We are planning a pilgrimage to Santiago— Alphonso, my brother Garcia, and myself." She nudged Jimena conspiratorially with an elbow. "An excellent excuse for an excursion, nights by the campfire, and all that. It relieves the monotony beautifully, and the priests cluck joyfully over our pious dedication to God."

Alphonso laughed and said, "Yes, do join us, Jimena. It is not good that you spend so much time alone. Will you?"

Jimena hesitated, stopping to look from one to the other doubtfully. "Well, I—yes. Yes, I would like that very much, thank you." As the words left her lips, Jimena felt an exhilarating uplifting of her spirits.

Santiago lay slightly more than two days journey from Palencia, in the heart of the state of Galicia. In this region the

first Goths had begun the reconquest for Christianity and Santiago was briefly their capital. When the bones of Saint James
were discovered there, a church was built over his burial place
and a bishopric established. Santiago became a center for pilgrims who came to pray at the feet of the saint. The road to
Santiago became almost as sacred as the road to Mecca was for
the Infidel.

The small group of pilgrims left Palencia at dawn. The sky
was cloudless, the heat already oppressive. But no one seemed
to mind the heat, least of all Jimena. Three male servants accompanied the party. No chaperones were necessary, since
Jimena's three companions were related and she was a member
of the family by virtue of her marriage to Rodrigo Diaz. Well
beyond the capital, Urracca reined in her mount and leaped
down from the saddle. She ran, skirts flying, a satchel in hand,
to a screen of bushes and small trees. When she emerged, her
black apparel was stuffed into the carrying case, and she wore a
white blouse, a loose-fitting leather vest, and breeches of a serf
that were snug on her shapely legs.

"Now, *this* is more to my liking," Urracca said. Then she
took a running leap up onto her horse's back and straddled the
saddle like a man, her heels digging into the beast's ribs. The
wind whipped her long hair back from her face as she sped off
ahead of the rest, kicking up a choking cloud of dust.

Since Jimena had never learned to ride, she was forced to
occupy the wagon beside a grumpy old manservant, who was
sweating so profusely his clothes were stained yellow and gave
off a rancid, suffocating odor. Jimena turned her head away
from him, trying to breathe out of the side of her nose that was
opposite him. Sweat ran in streams down the haunches of the
two horses, whose behinds were her sole foreward view. The
wagon bounced roughly over ruts and patches of weeds growing tenaciously in the roadbed.

Urracca rode back, coming at them at full speed, then jerking hard on the reins so that her mount came rearing to a halt.
How exciting she is, Jimena thought—so full of life and humor.
A truly beautiful woman, warm and good, not at all the witch
that a frightened, distrusting prisoner saw at that campsite.
Words from the Bible came to mind: "Let he who is without
sin cast the first stone." Urracca bathed herself, yes, but Jimena
had once tried to copy the Infidel Bible, a far *worse* sin. The
matter of bathing was between Urracca and God.

"Are you enjoying yourself, Jimena?" Alphonso had reined
in beside the wagon, looking windblown and very handsome.

Jimena glanced at the old man beside her, and her nose curled distastefully. "Well," she leaned aside confidentially, "I would prefer a horse, if that could be arranged."

"You said you do not ride."

"Indeed, but I see no reason why I could not learn."

"Are you certain?" he asked doubtfully. "I wouldn't want you to crack that pretty neck . . ."

"I will be quite careful, and ride extremely slow. I promise to land on a bush, not on the hard earth, if the horse and I feel we absolutely *must* part company."

Alphonso laughed appreciatively. "All right, if you insist. But I warn you, the drop from a horse can be far worse a jolt than tumbling down a flight of stairs."

The wagon driver sourly halted the vehicle at Alphonso's direction, grumbling unpleasantly, his small, black eyes glaring at Jimena's retreating backside. Alphonso untied a brown mare from the back of the wagon, saddled it and brought it around for Jimena to mount.

"My . . ." she exclaimed uneasily, "he *is* big, isn't he?"

"She. The horse is a she, Jimena. Discouraged so soon?"

"Oh, no."

"Then place your left foot in my palm; that's right. Now, swing your body up when I give you a boost. No! Jimena—do not clutch at my head—the reins—watch yourself!" Alphonso doubled over laughing, as Jimena clumsily dropped to the ground. Looking down at her in pretended disgust, he said, "Am I to be forever plucking you up from the ground, huh? Do you never stand steady on your two feet, woman? Now, Jimena, why don't you ride in the wagon? How can you expect to ride a horse, when you cannot even get yourself into the saddle?"

"Once more, sir," she insisted, grinning at him. "I shall manage this time, I promise you. I will ride this horse or *die* in the attempt!" She giggled foolishly, which brought on hiccoughs. She had not enjoyed herself so thoroughly in a very long time.

"Stubborn," he said, then set himself in a kneeling position, palm outstretched for her foot.

It was finally accomplished. Jimena bounced down the road for over an hour, until her teeth seemed about to come loose from her jaw, and her rump felt as if it was landing on spikes each time it slapped down on the saddle.

Urracca sped up beside her and reined in, slowing her mount. "Had enough, Jimena?" she asked playfully. "I have to tell you that you look a little the worse for wear."

Jimena glanced back to the wagon, and that detestable, reeking old man. She shook her head. "I am doing very well, in spite of how it may look to you, Urracca." But it was still early in the day. How severe the pain and how large the blisters, if she kept this up much longer? Another hour passed. Urracca and her two brothers were far ahead, nearly hidden from view by a grove of trees; even the slow, creaking wagon had left her behind. Jimena kicked the horse vigorously, as if it was the beast's fault they lagged so. With a relieved, enthusiastic whinny, the mare surged ahead. Jimena wobbled dangerously in the saddle, barely keeping her seat.

"Enough!" Jimena screeched, as she came up to and passed the others. "Stop this blasted animal. I have had enough, I tell you!"

She heard a chorus of laughter behind her. Then Alphonso rode up and took hold of the reins, bringing the beast to a halt. Jimena returned to her seat beside the wagon driver, grateful for small comforts and willing to put up with the man and his stench again. She was having a wonderful time.

Jimena had thought she would be lonely and unhappy at Palencia, with or without the presence of Rodrigo Diaz. She had requested that she be allowed to return to Gormaz, but had been refused by the king. Jaime had decided to lead the Gormaz knights at Barbastro, leaving Don Manuel Gonzales in authority, so it was considered unsafe for her to return so soon after her marriage to Diaz. If she went anywhere, it would have to be to the house of Rodrigo's mother, and that she would not do. She was quite pleased now that she had been forced to stay at Palencia.

At day's end, they camped near the banks of the Sarela River, several hundred feet from where it tumbled and churned over boulders, to join with the river Sar. The servants busied themselves setting up the tents for the night. The smell of goat roasting on a spit mingled with the clean, green-sweet air had set Jimena's stomach growling; never had she been so hungry, nor felt so pleasantly tired and invigorated. The moon was full in the sky, peeking coyly through the tall trees, spreading a sparkling path across the gently flowing river. Jimena sat leaning back against the trunk of a tree, sighing with pleasure and contentment. Urracca and her brothers were splashing in the river, playing like children, their naked bodies gleaming in the pale light.

"Jimena," Urracca called out, "do come and join us. The water is marvelously cooling."

"No—oh, no, really, Urracca, I couldn't."

"Coward!"

Jimena smiled wanly. True enough, she *was* a coward. She only needed to be beaten once to know better than to deliberately commit a mortal sin. The bishop, Don Pedro, had always said that the beauty within a person bloomed, rainbow-hued, when bath waters were avoided. Jimena ruefully asked herself now, if as the lice and grime accumulated upon her over the years, the beauty within her had *truly* blossomed. Watching her new friends leaping and splashing, diving like ducks, pushing each other under—she began to doubt whether she was more pure than they were in her abstinence. They were having such fun. Why, she asked herself, are the sinful things so often the more pleasurable? She guessed one simply was not supposed to enjoy this life on earth; only God knew why.

A servant called out that the meal was ready to eat. The three came running from the riverbank, wrapped in fur-lined mantles, the brothers chasing Urracca. Alphonso made a dive just as Urracca reached the center of the campsite, catching her ankles, throwing her flat on her face. Wrestling, rolling, playing, Garcia jumped in and began tickling her, while Alphonso pinned her arms to the ground. Urracca's happy screeches of protest, the laughter of her brothers, were like music, vibrating on the quiet night air.

The three children of the king sat in a semicircle around Jimena where she still leaned against the treetrunk, eating with lip-smacking enthusiasm. After the meal, tired and feeling very content, they lay around the fire on their backs, gazing up at the stars. Urracca began to hum a sweet melody. Alphonso, leaning on one elbow, looked adoringly down into his sister's glowing face. Jimena wished the day would never end, that this excursion could just go on forever.

Garcia, only sixteen years old, could not remain still for long. Suddenly he leaped to his feet, gesticulating wildly. "Look at me. I am the king—see?" He managed a perfect imitation of his father, even causing his jowls to sag, one twitching spasmodically.

"Stop. . . ." Urracca protested over-dramatically. "I wish to continue enjoying myself and cannot do so if you persist in reminding me of one as foul as our father!"

"Foul?" Garcia wailed. "My dear sister, he is not foul, who gives to me, who never thought to rule, a kingdom."

"A kingdom? You? Hah! Sancho will cut you down within a week of our father's death, my silly little brother. And if he does not, then maybe I will, hmmm?"

"Ah, Urracca, your tongue wounds me deeply. Come, let us not weep over the grave of Garcia, until he has breathed his last. Tonight I am a king!" He began leaping about, pretending he held a sword in his hand, slashing to left and right, a thrust, an agile leap back. "Die, Infidel, die," he roared, heaping up the imaginary bodies of his enemies around his kingly feet. "I shall slay so many of the vermin when I am king, there will be none left to scourge our land. I will take off their heads and put them on stakes and set the stakes upon the walls of my castle, and plant them in my courtyard; a garden of infidel heads rotting in the sun so that all who pass that way will know which of the sons of Don Ferrando is the true hand of God against the unbelievers!" More thrusts and slashes, then. . . "And I shall burn at least one thousand of them—no, ten thousand, in one great pyre that will be as a mountain peak of flame, close enough to the sky for God and His Host to take notice . . ."

Jimena abruptly stopped laughing. Without consciously thinking about it, she opened her palms and studied them, noting the scars left by the bishop's chain. He had been just a *man*—an ordinary-looking man.

"Garcia," Urracca purred reprimandingly, "you cannot kill *all* the infidels, or what shall I do for silks and jewels?"

"I will take wagon loads of jewels and silks, my sister, and set them at your feet." He bowed deeply to her.

"Ah, then slay them all, Brother—if you have the stomach for it."

Jimena's eyes darted to Urracca, thinking she had heard a sincerity in the words under the humorous tone of voice. "You do not approve of the slaying of infidels?" she asked hesitantly.

Urracca turned to Jimena curiously. "I do not approve or disapprove. I am simply appalled by the lust of men for slaughter. Infidel, or Christian—it makes no difference. I approve of killing only as a last resort."

"But the Bible says 'Thou shalt not kill,' Jimena offered questioningly, "which should apply to all men under all circumstances . . . ?"

Urracca shrugged. "The Bible is filled with words, every one of which I consider to be completely absurd."

Jimena's eyes widened in amazement. Urracca spoke with such assurance and ease, one would suppose everyone in the world thought exactly the same way. Suddenly an uncomfortable certainty that God was listening and taking note agitated Jimena. She saw Him automatically placing Urracca on His scroll for future punishments. Obviously, He did not intend taking any immediate action, since Urracca was sitting there before her unscathed and smiling. "Urracca," she said at last, "have you *no* fear of Hell—none at all?"

"Rubbish! If I guided my life by that redundant list of sins the priests carry around with them, I would deny myself all there is to living, and might as well cut my throat. I am twenty-seven years old. My father has decided my future. There will be no husband for me, not ever. You obviously possess the strength to deny your womanhood, Jimena, but my blood runs hot. I may deny the Bible, but I never deny my passions!" At Jimena's obvious pious indignation and wounded feelings, Urracca softened. "Ah, Jimena, forgive me. I was unkind and offended you." She reached out and stroked Jimena's hair maternally, smiling at her. "Remain as you are. Do not listen to me. Truly, you are worthier than I, who will surely if there is such a place, taste the ashes of Hell upon my tongue."

By midnight the exhausted pilgrims were all in their beds. The full moon spread an exquisite illumination over the campsite. On her mattress inside the tent she shared with Urracca, Jimena lay unable to sleep. She was very tired, but her eyes would not remain closed. Her mind was running over the events of the day, every word spoken repeating in her head, every sight vividly flashing back to be enjoyed again. Jimena's mind wandered to the fact that both Rodrigo and Jaime were marching toward Barbastro this very moment, knights in the same army, against the same enemy. Rodrigo was Jaime's commander; she prayed Jaime would not defy her husband and get himself killed. She shuddered, seeing for a moment the head of Jaime Martinez at the feet of Rodrigo Diaz, and then the face of Leonora weeping and the children. Garcia's childish imaginings of slaughter returned, and she saw the bodies of the people of Barbastro piling up as he had described. Thoroughly depressed now, she rolled over and pushed her face into her pillow, groaning softly, trying to force her earlier more pleasant thoughts back into her head.

Jimena heard Urracca stir softly, so she closed her eyes and pretended sleep because she did not wish to talk. Out of the slits of her eyes she saw Urracca standing over her, unmoving for long moments. Then Jimena watched Urracca turn and step silently toward the tent opening, disappearing into the night. Jimena relaxed and flopped over on her back, staring up at the roof of the tent.

A sudden, warm optimism washed over Jimena. She would

find *some* way to her husband's heart, surely she would . . . and
begin her first child. It would be nice to have a girl child first,
she thought—a girl with golden hair, or as white as her
father's, who would grow up as lovely as Urracca.

Uplifted by the pleasantness of her vision of the future,
Jimena flung the light coverlet back and jumped from her mattress. She wrapped herself in a mantle, thinking she would join
Urracca, who was obviously having the same trouble sleeping
tonight as she was. Emerging from the tent, Jimena stepped
surefootedly to the center of the camp, where the fire had
burned down to embers. A soft red glow lit the space directly
around her feet. She turned in a full circle, searching the moonlit campsite for a sign of Urracca, but she saw nothing but
shadows. The wagon driver and servants were asleep in bags
just away from the fire. She moved toward the river, stepping
more carefully as the ground became rocky, the brush more
dense. Urracca loved the water as much as Jimena did and was
probably sitting somewhere along the bank, watching it and listening to it.

Jimena walked along the sandy riverbank for some distance, turned and retraced her steps, then moved the same distance upriver. Frowning, she returned to the banks near camp,
worried that something might have happened to Urracca. She
thought perhaps she should go to Alphonso and Garcia's tent
and tell them but decided against it; she did not know another
person as self-sufficient as Urracca, and pitied the man or beast
who might attempt to accost her. Smiling at the picture of Urracca beating an attacker half to death with a fallen tree branch,
Jimena leaned and pulled off her felt shoes, so she could put her
bare feet against the sand and see what it felt like. Since Urracca
had given her the black gown to put on, she had secretly forsaken long woolen underwear, grateful to the length of her skirts
that hid the fact. The damp sand squeezed between her toes deliciously. She lifted her skirts and ran along the river's edge,
kicking sand in the air with her toes, jumping into the water
and out again. Winded, she came to a gasping halt a long way
from camp. To catch her breath, she trudged through brush and
brambles to a great tree, falling down at its base and leaning
back against the trunk. She experienced a most delightful sense
of aloneness. How often she had sat in her chamber at Gormaz,
with Aunt Galiana and the servants, feeling desperately alone.
This was a different kind of isolation; she felt as if she owned
the world and lived alone in it, with no other soul existing to
make demands, to nag, to threaten. She speculated upon the

possibility of coming to this wood and remaining here, living out her life without ever seeing another human being, one with the birds, the fish. She yawned, feeling suddenly very sleepy. She began pushing herself to her feet, but suddenly froze, startled.

"I will *not* stand meekly by and suffer it, I tell you!"

Jimena's entire body was jolted at the loudness and bitter quality of Urracca's voice behind her, emerging from somewhere in the woods close by.

"As the first born, I, not Sancho, am the true heir to the throne of Castile. But I am a woman! That damned tyrant intends leaving me only the monasteries, intending that I rot in one of them, still the pure, virgin Infanta; she must not produce a rival for his son's thrones. Damn his filthy soul to hell!"

Jimena flinched at the pain in Urracca's voice and slid down the tree's trunk, back to a sitting position. She could not interfere, and if she moved to walk away, her footsteps might be heard. She was uncertain whether Urracca was talking to someone or crying out to God.

"Urracca! You gain nothing by condemnations and bitterness. Accept your fate. You cannot alter the fact that you were born a woman, nor go against the will of our father, of the law of Castile."

"My dearest Alphonso! Only when I look upon you, touch you, then and only then, do I thank *God* I am a woman!" Urracca's voice was thick with emotion.

Jimena lunged away from the tree, emotion gagging her; something in the tone of Urracca's voice had sent shivers up her spine. She crept down the slope to the riverbank, hoping her bare feet would be completely silent on the sand as she escaped. But a thick wall of underbrush blocked her way. Frantically she looked back to where she had been sitting. Alphonso rushed into view, taking the place she had vacated only moments ago, his back to her, his forehead leaning to press against the tree's trunk. Jimena eased herself quietly into the brush, praying she would not be seen or heard. Unreasonably, her heart was banging against her ribs. Impossible for her to escape now; she could only hide herself and wait.

Urracca moved into the open, stepping to Alphonso. She put her hands on his arms and turned him to face her, then wrapped her arms around his waist, resting her head against his chest. They stood very still for endless moments, Alphonso gently stroking her hair as if she were an unhappy infant. Then Urracca stepped back, turning her face up to him, her eyes melting into his. The breeze pressed the dark cloth of her gown tight to her body. A muffled cry, a groan, and Alphonso's arms clutched her to him, their lips meeting in an explosion of loosed passion.

Jimena flushed when she heard the gasping sounds as they caught their breaths. She had covered her eyes with both hands, and was praying to God that what she was thinking was just ugly suspicion. When she heard a small cry of pain, curiosity compelled Jimena to look again in their direction. Alphonso had pushed Urracca from him. Her back was arched against the tree's trunk. His face was buried in his hands; he was weeping.

"For Christ's sake, Urracca, how can you torture me like this, how *can* you?"

"Fool!" Urracca wailed. "I offer you love. Is my love such torture to you?"

Angrily he reached out and caught her arms roughly in his two hands, shaking her so violently her head snapped on her neck. "Damnit, Urracca! I am your brother! Your brother, for God's sake. Incest is the word. Have you never heard that vile word, Sister? Have you never heard it, Urracca? Answer me, goddamn you! Answer me!"

"My brother," Urracca echoed, her voice breaking. "So does my birth continue to plague me. God and His almighty justice! When you first looked upon me, Alphonso, I stood on the balcony of my chamber and you sat on your horse in the courtyard below. We had never laid eyes on each other before, because our father had consigned me to the monastery from the age of five. You loved me, entreated me to speak my name. Then, when you learned the same blood ran through our veins, you cringed from me as if I was diseased! Why! Had we met in another place and you had never known, could you have denied the love I offered you? Could you have, Alphonso?"

"I do not argue with fate, dammit! Why must you persist in this constant opposition with your lot in life? You are a woman, my sister—never can you be my lover, my wife; never will you reign over Castile, Leon, or Galicia. Look these facts squarely in the face, and make what you can of your life, for the love of God!"

"Hah!" Urracca shouted. "You shall see what Urracca can make of her life. You preach to me about accepting. Talk, just idle talk. Look at yourself—trembling in fear, refusing to admit you love me, desire me—tortured by your conventional, cowardly mind. I *will* be your lover, Alphonso—such a lover as you have never known before, nor will ever know after me. I shall not be a nun. And I will have some share in my father's estate. These things I swear to you!" Her voice had reached a near-screaming pitch. "Before God, Alphonso, I swear these things!"

Desperate, Urracca hungrily clasped her brother's face in her two hands, pushing her mouth against his, her lips moving, sliding, until, with a groan, his arms swung around her, unable to deny his love any longer. Then, as swiftly as he had succumbed, Alphonso wrenched himself from her, stumbling backward. He stared at Urracca, then with a cry of pain bolted, running headlong into the dark of the wood.

To his retreating back Urracca cried, "There will come a day, beloved. There will come a . . ." Her words ceased when he vanished from her sight. She stood motionless, hands gripped into fists at her sides, then in a demented fury kicked at the trunk of the tree with a foot, over and over again, until she cried out in pain. Her head arched back and she screamed at the night sky, "Damn you, God! Damn you! You are merciless and cruel to plague me so with pain upon pain!"

Sobs overcame Urracca, and she blindly ran toward the river, passing only a few feet away from where Jimena cowered in the brush. With a leaping dive, she threw herself into the river, swimming across its silver surface with violent, pulling strokes of her arms.

"Holy Mary . . ." Jimena gasped, a fist tight to her mouth. She lurched to her feet, ran to the riverbank, and kept running until she was at the edge of the campsite. There she stopped, afraid that if she ran to her tent she might bump into Alphonso. She stood there, breathing heavily, tears filling her eyes.

"Charity shall cover a multitude of sins . . ."

Garcia had said the words softly behind her. Jimena whirled around to face him.

Garcia stepped to Jimena and put a comforting arm around her, hugging her tight to him. "Be charitable, Jimena," he murmured in her ear. "Neither you, nor I, can say what we would do under the same circumstance. *Es verdad?*"

"It isn't *possible*. I refuse to believe it," Jimena said between sobs, her face buried in Garcia's shoulder.

"If Christ could forgive the harlot, surely you can forgive Urracca and Alphonso?"

It had been a question, but Jimena heard it as an accusation. "I am not Christ, nor anything close," she exclaimed.

"Nor am I. But I have managed to accept it, and forgive. And generosity is not exactly one of my virtues. I love them both. My heart aches for them so much, that I find it difficult to condemn them."

"I am not condemning them!"

"No . . . ?"

Jimena jerked herself away from him, lifting a hand to wipe tears from her eyes. She opened her mouth to protest, but the sound of footsteps moving fast through underbrush caused her heart to skip a beat. She stiffened, keeping her back to the sound, knowing she would not be able to meet the eyes of either Urracca or Alphonso without revealing what she had seen and how she felt about it.

"A grand night," Garcia said lightly. "Jimena and I have been standing here for an hour or so, drinking in the moonlight and discussing the pros and cons of killing infidels. Our friend, here, is too softhearted, I think—far too much so for any good Christian."

"I was unable to sleep," Alphonso said behind Jimena, "so I took a stroll. Indeed, it *is* a beautiful night." After an uncomfortable pause he said, "I will say a good night to you. Enjoy yourselves."

Garcia said good night to Alphonso, then gave Jimena a kick against the ankle. She turned automatically and said, *"Buenas noches,* Alphonso." He did not acknowledge her words, but ran toward his tent and disappeared through the opening.

"Jesus . . ." Garcia exclaimed, "I thank the good Lord I was not born good, like Alphonso, because I think the pain of it would be too much for me. A man with no conscience would not be suffering as he is now, but would be laying with his sister!"

"Urracca has no conscience," Jimena shot back at him.

"You are right. Urracca is not good and she is not greatly subject to conscience—but she loves him, deeply and desperately. What Urracca is is *honest,* my dear Jimena. She has an enormous capacity for love and friendship. But, come, it is late, and we depart just after dawn. So we had best get some sleep, eh?"

Garcia took Jimena's hand and led her to her tent. He gave her a kiss on the cheek and an affectionate wink, then left her. He quickly stepped to the tent he shared with Alphonso and disappeared through the entrance. Jimena numbly turned and entered her own tent, moving to her mattress and falling face down upon it. Her mind was spinning as she struggled for an answer to the inevitable question. Should she shun them, refuse to spend another moment in their presence, because to know and not deny them was sin by acceptance and association? Did she love them enough to risk hell by condoning their sin? Time. She had to have time to think this out.

Exhausted, Jimena fell asleep where she lay, face down on the mattress, her mantle over her like a coverlet. When she was awakened by a servant at dawn, she glanced to Urracca's bed. It was empty, and her carrying case was gone. Jimena's heart sank, thinking Urracca had taken to her horse in her rage, leaving them to continue on without her. But when she stepped out of the tent, squinting in the glaring light of the sun, there Urracca stood by the wagon, a radiant smile on her face.

"Good morning, Jimena," Urracca sang out to her. "A perfect day, just perfect. I have decided to ride in the wagon beside you for a while, to keep you company. Come, you overslept. I have something here for you to eat as we travel." She held up a bulging leather bag that was giving off steam in the morning coolness.

Jimena smiled with difficulty and stepped to the wagon, awkwardly climbing up and onto the bench. Because she had to make room for Urracca, she was forced to sit much closer to the driver than she wanted to. Urracca was quickly beside her, talking nonstop. Alphonso and Garcia had mounted their horses and were trotting toward the road. Suddenly a massive, dripping slice of mutton was under Jimena's nose.

"Take it—eat," Urracca insisted. When Jimena gingerly took the meat from her, she said enthusiastically, "We will reach Santiago by this time tomorrow, Jimena. One more night by the fire. We will stay three days, then we will enjoy more nights in the wilds on our way home. I do hope you are enjoying yourself, my dear." Abruptly, she reached out a hand and put the palm against Jimena's cheek. "You are a dear, you know. I was so impressed with you that night—when you sat there across the fire from me all eyes, like a frightened doe, and equally brave. You could have accused them both, but you did not. Truly, I am honored to call you my friend, Jimena. I have very few friends, you know. I fear I am not the most likable person in the world." She looked away from Jimena, then whispered, "Nor am I lovable." Her shoulders straightened and her smile regained itself. She turned again to Jimena and said brightly, "You have not answered me. You *are* enjoying yourself?"

Jimena's resistance had completely melted. She took a huge bite off the meat in her hand and said around the mouthful, "I most certainly am, Urracca. I am having a *wonderful* time!"

The pilgrimage to Santiago was over. Jimena moved with the days, the months, without happiness or any lack of it. Life was merely a succession of reasonably satisfactory days. As a concession to Urracca, she took all her meals at the king's table now. She was still uncomfortable among people of the court, but time and new scandals had cooled down the heat of the gossip about her and Rodrigo and she had learned to ignore most of the slights and whisperings. Jimena enjoyed many pleasant afternoons with Urracca. They would spend hours animatedly handling the treasures of silks, velvets and jewels in Urracca's ornate chests. The Infanta closed the ten-year gap in their ages, acting as if she too were only seventeen years old. But there were those other days when Urracca could not bridge the gap, and anger and worry burdened her into a brooding silence. Then she would not speak to Jimena, who would sit quietly with head bowed, knowing the depth of her friend's pain but unable to heal it. Urracca would suddenly cry out, in a stricken voice, "My father lies dying on his bed, may the Devil take his rotten soul to Hell! So help me God, I shall not be condemned to a monastery. I will have an estate of my own, Jimena—I must. I *will* have it! I will!"

Jimena could not solve the dilemma of Urracca's destiny; her own was complicated enough. Alphonso alone offered Urracca respite from sorrow, and Jimena blessed him for the gifts of love and comfort which he gave so generously to his sister, gifts she herself would have given except that she could not completely escape her instinct to pass judgment. She simply could not forget that their love was sinful; she could only forgive them. The awareness of the sin, the knowledge of her own jeopardy, caused her to hold back a part of herself, which made the friendship she gave them a dreadfully shallow offering. Oh, but how it gladdened her sometimes, to see them riding side by side in the blazing sunlight, she so proud and lovely, looking every bit the queen she might have been, he the king he would soon be. There was no doubt in Jimena's mind that Alphonso had succumbed to his feelings for Urracca. As she would watch them from one of her chamber windows, Jimena would wonder what it was like to love someone so much, to feel so strongly about another person that it could shine from your eyes like a light. Though a great deal else had been denied her, Urracca had been given this, at least. At such moments Jimena saw a rather miraculous purity in their love, which she sincerely hoped God would note.

In the dark of night, awake on her bed, Jimena would guiltily dream of just such a love for herself, an uninhibited passion that would one day exist between herself and Rodrigo Diaz. The light she had seen in Alphonso's eyes was transmitted to the eyes of her husband: he would touch her tenderly, speak soft words to her, his kisses soft as silk against the flesh. He had been gone four months. A courier from Barbastro had brought word that the city had weakened under the siege and would soon capitulate. He would return soon, then. She closed her eyes tight, trying to recall his features. She wondered what he was doing at this very moment, if he was safe. Did he think of her, as she dreamed of him?

Chapter

✠ *SIX* ✠

The Muslim city of Barbastro had fallen. No man, woman, or child could escape the pious slaughter of the knights of the Holy Cross. Where months before the air was filled with music, laughter and the heady scent of a million flowers, now it was shattered by the wails of mothers watching their children being burned alive and the groans of husbands forced to see their wives and young daughters the pitiful victims of men's lust. The smell was not that of flowers now, but the stench of burned flesh and death. Fifty thousand human beings lost their lives in one day.

After six months of siege, the Muslim king sent a messenger to the crusaders; the people were weak from hunger and sick at heart and would surrender all their gold and send their leaders and rich merchants as prisoners, on the condition that the Christian knights take their city intact, without burning or pillaging. William de Montrueil had readily agreed, sitting upon his stallion like a miniature lion stalking its prey, wary and watchful. Six thousand Arabs filed out of the gate, some on horseback, others on foot. They had left their families, their whole lives behind them, and it showed on their drawn and stricken faces. They walked into certain death; their only crime was that they could not acknowledge the gentle Jesus. In their hearts they were true Spaniards; they had known no other land, nor had their fathers before them.

"Kill—kill—kill," the representative of God upon this earth cried out, and he himself was the first to do his own bidding. Covered with the blood of the Muslim prisoners who lay now butchered upon the earth outside the city, he led his horde through the open gates. He did not rest that day until he could find no one left to slaughter.

Rodrigo Diaz and the Infante Sancho had a mission of their

own. They pressed their way through the mob and clatter toward the king's palace, their coats of mail and helmets shining bright in the sunlight, untouched by the stains of battle, for there had been no battle; they had left the slaughter of the defenseless hostages to de Montrueil and his kind. The stench and smoke was unbearable. Rodrigo rode with a kerchief to his face in an effort to keep out the awful, choking odor. The foot soldiers, roused by de Montrueil, had swarmed into the city with butchery in their hearts. Everywhere Rodrigo looked he saw another gastly act of violence. The hooves of his mount were red with the blood that ran like a stream down the cobblestone street.

"Turn here, Sancho, this way"

But as they came around the bend in the narrow alley, a huge fire blocked their way, a mountain of burning bodies. The smoke was a cloud, thick, stinking, striking their nostrils hot and sickening. Coughing and gagging, they tried another street and finally dismounted; the way would be easier on foot.

It took hours. By the time they were within sight of the palace, darkness had begun to fall. There still seemed to be no end to the Christian thirst for blood. Sancho's face was twisted in a kind of agony; he was determined not to let this touch him. Rodrigo knew that deep within Sancho there was a gentle spirit that the king called weakness. Sancho despised this thing within himself so much that he covered it with a facade of cruelty. But this massacre of women and infants must touch his very soul, for it touched Rodrigo's and he did not consider himself a gentle man. Sancho's face was covered with splatters of blood and soot. His mail and helmet were no longer shining, but ornamented with rust-colored badges of death. A six-foot whitewashed wall surrounded the rather drab two-story palace. Illuminated by the light from the fires, immense trees could be seen rising against the night sky from beyond the wall.

"Pray God the men obeyed our orders," Sancho shouted, "and have not plundered it." With relief they saw that their knights and soldiers had posted themselves at intervals completely around the wall, holding off a shouting mob of Italian knights with raised swords and lances.

"Ah, thank you Satan. I shall reward these men well, Rodrigo. Perhaps this day will be to some avail after all."

Within an hour it was fully dark, and the knights of Don Ferrando, over a thousand strong, surrounded three deep the palace walls of the infidel king. Word reached de Montrueil, and in delirious fury he descended upon Rodrigo and Sancho, his squinty eyes blazing. "Here! Here now, what do you men think you are doing? Move away from that gate there—I command you. In the name of Alexander, as God's representative, I command you!"

Rodrigo squalled back, "And in the name of Ferrando, ruler of all Castile, I command *you*. Go to *hell!*"

"Swine! Godless, filthy swine! You shall reap the vengeance of the Lord. Your souls will burn in eternal fire. Here! You there. Charge that gate."

But the small group of Italian knights to whom he spoke only glanced apprehensively at the solid wall of men guarding the gate and remained motionless, sending their leader into another screaming tirade. De Montrueil finally rode off, passionately vowing reprisal. Behind him trudged his knights, heads bowed in shame as they listened to his condemning words, denying them forever the sanctuary of Heaven.

"Jesus!" Rodrigo laughed, "thankful I am that *that* is done with. Now—How might we enter this place? That gate seems to be forged of solid iron."

"Over the wall, my lad. And to you, Rodrigo Diaz de Bivar, beloved friend, I give that dubious honor." Sancho gave the gate a hard bang with the end of his sword, "Open it from within, while we rest a bit without, where it is comparatively safe."

"Ho-ho! Thank you, Sancho. I take it my usefulness has already run itself out. Ach, you send me to the king's guards, defenseless, helpless creature that I am—"

"Enough of your dull wit, man. Over you go."

Two men made a chair of fists and arms upon which Rodrigo placed a foot. With a great heave he threw himself over the wall to land flat on his face on the other side. He lay motionless for a long moment, slowly becoming aware of something strange and soft beneath him. It was grass, clipped short and as soft as a carpet. It smelled sweet and clean. The sounds of screaming and death from the city beyond the wall became dulled and faded. Now he heard the rippling of running water, and the occasional chirp of a night bird. There was an odd perfume in the air, carried on the wind over the stench of smoke and burned flesh. The stillness was almost frightening. For God, had he jumped into Paradise? No—no such angry God as he had witnessed today would have such a heaven as this.

"Good evening, sir."

The voice was deep and soft, but forceful. Rodrigo leaped to his feet, instantly drawing his sword.

"Ah, no need of that, my lord—I am unarmed."

With difficulty Rodrigo focused his tired eyes on a dark man of about thirty, who stood illuminated by firelight from the burning city. The Muslim was bowing to him, his black embroidered turban glittering with sparks of gold thread. He wore a flowing violet tunic and a mantle of gold; on his feet were silver shoes, buckled and jeweled with stones of red and blue. The infidel's hands were graceful as a woman's, his fingers long and slender. A huge ring of an irregular design circled his right thumb. Rodrigo stared at him openmouthed.

"Come, I will escort you to the lord." The man spoke fluent Spanish, and pointed in the direction of the palace. Forgetting about the still-locked gate, leaving Sancho to pace and fret, Rodrigo followed with hungrily curious eyes. He passed a fountain that shot water skyward ten feet or more. The perfume was overpowering now and Rodrigo suspiciously eyed the gushing water of the fountain, which seemed to be the source. Scented water?

"This way, my lord."

Turning a corner in the wide, graveled path, they walked between columns of marble pillars, and Rodrigo's boots struck tile. The man stopped before a door and knelt to remove his slippers, looking questioningly to Rodrigo. The infidel shrugged and opened the door wide, allowing Rodrigo to enter first.

"For Christ!" The words exploded from Rodrigo's lips, his eyes widening with amazement. He had stepped into a splendor that nearly blinded him. From the outside the palace was a windowless, drab, misshapen clod of a building, but on the inside, the walls were completely tiled in beautiful colors of every hue imaginable. Tapestries embroidered with gold thread and beaded with jewels hung over the tile here and there about the cavernous room. In the center of the room was a fountain, smaller than the one in the garden, made in the image of a tiny lion, from whose mouth spouted water; no, by Jesus, it *was* perfume. The little lion sat on its haunches, its ruby eyes staring indifferently into Rodrigo's startled face.

As he followed the infidel, Rodrigo noticed an old man at the far end of the room who sat upon a colorful, billowing cloud of silk bejeweled pillows, with his legs twisted under him. Rodrigo's escort made a quick bow from the waist to the elder and spoke, still in expert Spanish. "This is one of our captors, Yosuf. I found him in the garden and so that he did not lose himself in such a place as this, I brought him directly to you."

The wizened old man stared blankly at Rodrigo, no emotion showing in his half-closed eyes. He uttered a disgruntled snort and nodded his head. The younger man turned to Rodrigo and said, "This is the lord, as you say it, king of Barbastro, and I am Abu l Hasan ibn Al Hamman of Cordova, a guest in his house. And, if I may, I offer you our humble hospitality."

Rodrigo eyed the man coldly. "You are too kind, my lord. I must inform you that Yosuf is to be held for ransom in the name of Ferrando, king of Castile."

The Muslim king broke his silence. In a frail but smoothly polite voice, he said, "And who, if I may inquire, is expected to pay this ransom?"

"Maktadir. Your brother."

"Ah, indeed." A slight smile turned up the corners of Yosuf's quivering lips. "But my brother values his gold highly, young man, and Christian blood is cheap to him. You may find the mighty Maktadir more eager to cut your throats than to buy my freedom."

"And Muslim blood is cheap to *us!*" Rodrigo exclaimed belligerently, angered by the man's calm effrontery in the face of almost certain death.

Yosuf bowed his head to Rodrigo. "Allah forsake me, sir, if I have offended thee."

It was a polite phrase, but used as it was under this circumstance, it became a slapping insult. However, as the old man continued, Rodrigo's rage was subdued.

"My house is yours, and I am your humble servant, my lord. Abu l Hasan, show this young knight to proper quarters, and see to his every need."

Rodrigo studied his companion as he was led through the magnificent palace. The man's back was straight as a rod. He had always thought of the Muslim as a blacker man, but this strikingly handsome infidel had flesh of a light bronze, no darker than Rodrigo's, burned as he was by the sun.

"I sincerely hope that these rooms will suit your needs, my lord?"

A curtain had been drawn aside, revealing a room that more than adequately suited Rodrigo's needs, for he had never slept in such a bedchamber. It was not an overly large room, but the walls were tiled in a wild array of colors, blending in perfect harmony with the thick carpets that covered the floor from wall to wall. There was no bed, no furniture of any kind, only a mattresslike affair on the floor in one corner, covered with bright yellow silk and surrounded by enormous, embroidered pillows. The outside wall was made entirely of opaque glass cut into odd shapes, in beautiful shades of green and yellow. Abu l Hasan stepped close to one corner of the glass wall; finding an invisible latch there, he pulled one half across the other to reveal a garden but a few steps from the bed.

Suddenly Rodrigo became painfully aware of the dirt upon himself, the sweat that oozed beneath his coat of mail, the lice that ran their usual races up and down his spine. Everything was so damned clean here; how in hell did they manage it? His host stood at the garden entrance, staring coldly at him. Rodrigo had never known self-consciousness before. He was certain the man felt superior to him. Arrogant bastard.

"You! Who *are* you?" Rodrigo avoided using the title "my lord," though it started automatically to his lips—he did not know why, except that the man had the bearing of a king. "You introduced yourself as a guest. What are you actually? One would think you owned the palace."

Hasan's face did not lose its expression of calm indifference. He smiled pleasantly. "As I told you, my name is Abu l Hasan, of the city of Cordova. My home rests upon the banks of the Quadalquivir River. There, in that city, I am a teacher of philosophy, mathematics, and astrology. I am a guest of the great Yosuf at his invitation, for he had heard of my knowledge and imagination. I tell him tales of fancy to cheer his heart, and discuss with him the great men whose works teach us how to live, which stimulates his mind. For this humble service Yosuf repays me in gold each day. Invitations such as this have made me a wealthy man, my lord." He finished with a quick, polite bow, the question answered completely in an almost singing voice.

But Rodrigo had understood very little of what had been said to him. "What is this—this *mathematics*?"

"Numbers, my lord. Calculations, formulas and simple addition and subtraction."

"Ah . . . the keeping of ledgers."

"Much more than that. There is a branch of this science that deals with the properties of solids, surfaces, lines, and angles; it is called geometry. Another very new principle of numbers has recently been developed—*Al Gebra.*"

Rodrigo frowned. Only a priest or a monk could teach. But the Muslim had no priests. A teacher? He wanted to ask what philosophy was, and astrology too, but did not want to appear altogether ignorant. "And just who do you teach?" he asked testily. "Are the children of Islam all so familiar with these numbers you speak of?"

"Some are. But I do not teach *children*. I instruct adults, in a very large building that we call a college, or university."

It was too baffling. Rodrigo tried to envision a group of adults gathered together expressly to learn what this man had to teach them. It was too ridiculous; had they nothing better to do with their time? To what possible use could they put such useless knowledge? "Then what subject *do* you teach the children?" he asked, recalling his own schooling. The monks gave him a solid background in religion and elementary reading and writing. He had always considered himself highly educated and superior, armed with this vast amount of knowledge.

"It is quite involved, my lord, but I think I can briefly describe it. First, the child must learn the Koran, which is our Bible, then the Sunnah, or traditional comment. Next he learns the Hadyz, that is, the historical tradition of Islam. There is grammar, of course, and poetry. Arabic, naturally. Proverbs. The lives of princes. The science of government, and other sciences, such as those I have already mentioned to you, particularly biology, which is the study of living creatures." He hesitated to go on, but Rodrigo was engrossed and made no attempt to interrupt him. "The boy must also learn to groom a horse, draw a bow, wield a lance and sword, manage all weapons, and understand all strategies of war."

"This—" Rodrigo began in amazement, "this was the manner of your own education?"

"Yes, my lord."

So, Rodrigo thought, he can manage all weapons and understands all strategies. He might not have a muscular arm, but his lithe frame would render him a formidable adversary with a sword. He warned himself to keep a careful watch on the man. Deciding not to further reveal his ignorance, Rodrigo said commandingly, "The main gate must be opened immediately. The Infante Sancho awaits without. He is the son of the king of Castile, but I am equally in command here; understand that."

"Indeed. If there is nothing more, I ask your permission to withdraw?" He was backing up and bowing, moving toward the curtains.

"Wait! Tell me—why do Yosuf and yourself treat me so graciously! You could easily have had my throat cut. At the moment I am quite alone and helpless against you."

Hasan smiled. Holding back the red curtain with a hand, he purred, "Outside the walls of this palace you have many comrades who might be inclined to forget ransom, if one as noble as yourself were to have his head severed from his shoulders. We have a saying, my lord. When your enemy extends his hand to you, cut if off if you can, or *kiss* it." With that he quickly turned around to slip quietly out of sight behind the curtain.

Two days under a hot sun had created a stench of decomposing bodies that was unendurable. Thus the very soldiers who had slain were forced to pile their victims onto carts and wagons, hauling them beyond the city for mass burial in pits dug by other Christians for that purpose. When the streets of Barbastro were finally cleared of bodies and gore, an ominous quiet fell upon the town, a great depression upon the Christian horde. Even de Montrueil had ceased his incessant ravings about the loss of the palace, and sat now in brooding silence amid his sulking troops. Guards were posted in the city, but the men would not sleep there, for at night the screams and wails of the prisoners could be heard; they remained encamped outside the walls of Barbastro. Rodrigo Diaz had gathered together all his own men, billeting them at the palace.

In the dungeons, the Muslim captives suffered living hell, crammed into cells so thickly they could not lie down or sit. They stood and held each other up with weakening arms, and when one died he remained where he was, leaning grotesquely upon his neighbor, all those near him looking with horror into his dead and staring eyes.

But there was no misery, no brooding silence in the palace, the men quartered there having no reason to be depressed or sorrowful. Day and night laughter and sighs of delight could be heard. The harem wenches had been magnanimously freed from captivity. Some of the ladies were foolish enough to weep, others grimly set their delicate jaws and bore whatever they must, and there were those who smiled winningly, giving themselves with abandon.

Rodrigo Diaz did not exclude himself from the pleasures of harem women, as he had the murder of women and babes, for there was a woman so golden and soft, so exquisite of body that each time he looked upon her a volcano of emotion erupted in a consuming heat within him. He would take her, but never satisfied himself of her, so that in a little while he again felt the heat and his hands, his mouth, his body, would find her. She gave herself with such complete passion that it drove him to near madness.

He saw her first only two days after the palace was taken. It had been an extremely close night so he had left the glass door open. He did not know how long he had been asleep when something woke him. He opened his eyes slowly, and there she stood in the garden, the woman of every man's imagination, clothed in pale violet trousers caught tight at the ankles, topped by an embroidered vest. On her tiny feet were yellow slippers with pointed toes. Her dark brown hair fell in a curling cloud to her waist. She watched him, unaware that he also observed her. He became uncomfortably conscious of his nakedness and reached down to pull up the satin coverlet. In an instant she vanished.

Next day Rodrigo called Abu l Hasan to him. The man came obediently and Rodrigo felt a cloying irritation. Why did the man so humble himself? Just once he might defy, and then his captor might have some little respect for him.

"Abu l Hasan, I seek one of the harem wenches. I saw her in my garden last night. A lovely girl, about twenty-five, with eyes of deep green. Short—oh, no higher than this." Rodrigo raised his arm in a suggestion of height, "and I have never seen such hair, the color both red and brown. Find her for me, Hasan. She is not one of the wenches given over to my men. I want her."

Hasan stood before Rodrigo, quiet and stiffly controlled, his eyes fixed on his folded hands. He did not acknowledge the command. When he looked up there was a new brightness behind his eyes. Rodrigo thought, Ah, he will defy me at last. But the answer finally came, in a voice as polite and submissive as usual.

"I most humbly beg your pardon for my hesitation, my lord, but I could not find words, emotion closing my throat. You see, the woman you have described is my wife."

"Your wife! I thought you were from Cordova?"

"I do not travel alone across mountains and deserts. With me I bring my wives, foot soldiers for protection, servants, and much of my personal belongings, for it is often a year or more before I again see my home."

"Wives . . . ? And how many wives do you *have*, sir?"

"Four, my Lord, all of whom I cherish, though the one of whom you spoke is my favorite. As you have seen, she is of rare beauty and, in addition, possesses great intelligence and charm." He looked icily at Rodrigo. "I would not relish the loss of her."

"Ho! Four wives, eh? Then you will not miss this one, my barbarous friend." Rodrigo's voice took on sharper tones. "Send for her, Abu l Hasan."

Hasan's facial muscles strained as he held control. He sighed and said, "I can see you are determined. Then I shall make you a gift of her—such a gift as will rend my very soul. I will divorce her, so that she will not suffer the shame of being named adulteress. She is yours, Rodrigo Diaz. But," it came a definite warning now, "if harm comes to her, you will live to regret it." With that he turned and left the room.

Rodrigo was confounded. For Jesus Christ: a gift! Divorce her so she will not suffer the shame of—for the love of God! What a miserable excuse for a man, this Hasan. Such barbaric customs simply left a civilized man dumbfounded.

Rodrigo did not see Hasan again that day, nor that night. Suspicion clawed at him. Could the man have somehow escaped the palace with his favorite? Impossible. The next morning Rodrigo was at the main gate speaking to a group of knights when Hasan approached him. Hasan stood patiently aside as Rodrigo gave each man his instructions for the day. When he had finished, Rodrigo whirled upon Hasan with, "Where the devil have you been? Where is she? I will find her for myself if you do not bring her to me, and it will not go well with you if you have hidden her or helped her to escape."

Hasan avoided his enemy's eyes. "If you will follow me, please?" He led Rodrigo through the gardens to a secluded grove of barren trees, where the lady of Rodrigo's vision sat upon a bench, her face veiled now, her hands folded demurely in her lap. Hasan smiled wanly, reached down and took one of her hands in his, drawing her up to stand before Rodrigo. "My lord, her name is Sabíhah," he said softly.

Rodrigo stepped closed to the girl, grinning smugly down into the emerald-green eyes that stared back at him from above the veil. "You are exquisite. Sabíhah. That is a lovely name."

"She does not speak Spanish, of course, Saíd."

At the sorrow in Hasan's voice, Rodrigo laughed rudely, "Ah, Abu l Hasan, there are three more who await you in your bedchamber this night. Surely you are not such a man as can satisfy four at once!"

"*YAHRAK KIDDISAK man rabba-k!*" the curse slashed out at Rodrigo with a hissing fury. Hasan's eyes blazed at Rodrigo. Then he turned quickly and spoke in Arabic to the girl, his words low, his temper reined. She nodded slightly, watching in solemn regret as he left her alone with Rodrigo Diaz.

That night Rodrigo took her and she submitted to his embraces with warm, moist lips, quivering flesh and sighs of delight, teaching him ways of love that he had never known before. Such a woman, good God. A black passion raged through him, blinding him to all except the paradise of her pulsating flesh.

Thus Rodrigo left the management of the palace and all other duties of the garrison to Sancho. He spent the better portion of each day, as well as all the nights, with Sabíhah. Her eyes said she adored him. He was certain the girl deeply loved him. Of course. She was with a man, now. Indeed, what woman would prefer a Hasan, near-woman himself, when she could be cheered by the real article—a lion as compared to a puppy dog. He saw little of the poor husband after that last meeting. The man seemed preoccupied, spending much of his time with Yosuf, deep in conversation; Arabic was a God-detested language that neither Rodrigo nor any one of his men spoke or dared to learn. Whatever was discussed so seriously remained Hasan's secret.

Sancho burst into Rodrigo's bedchamber that was now littered with grime and debris. Breathlessly he began to speak, then he noticed the girl clutched in his friend's arms. "For God's sake—rid yourself of that slut. There is important news."

"She speaks no Spanish, Sancho. Proceed." Rodrigo had had too much wine and was laden down by a recent heavy meal. He felt lazy and content. He held on to Sabíhah and grinned foolishly at Sancho.

"I am uncertain if I should leave you, my lad." Sancho's tone was sarcastically humorless. "For the rest of your days you will be fighting your own blood . . . you will have left so many half-breed brats behind"

"Ho—good jest," Rodrigo smirked. "What is this about leaving me? Going somewhere?"

"Enough. I am in a hurry. I cannot waste time discussing your lust for Muslim women. My father has been struck down by illness. I must depart immediately for Palencia. The army will follow tomorrow. The crusade that was to follow this one, against Toledo, must be postponed until the king is well enough or . . . You are in command here. I will not be here to carry your burdens, so, for the love of Satan, Rodrigo, curb your lust, or you will find a Muslim knife in your back!"

Rodrigo unwound himself from Sabíhah's arms and rose unsteadily to his feet. He strode over to Sancho and wrapped an arm around his shoulder. "I am deeply sorry about your father. Go, and have no fear, Rodrigo Diaz will be diligent. I will await Maktadir's gold and guard the Arab king well, and," he smiled drunkenly, "I will try extremely hard to curb my lust, as you so aptly put it." He slapped Sancho's back affectionately. There was love in his eyes, which was mirrored in the eyes of his friend.

"If my father should die I will send for you, for I could not rule a single day if you were not at my side, Rodrigo."

Rodrigo was overwhelmed by the compliment, warmed again by the future he saw outstretched before him.

Two days after de Montrueil's army marched away from Barbastro, leaving the city to Rodrigo's Castilian forces the awaited message from Maktadir arrived at the palace. The gold would be delivered within the week. Rodrigo faithfully tended to the business of the garrison, saw that the guards on duty were not too drunk to carry out their own duties, and confined the harem sluts to narrow quarters for knights off duty. He saw Sabíhah only at night now—but such nights. That frigid, pale wife of his could never afford a man such abandoned passions, such ecstasy of heart and flesh.

Rodrigo paced slowly around the palace walls on his evening tour of the guard. There was a chill in the air, and the wind pressed hard against his body, so that he was forced to lean against it to keep his balance. The week was near an end. He felt restless and uneasy. Maktadir's gold would at last arrive, and he would be so damned relieved to be in the saddle again. This inactivity was becoming a grievous annoyance. Six months of siege, of waiting, with nothing to do but eat and sleep, then a brief excitement—and now this. But for Sabíhah, the days would be a total waste. By Jesus, he would miss the wench. It was a pity he had to leave her desolate. What would happen to her when her lover departed for Castile? Hasan might take her back, but not likely, for each time he looked upon her he would know that Rodrigo Diaz had been in her, and that she had been willing. The barbaric fool would probably sell her to the lowest bidder.

From a distance Rodrigo heard shouts and the sound of running horses. He jerked erect, listening, then ran swiftly toward an oncoming rider.

"Ruy Diaz!" Don Jaime Martinez cried out, leaping from his mount. He clutched at Rodrigo's arm, gasping for breath, trying to be coherent. "Out there, thousands of them, like ghosts all in white—as far as the eye can see!"

Rodrigo listened intently, attempting to piece together Jaime's breathless story. "I was on guard duty at the main gate when a small party of Maktadir's soldiers approached with a wagon, presumably the gold. Just in case, I sent a scout . . . and over a rise several hundred yards from the city walls he saw them, thick as wheat in the fields. A guess is six thousand, conservatively!"

"Damn!" Rodrigo cursed. Maktadir was a legend among the Castilians, the most ruthless, ingenious infidel they had to contend with near their borders. Rodrigo's mind raced over all possible avenues of escape. He had perhaps a thousand men who were not drunk or dead asleep. One thousand against five? Ten? "The swine—filthy swine!"

Shouts echoed from the city gate. The wagon with the gold had arrived. "Don Jaime!" Rodrigo shouted at the man, who was still gasping for breath. "I must have *time*. Increase the guard, hold them off, do not allow them to enter the city. Keep those goddamned gates closed! Tell them we will come out for the gold, that there is no need for them to enter the city. Go! And wait for me with your two hands on the gate blocks!"

Rodrigo raced through the palace, the gardens, the stables, roaring orders to all he could find or wake, ordering them to find horses and meet him at the city gates in full armor. Rushing to his own quarters, he exploded through the curtains and grabbed his suit of mail from a hook where it had hung unused these many weeks.

"Hah! He runs. The brave Christian pig runs like a frightened goat!"

Rodrigo whipped around, stunned.

"Sabíhah!"

"Yes—Sabíhah. Filthy pig! Did you think me so ignorant that I could not speak the childlike dialect of lowly Christians? Did you think that I could possibly admire such as you? Ach! You are not fit to wipe the backside of my Hasan. You smell like a dead goat! I sicken at the thought of you ever touching me again!"

"No, no," Rodrigo protested, shaking his head hard. She despised him. He could not believe it. But it gradually penetrated, and rage moved within him until he felt it flaming in his head. "Get from my sight," he screamed out at her, "get out of here! Harem slut!" He heard his own words as if from a great distance. The wine, this rotten, maddening woman, the luxury, all of it had softened him, made a weak-kneed fool of him. He shook his fist in her writhing face. "So help me God, such as you will never weaken my flesh again. Whore! Harem slut—get from my sight!"

Unexpectedly, in a blur of motion, the girl rushed at him, wrenching his knife from its sheath. She stood poised before him, eyes lit by a fire of hatred, the knife upraised in her hand. Her voice was cold and venemous, "I am going to kill you. Oh, how I have longed to cut your foul throat."

"Insolent bitch!" Rodrigo's arm shot out and caught Sabíhah across the head. The blow raised her from the floor. She fell forward with a lurch, uttering a faint grunting sound, then lay still. Her back heaved in a last, gasping breath, and she was dead. With the toe of his boot Rodrigo reached out and rolled her over. His knife was imbedded in her breast, on her blouse a red wetness was widening and moving down upon her trousers. There was no pity in his heart. He looked upon her, fastening the impression of her in his memory. He did not intend to ever forget Sabíhah. She would remain before his eyes the rest of his days, a constant reminder that the Muslim was and always would be his enemy; insidious, creeping demons with ways that softened a man until he could no longer call himself a man, able only to love and laugh and degenerate. Never. Never again would Rodrigo Diaz be so duped.

"Slut! Goddamned slut," he hissed at Sabíhah's lifeless form. "You listened and made your reports. You played the spy, used that face and flesh as a weapon against me—well, good *riddance!*" He kicked and pounded her face with his boot until it was only a mass of broken and bloodied flesh and bone. "That! That is what I think of your face. Slut. Oh, God!" He felt his shoulders quaking. He had to get hold of himself. Hands trembling, he clumsily yanked at his suit of mail, breaking a fingernail on a sharp edge as he pulled the coat over his head. Without a glance in Sabíhah's direction, he ran out of the room. He left behind him not only a dead Muslim girl, but his youth, the last sweet remains of gentleness and compassion. He went to the battle with a heart filled with loathing. That the soldiers of Maktadir failed to kill him that day was a tragedy, a miracle, or a blessing . . . depending upon the viewpoint of those who considered the matter during his time, and long after it. He was fully equipped now for the role he was to play in his country, that of a professional killer of men. Christians and Arabs alike would feel the cold stab of his sword for years and years to come.

Only eight hundred men had responded to Rodrigo's call to arms. He plunged through the mob, enraged by the terror and confusion on the faces of his knights and soldiers. Jaime Martinez was at his post with three other knights, hands ready to release the gate blocks. Rodrigo's mount awaited him, nervous and skittish, barely kept under control by his squire. He leaped upon the horse's back and cried out to the men, "Meet them as *one body*! Do not scatter! We are not out to win a battle, but to escape with our goddamned necks! Don Jaime! Open the gate."

Jaime and the three knights instantly obeyed, pulling hard on the heavy wooden blocks, sliding them out of the bolts. The gate swung open. Rodrigo was the first to ride out, plunging his lance through the heart of the first infidel he saw, then the next, until all the men who had come to the gate with the wagon were dead. Then he reined in his mount and shouted at the eight hundred to move. He waited, watching the ridges of the low hills in the distance. It came within seconds, a loud thundering that seemed to come from everywhere at once, a rumble of hooves that drowned out all other sounds. Then a white tidal wave of horsemen swept toward them. When the last of his men rode or stumbled on their two feet out of the gate, Rodrigo whipped his mount around and reentered the gates, hoping to arouse some of the stragglers. A groan to his right stopped him. Don Jaime lay on the cobbles, blood a pool around his crumpled body; one of the massive gate blocks had fallen over his legs and pinned him there. He had been trampled half to death by the terrified soldiers and knights.

Rodrigo leaped from his mount and was beside the man in a second. With a great heave, he lifted the tremendous weight of the block and threw it aside.

"Go," Don Jaime moaned, curling up his body in pain. One of his legs was limp. He lifted his head and stared down at the limb, looking more annoyed than horrified. "Jesus Christ!" he swore. Then he swung an arm at Rodrigo and shouted, "Will you get the hell out of here before you get an arrow through your skull!"

Rodrigo laughed. As he picked the man up to throw him over the neck of his horse, he said, "But I thought you *wanted* me dead, sir." He swung himself into the saddle. Glancing around for stragglers, he saw only one small group of smirking drunks staring at him. He viciously spurred his mount, speeding through the gate toward the point where his men had chosen to break the infidel line.

With a crash of Toledo steel against Christian iron, the eight hundred met the Muslim horsemen head on. The Christians fought their way savagely forward in a desperate effort to escape, as many as fifty falling dead at once. Rodrigo's mount was run through with a lance, sending him and Don Jaime sprawling to the bloodied earth at the very moment the break in the line was finally achieved. He swept Don Jaime up in his arms and ran with him, gasping for breath and stumbling, but not stopping until he reached a rocky, tree-sheltered slope. He climbed the hill backward, dragging Jaime up with him, careless of his injured and oozing leg. At the top of the rise he swung Jaime in under some trees, flattened himself, and lay there hidden. Every breath was another slash at his lungs; it felt like his chest was being ripped apart by knives from within. He glanced over to Jaime. The man was unconscious, perhaps dead. He crawled over to him and felt his throat. The pulse was strong. Then he examined the man's leg. It was almost completely severed above the knee. The bleeding had to be stopped. He yanked off his armor and then his shirt, ripping the cloth into strips. He tied the cloth tight above the wound and held it fast until the blood ceased to flow.

Rodrigo eased his body upward a little, attempting to see through the cover of trees down to the battle that still raged below and several hundred yards distant. "Good Christ!" he swore under his breath, as he saw the field scattered with the bodies of Castilians. Perhaps a dozen men could be seen speeding west on horses, leaving the massacre behind them . . . a dozen at most. He collapsed backward, laying on his back, staring up at the cloudless sky. "Damn! God damn!"

Rodrigo's room at Yosuf's palace was dark now. Sabíhah lay just as Rodrigo had left her, the knife jutting out of her breast, her blood a wide stain all around her, her face gone. Beside her knelt Abu l Hasan, tears streaming down his bronze face, one hand covering his mouth in horror and grief. Then he moved to gently remove Rodrigo's knife. He held the knife in his shaking hand for a brief moment then recoiled and dropped it to the carpet. Moaning, he lifted her in his arms and hugged her to him, burying his face in her wounded breast, weeping unrestrained.

"Sabíhah! My sweet, my lovely Sabíhah!" He shrieked in

anguish, his dark eyes black with hatred. "Allah give me the strength! Somehow! Some way! Oh, omnipotent Allah willing . . . I shall retaliate against this murder—and such a retaliation it will be that he will never forget it! Not as long as he lives!"

Chapter
✠ *SEVEN* ✠

Spring struggled impatiently, here and there sending a green shoot up from the barren, cold ground, a fragile blossom out upon the desolate branch of a tree. Life was fighting its always victorious battle against the death of winter. At the very moment this first soft murmur trembled the earth and made itself known, a man gasped for breath in a desperate, futile effort to hold on to the thin thread of his existence. The winter of his years was over. There would never be another spring for him. The king, Don Ferrando, took his last breath, and died. He drifted out of his world, not as he had lived, dramatically and forcefully, but quiescent in sleep, and there was no one left behind who would mourn him. His daughter, Urracca, smiled; there was a deep contentment within her, a new hope, a new bloom on the desolate branches of her own tree of life. His three sons were now kings, and within them the specters of distrust, jealousy, and greed emerged as Ferrando's legacy to them; a monumental part of himself would go on living long after him, destroying as he had destroyed and hating as he had hated. The character of King Don Ferrando was preserved in the hearts of his sons, who were still in the spring of their lives.

Jimena stood quietly, watching Urracca and Alphonso; Urracca was leaning upon the back of his chair with her arms entwined about his neck, her cheek pressed against his sand-colored beard. Urracca was glowing with happiness. Her vows were fulfilled. She was countess of Zamora, mistress of all the monasteries with their fields and granaries, and beloved by the man of her choice. How she had convinced her father to alter his will, Jimena did not know, but that it had made her friend gloriously happy was obvious.

"And what great things have you accomplished this day,

my lord, my dearest king of Leon?" Urracca asked playfully, as she roughly mussed Alphonso's straight, bristly hair.

"Ah, worth history noting. I settled the matter of twenty stolen goats, had the thief horsewhipped. And I have put a new law into the books, rendering incest legal, for every man should find such a one as I have found."

"Alphonso!" Urracca had bolted upright. "That is not funny! What a mean word to use. Oh, you have the worst manner of teasing. For one who was, at the beginning, so reluctant and . . . Well, you are truly a curious, unpredictable man."

Alphonso laughed wickedly and gave her a quick, affectionate kiss on the end of her nose. As his eyes turned from Urracca, they rested upon Jimena, who had been watching them from across the room. "Jimena, we embarrass you. I am sorry. Come here to me. I wish to speak to you a moment. Come, do not stand back in that corner like a punished child."

Jimena forced a smile. She walked toward Alphonso with hesitation because he was a king now and she was awed by his new status. His shoulders seemed straighter, his manner far more regal, or was this merely her imagination? Alphonso could never be described as truly handsome; his features were too irregular, his eyes too small and close together, his nose much too small for his large, heavy-jawed face; but his easy charm, basic kindness and his strong, well-proportioned body made him very attractive to women.

"Jimena." Alphonso took her hand and drew her close to him. Continuing to hold her hand, he said seriously, "It has been a happy year. I place great value on our friendship, I want you to know that."

His hand felt warm, a warmth that passed through to her heart. She did not love him as Urracca did, but, truly, it was a kind of love, this affection she had for Alphonso, the only man who had ever made her feel necessary, accepted, and loved.

"Rodrigo Diaz will return to Palencia soon," Alphonso continued solemnly. "Sancho has already sent word to him of my father's death. You realize, of course, that your husband is committed to Sancho's cause, whatever that may be. I want to assure you that no matter what happens, though Rodrigo Diaz becomes my mortal enemy, you, his wife, will always be my friend. You will always be welcome in my house, and if you ever need assistance, you have but to ask."

Jimena was warmed to tears by the honest affection in Alphonso's eyes, the regret in Urracca's. How she would miss them both. Soon they would go in separate directions, Urracca to her city of Zamora, she with Rodrigo to Castile; Alphonso would remain in Leon. Everyone at the castle said that Sancho would not rest until Garcia and Alphonso were dead, until he was king over all three countries, and that Urracca, too, would fall beneath the wrath of her brother, unable to keep what she had gained. Jimena was appalled at the thought of Rodrigo slaying such a man as Alphonso, killing her dearest friend. By what right did he play God with the lives of men?

The months had seemed to pass slowly but now she felt that they had flown by. The moment she had so dreaded and at the same time anxiously awaited was at hand. She anticipated the ordeal of living in Castile, away from her new and only friends, watching helplessly as her husband made plans to murder Alphonso. God! How could she bear the future before her, how could she possibly?

"I pray to God it will never come to pass that you become the enemy of my husband, Alphonso. You will always have a place in my heart, too. And you, Urracca—I *do* love you both." Jimena flushed, feeling painfully shy, but she was glad she had been able to say the words.

"Yes, Jimena, do pray to God," Alphonso said. "It is a heavy burden that has been placed upon my shoulders. I had not expected to rule. Gladly would I have had Sancho be king over all the kingdoms. Still, I cannot surrender that which has been given me, for I, too, have a certain amount of greed within me. I am not altogether averse to being crowned a king. That I must kill my brothers to keep this little country, however—God forbid."

Urracca quickly threw her arms around his neck and hugged him intensely. "Beloved, you will prevail. Our father knew that you were the one best suited to rule. One day you will be king, as our father was, of all three countries—I know it!" With words she was trying to give Alphonso the confidence and peace of mind he needed; she desperately wanted to ease his, concern. He was the only gentle, kind, loving thing in her life, and no one would destroy him, not as long as she lived. She would place her own hard and unrelenting soul beside his, like a rock, and whatever he lacked—she would provide.

Alphonso smiled indulgently at Urracca's earnestness, then rose from his chair. "I would very much enjoy remaining here with you two, but I am a king now, and have duties to perform. I must go." He turned to Jimena and said softly, " . . . remember what I have said to you. And have no fear.

Rodrigo is a fine man. He will be a *great* man one day. I am certain you will learn to love him well, in time."

When the door closed behind Alphonso, Urracca shouted, "Oh! Is he not the most wonderful man that ever lived on this earth?"

"Oh, yes, he is, Urracca. I wish my Rodrigo were half the man, then I would not quake so at the thought of seeing him again. I have prayed to the Mother every day to give me the strength. . . ."

"For God's sake, Jimena," Urracca interrupted scoldingly. "You have had almost a year to prepare yourself. Surely you are not still determined to hold on to your virginity? I mean, what are you planning to *do* with it? You cannot see it, touch it, feel it; it is no more than a badge of stunted growth, confirming that you are still a child and not a woman." At Jimena's wide-eyed, pained expression, Urracca laughed and playfully brushed her friend's cheek with her fingertips. "What a nightmare, if one day you should lose your faith and have to look back on all the pleasures forsaken while under a false impression, mmmm? I will love my dearest Alphonso until he leaves me, and then I will make confession and my bid for Heaven. Pray I do not die in the meantime. But who cares; if I lose Alphonso I shall be as good as dead and already in a hell."

Jimena shook her head in mock exasperation. "Urracca, you are just impossible! Lose my faith, indeed. What nonsense." Her words broke off at the sounds of shouting coming from somewhere outside the window. "What is it? Do you hear that, Urracca?"

Urracca rushed to the window and looked down. "Well, speak of the devil," she exclaimed, "and there he is! Your husband is riding hell-bent toward this castle. Your moment has come. Have courage; it will be better than you think.

Jimena was quickly beside Urracca, craning her neck to see. "Oh, my God—he looks terrible!" What she saw was a ragged, exhausted, angry stranger. Surely she was not married to that man; it was impossible.

Rodrigo viciously brushed aside everyone who attempted to greet him or question him as he rushed toward Sancho's quarters. He found the room empty. Exhausted, he threw himself on the bed, burying his head in weary arms. Every bone and muscle screamed for rest. The nerves in his thighs and calves jerked spasmodically. It was an effort to keep his eyes open. His eyelids were weighted not only by exhaustion, but by the dust that rains had turned into caked mud. He had not slept in—Jesus, it had been at least three days. Living hell. That first night he had dragged Don Jaime with him on foot; it was almost dawn when they reached the Christian village of Corina. He had left Martinez, whose leg was festering badly, in the hands of the local priest, and had taken horse to catch up with those who had escaped and were heading home. A force of Muslims, searching for survivors, waylaid the company of several hundred Christians at Gravalos. Caught off guard, eight out of ten were slain.

Rodrigo groaned and rolled over onto his back, covering his eyes with an arm. So this was that great, that glorious future he had tasted so sweetly? Jesus, how he had hated to ride into Palencia today. The events of the past months crushed him in a wild confusion of a thousand separate thoughts, one piling atop the other until he could bear it no longer. Beating his fists against the bed, he cried out, "So help me God, defeat will never be mentioned in the same breath with my name again! Damn you, Sabíhah. Damn your black soul to hell!"

"Christ! Are *you* a sorry sight to behold."

Rodrigo reared up on the bed. His bloodshot eyes strained to focus on Sancho.

Sancho rushed Rodrigo, yanked him to his feet, and threw his arms around him, slapping his back enthusiastically. "Damn me, it is good to set eyes on you again, you bastard. I did not expect you so soon. I only sent the message two days ago . . ."

"Message? I received no message."

"My father. He died, Rodrigo! Our future has begun. I, my dear friend, am now a king, and you are ensign to me." Seeing the grim expression on Rodrigo's face, he asked, "Is there bad news? Come, it cannot be that bad. Tell me."

Rodrigo could find no words of justification. He could only put the facts to Sancho. "Barbastro is lost. I bring no gold with me, no splendid victory—just myself and a handful of wounded, death-tired men. I have failed you in my first important command. So I think that you should give serious consideration to my appointment as your ensign, sire." His voice had dropped to almost a whisper and his eyes were cast down to his boots. "I have made a pledge to myself, and to God, Sancho, that I will never be so duped again."

"Maktadir, I take it, brought an army with him, instead of gold."

"He did indeed."

"I see." He studied Rodrigo closely, then said, "Rodrigo, I cannot say I am pleased with you, but I beg you not to take this defeat as anything more than a lesson." He smiled warmly. "Perhaps Alexander's cause was insufficient to stir the flames of conquest in you, hmmm? I know that you would never allow a cause of mine to fail. That is why I must insist that you be my ensign as planned. Forget Barbastro, Tigrito. Let us not brood over battles lost, when there are so many ahead of us to be won."

Rodrigo collapsed backward onto the bed, relieved and grateful. Together they would overcome the brothers and rule a reunited Castile. They talked for hours, laying their plans. Sancho was confident. Within the week they would depart for Castile and establish a court at Pamplona.

Then Sancho spoke to Rodrigo about a serious complication. Only the day before the Queen Mother had called all her children to her. His voice was bitter, "She begged us to ignore greed, to honor each other's rights—and forced us to vow to her that we would not attack one another. I mouthed empty words, Rodrigo. Alphonso, I believe, meant what he said, Garcia too. But there was one other at that meeting whose lips spoke lies. Urracca."

"What the hell does Urracca have to do with the matter of kings and kingdoms?"

"This you will not believe. My sister is countess of Zamora and sovereign over the monasteries of all three kingdoms. The power this gives her is beyond measurement!"

Rodrigo lifted himself onto one elbow on the bed, staring at Sancho in disbelief. "But your father spoke to me about his will. He said that it was signed, and that it would never be altered."

"She is a goddamned devil! She stood beside our father's deathbed and cursed him with such blasphemies that the wrath of God should have descended upon her right there and then. But it did not. I think the old fool, in his delirium, saw a witch and thought he was being cursed into hell for certain, so he gave her everything she demanded."

"Christ! Her ruthlessness combined with Alphonso's power as king of Leon constitutes a hell of a formidable enemy."

"Formidable is hardly the word for it! You should have seen her standing before our mother, dressed in that infernal black; the devil's bride. I swear she would slit the throat of her own mother, if it suited her purpose. But enough of my sister. We will face her when the time comes, and destroy her. Hmmmm?"

Rodrigo nodded and dropped back, putting his arms over his eyes. The sight of his men strewn upon the plains around Barbastro came back to him and he shivered. Quickly he put his mind to the better times ahead of him. Defeat would never be allied with his name again. Urracca did not frighten him, nor the pope, nor God himself.

When Rodrigo entered his wife's room in the blackness of night, she was sitting in a chair, eyes wide with fright and anxiety. He stood in the open doorway with hesitation. He had clothed himself in a white tunic and soft leather shoes.

"Jimena . . . ? Might I enter, Wife?" He could not see her clearly, in the dark corner. His manner was sober and subdued, almost apologetic. He raised the candle he held, glancing about the room. The flickering light illuminated his wife's dark brown eyes; he met them with a gentle smile. Softly he closed the door behind him and went to her, sitting himself in a chair opposite hers.

She is not beautiful, Rodrigo thought, studying her constricted face. Strange, but it seemed urgent, now, that she be just what she was—sweet, innocent, the blood running ice through her veins. Jimena was safe. In her he could find all he required, satisfaction without passion or lust. He must be gentle with her, not frighten her again. Safe. Never would this plain, pious woman drive a man mad with her flesh, demanding from him so much that she emptied him of all else. Sabíhah's battered face became a living image before him, superimposed over his wife's, and he recoiled for an instant, wrenching the ghostly apparition from his mind with a violent shake of his head.

"We begin again, my wife."

"Yes, Husband." Jimena whispered, then stumbled for planned words. "I . . . I would humbly beg your forgiveness, my lord—I did not mean to be so. . . . I vow that from this day I will be a truly loving wife to you."

Rodrigo reached across the space between them and put a big hand on each side of her face. "I forgive you, Wife, and in turn beg *your* forgiveness. I do not blame you altogether for what was both our faults." He leaned forward and kissed her lightly on the mouth, as a man would kiss his daughter.

Jimena felt a spark ignite within her at the touch of his lips, and a faint groan escaped her throat. Dear God, it was a flame already, and with only the slightest fanning wind of touch and kiss. A harlot. God save her from this iniquity. She whirled away from his touch, leaping from the chair to run and throw herself across her bed, her face hot with shame. Long moments, tears wetting the coverlet, then the touch of his hand upon her hair.

Rodrigo was gentle with her, hands moving little, lips undemanding, patient. He made no attempt to completely unclothe her, as she lay rigidly submissive; he merely moved up over her and took his release quickly, with no effort at prolongation or intensity of climax.

For Jimena there was only a dying down to embers of an inexplicable, momentary conflagration—no release of the bonds that imprisoned her desires. Only the dull sensation of flesh against flesh, a small pain, discomfort, then an agony of insoluble dissatisfactions. The silent scream caught in her throat was out of a new objection against the emptiness of the act. Yet, was this not what God required, restraint? Then she preferred continence. When her husband left her, Jimena wept and beat her fists against the bed, despising herself and life.

When word of the fall of Barbastro reached him, William de Montrueil flew into a rage and made his usual threats, but in the end gathered his army of knights together and departed Castile. He promised another army of zealous Christians would descend upon Castile in retribution for its failure—a failure so great that he was forced to beg extra wagons from Alphonso for his journey, since his own men and equipment could not carry the one thousand five hundred Muslim maidens, the five hundred loads of household goods, jewels, and clothing, nor the seven thousand prisoners, all to be presented to the pope.

Rodrigo Diaz and his king departed for Pamplona with minds filled with optimism. Jimena accompanied them as far as Logroño, then took a separate train on to Gormaz. She had asked that she be allowed to return home, and Rodrigo had readily agreed. Jaime was there, recuperating from the loss of his leg at Barbastro, and she longed to see him again. But she looked back upon Palencia with some regret as the city fell behind her; she would miss her friends. Gormaz. A year since she had left home. Her old room would be waiting for her, as drab and colorless as ever. Now it would be Rodrigo who came home to her every year or two from the outside world; he had firmly stepped into the framework of her father's fading image. She had barely known her father; it appeared doubtful she would ever come to understand Rodrigo. She lay her head back upon the seat of the carriage and eventually dozed off as the vehicle rattled and jarred over the precarious road to Gormaz.

The presence of Rodrigo Diaz in Castile as ensign was felt like an earth-shattering quake. The attacking hooves of the war horses of his knights were like claps of thunder that left death and destruction in their wake. An angry God spoke to his people through the deeds of just one man, who slashed, robbed, and killed his way to immortal fame. Charging like an enraged lion upon the white stallion he called Bavieca, he led his army across plains and mountains from victory to victory. Arabs and Christians alike began to tremble at the mention of his name. In the list he fought the famous knight, Jimeno Garces, of Navarre, a man of no small proportion and no little strength and so powerfully, swiftly, and efficiently subdued him that all who watched, friend and foe alike, stood and cheered. Even the army of Count Remon, Lord of Savoy, with twenty thousand men and the power of the king of France, could not defeat him, nor could the German emperor, or anyone else that was sent by the pope seeking tribute. Again and again he rode against the Muslim kings near the Castilian border, taking from them their lives and their gold. So it was that one day he stood upon the crest of a hill and looked down upon Zaragossa, the city of Maktadir. This city was famous throughout all Islam for its strength and its beauty. The city wall was of tufa blocks, all keyed together, rising on the outside to a height of seventy feet from the ground, but on the inner side the wall was no more than nine feet above the level of the streets, so that the houses topped the ramparts. Because they were whitewashed, the houses stood out clearly, even in the darkness of night. The White City of Islam it was called, and Rodrigo Diaz lay siege around its massive walls with all his engines of war. Thus even Maktadir the Mighty, undefeated warrior-king, pledged in writing to pay tribute, which he had never done before, in return for the assurance of his conqueror that he would be protected against Muslims and Christians alike.

Ruy Diaz rode on, destroying all who stood in his path. People began to say that he was unconquerable, for none seemed able to touch him with their sword. The Muslims began calling him Al Saíd, The Lord, and his own people called him Compeador, or Champion. Quickly the Muslim and the Castilian titles were combined and he became known as El Cid, Compeador . . . The Lord Champion. Tales about El Cid multiplied daily, swelling his image out of all proportion to fact. A national hero, a legend, had been created.

As the power and influence of El Cid grew, so grew the power of the king in whose name he fought. The two brothers watched with concern. But, biding his time, Sancho did not attack.

Garcia, now twenty years old, was still a gay, carefree youth and was considered weak by his subjects. Garcia, who had no men on his staff like Rodrigo Diaz, placed his faith and trust in a poor adviser, against the better judgment of his few loyal friends. Thus it was the boy, and not Sancho, as their father had predicted, who was the first to strike. Garcia rode against his sister Urracca and took from her all that she possessed except the city of Zamora.

At last Sancho had the excuse he had been waiting for. He sent a messenger to Alphonso, begging him to join with him against Garcia for Urracca's sake. But Alphonso, even for Urracca, would not go against a brother. Instead, he gave Sancho permission to take his army across Leon to the Galician border. The first test of strength had begun, two and a half years after the death of Ferrando. Garcia's men fought well, but they were swiftly defeated. Sancho had his young brother bound in chains and sent to a strong castle at Luna, where he died twenty years later, still in chains.

Now the victorious Castilian army hovered over the land of Alphonso like locusts. The battle against Galicia won, they refused to return to Castile. After gathering his forces together and bringing in new supplies and engines, Sancho demanded the reuniting of his father's lands. He sent a messenger to Alphonso, commanding him to give up Leon. Then, without waiting for a reply, he rode against the land, burning the fields and killing the innocent. Alphonso could no longer keep his vow to his mother. He begged Sancho to cease this plunder and, instead, face him on a battlefield.

The first battle was indecisive, the second conclusive. In the furious struggle and confusion, Sancho found himself inadequately guarded. He was taken prisoner by thirteen of Alphonso's knights. But Rodrigo Diaz was near and galloped after them. Rodrigo was alone. He had no lance, having lost it in the battle. Overtaking the thirteen who guarded his king, he cried out, "Knights! Give me my lord!"

"Ruy Diaz," a knight shouted back, "return in peace. Seek not to contend with us, otherwise we will carry you away prisoner with him."

Rodrigo leaped from his horse and stood before them, feet spread wide. He reached out a blood-stained hand, "Then give me a lance and I will, single as I am, rescue my lord from all of you!"

A lance was tossed to him and sly glances passed in his direction, for these knights did not believe the legend of El Cid. He had killed eleven of them before the other two begged for mercy. Thus was Sancho delivered by his ensign, and the day was eventually lost by Alphonso. He was exiled to Toledo, the Muslim city of Al Mammon, because his sister had pleaded for his life, and Sancho, wishing to please Urracca for his own purposes, gave her what she wished.

Sancho had prevailed. He placed a crown upon his head and named himself king over the three countries. But there was still a great discontent within him. Zamora remained in Urracca's possession, and he greedily coveted it, declaring "Neither Muslim nor Christian can prevail upon it. If I could have Zamora, either for money or exchange, I would truly be lord of Spain." So he sent his ensign to Urracca with his demands, and she replied, "No, Ruy Diaz, I will *not* relinquish what my father gave to me. And tell my brother to think carefully before he stirs the wrath of Urracca."

A siege was immediately set about the walls of Zamora. Urracca stood alone against her brother. He had prevailed against all except her. This was the final test of Sancho's strength and ability to rule.

Urracca stood upon one of the city wall ramparts, just above the south gate, her red-rimmed eyes scanning the scene outstretched below her. Zamora was indeed a well-fortified city, built upon solid rock, the river Douro running around one side. On the other sides were seven walls, one inside the other, each with a moat and massive towers. Built in the year 893 by a wealthy Mozarab—a Goth who was a citizen of Islam—it was destroyed by the plundering armies of Al Mansur, then rebuilt by her father.

The river was black and moved sluggishly, suffering from the drought of midsummer. The sun blazed down, as it had for weeks, relentlessly, without mercy, burning away all the feebler spirits of green; only the fittest, hardiest plants had survived. The tents of Sancho's army lay all in a group, like a grove of brown shrubs, blending into the brown, sun-scorched background. Smoke from the campfires hovered lazily over the camp, unruffled by the breezeless air. Urracca sighed. Alphonso, dear Alphonso, gone from her these many months. How she longed to see, to touch the sweet flesh of him. She despised Sancho with a passion that lay within her like a cancer.

Zamora was dying of famine. The people ate rats and dung and killed one another for a crust of bread. They were sick with fear and hunger, and screamed out in agony to Urracca for an end to their suffering. It could not continue much longer. The time for her to fight had come, or she must forever surrender what she so treasured. She had sold her soul to the Devil over and over again. She had leaned over her father's dying carcass, cursing him and his God. Now she clung frantically, helplessly, to what little was left of his bequest. The tyrant, the swine. He had known, even then, that she could not keep what he so begrudgingly gave her. If there were some way—if Alphonso were king over all the land—then she might find, and keep, that place in the world she required.

Through the heat-haze and dust, Urracca watched Sancho ride into the camp. A shiver ran up her spine, sending a rush of gooseflesh over her body. "Get yourself from my land, Brother," she had screamed at him that first day when he had approached the gate to plead with her to surrender the city, "or I shall have your head! You will not steal from me as you have from your brothers. It is *you* who will be destroyed if you persist."

"God," Urracca cried out now to the hot summer sky, "you who have always forsaken me; I plead now, I *beg* of you, do not take this, too, from me . . ." Hot tears rushed to her eyes. If there was a God, then the sin she now contemplated would be the ultimate. If He did exist, if He were forgiving, she knew He would never forgive her this. Urracca seldom experienced fear, but it lay now like an icy wall around her heart. But it was done. . . .

At the sound of shouting voices from below, Urracca leaned over and watched the knight as he dashed across the lowered drawbridge toward Sancho's camp. Vellido Adolpho loved Urracca; he would forfeit his life, forsake his God, for just a smile from her.

"Oh, my God! Vellido, come back! Vellido, please." But he could not hear. With a deep sigh of resignation, Urracca turned and walked away. There was nothing to do now but wait.

Vellido Adolpho stood before Sancho in the tent. Rodrigo

Diaz stood behind him, near the entrance. The knights who had brought him to the king turned and left them alone.

Sancho eyed the captured enemy closely, "What is this that you must say to me? Quickly! But rest assured that nothing you say will dissuade me from cutting your foul throat . . ."

"Sire," Vellido began, as he leaned to kiss Sancho's hand, "because I said to the council of Zamora that they should yield the city to you, the men of the town would have me slain, even as you have seen. Did they not pursue me out of the gates? Therefore I come to you, sire, and would be your vassal, if I might find favor at your hands." Vellido paused. He glanced over his shoulder to Rodrigo Diaz; he had felt those cold eyes against the back of his neck. He believed in the legend of El Cid, and was more than a little afraid of the man. Uneasily he turned back to the king, continuing, "In a few days I will show you how you may enter and take Zamora. If I do not do this, then slay me."

Sancho was inclined to disbelieve the man, but he could not forsake a chance to take the city. He could slay the fool after he knew his secret. He looked past Vellido Adolpho to Rodrigo, and their eyes met. Rodrigo shook his head emphatically in disapproval. "I cannot be satisfied only upon your claim that there is any way to take this city, except by starving the people into surrender. By what means might we enter . . .? Speak, or I shall have your head this instant?"

"Sire," Vellido purred, "you wrong me. I ask only for your favor and would serve you well. But—if you insist. There is a hidden underground entrance to the city that is never locked. It was once the private entrance of a queen. When it is night you shall give me one hundred knights, well armed, and we will go on foot. The Zamorans, who are weak with famine and misery, will let us conquer them. We will enter and open the gate and keep it open until all your soldiers have entered. Thus will you win the town of Zamora."

Again Sancho looked to Rodrigo, who was standing with his arms folded across his chest, his expression glum. "Do not listen, Sancho; the man is lying. Urracca has sent him to do you harm." Rodrigo moved now, slowly, toward Vellido, who swayed nervously from foot to foot. Swiftly and viciously he grabbed the man by one arm and whirled him around to face him. His hand shot out and caught Vellido's face with a hard, cracking blow. "Tell the king that you are a liar; tell him—you son of a bitch. *Tell* him!"

"Rodrigo," Sancho cried angrily, "leave the man be. I

would see this postern he speaks of. I do not relish another month of this miserable inactivity. Unhand him, Rodrigo."

"For Christ, Sancho, this man is after your head. Better you heed my advice, or—"

"Enough! I will see the secret entrance; that is my final word."

Rodrigo scowled and reluctantly let loose of Vellido Adolpho, who gave a great sigh of relief, straightened his shoulders, and brushed at his rumpled clothing. The first step in his plan had succeeded. Now he must wait until Rodrigo Diaz was off guard.

A week passed. Vellido managed to put Sancho off with one excuse after another, for Rodrigo never left his king's side, his cold, distrusting eyes glaring at the stranger in their midst. Then, on the seventh day, Rodrigo Diaz left camp. Sancho had ordered him, against his protest, to Palencia on matters of state. They had been at Zamora for many months; there were matters that needed attention. The next morning, following Rodrigo's departure, Vellido Adolpho went to Sancho and said that the right moment had come. They took horses, riding off alone around the city. On the northernmost side of the town, only a few feet from the wall, there was an ancient well. They dismounted, and Vellido showed the king how the well was not what it seemed, how a secret door at the base led under the walls and moats to the city streets.

Rodrigo Diaz had not gone far from camp. He sat upon his horse at the top of a rise overlooking the tents of Sancho's knights, and from that distance he saw Sancho riding off alone with Vellido. Fear set his heart racing. There was trickery here, he was certain now. He spurred his mount viciously, and the palfrey raced back toward the camp.

Sancho and Vellido Adolpho left the well and headed back toward camp. By the bank of the river, Sancho reined in and dismounted to relieve himself. He carried in his hand a light hunting spear and with childish trust, handed it up to Vellido Adolpho to hold for him. The instant his back was turned, Vellido thrust the weapon between his shoulder blades, driving it with such force that it tore through his body and came out at his chest. Sancho whirled about, his eyes shocked and frightened, and made a pathetic attempt to attack his foe, but his knees gave and he fell mortally wounded upon the riverbank, upon ground that by right of inheritance belonged to his sister Urracca.

Vellido spurred his mount and yanked the reins around,

racing for the postern just as Rodrigo Diaz charged into view. It was a furious chase. Rodrigo did not have his lance, only a sword sheathed at his side. If he had carried his lance, he might have thrown it and felled the murderer. Vellido Adolpho jumped from his saddle, climbed into the well, and disappeared.

Rodrigo, hoping Sancho might still be alive, did not follow Vellido into the city. Quickly he turned, rushing toward the river, his heart pounding erratically. Sancho was not yet seven and twenty. Pray God he was not dead.

Sancho lay awkwardly on his side, fumbling weakly at the spear jutting out of his breast. He was fully conscious. Rodrigo knelt beside him and lifted his dark head into his hands, "For God, Sancho, what has he done to you?"

"I—I am slain, Rodrigo. I pay for my greed, my sins. I broke the oath I made to my mother. Jesus, the *pain!*" His face twisted in agony.

Rodrigo ripped at his tunic and wet a piece of it in the river. He then placed the cool cloth against the sweating brow of his king. "Do not speak, beloved friend, save your strength."

Sancho smiled through clenched teeth, "I have not done well by you, Rodrigo. My father commended you to me when he divided his kingdoms, and you have lost the love of my brothers for my sake. Now you can neither go before King Don Alphonso, nor Urracca, because they hold that whatever I have done against them was by your counsel. . . ."

"It was of my own choosing. If I had known that you would die this way, I would have done the same!"

Word had spread, and now, all around, a quiet group of mourners stood with heads bowed. A priest knelt over the king, and gave him the last rites of the church, his voice mumbling monotonously on and on.

With a last surge of strength, Sancho pushed himself up on one elbow, brushing aside the priest. "I beseech all of you who are present, counts, knights, and all my vassals, if my brother, King Don Alphonso, should come from the land of the Muslim, beseech him to show favor to my Rodrigo, and always be bountiful to him and receive him as vassal; for if he always does this and listens to Rodrigo, he will never be badly advised." Exhausted by the effort, he lay back upon the ground. "Rodrigo . . .?" He reached out a wavering hand, his eyes unseeing now. When he felt Rodrigo's hand warm upon his own, he whispered, "Rodrigo, beg my brother Alphonso to forgive me the wrong I have done him, and pray to God to have mercy . . . on . . . my soul."

Urracca did not weep over what was done and could never be altered. Secretly, and immediately after Vellido Adolpho brought word, she sent messengers to Toledo, telling Alphonso of his brother's death. She entreated him to come as speedily as he could to receive his kingdoms.

The war of the brothers was at an end. Ferrando had refused to make the decision, leaving fate to decide for him. As he had so callously predicted, Sancho was the first to die. Rodrigo stood alone in his world now. There was not one to whom he could give his allegiance. He walked away from the lifeless body of his friend, his king, head bent with grief, heart heavy with hatred. There was one thing he must do. Alphonso had planned this death, curse his black soul, with the aid of a devil—Urracca. If there were any way, any way on earth, he would see that Alphonso never sat upon the throne. He would journey to Gormaz, and await word of Alphonso's return.

Chapter
✠ *EIGHT* ✠

The infant squirmed, throwing her little arms gaily about, her bright blue eyes laughing up at Jimena.

"Oh, now, do not flirt with *me*," Jimena cooed, playfully tickling the baby, "mother's little kitten. Are you mother's kitten, sweet pretty girl?" She hugged the baby tight to her breast, pressing her cheek against soft yellow hair, the miracle of her baby sending a warm glow through her.

Out of a drab, frigid winter night, after the final, tearing pain, there had come from within herself this golden dream of life and love. Her eyes were as blue as Rodrigo's, her hair the color of acacia blossoms. If only she could take the child with her, but the journey across the plains in late summer would be too dangerous for one so tiny.

Jimena turned to face the old woman idling behind her. "Now, Aunt Galiana, remember my instructions. A little goat's milk after she wakes, and leave a candle burning by her cradle at night. She does so hate the dark."

The old woman grunted unpleasantly, "For God! I have cared for more children in my day than I care to recall. You, but child yourself, need not tell *me* how to manage them! Afraid of the dark? It is you who fear the shadows, and you teach it to her!"

Jimena stared coldly at the woman. The same grumpy old witch. But there was none other she could trust. Aunt Galiana might be obnoxious and overly severe, but she would tear anyone apart who even suggested harm to the child. Perhaps she should not accompany Rodrigo to Zamora, though she wanted very much to see Alphonso and Urracca again. It was nearly three years since she had returned to Gormaz, and, except for the birth of little Urracca, it had been a lonely and uneventful time, the present blending wearily into the past.

Rodrigo had come home to her but once in the first two years, long enough to leave within her the seed that was now her beloved daughter, then was off again to his battles. He had been home now nearly two months, the longest time they had ever been together. But he brooded so over the death of Sancho, a death that held no sadness for herself. Alphonso was soon to be crowned king of Castile, Leon, and Galicia.

That Urracca had had any part in the murder of Sancho was an absurd accusation. What a monstrous plot against her. Urracca was no saint, but that she would murder her brother was inconceivable. How hurt she had been, when Rodrigo looked down upon their sleeping child for the first time and snarled, "Urracca! You gave her the name of a she-devil. Like a sleeping angel she appears, just as her namesake covers her evil with a mask of beauty. Take her from my sight and change her name, Jimena. I will not be constantly reminded through my own flesh of a murderess!"

Rodrigo waited, grim and impatient, for news of Alphonso's return to Leon, hardly speaking to Jimena, lying beside her at night without sleeping, his eyes staring at the ceiling. He did not often demand from her his rights as a husband, for which she was grateful. Their days were spent with him pacing restlessly, and she devoting her time, love, and energies to little Urracca. His anger was so great he seemed about to explode from the weight of it within him. Jaime had assured her it was true, that Rodrigo was the most powerful and feared man in Castile, so she was worried that he might have sufficient power to do Alphonso injury.

One night as they sat silently before the fire in their chamber, Rodrigo suddenly began to rant, and Jimena listened tensely until he had concluded. Then he beat his fists against the arm of his chair, raging, "Vengeance is mine sayeth the Lord! God! Can I wait out the eternity of time it will take you to punish this man? Give *me* your vengeance to perform, and I will cut his fiendish head from his shoulders in one mighty blow!"

"Rodrigo" she had wailed, "you cannot believe what you say. Alphonso did not slay his brother. I know it. Once he said to me, 'That I must slay my brothers to . . .'

"Shut your mouth, woman! What do you know of kings and their thrones? Tend to the business of your daughter and your duties as my wife—and I will tend to mine!" His eyes bared his dislike for her.

She had said no more. Now Alphonso had returned. His army lay encamped outside Zamora, and he resided at the castle with Urracca. The news had come only yesterday.

"Curse his murdering heart! Damn him to hell!" Rodrigo
had exploded, "I go immediately, Jimena." His face was dark
with his intent. She had begged him to take her with him but
could not tell him why she wished to go, that she would stand
by Urracca and Alphonso as a good friend should. At first he
brushed her off impatiently. "Do not pester me so with your
squalling, woman—my mind is full. Ach! Do as you like. But
remember that I have business. You will have to shift for yourself. I cannot promise that I will even return with you. God
knows where El Cid will be a month hence." She had answered
in her most subservient voice, "Thank you, my lord. Tell me
the time of your departure and I will be prepared, and will remain as inconspicuous as possible."

Jimena kissed little Urracca upon the cheek and purred,
"Goodbye, little flower, sweet dream of my life. I will return to
you as quickly as possible. Be a good baby now." She handed
the child over to her aunt. At that moment Jimena was overcome by an inexplicable, stunning fear. She clutched out frantically, dragging the baby back to her heart.

"For God! What *ails* you?" the old woman gasped, "you
near broke the babe's back, clutching her so."

"I—I do not know. I suddenly had the most frightening
feeling that something terrible will happen if I leave her. I
might never see her again!"

"Praise the Lord! Really, you are the most dismal person,
forever brooding and thinking wild and morbid thoughts. Say a
prayer to God, Jimena, for you must have sinned greatly to be
so plagued by demons of the mind."

Don Jaime was waiting for Jimena at the bottom of the
long flight of stairs, leaning against the railing post to relieve
the strain of the wooden peg against the stump of his leg. When
he saw her coming, his face brightened and he stepped back,
holding a hand out to her. "Jimenita . . ." he said, as she
swiftly descended, her skirts held up by a pale hand, "I am so
pleased that you are making this visit, Sister." He leaned and
planted a solid kiss on the cheek she turned to him.

"What? No warnings, Jaime, about the dangers rampant at
Zamora these days?"

"None. Alphonso will protect you. Come, your husband is
roaring. One of his wagon drivers disappeared during the night,
and he has been forced to find a replacement at the last minute." He took her elbow and began walking quickly toward the

courtyard door, the thump of his wooden leg against the granite floor rhythmic like a beating heart. "If you are seated in your carriage, ready when he is *not,* you will have defeated his reprimands before they can start."

Jimena laughed. "You know him very well."

"I told you that, the first time you asked me," he said, grinning at her as he reached to pull open the heavy door.

Jimena came to a halt in the open doorway, the dawn wind blowing her skirts. "You also said to me that you would never accept him as your lord."

"Ah, that was before I owed him my life." His smile was unfaltering. "And before he was gracious enough to leave the city to me, to rule as I please. He never interferes, Jimena, never. I am content. What else could I do with *this*?" He kicked up the wooden peg, banging it good-naturedly against the door frame.

Jimena smiled at him and quickly planted a kiss on his cheek. She ran toward her carriage so he would not see the tears in her eyes.

Jimena sat in brooding silence in the bouncing carriage, crossing and re-crossing her legs in impatience. What an endless, monotonous ordeal it was, traveling. How she regretted her decision to make this visit. Rodrigo paid no attention to her and would not allow anyone rest. He was racing to Zamora with murder in his heart. He would not camp until it was already dark, and his great, howling voice woke them before it was light. She was tired, and her clothes stuck to her flesh, wet and wrinkled. She glanced out of the window. Far in the distance she could see a thin, gray sliver that was the river Douro, the scenery there more wooded and green. The driver had said they would reach Zamora by midday tomorrow.

The driver. What a strange, unpleasant man he was. Jimena bent her head to look up through the opening in the carriage, staring at his broad back. He was extremely short and had long arms that hung loosely at his sides. His face was so homely it startled one to look upon it. He had a great, bulbous nose, and small, colorless eyes. The clothing he wore was ragged and soiled, but somehow seemed wrong on him, as if he wore it to make an impression. Ugly as he was, his bearing and manner was too proud for that of a bondsman. Bending further, Jimena asked, "How much longer before nightfall, Estiano? I swear this day will never end."

He turned his heavy, square body around and looked down

contemptuously. There was no subservience in his tone. "An hour, perhaps two, my lady. If you will look to your right, you will see the sun now passing from sight behind the mountains."

His voice was strange, Jimena thought, or was it the manner in which he pronounced the words? An odd accent. For God, the man was not to blame that he was ugly. If everyone distrusted him so because of his appearance, what a sad and lonely existence he would have.

It was fully dark when they stopped to make camp by the river. The cool moisture of the water rose in a mist, freshening the air near the banks. Jimena stepped down from the carriage, her bones creaking. Her bottom throbbed and was numb from all the hours of sitting. She gulped in deep breaths of the clean air. Estiano did not move from the driver's seat, holding the reins loosely in his stubby fingers. Jimena could feel his beady little eyes hot against her shoulderblades. She whirled around, forcing scorn, "Well, do not sit there, man, prepare my tent. I am desperately in need of rest. And do not take all night about it, either!"

"Yes, my lady."

She stood back haughtily, watching him erect her small tent. He was very efficient. After he had completed her shelter, he meticulously brushed away every stone and twig that lay upon the ground within. He stretched out her coverlets and brought a bucket of water and a dipper, placing them inside near the opening. Then, scanning his handiwork, he turned and made a polite bow "My lady?"

"Very good."

He did not leave, but stood looking at her. "Doña Jimena? How long a stay do you plan at Zamora?"

"How dare you question me in this way! You are impudent, man."

"My lady," his voice very humble now, "forgive me, but I am concerned for one as frail as yourself. There is much anger and bloodshed to come. The land will not quickly fall into a peaceful union. There are those men who so despise El Cid that it is like a consuming disease, and though they might fear to attack his person, they could find it expedient to wound him by a vicious attack upon yourself. Zamora is an unwholesome place these days. Forgive a further insolence, but I would not remain there long."

"Insolence indeed. No one will harm Jimena Gomez at Zamora," she said indignantly, "King Don Alphonso is my dearest friend, as is his sister, Urracca. For your concern, I thank you, but it is unnecessary. You may take your leave."

She watched him as he walked away from her, thinking there had been a start in his eyes when she spoke of Alphonso as her friend. There was something else about him, a strange air of strength and purpose, gentleness, too. It was possible, however—yes, it could be that *Estiano* was planning some revenge against Rodrigo. For God, another worry. She was much too weary this night to contemplate doom. She would have all the morning to let it fester in her mind. Tonight she would sleep like a baby.

Zamora's innards were so swollen she belched out the overflow of people from every city gate and doorway. Knights clogged the streets, and the curious rushed out of every house and inn. All the knights who had been vassal to Ferrando were gathered here to decide if Alphonso should be their king. As Rodrigo Diaz passed through the streets, their voices hushed, and they turned one and all to watch him ride by. They knew what purpose had brought him to this town; the death of Don Sancho was still black upon his face. The wagers made after El Cid was out of earshot were enthusiastic, giving Alphonso all the odds. It was the considered opinion of the majority of the multitude that the career of Rodrigo Diaz, El Cid, was finished.

"Urracca!"

Jimena rushed at her friend, throwing her arms around Urracca's neck, kissing her on both cheeks. Then, holding on to Urracca's smooth, bare shoulders, Jimena backed off a little. As lovely as she remembered, but there were lines about that sweet mouth, and the eyes had the old sadness in them. Of course, she mourned the death of her brother. Surely, though, her grief did not overshadow her joy for Alphonso's good fortune. "It is wonderful to see you. You look lovely, Urracca. How is our dear Alphonso? I am so anxious to see him."

"He is well, Jimena," Urracca replied flatly. "You are looking well yourself. I hear that I have a namesake. I congratulate you and thank you for the compliment. I . . . " her words broke off. She stared at Jimena for a long moment, then tears filled her eyes.

"Urracca! What is it? Can I help you?" Jimena reached out a hand in a helpless gesture of sympathy.

"No, God, no. There is no one to help me. It is only that when Alphonso came here to Zamora, I had not seen him in, oh, nearly a year. . . . He stood before me with cold and staring eyes, accusing me. He thinks *I* killed Sancho!—and nothing I could say would dissuade him."

"Ah, no! For God, my Rodrigo saw the man who did this murder, saw him put the lance into Sancho, and chased the brute. Everyone knows that. Have they not apprehended the man? Surely they have, and he has confessed?"

Urracca's eyes turned cold. "Vellido Adolpho will face Alphonso and the court tomorrow. He will confess his crime, and I pray God he will convince them that I was not to blame in any way."

Jimena saw that coldness of eye, and a flicker of doubt stabbed her. Her own eyes, with detached objectivity, slid over Urracca, searching for a deeper knowledge of this friend's soul, but there was only the masked face, the spoken words, to rely upon—and Jimena's intense desire to believe in Urracca's innocence. No wonder the tears came, no wonder the icy wall behind the eyes, for if this murderer did not confess, if he wanted to harm Urracca and spoke lies, then all Urracca had fought so hard for all her life would be lost.

Jimena wrapped her arms around Urracca in a sudden, surging pity, "Oh, my dear friend, do not grieve. The man will not involve you. His grievance was against Sancho, not yourself. Come, let us talk of brighter matters. I will tell you of your namesake. Do you want to hear about her?"

Urracca straightened her shoulders and brushed at her eyes, "Yes," she smiled wistfully, "do tell me of her? Is she quite beautiful?"

"Indescribably so! But I should never begin, or I will keep you all day. I have never known such a love as I have for this child." Jimena smiled secretively, "I hope that I shall love the next half as much. . . ."

"Another child? Oh, how I envy you, Jimena! How I have longed to bear a child. But what would this child that I would bear be to me? Nephew—or son? Jimena, even if I should escape this accusation which plagues me now, a child will be the one thing that I will not be able to give Alphonso, and that will destroy us. No one in this land, particularly the priests, would accept such blood upon the throne. They abide such blood upon the papal throne—but not on Castile's! Ah, forgive me. How I press you with my miseries. Tell me, is Rodrigo pleased with this expected event? This one might well be a son."

Jimena laughed bitterly. "Rodrigo is not pleased about anything these days. I have not told him. I have only missed two periods of confinement; there is time and a better day for such news. But I am happy about it, of course. There is no love between Rodrigo and myself, nor is there hope for it in the future. I will give to my children that part of myself I cannot give to a man." At Urracca's quick raising of the eyebrows, she added defensively, "It is sufficient, really it is, Urracca. I have become adjusted, and my life is adequate. Passion, indeed, is not for me, and better so. I have my virtue reasonably intact and look to Heaven as a reward. I bear what I must and am less plagued by the stirrings that once tormented me."

"Ach, nonsense! You suffer from lack of choice and opportunity. Given a new face, a different sort of man, more adept, you might be amazed at your reactions."

"Little comfort, I fear, since I am bound to Rodrigo for eternity. I will never know what I might have been, will I?"

Urracca gave a start, leaning to glance out the window. "It is late, Jimena. I will show you to your quarters. I have a thousand matters to attend to. Tomorrow is the day I have dreamed of for almost all my life. Together we will see our dear Alphonso crowned king of Castile."

Alphonso sat straight in the large leather chair against the end wall of the hall of audience. To his right stood a cardinal, two bishops and a monk, and all around him and before him were his faithful vassals. Scattered about the hall, in groups of three and four, were the counts and most famous knights of Castile and Galicia. One by one they came forward, and each in turn kissed his hand and called him their king. When the ceremony was finished, only one man had not so acknowledged him. Rodrigo Diaz stood in the center of the room, all eyes upon him.

No one seemed to breathe. Alphonso sat immobile for a moment, then slowly rose from his seat and in a loud voice cried, "You have all received me for your king, and given me authority over you. I would know of El Cid, Ruy Diaz, why he will not kiss my hand and acknowledge me, for I would do well by him, for my brother's sake and my father's, who commended him to my brethren. Speak, Ruy Diaz. Why do you refuse to kiss my hand?"

Rodrigo fought for control. He had not expected such unanimous acceptance. Even those who had been Sancho's most trusted advisers and knights had not spoken out against the murder. Vellido Adolpho had sworn upon the Bible that he had committed the crime of murder singly, no man or woman had been his accomplice. The lout would die carrying Urracca and Alphonso's guilt with him to the grave. The fool!

"Sire!" Rodrigo shouted, "all whom you see here, though they will not admit it, suspect that by your counsel the King Don Sancho came to his death. Therefore I say unto you, that unless you clear yourself of this, as by law you must, I will never kiss your hand, nor receive you for my king."

Alphonso let his eyes slide across the sea of faces, trying to read their thoughts. Indeed, many agreed with Diaz. "I swear to God and Saint Mary that I never slew him, nor took counsel for his death. And it did not please me, even though Sancho had taken my kingdom from me. I beseech you, therefore, as my friends and true vassals, that you tell me how I might clear myself totally of this charge."

"Before God," Rodrigo cried, "you will swear that what you have just said is the truth. If you lie, His vengeance will strike you down where you stand."

Alphonso was led to the church, where he stood upon a high stage so that all might see him. The building was full to overflowing, and some knights were forced to stand in the street. They waited, hushed.

Rodrigo walked determinedly up to Alphonso with a Bible in his hand. He opened the book and roughly tossed it upon the altar. "Place your hands upon this Holy Book, Don Alphonso," he commanded. "You come here to swear concerning the death of King Don Sancho—that you neither slew him, nor took counsel for his death. Say it again now, before God and all this host, that you did not do this deed."

Alphonso flushed. His anger had been building slowly; now the pressure of it was almost more than he could bear. "I swear," he murmured, glaring at Rodrigo.

"Speak up! We cannot *hear* you." Rodrigo's voice was sharp with sarcasm.

"I swear," Alphonso fairly screamed, "I swear—I SWEAR!"

Rodrigo looked straight into Alphonso's eyes, then turned slightly so that all would hear him clearly. "If you knew of this thing, or gave command that it should be done, may the lance of one who is your enemy cut into your back and through your heart—like that lance which pierced the heart of your brother." Rodrigo forced Alphonso to this same oath three times.

The reins of Alphonso's temper snapped. He clutched at Rodrigo's arm and held it with digging fingers. "Why do you press me, man? If it is a duel you seek, you will be disappointed! You swear me today. Tomorrow you will kiss my hand and call me king. King! Tomorrow? *Now*! Kneel before me, Ruy Diaz. I have sworn. Now kiss my hand and acknowledge me as is my right. I command you!"

Rodrigo did not move. Holding the Bible up before Alphonso's reddened face, he smiled defiantly, daring the man without words.

"You refuse? You have the gall to. . . ."

"I *refuse*!" Rodrigo roared.

Alphonso whipped round and shouted to the crowd, "Let me hear your voices! Am I your king?"

A resounding, "Aye."

"Then hear me. Ruy Diaz. Quit my lands! Go out from my kingdoms without delay. You are banished. Exiled! If you are not gone within nine days—nine days—I will seek you out with an army and I will have your goddamned head! Nine days!"

Rodrigo made a swift movement toward his sword, then thought better of it. He turned away and left the church, slamming his elbows into ribs, shoving knights from his path, the clack of his heels echoing through the house. He was twenty-three years old. Behind him was a successful career as ensign to the court of Castile—before him still another career. With him rode a legend that was only half created. As he strode out into the sunlight, a few knights turned to follow him and they were joined by others, their eyes reflecting the greatness they saw in him.

Don Alphonso crowned himself king of Castile and Leon and Galicia. He called himself emperor of all Spain, even as his father had before him. And in the beginning of his reign, he did in all things according to the counsel of his sister, Doña Urracca, who reigned beside him as queen.

A knight rushed down the lamp-lit corridor. When he reached the door he searched for, he pounded roughly upon it. Jimena opened the door wide, and he unceremoniously shoved a note into her hand. She remained poised there, puzzled, staring blankly into the man's eyes. "Sir—I do not read."

"Of course," he muttered unpleasantly. "Forgive me, my lady."

Rudely he caught the message back into his own hands and unfolded it. In a voice hurried and bored, he read, "Wife. I am exiled. Take yourself immediately to Gormaz. I will forward monies to Don Pedro for your needs. I do not know how long a time it will be before I can send for you, if ever. Take care. Go with God. Ruy Diaz."

Jimena's eyes widened, then her face crumpled and she whirled away from the door, running to her bed, sprawling herself out upon it, screaming in rage and grief.

Embarrassed, the knight reached out and pulled the door closed. He must make haste if he was going to catch up with El Cid. Her muffled cries followed him all the way down the long corridor.

Jimena pushed one hand into her mouth and bit herself, then beat both fists against the bed in a fury. He was gone— gone. He did not even wait to see her, but sent a piece of parchment with words upon it. She would bear his second child alone in that foul, empty castle.

"Jimena?"

Urracca hesitated in the doorway, her expression a mixture of happiness for herself and pity for her friend. Alphonso, only moments ago, had held her close to him, begging her to forgive him. Her heart went out to Jimena. She closed the door softly and moved to the bed. Reaching down, she smoothed back the girl's hair. "Try not to grieve, Jimena, dear. Alphonso has kept his word to you. He asked me to come to you, to give you his assurance that you are still his good and dear friend, if you are willing to accept his friendship now."

Jimena sniffed, and covered her eyes with an arm. No words came. No matter how hard she tried for control, the tears and sobs would not subside.

"Jimena, look at me."

Her eyes wavered to the ceiling, the walls; at last she managed to meet Urracca's penetrating gaze.

"At times your foolishness astounds me, Jimena! What is this? You grieve for a husband you do not love, who is better gone from you?"

Jimena swallowed and blew into a kerchief handed to her by her indignant friend, her sobs becoming less violent. "Oh, it is just that—well, there seems to be no end to my miseries. The very *thought* of returning to Gormaz castle. I. . . ." New tears rushed forth.

"Then do not go back to Gormaz. Come to Palencia with Alphonso and me. Stay with us a few weeks, and all will look better to you."

"Ah, no, I cannot. I miss the baby so much, and Rodrigo, in a message to me, ordered me to return immediately."

"Bother! What he does not know will never excite him. You need a rest, people about, laughter, and a change of climate. Besides, we have had no opportunity to renew our friendship. We will have a grand time of it, Jimena. And—" she slapped her hands together excitedly, "I will send a courier to Gormaz each week who will bring back word of your daughter's welfare. Agreed? A bargain?"

Jimena hesitated, greatly tempted. Only for a few weeks. Aunt Galiana was really quite dependable. Jaime was near, in case of emergency. "I will! That is, if you are certain Alphonso would want me now."

"He will be delighted. Come now, let us gather your things together. I did not tell you, but we leave within the hour."

As Urracca had said he would, Alphonso took Jimena into his household as an honored guest. Not once did he give the slightest hint that her husband had wounded him or was his enemy.

Jimena did not blame Alphonso for what he had done, nor would she plead with him for Rodrigo's release from exile. He was a good king; fate had been kind to Castile. At Palencia Urracca sat beside him at every council. If she had ever been vicious or unfeeling, there was no evidence of it now. The advice she gave to Alphonso was unfailingly benevolent. The anger of the past had vanished; Urracca had completely subdued the fear that had always haunted her, fear of personal destruction. Her place in life was now secure. If her life was not altogether perfect, it remained far better than that which her father had planned for her. The protective armor of cruelty, and all other of her defenses, gradually slipped away, leaving her emotionally naked and quite pathetically vulnerable.

"What!" Alphonso shouted, "Priest, take care! Guard your evil tongue. Do not speak to *me* of sin. I am your king. My life is my own."

The small group of priests shuffled nervously. The one to whom Alphonso spoke looked uncomfortably to the others for support, but received none. "But, sire," he said smoothly, "there must be an heir. Even if you are not concerned with the example you set before the people, or with your own salvation, surely you will agree that you must have a son?"

"I am but twenty-six years old, you fool! There is an age before me yet. I refuse to think of an heir at this time. And," he shook a defiant finger, taking in all six whose eyes glared at him, "and which of you will surrender up his wife, eh? The pope has often expressed his desire that all priests, monks, and clerks in Castile rid themselves of those baser commitments, those treasured representatives of bodily desires and lust. You, Don Romiro," he jabbed at the spokesman, "would you press me further and force me to comply with His Eminence's wishes, eh? Eh?"

There was a flutter of excited conversation among the priests, who huddled together in nervous uncertainty. Don Romiro finally emerged. He faced Alphonso's amused eyes courageously and said with controlled, deliberate words. "Sire, you drive a cruel bargain with us. It is for God to decide. We capitulate. But," he pleaded mournfully, "would it be too much to ask that your sister sit *behind* you in church, as is her proper place, and not at your side as if your queen? Really," he splutttered, "it is most humiliating for us to preach of sin, with the two of you sitting there together, rendering us jibbering fools—for the king does not heed our word."

"Ha—ha," Alphonso roared, "*are* you fools, Don Romiro? A tantalizing supposition." With an impatient shake of his head, Alphonso cried, "Be gone, wretches that name yourselves priests! Go to your wives and sin with them this night; look upon the faces of your children whom you love and cherish, and know that Alphonso will have *his* love, or you will lose *yours!*"

"Bravo!"

Urracca burst into the room, just as the door closed on the last retreating priest. "You are a most grand and noble man. And I adore you." She stood in the center of his chamber shouting the words as if making a speech.

"Indeed, I am. Come here to me, wench, I have not kissed you in, hmmmmmm—at least three hours."

Urracca, cuddled in Alphonso's arms, felt relaxed and happy. She smiled up at him, "I had the honor of a visit from Don Romiro just yesterday."

"What? Damn him, I—"

"Ah, now, love, you know me well—I was not upset. But oh, how he carried on. You know the dialogue. I must admit, however, that I feel a trifle uncomfortable, when I consider the grim possibility that what the Church contends is the truth." She sighed deeply, "But, then, I do not believe I could do otherwise than love you. Promises of a reward in the hereafter, as an alternative? Laughable."

"I am deeply touched," Alphonso murmured, kissing her soundly, "and grateful to you. I do not know how I could continue to exist without you here in my arms. That I near destroyed our love . . . how could I have thought that you would . . . your own brother—I. . ."

Urracca's face drained white, then flushed. Her eyes screamed out in pain. When she spoke, her words were stiffly controlled. "Alphonso, never mention this to me again, I mean it, not ever, not as long as you live." She placed her hands on his face, looking deep into his eyes. "There is no past, not for you or for me, and no tomorrow, only this day. Don Romiro will eventually win out over us. You will have to give Castile a future king, you will have to marry. I pray God, my dearest, that I will have the strength to face that day bravely."

"No. . ." he stopped her words with a gentle hand over her mouth. Alphonso leaned over and whispered in her ear, "Have an heir for me, beloved, and in my eyes, my heart, he will be heir to the throne of Castile, he and no other. To hell with priests. They can never marry us, but you are my wife—my wife, Urracca, until I die."

"Dear God," Urracca groaned.

Again he stopped her words, covering her mouth with soft kisses. They sat thus, silent, huddled together in the huge leather chair that was a king's throne, sheltering themselves behind a screen of love from a hostile world and a vindictive God.

Next morning, in the church, as Urracca stubbornly sat beside Alphonso, Don Romiro stood before all who were gathered there, his eyes resting upon the Infanta Urracca, and he said, "Let him who has hitherto lived in sin, quickly correct himself and repent before he departs from this life, for if he dies without repentance he will not enter into rest but will be cast into hell fire. Consider it is the last hour. Therefore do not love the world, for it soon passes away, and all the lust thereof with it."

Urracca did not move, nor did her facial expression alter, but a cold breath passed over her. She felt the accusing hand of God press down heavily upon her, throwing her into a dark and icy depression. The coldness did not leave her but remained with her forever after.

Chapter
✠ *NINE* ✠

News of the banishment of Rodrigo Diaz from the lands of Alphonso traveled swiftly. The sorrow of those who worshiped him was great. Some left their houses and their wives and children to follow him; others forsook the honorable offices they held. They would meet at the bridge of Arlanzon, then seek out El Cid. Within a week one hundred and fifteen knights had assembled at that place. Rodrigo Diaz awaited them at San Pedro, church of Bivar. Seven days of his allotted time had passed. They must make haste.

Rodrigo crossed himself. "God be praised for all things," he prayed, "Holy Mary, Mother of God and all Saints, pray to God for me, that He may give me the strength to destroy all the pagans and to win enough from them to repay my friends and all those who follow and help me." He rose quickly and strode out of the church, standing still in the bright sunlight, shading his eyes with a hand. There they were. Standing, sitting upon their mounts. Waiting, silent. The knights with their banners, and five hundred foot soldiers, and more coming even now. But the others must follow his trail; he could delay no longer. Alphonso, in his rage, had sent letters throughout Castile, saying that no man should give the Cid a lodging, food, or monies. He must find funds and supplies, and quickly, for this host that had pledged its allegiance to him.

Just as Rodrigo caught his breath to call out the order to march, he saw a boy running down the street, pushing excitedly through the crowd of foot soldiers. It was Alvar, his nephew, the son of his eldest brother, Faño. Faño, Rodrigo thought in disgust, that son of Diego Lainez who had without conscience broken their father's heart with his weakness and cowardice. Faño was nothing—less than nothing. He was neither knight nor priest. He tilled the soil like a serf and held such a ruling hand over his sons that they too rotted away their lives singing psalms and digging in dirt. What demon purpose was it that now chased Faño's son with such urgency toward his uncle?

Alvar Fañez fell breathlessly to his knees before Rodrigo. His handsome young face looked up with adoring eyes. He was seventeen years old, and there was nothing in the world he wanted so much as to be a knight under the leadership of the champion of Castile, who was, by a wondrous miracle, his uncle. "Uncle . . ." he pleaded, "I would go with you this day and be your vassal. Grant me this wish, I beg of you. . . ."

Rodrigo smiled down at the boy. Alvar was a fine lad. A little thin and wanting for muscle, perhaps, but training and experience could make a powerful man of him. His face was too pretty; the soft, curling brown hair that fell upon his shoulders was as fine as any woman's.

"What of my brother, lad? You wish me to add his wrath to the already heavy burden of hate I bear?"

"I will never return to his house, my lord," the boy replied emphatically, "whether you grant my request or not. I will be a knight! I would rather be with you, but, if I cannot, I will go to Alphonso's court and . . ."

"Enough," Rodrigo laughed, "I will have no kinsman of mine pledging himself to Alphonso. You there!" Rodrigo shouted at a foot soldier who stood nearby, "fetch this lad a horse. He is my squire as of this moment." Rodrigo looked down into the boy's beaming face, "And if he handles himself well, he will be a knight within the year. Satisfied, Alvar Fañez?"

Rodrigo led his men out of Bivar like a king before his army, and even as he did so more knights came from all directions to join him. They rode all day and encamped outside the city of Burgos that first night. There Rodrigo called the knight Don Martin Antolinez to him. "Don Martin, I have a task for you. You are my best man. If you do this for me I will double your pay."

"Anything, Cid," the man answered without hesitation.

"Good! You see that I have nothing with me. But I must provide for my companions. There are two men who live in Burgos, rich moneylenders. Go to them in secret, let no one see you. They have, no doubt, received a letter from Alphonso, but if no one knows of my contact with them, they will do anything if they think it will profit them. Tell them that I have two chests of treasure and gold that I cannot take with me because of their weight. Tell them I wish them held for me for one year and would ask the loan of only six hundred marks upon them."

Don Martin grinned, "It is as good as done, Cid."

Later, in his tent, Rodrigo and Alvar Fañez took two chests that were covered in red leather and gilted with gold nails and filled each of them with sand, fastening each with three locks. Then they sat down to wait.

Rachel and Vidas, the two moneylenders, entered Rodrigo's tent, smiling broadly. For only six hundred marks they would have the treasure that belonged to the great warrior, El Cid. They remembered all the battles he had fought and won against the Muslim, and imagined the extent of the wealth that would be in those chests.

Rodrigo smiled warmly upon them. "Ah, welcome, Rachel and Vidas. I hope your presence here means that we have struck a bargain?"

Rachel, the older, more wizened of the two, spoke in a voice that was whining and high-pitched. "A bargain? Perhaps, sire. But the figure of, uh, six hundred marks seems a little high? Do you not agree, Vidas?" He turned his anxious eyes to his companion, smiling uncomfortably.

"Ah, Rachel, you do drive a wicked bargain." Rodrigo shook his head helplessly, "Let us say, then, five hundred and fifty marks."

"Agreed!" Rachel cried happily.

"Fine. But you understand, of course, that I am in great haste because of the wrath of Don Alphonso." Rodrigo held out his hand, still smiling, "Give me the marks and we will call it a bargain."

"Forgive me, my lord, but this is not the way of business. We must have the chests first."

"Hah," Rodrigo laughed, "You *are* a shrewd one, sir. Alvar, remove the robe there and show these men my boxes of treasure."

Alvar leaped to his feet from where he had been sitting upon the earth at Rodrigo's feet. With a great flourish he whipped off the coverings. The two moneylenders gasped in unison at the richness of the chests' outer embellishments. Rachel reached into his tunic, removed a small leather bag, and slowly counted out three hundred marks of silver. The rest Vidas produced from his own purse, in gold.

The chests were so heavy that Don Martin and Alvar Fañez had to help the two men carry them to their wagon. Don Martin returned, pleased and excited. "We have done well," he roared, holding out one hand. "You, Ruy Diaz, have gained five hundred and fifty marks and I, thirty! I told them that since it was I who got these chests for them, I deserved a reward. Ah, Rodrigo Diaz, we have made a good beginning. . . ."

"Indeed we have, Don Martin. Now let us strike these tents and leave this place quickly. They promised not to open the chests for a year, but it just might enter their minds that I have duped them." Rodrigo began to laugh lightheartedly. All was well. "Alvar! Come here, boy."

"Yes, Uncle?"

"You are my squire, but I will have no time to instruct you. I place you in the very capable hands of Don Martin, here. When we do not fight but are at rest, he will lesson you in the art of combat. You are a fine lad. I am happy that you are with me. . ." He turned to Don Martin, putting an arm around the man's shoulders. "Teach him well, Martin, and protect him."

When the two had left him alone, Rodrigo reached into the box that held his few possessions, placing a sheet of parchment and a quill on the table. He would write a letter to Don Pedro, bishop of Gormaz, to be read to Jimena.

> Dear Wife:
>
> I pray this finds you well and safe after your return and beg your forgiveness for not seeing you once more before I left, leaving but a curt and unkind message for you. All is well with me, and as things look, perchance I will be able to send for you within the next year or two.
>
> I enclose one hundred marks of silver. You will please give the usual portion to the church; the remainder is for your needs.
>
> God be with you, until I can once more be husband and protector to you.
>
> Ruy Diaz

As the men dismantled the tents and readied the wagons for the journey ahead, Rodrigo stood far from the campsite, looking back toward Castile. His life, it seemed, was to be divided into parts. The first had ended. He turned and looked to the Sierra de Miedes, the border of mountains separating Castile from the land of the Infidel, where his future, whatever it might be, lay. He felt exhilarated. He would not look back again. He was a citizen of the world now and owed allegiance to no man. He was free, more truly free than any man alive. He raised his arm high over his head, and shouted out to his men. "To the future, *Hidalgos!* March!"

The caravan that slowly pressed its way across the narrow mountain trails had swelled to a company of three hundred lances, and a thousand foot soldiers. An army, with no king and no home, without means of any kind, except their courage, for survival. In earlier times and in other nations men like these had been called bandits, privateers, or marauders, but these self-exiled Castilians were known as *Hidalgos,* brave and noble fighting men, who fought for two gods. . . Rodrigo Diaz first, then the one who dwelt in Heaven, both of whom they called Lord.

At daybreak Rodrigo's small army was near the brow of the Sierra and he called them to a halt there. They would give barley to their horses and rest until evening.

"There it is, Alvar my lad," Rodrigo said, pointing down into the distance where the green fields of the valley lay like a patchwork cloth, dotted with hamlets and farms, with a walled city in the center. "The land of the Muslim and of our future. Their cities are like giant, juicy plums, waiting only to be plucked."

Alvar beamed in adoration, his stomach swirling with excitement. "That city, there," he pointed eagerly, "what city is it? Will that be the first to feel the sting of El Cid?"

Rodrigo grinned at the boy's eagerness, remembering when he was the same age. "That is Castrejon, a small plum to be sure, but sufficient for a beginning. Yes, my lad, Castrejon has the honor of being forever called the first."

That night the army of Rodrigo Diaz continued its way down from the top of the mountains, leaving behind them the sharp, clean air, moving deeper into the cloud of dusty, hot breezes that hovered over the valley. They passed through the fields quietly so that no one would hear or see them. In the moonlight the trees looked like they were jeweled, they were so heavily laden with ripened fruit. Under the feet of the foot soldiers the earth was soft and spongy and dark of color, so well was it irrigated and tended by the infidels. It was a green and blooming paradise that had been created from dry, sandy plains, urged by tender care and water to produce in abundance.

The men positioned themselves around the city walls in ambush. As morning lightened the sky, the people, knowing nothing of the danger that surrounded them, opened the gates and went out to their work as they did each day.

Rodrigo leaped from his hiding place and shouted, "Attack, Hidalgos! The time is here. Go with God, men . . ."

There was an instant cry of warning within the town. "The Christians are upon us. To arms!" Those who were within ran to the city gates to defend them. But when they laid eyes upon the raging giant swooping down upon them, they froze with fear, then ran for shelter. Rodrigo Diaz killed eleven men who could not run fast enough, leaning from his mount, cutting through them with his sword as they scurried in search of a hiding place where this monster and his horde could not find them. Some did get away, but to no avail. The city was easily won, and all the captives were herded together in the castle courtyard. Rodrigo's knights ransacked the castle, houses, and shops of Castrejon, routing out stray citizens, heaping up the spoils of gold and silver and whatever else they could find at the feet of El Cid. The conquering hero sat watching upon a high wall, extremely pleased with himself.

Rodrigo looked down with intense satisfaction at the immense mountain of wealth below him. "You . . . you . . . and you," he called out, pointing to one, then another of his knights, "to each and every horseman, one hundred marks of silver, and half as much to each foot soldier." He smiled with pleasure at the roaring cheer that followed his announcement. "You there," he gestured to a proud, royally dressed infidel, who stood among the crowd of prisoners, "come here to me."

The man walked slowly to him and made a deep bow. "I am at your service, Saíd." The man's tone was soft and humble.

Rodrigo winced. The memory of a dead girl returned briefly, and he accepted the warning with gratitude to God. "Send a messenger to the cities of Fita and Guadalajara," he growled, glaring down into the man's eyes, "and tell them we have taken your city and have prisoners for sale, and spoils. They may safely enter this city and bid with me for merchandise that I have no use for." Rodrigo waved an arm to emphasize his point. "And spread the word, after I leave this place, that Rodrigo Diaz, The Lord, does not rape your women, nor keep any prisoners because of his distaste and contempt for your sinful persons. But," he shouted now, "tell them also that they will do well to tremble in fear of me, for I will descend upon them one by one since I have *no* such distaste for their gold."

By sunset that day men came from Fita and Guadalajara and valued the spoils and prisoners, giving Rodrigo Diaz three thousand marks of silver for what was the property of their neighbors. Then they left the town, looking fearfully back over their shoulders, for their own cities lay within the probable route of this menace to their peace.

"Well, Rodrigo Diaz," Don Martin exclaimed, as he hoisted himself up upon the wall beside Rodrigo, "it has been a good and profitable day, worth waking in the morning for, I would say. What next, Cid? Surely we will not stay here?"

"No, Don Martin. There will never be a place in these lands where we can stay for long." Rodrigo laughed and pulled at his beard, his eyes dancing with amusement. "Alphonso has a treaty with this town. Christ, if he heard that we had taken it and that we were still here, he would descend upon this place with an army. Contrary to popular opinion, I am *not* unconquerable. No. We must go on, Martin, tomorrow."

The weeks passed swiftly. Thousands more, having heard of the feats of El Cid, rode out of Castile to join him. It was said that he was generous even with the foot soldiers, who were all rich men by now. His growing army sacked the cities of Alcocer and Calatayud, then Teruel and Monzon. Rodrigo then returned to Zaragossa, which he had conquered two years before as Sancho's ensign; he demanded that he be paid the tribute that was being paid to Alphonso, which by right of war was El Cid's. The people of Zaragossa received him with a cheerful welcome because he had spared them his sword. He stayed there for three months.

Rodrigo moved restlessly in his tent. He went to the opening and looked out upon the white walls of Zaragossa, gleaming in the sunlight. Damned if he knew why he could not bring himself to find an abode with more comfort within the city. Living in this rat's nest! But he was outside the walls, and his scouts were keeping him informed of any troop movements in the area. He would never be caught off guard out here on the plains. He would leave Zaragossa, soon. Winter was nearly over. The men were becoming restless. It was time for another march.

"I have done it, Uncle!" The boy leaped through the opening of the tent and stumbled right over Rodrigo's foot, falling flat on his pretty face. He rolled over and grinned sheepishly up at his uncle, "As I said, Uncle, I have done it. I have passed the last test. Don Martin says that I am ready. And in only these short months. Am I . . ." he queried hopefully, "am I ready, Uncle?"

"Damn me, yes," Rodrigo shouted, laughing. "A shame it is that spirit is not enough, if so you would put El Cid to shame, lad. I will knight you. But you need more muscle, boy, more muscle. When you hold a thirty-pound lance in an arm encased in five more pounds of metal, you need a great bulge there, to hold that weapon steady. And the legs. Develop those leg muscles. You must guide your mount with your knees, while one hand holds a sword, the other a lance." Rodrigo reached down for the boy's hand and jerked him to his feet, "Lift the weights, Alvar, day and night, then you will be the match of your proud uncle."

"Oh!" Alvar screeched as he ran from the tent, his cheeks flushed with excitement. "Don Martin, I have been *accepted!*"

The ceremony was brief and serious. Alvar Fañez knelt before his uncle and was knighted. His banner, his armor, and his sword were blessed by the priests. When he arose there was a new look of pride and maturity about him. Rodrigo kissed the boy on each cheek, tears hot in his eyes. Jimena had had a daughter, not a son, and he saw little hope that she would bear another child in the near future, since it would be impossible for her to come to him. Terror overcame him, but he quickly subdued it; he might die in the next battle, before he could immortalize himself in the flesh of a son.

Jimena slumped deeper into her chair in her silent chamber, thinking that there were moments when time seemed to hesitate, almost stop—and in those moments one's mind became supersensitive to the most trivial incidents. Even while one was living these suspended moments, somehow one knew that they would vividly return in some far-off place and time; the sweet scent of a flower held to the face long ago comes back so clear and real that one feels the tang of it upon the nostrils again. And there are those plans for the immediate future that are so eagerly anticipated and imagined they are already reality; even when they fail to come to pass—they, too, come back in later years as treasured memories.

With this vivid sense of stopped time, Jimena gathered to herself every minute detail of this day, knowing she would remember forever even such small things as the gentle stirrings within her of the child she carried, and the scent of the breeze entering through her chamber window. To be sure, it was a special day, the day of her return to Gormaz.

How she missed the baby, and how clearly she could see Aunt Galiana handing the child to her. The old woman would say, "Hah! Afraid of the dark? Not once did I leave a candle by her cradle and never a whimper from her." She would hold lit-

tle Urracca close to her breast, feeling again the warmth of her
sweet flesh against her own. Just thinking about it, she could
feel that warmth. Urracca would have a tooth, perhaps. She
might even be walking!

Jimena sighed and eased out of the chair. She moved toward the window, where bright morning sunshine spilled into
the room. These past four months she had received only one
message from Rodrigo, sent to Gormaz and brought by fast
horse to her here at Palencia. Shivering as a crisp wind swept in
from the window, she clasped her arms tightly across her
bosom. She shuddered at the prospect of Rodrigo being
marched upon by an army of Castilians. Word had reached the
castle just this morning that Count Ramon Berenguer of Bar-
celona had begun a move southward with an army of ten
thousand; his tributaries of Huesca and Montalban had been stolen by Rodrigo. Rumor was that there would be a pitched battle
at the Pine Forest of Tebar. Rodrigo's army was no more than
three thousand strong. She shrugged, thinking that Rodrigo,
since he was apparently unconquerable, would more than likely
prevail against this ten thousand, even against twenty thousand.
God did seem to ride with him.

Jimena erased all thought of her husband from her mind,
thinking once again of the journey to begin within the hour.
Where in the *devil* was Maria? She stepped closer to the window
and glanced down to the street below. A few people milled
about; it was still early morning and most people had not yet
begun the day's endeavors. Then she saw the girl, pacing back
and forth as if waiting for someone. For God, a thousand things
to do, and there she dallied. But Maria was a good girl, sweet.
She had begged to serve her again on this visit, and Urracca had
generously agreed. No older than I, Jimena thought. Pathetic.
Sold as a servant before she had reached ten years. It was certainly true that no matter how dark one's own lot, there were
others who contemplated an existence vastly more depressing,
which was some little comfort.

Jimena had just caught her breath to call out to the girl
when she came to jolting attention. Every nerve became keyed
to what she now observed. It must be—that man who walked
down the street toward Maria was Estiano, her carriage driver
to Zamora. Her heart flipped over in her breast so hard it took
her breath away. Nonsense. There were hundreds of expla-
nations as to why he might be in Palencia. But the coincidence
of his being wherever she was for the past four months. . . .

She watched, transfixed, as he stepped up behind Maria, then was stunned by the girl's pleased, bright smile when she turned and saw him there. "Great Heaven!" Jimena exclaimed out loud. Whatever did Maria find to admire in that offensive little man? But, no need for concern; Maria would be leaving for Gormaz this day, to remain with her permanently. Don Pedro must find a good husband for the girl. By the look of things it was time Maria was wed.

Maria busily rushed about Jimena's room, packing all the remaining articles and clothing into boxes. Jimena called excitedly from across the room, "Do not forget the shoes, in that container there, and that bolt of silk the Infanta gave me yesterday, though God knows I shall never make use of it. But it *is* lovely to look upon, to touch. How do you suppose the Muslims create such fabric? Quite amazing."

No reply came from Maria. She methodically did what she was told, her face a mask of grim purpose and weakly hidden misery.

"Whatever ails you, Maria?" Jimena asked impatiently. "Would you prefer to remain in the service of the Infanta? I would release you, of course, but I thought you wished to be with me."

"Ah no, my lady, it is only that I . . ."

Jimena glanced up from the packing box she was leaning over and eyed the girl suspiciously. "Maria? I saw you with a man not more than half of an hour past; is it he who grieves you so?"

"Oh-oooo," the girl wailed, her features breaking. "Oh, my lady, I gave him everything. I love him so. And," she choked on a sob, "and when I told him this morning that I would depart this day for Gormaz with you, my lady, he—he said that he thought I would never leave. He refused to meet me at Gormaz. He laughed at me! I begged him, pleaded, and he laughed at me."

"But," Jimena said sympathetically, moving to the girl's side, "you cannot expect a bondsman to travel where he pleases. Surely you are being unreasonable, Maria."

"He is *not* a bondsman. He was freed by his master and he is now a scribe . . . and sells his service in the market square!"

Jimena flinched. That curious, ominous man. First a carriage driver, vassal to Rodrigo, now a scribe and free. She wondered what he had pretended to be at Zamora? She observed Maria's face, all agonized over the loss of this man. "Maria, there is time. Go to him. Perhaps you might bring about some kind of reconciliation."

"I cannot," she wailed. "He has left the city. I watched him ride from the city gate, and he did not look back at me, or say goodbye. Oh-ooooo," she was howling now, weeping into her hands.

"What goes here?"

Urracca swept into the room, her violet eyes resting first upon a bewildered Jimena, then to the weeping servant girl. "What have you done to my girl, woman? Do you make a practice of torturing your servants—have you beaten her?"

Jimena smiled, relieved by Urracca's cheerful presence. "Ah, no, Urracca. Maria has lost in the game of love, and suffers a broken heart."

"I see."

Urracca moved briskly to Maria and placed an arm about the girl's quaking shoulders. "Come now, girl. Doña Jimena will leave you behind, if you persist. You cannot work while you weep. Console yourself with the fact that there is an abundance of men in this world. Come, pick up that box and carry it to the carriage—that is a good girl."

When Maria had left, still sniffling and miserable, Jimena and Urracca burst into instantaneous giggles. There was something so tragically amusing in Maria's misery, as if their own depths of emotion could not possibly be experienced by a mere servant girl. "And what a brute of a man he is," Jimena laughed, "quite monstrous, my dear—and how she wept over him."

Together the two women walked through the halls of Palencia castle, down the long, circular staircase, into the main entrance lobby, then out through the huge archway to where the carriage waited in the courtyard. They did not speak. To Jimena there was a strange sense of finality about this somber walk; every crack in the granite walls loomed before her eyes to imbed itself in her memory. She counted the stairs and would never forget that there were seventy-two of them. A cloud hovered in the sky as they stepped into the yard; it passed over the sun so that a sudden gray shadow erased the brightness of the day.

Maria was already seated in the carriage, pushed into one dark corner, her muffled sniffling clearly audible.

"Well," Jimena sighed, turning to Urracca, "it is time for us to part once again."

Impulsively Urracca grabbed Jimena's face in her hands and

kissed her. "Take care, Jimena, my good friend, and come again soon, very soon."

Tear-blinded, Jimena was moving to step into the carriage, when she heard approaching footsteps. Alphonso swiftly strode toward her, two knights at his heels. He took her hands in his, smiling down at her. "Jimena, my dear, we will miss you very much. I wish you would accept my house as yours, but," he shook his head sadly, "under the circumstances, it would not be fitting, I suppose."

"I thank you, Alphonso, for all your kindness to me." At the quick light of guilt in his eyes, Jimena reached up her hand and set it upon his cheek. "Oh, do not regret what you have done to my husband for my sake. Forced to choose where my loyalties lie, they necessarily fall to you—my friend and my king."

His affection for Jimena warmed Alphonso, smiling, he turned to the men who accompanied him. "Doña Jimena, these gentlemen have the honor of escorting you to Gormaz. This is Don José Gonzales, Don Diego Salvadores, knights of my court."

Jimena nodded shyly in their direction. They looked so awesome, decked out in all that metal. She smiled, "I fear you will find this journey quite dull, compared to your usual assignments."

The younger of the two grinned. "That is what we are here for, to guarantee a journey without incident. But if there be anyone who wishes it, trouble is what we will give to him."

"Farewell, Alphonso, Urracca!" Jimena called out, leaning half out of the carriage window as the vehicle lurched forward at the snap of the driver's whip. "I promise I will visit again soon. Soon." She watched them standing side by side, until the carriage turned and they were lost to her. That image of a king and his sister, with arms entwined, love and friendship in their eyes, was another of those living visions that she knew would return to her over and over again for many years to come.

Jimena settled back against the hard, wooden seat, content to watch the houses of Palencia pass by. Maria sat across from her, sulking miserably. Foolish girl, she was well rid of that unpleasant Estiano. Now *where* could he have ridden off to? At least it was certain he was not following, since he had left the city more than an hour ahead. But it would not amaze her a bit to see him on the streets of Gormaz one day.

Night fell softly upon the tents, bringing with it a chilling breeze. Jimena sat quietly on a chair outside the entrance to her small tent. The campfire a few feet away flickered dejectedly. She could hear Maria busy inside, preparing her bed for the night. The wagon drivers were already asleep and snoring beneath their vehicles. Don Gonzales and Salvadores sat together by the fire, talking in low voices. All was peaceful, yet ominously quiet, beyond the campsite. Jimena had tried very hard to shake the morbidity that had begun to plague her early in the day but fear was alive in her now and refused to be dispelled. Simply absurd, she thought, to be so irritated by nerves and dread; returning to little Urracca was an occasion for high spirits.

Maria appeared behind Jimena. "It is late, my lady. Come, I have your bed prepared. You must sleep. Tomorrow will be long and tiring."

As Jimena disrobed, Maria darted about the small enclosure efficiently. It relaxed her just to watch the girl, the childlike satisfaction she took in the simple tasks of placing her mistress' shoes neatly by the bed, of folding each article of clothing carefully and placing it for quick dressing in the morning.

Jimena lay a long time on the hard, makeshift bed without closing her eyes. The strangeness of her surroundings only added to her apprehension. Maria was curled up on the earth, smothered in heavy coverlets, at the entrance of the tent. Jimena could see past her through the opening. The two knights no longer talked, but nodded their heads. The stillness continued to disturb her. Her breath came in short gasps as unidentifiable shadows seemed to move all around her, pressing closer. At the faintest sound her heart would cease to beat for an instant, her breath caught in her throat. But sleep came at long last. It had been an exhausting day, from Palencia to this spot on the plains near the Castilian border, only ten miles from the Muslim town of Soria.

A piercing scream vibrated and shattered the heavy silence of the night. Jimena leaped from her bed, wrenched from sleep. "Maria! Maria?" she screeched, but no answer came. She was alone in the tent, a confusion of terrifying sounds falling upon her ears—cursing, struggle, then the crash of a wagon overturned. The darkness pressed against her; she could see nothing, and could only stand there rigid, unable to move.

Another scream. Jimena could do nothing but cower in terror against the wall of the tent. Then flames erased the blackness. Fluttering, hideous tentacles of light spread over the walls of her tent. She found her strength. Pushing wildly through the entrance she stumbled out into hell fire, a ghoulish nightmare. Alphonso's knights were still by the ashes of their earlier campfire, but were lying grotesquely on the earth. From their chests protruded the handles of the knives that had been plunged into their hearts.

"God in heaven! Maria! Where are you?" Her eyes flashed over the scene, until she saw Maria's body jutting out from under an overturned wagon. She ran to the body, her fingers tearing at the burning vehicle. She could not budge it. It was then she saw Maria's face—smashed beyond recognition, blood-smeared, with broken pieces of bone shoving out at awkward angles. "Aiieee!" She lurched back, staggering from the flames, from that monstrous corpse. "Oh God! God help you, Maria," she groaned, burying her bleeding, burned hands in her face, sobbing. Then her eyes slid away from trembling fingers and she looked out and about her. Not a living creature was left. Where were the devils who would commit such acts of murder and terror? She whipped around and around, hysterical. "Where are you? Do you spare me, only? There is one left: come kill me also! Where are you? God in heaven, where *are* you?"

She stood quietly then, hands over her face, her chemise in tatters, her hair and exposed flesh singed and smeared with soot. The burning wagons slowly died down to ashes. Silence. All had been demolished except her own tent which stood untouched, while all around there was smoldering destruction and death.

A hand reached out from behind and rested upon Jimena's shoulder. Numbly she turned, prepared to face sudden annihilation.

"Holy Mary!" she gasped.

Her would-be slayer was wrapped head to foot in white robes; she stared into dark eyes that were black pits of abhorrence. The white of his robes stood out against the night, framing his terrifying eyes. He was a ghostly apparition with living eyes that spit out flaming daggers from hell fire, a demon that moved, took hold of her, its fingers digging into the flesh of her arm.

"If I had intended your death, woman, you would not be standing before me now," the demon said, in a voice trembling with loathing.

The words struck Jimena's mind like an arrow piercing her heart. He would not kill her—not kill her. Why not? What worse torture did he have in mind? Dear Jesus, who was it behind those veils? Totally confused, frightened and exhausted, Jimena could only stare back at him.

A stabbing pain suddenly struck her—sharp, tearing her abdomen apart. Jimena's eyes widened in disbelief. She doubled over, clutching at her bulging stomach with frantic, clawing fingers, "Mother of God," she screamed, "help me, please, *whoever* you are. My—my baby. My *baby*!" She felt ripping, tearing, pushing, then a mist before her eyes that became darker and faded. With a groan Jimena fell unconscious at her captor's feet.

Chapter
✠ *TEN* ✠

Through a black blur of pain and semiconsciousness, Jimena was only occasionally aware of her surroundings. She did not know how much time had passed when the first wave of total consciousness came. Her eyes weakly opened and a glare of sunlight bruised them. She vaguely noticed a monotonous jogging motion and strong arms holding her tight, her head resting against the firm, white-enshrouded chest of her captor, the sound of horses' racing hooves thundering in her ears. The pain came again, and she prayed for that sweet oblivion to return. It was an endless nightmare. Again and again she passed into unconsciousness; each time she awoke those arms were still about her. Once she heard her captor call out in the language of the Devil. If she could only die—blessed, rewarding death. Then that tantalizing, color-sparked dream returned and she ran toward the sparks of color to a place where there was beauty and happiness. She would find that place someday, she knew she would, so she could not wholly give herself up to death. Jimena drifted in her dream, clinging precariously to a fine thread of hope.

Emerging from a whirlpool of exhaustion, pain, and burning fever, Jimena felt arms lifting her, carrying her, and voices murmuring in that devilish tongue. Then came the sweet relief of a bed beneath her tortured flesh. She heard agonized screams. They came from her own lips, she thought, but there was no reality, only a black chasm of terror and abortion. "Damn you," she cried out, delirious, "damn you—God! Urracca spoke the truth! You *are* cruel. Cruel to plague me so. Damn, damn—oh, help me, someone help . . . me."

A soft, musical voice entered Jimena's peaceful oblivion, then faded, then became clear again. Cool hands gently stroked

Jimena's brow. If she opened her eyes she would have to face her predicament that wavered uncertain and painless now behind eyelid curtains. The pain was gone now, and the fever, too. There was no longer any hope for death as an escape. Cautiously she slightly opened her eyes, peeking through slits.

"Ah, you are awake, my lady. Do you feel better?"

The voice was very clear now and it came from the painted mouth of a beautiful, dark-skinned young woman. An *infidel*!

"No!" Jimena gasped, throwing both hands over her eyes. She reared up blindly, screaming, "Where is my baby? Where is he? I want my baby!" The tears came and she wept for a long, long while, draining her body and soul of their last agonies, leaving her clean and renewed, prepared for whatever she must face. A demon creature all in stark white, with eyes full of hatred, had swept her up for a reason known only to himself, and had carried her away from the predictable future, from the anticipated joy of seeing a golden baby once more.

When she next opened her eyes, Jimena was alone. She glanced curiously about her. She was in some kind of tent, but it was enormous, its material striped and richly decorated. Covering the earth, making a velvet cushion on which to walk, was a rug, richly woven in a curious design. Even Alphonso did not have a rug upon his chamber floor, and here they placed one upon the earth. Her fingers slid smoothly across her bed. With a start she looked down. The colors were blinding. She lay upon purple velvet, and the pillows beneath her head were of yellow silk brocaded in threads of silver and gold. Her body, which in her first waking moment she had thought to be naked, was clothed in a linen so soft and fine she could not feel it against her. Long, billowing sleeves were clasped tight at her wrists and the bodice was cut very low upon her breast, over a bosom dismally flattened as a result of her illness. The yellow gown was cinched tight at her waist with a band of carved silver, then flowed out about her legs in trouser fashion. The yellow of all this blended in shocking harmony with the deep purple of the velvet coverlet. "For God!" she whispered and squeezed her eyes closed again.

Jimena awoke with a pleasing, unexpected sense of physical well-being and health. Only the night before illness had still been with her in weakened limbs and a listless disinterest in life. But now she stretched luxuriously and smiled with pleasure at the feeling of new strength in her legs. She felt marvelous and starving. Sitting up, she threw back the satin coverlet and swung her feet to the rug. She stood up, then cried out as her knees gave way to drop her back upon the pillows.

The same girl pushed through the curtains that covered the opening of the tent, holding back the silk drape with a pretty hand. A black manservant walked, head lowered, to the center of the enclosure, carrying a huge, round, jeweled box. He set it down and retreated. Jimena eyed him curiously. He was the first person other than the girl that she had seen in all these long days. She wondered what the box was for, and looked questioningly at the woman, who walked purposefully toward her.

"A good morning to you, my lady," she said crisply. "My name is Acacia. If you will please remove your clothing?"

Stunned for a moment, Jimena stared at the woman rudely. She had not expected perfect Spanish, and that name brought forth cruel memories. "Acacia?" she whispered. "There is an acacia tree in the—that I loved so as a child. I . . . " She faltered, recalling that nightmarish burning. Infidel or not, it was a ghastly act to commit against a man. She remembered also the two knights by the ashes of their campfire, Muslim knives in their hearts. Bewildered, she began to work at the fastenings of her bodice but clutched the vest back to her as the black servant popped back in. He carried a heavy pail of steaming water and dumped it into the jeweled box. He made six such trips as Jimena watched in silent fascination and growing dismay.

"I said, remove your clothing," Acacia said, hands on her hips, tapping a toe impatiently until Jimena had complied with her demand. Then, with a casual wave of her hand toward the box, she ordered, "Get in."

"In? In there?" Jimena spluttered, "No—no, I most certainly will *not* get in there."

The girl eyed her coldly, "Are you going to step into the water, or must I call the black man and have him *put* you in?"

Jimena fairly leaped into the box, standing up to her thighs in the wetness, embarrassed and fearful, holding her arms tight across her breasts in an effort to cover at least a part of her nakedness. "Holy Mary, Mother of God," she whispered to the tent roof, "forgive the sin I am about to commit." The water felt warm on her flesh, and a heady scent of perfume rose from it.

"Sit. For the love of Allah, sit." The girl placed firm hands on Jimena's shoulders and pushed.

"But," Jimena protested, unable to find a more reasonable argument, "I will get all wet."

Acacia threw back her head in a silent laugh. "Indeed you will, but when you step forth from your bath a far better aroma will surround you, I think. All Christians smell like goats, and you, my lady, are no exception."

"Oh-oooo!" Jimena plunked down into the tub, sending a furious wave up over her shoulders and out over the edges of the box. The gall of that girl, a crude, vulgar barbarian, believer in a false prophet—to say that Jimena Gomez smelled like a goat. Even if it were true, she need not have said it.

A soft cloth was handed unceremoniously to Jimena, then a white, yellowish lump of a substance that she had never seen before. She looked blankly up at the girl.

"*Alhomdalillah!*," the girl shouted, "That is soap! Merciful Allah was kind to me. Allah forbid I should have been born a Christian. Have you never used soap in *all* your days?"

Jimena's face flushed at the distaste in Acacia's voice, but still she did not know what to do with the articles. The *soap* was probably for eating, but what was she to do with the cloth?

She was immediately instructed in their use. The objects were wrenched from her hands and the soap rubbed briskly against the wet cloth until a mysterious foam appeared. Then, to her amazement, the girl began to rub the sudsy cloth over her arms and shoulders.

"You see? We *barbarians* call this washing. Do it, all over." And after Jimena had obeyed, "Do not forget the hair. We must drown a few of those lice you have allowed to make a home upon you." At Jimena's quick objection, she laughed heartily. "Yes, your hair. Wet it first, then soap it. Try it. Perhaps you will discover that beneath all that dirt a lovely woman has been lurking."

"Oh-oooo," Jimena raged, sliding under the water. She came up spluttering and spitting, her eyes blinking as water ran into them.

She bathed every day after that, though how one could become unclean in but a single day— Even more absurd, clean clothing after each bathing, a most shameful waste of perfectly good apparel. Each ensemble was more lovely than the last. Since she never wore the same gown twice, she naturally assumed the used ones were thrown away.

From her first moments of consciousness, Jimena had made herself miserable wondering who could have done this to her, and why. It was common practice, she knew, for Muslims to steal Christian women, who were usually never seen again. It was said they were sold on slave blocks, like cattle or goats, living lives of unimaginable horror, victims of lustful men who asked nothing more from life than satisfaction of their carnal desires. She did not dare question Acacia, preferring to leave her fate in obscurity, clinging to a small hope that in this instance it was ransom the infidel had in mind. Ransom was not common practice, but was known to have occurred. After all, Rodrigo was a wealthy man. Her composure hung on the balance of this hope; she could not know that her husband's wealth, when compared to Arab standards, relegated him to a status not far removed from a pauper.

Often at night, when she could not sleep, a possibility repeatedly leaped to the forefront of her mind—that she might *never* return to Castile. It was only a word, *never,* and its meaning seemed vague now. She grappled with it, her mind numbly defining it. Forever, the remainder of her life, not ever again. She could not visualize any other future than what was predictable according to the pattern of the past; therein there was at least a dim knowledge of what was to come . . . more of the same. This suspension was like walking slowly toward a cliff edge and stepping off into nothingness, falling end over end, with no jutting ledges to grasp hold of, nothing upon which to support herself—an empty, black, bottomless hole out of which there was no escape. But there were a few grim certainties. Her sister Leonora had told her all about the dread slave block, and about harems. A savage barbarian. His leering face. His pawing, lecherous hands would clutch at her; that experienced horror, brutal rape, would happen to her again. And not once, nor twice, but filling up the black hole that was the future. Mary Mother of God, she would kill herself, choose hell in eternity, rather than suffer such a hell on earth.

Still encamped outside Zaragossa, directly following sunrise mass, Rodrigo waved Alvar to him and said, "I have a mission for you, Ruy Fañez, your first as a knight. Go to Gormaz and see my wife, Doña Jimena, and my daughter. Tell them how well I am, and that, if I live, I will make her a rich woman. Salute for me the bishop of Gormaz, Don Pedro. Give him fifty marks of silver from the monies I give you, and the rest give to my wife." Rodrigo hesitated, searching for words. He did not know the woman to whom he sent word; the sacrament of the church was the only real tie between them. Jimena would probably feel herself well rid of him. No need of a chastity belt with that one. The ice in her veins was all the belt she needed, and it

would never be unlocked by any man, including himself.
Though penetrated, Jimena remained a virgin.

Rodrigo felt an annoying jab of pain and heat in his groin.
Damn, what he would not give for a Christian woman right
now, even as cold a one as Jimena. He was surrounded by
dark-eyed Sabíhahs but was constantly in this state of painful
dissatisfaction, because if he touched an infidel woman again his
present success would be shattered by the wrath of God; a God
who at this moment blessed his deeds against the Infidel.

"Is that all, sire?" Alvar asked hesitantly.

"What? Oh, yes, Alvar. Come with me to my tent, and I
will give you the monies you are to deliver."

Rodrigo handed the leather pouch to the boy and slapped
him soundly upon the back. "God speed you, knight. If, when
you return, you should not find us here, you will hear where
we are, no fear of that. Go now, and make a quick return, for I
will truly miss that pretty face of yours."

Rodrigo paced for a week, then called his knights and soldiers together. He stood before them, looking from face to face,
but there were so many now that he could not see those faces in
the rear. Two thousand knights—a fair army for the lonely one
of Castile.

He jumped up upon a wagon. "You know," he shouted,
so that as many as possible could hear, "you know, my friends,
that for all who live by their arms, as we do, it is not good to
stay long in one place. Let us be off again tomorrow. What do
you say to that, eh?"

Loud cheering and shouting was the reply. The next day
they moved away from Zaragossa to the Puerto de Alucant, and
from there they rode upon and destroyed two more cities belonging to Count Ramon Berenguer.

News of these most recent deeds of El Cid sped swiftly
from mouth to mouth, ever northward, and within two days
reached the headquarters of Don Ramon. Enraged and determined, the count struck camp, driving his army swiftly toward
the first confrontation of a Christian army with El Cid since his
banishment. Castile was about to rid itself of the rampant pest
that so plagued it.

Three days later Berenguer made camp near the Pine Forest.
Within hours he received a message from El Cid. "The booty
that I have won is mine, and none of yours. Turn yourself
around and leave this land, or I will slaughter you one and all."

But the count was confident; he had over ten thousand
men with him.

Rodrigo laid his camp out in the valley that was surrounded on all sides by the Pine Forest. Upon the encircling
hills his bowmen sat, hidden from view in the tall trees. The
foot soldiers lay in wait where the pass between two rocky
crags entered into the valley, turning sharply, so that anyone
who rode in would not see them until it was too late. Other
soldiers stood behind screens of brush on top of the crags, with
boulders and bows ready to rain death upon the enemy.

To the observer looking down upon the camp from a distance, everything appeared ordinary and unprepared for attack.
Knights sat around their fires laughing and unarmed. When
Count Berenguer confidently dashed through the pass, certain
that the great Cid was now destroyed, he was allowed to pass
by. But a wall of men closed in behind him, stopping short the
knights who followed him.

"What in . . . what *is* this? I—" The Count reined his horse
in hard, and whirled around in bewilderment.

"I greet you, Don Berenguer. Welcome to my humble
camp." Rodrigo was laughing, forced to shout over the shrieking, crashing noise of the battle that raged only a few yards
away. He ducked quickly away from a whistling arrow. The
count had ridden right into his trap, while Rodrigo had sat
upon his horse at the mouth of the pass, waiting. "Sir," Rodrigo grinned, "you are my prisoner, or had you already guessed?" He doubled over at the humor of his own joke and at the
stricken expression on the count's face. "Ah, sir, you might
well have listened to those who spoke of Rodrigo Diaz as unconquerable. . . ."

"Robber! Thief!" The man's anger shook him so that he
was nearly gibbering.

"Count Berenguer, you offend me. Call me knight. Or
hidalgo. But *never* thief. Would you have me starve? Leave my
dear wife and child without means? I save Christendom from
the Infidel. I am a hero. A legend. But I am *not* a thief." Rodrigo unsheathed his sword and placed the sharp edge threateningly against the count's trembling Adam's apple. "You have
insulted me, sir. My anger is great. Now, I think that you
might best apologize to me and call me El Cid." He pressed the
blade a little harder against the man's throat, drawing a thin
sliver of a wound from which trickled a stream of red Christian
blood.

Count Berenguer was a stubborn man. He stared coldly
into Rodrigo's eyes and did not move or speak.

Rodrigo slowly lowered the blade. The battle was dying

down. Most who had not been trapped had run like frightened
dogs; the others were dead or prisoners. "You are not a coward, Don Ramon. You beg for no mercy. You refuse to call me
lord, even with my sword at your throat. I think I will spare
your life; yes, I will." With a flourish Rodrigo shoved the
sword back into its sheath. "By God, I *will* let you go free. But
what I have taken from you is mine. You have no claim upon
it, in my mind. Besides, we want it for ourselves, being
banished men who must live by taking from you and others
like you. You will agree to this, my dear count?"

The count looked upon Rodrigo now in shocked admiration. He saw a devil, a thief—and a god. "Sir," he began, "if
you do this that you say, I will marvel at you the rest of my
life." He smiled, "Though I am hesitant to return to my home
with the news that I was so easily subdued by such a ragged
band of fellows."

"Hah! Then you agree that what I have taken, I may
keep?"

"You may keep it."

"Then choose two of your knights and leave, sir. And I
thank you for your, uh, generosity?"

Rodrigo followed the count and his two companions out of
the pass. He held his hand out to his enemy, an arrogant smile
turning up the corners of his mouth, "Go freely, sir, and if you
wish to play for the spoils of Montalban again, let me know
and you shall either kill me or find your head severed from
your shoulders."

Count Berenguer laughed. "You jest safely now, Cid, since
I have left with you a thousand men, and much gold. You have
been well paid for this day's efforts. No, I will not be coming
to see you again soon." He shook Rodrigo's hand heartily. "You
are indeed El Cid, Rodrigo Diaz."

The count looked back many times before he was out of
Rodrigo's sight. A small fear was within him that the lord of
Spain might repent his hasty decision. He need not have wor-
ried. Rodrigo was well satisfied with himself and of that day.
He reined his horse around and headed back toward the camp.

"Don Martin!" Rodrigo shouted as he saw the knight riding down from one of the hills, "How goes the battle, man?
How many Christians have this day joined our army, eh?"

Don Martin pulled up and rode alongside Rodrigo. "We
have twelve hundred prisoners, Cid, and a thousand to bury."
He looked at Rodrigo admiringly, "The marvel of your
achievements will go down in history, Rodrigo. Damnit, if

that was not clever strategy. We picked them off like flies under a swatter, fifteen at a time. Goddamned clever, I say." Don Martin slid agilely off his mount, then reached up and pumped Rodrigo's hand enthusiastically.

Rodrigo grinned and said . . . "Come into my tent, friend. I feel the need of talk."

Don Martin Antolinez was a short man beside Rodrigo's unusual height, but his legs were like steel ramrods, his arms so wide and bulging that he might have carried two lances and handled each well. His hair was long and unruly, his beard braided. Above his left eye there was the beginning of a purple scar that ran down the length of his face to his chin, and the forefinger of his left hand was missing.

Rodrigo flopped himself down upon his blanket and leaned his head against his folded arms. "Rest yourself, knight . . . "

As Don Martin sat leaning against a chest, Rodrigo said, "Tell me of yourself, Martin. You are from Galicia, are you not?"

Martin's mouth twisted down on one side in a crooked smile. "Tell you of *myself*? Christ, I am dull fare for conversation, Cid. I was born in a little hamlet near Santiago. I had eight brothers—nine counting the lost one—and four sisters. Ferrando accepted me as page when I was twelve, knighted me at twenty, and as proof of my super-human strength," he grinned, "I am still alive today."

"Thirteen children!" Rodrigo cried in amazement. "Your father could not have been a knight, or the key to your mother's belt fell into untrustworthy hands. I have not seen my wife the past four and one half months and in all our near five years of marriage, have spent no more than three, perhaps four months with her.

Don Martin stretched his short, stocky legs out in front of him, struggling to remove his boots. His feet throbbed and were wet and itchy with sweat. "Three, Cid . . ." he grunted, as he gave a great heave at his left boot, "three times have I visited my wife, three children have I left behind—in five years. You know, Rodrigo," he leaned forward, shaking his finger "these pagans have the right idea. Take women along with you to the battle. I tell you truth, man, there is a great, swelling heat in my groin these nights. You would do well by me if you lifted your ban upon their women. God, man, the wife is a hundred miles in that direction," he pointed and made a mock grimace of pain, "and here is that great swelling boiling in me. A man can bear just so much . . ."

Rodrigo tried to smile, but felt a scowl creasing his forehead. "No infidel women, Martin," he said emphatically. "The first knight I catch will lose that which he values as a man!" He sat up then, leaning upon one elbow. "Cheer yourself with the thought of Alvar Fañez, sleeping even now by the side of a yellow-haired Christian maiden. Mother of God, how I wish he would bring her back with him; you would have to fight El Cid for her, Don Martin. I share your pain and swelling."

"Ah, Cid. Do not torture me so with talk of Christian maids." Don Martin shook his head in pretended agony, then threw himself over on his stomach, resting his chin in a palm. "We will change the subject. Back to my life, eh? Out of the nine brothers, six are knights, two are priests. The ugly one is lost. I do not know what he is—dead, I suppose."

"Lost? That is the second time you have mentioned this lost brother. Tell me of him."

"Estiano? He was the last of the boys born to my mother, the last of her children, in fact. She was strained out, I think. That was the ugliest creature I ever saw. He was so ugly that the old woman would not even suckle him, crying out that a devil was born to her. When he was two there was not one of us who could love him. He did nothing but cry for days on end, until, in desperation, we stuffed his mouth with rags. I am not boring you, am I? Tell me and I will shut my mouth."

Rodrigo became more relaxed by the moment, listening to Martin's voice rambling on, barely hearing what the man was saying. Hunger for human friendship and companionship had been within him of late. He missed Sancho. "No," he said vaguely, "go on, man. Tell me of this ugly one. But, I ask you, where were the teachings of the priests in your household, that inward beauty is found beneath the rough exterior? Perhaps this—was his name Estiano? Yes? Well, there may have been the holiness of a saint beneath that ugly face . . . eh?"

"Hah! Not within that one. When he was, I think, eleven, there was a girl, daughter of the local metal smith, and this foolish little freak was so enamored with her that he fell upon her one afternoon in—you will not believe this—in the church. He kissed her good and sound. Well, that poor, terrified bit of female stuff just sat there screaming at the top of her lungs!" Martin beat the ground with his fists in hysterical laughter. "And," he choked, giggling, "and that boy bawled like a baby when her irate father descended upon him with a stick. After that Estiano was known, affectionately, of course, over all the countryside, as the romantic monster. He became morose, mean of temper, and would fight at the slightest provocation. Then, when he was fourteen, he disappeared . . . "

"Disappeared?" Rodrigo asked, his interest quickened.

"That is right. He took himself for one of his blasted walks and methinks he still walks, because none of us has ever laid eyes upon him since. So much for the ugly little brother with a face that was all nose and no eyes. A sad, sad tale I tell this day, eh, Rodrigo?"

Rodrigo said nothing, pulling at his lower lip thoughtfully, a vague memory disturbing him. "Jesus Christ!" he roared, sitting upright, "I have it now. I took on a wagon driver at Gormaz not more than five months ago to drive my wife to Zamora. The man had the meanest face I have ever seen; about twenty-seven years old, with long arms that seemed to dangle uselessly when he walked. And yes—his name was Estiano. For God, man, could this be the lost one?"

"Oh, *no!*" Martin cried, "there is no end to the coincidences of this life. You have described him perfectly, and this brother of mine would be twenty-eight this very month."

"Well then, I have solved the mystery for you. Another worthy event on this day of special events."

"But where did he come from? How did you happen to come upon him, who did he belong to, before—"

The two men started as the tent flap suddenly flew open, and Alvar Fañez stepped into the enclosure. His young face was as white as paste; sweat ran in rivulets from his forehead, dripping dismally upon his breastplate.

"Alvar!" Rodrigo leaped to his feet. He threw his arms roughly about the boy, giving him a great bear hug of a greeting. "Don Martin, look what else is good about this day; our beloved Alvar has returned. Christ, man, it is good to see you."

Alvar stood, head bowed before his uncle, unable to speak. The news he brought hurt him so much that he could not begin to speak of it. He stood away from Rodrigo remaining silent, and held out the letter he carried in his shaking, weary hand. He had not slept in three days.

"What is *this*, lad? What news is it that brings such pain to your young face, eh?" Rodrigo felt a vague apprehension. He broke Don Pedro's seal with suddenly nervous fingers. A small, multifolded piece of paper fluttered out and landed upon the sand at his feet. He paid it no mind, but began to read the message from the bishop. The words were such that his mind did not absorb them the first time.

He shook his head and began again, slowly.

Ruy Diaz:

It is with most sincere regret that I send to you this tragic news. Your beloved wife, Doña Jimena Gomez, is dead. From Zamora she traveled to Palencia and there stayed with the King Don Alphonso for a period of four months. She left that place two weeks ago, on the first day of the month of February, for Gormaz. Infidel bandits descended upon her train, and all were killed save one servant girl, who must have been taken prisoner.

Your wife's body was brought here to me; and may the Lord forever curse those hated infidels who could commit such a sin against one such as she. I will tell you that there was no other way to identify her but by the ring you gave her in marriage—her face was gone from her.

There is naught else I can say, except that I know, though the last sacrament could not be given to her, God has surely accepted her soul, for your good wife was well loved by Him. We will pray together that she now dwells in Heaven at His right hand. I hope this will be of some little comfort to you.

There is, enclosed, a letter that was delivered here for you, by one Estiano Antolinez, who vowed he was friend to you.

May God go always beside you.

Don Pedro, bishop of Gormaz

Rodrigo stood poised there, staring at the carefully printed words, reading them over and over again. Then he whirled upon Martin and Alvar, his eyes wild, "Get from my sight, both of you. Leave me alone! Get out of here!"

Alvar immediately burst into exhausted, pitying tears, and turned on his heels, running as far from Rodrigo's anguished cries as he could. Don Martin picked up his boots, completely bewildered, for he did not know what the letter said. He quietly left the tent, boots in hand.

Rodrigo leaned down now, numbly picking up the tiny message that had fallen at his feet. Somewhere within his mind were the words he expected to read there; instinct telling him that it had come, his last punishment for that one inexcusable sin of laying with Sabíhah. But when the words actually crossed his vision, the shock of them knocked the breath from his body.

"AN EYE FOR AN EYE, A TOOTH FOR A TOOTH— A WIFE FOR A WIFE."

Rodrigo let the words roll across his tongue, over and over. Then he tore up the detestable note into a hundred pieces, stamping them into the earth with his boot, as if he could in this way destroy the reality, grind it into the ground, rid himself of his helplessness and defeat. The great, unconquerable Cid had not been able to protect one frail, helpless woman who was his wife. "Oh, *God*," he cried out, as the true implications of this event overwhelmed him. He ran to the entrance of the tent and screamed out, "Get me a priest! Goddamn you—someone get me a *priest*!"

"Blessed Mary, Mother of God, pray to God that he accept the confession I have this day made. I have confessed to adultery and to indulgence of my flesh and to the touching of God-detested flesh. I have confessed to the murder of my wife—God forgive me, the murder of my wife. It was through my sins that this dread fate befell her. Know, blessed Mary, that I repent these sins that I so faithlessly committed."

Rodrigo knelt before the priest, his eyes dry, his heart bitter with hatred, as much for himself as for the Arab Hasan, whose image stood before him, triumph shining from his dark and savage eyes. Rodrigo raised his eyes up to heaven, "God, give me even more strength than you have already so generously endowed me with, that I might cut out the heart of this land, these pagan people—and the infidel murderer of my wife!"

Rodrigo rode out against the Infidel without waiting another day, Don Martin Antolinez to his right and Alvar Fañez to his left. The deeds that followed, day after day, week after week, year after year began to fill the pages of El Cid's contemporary chroniclers with a monotonous sameness. He laid siege, he pillaged, he killed, he wounded, he hated, and he became more feared, famous, and infamous every day that he lived. Though he had never loved her, his dead wife grew vastly more dear to him where she lay entombed in his memory beside Sabíhah; two faceless, dead reminders that served as excuses for his treachery and the justification he needed for his continued existence. El Cid had become the mad sculptor of the destiny of

Muslim Spain. There was more than a threat in his war cries now, there was also finality.

PART
TWO

✠

HASAN

Ah Love! could you and I with Him conspire
To grasp this sorry Scheme of Things entire,
    Would not we shatter it to bits—and then
Re-mould it nearer to the heart's desire!

Omar Khayyám

Chapter
✠ *ONE* ✠

A capricious, fateful wind sends its whistling breath across the earth and an innocent seed just loosened from the womb of its protecting husk, intent upon identical sustenance and form beside its towering parent, finds itself whiplashed up and away into the terror of unfamiliar environment. It comes to rest upon a rocky hillside and is desolate, forever divided from its original destination. Where is the dark and spongy bed of a valley floor; where are the gentle rains and whispering breezes? Yet its roots take form in automatic acceptance, the green twig of its body leaning backward for balance, twisting tentacles reaching from its base to grasp hold of rocks and minute particles of earth for support, because it knows instinctively that the secret of life is not in the choosing of one's destiny, but in how well one adjusts to the inevitable, how gracefully and well-formed one can grow in spite of the whimsical winds that guide each living destiny.

From where Jimena first awoke out of illness, she was swept up and carried deeper into a fearsome unknown, traveling ever southward through the rugged Sierra de Guadarramas. With Acacia, she rode like a dead woman, a ghostly apparition tied to the earth, wandering unseen amid foreign peoples, hidden within a curtained box wielded by camel, or by men when the terrain was too steep and rocky. Each night the caravan halted and luxurious tents were raised, soft beds laid out, a bath prepared, a lovely ensemble exchanged for the one worn that day, and rich foods brought on ornate silver trays.

On the third night of travel, after her bath and evening meal, Jimena snuggled back into her pillows, lounging comfortably. She listened to the now familiar shrill and laughing voices coming from outside her tent. At night she often enjoyed a pleasant singing that vibrated like an angel's harp through the black, fearful hours.

Acacia pushed through the opening, carrying a crystal bowl of fresh fruit, which she offered to Jimena with a pleasant smile.

"What is that?" Jimena asked, pointing to a furry, pink ball in the center of the bowl.

"A peach. Try it, my lady. They were rushed here from the south to cheer our wintered hearts."

Jimena carefully tested the fruit with teeth and tongue, and was amazed at the sweetness of it, the nectar that poured out upon her lips. She had already come to relish the foods that were brought to her, combinations of meat and vegetables in rich sauces, that Acacia had instructed her to scoop up with her thumb and first two fingers on a piece of bread. She finished the peach, rinsed her fingers in a cup of water, and sighed miserably. She did not know where she was, where she was going, or why. How long could she continue suspended thus, not knowing if tomorrow she would live or die? She looked to her silent companion, steeled herself for the answer that would follow, and asked, "To what place do we go, Acacia?"

"To Toledo. And from there to Cordova."

"Cordova! That cannot be. Cordova is—is a great distance, is it not? I mean to say . . . am I not being held for ransom?"

"No! Of course not."

"But why? Who spared my life when all the rest were slain? Why—why—why?" Tears of fear and frustration filled her eyes.

"Ah," Acacia said sympathetically, moving to put a small hand over Jimena's clenched fists. "My master planned your capture with great skill, patience and deliberation, for in his heart there was a passionate desire for vengeance. His quarrel was not with you; it was your grievous misfortune to be the wife of Rodrigo Diaz."

"Rodrigo! What could my husband have done to your master, that I was so ill-treated, all with me slain, my unborn child, child . . . " her voice broke, "my entire life destroyed."

Upon reflection, it did not seem fair to Acacia, either. But she had seen the agony on her master's face that night four years past as he carried Sabíhah's shattered body through the palace garden. Silently he had watched as they placed Sabíhah on the funeral pyre, tears in his eyes; as the flames consumed her he had screamed out in protest, and had to be restrained, or he would have thrown himself into the fire to die with her. When Abu l Hasan loved, it moved deep in him, so generous was his capacity for enveloping those about him with his kindness and affection.

Acacia shivered, thinking again of Barbastro; she had been there, following Hasan's instructions in his plot for destroying the Christian captors. For weeks she had sickened at each touch from the swine that took her, filthy, reeking men who condemned the Infidel for his lust, then wallowed in it themselves as no Muslim would. With intense satisfaction she had watched the soldier of Maktadir steal up upon the pig who slept drunk in her arms, and with exceeding pleasure saw the blood spurt from his severed neck as he died.

Obeying his ardent temperament, Abu l Hasan's first and only consideration was vengeance, which drove him year after year. On information provided by his tenacious spy, he had ridden across the plains of Castile, his men clothed as Castilian soldiers; in truth they were Spanish by descent, their fathers or grandfathers having been conquered and quickly absorbed into the new society that grew around them. These Spanish Arabs, called Mozarabs, disguised themselves as Christian soldiers. Abu l Hasan wore his native garb. Together they rode through Castile, planning to say, if halted, that they had here a captive held for ransom and were taking him to a certain Castilian count for imprisonment. But they were never stopped: the fate of Jimena Gomez was already decided by whomever held the almighty pen of life in his hand.

Acacia snapped out of reminiscence. She must inform this captive of what to expect. The anguish in the woman's eyes was pitiable. She said, "It surely is a tragedy, my lady, that you, who have never harmed my master, must suffer for the black deeds of your husband. But that is why you are here. Rodrigo Diaz, at Barbastro, took my master's wife from him and used her for his most base pleasures. Then, so that my master could not have her back, he stabbed her through the heart with his knife, and stomped her face with his boot until she was unrecognizable."

Jimena sucked in her breath and gasped, "I do not believe it. No!" Then she recalled her wedding night, how Rodrigo had lunged at her like an animal, and she knew that most certainly he was capable of such a murder. Then this was to be the husband's punishment, his vengeance, a life for a life. Dear God, she would be killed.

"As I have said, my lady, my master's quarrel is not with you. He is not the kind of man who would slay an innocent woman as vengeance against a guilty person. This would degrade him, lower him to the brutish level of your husband. You will not be harmed in any way, I assure you."

Jimena whispered, "If he intends no death for me, when will he return me to my husband?"

"Never."

Jimena shivered, chilled by Acacia's emphatic pronunciation of the word. She met Acacia's pitying eyes for long moments. Suddenly she was angry. "You *lie!*" she cried. "Not slay an innocent woman? I saw with my own eyes what he did to my servant girl. He is a beast, like *all* infidels! An infidel, that is what you are, detested by God!"

"Detested by Jehovah—loved by Allah."

"What?"

Acacia smiled tolerantly, and said smoothly, "Your servant would not have been killed had she not fought so to save you. When the carriage fell, she stumbled beneath it. No one could prevent it. It was an accident. My master intended only to take a wife for a wife."

"And how do you know this? Were you present?"

"No."

"There you are!" Jimena exclaimed triumphantly.

A long silence ensued, which gave Jimena time to collect her thoughts. A thousand questions formed in her mind, the answers to which might help enlighten the darkness that was tomorrow. She spat out defiantly, "Are you a slave?"

"Slave?" Acacia laughed. "I think, perhaps, that is a poor choice of words. But you could call it that; or concubine. I was purchased in the market square of Cordova, seven years past."

"How dreadful! How ghastly for you—"

"Dreadful? How so? I bless the day Abu l Hasan purchased me, get down on my knees and thank Allah for his kindness and mercy. Hasan is a good and gentle master, and a beautiful man to look upon. I am proud to be his."

"Truly? You are happy being a—a *slave,* to such a man?"

"Slave, wife, concubine, call it what you will, it is all the same. I am a woman, he is a man. Indeed, I could not be more content."

"Oh." Jimena frowned intensely, disturbed by the girl's arguments. She had always thought of infidel women as a most tragic lot, collected like beads upon the string of a man's lust, used and abused, then discarded for newer, brighter gems. She did not believe the girl.

One more question had to be asked. "Do you know who it was that informed your master where I would be and when?"

"Of course. It was Estiano Antolinez, a great friend of my Hasan."

Jimena was not surprised. "But he is not an . . . He is Castilian."

"No, not Castilian. Once, perhaps, but not today. He has lived in Cordova since the age of sixteen and has risen to the position of chief scribe at the library scriptorium of the University of Cordova. He speaks and reads seven languages, writes them, too. He is considered a great artist in that city . . . and as far away as Damascus. His works are famous."

"Library?" Jimena asked dully.

"A large building where over one million manuscripts are stored and read. Traveling men seek out great works over the face of the earth and bring them to Estiano to translate and print in Arabic."

"Of course," Jimena murmured, but she had not comprehended a word of it. The Infidel had a Bible and Christians had a Bible, which put *two* books in the world. Her mind could not conceive *one million*; her ability to count was limited to the fingers and toes and round again.

Estiano. That mean little man, hounding her for months, using Maria as his source of information. She had suspected something, but what could she have done if she had known his true intent? Nothing.

The image of little Urracca came to her and she clung to it longingly, then pushed the vision away. It was no use brooding about the baby, which only made her more miserable. Somehow, some way, she would return to little Urracca: she must. Rodrigo would not sit back and do nothing about this. Everyone called him "The Lord." The Infidel was terrified of him. He would sweep across Muslim Spain, seek her out and rescue her.

Acacia interrupted Jimena's thoughts, and with a few words destroyed forever all hope of rescue. "My lady, there is something you must know. Your servant was remarkably similar to you in appearance, I was told, in height, weight and coloring. Her body was clothed in purposely burned articles of your clothing and your marriage ring was placed upon her finger. Do you understand? My lady—you were *murdered* upon the plains of Castile six weeks past. You were buried. A gravestone with your name upon it rests in the cemetery of Gormaz castle. Estiano Antolinez remained long enough to attend your funeral, to see it done with and accepted by all who knew you. It was not planned this way, but afforded my master a far better triumph than he had anticipated. As far as your husband is concerned, my Hasan retaliated in kind, with a murder for a murder."

Jimena, beyond emotions now, could express no more shock or panic. She calmly absorbed Acacia's revelations. Soon she was aware of a kind of actual death. The person she had once been was gone and buried, and she was not altogether certain she regretted it. A new life was before her. Could what was ahead be more dismal than what was past? She offered Acacia a slight, wistful smile. She felt somehow relieved of a burden that had always been too heavy for her to carry. Resignation, still a significant element of her character, had come to her rescue. Her eyes roved up and around the tent. Her imagination saw through the canvas walls, out and into the future, and for the moment all fear was gone from her.

"Acacia," Jimena said on a sigh, "Can I not leave this tent for a few moments, even for a stroll? Am I to be imprisoned forever in a tent?"

Acacia frowned. She had received one very emphatic order from Hasan, "Under no circumstance is she to be allowed the freedom of this camp. The fewer who know that I have a captive Christian woman in my tents, the better, at least until we reach the safety of Toledo." She smiled maternally and shook her head. "It is but one more day to Toledo. There you will have a suite of rooms to wander in and a garden with many pools and fountains. Here you will find only desert waste and many rough men only too eager to offend you. And my master and yours would be most upset if he was forced to lash someone who was too curious about you. Understand?"

Annoyed and irritated, Jimena retired to her bed. For hours she lay on the mattress thinking about herself and her present situation. She thought about her father's admonitions about her shrinking spirit; it was true, lately she had not been very courageous. But tonight death held no significance other than as an escape. The nagging fears that usually prevented her from asserting herself were strangely stilled. Curse Acacia's master. She would do as she pleased, and walk if she felt so inclined!

Darkness closed in slowly. Impatiently Jimena waited for Acacia to fall asleep. Soon the woman's rhythmic breathing revealed her retirement from this world for the night. All camp activity and noises had subsided. Jimena dressed quickly, pulling up the trousers that she had become accustomed to, expertly fastening the snug gold vest. Then, wrapping silk veils over her hair, she tiptoed to the opening. She halted and held her breath as Acacia stirred in her sleep. For long moments she devoured the delicious sensation of pure adventure. It was safe now, and she pushed aside the heavy drapery to step boldly out into the darkness.

All that could be seen was a complete circle of tents exactly like the one she had emerged from, forming an opening that was the semblance of a gate. There was not a soul in sight. Surely there was a guard. She glanced around cautiously, but no guard was in sight. Furtively she moved toward the opening in the circle of tents, silently stepping past horses and camels tied all together in the center of camp.

A horse whinnied loudly directly behind Jimena and she reared forward, gasping and clapping a hand over her mouth. Instantly she identified the sound and turned to face the restless herd of assorted beasts, noticing one golden stallion that stood out from all the rest. Suddenly her mind went giddy with an idea, and her eyes darted around the shadowed circle again in search of guards. This stallion; she could ride him . . . she would fly through that opening and gallop triumphantly into the protecting arms of her husband. Impulsively she stepped close to the lovely, soft-eyed creature to hesitantly stroke his nose. Fumbling with the leather straps that tied him to a wooden post, she loosed the bonds and led him a bit away, then stood perplexed as to how she could mount him. A wagon was close and she eyed it. Her heart was drumming in her breast, her breath short.

"Come . . . come," Jimena hissed at the stallion. Yanking on his white, silken mane, she noted the decidedly disdainful expression in the beast's eyes, but he obliged her by sidling neatly against the wagon.

Jimena climbed awkwardly into the wagon, catching her trouser leg on a rough edge. She gave a great heave that hoisted her into a precarious position in the hollow of the stallion's back. She sat properly sideways, since it would never occur to her to straddle like a stablehand.

"Go! . . ." Jimena hissed, becoming frantic when the beast ignored her kicks in his side and merely turned to study her with amused curiosity. Impatient with him, she kicked the horse severely with both heels.

The beast lunged forward, nearly unseating her, and sped like the wind toward Castile and the security of predictability. Jimena gasped as her veils were whipped from around her face, and she leaned forward to clutch the animal around his neck. She thought she heard startled cries, then she saw a blur of tents before her eyes. Dear God, the dumb beast was not headed for the gate at all. How could she turn him? "Turn, horse!," she screeched, terrified, but he ignored her.

"Oh, *no* . . ." Jimena wailed, squeezing her eyes tightly closed against an imminent disaster.

The stallion, realizing that he could not run straight through a tent, decided that the single intelligent thing to do was stop, which he did. Bracing his forefeet solidly in the earth, he came to a sudden, complete halt. But his small rider, without anything to brace her, kept right on going, hurtling through the air to drop like a falling stone upon and through the wall of a tent.

There was great confusion. Apparently the camp had been attacked. Men came running half asleep to the rescue, swords and knives in hand. Cries of anger and frustration could be heard. Horses squealed and whinnied in fright. Camels hissed and growled, furious that their night's rest had been disturbed. When the clamoring soldiers reached the tent they found a mass of twisted canvas, broken stakes, and under it all their master, who was obviously fighting off his attacker.

Inside the collapsed tent, Jimena fought to free herself from a tangle of draperies, pillows and canvas. "Damn me," she wailed, tears in her eyes, her long hair falling all over her face and into her mouth; she could not see. She was unhurt, luckily having dropped upon a very large and resilient pillow. She ceased thrashing about as she became aware of curses emerging from a few feet away.

"Get me loose from here, for God, somebody . . . get me *loose!*" she shouted to whomever it was, and thus informed all who were near that it was a woman, a woman who spoke Spanish, therefore a Christian, that raised such havoc in the middle of the night.

The debris was jerked from about her and Jimena was dragged bodily from what was left of the tent. Abruptly and roughly jolted to her feet, her hands were held tightly together behind her back in an iron grip. Jimena was facing the staring eyes of about thirty Muslims, some smiling, others coldly glaring. Not a word was uttered for a long, painful moment. Then the man who had dragged her from the tent and who had kept his grip upon her arms yelped out a command to the men, who then wandered off reluctantly in small groups, some muttering to themselves, others laughing wickedly.

Jimena was alone with her captor. She was terrified and defeated, but this was her night for courage. Whirling around, she wrenched her arms free and faced him for the first time since her capture.

Jimena's stomach lurched and her eyes widened. She did not know what she had expected to see, only that she loathed this man for what he had done to her. But before her stood a man of devastating good looks, unveiled, dressed in the briefest of attire, a diaperlike affair which covered only his groin. In addition to the remembered dark eyes, she saw a face perfectly proportioned, a fine straight nose and full, sensuous lips. His mussed black hair waved softly to his shoulders. His beard was short-clipped and quite neat, even after a skirmish with a collapsed tent. Unlike the men of Castile, his body did not bulge with muscles, his legs were not like those of a mighty warhorse. His waist was, to be sure, no thicker than her own, his hips smaller than a woman's, but he widened perceptibly at the chest and shoulders, testifying to certain strength. His hands caught her attention. They were not roughened by weather and the handling of a lance, but smooth as a child's and gracefully slender. Something about those hands fascinated Jimena, and they held her gaze until they reached for her, catching her by the wrist and whipping her around. He ran with her, she stumbling and falling behind him, until they reached her own tent, whereupon he shoved her roughly into the enclosure and threw her bodily upon the bed she had left so defiantly shortly before.

Hasan stood glowering over Jimena, breathing heavily. Then he shouted, "Now *remain* there!" and strode off into the night.

Next day the caravan departed at dawn. When the drapery of the box she rode in was pulled aside it was dark and she was outside the wall of a building. Veiled, Jimena was stealthily ushered by Acacia through a garden and into a luxurious suite of rooms, rooms that for two long months were her new prison. Nothing but eating, sleeping, the annoying, degrading baths, and her own thoughts occupied her days. Acacia tried to amuse her in the evenings with stories. She would tell her of Cordova and of Hasan's home there in the beautiful suburb of the city called Medina Al Zohra, which meant, in Jimena's tongue, Town of the Flower. Night after night Acacia related to Jimena the wonders of this town that rested in a lush valley on the banks of the river Quadalquivir, five miles outside Cordova.

"I will tell you the story of Al Zohra, my lady, of how it came to be. In Andalusia, which is what we call our country, there once lived a great caliph, named Abd el Rhaman, who was a descendant of the great caliphs of Arabia. This caliph owned a ravishing slave girl named Zohra, whom he loved as Allah loves the angels of heaven. She was so lovely and of such wit and charm that he wished her to no longer be a slave, and he built for her a splendiferous palace upon the Roman ruins outside Cordova. In this palace are four thousand three hundred columns of precious marble brought from the ruins of Carthage; the floors and all walks in the gardens are paved with marble. In all rooms he placed fountains, some sending a delicious spray of perfume into the air. In one pavilion he built a fountain of quicksilver and in Zohra's own room he placed a fountain more splendid than all the rest, made of jasper, with the water spouting from the bill of a golden swan. Over the fountain he hung a canopy of silver and gold cloth, in the center of which was a pearl, a pearl of such magnificence it cannot be described. When this palace was completed, he set her free—and there Zohra lived out her life amidst glorious gardens and pools.''

Acacia sighed, her tale finished, and both women sat in a stupor of romantic daydreaming for the remainder of the evening.

Then came the journey to Al Zohra; the same pattern of tents, camels and monotony. Jimena was again ushered through a dark garden and a shadowed house, and was locked into a splendid room, the wonders of Al Zohra unseen.

No further displays of courage were possible, for outside her door stood two huge black eunuchs, day and night. Her window was dangerously high above the court, being on the second story of the house. A flat-roofed overhang, about ten feet by twelve, heavily green with potted shrubs and blooming vines, was her garden; there was a door leading out upon it from her room.

In this splendid room, Jimena languished for a full year and most of another. The concubine, Acacia, was her single companion.

Small boats and rafts floated languidly on the river, the listless current lolling them slowly past the grand houses along the banks. Music soared and faded, as boat after boat slid past the house of Abu l Hasan. Poplar and myrtle trees danced an elegant ballet in the garden, encouraged by gentle breezes. A flower bedecked barge slipped into view, young people, arms entwined, gathering to themselves, as only the Andalusians could, the joys that were to be reaped from each and every waking moment. As long as one could breathe, think, and feel, there was pleasure to be had, and they spent their lives in search of it.

The Quadalquivir was especially lovely this night, Jimena thought, as she sat upon the window seat leaning her elbows upon the cool tile sill. With a sigh, she turned her head away and a playful breeze caught her hair and sent it dancing about her face. She reached up a hand and pushed a wisp of hair away from her eyes, glancing about her room. How often she had sat thus at windows, in prison rooms, forever separated from life and the living. She rose from the seat and wandered aimlessly to a large mirror inset in the wall and stood brooding upon her reflection. There had been no mirrors at Gormaz castle. Only a small hand glass belonging to Doña Urracca had spoken of the gaunt, gray homeliness that had been her image two years past. Now the face was altered and foreign to her, full and no longer haggard, her hair white-gold, falling down in loose, fashioned curls to her waist. Extra flesh padded out her thighs and buttocks; her bosom was more rounded and out-pushing. Acacia had insisted upon lightening her hair with a foul-smelling liquid, and daily forced upon her the darkening of her eyelids with kohl, the reddening of her lips and fingernails with paint.

Jimena rashly conceded that the image in the mirror was fair to look upon. Acacia was forever squealing out compliments such as "stunning," and "ravishing," and Jimena withstood them frozenly. Now, with no little guilt, she executed a half turn to examine her profile, then quickly rushed away from the plaguing reflection. Physical beauty, she reassured herself, was of no significance; vanity was self-love and God-detested.

Stepping to a low table, Jimena picked unenthusiastically at sweetmeats spread out over a silver tray. She chose a large gooey one and popped it into her mouth, chewing furiously. Then she strode to her bed and threw herself petulantly down on her stomach. She had been pacing this room for hours— days—months, restless and wanting to scream from the torture of absolute inactivity. "Oh," she cried aloud, "if there were only something to *do*!"

At just that moment, Acacia entered with the evening meal. Jimena leaped to her feet eagerly and they ate together sitting on pillows, one on each side of the low table. Jimena chewed her food and swallowed, but did not taste it. Her mind was crowded. Perhaps Acacia could plead with the master to allow her more freedom. But no, it was of no use even to ask. "Acacia," she murmured, "is there not something that I can do? I am so weary of this emptiness, this *boredom*!"

Acacia pondered the question seriously, picking through

the bowl of fruit, selecting a bright red, plump apple which she promptly bit into, crunching off a huge chunk of the juicy pulp, chewing with intense concentration. "Well," she said, swallowing, "you, uh—why do you not learn to read, or something like that? In our land many women find pleasure in the pastime, and even learn to write." Then she said, more enthusiastically, "There are many famous poets and storytellers in Cordova that once were harem slaves; they were freed as a reward for their prowess . . . some are even teachers at the university. Why do you not learn to read? Books would surely entertain your lonely hours."

"I would not be entertained by the Bible," Jimena said sarcastically, "neither yours, nor mine. I cannot imagine anything sillier than collecting a million copies of a Bible."

Acacia laughed loudly, throwing herself down on the carpet and rolling over delightedly. "Oh, blessed Allah, but you are ignorant," she giggled. She sat up quickly at Jimena's hurt expression. "Forgive me, my lady, you could not know. Each book is *different*. Each tells a different story, or fact. The stories I tell you in the evenings are all written upon paper for you to read. Understand?"

Jimena frowned, now convinced the girl was not making fun of her. "I have often longed to write," she admitted, "if only my name. I would watch my husband writing pages and pages of words—he could write, you know, Rodrigo was especially clever in those ways, my father, too. It seemed to me the most fantastic of miracles, that he could so easily take the thoughts from his mind and transform them into scratches upon paper." Jimena leaned forward eagerly. "Do you think I could? I mean . . . am I clever enough? Will you teach me? Will you?"

Acacia's expression drooped, "Ah no, forgive me—I never did learn, myself."

"For God! Then why torment me with the suggestion? You know you are the single person I am allowed to see."

"I know," Acacia scowled. Then, more brightly, "I shall speak with Abu l Hasan. I will beg him to send you a teacher." She stood up, the half-eaten apple clutched in her fist. She shook the apple determinedly, sending a spray of juice into Jimena's face. "I will insist! I will *demand* that he do this."

Jimena scowled, then laughed at the girl's wild speech. Acacia would have no influence on her stubborn and vicious master, but her mind dreamed a small hope for release from imprisonment.

Chapter
✠ *TWO* ✠

The bishop hesitated, his hand resting upon the gate latch. He was trying to decide whether he should walk or ride the mule. Without actually coming to any definite decision he trudged wearily away from the church. It was a warm day and he felt more fatigued and irritable than usual. He tugged at his belt, loosening it from around his ample waist, his hand resting for a moment upon the large metal *C* that formed a buckle, telling all who watched him pass that he was a Christian.

"One hundred ounces of silver," he muttered to himself. The tax was too high for this diocese in the middle of the poorer section of the city. The only Christians who had not gone over to the Muslim faith were those not rich enough to pay very high taxes; the others, as their fortunes grew, greedily and sinfully took advantage of the fact that a Muslim paid ten percent less tax than a Christian. A twenty percent tax was a burden that the Andalusians had placed upon all Christians as the price for their faith in Jesus Christ.

Where was he to acquire one hundred ounces of silver for the tax collector by tomorrow? You would think, he thought, that His Eminence, the pope, would provide for his faithful flock in the Muslim world. How could he go on keeping all these little churches in existence, without sufficient monies to even pay the *taxes*? All the bishop received from the pope were complaints and threats. Last month he received a communication from His Eminence, demanding that all Christians in Cordova refrain from such bodily pleasures as baths and the wearing of silks and jewels, and that no further marriages between Christians and infidels would be tolerated, unless the infidel denied his prophet, his false God, and became Christian. This was impossible, simply impossible to enforce. The Christians treasured their silks and jewels and could afford them. When he

213

had demanded, at Mass, that his flock refrain from the sinful ablutions of the Infidel, there had been an instantaneous murmur of angry voices. The next day at least twelve of his congregation were missing and would probably never return. Now even less would be given in tithes to an already poverty-ridden church.

The bishop stopped at a wayside fountain and leaned over to drink. Standing erect again, he glanced about him. The street cleaners were charging down the slight hill to his right, water showering from their wagons, their brooms swishing playfully, haphazardly; anyone who did not leap out of their way got their skirts wet. The bishop moved quickly into a gateway and glumly watched the men as they passed by him. Damned Arabs.

Water, water, water, they were water crazy. It was not enough that they washed their bodies two or three times a day, but the streets also, and their clothes and every building inside and out. The *indulgence* of corrupt men! . . "Damnation," he swore, as a stream of icy water spilled down the back of his neck and into his robe. He turned peevish eyes up and saw that he had placed himself directly under a flower basket that hung from a lamp post. One of the infidel street cleaners had the task of watering the blasted things, dashing ahead of the rest, carrying a short ladder and a watering pail with a long spout. "Flower baskets from every lamp post," he snorted. They might better beautify themselves from within, by recognizing Jehovah and the Saviour and the beauty and peace of the True Faith.

It was a grievous burden, this living among the infidels clinging to truth, to your own salvation, against the cruelest of temptations that took a thousand forms. The faithful would indeed find untold rewards in the afterlife, and each and every pagan would go to hell fire, but, as far as this earth was concerned, the Arab already *had* his paradise, at least that was the feeling shared by most Christians. The Christian merchant mixed of necessity with those of his own station that were Muslim, but was denied the luxury of jewels and perfumed baths, and silk against his flesh. Sometimes he looked upon his one wife with resentment; his friends could have as many as four. When he was pressed by nagging, or his wife refused him comfort or love, he could not say three times, I divorce thee—and get himself another woman.

The bishop kicked furiously at a white pebble that lay in the street, sending it spinning into the air to bounce off the wall that surrounded the library. He turned and walked through the open gate. The library was crowded as usual. Everyone in Cordova spent at least some part of every day here, or so it seemed. They all had a great deal of leisure time. When they were not sinning grossly, they were reading, or jabbering their fool heads off in what they called "discussions."

He moved slowly down the brightly lit hall, peering into room after room that was jammed to the ceiling with books, the benches filled with silent, absorbed readers. "Filth," the bishop grunted, "nothing but filth, and lies." They read the words of the Devil, drinking in all the evil thoughts man had conceived since the beginning of time, ignoring Truth, deliberately choosing Hell as their reward. As he approached the door of the study, he paused, hoping Estiano was in a pleasant mood today. The man could be so damned belligerent at times. He probably felt uncomfortable with a Christian bishop, and well he should, since he himself had recently converted to the Muslim faith, to reduce his own taxes by ten percent. How could a man deny his God for a few ounces of silver?

Estiano's forehead was slashed by a deep frown as he leaned over the slanted easel, meticulously placing the finishing touches upon a Greek letter *A*. He did not hear the bishop enter, or notice him until the bishop stood coldly staring at him over the top of the easel. "Ah, Bishop," he said cheerfully, setting his pen down, "Good afternoon. Your manuscript is completed. It has been ready for over a week." Estiano got up from his stool and strode over to the wall of shelves, reaching for a black leather volume that was decorated in gold letters with a single cross in one corner. He brought it to the bishop, handing the book to him, a slight smile turning up the corners of his wide mouth. "It is grimly plain, Bishop. I might have covered it in velvet, embroidered it with gold and silver, but . . ." he shrugged disinterestedly, "it is as you ordered."

"The Bible needs no outward embellishments, sir," the bishop grumbled. "What is inside is beauty enough and speaks for itself." He tenderly opened the hard board covers and scanned the first pages. He looked up angrily, "This is very sloppy work. Your copyist wasted no time on it, I can see that."

Estiano sat back on his stool, picked up his bronze pen and placed the end of it between his teeth, "Bishop," he said patiently, "my scribes are Muslims. You cannot expect them to put their hearts and souls into a copy of the *Infidel* Bible. You might find whole passages missing when you read further; I cannot guarantee you perfection. For example, the virgin birth of Jesus . . . " Estiano grinned agreeably. "Once I chanced to read over a copy of the New Testament that one of my apprentice scribes had been working on, and where it says something about Jesus being the son of God he had inserted after it in parenthesis, *'That God should beget children, God forbid.'* " Estiano controlled a laugh and waved his hand in the air helplessly, "What can I do, eh?"

The bishop did not answer. He slammed the Bible closed and buckled the leather straps tight. He looked broodingly down at his hands for a moment, then said, "Estiano, I cannot, uh . . . " His face flushed with humiliation and anger. "I cannot pay you for this book until next week. The tax collection is tomorrow and . . . well, I . . . "

"Ach. Think no more upon it. Consider the book paid for. My donation to the church. Agreed?"

The bishop shuffled wearily to the window and fell down with a sigh on the bench there. "Estiano, matters become worse every day. Soon there will not be a Christian left in Andalus. The pope presses me to recruit new followers even though he *knows* recruitment to be the one practice of our faith Muslim law does not permit, tolerant as they profess to be." Throwing his hands in the air helplessly, he wailed, "I could be *executed* for doing that!"

Estiano leaned back, studying the bishop thoughtfully. The man was, he guessed, about forty, but there were many lines in his face, creasing his forehead, cutting deep crevices on each side of his mouth, causing the flesh of his jowls to sag mournfully. The bishop stubbornly wore rough sackcloth robes and his head was shaved and fringed like a clerk who had just taken the tonsure, even though most priests in Arab Spain had, by this time, given up such austere symbols of the Cloth for more conventional materials, such as fine linen and sometimes even silk, and hair long upon their shoulders. A curious man, the bishop. How could he have been born in Andalusia and his father before him, and decide to become a Christian priest? Though the Arabs were extremely tolerant of other religions, it was certainly a vast disadvantage to be a Christian.

Estiano recalled his own decision, only a year past, to become a Muslim. It had not been difficult. Actually, it was merely a matter of pledging oneself no longer Christian. The Arab had no organized, profit-making church, no priests to threaten and collect tithes; it mattered little what was stated in the Koran—the people of Spanish Islam lived as they pleased.

Estiano's mind wandered. Sixteen years . . . sixteen years

since that fresh, clear summer day. He had walked away from his home for a stroll, but when he stood upon the crest of that hill, there before his eyes was the earth stretching out before him. He knew instinctively that he could walk all day toward that distant horizon and there would still be unlimited land before him. He had looked back to the house that had been his home for fourteen years. It was a little house with so massive an ugliness swelling within it that it poured miserably out the windows and through the cracks, permeating the surrounding countryside with its unendurable stench. God had created man in his own likeness, he had thought, but if this was true, then what a cruel, unloving creature He must be. The baby pushed itself out of the warm comfort and security of his mother's body to emerge into a terrifying holocaust of noise, neglect, and hunger—hunger for soft arms around him, a desperate need for love. But the mother could not find it in her soul to love him, there were those needs of her own that had to be satisfied, so her child lay alone and helpless; she did not hear his cries for help, for love, for a kind word. When the mind began to function and awareness was with him, he came to know that that hostile human being, his mother, not only did not love him but actually despised him.

Estiano did not see a reflection of his own features until he was eleven years old, when his heart was already broken beyond repair. A little girl had looked upon him in horror when he touched her. He ran from the beating her father gave him to the shop of the glass maker. Oh, how he had *loved* that sweet little girl! He hovered outside the shabby little shop, his stomach heaving, his heart racing, tears streaming down his face.

After the shopkeeper had placed a lock upon the door and left, Estiano had waited there until no one was in sight on the dark street. Clutching a stone in his hands, he had pounded and beat against the lock until it gave.

Inside, he had leaned against the closed door, breathing hard. For the first time he would know why all who had ever known him—father, mother, everyone—why they could not bear to look at him, why they could not love him. He held the glass in trembling hands without looking into it. No, he could not do it. He did not want to know how he looked. An awful image would be imbedded in his mind to haunt him, always before his eyes, a constant punishment.

Estiano thought now that had he not already convinced himself that he would see a terrible, monstrous face, he might have observed that there were many things more ugly in the world than his face. He had looked upon his image, not through his own eyes, but through those of his mother and those of a little curly-haired girl whom he loved. "Aieeeee. . . ." he had screamed, hurling the glass across the dark room. And before he left that place there was not an unshattered mirror in the shop.

He had kept quiet when talk of a maniac loose in the village passed from the lips of gossips, someone who had broken every piece of glass in the glass maker's shop. After that he had withdrawn completely from the world of people, speaking only when spoken to. He walked through the woods in spring and found the first blooming wild flowers. He would pluck one, and press it against his beating heart, then carry it inside his tunic for weeks, until it turned brown and crumpled into nothingness. Brief flashes of beauty, continually fading, dying. But the ugliness and misery always remained unchangeable. He watched the sunsets on warm summer evenings, felt soft breezes against his flesh, caught the sweet scent of a lonely wild rose, forever dreaming of a world without pain and lonliness, a world of beauty and peace.

Thus he stood poised on that hill, his eyes resting first on the distant horizon, then back upon his home; until his feet began to move him in the only direction possible for him to go. He walked straight southeast and never looked back again or ever regretted his decision. That little stroll on a warm summer day blossomed into a hike of almost five hundred miles. He was just sixteen years old when he reached his goal. He had slept the night before in a crevice on the steep, craggy slope of a mountainside. When he awoke the sun was stretching colorful arms across the sky, painting the clouds with red and pinks. He sleepily got to his feet, yawning. Then his breath caught as his eyes fastened upon a mirage. The city of Cordova lay cuddled in the lap of a rolling green valley, her towers and minarets white and sparkling in the morning sunlight. A blue-green river wrapped its twisting arms completely around her like a halo of jeweled water and lush growth. For her gown, flowers in orange, pink, blue, and yellow, a billion floral maids for the bride of Andalus. She was so vast that her walls could not hold her glory in, suburbs spilling out in all directions. There were grand houses along the riverbanks with pools that looked like shimmering diamonds from that distant mountainside. He had left his dark world knowing there was beauty somewhere, certain that no matter *what* he found it could not be worse than what he was leaving behind. Now before him was a heaven on earth and he knew that he was home at last.

"Forgive me, Estiano, you have much to do. I keep you."

"What? Oh, Bishop—no, I am finished for today."

Estiano found it difficult to shake off the prodding past. The boy of fourteen would never be entirely forgotten, but he lingered upon the past very little lately. It was best to deny it. The less remembered, the happier he would be. "Bishop," he said, turning a curious eye upon the priest, "will you tell me why you chose to become a priest? What led you to it in a country where you could have been a doctor, a lawyer, a teacher, anything a man might want to be."

"My mother, sir, God rest her sainted soul." The bishop nodded his head in a quick, reverent motion of prayer. "Indeed, my beloved mother set me upon this noble path. She was Leonese by birth. My father bought her—at the block. A captive."

Estiano made no effort to disguise his amazement. He had known the man for years and would never have suspected. "Then you are half Arab! All these years I—"

"No! Lord have mercy on me, no not half. My grandfather, on my father's side, naturally, was half Arab. She never strayed, never, a devout Christian to the day she died. No marriage, no love for her, outside the Church. She . . . "

"But *why*? You could have been a devout Christian without going to the extreme sacrifice of priesthood."

"I was born to it. God needed me in Cordova. So much to be done. I . . . ". His voice sank to a discouraged whisper. "But I have accomplished so little."

"Ah, now, Bishop, you do what you can, considering the odds against you."

The bishop nodded and shrugged, looking miserable. "You ask me why I am a priest. May I ask you, sir, why you left the Church? How could you deny your God, your salvation? For a few marks of silver, surely not?"

"Oh, no," Estiano protested, raising both hands good-naturedly to the bishop. "You will not drag me into a religious argument *today*."

"I have no wish to argue. I just want an answer to a simple question, no more. I want to know how once a Christian, you could ever deeply be anything else?"

Estiano grinned at the man and said, "I do not think of it as having denied God, Bishop. I do not presume to say that

Islam is the light of truth, any more than Christianity. Say this; it is simply more expedient for me to be a Muslim, than to be a Christian. I find not enough difference between the two religions to be particular."

"Difference! Difference? The difference is that one is the Truth, the other lies. That is the difference. By denying your church you will go to Hell. It is a sorry trade you have made, Estiano Antolinez!"

"Perhaps," Estiano said amiably. "Heaven, for me, is Cordova. Whatever comes after I die, I leave to the Almighty."

"Ach!" The bishop squawked, exasperated. "You are like all the rest, the disease of earthly pleasures destroying you." He stepped closer to Estiano, shaking a finger at him. "This will not last, this paradise you wallow in! Cordova is like all earthly attachments, swallowed whole, and quickly, by eternity. The Christians in the north press closer to us each year. The Muslim fanatic to the south leers at Cordova with a lust to possess it. This paradise is a *mirage* existing, for a brief instant, in the midst of the real world. Tomorrow—who will remember that it existed? No one."

Estiano winced at the unwelcome truth in what the bishop had said. Cordova was a brilliantly burning torch within what history could only call a Dark Age. Never before had a million people lived in one city. There were over three hundred thousand privately owned homes, and the common man enjoyed a freedom and security that defied history. If, as the bishop predicted, it were to be destroyed, a thousand years might pass before anything like it appeared again on the face of the earth, if ever. Estiano loved every brick, stone, scent, and citizen of Cordova. He loved the public parks set aside for the rest and recreation of the people, one in every neighborhood; the library that was his second home; the college, where a thousand happy hours had been spent in vigorous debate on a hundred different questions; the peace of his own garden that was crowded with leafy creepers and shrubs interspersed with masses of flowers—roses, jasmine, violets and pinks; the dancing, singing spray of water that sprang from thousands of fountains; the music and poetry; the flowing silk robes and perfumes; the riverbank lined with palms and myrtles; the sweet song of the nightingales; fine carpets, elegant, graceful architecture. Andalusia was a wealthy, splendid land surrounded by an impoverished, moldering contamination. Estiano sighed, silently praying that it would not pass away while he still lived.

The bishop, receiving no response from Estiano and noting

the faraway expression in the man's eyes, assumed the conversation was at an end. He shoved the Bible under one arm and, without another word, strode sourly away, slamming the door of Estiano's study behind him.

A fall evening was a beautiful thing in Cordova. The sun set behind the mountains early, but the sky remained light, and pleasant warm shadows fell in intricate patterns upon the streets and under the trees. The scent of flowers became strong when the soft breezes pressed their heady intoxication into the lungs. The work day over, the voices of the people rose in song and laughter. The muezzin's shrill, musical voice echoed through the air, summoning the faithful to evening prayers. "Come to prayer. Come to prayer. There is no God, but God. Come to prayer. . . ."

Within the houses families and friends gathered together for the evening meal of perhaps lamb, or kid, sweetmeats, fruit, red wine that was boiled and strained, or lemonade for those who were religiously strict. Then games of backgammon or chess, and sometimes drinking bouts and dancing exhibitions. Or, before dark descended, the man of the house would go out into his garden and dig among his treasured flowers. Even the most highly placed man worked in his garden with his own hands, because it was said in the Koran that "he who planteth and soweth, and maketh the earth bring forth fruit for man or beast hath done alms that shall be reckoned to him in heaven."

Estiano strolled at a leisurely pace down the narrow street toward his home, drinking in the sounds, smells, the feel of this so-familiar pattern of his life. A lamplighter raced swiftly down the street, his ladder held with jaunty pride under his arm. Estiano had never become really used to or could quite take for granted the sight of a city street lighted at night. From any distant hilltop the entire city could be seen alight. It was a miracle of man's ingenuity and creation, and took one's breath away.

He turned into a narrow alley and stopped before a heavy, brass-decorated gate that proudly displayed a huge, ornate lock. He reached into his blue silk tunic and produced a key of equal proportion, pushed it into the lock and swung the gate wide. It was not a lavish house, but the usual middle-class dwelling; an irregular quadrilateral, on three sides of which ran long rooms, not more than ten or twelve feet wide. The fourth side was occupied by the kitchen, the same in width, but shorter. There was a rear entrance passage, stairs, and the sanitary convenience. (Another miracle of ingenuity, that wonder of wonders—the toilet. A large bucket of water was kept beside it and all one had to do was pour a fair amount into the tile box, and the body's waste was washed down into the sewers tunneling under the city, sewers so wide a man could ride through them with a horse and wagon.) A central court was formed by a building built in this shape, and all rooms looked out upon it.

Estiano walked straight through to the open court, as he always did, for he loved his garden as much as any Arab. The cool water from the fountain, picked up by a swift, down-sweeping breeze, blew a soft spray upon his face. He noted with pride the size of the blooms on his tree rose and, with tender care, snipped off a stubborn shoot trying to grow from the bottom of the trunk where it did not belong.

A black servant stepped up behind him and took the manuscript he carried from under his arm, then helped him remove his mantle.

"Ah, thank you, Masrur." Estiano stretched his shoulder muscles in an attempt to relax. "I will have my evening meal in the garden tonight. And do not boil the wine, please. I prefer it in its natural state." He smiled as the man left him. No matter how often he had already told Masrur, he had to repeat it every night. The Arabs insisted wine must be boiled and, he guessed, Masrur was determined that in this way too, he should be an Arab.

His meal finished, Estiano went to his library, where he lit a lamp that burned a scented oil. He sat himself down to read the manuscript he had brought home with him. It was an ancient copy, in Greek, of the Ethics of Aristotle. Though he had read it many times in Arabic, there was an exciting anticipation in knowing he would now read it in the original.

An unexpected loud knock at the door broke the pleasant quiet of the house and Estiano's thoughts. He waited for Masrur to come and tell him who it was.

The servant stuck his black face through the curtains, a sly smile wavering there. "A lady to see you, master."

"Well—what lady, man? Speak up."

"Elvira Rodriguez . . . " he said, his tongue twisting over the cumbersome Latin name.

Estiano started. What in God's name was Elvira doing here? "Show her in. And keep your flapping ears away from the curtain, or I will blister your backside.

Elvira walked silently in on bare feet, her colored toenails flashing bright red in the dim light. She laughed as she pushed the curtains aside, "The least you could do, if you expect me to obey the custom of removing my shoes, would be to keep your floors a little warmer. Ah, this rug is better. That tile in the hall was like ice."

Estiano eyed her cautiously, not moving from his pillows. "Well, Elvira, what brings you to my house this evening?" He had never gotten over his distrust of women. If his own mother could not love him, and a girl of ten was so horrified by his face, it was certain no woman in her right mind would ever care for him. He felt uneasy in their presence, and never made any advances until he was completely sure they would be welcomed. Consequently, his sexual adventures were dismally infrequent. Prostitutes were few and far between in Cordova, but one could be found if one had the price and knew the right people. He had never married simply because no woman had ever asked him; he would never presume to think any woman would wish to share her whole life with a man as monstrously formed as himself.

"I seek professional advice, Estiano," Elvira murmured sweetly. "I have written a new book of verse and wish to have it printed for my classes and, of course, for anyone else who might care to read it." She moved her dark head about in mock displeasure. "Is there no pillow for me to sit upon, or must I stand throughout my visit?"

Estiano blushed and leaped to his feet to move a few pillows into a corner, near the lamp that hung on the tiled wall. He watched Elvira's body move in that soft musical way she had, her hips swinging appetizingly. He had to make an effort to keep his eyes on her face as she lounged comfortably into the pillows. Her breasts were large and well formed and they moved in hypnotic rhythm, up and down. Stepping backward to his own pillows, he sat down with a thud, a lump of anguish and desire in his throat. Swallowing hard, he said weakly, "What advice can *I* give you? I will have my copyists print it for you, most certainly, but I do not see . . ."

"It is your expertise in the Arabic language that I seek, Estiano. I have never, in these twelve years since I came to Cordova, been able to completely put my thoughts into Arabic. I think in Spanish, then attempt to write it down in Arabic, and only manage a terrible confusion." Elvira sat up, hugging her knees with bare arms, her inviting eyes fastening upon Estiano's gaze and holding it. She went on. "For example, here is a bit of one verse." Speaking the words in Spanish, she said, "Love at

first sight is a spurt of spray, but a spreading sea when it
gaineth sway. I loved him soon as his praise I heard, for ear
often loveth before the eye surveys."

Estiano fidgeted uncomfortably, refusing to find meaning
where none was intended. Elvira taught poetry and literature at
the university. She was considered by many to be the most accomplished woman in her field. Somehow he could not envision her ever being confused. Another of those miracles, the
emancipated woman. There were many who still went about
the street veiled; many men who, out of religious piety, still hid
their women from view, but most were more free than women
anywhere in the world. Teachers, poets, artists, all making a
living for themselves, owning their own homes, like Elvira,
who was a wealthy woman. She was not only intelligent, but
beautiful as well, so that teaching was not the only service for
which she was well paid. No one would call her a prostitute,
merely a free woman, unwed, who sought pleasure and love. If
a man were willing to pay her in jewels or money, she accepted
gratefully, but she never complained if unpaid. She would
probably say that she gained as much as she gave, rendering any
payment totally superfluous. A truly stange kind of woman, in
this land that abundantly propagated strange phenomena.

"I would be most happy to assist you in your translations,
Elvira. Where is your manuscript?"

"Oh," Elvira exclaimed in pretended annoyance, "I forgot
to bring it. But tomorrow, perhaps? I might bring it to the library, and we could work together for an hour or so?"

"Of course."

Neither said another word.

Estiano's eyes moved from her green eyes, down the length
of her and up again, stopping to rest upon that fascinating creation of nature, a woman's bosom. As the eternally romantic and
descriptive Arab would say, full and upright, like two snowy,
ripe pears. No one appreciated a woman's body more, or wrote
or talked so much about it, as the Arabs. Quite understandable,
Estiano thought now. Quite understandable.

Elvira leaned forward and rose from her pillows. She stood
looking down at Estiano, a challenging smile in her eyes.

Stunned, Estiano did not know what to do with his hands,
or what to say. The invitation was clear. But, *Elvira* . . . ? So
beautiful, so . . . He had known her for years. Now, all of a
sudden, this bold advance. Had she lost her eyesight?

Elvira kneeled before Estiano and leaned forward a little.

"Estiano," she said matter-of-factly, "I have tried a thousand ways to make you ask me. I surrender. Now *I* ask *you*."

"You . . . " he stuttered, "you are—are asking me?"

"Yes. Do you find that so difficult to believe? Your face may be ugly, dear Estiano, but I wager there is a part of you that is as attractive as any other man's. You do not make love with your *face*, do you?"

Estiano threw his head back, then doubled over with laughter. Suddenly he felt a warm breath blow gently against his cheek and soft fingers sliding into his beard. He turned his face quickly, and hungrily pressed his mouth against Elvira's soft, reddened lips. Her body pushed closer; her breasts felt hot and hard against his chest. When he heard the groan of pleasure that passed from her lips, he knew the power of his maleness and the features of his face softened before his inner eye until he was the handsomest, most attractive of men, driving a woman to near madness by the mere touch of his mouth upon her breasts, her eyes, her lips. Thus armored with an illusion of outward beauty, Estiano forgot all distrust, all fear. A blind, innard-splitting urgency shattered all inhibitions, and he moved against her, kissed her, loved her, until she cried out for release, and then lay moaning and weak in his arms.

Elvira sat patiently waiting on the bench, her hands folded demurely in her lap. Her thoughts lingered over the night before, causing her to shiver in recalled ecstasy. Estiano as a lover had been all she had expected, and much more. It was a shame that his face did not mirror the beauty that lay hidden within him. How often she had watched his inelegant face, how many times she had marveled at the gentility and intelligent sensitivity expressed in his words, in that soft deep voice of his. How she loved him—she loved every irregular twist of that face, every line of care that creased his forehead, every swift, expert movement of his hands that could create pure beauty, almost as if he were trying to make up to the world for the little ugliness he had brought to it. Like the scarred, black face of the blind beggar who raises his voice in song on the street corner, the music, the beauty of his soul, poured out into the world. In truth there was no man all mean and ugly; somewhere within each of us lay the germ, the seed of pure loveliness.

With amused interest Elvira began to watch the people who walked past her in the hall. Handsome young Arab students in gaily colored silk robes, their dark beards thin and not yet full grown, but tenderly combed and clipped. An obese young girl waddled into the lecture hall and Elvira wondered to what use she would put her newly gained knowledge of physical health. She might do well to pass up that second portion of iced sherbet or sweetmeats, for it was a well-known fact that most rotund people ate like horses. Looking down at her own trousered legs, Elvira noted with satisfaction that there was not an ounce of extra flesh on her bones. Then she allowed her eyes to move up and around her, examining the muraled walls that were so familiar they were seldom really seen, walls that had watched so many students enter, pause, and leave. This college was the abode of the learned and the place of resort for the studious, the eminent, the noble of all countries, offering every branch of science, poetry, divinity, law and medicine; not since Galen had there been so many miraculous discoveries in the field of medicine; Abu 1 Kasim Khalaf, the surgeon and Ibn Beytar, the famous botanist, had begun their studies here.

Elvira recalled a passage from a book recently printed, by a noted historian.

> . . . Cordova is the Bride of Andalusia. To her belong all the beauty and the ornaments that delight the eye or dazzle the sight. Her long line of Sultans form her crown of glory; her necklace is strung with the pearls which her poets have gathered from the ocean of language; her dress is of the banners of learning, well knit together by her men of science; and the masters of every art and industry are the hem of her garments.

"Halwa?"

Elvira turned quickly. Hasan stood in the doorway and was motioning her into his study. She got to her feet, smiling, and swiftly entered the room, which was large and richly decorated with deep, thick rugs and tapestries on the tile walls. One tapestry in particular caught Elvira's eyes, as it always did. It was a beautiful work of art, a portrait of Sabíhah, done stitch by stitch in life colors against a background of soft green and silver. She gazed at it for a long moment, then sat down upon the cushion Hasan offered her.

Hasan moved papers around on his low worktable with nervous fingers. He was uncertain how to begin. It was an unpleasant task, but the matter had been pressed and he had admitted that this was the least he could do. He leaned back and looked at Elvira, his great respect for her clear in his eyes. Halwa was Elvira's Arab name, the one she used as teacher and poetess, the name meant "sweetmeat" and suited her well. He leaned forward, folding his hands together on top of the table. "Halwa, I have sent for you regarding a very delicate matter. You may refuse my request if you wish, I would have that clear from the beginning." He coughed uneasily, "There is a woman in my house, a Christian woman, and she wishes to learn to read and write. She is, to be honest with you, a prisoner who is not allowed out of her rooms; therefore time lays heavy upon her. I would have you come to my house each day for four hours and be teacher and companion to her. I will pay you well for this service, of course." He looked down at his hands, and said in a whisper, "Do you accept?"

Elvira could not conceal her amazement and felt it naked upon her face. Hasan had been absent from Cordova for nearly four years. He had returned from the north about eighteen months ago. Estiano had made a hasty departure over two years ago, and had returned with Hasan. There had been rumors of a prisoner taken, but a *woman*? Who was she that she was not allowed the freedom of Hasan's house like any other captive?

Instinct told Elvira there was something here that held grave significance for herself, for Hasan and perhaps for Estiano, who must have had some part in it. She moved uneasily on the pillow, glancing up at the girl in the tapestry. Sabíhah had not returned with them and when she had asked Hasan about her, he had said, with a dangerous gleam in his eye, "She is dead" and she had questioned him no further. What a tragic waste of a beautiful life. Sabíhah had been everything that was lovely, in form and soul, and had been one of Elvira's dearest friends.

She sighed, glancing back to Hasan. She said, "Who is she, Hasan? Speak her name. She will most likely tell me herself, if I accept."

Hasan grimaced, then frowned, and began drumming his fingertips on the tabletop; he looked deeply troubled. When he spoke, his voice was calm, but stiff. "She is the wife of Rodrigo Diaz, the lord of Castile . . . slayer of infidels, hero of the hour, murderer of women and children, Jehovah's avenger on this earth—and *she* is what I have taken in exchange," he waved an angry arm to the tapestry, "in exchange for my lovely, sweet Sabíhah. Sabíhah was murdered by El Cid, coldly, deliberately, and brutally stabbed to death."

"Oh, no." Elvira struggled with his revelation, unable to

conceive of a man who could destroy a woman who was perfection itself. A man would steal her away, perhaps, desire her,
surely, but murder her? Impossible. She stared into Hasan's eyes
in disbelief, then was overcome by a new shock. "You . . . you
cannot mean that you abducted this innocent woman and keep
her prisoner for what her husband did to Sabíhah? I do not believe it, Hasan! The poor creature. Surely . . . "

"I did not ask for your judgment, Halwa," Hasan spat out
angrily. "I seek your services—for pay. If you do not want the
position, tell me, and I will find another who is less sensitive to
Christian feelings and . . ."

"Hasan! That is unfair. Do not insult me with accusations
of prejudice. We have known each other a long while. You
know I am as much against the Christians of the north as you
are."

Hasan flushed. "Forgive me. It is a very uncomfortable
situation. I want to solve the matter with as little discussion as
possible. I want someone to instruct her, not to analyze my motives, my ethics—my crimes."

"Indeed. Rodrigo Diaz. Of *all* men, you steal *his* wife.
Most fortunate for you, for all of us, that so many mountains
and miles are between you, or he would descend upon this
place and cut all our throats."

"Ah, no . . . " Hasan murmured, finally able to smile with
some satisfaction. "You see, a body was buried that was
thought to be that of his spouse. He thinks her dead. In fact,
Estiano attended her funeral."

"For God! Where is satisfaction, if he does not know that
you have her?"

"Ah, the satisfaction is *mountainous*. A twist of circumstance
provided a faceless corpse. A note from me was delivered to
him informing him that I had taken my vengeance. He thinks
I murdered her, just as he killed my wife. Poetic justice, I
say . . ."

"But why keep her prisoner?"

"Because she is of a high-strung nature and would scream
to the mountaintops who she is, until the whole world knew,
including her esteemed husband. Besides," he added roughly,
"there is a great need within me to punish—punish," he slammed a fist down on the table. "Punish! And she is, shall we say,
convenient?"

Elvira gaped at Hasan, dumbfounded. It could not be
Hasan speaking: the words were completely incongruous with
her image of him. Hasan was never vindictive, or cruel. He was

the most patient and tenderhearted of men. The death of Sabíhah must have cut him deeply to cause this black decay of hatred.

Elvira came to a quick and determined decision. "I accept your offer of this position, Hasan. I will do my best."

"Thank you, Halwa," he sighed, relieved. "I ask of you but one more consideration. Keep silent about her identity." His eyes narrowed and his voice raised sharply. "Do not come to me with any problems you might have regarding her; make your own decisions. I trust your judgment completely. Understand?"

Elvira left the room filled with curiosity about the woman she was soon to meet and teach. It would be an interesting assignment to say the least. But she did not dwell long upon the matter. She had to hurry if she was to keep her appointment with Estiano. Her heart began to beat a little faster and she moved smoothly down the hallway, and out into the street, where she walked swiftly toward the library.

Jimena paced the tile floor of her suite, nervous and excited. Acacia had come running into her room two days ago, her face alight with triumph, shouting that she had obtained the master's approval, after tremendous insistence and demanding on her part, of course. "He is greatly pleased that you wish to improve yourself, my lady, and would be most happy to send you the best teacher to be found!"

Bless his benevolent heart, Jimena thought bitterly, as she continued her furious walk from corner to corner of the large room, skipping over pillows if they were in the way. A teacher. She was uncertain as to exactly what a teacher *was*. Someone, she thought, who knows what you do not know, and in some ways helps you to know what you would like to know? She shook her head, exasperated. This teacher would be the first person with whom she would come into close contact since her capture, except for ever-present Acacia. To read and write? She stopped abruptly, as a flash image leaped to the front of her mind, obscuring reality. She saw a little girl at a table, making scratches on parchment with a stolen quill. *"This child has been reading—and copying—the Infidel . . . BIBLE!"* She shivered, shaking the memory from her mind. This very day an infidel would enter her quarters, intent upon giving her a quill and parchment so that she could commit the same sin all over again. Preposterous! She had to have been out of her mind to tell Acacia she wished to learn reading and writing. Her stomach was filled with butterflies, and she was certain she felt pain in her hands, where the bishop had beaten her so severely with the chain.

The door opened behind Jimena and she whirled around. She stood frozen, openmouthed. A *woman*! And beautiful. She looked Castilian, rather than . . .

"Do not stand there with your mouth open, young lady," Elvira said brightly, striding toward her new pupil. When she was close to Jimena, she leaned forward and whispered in her ear, "You will catch flies!"

Jimena blushed and said, "Forgive me, but—but, I did not expect . . . You are so beautiful. And so *young*!"

Elvira laughed heartily. "Young! I thank you. Lately I have forsaken the word 'young' in referring to myself. I will be thirty next month, and I think of that age as more . . . mature? Or middle-aged, if one is forced to be exact. Certainly not young." She laughed again and said, "Here I have told you my age before I have even introduced myself. My name is Elvira Rodriguez. I am a teacher at the college. I believe I am well versed enough in the various elementary subjects to teach you anything you might wish to learn." She promptly dropped onto a low table a portfolio jammed full of books and papers. She leaned over and rummaged through it until she found a small, velvet-bound volume, which she handed to Jimena. "We had best begin with grammar and learn to speak Arabic first, then to read and write it. No sense, it seems to me, in beginning with Spanish, since you will be living in Cordova. Do you not agree?"

Jimena was overwhelmed by the woman's vital personality. "Uh, oh yes, certainly . . . " she stuttered.

The weeks and months passed swiftly. Each day Jimena eagerly awaited the arrival of her teacher and new friend, a fascination for learning having totally and quickly overtaken her. She no longer dreamed of the past. Each moment of every day was filled with a kind of magic. In the evenings, after her meal, she would sit down to practice, practice, practice, until, after only two months, she could read well enough for Elvira to bring her some books from the library. At first they were only simple stories written for children, and poetry, but lately they were great volumes of history and chronicles, which Jimena dove into with determination and enthusiasm. She learned quickly, because her native intelligence, combined with her enormous longing for knowledge, expanded her ability. Hour after hour was spent in the miracle of creating words and thoughts upon the endless supplies of paper furnished by Elvira. Then she began to scribble simple pictures, showing a decided talent for drawing that Elvira quickly recognized and encouraged. Paints were provided, and the long hours which had been spent in gazing out her window were now spent in preserving the scene upon her canvas.

Elvira communicated very little of herself to Jimena. In she swept each morning, bright and cheerful, eager to share with her pupil the knowledge she possessed. Jimena wondered where Elvira had come from and why she remained in Cordova; she was obviously free to move where she pleased, neither slave nor wife. All she knew had been gained from questioning Acacia, who knew very little herself, only that Elvira had once been a slave in the house of the wali of Cordova, and that she had been freed. Elvira did seem content with her lot, never showing the slightest evidence of regret or despair.

Elvira was well pleased with her pupil's progress, and always sensed when Jimena needed to move ahead in her studies. When Elvira brought the Ethics of Aristotle, it was in recognition of Jimena's desire for knowledge of a more intangible quality. Jimena turned the book over and over in her hands. If what was inside was half as beautiful as its outer coverings, Jimena was certain she would love this book above all others. The velvet cover was embroidered in gold thread in a geometrical design, the straps were of the most artfully tooled leather which matched the deep blue of the cover. She opened it with reverence, leafing through the thick pages. "Divine," she exclaimed. "Never have I seen a book so perfectly printed. And the illumination—a miracle of artistry!"

Elvira smiled, a new light in her eyes. "Yes. A true artist did the work, a man whose beauty is reflected in those pages you so fondly finger."

Jimena gave Elvira a quick, curious glance, then set her eyes upon the book again. "How I would like to learn such an art, to hold in my hands a book that I have printed and illuminated. You *must* teach me, Elvira!" Without waiting for her teacher to answer, she began to read, becoming lost in the thoughts and visions of Aristotle. The philosopher reasoned that happiness was the true aim of man, that we chose happiness for its own sake and never with a view to anything further. We sought honor, pleasure, intellect, even Heaven, because we believed that through these things we would be made happy. God's Heaven was a dream fulfilled, not in this life, but after death. The happiness that was lost to us on this earth, we looked for in that dark, empty unknown, the search of the desperate and of those who had nothing . . . a have for the have-nots. To Jimena it was an amazing expression of ideas, and difficult for her to grasp. Heaven had to be more—more than a hope, surely.

After Aristotle, she read the works of Hippocrates, Euclid, and Galen, drinking in the words and thoughts that they had put to paper so long ago; they were teaching her how to think, and thinking altered Jimena, in ways too subtle for her to notice. She began putting her own thoughts, as they developed, to paper, keeping the pages secreted from Elvira—bits of incompleted rhyme, sentences whose meanings escaped her own comprehension sometimes; it was as if another woman had entered her head and was attempting to tell her something.

Jimena had become so involved with her studies that she forgot she was unhappy. Books had become her escape.

Chapter
✠ *THREE* ✠

Elvira sat upon a stack of pillows across from Jimena, as she had every day without fail for almost two years. She looked especially beautiful today, Jimena thought. Her green eyes were sparkling with intelligence and enthusiasm and her graceful body was relaxed against the pillows. Her shining black hair was curled in Arab fashion in tiny ringlets about her face.

"I think," Elvira was saying, "that the Arab people, especially here in Andalus, are true Epicureans. Though they are Muslim in faith, they do not embrace their religion with a whole heart. Music is denied them by Muhammed, but they sing; the art of painting, re-creating nature in human, animal, or plant form, is strictly prohibited, but they cannot suppress their creative instincts. Truly they are the most wonderful artists and musicians. They have an instinct for joy. It is pleasure they worship, not Allah; they love, laugh, sing, bask in the joys of science and philosophy, and, though most have never read Epicurus, they are, nonetheless, true advocates of his philosophy." Elvira stopped her lecture and eyed Jimena, a tolerant smile on her painted lips. "Do you agree, mmmmm?"

Jimena jumped. "What? Oh, forgive me, Elvira. I was not listening, not with any concentration."

"And where were your thoughts? Pondering some great philsophy of your own? I seem to have reached a point where I am no longer needed. No more for you to learn from me?"

"Oh no, Elvira! I do so appreciate your coming each day. I cannot imagine what I would have done all these months without you. It is only—I have grown so fond of you and, well, every day I find I know less and less. There is so much to be learned, even about each other." She hesitated, but was no longer able to smother her need to know. "Elvira," she blurted out, "I have to know what happened, what brought you to

233

Cordova, and why you do not leave! You are Christian, the same as I—and Acacia tells me *you* were abducted, too."

Elvira's eyes had lost their amusement. She reached out and clasped Jimena's hands in hers, holding them tight. "I know, I know, Jimena; it is a terrible thing that Hasan is doing to you, keeping you prisoner this way." She glanced away for a moment, then said, "I, too, was unhappy, for a very long time. I do not often tell my story, as it is necessarily painful for me. But I think if I tell you, it might help."

Elvira's story began with her early life as Doña Elvira Margarita Rodriguez, in a city only a few miles from Zaragossa, just across the Aragon border. She was the only child of a rich and powerful count. Her father, she confided, was not a religious man and he blasphemed God most of his life. He gave nothing to support the local monastery, the result of which was its collapse. In his old age, however, as Elvira began to show great promise of beauty, for all her twelve years, the count, overnight, became a devout Christian. Hoping to pave his way to the Heaven that was fast approaching, he took the tonsure and became a monk, giving his daughter, as if she were a discarded piece of furniture no longer needed, to the Church. There, hidden from the world in a monastery, Elvira grew up.

"I was given no choice, Jimena; that life was forced upon me. But at the time I did not question. The nuns were kind to me, and I enjoyed many happy hours."

Elvira learned to read at the monastery, so that she could study the Bible, the single book available. She learned the laws of her faith; to be a Christian was to live; to be without her religion and the daily practice of it, worse than death. Her hours were spent in prayer, hard work in the fields, and weaving cloth. She took her vows with thanks to God for the privilege of serving Him.

"I had been a nun only six months, and had just passed my eighteenth birthday, when it happened. Maktadir swept across the border with his army. Though the monastery in which I dwelt was far from any sizable city, it was directly in the path of the marching invaders. They rushed through those sacred halls, defying the laws of the Christian faith, folding the ladies of the monastery up in their arms—and carried us off to a fate we supposed would be worse than death." Elvira paused, moving into a more comfortable position, her face expressing the pain she felt as she recalled the experience. "You can imagine the shock. My whole world had crumbled beneath my feet;

nothing that represented peace, security, or protection was left to me. It was a never-ending stream of separate, awful nightmares for a long while after that. I found myself upon the slave block, before the leering eyes of barbarians, my skin crawling at each testing touch of their hands. . . ."

She was sold, the first time, to a merchant named Al Rashid, who spent the majority of his time traveling at the business of selling his textiles. The mysteries of life had never concerned Elvira, the art of love was beyond her comprehension, so that nights with Al Rashid were terror-filled and disgusting. But it was in the house of the merchant that she had learned to read and write Arabic from her harem companions; as escape she had read every book in Al Rashid's library. She also learned how to beautify herself, and she began to enjoy soft silk against her flesh, cleanliness, luxuries she had never before imagined. One evening Al Rashid entertained an important gentleman of the wali's guard, who became so enthralled with Elvira's beauty that she was given to him as a gift. His name was Yosuf and he was kind to her. With him the act of love began to have more meaning than mere toleration of a man's lust, became an anticipated and longed for pleasure. Yosuf was a physically pleasing man, with great patience and tenderness, and she grew to love him.

"When Yosuf was killed, Jimena, a part of myself died with him; but his death is another story. I was then sent to the slave block, where I was purchased by the wali himself; I had often entertained him at Yosuf's house with my poetry recitations. It was he who, only a year later, gave me my freedom. Since then I have lived in Cordova in my own home by the river. I have two servants. I teach at the college, as you know." Elvira sat forward intently, looking hard at Jimena. "Now, you want to know why I did not return to Aragon when I was freed, and why I appear so content. I think it can be explained this way: what I did was weigh what I had here and could hope for, against what I would gain by returning. In Cordova I had as much true freedom as anyone in this life can possibly obtain. I had been given the miraculous gift of alternative, which one must have to make a truly free choice, to actually exercise the will. I visualized the girl who had been brought to this land, an ignorant, graceless lump and I found it simply inconceivable that I could once again tolerate layers of dirt on my flesh, nor could I any longer imagine conforming to any of the demands of the Church. The choice was not really difficult, Jimena."

Jimena's mind tried to block out the implications of Elvira's explanation. Indignation was hot in her breast. A nun. She had denied her *vows*. Then she experienced a sudden urgent need to understand and forgive.

"Jimena," Elvira said earnestly, reaching out to lightly touch her pupil's trembling hand, "I know what you must be thinking—that I have chosen hell by defecting. It is my opinion that our Church distorts Christian ethics when it demands that we have faith in precepts that Jesus did not preach, nor imply. I have learned more about Jesus Christ here in Cordova than I did in my church. The Arab greatly admires Jesus as a philosopher and prophet and much of what he taught can be found in the Koran. I am still a Christian, in that I continue to believe in Christ, not, I admit, as the son of God, but as a true spokesman for God on this earth. I prefer the unrestricted life of Andalusia to the cruel, unrewarding world of Christians. It is that simple. I have never regretted my decision. I study. I teach. I find much pleasure. I love, I live, and I *let* live." She sighed and leaned back into her pillows. Noting the bewilderment on Jimena's face, the concern, she said, "It can be as simple for you, if you let it. Forget the past. Think that you have been born again into a new world and accept that life, see the goodness in it. Oh, I know there are evils here. I would not wish to stand on the slave block again, a cruel and barbaric custom, but in any land, any religion, in any government, there is good, if you are willing to look for it."

"Then there is good in the Christian world. If one were to look for it, it *could* be found."

"How long did you dwell in that place, Jimena?"

"Nineteen years; no, twenty."

"Were you ever content—happy? Did you ever find what you sought? All of us are searchers from the day we are born."

Jimena did not answer. Her mind whirled with thoughts that piled one upon another. There was fidelity to the principles taught her as a child to contend with, a surge of belief in the old, then quick jabs of doubt . . . a longing to see a sweet, golden-haired child, but, pushing forward too swiftly for her to prevent it, there were the recalled strains of haunting music, a vision of velvet-covered books filled with men's thoughts and soft silk against sweet, clean flesh. Her eyes flew about the room, the brightness of color blinding her . . . silk draperies, richly embroidered pillows on her bed and the wide expanses of window letting in the clear, fresh air and sunlight. "Oh God," she cried, "I am so lonely, so terribly *lonely*! And I miss my baby. Do you know that she is four years old, Elvira? Four!

And I have not looked upon her since she was eight months old!"

"Oh. . ." Elvira said pityingly, "and the longer you are away the more difficult it will be to return, for so many reasons. Your daughter would not know you now, and your husband . . ."

"You *know* something," Jimena exclaimed. "You know something you are not telling me. You have news of my child? Tell me, please."

"I have heard only what all Andalusians know, that your husband has been worrisomely successful in his wars against the Arab rulers to the north, and that King Alphonso will soon take him back; he cannot afford to do otherwise. It would be extremely unprofitable to keep an army like El Cid's his enemy. Much gold and land could be gained by returning Rodrigo Diaz to the fold."

"My daughter," Jimena whispered anxiously, "what have you heard of her?"

Elvira sighed and looked away from Jimena. Months past she had heard news of Jimena's daughter from a friend who had returned from a visit to Toledo, but she had thought it unwise to tell Jimena. It was best to be honest, now, but she wished the girl had not asked. "Yes, I have news of your child, Jimena," she began gently. "She was placed in a monastery, at La Coruña I believe, soon after your, uh, death, to be raised by the nuns; with El Cid's blessing, of course. After all," she reasoned, defending the man for Jimena's sake, "he could not care for an infant himself, hundreds of miles from Castile, constantly at battle, exiled."

"Of course." Jimena's voice was emotionless. She turned away from Elvira and stepped to a window. She sat down heavily, numbed—and stared unseeing out across the lawns to the river.

Hasan sat still in his university study, a book open before him but unseen. He moved slightly on his pillows, his dark eyes moving to examine the life-size portrait of Sabíhah. He sighed, wishing the superstition that to create a likeness of a person captured the soul of the model, tying it forever to this earth, were true. Then she might breathe again for him, be warm in his arms.

"Forgive me, Hasan, for this intrusion upon your privacy, but I must speak to you about something important."

Hasan turned his head to smile up at Elvira, where she

stood in the open doorway, waiting for him to politely insist that she was in no way intruding, was more than welcome. "Come in, Halwa. You brighten the hour and this room with your presence."

Elvira was not distracted by Hasan's charm. She had kept her bargain with him and had never annoyed him with talk about her pupil. But this simply could not continue. He must release her. Jimena was too fine a person to be kept in that prison suite; it was cruel and contemptible. She stonily moved across the room and sat herself rigidly down on pillows across from Hasan.

"I will come directly to the point, Hasan," Elvira began firmly, meeting his eyes with an icy directness. "I ask you to release my pupil and your prisoner, who has become a dear friend to me. I think that she at least deserves the freedom of your house and your gardens.

Hasan sat erect before her, his face expressing surprise and anger at once. "What is this? You, who, with Estiano, know her identity, ask this of me? Are you mad? One step out of that suite and she would, I have no doubt, be running through my front gate to be retrieved again and again. Vengeance sits warm in my liver. I will not disturb its peaceful rest by bothering with the wretch. Had she been any other woman than the Butcher of Castile's wife, I would have sold her to the lowest bidder."

"Wretch?" Elvira said, eyebrows raised. "You have not set eyes upon her lately, obviously."

"Ach, Christian women are loathsome to me in their pious frigidity; I would as soon suffer abstinence as suffer their cold bony flesh."

Elvira threw up her hands impatiently. "I would suggest you take another look at her, Abu l Hasan. You will be amazed, I assure you, at the miracles Acacia has performed; she's quite extraordinarily lovely. But that is irrelevant. Say that she promises to live in peace in your house, never speaking her idenity; say also that . . . and I mean no insult to your gracious and irreproachable person," her voice thick with condescension now, "that she had been deeply wronged by your vengeance, which might sit warm in *your* liver but eats away at her own with the acids of despair and loneliness. Her mind is a jewel, Hasan, of quickness and hunger for knowledge. Her face and form are of the kind loved best by Allah. And she decays slowly into old age within the cage of your revenge against her husband. Disgraceful, Hasan. Absolutely intolerable!"

Startled by a severe jab of conscience, Hasan sat quietly for long moments, his head swimming with defenses and regrets that threw him into utter confusion.

"I have never known you to be cruel," Elvira persisted. "Inhumanity is the way of brutes, not men of virtue, as you are and have always been."

Hasan groaned and threw himself back into his pillows, guilt overwhelming him. He cast his eyes to the ceiling and said, "Let me tell you, Halwa—when I saw her writhing and screaming in pain at my feet, her flesh being torn apart in abortion, I begged Allah to forgive me. But I could not undo what I had done. She was ill, her child dead, and I was forced to leave that place swiftly." He lowered his eyes to avoid Elvira's penetrating, accusing gaze. His forehead was creased into tight lines. "I imagine," he murmured, more to himself than to Elvira, "that I have kept her imprisoned so long, because I did not wish to daily face my shame. But what strange creatures we are—I still enjoy my revenge. I think about Rodrigo Diaz and my innards are set afire with loathing. He was so arrogant, so certain such as my Sabíhah could be slain, smashed beneath his heel like an insect and never missed. To him she was something to use to satisfy his lust, no more. Beyond that, he compared her, my Sabíhah—can you *imagine*—to a fly upon a heap of dung. So," he sighed, at last meeting Elvira's now softening eyes, "I must make a choice. Either I return her to her husband, or I keep her imprisoned so that I need not face . . . "

"No, Hasan," Elvira interrupted earnestly, "I am not asking you to send her back to Castile. In my opinion returning her would be an even worse crime against her than imprisonment! She has unlimited potential, which would be destroyed in Castile. I ask only that you allow her more freedom in your house. Forget your shame and guilt. Time has healed many of her wounds. I believe it is possible for her to adjust to her new surroundings. Give her that opportunity, Hasan—please."

"You can guarantee that she will not become hysterical, scream out to the world who she is? I will not tolerate constant recriminations and demands that she be released entirely."

"I am positive she can be convinced such attitudes and actions would be extremely unwise. Yes, I would be willing to guarantee it."

Hasan looked doubtful, then threw up his hands in defeat. "Agreed, Halwa. I will grant your request. I did not intend to kill her when I devised the plan. I will not slowly kill her now." He let out a great breath of air, feeling relieved of a very heavy burden. "She is free to live in my house as any of my wives or concubines, but please *assure* her that nothing will be expected of her that she is unwilling to give. I offer her a home, protection, and an education. I will clothe her, feed her, accept full responsibility for her." His voice had dropped to a near whisper. "Jimena Diaz de Gomez is no longer a prisoner."

Jimena sat on her bed reading a book called *The Marvels and Wonders of the Thousand Nights and a Night.* She had read it many times, but enjoyed leafing through it when in the mood for something highly romantic. Impatiently she flipped the pages, skipping the dull parts, seeking out those uncensored, detailed descriptions of love adventures. In delicious horror she read about a queen whose husband watched her from a distance as she enjoyed an escapade with her lover.

> She cried out in a loud voice, Here to me, O my lord Saeed! and then sprang with a drop-leaf from one of the trees a big slobbering blackamoor with rolling eyes which showed the whites, a truly hideous sight. He walked boldly up to her and threw his arms around her neck while she embraced him as warmly; then he bussed her and winding his legs around hers as a buttonloop clasps a button, he threw her and enjoyed her. They ceased not from kissing and clipping, coupling and carousing till day began to wane. . . .

Jimena's eyes left the page and she gazed blankly into space. Her body jabbed her with a sharp pain, reminding her that she was a woman. "Oh, God," she groaned, throwing the book aside, struggling to suppress the visions stubbornly coming alive in her mind—a man, his hands and lips and arms . . .

Elvira entered the room and Jimena rolled over on her back, stretching luxuriously, her eyes still full of pain and frustration. "Elvira?" she asked disinterestedly, to cover her true emotions, "what does it mean in this story—to "bepiss"?"

Elvira choked on a laugh. "What?"

"I was reading a story, quite romantic, and I was wondering what the word meant. Bepiss."

Elvira moved to whisper in Jimena's ear, "To urinate, dear. The Arab leaves no details from his stories."

"For *God*," Jimena cried, "they certainly do not. What a thing to say. Romantic, indeed!"

Elvira was bursting with her news, but held it secret with

delicious pleasure all through the day's lesson. She caught Jimena looking at her curiously several times, probably noticing the self-satisfied smirk on her face, but she managed to hold off until she had gathered all her materials together for departure. Then Elvira said, "It has been lovely, Jimena, and it is ended. I will not return tomorrow; this is our last day as student and teacher. I pleaded with Hasan for your release, and I was successful. The guards have been removed from your door; this house is yours to wander about in as you please, the gardens are for your pleasure. You may walk along the banks of the river, and do almost anything within reason that you wish to do."

Jimena sat dumbfounded. Only words, their meaning slipped by her for a moment. Then she screeched, leaped up from her pillows, and attacked Elvira, kissing and hugging her. "Oh! You miraculous, darling person. You angel from Heaven!" She kissed Elvira's face all over and squeezed her ribs so hard that Elvira cried out for mercy. Then Jimena stepped back dizzily, her stomach heaving with a great rush of emotion. She felt faint, and absolutely ecstatic. She clutched Elvira's hand, dragging her to the pillows. "Now, sit here and tell me how you managed the miracle. Tell me—quickly!"

Elvira related, word for word, her meeting with Hasan, then said, "I must make one thing clear, little one. When I say that you are free, I mean it only in a figurative sense. You are free to leave this room and wander this house as you please, but you are Hasan's possession; he *owns* you. A misfortune, but by the law of Islam you are his and completely subject to his will. He will rule and regulate your life."

"Yes, yes, I understand."

"Remember what I have told you. You are not to divulge your identity to anyone, or attempt any escape. If you do, you will be sent directly back into this prison."

Jimena could not concern herself at this moment with such unimportant details; she would agree to anything. Three years and it was over; she could begin to live again. She let her eyes wander around her room, from ceiling to windows to floor. Perhaps she might be allowed another room? But no. Actually she would miss every piece of tile, every shaft of sunlight that wavered a reflected tile-rainbow upon the ceiling. It was really a very pleasant room, now that it was no longer a prison.

Acacia proudly led Jimena through the house, a house that Jimena had lived in so long and had never seen. Its splendor and comfort was unbelievable. Never would she have imagined that people could surround themselves with so much luxury. In the main entrance hall there was a fountain that sprayed perfume, floating a heady scent throughout the house. But the chamber that interested Jimena the most was the harem. It was enormous, nearly forty feet in length; silk draperies marked off each lady's section. In the center of the outside wall a glass sliding door opened upon a pavilion, where there was a fountain, and rose trees in tubs, and several richly decorated mattresses spread about for lounging. As she entered the harem, Jimena's eyes flashed into every corner in self-righteous curiosity, her lower lip pouting disapprovingly. Three young women looked up languidly from their beds, and Jimena thought she knew what they were thinking: Ah, here is another rival for our master's affections. How shall we outwit her, how match her, outdo her charms?

Acacia waved the women over, and they moved slowly, the silk of their trousers making a soft rustling sound in the quiet room. "This is Zarífah," Acacia said, gesturing toward the petite, brown-haired girl who stood closest to Jimena, " . . . and this is Shawah. And Nuzhab."

Jimena was amused by the names of the women, knowing their meanings. The first was Miss Pretty, the second, of all things, Lewdness, and the third was named Delight, and quite appropriately, for she was the most beautiful of the three; her eyes were kohl-black and her equally dark hair hung thick and waving to her knees.

"And this," Acacia said pridefully, "is Raushana."

Jimena jerked her head around to look at Acacia in surprise. Of course, she could not use her real name, but—*Raushana.* Then she smiled warmly upon Acacia in thanks for the lovely compliment. It rolled softly on the tongue and it meant Splendid One, or Splendor.

Nuzhab spoke to Jimena in a sweet, lilting voice, "We are happy that you are with us, Raushana. You must join us on our pavilion one afternoon to play chess. I must warn you, however, that Zarífah is our unbeaten champion; none of us ever has been able to checkmate her."

"You will retain *separate* quarters?" Zarífah queried Jimena wonderingly.

"She will," Acacia replied, before Jimena could open her mouth, her tone emphatic in an attempt to end any further discussion of the matter.

"I see. Then you will not wed our Hasan?" Zarífah persisted, "Nor are you concubine. A curious arrangement." She laughed brightly, "But welcome, Raushana. No warmer welcome can I give than to a woman who will be no competition to me."

Walking away from the harem, the smiling, pretty faces of Hasan's wives still before her vision, Jimena leaned to Acacia and whispered, "I cannot understand how they reconcile themselves to sharing one man. For certain, I would rip out the eyes and tear a woman bald who took the man I love from me, even for one hour, or a moment . . . if I ever loved a man."

Acacia giggled, covering her mouth with a hand.

"And what do you laugh at? I think it is terrible, disgusting."

"My good woman," Acacia grinned tolerantly, "does not every Christian woman share her lord with other women? The single difference is that she never sees her rival, or knows of her existence. Fidelity is not a Christian gentleman's best virtue, regardless of what your Bible teaches, this you must admit." She waved an arm back toward the harem, "We all know our competition personally, which simplifies our lives considerably."

Jimena stubbornly shook her head. "I still say it is disgusting to live within the same house, the same room even, knowing that tonight he will ask for her, and tomorrow he will ask for another. Barbaric."

"You talk foolishness." Acacia stared at Jimena, amazed at such reasoning, her eyes losing some of their tolerance. Once a Christian, always a Christian, she thought; Jimena would never change. "The Koran clearly states that a man must share equitably with all his wives," she began to explain, her mouth twisted into what-is-the-use lines, "Each has her turn. We compete with each other, certainly, but we all love Hasan dearly. When our turn comes, it is with the happiest excitement that we prepare ourselves for the night, even assisting each other, all the while dreaming of the night that will be ours."

"But what of concubines, you, for example? It is not in the law that he must share equitably with you. Do you, too, receive your fair share?

Acacia smiled. "Well, it depends upon the man, of course. But I will tell you truly, our Hasan has sufficient to go around."

"Oh!" Jimena gasped, "that is . . . is . . . The love act cannot be separated from marriage, which is a holy union. Really, what you practice here is no less than—than legalized adultery, legalized lust and depravity!"

"Better to make it legal than to call it sin, thus condemning nearly every Christian to Hell. Why impose laws upon people that they are unable to obey? Your God created man in his own image, then condemned you for being what he made you. To me, much more disgusting."

Jimena clenched her teeth tightly together. Acacia simply did not comprehend. There was no use even discussing the matter with her. But how content Urracca would have been here in Islam. Surely she had been born in the wrong land. Urracca— Strange to think about her at this moment. Pray God she was happy, able to maintain against all the odds against her.

Acacia and Jimena spent hours wandering through the gardens. The fountains were a mirage of beauty, the river a glorious frosting upon an already painfully beautiful cake. There was a small grove of orange trees in full blossom, in the center of which was a carpet of lawn and a bench of white wrought iron on which to sit. There were oleander shrubs as high as trees, and roses that made a hedge along the path to the river, also slim, swaying cypress trees, green hedges and tiled walks. Jimena sat down on the soft green grass at the riverbank. The sun was warm upon her skin. Flowers from the magnolia tree over her head dropped their petals softly down upon the rich earth. The rippling water of the river moved in artistic designs as the gentle touch of a flower petal created a whirlpool, sending the pink fairy-raft sailing, swirling out of view. A tiny silver fish came up to the surface and stared unblinking at Jimena, then whirled away into the dark depths of the river. A nightingale warbled a song that set her senses reeling. She sighed, recalling something she had read recently; that Heaven and Hell were here on earth. Her eyes gazed into the clear water and she knew that Heaven could not be more lovely or offer any more peace than this garden. She reluctantly rose, following Acacia along the rose-lined walk toward the house. Her fingers slid over the flowers, and pulled one bright red rose from its stem.

Jimena halted abruptly, her heart thumping heavily in her chest. Hasan was walking slowly toward her with his eyes cast downward. He wore a dark-green silk tunic. About his head was a golden turban, in the center of which, over his forehead, sparkled a large emerald. Jimena began to tremble. As he drew nearer the trembling did not cease, but worsened, and when he stood before her, noticing the two women at last, her breath was coming in short gasps. Such a confusion of emotions overcame her that she did not know what to do, to think, or what in God's name she could say to him. She prayed he would not notice her and walk right on past her. But he came to an abrupt, surprised halt before her. She refused to look up at him, painfully aware of his dark eyes that examined her from head to foot.

"My lady?" he said in a soft, controlled voice, "I hope you are enjoying my gardens. I have a great fondness for them, and walk here every day at this time."

Jimena felt Acacia's elbow jab into her ribs, nudging her to respond, but she was voiceless. The only words that raced through her mind were accusations. . . . My baby is four years old! She lives motherless in a granite-walled prison. If I returned today she would not know her own mother, would shrink away in distrust as from a stranger. Damn you to hell! Then came a terror that if she did not respond with a reasonable politeness this infidel would lock her into her suite again and leave her there forever. She sucked in a breath and with painful effort lifted her chin, meeting his eyes. Ignoring the butterflies buzzing wildly in her mid-section, she said tightly, "You have a magnificent home, my lord." The idea struck and she instantly switched to Arabic, "I am sure Al Zohra is of equal beauty and I cannot with patience wait to see more of it."

Hasan covered his amazement with a solemn expression. He had expected unrestrained hatred, or cold aloofness; he certainly could not have anticipated charm, nor such expert use of the Arabic language. His eyes moved from her face down the length of her. *Alhomdalillah,* could this be the scrawny, ignorant savage he had picked up off the plains of Castile? He would have said she would never be beautiful, no matter what means of beautification were at her disposal. But what he saw now forced him to admit to having been grossly in error. A face full and round with flesh the shade of pale-pink magnolia blossoms. Her hair, that had been infested and colorless, was now so fair as to be considered white, waving down upon supple shoulders. Her nose, which in her too thin face had been pronounced, now blended into her features delicately, and her eyes were enormous, with lashes like upturned canopies, shading a brightness of eye that he found discomforting.

Cautiously Hasan said, bowing from the waist to her, "I might show Al Zohra to you." He quickly added a vague "someday."

It was an invitation to step even further beyond her prison and Jimena leaped at it. "I thank you, oh Father of Beau-

ty . . . " She dipped her head respectfully. "I will look forward
to that day with the same eagerness as Allah as he anticipates
your glorious presence in his Paradise."

Acacia slapped her hand over her mouth to suppress a giggle. She watched her master's face closely, noting the amused
smile that lifted the corners of his mouth. "Halwa has taught
her well, has she not, my lord?" she said to Hasan, with a
wicked, self-satisfied smile on her face.

"Indeed," Hasan murmured, his eyes resting upon Jimena
for a moment before turning his head to Acacia. "A good day
to you, Acacia—and to you, Raushana." With that he lifted the
"tail" of his turban, threw it over his shoulder and strode away
toward the river.

That night Jimena lay tormented upon her bed. The winds
of fate had blown her to this place, this prison house, like a leaf
torn from a tree. She seldom wept over what was impossible to
change; she had accepted her fate, but at the same time she had
never entirely forsaken a phantom hope of escape, of a rescue
from this waking dream in which she dwelt. Resignation was
not enough; she did not grow in this soil, but remained dor-
mant in original form. New philosophies that were presented to
her through her books slipped from her consciousness like rain
from the slick leaves of the eucalyptus. She allowed herself to
be swept along on the current of her days without resistance, as
she always had. She could not bear the thought that little Urracca was four years old and would not recognize her now, so
her daughter remained an infant before her longing vision; she
would hold her again to her breast, cooing affectionately into
her petal-soft little ear, then she would feel again the movement
of a child within her womb. . . .

Jimena stifled a cry by striking her mouth with a balled
fist. She bit into her knuckles, thrashed on the bed, and wept
into her pillows. Her fall into the flames of loss and tender
memories was brief. Within a few minutes she was once again
calm and determined to bear what she must, since she was helpless to alter any of it.

Chapter
✠ *FOUR* ✠

Hasan sat, as was his place as host, in the seat of honor, his back to the far wall of the banquet room facing the entrance. At his right sat the wali of Malaga, to his left Al Rakashi, chief adviser to the wali of Cordova. Fanning out and declining according to rank sat five other men. Estiano Antolinez was the very last, for he had no rank whatsoever aside from his close friendship with the host.

Estiano sat at the end of the circle with his back to the door, facing Hasan across the low table. He squirmed uncomfortably. He had never become used to eating while sitting on the floor; he did not know what to do with his bulky knees. It was impossible for him to maintain the Arab position of balancing on the heels. After only minutes pain would stab through every muscle of his legs. He leaned over awkwardly, dipping a morsel of bread into his bowl of harísah, a favorite, heavily spiced dish of his of boiled rice reduced to a paste then mixed with shredded lamb. It had a marvelous, mouth-watering aroma and Estiano was famished, but in the long journey from the bowl to his mouth he lost a great glob of the stuff somewhere upon his tunic. Red-faced, he made as inconspicuous a search for it as he could. Then, much to his acute embarrassment, the graybeard who sat next to him leaned over and politely wiped away the mess with his linen, it had been hidden in a deep fold of Estiano's sleeve. Estiano smiled sheepishly at the man and gave up on the harísah, contenting himself with a handful of raisins and almonds, his gaze passing hungrily and regretfully over the sumptuous table.

A cluster of candles had been placed at each end of the table, and in the center, for decoration, there stood a small silver statue of a nude young girl, feet apart, head bent gracefully back, her arms stretched outward and up. Covering her perfectly molded feet was a bouquet of pink and white water lilies, and all around her were bowls, platters, and baskets filled to overflowing with food. Besides the steaming platters of harísah, there were copper skillets raised over artistically designed, flaming braziers, round-heaped with sliced mutton covered with a blanket of glazed mushrooms; silver trays piled three high with tarts and fritters that were delicately scented with musk, pistachio nuts, pickled safflower, and olives in brine, apples, peaches, and cucumber slices cut in artistic designs, and woven, colorful baskets heaped with six varieties of bread.

"Wine, Saíd?"

Estiano jumped as Acacia leaned near with a crystal pitcher sparkling red with wine in her hand. He smiled up at her and held his glass beneath the pitcher, then turned up his nose in disgust. The wine was warm, as usual. Why must they always *boil* the stuff? Estiano vowed he would have his cook prepare his meal, no matter what time he arrived home; he would sit upon a *chair* and have a glass of wine that was chilled and inoffensive to the taste, and he would eat his food without spilling half upon his clothes.

Acacia moved smoothly behind the group of guests, and all accepted the wine except one, Al Rakashi. He was a pious man. He glared coldly at Acacia for forgetting he did not partake of the Allah-detested brew. Al Rakashi took great pride in his religious affectations and in the fact that all who knew him or came in contact with him recognized in him one of the Faithful; he was certain it showed upon him and surrounded him like a bright and holy glow.

"Forgive me, Saíd . . . " Acacia murmured, quickly hurrying away to escape the man's indignation. When she reached Hasan she leaned just a little closer than was actually necessary, allowing her breath to lightly blow upon his ear.

Hasan turned and smiled pleasantly into her eyes as she refilled his glass. He watched her hips with interested, gleaming concentration as she swished out of the room.

Hasan moved a hand gracefully, to scoop out of his bowl a choice bit of lamb upon a small piece of bread. Smiling, he offered the delicacy to the wali of Malaga. The man nodded politely and accepted the morsel, which was very gently placed upon his extended tongue. Then he in turn did the same, choosing from the table a safflower from the brine which he placed between Hasan's slightly, but sufficiently parted lips.

A mellifluous belch reverberated above all other sounds,

and Hasan, very pleased, turned his attention to Al Rakashi, who grinned proudly, rubbing his stomach with a large-boned, heavily jeweled hand.

"Your table, Saíd, is of a nature that one might expect in Allah's paradise," Al Rakashi said graciously, "lacking but the splendiferous maidens who are angels there."

Hasan bowed his head and smiled, then clapped his hands together sharply three times as a signal.

Nuzhab appeared in answer to the command. She moved silently, smoothly, through the draperies at Hasan's right. She began to dance, almost motionless at first, her hips undulating, twisting in circles, her long hair flying over her face as she bent her head in swift, graceful movements. Then she suddenly stopped, holding her arms in the classic, arched attitude of a statue and remaining as still as death. Three musicians slipped through the curtains and stood behind her, their fingers hoverig over the stringed instruments clasped to their breasts. A small black boy of about fifteen appeared, heralded by the crash of his two hands upon his drum. A wailing, pulsating melody began to take form, pulled into balance by the rhythm of the drum. Nuzhab began to move once more, but this time only her head moved, the enormous, looped gold earrings she wore swinging only slightly at first, then whipping, snapping, a yellow blur as her head spun round. The drummer boy's fingers snapped against the stretched hide of his instrument so fast as to show only a blur, a flesh-colored shadow. Now Nuzhab threw the black mane that was her hair around her in an arc, sweeping it round in front, then back again, the gold chains around her neck and her earrings flashing like Salome's. She bent, quivered, smiled, and exulted, her dance undisguisedly sexual, her face covered by the frenzy of hair that whipped about it, her body slithering like a reptile, until she lay outstretched upon the floor. The drum faded and the music died to a whisper.

"Sublime," Al Rakashi whispered, running his tongue out over his lower lip, his eyes fixed upon Nuzhab.

The eyes of every man in the room were so fixed. Reaching for food automatically, without watching what their hands were doing, they chewed seriously, busily, and did not take their gaze from Nuzhab.

Hasan was proudly smiling, his own eyes seeing beneath the blue trousers of her costume, the palms of his hands tingling in sweet remembrance. He reflected that the women of his house were of the most treasured kind, all lovely of body and feature, not one without charm, wit, or accomplishment. "Nuzhab," he said, waving an arm enthusiastically, "recite for us now."

Obediently Nuzhab rose and took a kneeling position. She bowed her head low and stretched her arms out to place her palms flat upon the rich, deep-piled carpet. As she sat up again, a pale, delicate hand swept across her brow, wiping away the perspiration there, then fluttered to straighten her tangled hair. She sat upon her heels and began to speak in a sweetly high-pitched voice. "Beware of losing hearts of men by thine injurious deed; for when aversion takes his place, none may dear Love restore; hearts, when affection flies from them, are likest unto glass, which broken, cannot whole be made,—'tis breached for evermore . . . "

The men listened in rapt attention as she spoke, their eyes following the flowing, rhythmic movements of her hands, her tiny, pink fingers fluttering in accent to the words. When she had finished the long poem she bowed her head humbly as a muffled groan of appreciation passed from the lips of all present. Hasan beckoned to her, motioning her to a pillow between himself and the wali of Malaga. Nuzhab sat down demurely between the two men, smiling in turn into the eyes of each.

Black eunuchs dressed in gay red and yellow costumes cleared the table of all but the silver maiden in the center. New clusters of candles were brought to replace those burned down. A large, ornately designed silver bowl filled with warm, scented water was passed and each man furnished with a fresh linen. Then, as the company leaned back, saying polite things about the meal to Hasan, the curtains at the right were again thrown aside and a trembling, painfully self-conscious Jimena stepped into the room. Her long hair was curled in tiny ringlets about her face, the back hair tied with a gold clasp to fall like a horse's tail to her waist. A white gardenia had been pinned behind each ear. Her whole costume was gold, the vest intricately and heavily embroidered, patiently beaded with thousands of pearls. Eight coral bracelets circled her right upper arm.

A low murmur of ahhhs was heard again, then silence, as every eye fixed upon the golden angel of Hasan's paradise. The silver tray she held shook in her nervous hands, rattling the crystal dishes of iced sherbet she was to serve. Somehow she managed to point her bare, pink toenailed feet in the right direction. She leaned over Hasan, offering him the first cup of sherbet.

Hasan frowned. She should have served his guests first. But no matter. He watched her face, so close to his own, unable to suppress the excitement she caused to rush through his innards. Exquisite, he thought, perfection itself. But her eyes would not meet his. She moved quickly away, offering a sherbet to Al Rakashi.

Al Rakashi shared Hasan's excitement; it showed in his unmasked eyes, but he was not content with a profile of her face. He reached out a hand and with a jeweled forefinger under her chin turned her face to him. "What is your name, my angel? Now I am *certain* this is Allah's paradise, for I have never seen one more heavenly, more intricately put together than yourself."

Jimena flushed, but was at the same time very pleased by the compliment. Her head turned slightly and she met Hasan's gaze at last. Looking at him, rather than at Al Rakashi, she said in Arabic, "My name is Raushana, Saíd," The soft beauty of the language added to her charms.

Hasan smiled warmly, his great pleasure bare upon his face.

Jimena then moved around the circle until she stood a few feet away from Estiano Antolinez, who was staring at her, his mouth open in disbelief. As she looked upon and recognized the man before her, Jimena's stomach lurched and her hands became so weak she nearly dropped the tray. She stopped still, staring into his colorless eyes, eyes that became a mirror to the past. The visions she saw reflected there enveloped her like cold, icy shrouds. Anger and hatred burned within her. This was the man without whose aid it never could have happened. The spy. The hunter that stalked her like prey, then attacked from ambush when she was insufficiently guarded. Murderer. He murdered Maria, breaking first her heart, then smashing her body as well. *And my unborn child,* Jimena's inner voice screamed out, her eyes communicating her emotions across the space that separated them, *you killed him too! Murdering, ugly little man, how I despise you for what you have done to me.*

Estiano sat very still, staring at Jimena in stunned amazement. The sight of her so excitingly lovely took his breath away. Why he had recognized her he did not know—she had changed so much. It was her eyes that were unaltered, he thought. Through the veil of grime and ill health she had worn her large brown eyes had sparked intelligence and a unique character, then . . . and now.

The past settled heavily upon Estiano as he recalled how he had deliberately and without feeling destroyed this girl's life.

Returning to Castile had been an ordeal; the mere contemplation of that land to the north brought with it a cold dread. He had sworn never to return, certain that black decay would place its slimy fingers about his throat and choke out his life, that he had escaped only just in time from the fate he had been born to. When he had looked upon Jimena Diaz for the first time, he had seen just another savage, like those that had surrounded him in his childhood, and he had felt no shame or guilt; no reservations threatened the success of his mission. Looking at Jimena as she was now made him realize for the first time that within the land from which he had run there was an abundance of beauty that was simply hidden behind an impenetrable veil. In Jimena, Estiano saw the beauty that he might have seen in his mother's face, the light that might have surrounded his childhood, and his heart reached out to her; he loved her and knew he would love her the rest of his life. This love was not an unconscious thing, but was painful and absolute in his conscious thought. His heart began to beat fast, and his hands ached to touch her. His soul cried out in anguish at the hatred he saw in her eyes.

Jimena forced herself to approach Estiano, avoiding his eyes. Quickly she leaned to offer him a sherbet, then she swiftly moved away from him, feeling his gaze hot on her back, just as she had on the road between Gormaz and Zamora.

"Raushana?"

Jimena heard Hasan speak, but for an instant did not associate the name with herself. She had served each guest and was now back to him. She turned her head and looked down at him uneasily.

"Sit here, Raushana," Hasan said fluffing up a pillow between himself and Al Rakashi.

Jimena sat down, meeting the eyes of Hasan's guests each in turn, but avoiding those of Estiano, that seemed to cut through the space between them like a sword.

"This is a *new* maiden in your household, Abu l Hasan," Al Rakashi smiled, leaning across Jimena to speak to Hasan. "Tell me, Saíd, where the slave market is that sells such merchandise as this, and I will give you half my fortune."

Hasan's facial muscles tightened. He did not return Al Rakashi's smile, but was polite, "That must remain my secret, Saíd, a secret worth much more than mere material wealth, do you not agree?"

"Indeed, indeed," Al Rakashi purred, a hand reaching out to pat Jimena's knee admiringly. Then his voice deepened as he once more turned Jimena's face to him with a finger, his eyes slightly accusing, "You are a Christian. Am I correct?"

Fear tied Jimena's tongue. She did not dare answer such a query. She clearly recalled Elvira's warnings. Helplessly she stared into the searching, questioning eyes of Al Rakashi.

"A pity," Al Rakashi whispered, letting loose of her chin, tapping her on the end of the nose with a forefinger as if she were a pretty but naughty child. "One as lovely as yourself deserves a religion of equal beauty. Surely those in paradise that write the pages of our destinies have erred, delivering such a lovely child into the world to be called by the vile name of Christian. Do you not know, child, that there is but *one* God? That the likes of you should worship pagan idols, dead, inanimate things, such as a cross, Allah forbid. You must come to the True Faith, my child. Allah will welcome you, for he loves beauty well."

"Tell me," Hasan said loudly turning to the wali of Malaga, "is all well with your brother, the sultan of Madrid? I wonder if he has successfully avoided annihilation by the Christians who prowl his borders?" He well knew the answer to his own question, had clutched at a straw in order to swiftly change the subject; the conversation had become dangerously centered upon Jimena.

The talk followed Hasan's lead and Jimena heaved a relieved sigh, settling down into her pillows to listen. Her eyes moved around the room curiously. The quiet conversation between Hasan and his guests brought to mind a bitter comparison. She vividly recalled her wedding day, the touch of drunken, hot hands upon her, a girl chased down the length of a table and a king falling into unconsciousness before his company. Hasan and his guests drank the same juice but it was sipped, not guzzled, and not one was drunk. They spoke to each other with a polite congeniality and dignity. What a vast difference there was in people.

"Ah, Hasan, I think that you are a sentimental man, beyond that which is normal for we emotional Arabs," Al Rakashi said with a pleasant smile.

Hasan laughed and refilled his wine glass from the pitcher near his elbow, "Yes, Al Rakashi, I am sentimental when we speak of Andalus. I love this land with a passion no woman could muster within me. I cry out to Allah in my prayers each day to save us from the wolves who howl outside our doors. My heart breaks that no Caliph sits in the palace to lead us and to save us from self-destruction."

"Destruction?" a man queried from Hasan's right. "Do you

believe that we will be conquered? I cannot envision any power in the world today capable of destroying Andalus. No, there is no such power."

"Anarchy is our enemy," Hasan answered sadly. "Our land is being destroyed by lack of central leadership. What do we have today? More than twenty independent dynasties; Seville and our beloved Cordova are separate republics. We war against each other, destroy one another and even hire Christian plunderers of the north to do a part of our killing for us. Can you honestly say we are *not* destroying ourselves by refusing to join hands against the Christian? The streets of Andalus run red with the blood of our people. Where is the peace our fathers knew? Where is the unity of yesterday?"

"Ah, Abu l Hasan," Al Rakashi sighed, "why this concern for the land as a whole when your position in it is in no danger? What is it to you that many kings rule in the place of one, as long as the gold in your own coffers keeps multiplying and your bed is soft, shared by the most lovely of companions? What is this strange love you have for Andalus? I care only for those things which are mine. I find much good in Cordova and have all that a high civilization has to offer a man: dignity, education, comfort, and wealth. And I will possess all these things for the rest of my days. After I am dead it will not matter if there is an Andalus or not. Not to me."

Hasan leaned his elbow upon one knee, and swirled the wine around and around in the crystal glass he held in his hand, trying to find the best answer to Al Rakashi's question. He raised his eyes, and he looked from guest to guest; they were all politely waiting for his reply. In their eyes he saw amusement and some curiosity. Only in the eyes of his friend Estiano did he see a light of understanding, and he gave the man a warm, thankful smile. "Allow me to change my plea, then," he said at last. "Say that I cry for the people, the people of the whole world. I believe Andalus is the solution for humanity, for the world. The ordinary man has found himself at last in this land of ours. Where else in the world could a maker of steel own his own house, have a private garden and pool, pay taxes of less than ten percent, enjoy public parks and provide his wives and children with more than mere subsistence? And where, today, or at any time in the past, could this average man so feed his hungering mind that he rises, through the magic of his own intelligence, far above the animal that he is?" His voice was becoming louder, and he waved his arm in graceful arcs to emphasize his words, "Out there beyond our borders there are untold millions of animals held captive in a veritable dungeon of ignorance and poverty. We, only three hundred and fifty years past, were no less savage. If we could progress this far, so might they. Yes, it is the *world* I would save, all humanity I would free from bondage. But to do so, Andalus must remain alive, must be the lamp amidst the darkness for the miserable ones outside."

"But, Hasan," the graybeard next to Estiano said, "no civilization can live *forever*. The way of Troy, Athens, and Carthage will be the fate of our Andalus, as it is for all civilizations, past, present, or to come. When Andalus passes away, so will the light you speak of. The man shrugged and threw his hands into the air. *"Kuzia Fakan,"* he sighed. "It was decreed by destiny; so must it come to pass."

"Why? Why must every civilization die? If it is good for all mankind, why can it not live forever, as immortal as the mountains and oceans? Will someone please answer this question, as my mind provides me with no answer."

The wali of Malaga cleared his throat loudly to capture attention. When all eyes were upon him, he began in a voice quivering with the hesitance of old age, "My heart rejoices, Abu l Hasan, at your words of love for this land. I share your affection. Long ago, for I am a very old man and have seen the beginnings of the destruction you speak of, I surrendered the dream of everlasting life for Andalus. Perhaps, I have told myself, a civilization is like a human body; in its infancy it is fragile and weak in its struggles for maturity; vigorous in its youth; dymanic and powerful in adulthood; weak and tired in its old age, decaying from within. As the beating heart of a man falters and stops, so does the pulsating heart of a nation. Andalus is three hundred and fifty years old; the dying process has begun. But this land will have its reward, its eternal life, in the pages of history. I think that that is all that can be reasonably expected. And perhaps those pages, read in the ages to come, will shed the light you dream of, Abu l Hasan; *Inshallah* —if Allah pleases."

"Then I cannot be called a reasonable man, Saíd," Hasan argued. "We cannot always dream in terms of ages to come. Eventually we must do today what we so haphazardly pass off to future generations. Our Andalus is what Allah planned for the human soul. We must preserve it. We must!"

"Abu l Hasan," another guest said, "I most humbly beg your forgiveness for this rude interruption of your profound and enlightening observations, but I must speak. I believe that you have hit upon the answer to your question, your searching, when you speak of *Allah*. To that ugly world outside the civilized nations, Abu l Hasan, there is no Allah. There is Jehovah and there is Zeus, Vishnu, Amen-Ra, and Baal. There is Buddha and the prophet Jesus, but there is *not* our beloved Muhammed. This then is your destroying factor and its name is religion. Remove the belief in Muhammed from this land and perhaps you will at the same time remove that which will cause them to destroy all they see when they come. The priests to the north keep the minds of their people in bonds of ignorance; it is calculated, in this way they more easily control the masses. They teach each child that our beloved prophet is the personification of the Devil. Give those savages you speak of a volume written by Hippocrates or Aristotle, and they will spit upon it and burn it, for you, the giver of the gift, are an infidel."

"One religion, then, is this the answer?"

"Or none at all."

"Impossible."

"Indeed, impossible. That is why Andalus *will* die. Not you, nor I, nor any sincere lover of mankind can prevent the hate that instinctively grows within the souls of men for that which is different from themselves, even as the white detests the black, the ugly the beautiful, the miserable the happy. Until men's minds meet, sharing ideologies of all natures, the world will be in flames, Hell rising up from the depths, casting its shadows of war, pestilence, and murder over the land. The peace of our fathers, you say. What peace? They fought their wars, the single difference was that they were always successful, were never threatened by annihilation as we are today. As the good wali of Malaga has said, Abu l Hasan, do not expect so much from life; be more reasonable."

"I concede," Hasan said, shrugging defeatedly, "but it seems reasonable enough to me that you would all wish to preserve what we have—at least long enough to cover the time span of your own lives?"

"Of course."

"Then we must lift our asses from our pillows and stand up and fight for what we wish to preserve. We must band together against the Christians, and cease this warring amongst ourselves. Alphonso means to press the reconquest. He is *not* his father! I warn you all, we are in mortal danger."

"And what, Abu l Hasan," Al Rakashi said impatiently, "what do you propose to do? Will you go personally to the sultan of Guadalajara and demand that he ignore Rodrigo Diaz, who breathes like a gigantic dragon against the back of his neck? Will you also tell him to forget that the sultan of Calatayud is his enemy, having stolen that part of his land left to him by his father? And Maktadir of Zaragossa, pray tell him to drive El Cid from his doorstep, the man who protects him and fights his battles for him. No, Abu l Hasan, there is no solution. We must protect and defend our own republic of Cordova and let the rest solve their own problems. Alphonso cannot in his lifetime take and rule the entire peninsula. It is an impossibility and we all know it. No, it will be his great, or great-great-grandson who will have that final and inglorious honor."

"Ach!" Hasan spat out, throwing his hands into the air in despair, "thus do you deliver us into the hands of beasts; thus do you give to that vile Diaz more power, clearing his path of all obstacles. You will not fight him. He is victorious before the battle *begins*!"

Jimena's forehead throbbed, a sharp pain shooting from the back of her head through her eyes. She had listened eagerly at first, enjoying the fact that fear had been put into Hasan's heart by her own people. She envisioned the armies of Alphonso storming the walls of Cordova, infidels fleeing like frightened animals. Alphonso would see her among the prisoners, and oh, his face would come alight with joy. Leaping down from his horse he would rush to her side and gather her to his breast, comforting her and wiping away her tears with a tender fingertip. Jimena Gomez would return to Castile triumphantly with the victorious Christian army and all would marvel at her strength, that she had survived so well the brutalities and vulgarities, the degradation and corruption of the Infidel world. Then she would speed to the monastery of La Coruña and take a beautiful, golden child into her arms. God in Heaven, how she ached to see, to touch and to kiss little Urracca once again. She would be a pretty child, she was certain. She tried to recall the miniature, sweet face that had been so close to her own that last day at Gormaz, but she could not see it. There was only emotion, a deep, hungry yearning to see the child of her flesh. But, in truth, that child she had so loved no longer existed; she would see a strange little face that she would not know unless identified by someone else. All dreams of joy melted away into depression and fear.

Then Al Rakashi had said the name Rodrigo Diaz and Jimena's heart had begun to pound, the blood rushing hot through her body, a pressure building against the veins of her forehead and neck. She had been unwillingly reminded of brutalities far exceeding any yet seen or experienced in Islam. It was confusing. Her mind leaped from country to country, from one man to the other. In truth, what was corruption . . . brutality? Each race of men placed these name tags upon those separated from them by racial or religious barriers. Who was the barbarian; who the infidel? She repeated her previous daydream, but from the opposite viewpoint. Alphonso again stormed the walls of Cordova. She was brought out and away from the other prisoners, but there was a great fire now and all those she had come to know these four years were burning and screaming as they were forced into the flames. Acacia was dead, Hasan, Al Rakashi, Nuzhab, and Elvira. God in Heaven, if Alphonso could be called a barbarian, then *all* men justly deserved the title. Was there no such thing as a truly righteous man? Was there no real truth the mind could cling to?

Jimena glanced quickly across the table. Estiano was staring hard at her but she could not read his expression. Was it sympathy, or a warning? She did not dare look at Hasan. She sat, face hot, hands tight together. Then, when she thought she could bear it no longer, she was startled by a warm, unexpected touch. A hand had reached out, firmly pressing down upon her clasped fists. When she looked up into Hasan's eyes, she saw both severity and gentleness there. He understood her pain, but warned against any foolish outburst. She twisted her mouth into an insincere smile and looked away from him, praying the conversation would end. Let them speak of anything, anyone—but not about Rodrigo Diaz.

Hasan let loose of Jimena's hands and slowly rose from his pillows, stretching his arms and yawning as a signal to his guests that the evening was at an end. Politely he bowed and extended his right hand to each man as they said their good-byes, "Heaven deprive us not of thee, pray I see thee often," he said to each, until Estiano stood before him. "Friend," Hasan whispered, holding Estiano's hand in his, "I saw in your sweet eyes tonight a pain as great as my own. We have a common mistress, you and I; we both love our Andalus. Thank you for your understanding, my friend."

Estiano's eyes moved down to where Jimena sat with her eyes cast away from him. She would not look upon him; she despised him. The pain of that hate showed in his eyes when he looked back to Hasan and said, "Yes, Hasan, we share a love, but I believe that I can love her even more deeply than you, having known so well that dark dungeon of which you can only speak."

"Truth, Estiano. You most probably speak the truth." Hasan pumped Estiano's hand affectionately, "Allah be with thee, Estiano; I will see thee in the morning."

Jimena watched Estiano Antolinez walk slowly from the room, his feet seeming reluctant, dragging against the thick carpet. She thought that no other person in the world had had so powerful an influence over her destiny. If he had made only one mistake everything would have been so different. In those huge, ugly hands had rested her fate . . . and Rodrigo's, too. Even little Urracca's and Hasan's.

When Estiano was gone, Jimena was alone in the room with Hasan and the quiet, patient Nuzhab. She glanced over to the girl, who sat within touching distance of her. Nuzhab was watching Hasan's face expectantly and did not move from her pillow. Jimena became more uncomfortable by the moment. Hasan stood above her, staring down at her just as Nuzhab stared up at him. Jimena watched only her fidgeting fingers. The silence was unbearable. She thought there must be some way to leave without speaking, without causing Hasan to speak.

"I excuse you, Nuzhab," Hasan said softly, "sleep well, lovely one, sleep well."

Jimena heard his voice as from a distance and when Nuzhab rose to leave, panic caught hold in her throat. She opened her mouth to call out to the departing girl, but no sound emerged.

"Oh," Jimena gasped, startled by the gentle touch of Hasan's fingers upon her upraised hand.

"Do not be afraid. I will not harm you." His voice was black velvet, his eyes kind and at the same time wary.

Jimena yanked her hand from his touch as if burned, but the warmth of his fingers remained. She closed her eyes tight to hold back tears.

"Raushana," he said, "I humbly apologize to you for the anguish you suffered this evening. I had hoped that the days of punishment had come to an end, but I see that that will be difficult." He kneeled down and arranged a number of pillows into a couch, settling himself down well away from her. He reached up and removed the gold turban from his head. Thoughtfully he ran his jeweled fingers through his hair that fell down in waves to his shoulders.

Jimena began to relax when it became obvious he intended

no vile advances. Out of the corner of her eye she watched him lounging there, gazing upon her own profile.

"Why did you serve? I did not request it. I was surprised, pleasantly, of course, when you made such an unexpected entrance."

She sucked in a deep breath, and replied, "I—Acacia said that it was my place as a woman of your house to be useful. I . . ." her voice gave way and her eyes roved over the walls, the table, and her own fluttering hands, finally managing to meet Hasan's. His eyes were like magnets that pulled her gaze into his and held it fast. There was a tremendous extending of himself, that self moving across the space between them, whispering what he would not speak. *You are beautiful. I think that I could love you one day, Jimena Gomez. Did you love your husband? Is it possible that such as you could love such as he? Ah, but send me one inviting glance, one wistful, affectionate smile—and my arms will reach out and entwine you. Do not be afraid of me, Splendid One—I would only love you tenderly, in compensation for the pain I have caused you.*

Jimena wrenched her eyes away from his, as she suffered a conglomeration of emotions—desire, fear, repulsion, and panic.

She must speak and break this spell. She blurted out, "I *begged* Acacia to let me serve. I thought it would be exciting, something to shatter the boredom."

"Ah," he smiled, "now that is better. But I would have you know that, since you are a woman of my house only by law and not in fact, if you understand my meaning, you are not expected to perform such duties. I cannot assure you that the conversations you hear will be free of unhappy reminders."

Jimena fought against a thousand pleas that formed in her mind. She wanted to cry out, Send me back to my husband, for the love of God and my beloved child. My soul teeters on the edge of a precipice—I will fall to destruction, into the dark abyss of God-forbidden sin and punishment, if you do not release me. But that locked and guarded door of only months past kept her silent.

"My lord, I would beg a consideration of you," she said, compromising.

"And what is that?"

"Now that my tutor has been discharged, I would like to be allowed a daily visit to the university."

"What?" Hasan exclaimed in amazement, sitting up.

"I would study at the college," she replied shakily.

"And what subject would you choose?"

"I . . . I am not certain. Perhaps—"

"We have an excellent course in *comparative religions*." His tone was sober but tinged with humor.

"That subject sounds quite interesting, Saíd," she said defensively. "I would like such a course."

Hasan laughed heartily. "Do you mean to say you are willing to stake your precious faith against all the arguments of a hundred different beliefs? Do you know it is a sin before your God to read such books as would be given you for such a course?"

"My faith is not so insecure," Jimena exclaimed indignantly, "that I need fear the arguments of misguided *fools!*"

"Bravo! Thou art a worthy Christian, Raushana. Jehovah will welcome you to his vast, underpopulated heaven. He has destroyed in the fires so many of his own that I imagine as pure a soul as yours will be a miraculous sight to his angry, vindictive eyes."

Jimena leaped to her feet, "Infidel!" she shouted, "I wish I were as worthy as I *might* be! If I could enter a Christian church again and regularly make confession I might be worthy of His almighty, tender mercies!"

"*Alhomdalillah!* Go. Go to church, woman. There is no law in Islam that denies you the right to your own religion. Allah hath said, 'Jews and Christians who believe in God and live good lives shall receive their reward from the Most High.' Seek out a church. A servant will escort you. I have no objection."

"Oh," she said flatly, speechless.

Hasan rose and moved across the distance between them, putting out a hand to her. "Come, Raushana, the hour is late."

Subdued, Jimena placed her hand in his and allowed him to pull her to her feet.

"I will accompany you to your quarters. You will need much rest this night, since you are to begin a course of study on the morrow. I will knock on your door the hour after morning prayers and you may ride with me to the university."

Jimena lay awake for hours consumed by dread, rather than joy, in reaction to Hasan's unexpected generosity. Church. It was over four years since she had entered a house of God, made confession, and taken communion. The dark, shadowed church of Gormaz came clearly etched into her mind. She saw Don Pedro standing at the lectern with his arms flailing about in zealous fury; she felt the dark curtain of the confessional all about her, heard the voice of the bishop comforting, warning,

threatening, dealing out penances for the petty sins of her childhood. Then the voice of another priest who mouthed words
that bound Jimena Gomez to Rodrigo Diaz forever, tied them
together for eternity with the constricting, unbreakable bonds of
religious sanction. My body and my soul belongs to Rodrigo
Diaz, she thought, I must never forget this fact. I can give sexual love only to my husband, and then reservedly. I must confess to all the evil thoughts I have allowed to play in my mind,
to the pleasure I took in them, to the wavering of my faith in
the True Religion. I must hold fast to Truth, must never lean
toward lust in this land even if it means for the rest of my life.

Jimena was swept up on a cloud of good intentions as she
desperately tried to maintain the image of herself etched in her
religious, wishful mind; she would like to be a saint like the
Virgin, with a serene, pure countenance. Only noble, sacred
thoughts would enter her head and temptations would not exist,
because anyone as perfect as herself could not be tempted by
any man, circumstance or philosophy. Her body would never
again writhe with desire.

Abruptly Jimena dropped back to earth. Church? Confession would be the worst of it; she could not imagine speaking
of the sinful lust that plagued her night after night or her blas-
phemous quaking of the heart whenever she was under Hasan's
gaze.

"Holy Mary, Mother of God," Jimena whispered to the
shadows that danced upon the luxurious tiles in her room,
"help me!"

In an elegantly outfitted litter Jimena rode stiff and silent
beside Abu l Hasan along the highway that stretched from the
suburb of Al Zohra to the walled city of Cordova. She was delighted by the luxurious scenes slowly passing her window, but
in the distance mountains kissed the sky; they were a surrounding, impassable wall between herself and Castile. Hopelessly she
thought of somehow getting a message into friendly hands, but
who in this land would take her side against this imposing lord
beside her? Not even Elvira, as devoted a friend as she was,
would consider disloyalty to Hasan. Elvira had made it quite
clear that she considered any wish to return to Castile nothing
short of foolishness on Jimena's part; not even a child was
worth that enormous a sacrifice.

Jimena tried to imagine what this "college" she approached
would be like. She would walk among infidels, speak with
them, learn with them; it was too bewildering.

Suddenly Hasan leaned forward and said to the driver, "Halt, Kasim."

Jimena gasped as she followed Hasan's prideful arm gesture, her eye falling upon the expansive view from his side of the carriage. Impulsively she threw open her door and jumped to the stone highway, running around the vehicle to stand entranced in the wind on the crest of a hill.

Outstretched before and below her in the valley rested a queen of cities, unreal in its magnificence, something straight out of an Arab tale of fancy. Until now the Quadalquivir River had only existed for her as a fragment seen from the windows of her suite, but from here it was the shade of pale emeralds and it twisted around the city like a necklace of precious jewels. Pomegranate domes darted the sun back into her eyes in lightning bolts. Spired towers and the ravishing colors of housetop roofs intermingled to create the effect of a rainbow over the entire city.

Trembling before such a sight, Jimena thought, From a dark, narrow, and colorless world I have somehow come to this fantastically lovely place; it is surely a mirage, the stuff of dreams and reserved for Paradise.

Hasan, well pleased, sat patiently back into the carriage seat, watching the woman closely until she returned to again sit beside him. They rode on in silence through the city gate, along narrow streets shadowed by overhanging, bare-faced houses, past city parks where children played and adults lounged amiably, past the polo arena and to the sprawling, vine-smothered university buildings and grounds.

Stepping nervously from the carriage, Jimena cried out as icy water dropped from above into the hollow of her bosom.

Hasan laughed and explained, pointing to the blooming flower basket swinging over her head, "The men have just watered them."

Jimena, still extremely uneasy in his presence, glanced shyly away. She asked, "What is that odd post from which the basket hangs?"

"A lamp post. At four the lamplighters will begin their stampede through the city to light the oil, and it is a sight to behold, Cordova illuminated like a star in the heaven of this earth."

"Ah . . . " Jimena exhaled, unable to imagine such a spectacle.

A few students in brightly colored silk robes, their beards tenderly combed and clipped, whisked past Hasan and Jimena on the white-graveled pathway that led through the grounds to the central building. A young man acknowledged Hasan with an abrupt bow from the waist. Jimena nervously followed her master's quick step, entering the awesome structure with wide eyes.

Hasan halted his step in the center of the cavernous, high-ceilinged lobby and faced Jimena with the question, "Now, which course intrigues you most, eh?"

She kept her eye upon the ruby glittering on his turban at the center of his forehead and twisted her mouth thoughtfully. She said doubtfully, "The art of illumination . . . printing, could I learn that in this house?"

He eyed her with amusement, then swept around and strode across the tile floor, his linen skirts rustling softly. She trotted nervously behind until they reached wide and swinging doors, whereupon Hasan halted and extended his arm for her to enter.

"Estiano, I have a new student for your class," Hasan said with a raised eyebrow and penetrating glance into his friend's alarmed eyes. With a look, he said—at your ease, Estiano, all is well.

Jimena recoiled at the sight of Estiano standing at his easel, paint and lampblack smeared upon his bulbous nose and craggy forehead.

Estiano rose as if drugged, staring at Jimena. He blinked, then whipped forward to clutch Hasan's elbow, dragging him aside. "What *is* this?" he hissed. "Have you gone mad?"

Hasan grinned broadly and leaned forward to whisper, "Delicious, is she not, eh? We clutched up pig iron from the northern desert and it has become pure silver, mmm?"

"You allow her to roam free, to bring hell fire down upon us? Think upon who she is, man!"

"She is meek and is in fear of me and of being again locked into her rooms; her lips are sealed. Look upon those lips. Like two garnets—"

"Enough!" Estiano barked. "For God, spare me your turgid romanticisms." Then to Jimena, who hovered back against the doors, "Can you draw a straight line, eh? Well? Speak up. Can you offer me any hope of success with you or shall I be expected to do no more than *amuse* you?"

"I will take another class," Jimena said shakily to Hasan, swallowing bitter tears.

But before either man could comment, the doors behind Jimena exploded open and a flood of young people poured noisily into the room, scrambling for easels and talking all at once. Hasan shrugged bemusedly, strode to Jimena and patted her hand paternally, "I will call for you at three," he said, and was gone.

"What is your name?" Estiano snapped at Jimena in a voice for all to hear, warning her with his eyes again.

She thought to run, to scream out her hatred for him, but twenty young men were now quietly studying her. She murmured weakly, "Raushana, Saíd."

"Sit there," he jabbed a finger at the easel to the right of his own that faced the class. "Abdullah, fetch ink and pens for the lady. Today, this phrase will occupy our pens, 'Dear is Plato, but dearer still is truth.' First lightly in charcoal. Do not touch pen to it till I have examined it. Proceed."

Chapter
✠ *FIVE* ✠

Summer came, then moved on, leaving behind an earth decorated with the fading petals of a million flowers. The skies that had been clear blue and cloudless for so many months, now dressed themselves in mantles of gray and white that took the shapes of a flock of sheep, a giant bird or an angel with outspread wings—always moving and changing shape to become something else even as the eye watched. It was a time of change, when nature was never content but always striving for perfection, erasing what she had painted yesterday to draw a new design for tomorrow. There was not a leaf, a clod, a dream, a soul in the world that did not move with this pattern that was and always would be the vital essence of life.

Jimena did not fully comprehend the forces at work within and around her. She noticed, of course, that the leaves were falling from the trees. She felt the sharpness in the air and knew that summer was gone. But the change taking place within herself was not apparent, because the process was so gradual and indistinct. The days moved so swiftly by that she was barely able to keep pace with daily rides to the university, luncheons with Elvira at a small inn nearby, the return home to hours of patient, intense study, then the evening meal in the harem with Nuzhab and Acacia and the inevitable games of chess and backgammon afterwards. Each night when she dropped into bed, sleep overtook her within seconds.

Jimena followed this pattern of life unaware that she was gradually becoming something other than she was before; it would be a long time before she would look in her mirror and see a completely new person. Not really contemplating the matter, she went on living, believing that she was still the same Jimena Diaz that had been stolen and displaced.

Jimena leaped agilely down from the horse's back, giving

the animal a swift, affectionate slap on the hindquarter. She watched the black servant leading him away to the stables, but her mind was far away. She sighed, then quickly turned and hurried through the open gate, moving swiftly through the maze of stone walls, then through a second gate that opened into the entrance garden. Gaily she let her fingers dance over the hedge of blooming oleander that lined the walk, knocking the white and pink petals to the earth, so weakly did they cling to what was left of summer. Humming a bright tune, she jauntily kicked off her velvet slippers and entered the house. It was very quiet inside, as it was every afternoon at this time. The manservants would have just finished their prayers and would be napping in their quarters, resting after a morning of cleaning, gathering new energy for the late day's tasks of meal preparations, the watering of the vast lawns and the killing of fowl and lambs for next day's table. A pungent, tangy aroma could be detected over the usual heavy perfume in the air. It was the kettle of wine boiling on the fire in the cook room. Jimena rushed up the long open staircase, taking the steps two and three at a time, her bare, pink-toenailed feet making a soft padding noise upon the carpeting. She rushed across the wide corridor, pulled apart the heavy draperies, and let her glance quickly scan the room. "Zarífah? Nuzhab?" she called. "Is no one about?"

"Here. Here, Raushana. On the pavilion."

Jimena smiled and walked across the room, pushing aside silk curtains as she passed through the different sections. The first partition belonged to Zarífah; upon her bed, piled one upon the other, there were more than thirty dolls. Zarífah collected the figurines, treating them like the children she had never had but so desired. Jimena stopped at the foot of Zarífah's bed, and her hand reached out to pick up a tiny-golden-haired baby doll. She felt a sudden constriction of her throat muscles. Quickly she replaced the doll and moved on.

As she passed through Nuzhab's quarter, Jimena hesitated again. Dear, gentle Nuzhab, her favorite of all Hasan's women, had been married to him nearly fifteen years. Once she had lived alone in these quarters, but now she cheerfully shared her man with four others. An amazing display of that elusive virtue—acceptance. Nuzhab did not foolishly cry out against what could not be altered, but moved with the waves of her existence as a ship sails into and not against the rolling seas. Nuzhab collected books as Zarífah did dolls, and had neatly placed her collection upon shelves beside her bed. She never wearied of reading, saying this was her only escape. But she was quick to deny there was anything to escape *from*, would not admit that her life was anything less than perfection.

A room was marked off by draperies between Nuzhab's quarters and those of Acacia, and at the end of it was an archway that led to the balcony. With a quick step Jimena joined her friends. "What? Chess so early in the day? Who is the victor, or need I inquire?"

Zarífah was leaning on one elbow, lying stretched out on her pillows with her forehead creased, her mouth twisted and caught at the side by her teeth. She did not look up, just grunted disagreeably. Nuzhab sat upon her heels across from Zarífah, glaring at the girl, her tiny fingers thumping impatiently against a thigh.

Nuzhab threw her hands into the air in exaggerated fury and cried, "Raushana! Zarífah has been as you see her now for over an hour. By Allah, I shall slit her throat one day, I swear."

Jimena laughed and sat down upon a pillow between the two women, taking in the positions on the board, realizing quickly why Zarífah studied it so grimly. It was impossible. Zarífah would not get loose from this one. But then again, she just might. "Nuzhab . . ." she whispered, not wanting to disturb the thinking Zarífah, "look." She held a book out to Nuzhab, almost reverently.

"Oh," Nuzhab cried enthusiastically, "you have completed it." She turned the bright yellow volume over and over in her hands, then quickly leafed through the pages. "Beautiful, Raushana. You are truly an artist. How did you ever learn so quickly?"

"My teacher said that there is not an imperfection in a single letter," Jimena said proudly, reaching out for the precious volume. "I wish I could frame it and hang it in some way upon my wall, I am so proud of it. You really think it good, Nuzhab? Do you *really*?

"Really, Raushana. It is a work of inspiration. Did you place each pearl upon the cover or did someone else do that work for you?"

"*I* did! It took weeks. My eyes were near popping from my head. But I persisted. There are two hundred and twenty-six pearls, to be exact."

"Ach!" The cry came from a suddenly upright Zarífah. Her thin right arm moved and she calmly lifted a piece and then triumphantly set it down. "There," she exclaimed, a self-satisfied smirk on her face as she looked up to the two whose eyes were now upon her.

"*Alhomdalillah!*" Nuzhab screeched. "Give me a knife and I will cut my throat, *then* you will be sorry, Zarífah, for once again making a fool of me."

After a hearty laugh the three settled down and leaned back into their pillows. Jimena thought that she had best go to her room to study before the evening meal, but she remained where she was, gazing up to the sky, watching the changing shapes of the clouds as they swept by. A bird twittered musically above her and she looked over to see it sitting cockily upon a branch of the magnolia tree that spread its arms out over the pavilion.

"Hasan returns within the month; had you heard, Raushana?"

"Really, Zarífah?" Jimena responded disinterestedly.

"I can see how overjoyed you are, Raushana. Even if you do not care, you could at least be pleased for *us*."

"I am. I am, Zarífah."

Zarífah slithered over on her stomach and placed her delicate chin into a pillow, gazing up at Jimena. "Really, I do not see how you continue year after year, Raushana, without intercourse. My intimates ache so that I swear I shall die of it if Hasan does not return soon. And my turn is *first*," she cried, shaking a warning finger in Nuzhab's face, her eyes dancing with amusement.

Jimena frowned, displeased at being reminded of what she tried not to think about. She forced a weak smile and said, "I have my aches and pains, Zarífah—I have them."

"Well, if it is men you cannot abide there is a charming member of this household of our own sex who would gladly oblige you."

"Zarífah," Nuzhab giggled.

"It is the truth. What is so dreadful? To each his own, I always say. It would certainly fill in those empty nights when. . . ."

"Hush," Nuzhab hissed, "she will *hear* you."

"So, she hears me. If Hasan does not return soon, I swear I shall seek her out. Hah. A good jest. I have been fighting her off for weeks."

Jimena felt her face burning. She would never become used to such frankness. "Where is Al Síd now," she asked, deliberately changing the subject. "Is he at Valencia still?"

"No," Nuzhab answered, "he is at Denia. Before he returns, he will travel through the south to Seville, and then come home."

"What does he *do*, I ask you," Zarífah pouted, "that he

cannot take us with him? Surely our Hasan is not so intense about affairs of state that he needs not the comfort of our passions?"

"Oh, Zarífah, your mind is always occupied with passion." Nuzhab scolded. "Is there nothing in this world more important to you?"

"Nothing. Absolutely nothing!"

"Well, for our Hasan there *is*. Gone these many months, he carries with him a grand dream and the hope that Andalus might be saved from the barbarians." Nuzhab turned to Jimena seriously . . . "No offense intended, Raushana, but I pray he so stirs up those complacent idiots to the north that they gather up as a swarm of bees to devour the beasts that threaten our borders. It is ghastly when you think they might come as far as our Cordova. I tremble at the thought." She threw her hands up excitedly. "Raushana, does it not frighten you to think you might be forced to live such a life again? How did you bear it, living amidst such—Ah, Raushana! I did not mean . . ." Nuzhab looked with sad, regretful eyes at Jimena's retreating back. "For the love of Allah, Zarífah, why did you not clap a hand over my foolish mouth. How thoughtless of me. She has a *child* in Castile!"

Jimena threw herself down on her bed and heaved a deep sigh. She reached over to the low table and chose an apple from the bowl of fruit and held it in her hand high over her head, turning it around and around as her thoughts wandered. Poor, sweet Nuzhab, she was probably suffering such pangs of guilt. Strange, that sudden need to run away when she was asked how she could bear living in Castile. It was not a ridiculous question. How *had* she borne it so long? No. Truly, life in Castile had not been *all* mean. It would be difficult for Nuzhab to believe it, but she enjoyed some quite fond memories. Her mind fondly settled upon the better moments of the past. She remembered Urracca; dark and lovely, gay and tragic. Pleasant afternoons spent playing games like small children, the talks, the confidences and that wonderful excursion to Santiago. Urracca was the best friend she had ever had and Jimena missed her very much. And Alphonso. Imagine, Alphonso such a mighty king now that this entire country was in turmoil, they were so frightened of him. There was even talk of importing the armies of Africa to help hold back the advancing king of Castile.

Of course there was Rodrigo, too. The better part of the

past did not include him, but in all her recollections of yesterday his image appeared. He was even more feared in Andalus than Alphonso. It was said, and Jimena shuddered to think of it, that Rodrigo burned all Arab prisoners alive on vast funeral pyres and sometimes roasted one on a spit to be eaten, so that the very mention of his name or the sight of him riding before his men destroyed his enemies with fear, rendering his sword unnecessary. How difficult it was to envision this fearsome warrior whose name was on the tongue of every Arab in Cordova as the husband of her past . . . and of forever.

Jimena rolled over and took a huge bite from the apple, chewing viciously, feeling a strange anger churning within her. Life was simply stupid. How could she be married to someone who thought her dead, who was hundreds of miles away, whom she would never see again, most likely, as long as she lived? Ridiculous. And why did God concern himself as to whether Jimena Gomez, tiny speck that she was upon the vast window of his vision, coupled with a man or did not. Surely all the complicated problems that must arise in the keeping of Heaven and Earth according to His desire—even the most *trifling* problems of the universe—must be vastly more important to Him than the insignificant temptations of Jimena Gomez. Jimena, she said to herself . . . you are becoming cynical and your mind is heavily burdened with sinful thoughts. Why, dear self, have you not sought out a church? Are you afraid? Yes, you are afraid. All the bleakness of yesterday might return along with the confessional. You are afraid of the penances, of the mortifying of your flesh for the sanctification of your soul, of all the demands that will be forced upon you. You are deathly afraid that the faith of your childhood will not satisfy you, now that you have a mind able to think and reason, which might leave you floating face down in an ocean of nothingness, of atheism.

Jimena did not study that day, but spent the entire afternoon in discussion with herself, never coming to any conclusions. That evening Nuzhab received her apology and she received Nuzhab's. All remained peaceful and serene among the women of Hasan's house.

The bishop halted in the middle of a sentence, his pale eyes narrowing as Elvira Rodriguez entered the room. He felt the flesh at the back of his neck crawl, and he cautioned himself about hate; but this was a heretic he was certain God could forgive him despising, even as God himself despised all infidels.

Revolting woman. A demon's soul glittered behind those green eyes, and she was allowed to roam free, to contaminate all who came in contact with her. If she lived in Christendom, she would have been burned alive long ago for the crimes she had committed against God. It was agony for him to stand looking upon this damnable woman, powerless to do anything except move away as she approached, recoiling as if she were an enemy he was in fear of, playing the role of coward.

"Estiano," Elvira said hesitantly, "I interrupt you. I am sorry, I . . ."

"No. No, Elvira. Come, sit beside me. The bishop and I will have concluded our business shortly."

As Elvira moved across the room the bishop backed even farther away, making no attempt to cover his abhorrence. He came to rest ten feet away, leaning against a shelf of manuscripts, his hands shoved up into the full sleeves of his robe as he glowered at Estiano.

"Actually, Bishop," Estiano said, turning from Elvira, "I think you would be more pleased with another bookmaker, one who is a Christian. The work done here is, you must remember, for the library and the university. I only take these special orders as an accommodation to certain friends."

"I know, Estiano," the bishop interrupted with an impatient shake of his head, "you need not inform me of matters I am already fully aware of. It is not the workmanship I complain about. God knows that is why I come to you, you are the best in Cordova. It is the tampering, the deliberate defiling of a sacred book that—"

"Bishop, I have told you, over and over again, these men do not have any reverence for your Bible." Estiano gave Elvira a quick glance, then placed a thumb between his teeth, chewing at it and trying not to get angry. "Come now, Bishop, take your work to another, and we will both be happier for it, eh?"

The bishop was dumb with indignation. His eyes moved back and forth from Elvira to Estiano and his facial muscles drew tight, his jowls quivering. Why? Why were men such fools? There they sat, two condemned sinners, and they were not afraid, could not be dissuaded. But it was his responsibility, his sacred duty as a bishop of the Faith to bring them both back to Jesus Christ. But how? He could do nothing if they would not listen. The Christians of Andalus were beginning to forget their own language. Only two days past he had had occasion to visit the home of Pero Ansuras, a weaver of silk, and when he spoke to the man's children in Spanish they laughed, jabbering in the dialect of the infidel. Pero's wife, Maria, wore paint upon her face and bracelets about her ankles. It was almost more than he could bear, but "Blessed are they who are persecuted for righteousness' sake, for theirs is the kingdom of heaven." Without this comfort, the bishop thought, I could not go on.

"Estiano? Could you help me with . . ." Jimena stood in the doorway to the scriptorium, her face spotted with green and black ink, a heavy canvas apron covering her silk gown. She hoped she had not interrupted something important.

Estiano smiled broadly at her and said, "Raushana, come in, join us. I would like you to meet a friend of mine."

Jimena smiled and nodded to Elvira in silent greeting, noting the wary expression in her friend's eyes. Then she saw more clearly the man who leaned against the manuscript shelves. For an instant her heart ceased beating, then began to pound frantically. It was a priest. A Christian *bishop*.

Estiano rose and moved to where Jimena was standing rooted to the floor, staring and apprehensive. He took her hand and gently drew her over to the bishop, whose eyes were transfixed by what he saw; a beautiful, golden-haired, Christian girl with a sweetness and purity on face that set his soul rejoicing. This one could be saved; he knew it. It was not too late for her. From the eyes of this girl shone that same light that he had seen so often as a little boy when he looked into the sacred eyes of his mother, God rest her soul. Here was another captive, a suffering victim.

"Raushana, this is a very old friend of mine. Bishop . . . Raushana."

Jimena was still speechless and shaken. For a moment she thought she was looking into the face of Don Pedro, of God Himself; about this priest she saw a too-familiar air of religious piety and zeal that gave her a sudden impulse to run. But the impulse was brief, replaced by a suspicion that God was showing her the way, reaching out a hand to her and offering salvation through this bishop. She would no longer be allowed to waver.

"You are a Christian." It was a statement that allowed for no denial.

"Uh, yes. Yes, I am, Bishop."

"And what church do you attend, pray?"

"None, Father. I, uh, you see . . ."

"None! My child, then you are *not* a Christian."

Jimena turned helplessly to Estiano, then to Elvira. Elvira's expression was blank; she shrugged her shoulders slightly, her expression saying "look not to *me* for answers." "Oh, but I have been *meaning* to attend, Father. I have been so occupied, you see. I do not know where there is a conveniently located house of God; my schedule is quite heavy, you see. . . . " She blushed, realizing she was making excuses that were weak and confused.

The bishop put his chin down and glared at Jimena through half-closed eyes. "My church is but half an hour's walk from this place. I would be most pleased to escort you. Right this moment, if you can fit worship into your heavy schedule?"

"I—I think that I might." She again turned questioningly to Elvira.

"I can eat alone, Raushana. Or Estiano will accompany me." Elvira smiled tightly at Jimena, making no effort to encourage or discourage her.

Estiano grinned in agreement, then quickly sobered. He watched Jimena closely as she nervously removed her apron and gathered her things together. Placing her portfolio under one arm, she hesitantly moved toward the door, forgetting the smudges of ink on her chin and nose. The bishop followed behind her disapprovingly. She wore silk. She bathed herself and painted her face. Indeed this was a wavering soul. He enjoyed an exhilarating confidence, certain that this time he would not fail to win his battle against the Devil. If he could save this one soul it would all be to some avail.

"Mmm . . . ," Estiano mumbled as the door closed behind Jimena and the bishop. He snapped the pen he held in half with tense, shaking fingers.

"You are worried about her," Elvira said softly.

"A little. Yes, a little. I think it would be a tragic waste if she let herself become enmeshed in the nets of religion again. She—Ah, I just hate to see it, hate to see it happen."

Elvira got up out of her chair and walked over to the window. She turned to watch Estiano as he scrubbed ink from his hands. She knew him well. A certain twist of his mouth, a subtle movement of his expressive hands, or a sudden change of expression in his eyes was sufficient for her to know his thoughts. She understood his fears and knew his loves. Estiano loved Jimena. At first it had not mattered because Jimena passionately and unreasonably despised him. But Jimena had wanted so much to learn the skills he could teach her that she agreed to join his class. Within a few weeks she was coming here to the library for extra lessons, confiding to Elvira that she had grossly wronged Estiano, that he was not at all what she had supposed him to be. It was then that Elvira became concerned. But she soon realized that Jimena was still unable to see in him what Elvira saw. Jimena's eyes saw only the surface of the man; it was not in her nature yet to look beyond the dreary masks that life sometimes put upon those who were most attractive. Jimena would never love Estiano in return. Though she was his second choice, whether he loved her or not, if Estiano wanted her, Elvira was his. "Estiano," Elvira said quietly, "I think you do not give Jimena enough credit. She has learned a great deal in the four years she has been in Cordova. The bishop will get only so far with her, then she will balk."

Estiano sighed. He straightened his shoulders determinedly. When he turned to face Elvira he was smiling. "Did you see the man's face? I have not seen him so glowing in years. It will indeed be a pity if what you say is true and Jimena dissapoints him. I do not think he could bear another sheep straying from his flock. The man hangs precariously upon a long rope over the cliff of defeat, and someday, that rope is going to break. No one can swim against the tide forever; eventually the strength fails and we sink."

Elvira laughed. Walking across the room to him, she placed both arms about his neck and kissed his forehead affectionately. "My, but we are philosophical today. Are you going to buy me a meal, beloved? I am famished!"

Kasim, Hasan's black servant and Jimena's shadow, slipped into step behind the bishop and his charge, his arms crossed over his massive, satin-clothed chest, his black eyes wary. He moved silently behind them, remaining several feet distant. His master's command had been that the woman was free to do whatever she pleased, but he was to be there when she did it.

Jimena walked solemnly beside the bishop, skipping occasionally to keep up with his hurried pace. She shivered, pulling her mantle tighter about her; the air was brisk today. It seemed an hour since they had left the library. If it were a mere half-hour walk, as the man had said, then it was at a running gait. The streets were becoming more narrow as they moved farther into the older section of the city; deep shadow surrounded them. The upper stories of the houses overhung the streets, almost completely shutting out sunlight. But it was a clean neighborhood. The stones of the road were washed daily, and the flower baskets from each lamp post had been carefully potted with new, blooming autumn plants. It was the time of prayer, so few people were on the streets. Those that did pass them nodded to the bishop, offering him a murmured greeting. Several people seemed reluctant to meet his gaze, and turned their heads quickly, as if their interest had been caught by something in just that instant that they must pass him by. By their features and coloring, Jimena guessed they were Christians, or at least Spanish by descent. Thinking about it, almost everyone they had met and passed was Spanish, some wearing the C that marked them Christians. Even after three hundred years of Muslim rule, tens of thousands of Spaniards remained in Andalus and not all of them had intermarried. Significant, she thought, that they did not swarm across the borders to join their own kind, remaining in Andalus as a necessary and important part of the culture. What side, she wondered, would these people take, if Alphonso did indeed overrun Cordova? An interesting speculation.

The bishop led the way, turning sharply where three streets met in an intersection. There before Jimena was the first Arab marketplace she had never seen. The street widened into a long cul-de-sac, and lining each side were wagons heaped with the produce of farms outside the city. Down the center, piled up in huge mountains, were mint, coriander, cumin, marjoram, sage, and celery. The combined fragrance was a delicious treat to the nostrils. And there were pyramids of oranges, apples, figs, and dates, and wagons filled with pomegranates. Behind the wagons, along narrow sidewalks, were the shops of silk merchants and rug sellers. There were leather products of incredible variety and color, slippers of bright orange, purple, and green, also belts, vests, and tapestries. Jimena tried to slow the pace, aching to take in every detail; she would love to buy something pretty and spend the rest of the afternoon looking, touching, and bargaining. But the silent priest pushed through the sparse crowd of shoppers, not looking to see if she was keeping up, moving toward a house at the curved end of the cul-de-sac. What a cold, resolute man, Jimena thought. She could not imagine his face ever cracking into a smile—the lines there were so obviously wrought by a lifetime of care and determined unhappiness.

The bishop finally came to a halt before a heavy, rusting gate, his foot tapping impatiently, his attitude that of supreme authority. When Jimena caught up with him, he ordered her to cover her head and she did so obediently, waiting for him to give her some indication as to where the church was. The priest made an arm, inviting her to enter the gate he now held open for her.

"But, Father." Bewildered, Jimena looked around her and through the iron bars of the gate. She saw only the naked front of another Arab house. There was no cross, no figure of the Christ. "But, Father, I see no church. Where?"

"What did you *expect*? The Infidel smugly brags of his tolerance, but does not dare allow us to place the symbols of our faith where his own might see. No crosses. No figures. But we may ring the bells on Sunday; bless them for their bountiful generosity." He had thought to receive sympathy from the woman, but she was smiling. "What did you find in my words that could even vaguely be construed as—as amusing?"

Jimena was silent for a long moment, uncertain whether to speak her mind, or not. Strange that such a thought should come to her. No, not strange at all; it was the truth. "Bishop," she said softly, looking the man straight in the eyes, "in Castile, where I come from, we not only forbid the symbols of Islam, but burn at the stake anyone even suspected of practicing that faith. There is no church but the Christian church. You are indeed fortunate, I was thinking, to be allowed the bells and the practice of your faith."

"Fortunate!" the bishop shouted, waving his arms. "More like degraded! It is calculated. I would prefer death at the stake to this—this so-called *tolerance*."

Jimena examined the man thoughtfully. His face was all twisted and snarling with hate, indignation, and frustration. Amazing, she thought, how many people choose those roads that can only lead to one result, suffering. She was abruptly overcome by a suspicion that she and this bishop were of one kind. Looking into his sad, defeated eyes was uncomfortably like gazing into a mirror. She turned away from him, quickly moving through the gate opening toward the drab little house.

Kasim remained behind. He would not enter a house that did not welcome Muhammed or his followers.

It was a typical Arab house, but had been stripped of all rugs and draperies and most of its inner partitions. An attempt had been made to make it as austere as a northern church, with a plain wood altar, unadorned pews, and a solemn emptiness, but the beauty of mosaic tile walls and floors caught and delighted the eye. The wide expanse of window that looked out upon a pathetic, neglected garden gave the room an air of openness and light that was like no church Jimena had ever seen. There was no gray, cold granite or glowering saints, no vast ceilings where shadows clung. There were no ghosts here, only gay flashes of sunlight dancing upon rainbow-colored tiles.

The bishop led Jimena down the center aisle, past the altar, then turned to his right. He opened a door and stepped aside, indicating with a nod of his head that she was to enter first.

Jimena smiled. This bishop was indeed a pious man. The walls of his chamber had been carefully draped with gray muslin to cover the radiant tiles. The windows were high and allowed in little light. A candle burned beneath the figure of the Virgin that sat upon his littered table. There were several manuscripts lying about on the table, a chair and on the floor, but they all contained the same text, the Christian Bible. Jimena had not seen so much dust and grime in a very long time.

"Sit, my child." The bishop waved her to a chair beside his table. He sat down himself, leaned back in his chair, and folded his flaccid hands together. "Now," he sighed, "we must see what can be done about you. Tell me about yourself. I must know when you made confession last and took communion. Then I will know what course to follow in bringing you back to God and His mercy."

"I—Father, I cannot reveal everything," Jimena began, feeling more than a little uneasy. "As for the church, I have not been to confession, taken communion, or been within a house of God, for over four years, nearly five. I—"

"Wait a moment, child." The bishop held up a hand to halt her words. "First tell me your name. I know it cannot be Raushana, which is the name of an infidel, not a Christian."

Jimena pulled her lower lip in, and pushed down upon it with her teeth. If she were anyone but the wife of Rodrigo Diaz, she could speak her name. If one wrong person were to discover such a secret, the news would travel like wildfire throughout all Cordova and on into Castile. But that could mean escape. Ah, no, only imprisonment again. There was no escape. But there is my darling child, my baby girl, she thought.

"Forgive me, Father," she said, swallowing rising emotion, "but I cannot divulge my full name. I can only tell you that my given name is Jimena."

"I see," the bishop said indignantly. "And will you be as reticent to speak in the confessional? If so, Doña Jimena, I cannot promise . . . "

"No, Father. I have nothing further to hide from God. I am willing to confess all my sins, to make penance; I only withhold my name."

"You cannot hide your identity from God! It is me you wish to deceive, is that not so? You realize, of course, that when you seek to deceive me, you deceive God? I am his servant. For you, this moment, I *am* God."

"Of course," Jimena meekly replied. But the bishop could not change her mind.

"As you will, then. Continue. Tell me of your religious life."

"I—I am married, Father . . ."

"Married! In Islam? To an—an *infidel*?" The bishop was rising to the occasion now. There was more sin here than he had guessed.

"No! I was married by a Christian bishop in Castile. My husband still lives. I have not seen him in a very long time."

"You *are* a captive, then?"

"Yes, Father."

"And what is your relationship with this heathen?"

Jimena's eyes darted up from her nervous fingers to coldly meet the bishop's accusing gaze.

"Fear not, my child," the bishop said kindly. "I understand. These people are savages, all animal lust and vileness. No wonder, you must agree, that God so despises them."

"But, Father—"

"No. No, my child, you need not explain. God truly understands your ordeal."

"Bishop, this man asks nothing of me. He has not touched me. I—"

"Jimena, must I educate you about what you must have learned at the age of five? I say again . . . when you speak to me you are speaking to God. Fear not. God will not punish you for what you were helpless to prevent. A woman is weak physically and cannot fight off the stronger male. Hold close to you, my child, *this* thought, that through suffering the soul is cleansed and the gates of Heaven are opened wide for the weak, the meek, and the ill-used of this world."

"Yes, Father." Jimena sighed in defeat. She did not wish to argue further. It suddenly became apparent to her exactly how generous Hasan had been with her. She thought, if God were so certain she had been used in this way and were so willing to forgive it, it was most awfully sad that it was not true. She almost laughed out loud.

Jimena made confession that afternoon, then took communion and accepted the penances, promising obedience and strict adherence to the Faith. She did not question herself as to possible alternatives. Even if she had thought about it, she would have assumed the matter of obedience to be beyond personal choice; she had strayed, sinned by failing to seek grace long after she was told her religion was open to her. Her faith was all that was left of what she had been, all that remained of her identity. She swore to herself, I am Jimena Diaz de Gomez, the wife of El Cid, mother of Urracca Rodriguez, and I am a *Christian*! God was with her again. She scrubbed the paint from her face, removed the bracelets from her ankles and wrists, and attended Mass every morning before classes, leaving Hasan's house an hour earlier than had been her habit.

Each morning the bishop saw only Jimena as he spoke the words of his sermon. There was a new vitality in him, evidenced in a slight increase in attendance. His warnings were vehement, his threats more fear-inspiring, drawing back to the fold those more tenderhearted recreants. His attentions sometimes embarrassed Jimena. On occasion he would embrace her, his small eyes shining, his hands warm and damp against the flesh of her bare shoulders. He also made an appearance every day at the scriptorium, to Estiano's extreme annoyance.

"What is this between you and the bishop, Raushana?" Estiano asked snappishly several weeks later. "Piety, or passion? Eh?"

Jimena laughed the question off as a joke. Ridiculous. The only passion the bishop had in him was for his God and for the sacred memory of his dead mother. When Elvira said, "You are looking rather homely these days, Raushana," she was deeply hurt. God did not love the vain. Her eyes did not need kohl and her lips needed no paint. When she had refused to let Acacia touch the darkening roots of her hair with the tint, Acacia had asked in all innocence, "But why does your God not love you if you alter the color of your hair? Hell is a rather gruesome punishment, I think, for such a small sin." Jimena had been unable to find an answer. She tried not to ask herself too many questions, it was dangerous, since answers too often failed to come.

Chapter

✠ *SIX* ✠

Hasan paced his library, to the window and back again to his pillows. It had been a thoroughly unsatisfactory trip. His friend, the wali of Malaga, had been the only man intelligent enough—No, it was not a matter of intelligence, all the men he had sought out were educated and enlightened; it was a matter of character, of values and of what was of immediate concern as against a vague possibility. Mo'temid, of Seville, was a prince of untold accomplishments, a poet, philosopher, writer of historical documents praised over all Andalus, and yet he kept a garden of staked Christian heads . . . mixed with a few heads not Christian, but Muslim. This sagacious yet barbaric man had listened quietly to Hasan's speech, "Let us be united and we shall be strong, strong enough to overcome the Christians. But let us not call into the delicious plains of Andalus the lions and tigers of the burning sands of Africa. They might break the chains of Alphonso, but would give *us* chains that we could not break."

Mo'temid had shrugged disinterestedly, replying, "It is better to be a camel driver in African deserts, than a swineherd in Castile." It was the same everywhere. Each prince was most anxious to halt Christian advance, but refused to give up a single possession, a single grudge; all were complacently certain that the Christian did not possess the intelligence, strength, or wealth to conquer such as themselves. And if they were by chance mistaken? There was always the fanatic fellow Muslim across the sea, waiting to be called, hired.

Hasan kicked hard at a green silk pillow, sending it hurtling across the room. Fools! Could they not see that all they had would be lost in any event? The savages of Africa were not preferable to those of the north. Andalusian women would again be enshrouded in veils, skepticism would be condemned, all thinking, questioning minds would become suspect. Or, he thought bitterly, am *I* the fool? Why do I burst my gallbladder over the lot of humanity, when they themselves have not sense enough to even recognize their precarious situation. In the end that is all I shall have for my pain, a broken, defeated soul.

"Oh Father of Beauty . . . ?"

Acacia stood with her hand upon the door drape, a worried frown creasing her forehead.

Hasan turned around and said sharply, "Where is she, woman? I expressly said to send Raushana to me immediately. Now get from my sight this instant, and go fetch her!"

"But," Acacia stammered, shaken by his unusual bad temper, "I tried. She—Raushana—she refused to come."

"Refused! In the name of the Prophet, *why*?"

Acacia flushed, "Well . . . what she said was, she is a married woman in the eyes of her church, and she refuses to sin against that sacrament." She sighed, and spat out the rest in a great, pushing breath, "She said that she absolutely will not share your bed, even if you beat her, or threaten to kill her."

"Enough!" Hasan roared, waving his arms in a fury. He moved across the room and stood an inch from the wide-eyed, cowering Acacia. Speaking in a stiffly controlled, confidential voice, he said "Now, Acacia. I want you to return to Miss Innocence and Purity and tell her that she can keep that which she so values. I do not *want* it! I am not interested!" He was shouting again, his nerves at the breaking point. "Tell her to get herself to this room within one hundred countings or I will have a strong servant drag her here! Do you understand? Go!"

In an instant Acacia was gone.

"For the love of Allah," Hasan yelped to the empty room, "all I need this day is a simpering, virtuous woman!"

But it was not all anger that he felt toward Jimena. Part of the pain he suffered, much of his frayed disposition, was caused by the news he must give her. If there had ever been a time when he might have undone the wrong against her, it was lost forever now. The circle of destiny was complete. He cursed himself for the twisted vengeance he had taken. How he wished that he had been a leader of armies rather than a teacher, then he could have performed a *true* retaliation, a sword straight through the heart of Rodrigo Diaz. It was not only Sabíhah that drove him now, but the uncounted thousands of butchered Muslims whose rotting flesh upon the northern plains, mingled with the putridity of burning bodies from El Cid's funeral pyres, was causing such a stench that it was like a great, ominous cloud darkening the light of Andalus. Soon that cloud would expand, because the army of El Cid had joined with that of King Don Alphonso. The king had made extravagant promises to that animal of destruction, in forgiveness and bargain. All that Rodrigo Diaz took from the Muslim, of land, monies, or goods, would be his and handed down to his descendants. No longer did El Cid pretend to kingliness; he was now, undeniably, a monarch, independent of both Christian and Arab. He had been hired by Alphonso, even as the hordes of Africa might be purchased by the Andalusians. Toledo was endangered, and Valencia. But the sultan of Toledo shrouded himself in delusion; he had a pact with Alphonso, made when the king was in exile in his palace; his city would never be taken while he lived. But the man was over seventy. Did he expect to live forever? Or did he care what happened to Toledo after he had gone to his reward? To hell with such a fool. Even Allah did not love a fool.

Hasan was standing tense and depressed by the window, when he heard the soft rustle of the drapery behind him. He knew that Jimena was there. He waited a long moment, steeling himself for the ordeal. When he turned, his stomach lurched over; for the love of Allah, what had she *done* to herself?

Jimena let her chin rest meekly upon her chest. She was thoroughly mortified. For God, what was she supposed to think? When Hasan wanted one of his women he simply sent for her. She could not imagine why else he would want to see her, so she had thought. . .

"Raushana?" Hasan said sympathetically, "have you been ill? You are quite drawn. You do not look well."

"For God!" she exclaimed, lifting her chin defiantly, "no, I am *not* ill. Why does everyone ask the same question of me? I simply no longer allow your servants to force self-indulgence upon me, but rather I purify and beautify my soul!"

"I see."

"You need not sound so. . ."

"So what, Raushana?"

She shrugged and refused to answer.

"I assume you took advantage of my generosity and found yourself a Christian church?"

"I have! I was never enamored with the image I presented, never!"

"Oh? Well, *I* was. But you need not defend yourself. I did not call you here to argue. Come. Sit down."

Jimena flounced to a pillow in the corner of the room,

plopping down into it like a spoiled, pouting child. She no longer quaked with fear when faced with disconcerting or dangerous situations, but she still lacked the ability to smoothly handle herself. It infuriated her when she became flustered and stuttered stupidly while all the words she might have said lay in a state of morphia somewhere in back of her tongue.

"Raushana," Hasan said moving to sit close to her, "how go your studies at the university? Do you find pleasure in them? Has the ride into the city each day been difficult for you?"

"All goes well, my lord," she replied less sharply. "And I thank you for your generosity. Estiano has been most kind, teaching me, busy as he is, extra hours of each day. I have completed my first manuscript." She was becoming enthusiastic now. "I must show it to you, someday."

"I would be most pleased to see it."

"And I have learned to ride the golden stallion, so that the ride to town is most pleasant. Kasim is always with me, according to your order, but I would not want to wander the roads alone, at any rate."

"No. Of course not."

"And in the spring a class in ancient poetry is being offered, which I will take. Did you know? *I* have written some poems." She fully expected him to be amazed.

"No! Really?"

"Yes, I have. I am copying them into a tiny gold manuscript. I should finish within the month, if you would care to read them?"

"Indeed, I would."

Jimena flushed. Hasan was smiling at her, laughing at her childish eagerness. "Forgive me for carrying on so. Was there something you wished to discuss with me?"

Hasan lost his smile. He hesitated, moving restlessly on his pillows. But she would hear it sooner or later, and it was better that it come from him. "Tell me, first, is there not some satisfaction in your days, some little contentment?"

She was staring curiously at him. He leaned forward and took hold of her hands. At first she flinched, and tried to pull away from his touch, but then she let her fingers rest in his.

"Raushana, I have news for you of a nature that tears my soul to tell of it. You have all these years suffered a great hate for me, I know, and it will increase a thousandfold now." He took a firmer grip on her fingers, and plunged ahead. "Word of your daughter has reached me. She is well under the direct guardianship of a bishop, Don Pedro. I must also tell you

Raushana, that your husband has taken another wife." He halted, having expected a reaction, but her eyes never left his, only widened imperceptibly. Then he felt her fingers tightening and his palms were being stabbed by her nails. "Allah knows," he whispered, "how deeply I regret—"

"When?"

"On the nineteenth of July."

"Who? Who is she?"

"Jimena Diaz, daughter of the count of Oviedo. She is Alphonso's cousin. It was he who arranged the marriage. Raushana . . . Jimena! They do not *know* that you live. I—"

"Jimena? Did you call me *Jimena*? You say that her name is Jimena?

"Please, do not . . ."

"Ah! How funny! Mary Mother of God, but this is too hilarious." Jimena threw her head back, screeching with laughter. She doubled over, choking, giggling, tears running from her stricken eyes. "Sir! You do not think it humorous? Eh? Good Christ, laugh! Why do you not *laugh*?" She could not laugh any longer either. She heard herself shriek like a madwoman. A ghastly night of shadows, fire, and death returned to her, and she saw Hasan now as he was then, the epitomy of terror, pain and loathing. Abortion returned, tearing at her abdomen and her two children, one dead, the other lost, came clear before her eyes, then swiftly vanished from her sight, leaving her floundering in a dark and bottomless pit. She wrenched her hands free of his touch, screaming, "Infidel! Do you *know* what you have done to me? Can you possibly comprehend what you have *done*?"

"Stop this!"

"Stop! Stop, you say. Dear God, you have killed me. Filthy swine! You have *killed* me!" She struck out at him, kicking and biting like a cornered, wounded tigress.

Hasan fought to hold her off, tears hampering his vision. "Raushana," he cried, "please listen to me."

"Oh, my god—god, my baby! A monastery is a grave. She is buried, and I am buried; you killed us both! My baby, my poor, poor baby."

Jimena fell to the floor, weeping as she had not wept in years. Hasan knelt helplessly beside her. He raised a hand to touch her, but drew it back without making contact. It took all his strength to quell his own sobs, he did so pity this weeping victim of his vengeance.

"Raushana, beloved, please do not weep." He took her

shoulders in his two hands and drew her to him. She did not
flinch or pull away, even when his trembling hands turned her
over and pulled her face into his breast. She lay in his arms and
wept unrestrained.

The house was dark when Hasan walked up the long flight
of stairs, carrying a sleeping Jimena in his arms. She had
exhausted herself and fallen asleep like a child. He placed her
gently upon her bed and leaned down to kiss her lightly on the
mouth. "Sleep well, Splendid One. Allah's blessing on thee.
Pray you find the happiness you seek. Allah forgive me for
what I have done, and may you forgive me, also."

A cold, whipping wind blew a gale through the narrow
streets of Cordova, forcing the citizens inside behind shuttered
windows. Though it was only midday, the sky was dark,
foretelling the storm to come. Jimena clasped the reins tight,
bracing herself against the wind. Her mantle would not stay
around her but flew open and behind her as the horse sped
through the alleys, its iron-shod hooves clacking a hollow,
mournful rhythm that mingled ominously with the wailing
winds. She had fled from Hasan's house by means of a
foolhardy drop from her pavilion railing and was nearing the
city gates before anyone realized she was not in her quarters.

Jimena leaped down from the stallion's back and ran toward the church gate, forgetting to tie the horse's reins to the
post. When she entered the church she slammed the heavy door
closed behind her and leaned back to press her head against it,
tears wetting her cheeks. She was alone. No worshipers sat in
the pews. She moved down the center aisle and stood before the
figure of Christ that was stretched in holy agony upon the
cross. She knelt before him, folded her hands together, and
prayed. "Blessed Mary, Mother of God, pray to God for me
that I may find my way in the darkness. I am forever bound to
this world of infidels. I am lost. My identity has been stolen.
Another woman lives in my place; Jimena, wife to Rodrigo
Diaz. Help me. I am lost. Help me. I am so frightened."

"Oh!" Jimena jerked her head around at the bishop's sudden touch upon her shoulder.

"My child . . . what are you doing in church at this hour?
Foolish question." He smiled adoringly. "It does not matter
why, only that you have come. I have been wanting to speak
with you. Come into my chamber, will you please?"

Jimena numbly followed him and sat down across from
him. Her red-rimmed eyes focused upon him, but were unsee-

ing. There were no thoughts in her head, only an agonizing pressure over her eyes, a vast, black emptiness of feeling.

"Jimena," he began carefully, "you have been progressing quite satisfactorily. I am proud of you. But there are a few matters that I have not wished to press. Jimena? Are you listening to me? Jimena!"

"What? What was that you said, Father?"

"What is it, my dear? Are you troubled?"

"It is nothing that cannot be discussed with you later, Father. Did you want to say something to me?"

For an instant the bishop thought to postpone the conversation, but sooner or later this child must accept her full responsibility to God and to herself. "As to your studies at the college. You realize, of course, that you must give them up."

Jimena was abruptly brought out of her stupor. "I beg your pardon? I could not have heard you correctly, Bishop."

"You must forsake your classes," he said emphatically.

"But *why*?"

"Now that is a foolish question; why, indeed. All the evil and sin produced by the minds of corrupt, depraved men is there inside that building of iniquity. You sin mortally when you read such works, and well you know it!"

"For God!"

"Guard your tongue, woman. You are in the house of God."

"Bishop. Where is it written that to read such works is sinful? Did Jesus say it? I would have you quote me the scripture."

The man lurched back in his chair, stunned by her vehemence. Fear touched his soul with icy fingertips. He must move cautiously, he told himself. He could not bear it if Jimena withdrew from him. No, not Jimena.

"I asked a question of you, Bishop!"

"Watch how you speak to me, woman," he warned, but more softly.

The pressure against her forehead was now unbearable. "Bishop," she said irritably, "I must say this to you. It is not my faith in *God* that is wavering, it is my faith in you and what you preach that is in jeopardy."

"Enough! Take yourself to the confessional and make your peace with the lord! When you deny me, you deny Him. Beg His forgiveness, girl, before another instant passes, else—"

Jimena lurched from her chair, sending it spinning over behind her. She fell forward over his table, placing her hands flat on the surface and glaring straight into the man's startled eyes.

"My husband has remarried," she screeched at him. "Advise me, Bishop. What am I to do about *that*?"

"Why, I—I," he stuttered,. "remarried, you say? Why, then, we must—you must escape, return to him. There must be a way."

"Escape! What possible good could come of that?"

"You became his wife before God. Nothing can alter that fact."

"And what about the woman who lives with him now and names herself wife to him?"

"Ah, now, God will not punish her for what she has done, since she was innocent of intent."

"And if she bears a child before my return?"

"Oh. Ah, now, the child would be another matter entirely. You see. . ."

"Yes! I *do* see. If I tell you that I despise the man and do not want to return to him and live within the circle of his foul destiny, what then?"

"Woman! He is your *husband*."

"I know! Forever and throughout eternity, my husband. A truly grim contemplation, hideous and insupportable."

The bishop's facial muscles quivered and his cheeks flushed. "Calm yourself. Perhaps I can find someone to aid you in your escape from this hellish place."

"For God sakes, man, have you not listened? There *is* no escape!" She choked on a sob and clutched at the table edge for support, "I would not be missing more than a few hours before it was noticed. I would never get beyond that first mountain range. Forget escape. Tell me what my life will be in Cordova. I have perhaps thirty more years to live. Tell me how I will live out that time, Bishop."

He chewed nervously at his lower lip, "Now, now," he muttered, gaining time to think, "perhaps a monastery. But you need not wear the habit to lead a life of sacrifice and suffering." He stood up and came around to her and embraced her warmly, "Live out the years in peace and prayer. Work with me in Christ for your personal salvation. Dear girl, think not so much of the perhaps thirty years ahead; know that that is but a moment in eternity. Think of the infinity of bliss after you and I are finished with this world. Together we will live in spirit for our God."

Jimena wrenched herself from his arms. "Damn, damn, damn!" she cursed, beating her fists on the table. It was hopeless. The hundred questions in her mind that had no answers slashed gaping wounds in her soul. She whirled around and rushed blindly across the room to the door.

"Where are you going?"

"I know not, sir. Anywhere. Nowhere."

"You will give up your studies!"

"Yes, I imagine I will, Bishop."

"Wait! Your confession . . . I . . ."

"Not now," Jimena cried, as she swung the door open and ran out of the church, into a raging storm.

Ignoring the rain and wind lashing against her face and soaking her clothing, forgetting the golden stallion waiting patiently for her return, Jimena blindly ran through the deserted market square and out into the streets of Cordova.

"Raushana! Good Lord, where have you been!"

Estiano took hold of Jimena's arm and whirled her around to face him. She stared blankly at him, not knowing where she was, nor why. She stood unsteadily in the drenching rain, slumping into his hands. He shook her shoulders to snap her out of the daze she was in. "What are you doing wandering the streets in this downpour? Hasan and I have been frantic all afternoon. He went to your church, but the bishop would not say if you had been there or not. Raushana! What ails you?"

Jimena could only shake her head and mumble incoherently.

"Damn," he cursed, undecided as to what to do with her. "Well, we will get you out of the wet to begin with. Come, my house is but a few doors down." He placed an arm beneath her shoulders to support her as they walked.

Jimena had been discovered just in time. She felt a black fog enveloping her. Suddenly she fell forward, but Estiano managed to catch her up in his arms. He carried her at a running gait to his door.

Jimena awoke feeling a pleasant, cozy warmth. She was wrapped completely in satin coverlets. The room was filled with scented clouds of steam that billowed up from pots set in the four corners of the room. Above the perfume was the delicious aroma of lamb and rice. Her stomach growled angrily; she was famished.

Estiano grinned as Jimena turned her head and saw him. "Feeling better?"

"Estiano! What are *you* doing here? Where am I, for heaven's sake!"

"You have no recollection of meeting me outside on the street?"

"For God," she groaned, "I do not recall anything much since—when was it, only last night?" She covered her eyes with the palms of her hands. Her blind rage was gone, and she felt much better.

"Are you hungry?"

"Oh, I am absolutely starving."

"Good. Try this. I have an excellent cook, who is, I am sorry to say, off on his own tonight. I cooked this myself. You eat at your own risk, my good woman."

Jimena laughed and sat up, leaning into the pillows Estiano had quickly placed against the wall behind her. She ate two bowls of the harísah and half a loaf of bread before she stopped. All the while she was uncomfortably aware that she was stark naked under the satin coverlet she was awkwardly holding up over her bosom. He must have disrobed her while she was unconscious. How humiliating. Estiano of all people. Still, she felt more relaxed with him than ever before.

"Estiano," she sighed, "it was so delicious I would have eaten a ton, but for the limited capacity of my stomach."

"I thank you, most generous and kind lady," he said with a gallant flourish.

Jimena studied him a long moment, meeting his eyes directly. Then she said softly, "We appear to be friends of a sudden, Estiano Antolinez."

He flinched and drew back, "And should we not be?"

"What you did to me," she whispered, looking down to her hands, " . . . was brutal."

"Are you absolutely certain?" he asked, his solemn eyes trying to catch her fleeting glance.

"Certain! Of what? That you took a knife in your hand and cut my *life* from me?"

"Or with my knife removed a tumor that *threatened* your life? Describe the deep love you enjoyed for your husband to me and tell me of the daily joys that filled your blissful existence before I came upon you with the knife. Then I will drop to my knees and out of guilt beg your forgiveness."

"Rodrigo has remarried," Jimena cried. She threw her arms up for emphasis, then clutched at the coverlet that dropped away from her bosom. "For years I have vegetated here neither dead nor alive. I should thank the Lord and you, sir, for such a blessing? I want to live. Dear God, I cannot bear this suspension any longer. In the north my place has been filled. In Andalus there is no place for me. It is you who are to blame, Estiano, and I despise you for it!" She choked on emotion and swiped away hot tears with a hand. "Cordova may be a paradise to you, but it is a hell to me!"

Estiano slapped his hands down upon his knees in exasperation, then threw his glance up to the ceiling. "Woman," he shouted, "when you are safely in Heaven you will languish and bemoan because you will have lost all chance for hell fire! How you enjoy your misery; it sickens me!"

"Heaven is all that is left to me, now! If I live as you do here, then hell fire will indeed be my reward. God does not allow me a life outside the sanctity of my marriage. Surely *you* can understand that; once you were Christian. Either I return to Castile or I remain dead. The bishop has ordered me to stop my studies; he insists that I live in chaste subservience, and . . . oh, I . . . " There was no way to verbalize her volcanic emotions.

"Then blame God. Blame the bishop, or your own mind for indulging in childish superstitions. But do not blame me, who had no stronger part in your destiny than the wind that blows the seed! Put down your roots and grow, or die on the vine: it is your choice. In truth there is no one for you to blame except yourself if life in Cordova, in Hasan's house, is less than rapturous."

Estiano swung to his feet and paced back and forth before her like a snorting bull in an arena, anger and indignation disarming his usual shyness with women. Suddenly he dropped to his knees before Jimena, leaning to take her bare shoulders in his two hands. "You are a lovely woman. See how your bosom rounds delightfully before my eye." One of his hands slid smoothly under the coverlet to caress what he described. "But see how you recoil with panic in your eyes. This frigidity is to blame, Raushana. Chase it from your house, together with superstition, and life will come to you in force." With desire bright in his eyes, he said huskily, "Shall I give back to you what I took away? Shall I give warmth to your flesh where there has for a lifetime been only chill?" He let his face brush close to hers, and his long arms drew her close to his breast. She froze in terror, squeezing her eyes closed, but he persisted. "Live," he whispered in her ear, "before you vow living to be of no significance. Feel, Raushana. Let down your armor. Tell the bishop it is *he* who will go to Hell, for blasphemies against life and the living."

"Let go of me," Jimena cried between clenched teeth. "Take your hands from me, you *ugly*—"

Estiano lurched away from her as if burned, and quickly turned his face to the wall.

"Oh! Forgive me. That was cruel of me, I . . . " She was furious with herself for allowing such a brutal word to slip from her tongue.

"Not cruel, just truthful," he murmured bitterly, keeping his face hidden from her. "I wear this carnival mask in jest; underneath it I am as fair as Hasan. But I am the only one who sees myself as I truly am. Once, when I had a mother who despised me and brothers who taunted me, I smashed every glass that spoke of the grossness of my features." He angrily whipped his head around and shouted, "But this face has not prevented me from tasting every joy of living that is God-gifted or Devil-inspired! Nor from molding my destiny according to my desire. Your character is weak, woman, thus you suffer a weak existence!"

"Saíd?"

Estiano and Jimena were both jolted by the servant's voice from behind them.

"What is it, Masrur," Estiano demanded, rising unsteadily to his feet, cursing himself for the senseless passion that this ignoble female aroused in him. Damn him, he had been plagued by illusions of her day and night for months now. There was little about her to admire or love, except those things sensed, as one imagines the finished jewel in the uncut stone. It was the woman she *could* be that enamored him, he reasoned; truly she was gifted artistically, a virtue in itself.

"I have fetched Abu l Hasan, according to your instructions. He awaits you in the garden court, Saíd."

Estiano ordered the servant away with a gesture, then glared down into Jimena's wide, haunted eyes. "Dress yourself, woman, your master awaits you. Will I see you in class tomorrow?"

"No," she whispered. "The bishop is my bridge to God, Estiano. Unstable as that bridge is, I must cross it, because I am so in dread of nothingness, which is worse than Hell."

Chapter

✠ *SEVEN* ✠

In the north there was a rumbling thunder of hooves; the combined armies of King Don Alphonso and Rodrigo Diaz were on the march. Eight-year-old Urracca Rodriguez wept upon the shoulder of a nun at the monastery at La Coruña; she was lonely and unloved. Rodrigo's wife, who was only nineteen years old, held in her arms a tiny boy-child, named Diego for both his grandfathers, and wept as El Cid departed from her for battle. A princess, daughter of Philip I of France, passed through the mountains separating her country from Castile with her train, to become the bride of Alphonso and the queen of Castile; her name was Constanza. And another princess, with a heart shattered beyond repair, rode away from Palencia never to return, carrying within her a secret joy and a profound despair. She rode to the monastery of La Coruña and by choice and as penance stepped into a prison cell from which she would never emerge, the sins of her life etched upon the outside door for all to see and know. *"I, Urracca, a miserable sinner, do confess to all the sins I have committed through pride, in thought, deed, word—of incest, murder, perjury. . ."* it said, and throughout the monastery faint wailing sounds could be heard at night.

In Andalus there remained a stubborn complacency; there was no uniting of forces; only a great fear that was enlarged by self-interest and indecisiveness. The armies of Yosuf of Africa began to gather in greater force now on the shores of the Mediterranean; they waited for what was inevitable, an Andalusian cry for help.

Elvira Rodriguez began and completed her class in ancient poetry, an empty chair reminding her of a lost friend. Estiano Antolinez buried himself in his work, remaining at his easel long into the nights, finishing tasks that could well have waited another day. But the bishop glowed, his joy knowing no bounds; Jimena had not disappointed him. Elvira Rodriguez and Estiano Antolinez had lost her because he had won her for God.

Jimena sat in her room overlooking the timelessly moving waters of the Quadalquivir watching the world go by, just as she had for so many years in the past. Her face mirrored the sadness she felt. There were no guards to keep her imprisoned, the door was unlocked, the prisoner, released years before, was shackled now only by invisible chains placed about her and locked tight by her frantic hold upon the promise of Heaven. She did not join Hasan's women for games and talk, and had entirely forsaken her studies. Jimena lived in another world from Elvira now, so there were no more lunches and stimulating conversations. No Estiano, who, with a graceful flick of his brush, so expertly taught her what she wanted to learn . . . no college, no books, no lampblack smudges on her nose and no sweet joy of accomplishment. Only this dense nothingness; life had ceased.

Jimena traveled to Cordova every morning to attend church, which was her only escape from the monotony of her life. Each day she prayed to God for guidance. "If I am forbidden to take delight in this life, God, then take life from me. If death is my reward, then send that black cloud over me and I will be happy with you in Heaven. But torment me no longer with ten thousand temptations. I am weak, hungry for the things of this earth and my grip upon the ladder to Heaven is loosening. I will fall. Fall. . . ."

Her only friend, the bishop, was always there encouraging her, clucking over her like a mother hen, his reminders never ceasing. In no way was she to mingle with, to imitate, or to speak with infidels, not unless she was forced, which would leave her innocent and God-forgiven. When Jimena's hair had grown out sufficiently, the bishop himself took shears to it, cutting off what remained of the sinful gold. He stood back from her that day with adoration bright in his eyes and exclaimed, "Jimena, the beauty of your pure soul shines about you like a halo; God bless you, my child. God bless you . . . "

Untutored, plain and unbathed, Jimena was herself again; at least the reflection in her mirror seemed the same as it had been long ago.

When Abu l Hasan returned from his latest travels, he was told about Jimena's condition by each wife in turn and then by Acacia. He heard more from an angry Elvira and then had to listen to a speech from Estiano. Hasan set aside his fears for the destiny of Andalus, to ponder the fate of Jimena Diaz. A message was delivered to the self-styled prisoner, commanding her to meet her master in the garden tomorrow morning, immediately following prayers. She was to make no plans for the day. No excuse would be accepted for her failure to appear.

The next morning Jimena walked obediently through the house, feeling extremely self-conscious; she prayed she would not meet Nuzhab, or Zarifah. She could not meet their eyes now. In her denial of them there was the unspoken insult . . . You are infidels, unclean, sinful, condemned to hell, while I am sweet and clean, especially chosen for Heaven; I am too pure and holy to fraternize with the likes of you. This was what was implied, but Jimena did not feel special, or selected, but rather like the only person in the world that God had overlooked.

As she stepped out into the garden she ran trembling fingers through her short, matted hair, her eyes casting about for Hasan. She tried to straighten her clothing, wishing she did not have to wear the trousers of infidels; the soft, clinging cloth was a painful reminder of past luxuries, of brief, joyful self-indulgences.

"Raushana. Here. Beneath the rose arbor." As Jimena walked toward him, Hasan studied her severely, a frown creasing his forehead. But for the extra weight filling out her form, she would be the same drab creature he had scooped up off the plains. But face paint alone did not render a woman beautiful. The glow that must come from within was what was missing. Unhappiness was dragging her facial muscles down into ugly lines. Her eyelids were heavy over eyes dulled by loneliness and defeat.

"Come here to me, woman," Hasan ordered, his voice purposely severe. "Let me look at you."

Jimena's face flushed hot as he took her shoulders in his hands and turned her around and around, his eyes examining her from top to bottom. She tried very hard, but was unable to convince herself that she did not care how she looked; she cared so much it was agony to feel his eyes upon her and know what he saw.

"Ach," Hasan spat out in disgust, "you are a wretched sight! What have we here, eh?" He flipped an angry finger under a straight lock of her unwashed hair, extreme distaste curling his lips. "Would you presume to call this *hair*? If you no longer wish to color it, at least be good enough to wash it and curl it. And this . . . " he clutched hold of Jimena's head, roughly pushing her chin against her chest, "By Allah, you could plant a pomegranate in the soil upon your neck! How long has it been since you bathed yourself woman? Eh? Speak up!"

Jimena choked on rising tears. She whispered, "Fifteen months, my lord."

"Fifteen months! *Alhomdalillah!*" Hasan threw his arms up in horror. "Listen *close* to what I say. This has gone quite far enough. You will immediately take yourself back to your room and wash the earth and animal life from yourself. And curl that stringing hair! I had planned an excursion. Do you recall? Years ago I promised to show Al Zohra to you?" He smiled, placing his forefinger beneath Jimena's trembling chin, "Come, do not weep. You cannot expect me to be seen on the streets with you in *this* condition. Abu l Hasan is known to possess the most beautiful women in Cordova. You would not make liars of those who make such claims, would you?"

"But," Jimena began.

"Ah. But *what*, eh?"

"I cannot bathe . . . because it is against my faith . . . and I cannot accompany you, because, you see, I—I must attend church. The bishop, you see . . . "

"I see *nothing!*" Hasan shouted. "Except that you wallow in misery and filth like a swine in its stall!" He shook a finger under her nose. "I am your lord, Raushana, your master. I give you commands and you must obey them. This is the law of the land in which you now dwell. I offered you free rein over your life, but I can see you cannot satisfactorily mold your own destiny. Thus I say to you that from this moment on you will be scheduled by me. You will return to your classes. You will bathe at least once a day. You will look presentable every waking moment." He hesitated, taking a deep breath. "And I forbid you to enter a Christian church again. If he is not careful, your bishop will lose his head. You are never to be seen with or to speak with this man again. Is that clear?"

Jimena's eyes widened. Speechless, she stared at Hasan. Somewhere in the back of her mind a soft voice cried out in answer to him, Thank you, oh blessed Father of Beauty, I was drowning and you have thrown me a rope. Force me . . . threaten me so I will be innocent of intent, so I will have the excuse I need to live as I truly want to. "Yes! Yes, yes, yes," she screamed, more enraged at herself than at him.

"Ah. The spirit has returned. Excellent. Now go, and vent

some of that anger against the dirt upon you. I will expect you back here within one hour . . . ''

"*One hour?*" Jimena gasped.

"Granted," he laughed, "that is insufficient time for what needs to be done. I will send Acacia and Nuzhab to you to speed the process."

"No. I—Not Nuzhab. I mean . . . ''

"Raushana." He shook his head sadly. "They do not hate you. Nuzhab pleaded with me to help you. It was Zarífah who was the first to tell me of your trouble, and there were tears in her eyes. Smile at them and they will know you still love them. . . . Do not toss aside even one friend, Raushana, because there are too few in the world who will love us to ever do that."

"Yes," Jimena murmured, and turned away from Hasan. Before she had reached the house she was running. Rushing into her room, she began tearing off her clothing, throwing pieces in every direction. Ransacking her closet, she brought out a gown of gold, the same one she had worn the night she served dessert to Hasan's guests. She threw the ensemble on the floor beside the long unused washtub, then selected golden slippers, pearl earrings and eight sapphire bracelets. From a leather bag brought down from a high shelf Jimena took out the jars of paint and kohl that she had hidden away months ago. She had thought at the time that she should throw them out, but she could not bring herself to do that; it was as if she knew she would use them again one day.

Jimena whirled around at the sound of water splashing into the tub. "Oh! Acacia, thank you." Then Nuzhab walked into the room, with her eyes cast downward, a curling iron in one hand, a brazier in the other. Jimena rushed across the room and grabbed the two of them to her, an arm around each, "Nuzhab, Acacia, forgive me, please. I love you both." She kissed each of them soundly on the cheek.

Jimena lolled and soaked and groaned with pleasure in her bath. "*Alhomdalillah,* Acacia," she cried, "I cannot believe you had to *force* me to bathe that day. How I cried and protested." Jimena splashed a spray of water up into the air, giggling foolishly. "And I was forced today. Allah bless me, I am a fool!"

"You smelled not *half* as bad today as you did then, Raushana. Whew!" Acacia put a dainty finger under her nose, "Such a stench came from you, that . . ."

"Enough!" Jimena shrieked in mock humiliation, "you

embarrass me. Nuzhab will think I was a savage, or something.
I was not as gross as you say, Acacia, admi— Ow!" She jumped
and almost fell out of the tub when Acacia landed a loud slap
on her bottom; Jimena had been standing up to briskly scrub
her legs.

"Stop dawdling," Acacia ordered severely. "You have only
half of the hour left and Nuzhab will have to be an artist-
magician to do anything with that hair of yours, it is *terrible*.
You look like a beggar boy."

The hour had passed and Jimena stood before her mirror
critically eyeing her reflection. Nuzhab had worked a miracle
with her hair. By pulling the short side hair back with a band of
bright flowers and pinning a false hairpiece at the back, no one
would suspect that she had recently been sheared. And the style
was good for her face; her eyes seemed rounder and her brows
more arched. The image in the mirror was pleasing, but she
wished her hair was white again. A sting of conscience disturbed her. But the bishop could no longer reproach or threaten
her because with a command Hasan had rendered him almost
nonexistent. The bishop was gone from her life, along with
Don Pedro of Gormaz and the rest of the past. She thought, It
is not the eyes of God that makes people apprehensive and
spineless, but the eyes of the priests.

Hasan was waiting beneath the arbor just where she had
left him. He stood quite still, leaning one hand against a slim
marble pillar. The outline of the arbor framed him as if he were
a portrait; the trailing pink and white roses about him dropped
an occasional petal at his feet. The sun was full in the sky now
and all the pleasant sounds and smells of late summer were in
the air. Jimena stopped behind a hedge of oleander to absorb the
scene before her and impress it upon her memory. Here was
heaven within reach of her vision; grass stretching out a thick,
green carpet, sunlight reflecting off the rushing water of the
river to send fairy lights dancing and leaping over intricately
carved benches, beds of flowers, and water fountains. And there
beneath a cascade of pink and white roses stood a man—a man
as perfect in appearance as anything of beauty that surrounded
him or met her eye.

Self-consciously Jimena looked down upon herself, making
a final check on her toilette. She was aware of a definite weakness in her knees and her heart was beating suspiciously fast.
She knew she looked beautiful, which in itself was enough to
panic her. There was a certain comfort in being homely and unclean; if no man asked her, she was spared the temptation of

saying yes. Now she had to parade herself before Hasan, knowing what he would see, certain he would desire her as he did Nuzhab and Zarifah. How far along this path of defiance could she travel? It had been relatively easy to bathe and paint her face. As for that greater sin, she could not bring herself to even contemplate the punishments in store for her if she should weaken.

Jimena stepped from her hiding place like a moth drawn to a flame, unable to resist Hasan's beckoning beauty. But unlike the moth, Jimena was fully conscious of what lay within the arms of that flame . . . the destruction of her soul. A sudden overwhelming fear demolished for her what might have been like the uncomplicated and joyful dance of a moth fluttering toward its destiny.

When Hasan saw Jimena approaching him, he straightened up quickly and threw his head back in an exaggerated gesture of admiration, the end of his white turban whipping back over his shoulder. "Ah," he cried, rushing to meet her, "lovely, enchanting." Taking her hands in his, he whirled her around and around for his inspection, his eyes verifying her fears; he did indeed find her desirable. Hasan turned her to face him, a sudden grimness tightening his lips. Giving her shoulders a firm but gentle shake, he said, "Raushana, never again allow that mask of grime and misery to hide from the world what you are." His voice became rough. "Allah created his most perfect work in you, a woman. Be proud. Preen like a peacock. Shout out to the world that you are you, a complicated and intricate machine: delicate, intelligent, and perfect. Use what you have been given and make Allah pleased that He created you." He placed a cool hand against Jimena's cheek and said, "Raushana, Allah gave you eyes the color of chestnuts when sunlight dances upon them, and a face sculptured with the profile of an angel as model; a form all round and soft as a new fallen snowdrift, the flesh that white and gleaming, and a mind as sharp as a blade of steel. Wondrous gifts. Do not be so ungrateful as to deny or destroy them. There is purpose in all things. Surely a part of your purpose on this earth is to help beautify it. If Allah had pleased, he would have created you ugly."

Jimena stood before him trembling, with her eyes cast down. Hasan knew a sudden impulse to slap her, to shake her, to beat sense into her. Here was a grim example of the brutes who lived in the darkness outside Andalus. Trembling before him was all humanity that stubbornly fought against enoblement of spirit and body, that desperately clung to a pestilent ignorance and misery. Like a wounded hyena devouring its own flesh, the human animal committed slow, agonizing suicide. How could one fight against such a hellish instinct for self-destruction? Even as this young woman destroyed herself, so would civilization go up in flames, the fire set by those who were burned.

"When you destroy the beauty on the outside, Raushana," Hasan pressed, digging his fingers into Jimena's shoulders, "when you allow your mind to deteriorate and rot away, there is nothing left to call *you*; then you have murdered *yourself,* which is truly the most abhorrent of sins. Live, woman. For the love of Allah, reach out your arms to life and enfold it. Take from this world all the pleasures that are available to you. Just as the earth gives us the gold ore, the diamond, and the ruby, it gives us life's riches, but you must dig for them." He abruptly let loose of Jimena, his expression apologetic. "Forgive me. I preach too many sermons these days. I might better have been a priest than a teacher, but then, what religion would I expound? I would have had to invent one, I imagine."

Jimena raised her eyes to look at Hasan with a new understanding. All the searching agony of her life seemed to have led her to this one moment. Her mind stretched out and examined the thoughts he had expressed. In an angry yet gentle voice he had shown her a truth. Just as God had created the fruit upon the tree, the grain of wheat, the cool rains of spring, He had created herself. What God did not wish to give, God withheld. Nothing on earth, no object, emotion, no thought or desire was without purpose. The apple did not refuse to become red, did not hide from the rains that nourished, washed, and polished it; the acorn would not refuse to become an oak tree, had never proclaimed a God-written taboo against its inherent destiny, accepted its existence and lived to fulfillment without ever asking the purpose of it all.

Jimena was awed by the wonder of these revelations. She did not know what to say to Hasan. He had turned away from her and was staring out across the lawns to the river, his hands tensely fumbling with the turban he had removed from his head. His dark hair waved down to his shoulders, his back was straight and stiff. She watched him, noticing every detail, the way his little fingers were gracefully upraised; the way he set his legs wide apart when he stood still; the slenderness of his waist; the softness of his black beard that shone with blue highlights, it was so dark.

She suffered a compulsion to take the few steps that separated them, to touch him, demand love from him, to drink him in as a bee sips honey from a flower. She knew she would be whole when she was blended with Hasan, when he had implanted within her that part of himself that was divided from her now. His life would flow into her own to wash away grief and fear, and replace them with love and new life.

But wanting him was not enough. She could not escape from the vivid memory of an act so brutal and distasteful that natural instinct and desires were powerless against it. Jimena remained frozen where she stood, with a gnawing discomfort in her groin.

With a determined sigh Hasan turned to face Jimena. He deftly rewound his turban around his head. "Enough of this dreary talk. The day is half gone and I had planned so much." He hesitated, and looked questioningly at Jimena. "Do you wish to go? I was rather harsh earlier. Really, I have no intention of making a total slave of you. I . . . "

"Oh, no. I mean, yes. Yes, I wish to go." Jimena blurted, flushing at such a display of eagerness.

"Excellent," Hasan said with a relieved sigh. He took Jimena's arm in his and led her toward the stables.

They rode side by side, talking very little. Jimena drank in the sights, sounds, and smells along the way, knowing it was a special day and determined to imbed the date in her mind so that she would always remember it. It was the fourteenth day of September, 1076. No—it was the year of Muhammed, *455.* She was Andalusian now.

The excursion produced a disappointment for Jimena. She was unable to see the palace of Al Zohra as Acacia had described it to her. A year ago it had been destroyed by Muslim fanatics on a rampage of murder and terror. The rebels were black men brought to Andalus fifty years ago by Al Mansur, the great caliph, to aid him in his wars with the Christians. The descendants of those blacks lived in many small colonies outside the city walls that were festering boils upon the face of Andalus, while their brothers in Africa anxiously waited to join them. They adhered strictly to the laws of Islam, veiling the women of their houses, never drinking the wine that flowed as water from the vines of Andalusia; there was not an artist or singer among them. The lives of these revolutionaries were devoted to the same cause as that of King Alphonso and Rodrigo Diaz—to bring to a close the Arab-Persian era in Spain. They were called Moors.

As Jimena's glance sadly moved away from the ruins of

Zohra's palace, her eyes fell upon a sight that caused her to gasp out loud with pleasure.

Hasan, following her gaze, smiled and said, "There is a story about that mountainside. Shall I tell it to you?"

Jimena merely nodded, her eyes fixed on the scene before her. She had reined in, stopping her mount close beside Hasan's.

"The caliph who built the palace for Al Zohra spent much of his time visiting his lady, and from the windows of his own rooms he looked out upon this mountainside. He ordered that it be planted so that it was covered like a carpet with flowers, for he wished to see naught but beauty no matter where his eye fell. A fantastically beautiful sight, is it not?"

"Oh, yes," Jimena sighed, "but how sad it must be in winter, when all the flowers are dead."

"No. Oh, no," Hasan laughed. "He came to her in winter, too. The slopes have been planted so that when one fades another blooms; in winter there are some blooms that surpass any flower of summer, and the color is equally spectacular."

"Amazing!"

"Shall we ride up? The horses will take us part way, then there is a path winding between hedges of roses and through fields of poppies and geraniums. I could show you the viaduct from there, the one that supplies Cordova with the water for its sewage system, and for the baths of . . . " he grinned charmingly at Jimena, "lovely ladies such as yourself."

Jimena laughed, "Your point is well made, my lord."

Hasan grinned and said, "A thousand pardons, my lady, if I said something to offend you."

Laughing, Jimena spurred her horse and sped down the road. Hasan immediately gave chase. The wind was soft and warm against her, pushing the gold silk tight to her flesh. Her legs were becoming sore from sitting so long in the saddle, but she did not care if the next two weeks were spent with salve and bandages, this day was too perfect to spoil with such worries.

It took more than an hour for them to reach the spot where the path up the mountainside began. They tied their mounts to a post and began the climb up the slope. It was not steep to the eye, seeming more a gentle incline than a mountain, but in only a few minutes Jimena's wind became short and she began gasping for breath. "For God," she gasped, "I cannot move another step." She stopped and placed a hand over her breast, fascinated by the monotonous, heavy pounding of her heart.

Hasan reached out and placed an arm under Jimena's shoulders to support her weight. "Here, I will help you. It is only a little farther. As long as we have come this far, I would have you see the viaduct."

She leaned back into his arm gratefully, and they walked slowly upward through fields of violets and past hedges of blood-red roses, until they reached a graveled clearing where benches had been placed for weary climbers. Jimena stopped and turned and the view struck her like a quake. Cordova lay below in all its splendor, illuminated by the midday sun. Just as that ancient caliph had desired, there was beauty wherever the eye fell.

"There," Hasan said, pointing to the east, "that is the via-duct. See the golden lion in the center? From his cavernous mouth spouts the water that speeds swiftly down into Cordova and Al Zohra. It is a masterpiece of engineering."

Jimena shaded the sun from her eyes with a hand, eager to see the viaduct that was famous throughout the civilized world. The lion was so enormous she could easily discern its form from this great distance. She was suddenly overcome by exhaustion. It was all too much. It had not been more than a few hours ago that she had stepped out of the house so de-pressed and frightened about meeting Hasan in the garden, but it seemed at least a week ago. So much in five short hours. Her legs were barely able to support her, so she walked a few steps from the clearing and dropped down upon an earth blanketed with violets. Lying flat on her back with her arms outstretched over her head, she gazed at a blue and cloudless sky. Birds winged past and the perfumed air lay over her a soft, warm coverlet. Her fingers lovingly plucked at the flowers they rested upon.

Hasan had followed her and now stood looking down upon her. She lay surrounded by a halo of violet flowers, her breasts rising and falling seductively. His eyes slowly moved down the length of her body and up again to her face. He felt tension knotting his muscles and thought, It will take super-human strength to keep my hands from her. He sat down beside her, careful not to sit too close, and deliberately stared at her, with his will demanding that she look at him, that she take her eyes from the sky and bring them to the reality of this moment. "Raushana?" he whispered, "Splendid One?"

Jimena's heart pounded as hard as it had on the climb up to this paradise in the sky. She was afraid to look at Hasan and afraid *not* to. To turn her head a few inches took every ounce of willpower she had. "Yes, my lord?"

"Hasan."

"Yes," she murmured. "Hasan."

"Have you forgiven me, Raushana? Have you?"

"For what, my lord; I mean, Hasan?"

"You suffered so terribly that night. I held you tight against my breast on that wild ride through the desert and each time you cried out in pain my heart bled for you. I asked myself over and over again—what kind of beast am I to inflict such torture upon an innocent woman?"

"Hasan please . . ." Jimena whispered. "The past is dead. I . . . I would prefer not to be reminded."

"But I want you to know what I am—I want you to understand me. I am distressed by the fact that you despise me."

Jimena fought against it, but the past returned to her. She did not want to think of Hasan as that beast of an old nightmare; that was another man and another woman and had nothing to do with the reality that was now. No past, no lost children, no husband, no priests, no terror, or loneliness, only flowers and sunshine and love. "Please," she pleaded again, covering her eyes with an arm as if to ward off a blow.

"*Do* you despise me, Raushana? Do you?"

"No."

"But I recall the night you struck out against me, calling me '*swine, infidel*'; you sobbed, crying out your hatred for me, your heart broken because your husband had remarried. When did you cease hating me? When, Raushana?"

Jimena pulled her arm away from her face, and looked at him, needing to see the expression in his eyes. Did he mock her? Was he trying to make her say things to humiliate and defeat her? But she saw only intensity and an urgent need, and her reply came easily. "It was at the house of Estiano, when you came to fetch me. You entered the room, and I was aware that all loathing had been washed away by the tears of the night before. I fought it, and refused to admit the fact, but I know now that my hate for you has been self-deception since that moment."

Hasan moved and stretched out beside her, facing her. He studied her face anxiously and said, "Regarding our conversation of this morning, are you willing to obey my commands? Now that my anger has passed, I feel you surely have a right to decide for yourself what you will do with your life. I left you little enough alternative, Allah knows, by bringing you to this land and keeping you prisoner. Know that I very much want you to be content and happy. I readily admit that I chose the wrong method of retaliation, but it cannot be undone."

"Yes," Jimena said on a sigh, "I am willing to comply with your demands. I wish, more than anything, to continue my studies at the college, and to be attractive and clean. I want so *much* from life, so many things. . . ."

"Name those things, Raushana, and I will give them to you."

She did not answer, could not tell him it was love she wanted most of all. But it showed on her face, in the uncontrollable tremor of her lips, the downward curve of her eyelids and the silent speech eyes can transmit.

Hasan could no longer control his hands. He reached out and lightly placed hesitant fingertips upon Jimena's arm. He caressed her hand and wrist, cautioning himself not to press her, to allow her to decide the next move. He did not want to cause her any further guilt or anguish; he wanted her to love him, to want him, to give herself freely with no taint of sin upon the act. Surely there was desire for him behind her eyes?

Jimena dared not move or breathe. Her stomach was swirling and sheer terror had weakened every muscle, dissolving her flesh into rivulets of perspiration. The day, the moment she had so often dreamed of, had come. She must immediately decide between her immortal soul's salvation and a moment of passion on a mountainside. As she might have expected, panic came, an irrepressible compulsion to run. Hasan's fingers that moved upon her arm were hot irons searing her flesh; in his eyes she saw a fervency and warmth that sent a hot rush of blood through her veins. Every muscle tightened and a stabbing pain began in her groin.

"Raushana?" He moved closer to her, his gaze holding hers.

There was such sweetness in his emotion-roughened voice. She felt herself to be a moth impelled toward him, the fire, and the flames were hot about her now. She watched his mouth moving closer, closer, felt his warm breath upon her cheek, her lips. Soft lips touched hers lightly, unmoving, waiting; his arms slid around her, holding her close, oh so gently. Pulling her mouth slightly away from his, Jimena groaned. "Oh, my God," she gasped, then threw her lips back to his; she was starving and had found nourishment . . .

Hasan no longer held back. Jimena had given him the signal he waited for. He kissed her eyes, her cheeks, her hair; he pressed his mouth against hers again and again, his gasping breaths mingling with hers. He felt her body tight against his own, the entire length of her, every hollow and curve of her.

His arms moved from around her and his eager hands caressed her trembling, responsive flesh. Then he suddenly went tense, as he felt Jimena stiffen under his touch. His eyes darted up to her face and he saw the panic in her eyes. "Raushana, do not be afraid," he whispered hoarsely, tenderly stroking her hair back from her face. "It is right, Raushana . . . *good*." He placed a hand behind her head, lifting her lips back to his.

Passion for her broke loose from the bonds of tenderness and restraint. He pushed her lips apart with his own, pressed his tongue against her teeth until they too gave way beneath his onslaught. His body automatically rose, moved over and rested upon her.

"No," Jimena choked. She began striking against him with both fists, unable to control the cold dread of what he was about to do to her. She gasped, "Damn you! Goddamn you to Hell, let me go . . ."

"No," he groaned, pulling her tighter against him, roughly now, forgetting his good intentions of only moments before.

Jimena fought him. She struggled, thrashed, kicked, and bit at him. Suddenly she was free and blindly she ran without knowing the direction in which she was going, imagining that Rodrigo Diaz was right at her heels. She was running away from yesterday's reality as if the years had not passed. She stumbled and fell, got to her feet again, then was so unexpectedly and roughly brought to a halt that her neck snapped back with a loud cracking sound, wrenching every muscle there. She was whipped about to face an infuriated Hasan.

"Did you think that I would force you?" he shouted at her. "Do you think I must *rape* my women? Look at me! I said . . . *look* at me!" He took hold of her and shook her hard, venting his shattered ego upon her, desire still raging unsatisfied within him. "Stop playing the part of virgin . . . you only make a *fool* of yourself! I thought you wanted me. Do I look like the kind of man who must take from a woman what she will not willingly give me? Eh? Answer me Señora Diaz . . . do I?"

"No! No, no," she cried, shaking her head furiously. The pins flew from her hair and the false hairpiece dropped dismally to the ground between them.

"Fool! Your Christian husband, animal that he is, probably attacked you, took from you what you would not give him, but before you feel *my* arms about you again you will come to me begging . . . on your knees. Did you hear me? You will beg me for it. I have three wives and two other women who are all most anxious to please me. I would not degrade myself with the indignity of rape!"

"You are hurting me," Jimena whimpered, sniffling and trying to pull her arms from his digging fingers. She refused to meet his eyes.

Hasan was breathing heavily, but his tone was calmer now. "I have not finished. You listen closely to what I say. You *will* beg me. For you there is no other man, not now, nor in the future. It will be me, or no one; remember that. Always keep this fact in your mind. You will take my arms, my lips, my love . . . or spend the rest of your life in abstinence like a nun! When you are willing, come to me. If I feel generous that day I might, *might* I say, give you a little, if you are not too old and ugly by then to appeal to me."

"Oh!" Jimena gasped, infuriated. "Oh, I . . ." Unable to speak coherently, she stamped her foot on the ground, twisting vigorously to get loose from his grip and away from the stabbing insults being thrust at her.

"Ah. You are insulted, mmh? How many more years will you wallow in piety? How many more years will your youth and beauty last? Eh?"

"Goddamn you! Shut your mouth! How *dare* you speak to me this way, you—"

"Twenty-six, are you? Twenty-seven? Ten years, perhaps fifteen. For you, hardly sufficient time . . ."

With a surge of anger-produced strength, Jimena wrenched an arm free and sent her hand slicing through the air to jar Hasan's head with a blow across the face that left the red outline of her palm upon his cheek.

He caught her wrist and jerked her toward and against him. "To refresh your memory," he hissed, his mouth twisted in anger, "so you can remind yourself of what you will be missing all those lonely nights ahead in a cold bed." He put his other hand at the back of Jimena's head and pushed her mouth to his, pressing his body against her, cutting her mouth with the moving weight of his own. Then he roughly hauled her up into his arms and carried her at a running gait down the mountainside like a sack of garbage he was about to dispose of on a rubbish heap. He threw her up onto her horse's back and gave the animal a furious slap on the hindquarter, sending him rushing wildly down the bridle path toward the road, and Cordova. Desperately Jimena tried to keep her seat, guilt, indignation, hate, and love mingling together in her head until she thought her brain would explode.

Early next morning the black servant Kasim knocked upon Jimena's door and when she opened it he told her he was ready to escort her to her classes.

Jimena gaped at the man from swollen, red eyes, not fully comprehending what he was saying. "Classes? But, Kasim, you know I do not. . . . I am *not* going to the college!"

Kasim bowed from the waist, a practiced smile cracking his face, "Yes, my lady," he said agreeably. "I will await you here in the hall. Please make haste. I have other errands in the city this morning."

Jimena reached up a hand to shove a stray end of hair away from her forehead. Exasperatedly she said, "Kasim, what ails you? I said, I am not going to the college today!"

"The lord has said, my lady, if you will not ride, nor walk, you are to be carried."

Jimena glared into the man's leering face, then surrendered. "For God," she cried, with an angry stamp of her foot, "give me half of an hour. And you need not carry me!" She slammed the door hard in his face and stamped across the room to her closet to angrily choose what she would wear.

As she dressed herself the anger and numbness of the long, sleepless night began to leave Jimena. It was not too late to join Elvira's new class in poetry. And she could see before her the tiny, unfinished volume of her own poems upon Estiano's library shelves, waiting for her return, for the loving touch of her brush and pen. How wonderful it would be to see Elvira again, and to enjoy those leisurely afternoon meals at the Inn of the Swan.

The bishop—Jimena's heart rolled over in her chest when she thought about seeing him again. He visited Estiano at least once a week, so he could hardly be avoided. Hasan had demanded she give up her church, then relented, then became angry with her again. He probably meant to hold her to that command. But the bishop would not easily surrender. He would have missed her at church yesterday and would soon enough hear of her return to the college. She hesitated, her fingers tightening upon the stick of kohl she held in her hand. The paint of the damned, she thought. I must face the bishop, must stand before him painted and dressed in silk, and tell him . . .

"Damn," she swore, her nerves threatening to snap like the tight, thin strings of a lute. She slammed the black stick down upon the table, and it broke it into several hundred pieces. When would it all end? Would her life ever settle into anything vaguely resembling contentment? What was she going to say to the bishop? The easy way would be to say the half truth that Hasan demanded it and she was helpless to refuse, but there was more to it than that. There was the ring of truth in the words Hasan had said to her yesterday morning. There was something within her soul, something that defied conscious expression. A faint inner voice seemed to be speaking to her, but too softly for her to make out the message.

"For God," Jimena shouted out loud, "I will say to him whatever comes into my head, whenever the need arises. I will not worry upon it now." She finished the painting of her face, placed gold bracelets upon her upper arms, inspected herself in the mirror, then strode out into the hall to the waiting Kasim.

Jimena hesitated outside the door of Elvira's office, her hand resting upon the latch. She took a deep breath, raised her chin just a little to give herself an air of confidence, then opened the door.

Elvira soberly looked up from her papers when Jimena entered. Her eyes were vacant; she was still concentrating upon what she had been reading. It took a few moments before Elvira realized who that was standing so hesitantly just inside the door of her study. "Well, for the love of Allah, . . . Jimena!"

"Am I welcome? Or shall I leave before you throw me out?"

"Ridiculous. Come in. It is wonderful to see you."

Elvira was smiling most charmingly, but Jimena thought she saw a certain tenseness in her bearing and behind her eyes. Or was she just imagining it?

"You are looking well, Jimena."

No, Jimena had not imagined it. Elvira's eyes were extremely wary, her tone slightly edged with ice. Jimena guessed Elvira was wondering what had brought on this sudden change. She nervously met Elvira's chill gaze and suddenly before her inner eye came a dim image in a black habit and veils; then the reality of green satin trousers and gold vest. She looked for a mark of evil, but the countenance was the same as ever, composed and beautiful, the habit of her imagery incongruous with what this woman was. But what *was* Elvira? Many things, none evil; teacher, poetess, friend, woman, and free spirit. Elvira is the woman I would like to be, Jimena thought. Standing before me is myself as I might have been—might still be, if only. . . .
"Can you ever forgive me, Elvira? For two days now I have

had the discomforting task of begging forgiveness from too many people." She held out a hand to Elvira in a pleading gesture.

"There is nothing to forgive." Elvira said softly. "I understand; believe me I do." But she did not move to grasp the offered hand. "Has your mind changed again, Jimena? Do you *know* your mind now? Or will you turn against us again . . . tomorrow?"

"Elvira! That is unfair. Really, I . . . "

Elvira moved a few papers about on her table with long, relaxed fingers, an easy smile turning up the corners of her red-painted mouth. "Yes," she admitted, "it was unfair. Forgive me." She leaned back in her chair, folded her arms across her chest and studied Jimena's stricken face. "My deep-seated sense of superiority was slightly *un*seated when I realized you placed your salvation above my friendship, Jimena. But who am I to ask that I be placed before God in the estimation of my friends?"

"Elvira, please."

"Well. What brings you here? I see paint on your face. Obviously you have bathed recently. Your bishop will not like what he sees. His indignation will be a sight to behold. I pray I shall be there to see it. Damn me," she exclaimed exaggeratedly, "that I absolutely *have* to see!"

Elvira's ludicrous glee in anticipation of the bishop's agonies brought a sudden giggle from Jimena's throat. Soon she was laughing, amused at what only hours before had seemed an ominous threat.

"Now you laugh," Elvira smirked, shaking a warning finger at Jimena, "but it will not be so humorous when those accusing eyes of his are directed at you. Correct?"

Jimena smiled and shrugged.

"Are you going to give up your religion, Jimena?" The question was thrown at Jimena like a swift, unexpected sword thrust. Elvira's gaze probed deep into her in search of signs of self-knowledge and confident independence.

"Hasan demands it," Jimena said weakly.

"Ach! What do I care what Hasan demands! Hasan cannot forsake your religion for you. Speak for yourself."

"I—I do not exactly mean to give up my religion; I . . . I want to—"

"Wear silk and paint your face and commit any number of other sins with the right hand, while with the left hand you cling to God. Is that what you are trying to say?"

Jimena exhaled a rush of air, exasperated by the truth of Elvira's words. It was certainly an accurate description of herself, clinging with one hand to the Church and grasping with the other for a free life. She stepped away from the table and threw herself down into a large mound of pillows. She clasped her hands tightly together in her lap, slumped down and stretched her legs straight out before her. "For shit!" she suddenly swore, kicking both feet into the air, then slamming them down on the floor like a spoiled child.

"*Jimena!*" Elvira exclaimed in amazement. "Such language is unbecoming."

"How am I *supposed* to react? What in the name of Christ am I to do? Hasan says 'You are never to enter into a Christian church again.' The Bishop will say, 'You must never again deny your God because the wages of sin is Death'; and you say to me that I must let loose of my faith or drown intellectually. Everyone with something to say. I am being batted about like a ball on a polo field!"

"It is of your own making."

"Of course! Tell me, Elvira, why is everyone so concerned about what I do and think? Why can't you just leave me be, I ask you? I include the bishop."

"An excellent question. The bishop is interested in your death. We care about the quality of your life here on earth. But since you are so annoyed by my interest, I shall withdraw it. Go to Hell, if you believe such a place exists, or to Heaven if you are certain you know the way."

"Oh, Elvira," Jimena groaned, "you make me so damned angry sometimes." She felt deeply sorry for herself.

"Do I?"

"Nothing ever flusters you or defeats you. The simplicity of your life in the face of untold numbers of complications— well, I imagine I am jealous."

"But, Jimena! You are the one who complicates your life. Your mind teeters back and forth, avoiding decisions as if they were plagues that might destroy you. Never allow more than five countings for any one decision, then accept any and all of the consequences. You learn from mistakes and soon have an uncanny instinct for what is right." Elvira grinned and said, "Never, I say, *never*, listen to anyone who gives free advice. Use your own judgment. After all, it is your life, not theirs'. And I do include my own advice in this advice."

"Well, thank you."

"It is the least I can do, Jimena, the very least."

"Now stop this, Elvira," Jimena giggled.

"Stop what?"

"Teasing me."

"Who in the name of hell is teasing?"

"For God!"

Elvira leaned forward, laughing, her guard finally down. "Would you like to join my class? I have room for you. I am beginning a course in ancient poetry again, predominantly Persian."

"I would adore to, Elvira. Can I start today, or . . ."

"Absolutely! Class begins at two. But if you do not allow me to finish my preparations there will be no class at all. Forgive my bluntness . . ."

Jimena reared up on her pillows, feeling suddenly light-hearted. She got up and strode across the room to the door in pretended indignation. "Well," she cried, as she opened the door and turned to smartly face her friend, "you need not tell me to get out a second time. I will be in my seat promptly at two. See *you* are as prompt."

Jimena walked swiftly down the long hallway and confidently burst into the room nearest the stairwell. There was no one about: the room was empty except for a certain vibration in the air, a silent expectancy. Every pen and brush seemed suspended outside its usefulness, awaiting the eager hands that would come soon, clutch them up, and create new beauty in the world through them.

She walked down an aisle between rows of tables, to one in front near the teacher's lecture stand. She sat down on the stool and eased the drawer open, pulling out the brushes and pens, bottles of ink and paint. Placing a small sheet of white paper upon the easel, Jimena quietly and with intense concentration began to put her thoughts and emotions into words and rhyme. "Unjust it was to bid the World be just. Ah, blame it not. It ne'er was made for justice: Take what it gives thee, leave all grief aside, For now to sweet and then to sour, its lust is." She frowned and scratched it out, beginning again. "By Allah, set thy foot upon my soul; Since long, long years for this alone I longed: And whisper tale of love in my ear; To me 'tis sweeter than the sweetest song!"

Estiano stood in the doorway staring at the woman at the front of his classroom. Irrationally his heart began beating faster; it was such a shock to enter and see her there. He had thought he would never look upon her again. There, just as though she had never been away, her soft young shoulders bent over her easel, that same intense expression upon her face as she worked. He stepped quietly and came to a stop behind her, then reached out a hand and placed it gently upon her shoulder. It was the first time he had touched her since that night when she was for a brief moment against his breast in embrace.

"Ah, greetings, Estiano . . . I am back," she said, not in the least startled by his sudden appearance.

He reached across her and picked up her writings. After studying them carefully, he set them down.

"Not very good are they?" she asked confidently.

"I have read much worse."

"I wish to complete my book of poems, Estiano. Can I come to the scriptorium after class today?"

"*Any* day."

"Thank you, sir."

"And how long will you continue your studies, Raushana?" he asked, trying to keep his voice disinterested, belying how much her answer meant to him.

Jimena hesitated, then said emphatically, "Indefinitely, Estiano—indefinitely."

Estiano's shoulders relaxed as if a weight had been lifted from them. He did not in any way acknowledge her reply, but silently walked away from her to the lecture stand, where he soberly began laying out and organizing his notes for the day's task.

Chapter
✠ *EIGHT* ✠

The bishop clutched nervously at the gatepost, trying to
keep his eye from the marketplace. But for only brief instants
would they rest upon the earth, the sky, or a winging
butterfly—they always cast upward and out once again, searching for that small figure that never came. There was a throbbing pain in his chest and his breath was short. He wondered if,
at forty-five, he should consider himself old. He certainly did
feel old today. The blood ran sluggish through his veins, his
mind was fogged, and there was a definite if minor palsy of the
right side of his face. Probably just strain. But that fluttering in
his chest at night, when sleep would not come, concerned him.
He placed a hand over his chest, listening, waiting for the reas-
suring throbs. He raised his eyes to the sky, an unspoken prayer
behind his tightly drawn lips. Please, Lord, let her be before my
eyes. But when he searched again through the crowd of milling
Arabs, Jimena was not there.

She was ill, perhaps even dying, he thought. That infidel
savage would not call him, would allow her to die without the
final sacrament. Sudden panic caused him to lurch forward, to
tightly grasp the carved iron bars of the gate with white,
clenched fists. He heard again his mother's gasping, shrieking
cries for a priest as she lay dying and he slapped a hand hard
over each ear to shut out the cries that emerged from the darkness of his childhood.

"Blessed Mary," he wept, clutching at his pounding heart. He
walked unsteadily away and entered his church. Jimena would
not come. For a few moments he stood indecisively in the entranceway, telling himself he must take action. But what? What
could he do? Suddenly he threw back his shoulders, turned and
swiftly walked out of the church and down the short path. He

shoved the gate open and out of his way. He would end this awful apprehension immediately. He would storm the house of Abu l Hasan and force the pagan to let him see her.

It was a long few moments before anyone answered the bishop's loud knocking at the door. He rocked back and forth from foot to foot, his shaking hands fumbling with the folds of his gray robe.

The manservant who finally responded stood with his lips parted to speak, eyes rounded in surprise, no words coming.

"I would speak with Doña Jimena!"

The servant looked at the bishop as if he were mentally deficient. "There is no one in this house by that name!," he snapped and started to close the door.

"Raushana!" the bishop shouted, his distaste for the name apparent in his pronunciation.

Again the servant's mouth dropped open. Men simply did not knock upon the door of an Arab gentleman and demand to see a woman of his house. "Go away, fool," he snarled. "You are *mad!*"

"Listen to me, you savage! Allow me to enter. I will beat upon this door for a week, if necessary."

Quickly the door was slammed shut in the bishop's face. He began knocking again, grim determination driving him on. Finally the door opened again and a now-smiling servant ushered him into Hasan's house. The bishop's eyes immediately scanned the entrance lobby half hoping she would be there awaiting him, but the entire house seemed deserted. He followed the servant up the stairs and to the left at the landing. His heart was in his throat as the servant pushed aside the curtain for him to enter Hasan's library.

Hasan sat upon a stack of pillows with his legs crossed. His eyes were cold. "What is so urgent, Bishop, that you must beat so upon my humble door?"

The bishop felt extremely ill at ease. Sweat was pouring from his palms and wetting his robe under the armpits. "I would see Jimena immediately," he commanded, trying to transmit superiority through his tone.

"You *would*? Ah, I think not, Saíd."

"But," he stammered, "but if she is ill, dying, you cannot withhold the sacrament from her—you cannot, I will not allow it!"

"My dear fellow," Hasan purred, "I assure you she is not

dying. In fact, I would say that she is most thoroughly *living* at this moment, for the first time since you set your pious fangs into her."

"Why have I not seen her this past week?"

"Because I forbade her to ever step foot inside your church again, sir. Does that adequately answer your question?"

"But—but you have no *right*! You cannot do this: she is Christian. Even your own—" he choked on the word—"your Koran allows her the privilege of choosing her own faith!"

Hasan moved smoothly from his pillows and stood erect, setting his feet wide apart and resting his hands on his hips. He glared straight into the bishop's retreating eyes and said, "The *Koran* allows it, Saíd, but *I* do not. Now, I think there is no more to be said here." He walked to the doorway, an eyebrow raised questioningly, silently asking the bishop to leave.

But the bishop remained immobile. He did not know what to say, but could not bring himself to give up.

"Bishop," Hasan said impatiently, "you are making a fool of yourself. What is one less sheep in your pathetic flock, one insignificant, frail young woman? You act as though I have stolen the month's collection from your box. Do you take all your souls so seriously—or is there more here than meets my eye, eh?"

"Swine!" the bishop exclaimed defensively, "good men of Christ are not like you; there are higher purposes than . . . than the flesh!"

"Ah, Bishop, I have insulted you; forgive me. How tragic for you, to so despise the stirring of your blood by this woman. I do admire your taste, Saíd. Raushana adds grace and splendid beauty to my house. I am grieved that you must be denied her company henceforth, but I am certain you will eventually find another just as comely as she to vent your sterile passions upon, poor man." He moved quickly and took hold of the man's arm. "I will escort you to the door, Saíd. I would not want you to lose your way, for my house is large, with many halls and stairs."

The bishop was totally defeated. There were no more words he could use against this man. His eyes filmed over with tears. He saw Jimena in this Arab's ravaging arms, screaming out in agony at every touch, threatened, forced, beaten into submission and helplessly following in the footsteps of this devil. And he saw white, soft arms, brown eyes bright with innocence, thin, lovely fingers entwined in prayer, that sweet head bent low before him. He saw his own hand touching the gleam-

ing gold that once had been the color of her hair, lingering over
the beauty of it, sad that it must be cut away, a sadness for
which he had paid severe penance. He remembered the disturbing scent of her flesh, the low resonance of her voice. Suddenly
fear closed his throat. The image of his mother's face faded, and
he saw Jimena upon her deathbed with her soul drifting, descending into the depths . . . the fire, the torturing, flesh-
devouring fire.

"Are you ill, Saíd?" Hasan asked concernedly as the
bishop's step faltered; he had felt the man's arm tighten and
knot beneath his fingers.

The bishop could not reply. His mind was searching frantically for and finding new courage. It was not Jimena's wish that
she stay away from him, away from the church; she was being
forced. Somehow he would see her and rescue her. She would
have her reward in Heaven if it took all the strength left in him,
if it cost him his life.

The bishop kicked at a puffy gray thistle of dust, disinte-
grating it into a thousand microscopic particles that dejectedly
settled back upon the floor. The single solution, he assured
himself, was complete escape. But was the gain worth the
price? It was not the money; God knew he would have paid the
man much more if he had demanded it, but he had stolen from
profits that were by right the pope's. Yes! Before God, it was
worth it. God understood that he had committed the theft with
noble purpose, and if there was no real repentance, God would
forgive that also, for one of His own was to be saved. Jimena
would be freed from slavery, and meaning and grand purpose
would be restored to her life.

A flutter of nervous excitement surged in the pit of his
stomach. One of his clerks had been sent to watch the house of
Abu l Hasan and had returned with a full account of Jimena's
daily movements. He had sent the clerk out two more days,
and the schedule was precisely the same. Totally ignoring the
clerk's aside that the woman appeared quite amiable to her situation, he steadfastly held to his illusion of enforced obedience.
He saw the joy that would light her sweet face when he told
her the news, gave to her this one supreme gift and sacrifice. In
worshiping gratitude she would kneel down before him, tears
wetting her cheeks, and kiss his hand. The bishop felt the anticipated warm touch of those lips and his fingers moved longingly.

Two days later the bishop crouched in dense shrubbery

outside the walls of the scriptorium, waiting. Not only the destiny of Jimena Gomez was at stake, but his own. He would save Jimena if he could, but there was no one in the world who was willing to save *him*. He waited with his head high and his shoulders straight with purpose and sincerity, on the brink of a dark abyss from which he could not escape. He had refused to heed the warnings, the signs along the road that told him he was taking the wrong path. He was too confident in his righteousness.

Jimena washed the ink from her fingers, then leaned forward to examine her face in the small glass over the marble basin. She wiped away a smudge of lampblack from under one eye and ran her fingers through the curls at the side of her face, wishing it did not take so long for hair to grow. It still barely reached her shoulders. She vowed that the next Friday, when there were no classes, she would have Acacia lighten it again.

Moving back to her easel, she picked up the newly begun book of poems and lovingly inserted the day's two pages. She leafed through the manuscript, counting the pages as a measurement of her accomplishment, glad that the work went slowly, because to finish was to end the anticipation of completion that was so exciting. How simple it had been, all the patterns of the recent past falling back into place as if those long, wasted months had never existed. How had it happened? One day she was beginning to enjoy life and within a few short hours a shroud had dropped over her that buried her inside herself. The why of it lay in the figure of a man, a man of God who had captured her soul and held it for ransom; the price for her immortal soul's salvation was her life. She wondered if her strength had grown, if she could ward off that black cloth when it hung over her head again, if she could defy the terrible wrath of God that would blaze from his eyes like the fires of Hell.

With a shiver, Jimena tried to force thought of the bishop from her mind. Weeks ago she had decided to face the situation when it confronted her and not before. But when would he come? At what moment of what day would she suddenly be face to face with him?

"Finished for the day?" Estiano smiled up at Jimena from his easel as she entered his study. He put his pen between his teeth while he concentrated on the mixing of a lighter yellow.

Jimena nodded in affirmation and stood behind him, eyeing his work like an expert viewing it for critical analysis.

"Well," he grinned, "do you approve?"

Jimena pursed her lips and frowned. "Mmm . . . it will do. Be patient. Work with me another year and you will be amazed at your improvement."

"Is that how I sound? God forbid!"

"It is beautiful, Estiano. I remember the first book of your printing that I ever saw. Elvira brought it to me. It was an Aristotle. I know now that it is your work, it could be no one else's. That book is still my most treasured keepsake, though today the words have more meaning for me. Then it was only the beauty of your illumination that I admired. I treasure it twofold now. You are a great artist, Estiano, not just a craftsman."

"I thank you," he said, his voice rough with the pleasure her compliments gave him.

"Do you mind if I sit and watch you for a little? Kasim is late this evening and I dare not travel alone, else Hasan would—Well, I do not know what he would do, but I cannot imagine it being pleasant."

"It is best to wait," he agreed and went back to his work. He was acutely conscious of her eyes on his fingers, which rendered them less sure. Just as his brush hovered over the parchment to make the final flourish upon a decorative effect, Jimena spoke, and the words so startled him that the flourish became a blob of yellow that turned the entire page into scrap paper. He put his pen down, turned his head to her and exclaimed, "What did you say?"

"I said, are you going to marry Elvira? Why are you so shocked? You have been seeing her for years."

Estiano threw up his hands. "God bless me, and Allah, too . . . and any other gods in earshot. That was about the most ridiculous question I have ever had put to me." He was laughing, but his emotions were in turmoil. He had denied himself all alternative treasures with a faltering hand outstretched toward his heart's true desire—that one perfect dream that could never be. He bent his head down and away from Jimena's searching eyes, letting his mind speak the words his tongue could not manage. *It is you I want, Jimena, Splendid One, only you.* He was so shaken by the vehemence of his unspoken declaration and the depth of his emotional pain, that he was unable to control the expression on his face. His feelings were clearly mirrored there.

"Oh, Estiano," Jimena whispered, resting a hand lightly on his arm. "I *am* sorry. My nose is too long, poking into things that are none of my business." Her heart reached out to him.

She was certain she understood his pain; it was the reflection of himself seen in every glass, and in every still pond or stream. How dreadful it must be to carry homeliness with you like an unremovable festival mask. Suddenly her understanding became something more, a complete *knowing,* so that she felt exactly what Estiano felt. A very young girl appeared before her inner eye, a girl so homely it was unlikely that any man would ever want to marry her. Then she recalled Hasan's words, that if God had intended her to be ugly, He would have created her that way. What purpose did God have when he designed poor Estiano with all his beauty hidden from the eye?

Jimena turned her eyes to the door. Kasim still had not come. She became restless, trying to decide whether to go off alone or continue to wait. She stepped to a window and looked out. The sun was low and shadows were beginning to form in the pathways. The clouds were already slightly tinted with the hues of sunset.

"He will be here any moment," Estiano said. Quickly he caught up his brushes and put them away; his fingers did not wish to work, dragging as if a weight held them back.

"I hope so. It will be dark before I reach home, as it is."

Estiano moved over to the window to stand beside her. "If he does not come before Elvira arrives, we will see you home. I would not allow you to ride alone. So do not concern yourself, all right?"

Jimena abruptly dropped down on the window seat. "Dear God," she gasped, "I just suffered the most dreadful sense of impending doom." She attempted to laugh. "When I was a girl I often had such premonitions." She shivered, hugging herself with her arms. "Oh, Estiano, I feel cold all over, and snakes of ice are wrapped around my heart." Suddenly Jimena remembered seeing little Urracca in Aunt Galiana's arms for the last time. She saw herself clutching the child back to her breast out of fear that she would never see her again.

"Nonsense," Estiano said, dropping a hand to her shoulder reassuringly. "You are just tired." He added thoughtfully, "I would say most people feel ice around the heart when contemplating their childhood—the most ghastly time of our lives."

"Amen," Jimena whispered. "I would not be a child again for anything."

"Nor I," he interrupted earnestly. "Any dismal today is worth the pain, as long as we know that black yesterday can never touch us again."

"Not touch you, perhaps, but my yesterday is a dark shadow that follows me wherever I go. I have never become separated from it. It is not a matter of touching me; it *is* me and I am it—the child and the woman are one and the same."

"No," he smiled, placing a hand on Jimena's clasped fists. "There is a greater gap between your two selves, child and adult, than you realize. I find it exceedingly difficult these days to believe that you are the same girl I drove to Zamora in a carriage."

"Ah, that is comforting. But I feel the same, I really do."

"No; you lie to yourself."

"Ach, of course I do!" she cried, slapping her hands down hard upon her knees. "I am not the same at all. Misery is just a habit with me, one I do not know quite how to live without; if not there, I manufacture it. But why would I do such a ridiculous thing like cling to a person and life that I despised?"

"Jesus, don't ask me. Better men than I am have tried to answer the whys of existence and failed. I am not God, or a philosopher, or very wise at all. I only know what is right for myself."

"Well, good evening. What are *you* doing here, Jimena?" Elvira swept into the room, rushed to them, and gave each a warm kiss upon the cheek. "For God's sake, why so *serious*? You both look like the storm clouds that I *thought* I left outside."

Jimena laughed and returned Elvira's kiss. Then she frowned and asked, "Is there a storm coming? If so, I had best start for home."

Outside the library stormclouds had indeed begun gathering. The bishop waited in the dark cover of shrubbery along the path Jimena would take. Kasim rushed breathlessly down a darkening alley toward the library; he had been detained by the mounted police because he had witnessed a theft in the marketplace. He was only fifteen minutes away, but he would be too late. Estiano, Elvira and Jimena were already walking briskly down a lamplit hallway, intent upon getting to their horses and to Hasan's house before the storm broke.

The bishop groaned and leaned back in exhaustion against the stone wall, not so much from the hours he had waited, but from tension. His earlier exhilaration had been replaced by morbid worrying. He must speak with Jimena alone, but the infidel's manservant might not allow it. He should have thought to include a thug in his plan, to subdue the servant while he talked with her. But all he had to do tonight was inform her that he was beside her in her time of need and despair and that he had news for her, grand news. She could slip away and come to him tomorrow, or the next day. No need for haste. The caravan did not leave until month's end.

Suddenly the bishop lurched to attention. It was Jimena. No one else laughed in just that way. But there were others. Estiano and Elvira Rodriguez. Quickly he stumbled backward deeper into the shrubs so that he was completely hidden. He watched the three walk out of the library gate. Talking and laughing, they moved down the street toward the livery stable. He followed them, keeping a safe distance behind. He hired a horse for himself only after they had ridden off. It was better this way. But he must be quick and catch Jimena before she entered the infidel's house.

Estiano's ears were keen, his senses acute. At first he thought it was his imagination. No, he was certain they were being followed. The hollow ring of hooves upon cobbles behind them was unmistakable. They had nearly reached the city gates, but after having made several sharp turns the steady rhythm was still behind. Recalling Jimena's uneasiness of an hour before, he hesitated to speak of it to the women riding ahead of him. But if a thug were to attack on the dark, shadowed highway to Al Zohra, he was not certain he could adequately defend the women. Better to face the villain within the city wall than in the more haphazardly policed suburbs.

"Jimena! Elvira?" Estiano called out as softly as he could and still be heard. "Rein in and dismount around the next turn."

"What?" Elvira shouted back over her shoulder.

"Sssst," he warned, shaking his fist angrily at Elvira as he brought his mount alongside her.

Elvira laughed, thinking it was a game, but she quickly grew serious when she saw the urgency on his face.

"We are being followed. Do not excite yourselves; it is probably nothing. Rein in around the next bend in the street." At Jimena's blank, startled expression he yowled, "Do as I tell you, for the love of Allah! You can think upon it some other time!"

Jimena leaped off the horse's back and ran for shelter, her heart racing. She threw herself down behind the marble drinking fountain that formed a square in the center of the street and covered her head with her arms. She felt Elvira's body lunge down beside her and heard the approaching sound of clacking hooves slowly moving closer to where Estiano lay in wait.

"You! What in hell do you think you're doing?"

Jimena heard Estiano's angry words and knew who it was, even though the reply was low and muffled.

"If you would speak with me, then approach me openly!"

Another muffled reply.

"No! You may *not* speak with her. You know as well as I do that Hasan has forbidden her to see you. What ails you, man? Go home to your bed, Bishop, and leave us be."

"Oh, my God," Jimena moaned, then felt the firm pressure of Elvira's hand upon her shoulder.

"Are you afraid, Jimena?"

"Yes."

"Do you want to see him?"

" . . . No."

"If you are not prepared to deny your faith, it would be unwise indeed to deny your bishop." Elvira strained her eyes to see in the dark. Taking Jimena by the arms she pulled them aside so she could see her face. "Well, Jimena?" she asked impatiently.

Jimena could not answer. Her throat was closed, her eyes filled with tears.

Enraged, Elvira shouted. "Damn you, where is your *backbone*? Have the courage of your convictions. Be a good Christian or do not be one at all!" She jumped to her feet yanking Jimena up with her. She shook her roughly. "Go, Jimena," she commanded. "Cease your sniffling, straighten your shoulders, and tell the world you are *proud* to be a Christian. Tell the bishop. Right now!" She gave a powerful shove that sent Jimena stumbling out into the street.

Jimena walked blindly down the street, her feet dragging as if shackled with weights. It was a terrible thing she must do. Elvira had misunderstood her tears, her hesitance. They had been tears of regret that the road to her own desires must be paved with the pain of another, not tears of fear or uncertainty.

"Jimena!" Estiano cried. "Go *back*. You cannot . . . "

"Shut your mouth, Estiano." Jimena's voice was hard and loud. She was angry now, angry enough to slap everyone in sight. "I have had enough advice and criticism for one night. The bishop wishes to speak with me, I believe?"

"Yes, but . . . " Estiano fell silent as she came closer and he could see the fury in her eyes. He reined in his horse, slowly moving away from the bishop and into the background where Elvira stood watching Jimena with a pleased expression on her face.

"Wonderful! the bishop cried emotionally. "Jimena, you were wonderful. I knew they could not keep you from me for long; your faith is too strong. God loves you well, my child. He loves you well!"

The bishop rushed at her and clasped her to his breast in an ecstacy of pride, his impassioned lips pressing hot against the flesh of her neck.

Jimena squirmed as gracefully and gently as she could from his embrace. Her anger diminished as pity for him emerged. "Bishop," she said softly, "please."

The bishop did not hear her. His head was spinning with how well it had gone and bursting with his news. He pulled her further away from Estiano, leaned forward confidentially and hoarsely whispered, "I have fantastic news for you, wait until you hear." He grinned like a small boy returning from school with a prize. "In less than a single month you will be on your way home." He darted his eyes from left to right to see if anyone skulked nearby that might hear. "Home, Jimena. It is all arranged. A caravan—no one will discover you beneath bolts of silk; there is a box where you can be hidden if anyone searches for you."

"What?" Jimena protested. "What in God's name are you raving about? Home? Could you mean—*Castile*?"

"Well, what other place do you call home?" he snapped.

"Bishop, listen to me. I—"

His face drained and he shouted, "I will travel with you!" His heart was going to explode. No. It was not possible. He would not listen to her. "We will be free, Jimena. Away from this hellish land of pagans and among the chosen of God . . . me at long last and you once again. We must be quick. Here is what you must do. Leave the scriptorium at your usual time . . . Bless me, I forgot to tell you the day. Three Fridays hence. Now leave at your usual time—"

"Bishop! Be quiet and listen to me!"

"No! Dear God, I will not listen!"

"Oh, yes, you *will*, sir; I have no intention of returning to Castile with you, or with anyone else. I want you to understand that. Forget your plans!"

"Not return! But you cannot mean—you cannot remain here and be, be tortured by that swine! I spoke with him—he is a *monster*. He had the . . . said that you would never step foot in my church again. I thought you were dying, and would not receive . . . the final sacrament. I—" he gasped for air and tears filled his eyes. "Jimena, Lord God, you cannot do this!"

"Bishop. Oh, Bishop . . . please," she pleaded, her heart constricted, tears of her own behind hot eyelids. "Please try to understand. I cannot return. The woman I once was is dead. Jimena Diaz lives with her husband to the north and has borne him two children. There is no path on the soil of Castile upon which I can walk. It is difficult for me—because my child is there—but I would be no fit mother for her in that land as I am. I hope to bring her here to me someday. This is my home now. This is where I shall live out my life, and I thank God for his mercy for giving me my escape."

"God! God, you say? You choose to live amidst *infidels,* and dare to speak of God?"

Jimena hesitated, gathering her new convictions together. She whispered sadly, "Your God is my God no longer, Bishop. We walk on separate paths, but"—she held out a hand to him—"but I would like to be your friend, if you would let me."

"Friend!" he shrieked. "Explain to me how you can deny all that you have held sacred, how you can ignore the flames— the flames, Jimena, the *flames!*"

Outraged, Jimena shouted, "There is the answer to your own question, sir! If all other arguments fail, you can always use the threat of hell fire against me. Well, you can no longer use such threats to maintain my submission. I need not beg or grovel before you . . . nor kiss your hand, or that of any other man who thinks himself His assistant, who thinks himself any closer to God than I am! This is the vile result of enlightenment, Bishop! In this land I have heard dissenting voices. I have been offered an alternative and I am accepting it. Go home to your church, sir, or depart on that Friday for Castile, I care not. Just leave me be. Leave me *be!*"

For an instant the bishop stood thunderstruck; then he charged like a maddened bull, lunging past Jimena until he was face to face with Elvira. "Devil!" he screamed at her. "Witch . . . see what you have done! Another soul destroyed, to fry beside you in the depths of Hell!"

Elvira had no opportunity to reply. The bishop's fists suddenly struck her with hysteria-increased strength. He hit the side of her head, then her now fear-stricken face, crunching, sickening blows that threw her head backward against the brick wall with bone-crushing force. Her eyes were instantly covered over by a rush of blood that ran into her mouth and down upon her breast. Elvira collapsed to the cobblestone street, unconscious.

Estiano had had no time to prevent the attack; he had been taken as unaware as Elvira. Released from inertia, he fell to his knees and clutched out in grief to lift Elvira into his arms. "Police," he cried out, his voice shaking with rage and fear, "in the name of Allah, someone call a policeman!" Then he turned upon the heavily breathing madman who was still standing in the position of his attack. "You fool! You miserable, pathetic fool! Get away from my sight before I *kill* you!" He moved to gently lay Elvira upon the cobblestones, his long arms swinging, his fists clenched tightly together—murder in his eyes.

The bishop backed away from Estiano, his eyes glazed. His heart was missing every other beat. His hands were numb and tingling from the blows he had struck at the Devil, but it was good to feel it. What other man of God could say the same. I have struck a mighty blow to the flesh of the Devil, knocked him senseless. Ah, God was proud of him today. But he must further prove his worth; the blows were not enough. The Word of God—that was the way; he would preach the Word of God to the multitude and save a thousand upon a thousand souls, or die. They would have to kill him to restrain him. "He who is persecuted for righteousness' sake." "You are all *sinners,*" he shrieked, flailing his arms in the air, turning around and around in stumbling circles. "Save yourselves before it is too late!" Then he ran, racing through gates, knocking upon doors, screaming his warnings at the city of Cordova. His voice echoed back to fall upon Jimena's horrified ears, fainter and fainter, until the sound of his cries was lost in the darkness of the city.

"What have I *done?*" Jimena wept, covering her face with her hands. "Dear God, Elvira—what have I done to you?"

A crowd had gathered. A doctor came and bent over Elvira, his gentle fingers pressing a cloth to her battered face, wiping away the blood to reveal purpling bruises and a deep gash in her skull; he shook his head uncertainly. Then the police came, mounted upon gaudily decorated horses. Within seconds, after hearing Estiano's tearful explanation, they rode swiftly down the dark street, following the bishop's path of destruction.

Another crowd, not far distant, watched the bishop in solemn, rapt attention. A Christian priest had gone mad. When a new arrival walked upon the scene, one of them would point to the minaret's balcony whispering that it was a great pity.

"Come down," a young Arab called, his mouth cupped by jeweled fingers, "before the police arrive, and I will help you to escape!"

There was no reply from the moving shadow on the balcony above.

"Someone should go up and bring him down," another said.

"I attempted it, but he has bolted the door. Look! See how he reaches up to the heavens, then leans over as if choking with a mighty regurgitation? He will allow no one to help him. A pity. A fine, pious man, he was, too."

"You knew him?" a woman called out, elbowing her way through the crowd to the man who spoke.

"Indeed. A bishop of the Christian faith. His church is but five doors from my leather shop. I would not have believed it, had any man predicted this sad event. Ah, he was indeed a pious man."

"Then Allah will welcome him, and Jesus Christ, Allah bless him, will meet him at the gates of Paradise."

"Quite true."

"Sinner!" a shrieking voice cried out, echoing through the night and silencing the whisperings of those below.

The bishop was breathing heavily. His hands gripped the balcony railing so tightly that his knuckles shone white in the darkness. "All those who wish to give themselves to God," he called down to a sea of dim faces, "come here to me, and I will hear your confessions and place you in His loving hands. Come! Damn you! Fools! Why do you not listen? Why?"

All else might have been forgiven, understood by the charitable Muslims, but the bishop had one last thing he would say before the police, now rushing up the long staircase, could stop him, "Muhammed is not a true prophet! He is false—a liar—a God-damned liar! When you follow his word, you follow the way of demons, the Devil himself! I—No! Take your foul hands from me, you swine. Let loose of me, I tell you. I am a bishop . . . I represent the Lord. You will burn for this, I must save those who are coming to me. See? Can you not see them filing up the stairs? It was I who saved them and I must hear their confes—"

A gay-colored silk scarf was stuffed into the bishop's mouth, choking off his frantic flow of words. His arms were tied behind him. Thus bound and gagged, he was led down the stairs by three policemen, his shoulders slumped, his head bowed, his chin resting upon his heaving chest. The crowd was still and moved apart, making a path through which he might be led.

On the twenty-fourth day of October in the year of Christ, 1075, the bishop was taken from his cell and brought before Al Rakashi, chief adviser to the wali of Cordova. As pious a man as Al Rakashi was, he offered leniency to the prisoner. He would release him, return him to his church, if he would give his vow, upon his own Bible, never to blaspheme the prophet of Islam again. But the bishop refused the Arab's generosity.

"Avenge your accursed prophet," he cried joyfully. "Treat me with all your barbarity. I will gladly die for my Lord in Heaven. Never will I cease preaching the Word, His word. Release me and within one hour I will be standing high over the heads of your people denouncing your foul, mock prophet!"

"The punishment is death," Al Rakashi warned.

"No, not death, infidel, but *Heaven*! 'Blessed are they who are persecuted for righteousness' sake, for theirs is the kingdom of heaven.' Do what you will with me. The followers of Christ will kneel down to me for all the ages to come and call me saint!"

"You fool!" Al Rakashi snorted, slamming his fists down on the table. "You are not a saint, a blessed martyr. You merely commit suicide, one of your mortal sins, when you deliberately refuse my leniency. Suicide! You would have me slay you so that all the Christians of Andalus might weep over your grave, despising me and the religion that condemned you. Am I not right? Answer me, Bishop!"

"I do not fear the vengeance of your false prophet." The bishop smiled triumphantly. "It is you who should tremble in dread, you who stirs the wrath of the Almighty by what you intend to do to one of his own."

Al Rakashi sighed and folded his hands together on the tabletop. He looked long at the man standing before him, pity in his eyes, shaking his head contemptuously. "So be it, then. What will be, will be. Allah be with you, Saíd. I pray your soul is strong enough to bear the bitter disappointment and suffering that awaits it."

On November the fifth of that year, on a Sunday, the bishop's head was laid upon the block and swiftly and efficiently sliced off with an ax.

"Vengeance is mine, saith the Lord. The destruction of Islam is at hand. God will prevail and Christ shall rule the earth. The false prophet of Islam will be destroyed for all time. Blessed Mary, Mother of God, I commend myself into your hands, that you may deliver my soul unto the Lord."

These, the bishop's last words, were committed to writing by the Christians who had watched his execution, and were delivered across the world to his Eminence, the pope. The name of the bishop was placed high on the holy list for canonization. And, as he had predicted, he was in time named saint, to live immortal in the minds of Christian men.

But one other had spoken at the same moment. Al Rakashi was standing near the block, sadly watching the sentence being carried out. As the bishop condemned his prophet, he whispered these words, "Love your enemies, do good to them that hate you and pray for them that despitefully use you and persecute you," words from the bishop's own Bible, mysteriously ignored by the saint who was about to die.

Chapter
✠ *NINE* ✠

Wine flowed from enormous silver kegs set upon the garden wall. Under the orange trees a table twenty feet long was heaped to overflowing with sliced meats, fruit, and sweetmeats. Musicians roamed through the halls of Hasan's house, from room to room, then out into the gardens, strolling along the riverbank, raising their voices in songs appropriate to each new scene they met with, a pair of young lovers behind an oleander bush entwined in each other's arms, a group of obese old men sitting upon the lawn with a chessboard between them, a cluster of dancing girls with bare, oiled flesh gleaming in the light of the colored lamps resting before once more taking up the task of entertaining Hasan's guests.

Jimena stretched luxuriously, feeling the soft coolness of the lawn through her gown. She lay flat on her back near the riverbank with her arms folded under her head. She listened dreamily to the sounds of this night—sighs, laughter, singing, the gentle rippling of the water near her feet, the breeze humming in the branches of the giant magnolia tree. She watched the full moon, slit in two by a branch, move ever so slowly until it was complete again and sent a shaft of silken light down upon her face.

"You are rather exclusive tonight, Raushana."

"Oh, Elvira." Jimena rolled over on her stomach to face her friend, leaning her chin in the palms of her upraised hands. "Just enjoying the night, watching the moon take its evening stroll across the sky. I had had sufficient wine and my throat was dry from so much talk. Come. Join me." She patted the soft earth beside her in invitation, guardedly observing Elvira's strained facial expression, uncertain if she should offer assistance or not.

Elvira awkwardly threw one stiff leg before the other in an

effort to sit down. "Damn me, Jimena," she laughed, "if the perch is not exactly where the ass is, I simply cannot manage the feat of sitting down. Help me, please?"

With tears hot behind her eyes, Jimena instantly leaped up, and helped Elvira swing around and drop upon the grass.

"Huuug," Elvira grunted, "what a jolt. A good thing these teeth are my own, or I would have swallowed them."

Jimena sat down on the grass, her heart wrenched by Elvira's struggle. One side of Elvira's face sagged and had remained purple and black. The doctors were helpless to explain why her left side was paralyzed, or why her condition steadily worsened; all agreed her injury would eventually lead to her death. Brain damage of some sort, they surmised. Elvira was dying. The bishop had murdered her, more brutally than his twisted mind could have conceived. It had already been months. How much longer? An enormous amount of suffering still lay before this woman. Now one arm hung limp. Her weakened left leg was braced with steel and, when combined with the thin, silver crutch she used, was strong enough to support her weight.

"Are you comfortable, Elvira?"

"I am, thank you."

"Can I get you a sweetmeat or some wine, perhaps?"

"No, nothing, Jimena."

"It is a fine celebration."

"For God's sake," Elvira exclaimed, "you act like we are strangers. Relax. I am not crying about it. . . . See *you* do not. Save your pity for someone more deserving."

"But," Jimena began emotionally, "I feel so responsible. I mean, if it had not been for . . ."

"That is plain nonsense. I happened upon the wrong place at an inopportune moment. That is life, and so it is."

"You are a saint, Elvira! I wish I possessed your capacity for accepting all life's tricks and meannesses with such stoicism."

"Rot! I am grateful to be alive. I still have a clear mind, thank the Lord for that, and I am able to walk, see my friends, attend a fine celebration, and teach my classes at the college. Well, nothing has changed that is of any significance, except the attitude of certain friends toward me. Instead of simply liking me, enjoying my company, now I am given generous doses of their pity. Ach, I have made a speech. I should pen a book, calling it Elvira's Ethics, eh?"

"Yes, do, Elvira. I will purchase the first copy." Dear God, Jimena thought, she does not know she is dying . . . or *does* she?

"Ah, here you are."

Hasan walked smoothly toward Jimena and Elvira where they lounged. Beside him walked Al Rakashi, resplendent in robes of ivory satin and a jeweled turquoise turban.

"Al Rakashi would see you once more, Raushana," Hasan said with no enthusiasm. "He confided in me that he thought to have seen a vision that long-gone night, and would prove to himself that you are real."

Al Rakashi stepped close to where Jimena sat and bowed to her elaborately. "Ah, 'tis indeed yourself, no other could it be, not a vision at all."

Jimena rose smoothly. Bending her head low, she folded her hands together and kneeled to Al Rakashi. "I thank thee, Saíd, for your kind and generous compliment. Heaven deprive us not of thee, grant we see thee more often."

"Ahhh," he purred, "lovely. Charming."

"May we join you?" Hasan asked. "You seem very comfortable. I have been standing on my two feet since—well, it seems a week."

"The lawn is yours, my friend," Elvira said, smiling, "sit upon it if you will."

Jimena said nothing. She became fascinated with the river and kept her eyes there. Her stomach quivered, which stirred up the sweets and wine in it until she thought she would lose it all. She sat down, and from the corner of her eye gazed upon an elegantly proportioned jeweled hand that rested close to her own. Then she looked to the bright gold buckle on her slipper, so that she could see Hasan without actually looking at him. She thought about what a fool she had been. All the tenderness of that day on the mountainside, months past, shattered by her own stupidity. How she wished she had accepted and returned his passions; what wondrous nights might have followed. He had meant what he said. He was barely polite whenever they met—in the hall outside the harem, upon the stairway, at the library, his attitude always aloof and contemptuous. How did a woman beg a man for love? She could not imagine herself striding up to Hasan and brazenly saying, "Please, my Lord, will you make love to me?" Ah, it would have to be on a moonlit night like tonight, with a river making soft music against the stones of its floor and a gentle breeze. She thought of a man and woman lying side by side, a touch, a whisper, a tender kiss . . .

"Are you still a Christian, my lovely? Or have you taken my suggestion and come over to the True Faith, eh?" Al

Rakashi was sitting upon his heels beside Hasan, his eyes devouring Jimena's tremulous face.

"He is speaking to you, Raushana," Elvira said. "Where are you? Raushana! Wake yourself."

"Uh? What? What did you say? Forgive me."

Elvira laughed and made a sweeping gesture toward Al Rakashi with her good arm. "She is with us once more, Saíd; pray continue."

"Have you converted to the True Faith, my dear, or are you Christian still, eh?"

Startled by the question, Jimena had to force her mind away from the contemplation of love, to a more serious matter.

"That is a double question, Saíd," she said with a smile, meeting Al Rakashi's eyes directly. "To the first, yes, I am partly Christian still; to the second, no, I have not converted to Islam."

"Partly? How can you be *partly* Christian? Either you are or you are not, eh?"

"Perhaps," Jimena said thoughtfully, "but I have my own opinions regarding religion. I no longer require the solace that religion of any persuasion offers. Religion is important to the individual, I think, only to a degree proportionate to the consolation he requires as a result of his abundance, or lack, in this life. I mean no insult to your beloved Muhammed, Allah bless him, Saíd—but he was, as a thinker, teacher and lover of mankind, a novice when compared to Jesus Christ, who was, is, and always will be my prophet. I will never convert to Islam. I merely withdraw from Christianity those more worthy and unquestionably sound philosophies and discard the rest, as do the majority here in Andalusia who are less pious than yourself and are skeptically unfaithful to the better portion of your prophet's dogma."

"I see." Al Rakashi nudged Hasan enthusiastically with an elbow. His face cracked into an admiring smile. "She is a thinker, Abu l Hasan. Indeed it is always a pleasure to find a woman with a capable mind, even if she is slightly misguided, eh?" When Hasan gave no reply, remaining glumly silent, he said, "Speaking of Christians, I have had a most trying time of it since that mad bishop was executed. Demented fools! They commit suicide by the hundreds, or try to. It is a disease, an epidemic of suicidal righteousness. Slice off the head of one of them and every fanatic clerk in Cordova would join the martyr in Heaven on the assumption that the same halo of righteousness will glow around his head."

Silence. Al Rakashi looked from Jimena's suddenly pale face to Hasan's. No response. Bewildered, he continued. "The bishop was a true fanatic, typically small-minded and vicious in his hatred for other beliefs. Take myself, now. I am a pious man, but if you would go to Hell by drinking the forbidden juice or worshiping a false prophet, that is your privilege. Glory be to Allah, but that bishop must be wailing now. Quite sad, is it not, that a man uses up his entire existence upon this earth following a lie, carrying that falsehood with him into the grave that he has dug with his own hand? A pity. And I did try to save him. But he would have it no other way. Another mystery! Why teach dogma that you cannot accept yourself? *Love your enemies*. What fools. Raushana, you do well to question a church that so contradicts itself."

Elvira saw Jimena's eyes turn moist, saw her swallow hard against the guilt she suffered for the bishop's death. In an effort to change the subject Elvira said, "Saíd, Raushana has many attributes in addition to those that so obviously meet your eye. I am one of her teachers and greatly admire the book of poems she has written."

"No!" Al Rakashi exclaimed, turning to Hasan, "poetry, too? Where is this—I suppose it is in manuscript form—book of verse? I would be enormously pleased to read it."

Hasan cleared his throat uncomfortably. He wished he could leave, but did not know how to do so tactfully. "I have not seen her books myself, Saíd, thus I could not give one to you."

"Recite a verse for them, Raushana," Elvira said, nodding her head in encouragement, "my favorite, please?"

Jimena sighed in relief. Anything, even reciting lines of love before Hasan, was preferable to talking about the dead bishop. She stood up and moved past Hasan, whose eyes followed her curiously. She leaned against the gnarled trunk of the magnolia and began her verse. Her voice was deep and melodious, and her eyes met Hasan's with some intent.

I longed for my beloved, but when I saw his face,
Abashed—I held my tongue and stood with downcast eyes,

And hung my head in dread and would have hid my love,
But do what I would, it would not hidden lie;
Volumes of plaints I had prepared, reproach and blame,
But when we met, no single word remembered I.

Oh you, whose name clings round me like a cloak,
Whose love yet closer than a shirt I drew,
Beloved one! how long this hard despite?
How long this severance and this coy, shy flight?

"*Alhomdalillah!*" Al Rakashi exhaled, whirling upon Hasan. "What price, Abu l Hasan? Name it and you shall have it! I would have this woman in my house and drive every cull there now out, for there is not one among them that can compare." Excitedly, he snapped his jeweled fingers under Hasan's nose. "Come! Name your price. A thousand dinars—two thousand— three, perhaps?"

Hasan smiled painfully and held a hand up as if to ward off a blow. He smiled and turned his head to look directly at Jimena. But his smile was superficial, affecting only his mouth; his eyes were extremely unfriendly. "Ah, your price is too high, Saíd. Your eye deceives you and her poem has bewitched you. Do not judge a book by its rich embellishments. Thou art too dear a friend for me to deceive you. I would agree to— mmmmm," he grimaced, pulling at his lower lip, trying his best to terrify Jimena, "oh . . . I would agree to—five hundred dinars? That would seem to coincide with her true worth, Saíd."

"You jest, Saíd!" Al Rakashi gasped, "and insult the lady with such a price. No, I will pay no less than two thousand di- nars, oh Father of Beauty. Is it a bargain?"

Hasan deliberately hesitated, searching Jimena's face for the fear that would be agonizing her by now. But she was smiling coyly. "No! I will not cheat such a man as yourself, else I would be exiled from Allah's paradise. No, Saíd, I insist. Five hundred dinars."

"Saíd?"

Hasan jumped at the sound of Jimena's sugared voice, un- certain if she spoke to himself or to Al Rakashi. He turned his eye to the man beside him, but he made no move to reply. In- deed, she was speaking to him. "Raushana?"

"Oh Father of Beauty," she sang, "you can end this argu- ment easily by sending me to the house of Al Rakashi. If he agrees, within one week, that your price is just, then that shall be the figure—but if I am all that he expects me to be, then he must pay the two thousand dinars. Is this not a reasonable and fair arbitration of your disagreement?"

"Indeed!" Al Rakashi immediately agreed, his tongue flashing out over his thin lower lip. "A wise solution, Abu l Hasan. Now will you agree?"

Hasan stared at Jimena in a state of profound confusion. The witch! She had skillfully forced him to admit he did not wish to sell her, not for any price. He smiled, then, telling her with his eyes that her sword had reached its mark, the point was hers. "No bargain, Al Rakashi," he said firmly, not taking his gaze from Jimena's face.

"Ah, hah!" Al Rakashi snorted, "I thought not! You cannot delude an expert like myself, Abu l Hasan. No price would be high enough, am I right? Eh?"

"You speak the truth, Saíd. I should never have attempted to mislead a man of your discernment, who, when it comes to women, has owned, does own, the very finest. Forgive me my little jest, Saíd. I meant no insult to you but taunted the lady as a result of a minor argument. You understand, of course."

"Of course." Al Rakashi sighed regretfully.

Hasan rose and took Al Rakashi's arm. "I must return to my guests, Saíd. Come, I will show you to the food."

"It is with sincere regret, Saíd," Jimena murmured, as Al Rakashi stood before her, "that I say farewell to thee. But there may come a day when Abu l Hasan is of a different temperament, eh? Until that day, Allah direct thee, oh most pleasing one."

"Well, well, well," Elvira said bitingly behind Jimena, "the cub has become a tigress. Masterfully done, Raushana."

Hasan and Al Rakashi had walked away, but Elvira's words were too soon uttered. Hasan turned his head and glanced back over his shoulder. He laughed and then began to ponder various exciting possibilities.

Jimena dropped back to the grass and said smartly, "It *was* rather clever of me, wasn't it? I certainly did clip his wings, the arrogant—The nerve, trying to make me think he would sell me. Five hundred dinars indeed! Can you imagine!"

"Forgive me, oh angry tigress, if I err, but I think you overestimate your worth. I would place your value at closer to zero."

"What!"

"Oh, do not widen those brown eyes at *me*. You are not worth one single alif to Hasan, and well you know it. You eat his bread, wear his jewels and silk trousers, you sleep in his bed—I *should* say in a bed *owned* by him—he shelters you and protects you. Pray what do you offer him in return for all this?

Answer me one insignificant thing, excepting all the trouble you have caused him."

"Trouble! I did not ask that he abduct me, you know!"

"But you are now grateful that he did. I heard you say it yourself to the bishop that night."

"I do not want to talk about the bishop! You know I cannot bear to think about him."

"Oh, cease the dramatics. You are avoiding the issue. Now that you intend, as you put it, to spend the rest of your days in this land, another forty years, perhaps, what are you prepared to give to this house? Or is your splendid presence sufficient?"

"Elvira!"

"What? Do you two argue? Do not start the new year in such a manner, or you will be at each other's throats throughout all the days that follow."

"Ah, Estiano," Elvira said, smiling up at him adoringly. "No, not arguing. That was righteous indignation you heard spouting from Raushana's throat."

"Oh! You are impossible, woman." Jimena giggled and leaped to her feet. She affectionately placed one hand upon Estiano's head and one upon Elvira's graying curls. "You two remain here and discuss me further. I have an emergency appointment at the house. My cup runneth over, so to speak."

"Well, make haste," Estiano gasped playfully. "I do not want it runnething over upon me!"

"Beast!" with that she hurried off toward the house.

Jimena lay flat upon her back on red satin cushions. The pavilion was heavenly quiet, the night wondrously sensual. It was indeed remarkable weather for the New Year; the forces of nature were cooperating splendidly for Hasan's affair. The sounds of merriment had gradually subsided, until only the voices of the servants could be heard as they cleared away the debris inevitable after such entertainments. Now only normal night sounds could be heard, but she could not sleep.

She sighed and rolled off her pillows. Standing up and stretching, she walked slowly to the pavilion railing and leaned upon it with her elbows, her eyes roving dreamily over the moonlit court, over the rooftop to the gardens. Then her eyes halted, coming to rest upon the figure swiftly making his way down the stone path toward the river. She watched until he was out of sight behind the foliage of a hedge. Without conscious thought or decision, Jimena moved away from the railing and walked across her balcony, through her room, out the door, and down the stairway, directing herself toward where that man might be seen more clearly, perhaps even touched.

Jimena stood silently watching Hasan as he swam lazily in the water. River water had been diverted and dammed at this spot to form a pool; water flowers lay upon the surface and the last dropping leaves from an acacia tree fluttered down to form miniature whirlpools. She was hidden from view by shrubbery. She did not wish to remain hidden, but she could not bring herself to approach him brazenly. Deciding to return to her room, she made a quick about-face then cried out when her trouser leg caught on a rose thorn and her thigh was scratched.

"Who is it? Who is there? Speak up!"

It was a moment for swift decision. Jimena decided to face him. She stepped out from her hiding place with her head held high and defiant.

"Bless me! If it is not Miss Innocence, herself."

Hasan stood shoulders and waist out of the water, about ten feet from Jimena. She could clearly discern the wry smile on his face and the sarcastic amusement in his eyes.

"It is herself," she agreed, then sat down, holding her drawn-up knees with shaking arms.

"And what brings *you* to the pool this time of night? Eh?"

"I could not sleep, simply felt the need for a stroll. Is there harm in this?"

"Ah, now, we must not quarrel." He raised both hands up as for prayers, "Peace, Raushana. Peace."

She tried to smile, but could not. "Peace," she echoed belligerently, "but to achieve that goal we must be a good distance apart, it seems. I shall withdraw." She made a halfhearted movement to rise.

"No. Do not leave. Can you swim? The water is a bit cold but quite invigorating."

"For God, no, I do not swim. Where might I have learned, I ask you—in the stagnant, infested waters of a *moat*?"

"Tch, tch, you *are* quarrelsome tonight." He fell smoothly into the water and swam to where Jimena sat on the bank, coming to rest at her feet. He placed both arms upon the bank and rested his chin upon them, looking up into her averted face.

The moon discreetly moved out of view. Hasan's body was covered by only the slightest depth of water and shone clear and outlined to Jimena's eye. She could not help but look at him. The droplets of water that clung to his hair and beard shimmered and sparkled like diamonds; she saw similar lights in his eyes.

Hasan reached out a hand. "Come. I will teach you. Ah, now," he laughed, noting her startled expression, "you may swim in your chemise. Remember, please, what I said to you upon a mountainside."

Jimena removed vest and trousers, her shaking hands barely able to work the fastenings. As she moved to the water's edge, her chemise so brief that most of her flesh was revealed, Hasan turned and swam back to the center of the pool, thinking that rape might not be so degrading after all; for Raushana a man might descend to that depth. His hands hurt with the need to touch her. But what was love when one played at it alone. Like the sun with no heat, water without wetness—the hand would do as well. To take and not receive rendered the act sterile and devoid of ecstasy. It was that giving of one's self, that pushing, squeezing need to be joined wholly with another, that set the senses reeling. Only then was the passion complete. Blessed Allah in Paradise, but he wished that she was other than what she was; how much of himself, soul as well as flesh, he might give to her.

"Walk out to me, Raushana, and I will give you your first instruction in *swimming*."

His voice rose suspiciously at the end of the sentence, and Jimena had an angry compulsion to show him she was not afraid of him. She leaped from the bank into the pool. The icy water sent a shock wave slamming over her. A gasping squeal emerged from her throat. She waded toward him. Suddenly her hands were caught and she was roughly shoved under.

"Oh! Damn. Damn you!" She came up spluttering and coughing, thrashing her arms as if she truly could drown in four feet of water.

Hasan laughed and splashed water into her face. Then she laughed in echo, beginning to enjoy herself. She plucked a pink water lily and placed it behind one ear, then dunked herself down to her chin, feeling as gay as any water sprite.

"Now it is time for your lesson in the art of swimming," he said, as he gently took her shoulders in his hands, "I will place my arms beneath you—thus. Now lie back and relax. That is right. Just float. See how simple it is? Now, when I let loose, do not stiffen. Relax and you will glide atop the water like a golden swan."

His words were inspiring. Jimena lay suspended upon the

water with a man's arms beneath her and a sky full of stars overhead, thinking it was another of her dreams. No, not a dream, but time was an enemy of the moment and was carrying her swiftly away; tomorrow this reality would be only a treasured memory. Time, please hesitate right here and make this moment last forever.

Hasan also regretted the passing of this moment, lingering over the warmth of her body against his fingertips. Her breasts, sharply outlined by clinging cloth, rose and fell with her breathing. His eyes moved upward to her face, a yearning in him that was like a weight pushing him toward her from within.

Jimena turned her head to meet his eyes, only inches away, and her breath caught. She thought the time for love had come at last and was eager now for the moments to move more swiftly. But he came no closer. His eyes told her he was waiting. She turned her glance away, and the spell was shattered.

"I will release you now. Relax and allow yourself to float."

For one miraculous moment Jimena floated atop the water. Then she was certain she would sink and with the conviction came the actuality; under she went. She could find no footing; the water was too deep here. Fear clutched at her throat and she opened her mouth to scream, but was choked by a rush of water into her lungs. She was quickly dragged up from the depths by a laughing Hasan, but this time she did not share his amusement. She coughed and gagged, desperately trying to clear the water from her lungs. Water had plugged her ears, stuffed her nose and blended with the tears in her eyes. She sobbed like a child, fear still cold upon her heart.

"Raushana, forgive me. Please, do not weep." He brushed her tangled, dripping hair from her eyes, then picked her up in his arms and carried her to the bank, where he laid her down upon the grass. He sat beside her, stroking her forehead and murmuring words of apology over and over again.

Jimena sniffed, smiled, and wept no more. Sheepishly she met his eyes. "I am terrible about such things," she apologized. "I only hope that when death comes, it will be quick. Oh, I should not speak of it. I thought for certain I was on my way to eternity."

"What? Did you think I would stand back and let you drown?"

"I did not think at all, that is the trouble. Surely, if I had relaxed, as you advised, I would have bobbed right to the surface again?"

"Indeed."

"How foolish of me."

"No."

They looked into each other's eyes and each leaned a little closer to the other. Impulsively Jimena reached out and placed a palm lightly upon Hasan's beard. Swiftly his own hand covered hers, holding it tightly to his face for a moment, then he turned the palm to meet his lips, pressing his mouth against the sweet flesh of her, breathing in the scent of her. But he made no further advance.

Jimena was drowning once more, drowning in eyes so deep with love and wanting that her mind and body screamed out with equal desire. The hand that held her own trembled with a fire that burned within him also.

"Raushana," he whispered, his lips moving on her palm, "say it. Tell me you want me as I ache for you." He kissed her hand again. "Say that you want my lips against yours, my arms about you—say to me that all you have you will give to me this night. Raushana, beloved, say it. For the love of Al-lah . . . speak."

"Yes! I want you." Her senses were reeling, the world about her fading into nonexistence; all that existed was his face above hers, his body so close, yet not close enough. "I have said it! Would you indeed force me to beg? Truly beg?"

"Raushana, kiss me." He still had hold of her hand. He waited.

She moved her face toward his, her heart pounding and her eyes captured by his. She felt his beard brush softly against her cheek, then his breath upon her lips. As her mouth touched his all reasoning and reluctance left her. She pushed her mouth hard against his, kissing him over and over again, but neither his body nor his mouth nor this arms responded. Clutching his hair with frantic, shaking fingers she cried out against his stubborn mouth. "*Damn* you, Hasan . . . I am *begging*! I want you so desperately I shall die, if you do not make love to me. Everything that I am capable of giving I will give to you this night. Please! How can you treat me this way! I want you, need you. Please?"

"You have been instructed?" he demanded roughly, pulling a little away from her intense embrace.

"I have!" In desperation she pressed her mouth to his again, softly, clinging, moving—until his arms at last swung around her.

Hasan whirled her over, returning her caresses now, hands

demanding, murmuring her name over and over in her ear, until she felt the solid earth leaving her, suspending her, floating her upon a wave of rapture. She experienced a need for haste, desperation to live the moment quickly before it raced away from her to become lost in the golden dust of her memories.

"Raushana, there is time. There is all our lives."

"Ah, no. The moments go so swiftly by. Now, Hasan. I have lived all my life for this moment; let it not pass by unfulfilled."

When she felt his lips pass over her, touch her in every aching, pulsating round and groove, and when his body at last rose and rested itself upon her, joining himself to her in body and soul, she did not think to run or scream out in fear, but melted into him even as a sunflower turns its face up to the blazing sun in gratitude for the life-giving nourishment that the sun alone can give.

The next morning, Hasan sent for Jimena and she went to him eagerly, the sparks of love still in her eyes. But his face was dark, none of last night's light was reflected there. He moved toward her across the room with a determination that struck her heart with apprehension.

"Raushana," he said roughly, "sit down, please; we must talk."

She sat upon a pillow, folded her cold hands together in her lap, and did not look at him as he sat across from her.

"Jimena Diaz, I am returning you to Castile."

Her eyes flew to his face; she was shocked not only by his statement, but by the use of that name. Jimena Diaz. It did not sit well on her, she thought confusedly. Raushana was her name, her identity. She cried, "What are you *saying*? Did I play the fool last night?

"No! Oh, no, Splendid One, do not think it is because I do not love you or want you. I offer you this escape so that I can know your true heart. I have kept you here by force. Nine years it has taken me to destroy all that was you . . . your faith, your marriage. You have a child in Castile. Last night was the final victory over you. It was inevitable that you would succumb to me." He reached out to take her hands in his. "This was not a satisfying victory for me, I want you to know that. Now, I set you free, now that it is nearly too late. But there are still some threads of a life in the north. I know that you are quite capable of weaving them together into a life that is something better than merely adequate." He stumbled over words that must be said. "According to Christian law you are still wed to Rodrigo Diaz. I am certain he would be delighted to have you back, that the love you have offered me, as a substitute for him, would warm his heart, as it warmed mine for a single night."

Jimena let out her breath, tremendously relieved. Laughing, she cried, "Substitute? Hasan, beloved—you cannot be serious."

"What is your will? Whatever it is, so be it."

She glanced away from him, complex emotions and vague longings disturbing her momentarily. "Hasan," she said at last, "the child is that one bright light amid the darkness of the past toward which I lean as longingly as any mother, but she is all there is. I think that I should not sacrifice myself, every hope, dream, and fulfillment of my life here for but one bright rose of yesterday. As for Rodrigo Diaz—His wife was slain on the sands of Castile nine years past, and he has taken another, a woman I can only pity because she must share her entire existence with such a man. Forget the husband. *I* have. I will bear other children, beloved, of yours, that will warm the cold loss I feel at this moment as I deny the sweet child of my flesh."

Hasan stared at her in speechless shock. He had assumed she knew about his deepest sorrow. He turned away, clenching his hands into fists against the memories that surged forth to torment him. How he had fought against acceptance of it in those years of early manhood, certain it was Nuzhab who was barren, quickly taking Zarífah into his house, then Sabíhah. But there came a day when no sensible man could any longer deny the obvious. He had looked down upon the physical apparatus that functioned in all respects normally, but lacked the seed of creation; it gave him pleasure and nothing more, Allah beginning him and ending him in the brief moment of existence that was a lifetime. He wanted to beat against it, stab it, curse it. The tears of his wives, the emptiness of his house where a dozen children might have laughed and played, were as heavy as iron in his groin. He had screamed out to Allah, 'Why? Why."

"Raushana," he said huskily turning to face her again, "I must tell you that . . . Surely you have wondered why no children grace this house, not Zarífah, Nuzhab, nor any of my women giving birth? There will be no children for you, if . . . if you remain in this house. I can give you anything else, my adoration, mind, and soul forever, but not a single child. This Rodrigo Diaz could give to you that *I* cannot."

Jimena's eyes widened in disbelief. "But the seed is with the *woman*, is it not? What have you to—"

"You speak foolishness," he said sharply. "If that were so, then what need of intercourse *at all*? I am without fertility. It is a fact. Now what is your will, Raushana?"

"No children," she whispered, fighting against tears of pity for Hasan, and for herself.

She was aware of an urgent need within herself to feel again the fluttering movement of new life in her long barren womb. But life could not offer all there was to each individual. One must choose from the assortment of goods available, this much she had learned in these nine years. But there was another obstacle that loomed between herself and this beloved man, one which nagged at her now and had to be spoken. "Hasan . . . will you divorce your wives for love of me?"

"Raushana!" he cried in despair.

She leaned forward quickly and kissed him lightly on the mouth. "Today we shall love, my Hasan. Tomorrow—another time—we will think upon these difficulties. Hasan, I love you very much and I am truly happy for the first time in my life."

But there was that light amid the darkness of the north, the bright eyes of a ten-year-old child, now eleven, twelve, then thirteen, that prevented Jimena's life from being absolutely perfect. She leaned closer and closer to that light as each year passed.

PART
THREE

✠

ESTIANO

Each morn a thousand roses brings, you say;
Yes,—But where leaves the rose of yesterday?

Omar Khayyám

Chapter

✠ *ONE* ✠

He was a tall man, with a heavy beard and black hair waving upon his shoulders. He was a young man, just thirty-four, and there was gentleness in his eyes, intelligence and sternness, too. He was two men, buoyant and quick-witted at one moment, resolute and solemn in the next; mathematician, free-thinker and astronomer. His name was Ghiyathuddin Abu l Fath 'Omar ibn Ibrāhim al Khayyámi, known as Omar, Son of The Tentmaker throughout all Islam.

He would have preferred to inspect the college with a single guide but the teachers and students of Cordova University flocked around him in worshiping admiration the entire day, because there was nothing they more admired than intelligence and fluent use of the Arabic language. Graciously he answered their eager questions, a smile turning up the corners of his wide, full mouth. With intense interest he surveyed the institution, saying polite things to each teacher. He was especially impressed with the scriptorium of Estiano Antolinez; he had seen none finer anywhere in the world. It had been an exhausting day. He was weary and hungry and wanted to be alone, but a dozen separate invitations were offered him, the houses of Cordova jealously bidding for his presence at their tables. Seriously studying the faces before him, he lifted a slim hand and pointed to Abu l Hasan ibn Al Hamman, Saying, "Saíd, with sincere pleasure do I accept your generous hospitality; pray do not trouble yourself with intricate and elaborate menu, for I am a simple man with simple tastes."

Within moments a servant ran frantically from the main entrance of the college and leaped upon a horse. He must arrive at the house of Abu l Hasan within half of an hour or there would be hell to pay. A hundred separate orders, given to him by an excited Hasan, whirled a great confusion in his head. Had the master said six kinds of fruit and three kinds of meat, or three kinds of fruit and six kinds of meat? And did he say *not* to serve wine, because the great Omar did not partake, or to *have* wine because he did partake? Bless Allah in his Paradise, he could not remember a thing. Ah, well, Ghanim, the chief kitchenman, would know what to do, would he not? Allah help him—he had better.

Jimena leaned to kiss the child upon his cheek as she tucked the silk comforter about his sleeping form, then brushed a wisp of red-gold hair from his forehead. Little Hasan. How she adored him. He was all pleasure, filling the house with laughter, tears and satisfying purpose. Sighing, she tiptoed out of his nursery into her own quarters, which were connected by a sliding door. She went to her pillows, picked up a book, but could not concentrate on it and put it down.

Elvira. If only she had lived to know the boy. Three years had passed since her death. The dear fool did not have the strength to bear a child, her body weakened so by the dysfunction of her brain, but she had wanted it so very much. Truly she had lived on will alone the last three months she carried him . . . bedridden and totally helpless. But the child grew strong and healthy within her. Her muscles refused to push the child forth, so a knife had been applied to deliver him. His mother was dead before his first cry. "It is all I can give to my husband," Elvira had said so often in those long months, ". . . the single lovely thing this broken body of mine can create now; my gift to Estiano, in gratitude for all the joy he has given me through the years."

Free-spirited Elvira had left this earth smiling, a winner in the game of life. Her last words were for Estiano . . . "The most beautiful thing in my life . . . has been . . . *you.*" She smiled at him, closed her eyes, and moved on.

Poor Estiano had been stricken with grief, actually taking to his bed with fevers. The doctors could do nothing for him; it was months before he was well again. It had been Estiano's wish that Jimena care for the infant and she had done so gladly, but she was at first sick with the knowledge that she herself would never bear another child. Dear Hasan, whose heart was so heavy with guilt, he knew her pain. Once she had said to him, "How could I love you less because you cannot give me a child? If that were all I wanted, I could lie with any man and be given such a gift. I love you exactly as you are." It was said to soothe him and was sincere, but tinged with regret and doubt. He had wept, "I did not know my father; he died before I was born, and I shall never have a son. I am suspended in the world, unconnected—and when I leave it, not one particle of myself will be left behind."

Estiano recovered, but he did not take the child. He left him with Jimena, saying, "He needs a mother, Raushana, and I know of no other I would rather have rear my son. I will see him as often as I can, but you and Hasan will raise him."

Though she adored little Hasan, Jimena's mind too often wandered to Castile, to the only child of her flesh. God in Heaven, how lonely Urracca must be. She remembered herself at the age of fourteen captive in a dismal castle, unloved and tormented by fears. If only the child could be brought to Cordova, but that was impossible. A monastery at the northernmost tip of the peninsula was not as accessible as that fateful campsite on the plain very near the Muslim border. Rodrigo was the father of three other children now, children who should never know of their illegitimacy. Completely hopeless. But she must see Urracca once more before she died, even if the child could not know who she was, even if she was unable to speak to her. Just to set eyes upon her sweet face would be enough. She was fourteen years old. Soon. It must be soon.

Jimena was abruptly brought out of her reveries as Acacia stumbled into the room squealing incoherently in her excitement.

"Acacia! What has you so excited? Praise Allah, calm yourself."

"Al Hamman says you are to—" She gulped, catching her breath. "You are to dress elaborately because a special guest will be at table and our master wants you to be present. You will never guess, Raushana, never guess who it is!"

"A special guest." Jimena smiled indulgently. "The emperor of France, perhaps?"

"No! The Tentmaker! Omar Khayyámi!"

"Good Lord!" Jimena leaped to her feet in surprise. Hasan had been boyishly excited this morning when he came to her rooms to say good-bye before leaving for the college. He had told her Omar Khayyámi was to visit the university, but not that he would bring the great man home for dinner. Omar. The genius adored by all Islam, the inventor of Al Gebra and the new calendar that was now five years old. Jimena was most impressed with the man's whimsical epigrams that were so popular in Andalusia.

For God, she must hurry; it took a great deal of time to

adequately beautify herself. Omar must see that Abu l Hasan's favorite was a rare beauty at thirty-two years of age. She rushed over to the mirror to critically examine her face. The lines there were not those of age, but of character, smile lines that did not detract but added to her beauty. In fact, setting all humility aside, she was more beautiful than she had ever been. Happiness was the best of all cosmetics. Diligently she set about the tasks of bathing, dressing and making herself up. Imagine. *Omar Khayyámi.*

For a simple man of simple tastes, the table being spread in honor of Omar Khayyámi would leave him completely without choice, for Ghanim, chief kitchenman of Hasan's house, had spared no effort. He was an avid devotee of the great man. Every intricate recipe, all those for which he was most proud, was being created tenderly and with temperamental insistence upon perfection. The best wine had been boiled exactly twelve hundred and thirty countings, meticulously strained and poured into pitchers of cut crystal rimmed with gold. Raisins were dipped into thick syrup, then in a powder of crushed pistachio nuts. And a hurried message was dispatched to the town, within the hour bringing two horses to the courtyard that carried thick leather bags filled with snow from the mountaintops. Omar must have a sherbet, and it would be a sherbet like no other he had ever tasted. Ghanim possessed a secret and treasured recipe that combined the heavy sweetness of very ripe peaches with the tartness of plump, crushed berries.

When Hasan arrived with his guest, all would be in readiness. Ghanim peered from a gap in the banquet room's draperies—a post he intended to maintain throughout the meal so he could gather to himself all the joy and satisfaction to be gleaned from the great Omar's compliments.

Soon after Hasan entered the house and went with Omar to the room for washing, Estiano rode into the courtyard. He had gone first to his home to change into more formal clothing. He had chosen to wear a white linen turban, although he despised turbans, but in honor of *this* guest he would suffer it. It was not only that he found turbans uncomfortable. Equally disturbing was how ludicious his face looked beneath them. Such headgear had been designed for the gracefully featured Arab and not for the Germanic, heavier visage. As he dismounted and strode through the gate he heard an immediate cry of "Father," and saw the boy running across the lawn toward him. As always, when Estiano looked upon his child, a lump of emotion stuck in his throat and he felt maudlin tears behind his eyes. How perfect he was. God bless the woman who could give a man such a gift. Then he felt a sharp stab of guilt, a guilt that perpetuated itself with each new lie he lived. His friends and the doctors all thought it had been love for Elvira, grief over the loss of his wife, that had sent him ill to his bed. The shame was still unbearable because the pity in their eyes and their sympathy was so undeserved. Good Jesus, if they truly knew his mind. She had lay there never screaming, but writhing in pain, struggling to push out of herself the growth placed within her by himself. Barely breathing, her scarred, sweet face already pale with death she had whispered, " . . . It will be beautiful, beloved. Nothing created by you could be anything but beautiful."

When she sighed her last sigh, he was struck down by the sin of omission. For over a year she had lived only for him, and was happy in death because she was so pleased at the giving of the child. And he had never loved her, had given her absolutely nothing of himself. Every secret dream of Jimena throughout that year was a part of the metal that had cut him to the point of near death. How unreasonable the human soul was. No matter what we wished to feel or thought we ought to feel, the soul went its own way, loving whomsoever it chose to love, completely unconcerned with matters of conscience.

Estiano reached down and swung little Hasan into his arms, a few tears escaping his tight control. Thank God the boy did not favor Elvira; he could not have borne that. Nor did he look like his father, another blessing from the Almighty. The child was an individual, looking only like himself, and named for a friend and for his mother . . . Hasan, or Beauty. Hasan Estianez; a happy combination of Arab and Galician. Hasan would speak the tongue of Islam and in all ways be Andalusian, except in blood. A worthy legacy to his son; it was for this he had traveled all those miles as a boy. "And what have you done today that was exciting?" he asked the boy, giving him a hug.

" . . . Ate dirt. Auntie Rau'thana spanked me."

"Ah so. But dirt is for the flowers to eat, not for little boys."

"Are you really my father?" the child asked, twisting at Estiano's beard with his grimy fingers and giggling.

"I most certainly am."

"Where's my mother?"

"She is—dead, Hasan. With the angels in Allah's Paradise."

"What's dead?"

"Hasan! I order you to cease asking so many questions. Do you hear? Eh?" Laughing, he kissed the child on the end of his nose.

With the child clutched under one arm, Estiano kicked off his shoes outside the door, opened the latch, and ran into the house to amuse his son, who squealed with delight.

"Ah, Estiano. Here you are. Hurry—Hasan and his guest are already at table. Child, go to Nuzhab. She will tell you a story and see you to bed. Go, go, go . . ." Jimena patted his rump a few times, and followed him partway up the stairs. She quickly returned to Estiano, who was soberly watching the child as he sulkily went off to the harem.

"You are a fine mother to him, Jimena," he said roughly. "You give him something of immeasurable value that he would have been denied had you not taken him. I . . ."

"I know. You told me the same thing last week, and the week before." Jimena smiled at him affectionately.

"Forgive me. I *am* repetitious but sincere—*sincere*. You will not accept money, so I repay in thank-you's. I will attempt to control my gratitude henceforth, agreed?"

"Gratitude. How foolish can a man be? It is I who am grateful; sentimental fool. Now come; this is no time to stand around admiring one another. The great Omar Khayyámi waits dinner for us and the likes of us have no right to keep the likes of him waiting."

As they walked arm in arm to the banquet room, Estiano leaned and whispered, "You are looking ravishing tonight; positively bewitching."

Jimena smiled her thank-you, pleased and silently agreeing with him. Why not? Had it not taken all afternoon to create the effect?

"Ah—what is this that enters like a vision, without veil or downcast eye?"

Entranced, Omar Khayyámi gazed upon Jimena as she entered the dining room and swept gracefully to a pillow beside his host, demurely seating herself.

"My favorite, Saíd," Hasan said proudly, but wishing that he might have said my favorite *wife*.

"Charming. A most interesting and agreeable custom, the freedom allowed your women in Andalus. Do you never wear the veil, lovely one, not even when out upon the streets?"

"Never, Saíd," Jimena sweetly replied, directly meeting his

eyes. "What is there to hide? If I were ugly, then I would wear the veil and be grateful for such a convenient custom."

All three men laughed at her remark.

"Indeed," Estiano said, still chuckling, "in the suburbs where fanatics dwell, I have seen women crossing a stream naked as newborn colts for all eyes to see, yet veils covered their faces. A curious tradition, to say the least."

Omar smiled, reaching out for the serving of lamb and rice a servant had prepared for him. "The world is full of curious traditions. But this custom I particularly admire; a woman is too special a creature to be hidden and imprisoned, as in old Islam. I beheld many women in the classrooms today. Excellent. Who nurtures the children? The women. When we plan education *they* should be considered foremost. I .will wager, Abu l Hasan, that your favorite is as intelligent as she is attractive."

"She is as intelligent," Hasan agreed.

Jimena balanced expertly on her heels and daintily ate her meal, careful to observe all the intricate details of proper manner, experiencing a delicious glow of pleasure at the great Khayyámi's compliments. "What brought you to our lovely Andalus, Saíd?" she asked in a voice sweetly high-pitched, "a holiday, or some business affair?"

Omar touched the corners of his mouth with a linen and replaced it beside his empty bowl. He leaned back, his sharp eyes moving around the room. "A holiday," he began, carefully choosing his words, "but I had not intended to travel this far, only to the Atlas Mountain region; I wanted to see the great waters that divide the world. There I met a leader of men named Yosuf, and saw great ships lying in wait, tens of thousand of soldiers gathered in cities of tents were also waiting. For what did they wait, I asked this Yosuf, and he said to me, 'For that time so near at hand when we shall be called to Andalusia to save them from the Christians,' and my eye wandered across the sea, thinking there was something I must see beyond the mist that veiled my vision. In the eyes of this Yosuf I saw the light of a conqueror, upon his forehead the brand of genius. Uneducated and totally without sophistication, unable to speak the Arabic language, this fanatic Muslim thought to rule that vast land across the sea. Thus I came to see the wonders of Andalusia while they yet exist."

A hollow silence fell. Jimena glanced worriedly to Hasan and saw the tightness about his mouth. She turned to Estiano and shrugged helplessly.

Omar looked from one to the other, a light of amusement in his eyes. "Ah," he murmured, "but those were perhaps cruel words. Of course, you dread the loss of what you possess here. A pity."

Hasan covered his mouth with a fist and coughed nervously. "Indeed, great one," he said flatly, "but, of course, you have never lived within such a civilization as this, and cannot know what it is to be free and to have that freedom threatened, bound as you have always been to the archaic traditions and strictures of the old world."

Omar smiled and with a nod acknowledged the truth in the man's words, watching the working of Hasan's face with interest as he continued.

"I have bickered and lectured for years against the calling of Africans into this land. I will continue the struggle until all hope is lost. Toledo has been under partial siege for two years now. If Toledo falls, the people of Andalus will cry out for a deliverer. They will not help themselves but bow to the might of Yosuf. Our last hope lies within the hearts of Toledo's citizens. They must *not* surrender, or allow themselves to be conquered."

"Hasan," Jimena said softly, "our guest is on a holiday; surely he is not interested in Andalusian internal affairs."

"No, no," Omar protested. "I am always interested in the struggles of men. You are a humanitarian, Abu l Hasan. Ah, the pain you inflict upon your soul with such noble purposes and actions."

Estiano had remained quiet, lounging into his pillows and eating very little as usual. He could not muster as much enthusiasm, expend the effort Hasan did, but in his heart were similar dreads. "Said," he said to Omar, "do you not believe that when all hope is gone from the breast of man, men will simply lie down, cease propagating, and become extinct; that all man is is hope, which is the guiding light of his existence, that without it we would all slit our throats?"

The reply to Estiano's query came poetically from the lips of Omar, for it was said that an Arab, lying in a pool of his own blood, would still be a poet, his last words in rhyme. " 'The worldly hope men set their hearts upon, turns ashes, or it prospers, and anon—like snow upon the desert's dusty face, lasts a little hour or two and is gone.' Indeed, we must have hope, but at the same time must realize that that hope is hopeless. It is the way of life—who can change it?"

"Then why live at all?" Hasan exclaimed impatiently, "if every dream and cause is lost inevitably?"

"Why, indeed."

"You are a rancorous man, Omar Khayyámi—the light of hope within your breast all blackened out. How can you cling to your existence without hope? How?"

"Simply by refusing to attach myself emotionally to any creed or cause, except that of *my* existence. This Toledo you speak of. Why do you not stand back disinterested and observe history unfolding before your eyes, leaving *causes* to more ignorant men, who in the long range decide the end result, anyway? How unimportant and insignificant is your Toledo, when compared to the ages that stretch ahead. Would you spend this spangle of existence, this brief instant that is your life, upon such trivial matters? You would? Ah, I would not."

Hasan was angry. There was too much truth in the man's words, which made any argument of his own seem fanciful idealization. Yet he would never be convinced. It was such men as this Omar, who would sit back amused and watch the horror of man's destruction unfold, that did most to thwart a cure. It was like a doctor standing beside his patient and refusing to administer the drugs or use the knife, curiously observing the progression of the infection. The disease was within man himself, the cure within him, also. Only man could save man, and standing back a disinterested witness was not the way to a solution. *Someone* had to struggle, had to believe the cure was worth the pain of search and effort.

"Let us say," Hasan said bitterly, "that Toledo's fall or survival may be insignificant a thousand years from today and to you—but *today*, to *me*, it is of utmost consequence. I do not think in terms of time. What is time? For me this moment of my existence is eternity and I will do what I can to make it better for myself and for humanity. Indeed, I would spend this spangle of existence upon such matters; to me it is a matter of Andalusian life or death, and all the passion I am capable of I will give to this cause in which I so deeply believe!"

Omar had listened intently, his head bent forward in concentration, all humor gone from his eyes. When Hasan had finished, he released a chest-collapsing sigh and said, "And you would forfeit your *life*, I suppose, for this heroic cause, this protection of your land from barbarians?"

"Ach! What dream is worth an intelligent man's consideration, if not worth the ultimate of sacrifices? A man is only half a man without such a conviction, without a cause that he would die for if need be."

"I agree," Estiano murmured.

"Forgive me, but I do *not* agree."

The startled eyes of all three men turned upon Jimena at her unexpected comment. Hasan was obviously stunned. Estiano was curious. And Omar was fascinated.

"I would be pleased to hear the opinion of the favorite of Abu l Hasan, for I think I have a friend within touch of my hand. Speak, lovely flower, and tell us of your thoughts."

"I think that my beloved lord does not choose his words carefully enough, so that the true meaning of what he says escapes us. When a man states he is willing to *die* for this cause or that, what he actually means to say is, that this cause is worth *killing* for, for to assert that you will give your life for a belief presupposes a battle in which either you or another will perish, so that the vow 'I shall die for what I believe in' merely becomes the excuse of the mind, a rationalization for the murderous intent of the soul." For a moment she hesitated, thinking she might better halt before too deeply enmeshed. Quickly she glanced to Hasan to see if he were angry with her. He nodded just a little, his eyes unfathomable. "If the Christians are willing to die for their church, and the Adalusians for their country, holocaust will be the only result, as always. When each of us discovers the right road for ourselves, but does not insist all men live the same, then the murders will cease. As much as I cherish Andalus and the life it has given me, I would not kill a single Christian to preserve it, nor dig my own grave with the shovel of righteousness."

Omar raised his hands and made a formal bow from the waist to Jimena in exaggerated compliment. "I bow to thee, my lady, in admiration, for I could not have said it better."

"Ah," Hasan laughed uncomfortably, "my sentiments have been profoundly refuted. But all the arguments of woman and scholar cannot alter a mind filled with conviction. Raushana has forced me to be more explicit, thus I say—Andalus is worth *murdering* for, despicable as this might be."

"Ah," Omar purred, " 'I sent my soul through the invisible, some letter of the afterlife to spell, and by and by my soul returned to me, and answered—I myself am Heaven and Hell.' "

Estiano again entered into the conversation. "Without such causes as set the human breast afire, Khayyámi, there never would be any progress. At some time, some men will hit upon that truly right idea, and the world will be a better place."

"No, Saíd, for other men will disagree, and all will perish."

Omar Khayyámi was gone, and Estiano, too. The house was quiet, with a scent of spiced lamb and fruit lingering on the air; the lamplit hallways of the house were warmly shadowed. Jimena felt a glow of well-being, as she slowly walked up the stairway, her fingers sliding over the marble bannister. Moving down the upper hall, she opened the door to her room and entered, deep in thought.

It had been very difficult the first year, when all the wonder of Hasan's love for her slowly ebbed. She had become confused and was unable to comprehend his reasoning. If he truly loved her, then how could he do those tender things he did with her with so many others? To her the act of penetration had evolved into the essence of love, her single means of expressing what she felt for Hasan; she wanted it to be the same with him. But he made no move to divorce his wives and even called Acacia or one of the other concubines to him regularly. Nor would he discuss the matter. Only one day of the week did he give to her. When he held her tight to his breast, whispering words of love into her ears, a pain was within her that divided them like a wall. He was insincere, speaking these same treasured vows to another only the night just past. Not enough, his vow that she alone shared his soul.

Finally she had found the courage to speak, and, oh, the humiliation when he laughed at her pain, saying, "What? You are not content with owning my soul? You would place a sign upon my penis reading 'keep away . . . this apparatus belongs to Raushana, not to the man who wears it, nor to any other woman, it is her sole possession' . . . Is this what you would have, eh?" She had wept, then, "But if you truly love me, how can you?"

Hasan's reply had come swiftly, his eyes amused and patient. "And what has love to do with intercourse? It is a game men play at, like backgammon or chess. I take Nuzhab, and the others, using her like a chessboard, moving my pleasure about until I win. Like the lutist, I might play adequately upon even the most flimsily put-together lute, but there is that one that is perfect, and when he plays upon that one his very soul is touched with the pleasure the resultant music gives to him. He will play upon the others, for he would not have them lie and waste, but his mind always lingers toward the day when he will

touch that perfect one again, treasuring the suspense and anticipation. Thus are you to me, Splendid One, the one woman I
truly love, the one whose touch cuts deep into my body, beyond the apparatus, affecting my mind and soul as well."

"But—but it is *immoral*," she had sobbed.

"Immoral! Ah, my love, you spout the jargon of Christians
again. What difference, the man with a single woman, or he
with two or three? Each has the same energy to outpour. To
concentrate it all on one, or to divide it among three—I see no
difference."

But he did allow her separate quarters, so that she need not
consider herself just another harem wench, if the harem was
that offensive to her. It was his single concession, and it did
soothe her. As the first year passed and she saw that she was
indeed his favorite, always at his side at dinner when all the
others must eat in the harem, sought out when he was troubled
or wished to talk, she had ceased worrying. But she refused to
marry him. What need? She was his in any case, by law of abduction. She would rather be called a concubine than falsely
called his wife. This was one Christian ethic that she was unwilling to forsake, that of one man for one woman throughout
eternity; an impossible ideal not even realized by those who had
created it and those who expounded it.

Jimena laughed out loud, as she recalled how embarrassed
she had been as Hasan fancied a sign on his penis. She had
never said it to him, but if intercourse were simply an innocent
game why was it he and his fellow Arabs so guarded their
women and so detested the woman who played the game herself. Men—A complicated, foolish lot. But the Arab, better than
the Christian male, at least protected, fed, and clothed the extra
women in his life. Hasan was a dear man; she loved him deeply. Enough of such matters that belonged only to the past.
This night belonged solely to herself. She must hurry. Hasan
would become impatient at her delay.

"*Auhashtani!*" Hasan exclaimed, mock pain upon his face as
Jimena at last entered in a lime green gown that had been his
gift to her on her birthday. "So long you have been away from
me, you have made me desolate."

"Ahhhh," Jimena purred, placing her arms tightly around
his waist; she pressed her mouth seductively against his bare
chest.

"Ach, it is good, Raushana, to feel you close." He pulled her
away slightly, holding her arms in his hands, his eyes roving

down the length of her. "I do believe that women should never wear trousers, only such Christian dress as this, the flesh shimmering half-seen behind transparent silk. Aieee, you are like a sherbet, good enough to eat."

Jimena giggled and pushed herself back against him, her heart beating a trifle faster, a tiny flame beginning. "Hasan! Wait now. There is all night. Stop it—"

"Ah, you are not as eager as that first time beneath the stars, eh? Now you would linger and play."

"I would! I have waited five long nights for this day. Why spend it all in a few quick moments? Once begun I cannot bear to . . . no . . . Now, Hasan!"

"Lovely as it is, remove that shadow of green that blocks my vision and my touch."

It was half of an hour of touch and tease and groans of pleasure, of sighs, of whispered demands and words of tender passion, until each lay exhausted in the other's arms, beads of perspiration on their brows, contented smiles upon their lips.

Jimena leaned her head and kissed Hasan lightly upon the mouth, "What a delicious man you are, my Hasan!"

"Listen to me, woman. If you were any more artful with me, I would indeed be tempted to throw aside all others and concentrate upon one. You render the others rags as compared to silk, goat meat as compared to tender lamb. Allah be blessed, I swear I shall be inequitable and call for you again tomorrow. Tomorrow? Damn me—what is wrong with right now?" He kissed her soundly, his arms locking around her.

"Hasan! You are ridiculous." She laughed gaily, struggling out of his arms and rising to sit upon her knees. "You have discovered my secret, eh? There is more than one way to rid one's self of competition. I shall so excite you, treat you with so much tender play and passion, that each other will bitter be, compared to fruit as sweet as me!"

"Come here!"

"No."

"Come, foolish one. I am forty years old, well past the age of twice a night!"

'Oh, I do not believe *that!*"

"Well, perhaps I might, but not this night. Come, Raushana." He held his arms out to her, his eyes suddenly pain-filled. "Let me hold you close. I love you deeply."

Cuddling down into his arms again, Jimena turned her eyes up to his, a worried frown slashing her forehead. "What is it, Hasan? Tell me."

He pulled her head to his chest, one hand holding it there, his chin resting in her soft, white hair. When he spoke his voice was unsteady with sadness and regret. "I depart for Toledo in three days, beloved. I will not return for·at least eight months. My sadness is that I will miss you desperately. I promise, sweet love—"

"Toledo!"

Jimena reared up, pulling herself back so that she could clearly read his eyes. "You cannot go to Toledo! You said that Alphonso has placed a siege about the city. Hasan! Whatever ails you?"

"Raushana, please."

He swung to his feet and moved to a chest near the window, picking up the robe that was thrown across it. Wrapping it around himself, he stood staring out the window into the darkness, his mind in a state of despair. All his efforts of the past ten years would be a total waste if he could not prevent the disaster about to fall upon Toledo.

"Well?" Jimena said impatiently behind him.

He kept his back to her, knowing her feelings and respecting them. "It is only a partial siege, the army coming in the spring to destroy newly planted crops, to ravage the countryside all around, to harass and deplete, to frighten and to weaken, then returning again in the fall, and in the winter on occasion. But in the interim, traffic is free to the city, visitors coming and going as they see fit. I will be perfectly safe."

"Oh, now, Hasan!" she cried, rushing across the room to pull him around to face her. "Do not lie to me; I am no fool. Alphonso might wage a full attack at any moment. How can you say you will be in no danger? Oh! I think this is just ridiculous. Why, Hasan? *Why?*"

He grabbed her shoulders in his two hands, his eyes now ablaze with fury. "You made your views quite clear tonight," he shouted, "but I thought to have made myself *equally* clear. I will cut the throats of as many Christians as I have to to further my ambitions. I will not stand by weeping about the state of the world, doing *nothing*! Let that penetrate your thick, Christian head! I am leaving for Toledo in three days, whether you approve or not!"

"Hasan!"

"Ah, forgive me. That was vicious, cruel of me—and I did not mean it."

Jimena swallowed, pushing back the tears that threatened. "Hasan," she whispered, "does it hurt that I was once one of them? When you look at me, do you see your enemy? For God, if my skin could be darkened, my hair made black, my blood changed to Arab, I would do it, if you would love me better."

"*Now* who is being ridiculous?" He let go of her shoulders with an impatient shove.

"Then you will go to Toledo. And what will you *do* there? Guard all the gates and walls *yourself*? Fight off the Christian army *singlehanded*? You are not a soldier—you are a teacher!"

"I dislike your tone, Raushana," he warned. "I go to plead with Sultan Yahia to cease his insolence that breeds hate within the hearts of his own citizens, as well as those who are governors or sultans of nearby cities. The man is mad to believe that he can succeed unaided. I will attempt to convince him that he errs, force him to see the danger that exists."

"Impossible, and well you know it. How can you place your life in jeopardy for—for what, Hasan, for what?"

"You have asked me, so I will tell you!" he shouted, thrashing one arm in the direction of the window. "Would you like to see Rodrigo Diaz riding across that lawn out there with a torch in his hand? Would you like to see me . . . Estiano, Acacia and Nuzhab upon a funeral pyre, being burned alive? This house, which you profess to love so deeply, in ashes? We are not protected here by city walls; this is a suburb, easy prey for marauders. I do not want them this close. And *you*—eh? My eyes can already see the bloodstained footprints of El Cid's boots upon this carpet! Glory be to Allah, but I think you dense at times. All that talk of goodness and gentility is all well and good, but impractical!"

"Yes, beloved, impractical," Jimena demurred, a hand reaching up to touch his cheek. "Forgive me. Do what you must. Allah go with thee."

Hasan groaned and tears welled into his eyes. He threw his arms around her, crushing her ribs with an urgent embrace. "Allah knows I am torn in two directions. I see your views, my dear one, and you are right, but a great pain is within me, a great pain, and all I can do this moment is weep."

They stood clasped in each other's arms for long moments, Hasan comforted by Jimena's caressing, maternal soothings, while a pain of her own emerged to bring a golden image from the past. Her mind's eye looked to Toledo, then across the mountains to Castile, but a few miles farther. Was this the moment? Yes, she was certain it was. It was time now for that undeniable cause of her own, the return to her heart of the one bright rose of yesterday.

"Hasan," she whispered in his ear as he held her, "I will travel *with* you to Toledo."

"What!" he cried helplessly, throwing both hands into the air. "What is it with us tonight? Have we both gone mad!"

"Just listen a moment. I will go with you to Toledo, then on to Castile. I *must* see her again, Hasan! I need to know that she is well. I only want to look upon her face one more time before I die."

"*Alhomdalillah!*" he wailed. Turning on his heel, he lunged out of the room, leaving Jimena tearful but determined to have her way.

Estiano thought the house was depressingly quiet tonight. Or was it his imagination? Nothing was different tonight, compared to any other evening of his life. No, by Jesus, there was something in the air, stuffing his ears so that all sounds of rustling trees in the garden, night birds, and the servant's footsteps within the house were withheld from him, leaving only this goddamned uneasiness. Estiano slammed down the book he had been pointlessly holding up to his eyes and sat staring at the empty tile wall across the room from him. A loud clanging of the door knocker caused him to lurch erect.

"Thank God!" he exclaimed, and leaped to his feet to see who his deliverer from silence was. "Hasan! Glory be to Allah and all Christian saints. I am pleased to see you. Come in, come in!" He pumped his friend's hand vigorously, practically pulling him into the entranceway.

"You need not attack me, Estiano," Hasan laughed. "What is the matter? The quiet life beginning to pall?"

"Truth you speak."

"Fret not, your quiet, peaceful nights may look brighter to you . . . in reflection."

"By Allah, if you have some adventure in mind, I am your man. I go insane from silence."

Estiano led the way into the garden that was lighted by oil lamps, and offered Hasan a couch, then sat down across from him and leaned forward eagerly. "Now what have you in mind? Tell me quickly, before my mind alters and I think myself a contented man again."

"Actually, it is a very serious matter," Hasan said sorrowfully.

"Well, what is it, man? Out with it!"

Hasan managed a weak smile. "As you know, I will travel to Toledo. I had planned my departure for tomorrow, but, Es-

tiano, Raushana insists upon traveling with me . . . upon returning to Castile! She would see her child again, and you are
the single man I can trust to—"

"Halt! Wait, friend. Raushana return to Castile? You are, of
course, joking and a bad joke at that."

Hasan shook his head helplessly. "I cannot deny her the
look at her child she so longs for! If I could have—if she had
had another, perhaps . . . Will you accompany her, Estiano? I
would not rest one single night knowing she was in that land
without a true friend."

"You fool. . . . She has no intention of just *looking* at that
child; she intends to *take* her! Have you any conception of what
the priests would do to her if she were caught? We are discussing his child, now! First you embroil me in a plot to steal his
wife, and now—"

"She will use a fictitious name" Hasan interrupted stubbornly. "The danger is actually slight, Estiano. She feels that
she must do this, that she will never forgive herself if she does
not go to the child. As it is decreed . . ."

"Goddamned rot!" Estiano shouted. "Do not offend my
ears with that destiny bilge! *You* decree it. You bring it to pass.
Your word is law in your house. She will not, cannot leave
Andalus without your sanction. Change your mind, I beg of
you!"

"No, Estiano. Raushana would not be foolish enough to attempt to abduct the child. I cannot deny her this mother's
dream, and will not."

"Jesus Christ!" Furious, Estiano paced the room, his short
legs pounding his bare feet against the cold tiles as he stalked
back and forth, around and around Hasan. "When? What day
do you propose to begin upon this road of folly?"

"If you agree to accompany her, I think all other matters
could fall into place by—say a week hence? Too soon for you to
settle your affairs?"

"No, I can well manage in a week," Estiano growled.
"How many men in the party, aside from myself?" His colorless eyes stabbing at Hasan.

"Eight, perhaps ten, all men of your race that I am paying
extremely well."

"Ten! The dear Lord have mercy on my soul!"

"Would you take an army, thus rendering the whole affair
an invasion?"

"A thought, a truly worthy contemplation."

"Any more than ten would attract undue attention to her.

She must pass through that land as an ordinary lady of distinction, with very Christian-looking knights. Too great a curiosity aroused could be fatal. None of these men I have hired know her true identity."

"And no ten Mozarabs can possibly save her, if the secret is discovered."

"No."

Estiano sighed and again sat down near Hasan. Placing one elbow on a knee, his chin dropping discouraged into the palm of his hand, he glared accusingly at Hasan. "Make your plans, oh Father of Beauty. I will be fully prepared within the week."

Hasan smiled in relief. "I have faith in you, old friend. I may not be fully at ease, but I will be far less concerned knowing you will be there to guard her with your life. Allah guide thee and protect thee every step of the way."

"To hell with Allah's blessings! Pray we do not run into Rodrigo Diaz, El Cid, Compeador, and so forth. That is what *I* will pray for. And that I might return your woman to you as whole in body as she is this moment, and unshattered by broken dreams.

Thus did Doña Elvira Rodriguez, daughter of Don Rodrigo Ordoñez, Count de Tudela, Aragon, appear one November day in Castile with her entourage. No one gave her carriage more than a casual glance as she made her way steadily northward toward Palencia. She was a pale woman, in mourning veils and a gray linen gown, with fingers smudged with grime. Beside her on the carriage seat rested a worn Holy Bible, around her throat on a heavy chain a cross.

Chapter
✠ *TWO* ✠

It was hot as hell. The air was thick with the outpushed exhalations of panting humans that mingled, jabbered and crowded the large hall, which was thick with vinegarish whiffs of rotting garbage and steaming dung, and the stench of sweat that wet a man's clothing to putrid, clinging discomfort. Alphonso slumped deeper into his chair, passing grimy fingers over his balding head. His eyes skulked around the room in search of some fool to reap his agitation upon. Abominations! All of them. Hovering around him in sadistic fear of missing something. Leeches! And the only friends of a king—fed by him, clothed by him, seeking favors from him like maggots picking at a rotting carcass, which indeed he was.

"You there!" Alphonso raised half out of his chair, his arm waving at a startled clerk who thought he had been tending most diligently to his own business, "Come here to my feet, you worthless, miserable lout! Ah, that is right, on your knees before the *king.*" He reached out a hand and caught hold of the clerk's fringe of hair, clunking the man's bristly, shaved skull with the forefinger of his other hand. "What is this, eh? My wife is dead, gone to her maker, her sly, conniving priests gone back to that land from whence they came, yet you flaunt the sign of Rome upon this fat head! No tribute do I pay as yet. No Roman liturgy do the priests of Castile spout, dividing into only three parts that which rightly requires nine. So do not play the game, my lad, or I will slice this monstrous empty glob from off your shoulders. Be gone! Get from my offended sight. Take yourself to Rome, if you would kiss the feet of popes, but get from my sight!"

The young priest stumbled away with terrified and bewildered eyes. The crowd of knights, ladies, and priests fell silent, all eyes resting expectantly upon the king, who glared back at them even more sourly than before. He passed both hands over his protruding abdomen, feeling the groans and gurglings of rampant air in his vitals. He belched up a good blast of it, then settled back. He was getting damned tired of this infernal waiting. Another wife? For what? Were not the two he was rid of enough? Thank the Lord for great gifts, both had seen fit to lie down and die, thus delivering themselves and their displeased husband from any further misery. Sullen-faced, weeping Constanza; what a miserable excuse for a woman. He belched again, the very contemplation of his first wife causing a mighty stomach upset. And that one still warm in her grave; one child and she had burst a gut, as weak as a starving goat. And she had had the face of a goat!

What manner of discarded trash would this new one be? The sultan of Granada wished to feather his nest with a gift of a daughter; profound sacrifice—the man had twenty-two of them and more than fifteen sons. Either the sultan had a dozen wives or he kept four damned awful busy. But then, he had a nest of his own to feather; a few Arab brats about the castle would be a pleasing aggravation to the priests, and would at the same time insure the cooperation of their esteemed grandfather, when the great march to the Pillars of Hercules began. Within the hour the wench would stand before him, poor thing. God have mercy on her, consigned to such as himself.

Bitterly, Alphonso leaned to touch a ragged, very soiled doll caught into the side of his chair. What a disreputable object it was, all chewed, with one arm missing, but how Urracca loved it. She held it in her arms each night of her life, and had since she was a babe. She would shortly come dashing in the door; she would not leave her cherished companion for long.

Alphonso sighed, thinking about his eldest child. No monastery for her. He would have her near him until she was grown, motherless or not. What manner of mother would a pack of meal-mouthed nuns be to such a one as she, whose eyes danced with eagerness and life, whose father loved her as he had loved only one other human being. Even if he had a dozen sons before he died, this daughter would one day inherit the throne and be queen of Castile. God knew a woman was as capable of ruling as any man; he would not deny her her birthright, place that knife of inferiority into her heart, as it had been driven into the soul of—. Damn, but even the giving of a throne could be a curse. To wish upon her this vacancy, this loneliness, without a friend, but with a thousand enemies all eager to have the chair you sit upon placed under their own covetous behinds!

He slumped into the chair, resting his head upon folded arms, trying to put to good use a few spare minutes. After meeting his new bride, he would meet with a representative of France to agree upon the joining of the Frankish troops with his own, for the coming attack upon Toledo. The Italians and Germans were already with Rodrigo Diaz where he lay encamped and impatient. Never in the history of Castile had so goodly a force of Christians been assembled, as for this great and Catholic war. Not another winter would the king of Castile be seated at Palencia, but forever after housed within the first, the true capital of Christian Spain . . . Holy Toledo, political Toledo, geographically strategic Toledo. Thank the Lord for the cause of reconquest, or this business of being a king would be unbearably futile. Progress, the molding of history, a man's name etched upon men's minds as long as these times were close enough to be of interest, was enough to convince a man that his life was worth living. And after Toledo? Ah, he would set his eye upon The Rock and drive every infidel into the sea. The Arabs believed it impossible, but soft living had softened their heads. He did not fear the might of African savages. What were they against the strength of all Christendom? It was a *world* crusade now, not merely an internal war. The dreams of popes were shoving a burr of zealousness up Christian rumps. Ah, yes, the pope—he was so pleased with this planned crusade that he found it unwise to further threaten Castile in his lust for tribute. There was time, endless ages of time. At least one problem shelved for another day; tribute to Rome.

"Jezebel?"

A small face, all eyes of violet blue, peered around the side door behind Alphonso's chair, and he turned quickly, his expression one of extreme pleasure. "Here! Here is your sinning woman, daughter, reclining upon my chair."

Urracca stomped into the room, her face scowling with angry disapproval, her small hands doubled into tight fists that pushed indignantly against shapeless hips. "You naughty, naughty girl," she scolded, shaking the doll so hard a wisp of stuffing flew out. "You did not attend Mass this morning. Now you must make confession . . . a hundred and ninety Hail Marys—you hear?"

"Why do you *tolerate* Jezebel, Urracca? She is hell-bent for certain."

"I love her."

"Ah, well. And what of your father? Might I have one of those kisses you so hoard, eh?"

Fully aware of her power, the child looked her father in the eye and said flatly, "No."

"Not even one tiny, bitsy one?"

"Father, I am eight years old. Must you treat me like an *infant*?"

Alphonso laughed, then sobered quickly. "Ah, forgive me, *Doña* Urracca. We might shake hands. I think that would be proper enough for a lady of your increasing years."

"Now you tease me," she pouted, her long double eyelashes fanning open and closing provocatively.

Suddenly the doors across the hall swung open and an aged servant hastened toward Alphonso, keeping his gray, palsied head bent low. "Sire, there is a lady in the courtyard who insists upon audience with you. I informed her that all audiences must be arranged through Don Bermudez, but . . ."

"That is the fact exactly. So why annoy me with buts?"

"But."

"There you go again! Be gone, before I beat open your empty skull."

"Sire, she insists that you will see her. Nine strapping young knights and one elder accompany her."

"Her name?"

"Doña Elvira Rodriguez of Aragon."

"Nonsense. Why would I see a woman I have never heard of? Take twenty men and shoo them away as you would stray chickens."

"I saw the lady, Father. She is very pretty."

Alphonso turned to Urracca, calming his miserable temper. "You did, eh? And where did you see this mystery lady?"

"In the courtyard as I was returning from church. She sat back into the carriage, but I peeked inside."

"Pretty, you say?"

"Well, for an older woman."

"And how *old* would you say? Fifty? Sixty?"

She twisted her lower lip thoughtfully, "Mmm, more closely thirty, or forty, I think."

"Ancient! How well preserved she must be, that someone as discerning as yourself can still refer to her as pretty."

"Sire?" the servant pleaded helplessly, "shall I . . ."

"Ach, I will see her. Who am I to refuse a pretty woman my esteemed presence? But only the minimum time. I have more important matters on schedule today than satisfaction of the whims of mystery ladies. We will see what she would have of the king of Castile, eh?" He took hold of Urracca's hand, giving her a quick, affectionate smile.

When the woman entered, flanked by a small army of knights, Alphonso sat forward, suddenly interested. She was dressed in black, veils of mourning hiding her face; a proud woman, striding confidently with her head high, shoulders straight with purpose. She halted before him. The knights stood back in a half circle around her. He looked from one man to the other and saw something in their eyes that reminded him of captives standing before a conquering general. Odd. They obviously were uneasy, wary, one in particular, whose inhuman face loomed ludicrous and unreal from under his helmet, his beady eyes full of distrust and caution.

"I am at your service, Doña Elvira Rodriguez," he said grandly, bowing a little.

"I would speak with Your Highness alone," the woman said from behind her veil, "if that can be arranged?"

"What?" he laughed, taken aback by such presumption. He strained his eyes to see through the veil, but could not. Damn him, if she could see through it from the other side, walking a straight path, why could he not see through from this end? "Attend me, woman," he shouted, proving his position, "you are fortunate to stand before me *at all*; now state your business or depart!"

"Forgive me, sire, I have angered you. If you recognized my voice, remembered me, you would not shout so, nor refuse my simple request . . ."

"Elvira Rodriguez! I know you not, today, or ever in the past. Enough!" He waved the old servant to him, bellowing "Have this lady escorted to her carriage and see her out of Palencia—immediately!"

"And you said to me, 'You will forever be my friend, always welcome in my house, and if ever you need help you have but to ask.' Now, I ask you, Alphonso."

Alphonso's eyes went blank. He gaped, then shook his head in disbelief. He well remembered to whom he had said those words. A dead woman, gone more than thirteen years. And he was reminded of better days, of youth, and love, and bravado. "Are you a witch . . . that you can so delve into my past and bring forth a memory?"

"Speak not my name, sire" she said low, "and I will tell you that I *am* that memory, absent from this land for many years."

"Impossible!"

Alphonso's eyes searched the faces of each knight until they rested upon those colorless sockets belonging to the ugly one, and they spoke, that absurd head nodding in reluctant affirmation. For a moment he sat unmoving, stunned. Jimena Gomez alive? Then it struck him full force, the tragicomical significance of this unexpected exhumation, and he broke into sudden, howling laughter. Marvelous! That arrogant bastard deserved this. To see Rodrigo's face when he discovered Jimena was alive. The entire world would feel the concussion, as the Lord of Castile exploded into a thousand protesting pieces.

"You there! The scurvy lot of you," Alphonso shouted to the stragglers still lolling in corners of the hall, "out! All of you." He waited, still smirking, until the last of them was gone. Then he turned to Jimena's armed guard, scowling furiously. "And what roots your unhearing selves to the floor, eh? Be gone, fools—this woman needs no protection under my roof. I am indeed her friend. Scat, bothersome vermin, superfluous wretches!" All left save one, who remained close beside the woman, glaring distrustfully up at him. "What ails *you*, eh?" he spit out at the ugly brute, then forgot the wretch, and turned to speak gently to his daughter, who stood properly silent beside his chair. "You will be late for meal, child. Anna will be searching for you. There is nothing here of any interest to you. That is my good girl—give your father a kiss and be off."

The child pouted, wrenched her arm away from his touch, then quickly gave up the attempt to alter his decision. But she did not kiss him. She turned a long and withering look upon the veiled woman, then pranced across the room and out the door, slamming it closed behind her.

"Independent child." Alphonso laughed uneasily. "But I adore her. One speck of perfection amidst the . . . Ach. Come now, remove that accursed veil and let my eye see this miracle. In truth, is it you, my old friend?"

Jimena quickly pulled off the smothering cloth and her white hair, loosened from its ties, fell soft and thick down her back and over her bosom. "It is myself, Alphonso, but I again beseech you not to say my name aloud; the walls have ears. I would not have recognized you. So rotund you are, and bald."

Again Alphonso stared with collapsed jaws, his mind stumbling over the implausability of what his eyes beheld. Such events simply did not happen in this life; who was dead, remained dead. But he did not believe in ghosts, either. The face was fuller, older, but undeniably the same; her voice, too. "Trivialities! Christ, woman tell me how this can be, how you managed such a perfect escape for so many years, where you have dwelled. Do not be a fool. Remain in your grave—there is nothing here worth returning to." He was excited and depressed, the weight of his own dead past heavy in his rumbling gut.

Jimena laughed. "How does one put into a few sentences thirteen years of living?" She threw her hands up helplessly. "To begin with, it obviously is not *me* in that grave at Gormaz; my servant girl is there. I was taken south and have dwelt there ever since. Now that was the greatest oversimplification that has ever been mouthed by mortal." She turned to smile at Estiano but received no response; he was sour and disagreeable about this entire venture, certain Alphonso would have her burned at the stake rather than envelope her in welcoming arms.

"You have survived the ordeal amazingly well, it seems. You have been content?"

"Content? Not at first. But lately . . . indeed, yes. But let us come to why I have returned."

"The child."

"Exactly.

"But what about the *man*, eh? He will be more than shocked, I can tell you. He will be thunderstruck. Hah! To be near and see his face—" he cut off his words, awaiting Jimena's reply. Her return was strange enough. No stranger would it be for her to pronounce undying affection for her husband.

"Man? What man, sire? In a garden of Castile I once planted a bright yellow flower, that I want to transplant to more fertile soil. Since I no longer own the soil in which its roots are fixed, I must dig it out secretly, you see, and slip away. It is only a weed, actually, untended, unadored, but it is mine and I would take it where it can flourish into something more than a weed. Have you understood me, Alphonso?"

"Easy enough to do, I would say, since few in this land are even aware that your flower exists. The man has three other blooming trees which suit him better; this one has been forgotten. But . . . *must* you keep your identity secret? Six years of persistent adultery, eh? Hilarious! All other of his crimes he has justified before God. But *this*!"

"I must."

"So be it, then," he shrugged.

"You have changed so much, Alphonso, as we all must I suppose, but you seem . . ."

"Ah, the young are blind. The old see no better, but feel the pressures more. Nothing has changed except my attitudes. Life was no less absurd before; I simply refused then to accept what I did not wish to believe. Nothing has changed."

"Urracca is an anchoress?"

It had come, the inevitable question. Alphonso's throat constricted, his tongue becoming thick, choking him. He turned his face away, his emotions uncomplicated. He had loved Urracca then, and he loved her now, and he would love her through eternity. "She left me," he whispered hoarsely.

"No, Alphonso . . . she would never have left you. No truer love could any mortal give than that which she showered upon you."

Alphonso leaped to his feet in a rage. "Presume not upon my friendship, woman . . . come creeping back into my life like a ghostly, accusing finger. You have your tragedies and I have mine. Now let it lie! For Christ's sake, let it lie!"

Jimena flinched. She saw in this king's eyes the same bleakness she had seen on too many faces from the border of Castile, in the fields, at an inn—knights, priests, now even a king. A nation with a single purpose, that of annihilation, the cause of restoration their only weapon against a guilty inner voice that whispered words from their Bible, "Thou shalt not kill." On their faces she had seen a general pallor of despair. They wore rags and ate the humblest of fare, kneeled before their saints to pray for sons butchered before their beards were grown, and went forth from churches to send another son to die. For what? A handful of earth. What cause would drive them when the peninsula was entirely regained? Enlightenment, the arts, or Christian goodness? No, they would reach across the sea for more of the earth, continuing the destruction, the voices of their priests always encouraging and justifying. And somewhere beyond consciousness that inner voice would weep, "I have forgotten to *live*." They would burn the library of Cordova to the ground and the university, and cry out, "Where is meaning, joy, and peace?" Their armies would trample down the orchards, farms, gardens, and parks, the great viaduct, and they would wail, "We are starving." There were unanswerable questions in Alphonso's eyes. Inside he was weeping, "Where is love?" It was gone from him; he knew only despair. "Where is joy?"—gone with his youth. He longed for personal peace, but

wanted it not for his people, his single weak joy was the exter-
mination of better men than himself. Alphonso was, after all, a
barbarian, a ruthless, uneducated tyrant, Hasan's detested destroyer of civilization. Pity and revulsion replaced friendship.
Once she had loved this man, now she would be kind and tolerant and use him for her own purposes.

"Sire," Jimena began in cold tones, "I require a letter of
safe conduct, one that will allow me all the privileges of a rela-
tive as regards Urracca Rodriguez. I am her mother's cousin,
from Aragon, and ask to be allowed audience with her, and request that I be given the power of decision as to what is in her
best interest. I will remain in Castile only a few weeks, then
will return to Toledo, and from there to my home."

"Toledo!" It had taken a moment for Jimena's words to
penetrate Alphonso's self-pity. "Why in the name of the Mother
do you travel to Toledo?"

"A man awaits me in Toledo, sire. This man I speak of is
of great interest to me."

Alphonso's eyes widened in surprise. He pulled at his lower
lip thoughtfully, his mind stumbling as he made a futile effort to
connect her statement with the recollections of her that dimly
came to him out of memories. Religious to a fault; a frail, skittish bird who was plain, shy, sweet, and excessively pious. Yet
she now admitted to adultery as one might matter-of-factly
state that white was white. He knew a nagging envy. Would
that he might just as openly say the truth, let the world go
hang. Where did Jimena dispose of guilt? Upon what rubbish
heap? There was not a hint of it in her eyes or manner.

"I would advise you to avoid Toledo, woman," he said.
"Rodrigo Diaz will attack within four months. He has a free
choice as to the exact date, being in full command."

"Goddamn!"

Estiano whirled upon Jimena, no longer content with silence. "I have listened to enough. We will take ourselves to Toledo immediately, and remove that fool man from the trap. Do
you hear?"

Jimena was dazed. Her heart was beating fast, fear for
Hasan sending the blood rushing hot to her face. She did not
heed Estiano's outburst, but looked to Alphonso. "Attack. But
not until the end of winter."

"He will not attack in winter. At least no one *else* would.
No, not until spring, even early summer; his army is not yet
complete."

"Four months," she whispered, intently chewing at her

lower lip, suspended between Toledo and a monastery. She glanced to Estiano's raging face, then again to Alphonso. A quick decision. "We leave for La Coruña immediately, Estiano. We will easily be in Toledo and away before any attack. I *must*. Can you not understand? I have come this far. I will not turn away now."

"Damn!" Estiano barked. "Are you willing to gamble against such odds? Willing to walk straight along the path Rodrigo Diaz makes, to be caught within an embattled city? Have you any conception of what Toledo will be like the day after it is won by the Christians? You are a fool chasing rainbows!" Estiano threw up his hands in disgust. He vowed to send Juano, one of his knights, to Hasan warning him of the danger, pleading with him to leave that place as soon as possible.

"May I have the letters, Alphonso?" Jimena persisted, every muscle taught, urgency pushing at her as the clock of fate ticked off precious moments.

Alphonso sighed. In had walked a ghost from out of that happier past, bringing with her sweet memories not often brought to mind today. Now she would evaporate into the lost so soon again, taking with her those memories, leaving him cruelly reminded and all the more desolate. He saw violet eyes bright with love, shining close, heard a lyrical voice whispering his name over and over again.

"Alphonso?"

"Eh? Ah, yes. Yes. Wait in your carriage. The letters will be brought to you. A letter is all the aid I can give to your floral transplanting, you understand. I would of course be expected to allow my dead friend's cousin the privilege of audience, and action as kin in her regard, but if you fail and are apprehended I will be forced to treat you as a criminal and a fraud."

"Of course," Jimena agreed, looking long into the dead eyes of a king. Then she turned and moved toward the door.

"Doña Elvira!"

Her hand upon the door latch, Estiano close beside her, Jimena turned back at the sound of Alphonso's voice. She gazed across the vast hall to that slumped and lonely statue of a man. "Sire. . . ?"

"It will be of no use warning Toledo. They have known for three years that I would attack and no help has come to them from their brethren. It will not be offered now, even though the date is more certain. Toledo is only the beginning.

After that—all of Andalus! You shall see. It is a Holy and Catholic crusade now and—"

Jimena softly closed the door on Alphonso's desperate protestations.

Seven precious days had been spent, three in travel to La Coruña, another lost in settling into Garcia Castle—which Alphonso had thoughtfully ordered open to her party—and another three days consumed in bickering with an icy-faced clerk who guarded the monastery and Urracca Rodriguez from intruders. Alphonso's letter was not questioned, but the child was in Retreat, retired from the world in constant communion, through prayer and meditation, with the Lord. It would be another week before Jimena would be allowed entrance. Estiano kept pestering her to give it up. The days were monotonous and uncomfortable, depressed by disappointment and frustration. Two months of grime had collected upon her; lice were crawling over her scalp and under her clothing and there was not a single opportunity for an illicit bath, with a castle full of already distrusting servants. Jimena suffered a nagging suspicion that she had made a terrible mistake in attempting to undo what was already done, to alter the unalterable.

For two more days Jimena paced. God in heaven, how slow the moments passed. In Cordova she had almost wept these past three years at how swiftly time flew. How had she borne it as a child and young woman without going mad? If she could read a book, compose a few poems, something, but Estiano, eternally wary, forbade it. She was to be Christian exemplified, without any extraordinary little habits to stir curiosity. Thus she sat, paced, slept, and worried. What would her Urracca be, what manner of young girl? To be sure, she would be ragged and unclean, devout and superstitious, uneducated, but did she dream of better things as her mother had? Or was she content with her lot? Did she deeply desire the life of a nun, or was it lack of choice that moved her? And would she depart with a strange woman, turn her back on the familiar, walk into a circle of infidels? Of course not! But she could not turn her back on her daughter, leave her behind in this darkness of time, knowing that the light of civilization was open to her child and her grandchildren. Grandchildren, she thought wistfully—that extension of one's self into the future; how we long for them to know a better world. Grandchildren were flesh of our flesh . . . our immortality.

A light tap at the door jolted Jimena to attention. She paused to collect herself. She was always on guard with the servants. "Enter," she called out and sat herself down in a chair with hands properly folded.

The boy opened the door wide but remained standing speechless in the corridor. He was a shy lad, son of the cook, whose duty it was to run errands, carry messages, and any or all other tasks not specifically assigned to anyone else.

"Yes, Jaunito. What is it?"

"Th-th—the bishop is c-c-calling, mmmmmm-y lady," he stuttered, his small, nervous hands leaping about as if the gestures might aid him in pushing forth the words.

"The bishop?" Jimena kept her expression fixed, but her heart leaped into her throat. Her guard was up and fully armed.

Juanito had no opportunity to reply. He was shoved roughly aside by a very grim and rushing Estiano and the door was rudely slammed in his face.

"Estiano! For God—"

He leaned back against the door, glaring across the room at her, breathing heavily. "Oh, it is nothing at all. Just a man in the entrance lobby awaiting the presence of Doña Elvira Rodriguez. A Christian bishop to be exact, and to be even *more* precise than that, his name is Don Pedro. Familiar, eh? Bring to mind anyone in particular?"

Jimena glared back at him for a moment, then slapped her hands down on the arms of her chair and cried, "Oh, *bother*! How revolting. That is all I needed this day to make it totally unbearable. Don Pedro of all people! Another damn complication."

"Complication!" he yelped. "Have you lost your mind completely, woman? It is more than a mere complication; it could mean your death warrant!"

Jimena waved a hand in the air impatiently. "Don't be silly, Estiano. What would that Don Pedro be doing in La Coruña?"

"As guardian of Urracca Rodriguez, of course!"

"Oh— Yes. Damn him, why did he not stay at Gormaz where he belongs? He should have died long ago—he must be very old by now. I recall that he was gray and aging when I was a ch—"

"Stop it!" It was a desperate plea. "We must leave this place immediately. He asks to see Doña Rodriguez, thinking her ill, because she has not attended church since her arrival at this castle. Do you intend to prance down those stairs and greet him like—"

"Yes! That is exactly what I intend to do!" Jimena jumped up from the chair and went to her bed. She grabbed up the thick mourning veils and plopped them askew over her face. "Like *this*. And he will not know me, nor suspect me, for I will excuse myself, saying I grieve for my dead father only recently departed. Then I will take myself to his blasted church, receive communion, make confession, if I must; I will do anything to get to that child. Is that clear? Now come along, Estiano, we will face him together, eh? Have courage, sir, it will all be over soon."

"Ho-ho, not me, courageous one," he said with a flourishing bow from the waist. "You can hide beneath veils, but I cannot. He will remember that it was I who delivered the note to Rodrigo Diaz, I who attended a certain funeral. A face like mine no one could forget."

Jimena smiled under her veils. Courage, she thought. There had been a time, to be sure, when she was anything but brave. Courage. What was it actually? An empty word. One does what one feels one has to do, regardless of obstacles. Too many people had not sufficient courage to take even one more breath, or to dream, love, or challenge life in any way; the living dead. She waved Estiano out of her path with a purposeful gesture, and marched confidently down the stairs to face Don Pedro.

Horrified, Estiano rushed to the rooms where his knights were quartered and made hasty plans to have Jimena watched and followed every single moment, if they must storm the walls of that blasted monastery to do so. Meanwhile Jimena calmly met Bishop Don Pedro. Her heavy veils were unnecessary, she quickly realized, because he was nearly blind, hobbling miserably, resting his frail weight upon a stick. She explained her trouble and promised an early appearance at church. Don Pedro was most gratified to find her well and would be looking for her soon at Mass. Not more than a few moments did it consume. Jimena was returning to her rooms before Estiano's knights were fully awake and aware of what he was shouting about. As two of the knights rushed headlong from the room, they met Jimena returning, very pleased with herself. Grumbling and complaining, they took themselves back to their beds, disgusted with her overly zealous protector, certain now that this woman of Abu l Hasan's required no one to guard her—indeed, she might well be the one to protect them.

Chapter
✠ *THREE* ✠

Jimena hesitated, her eye roving up the moldy walls to the debris-strewn tile roof of the convent, and up to a blue sky, the same one that curved a crown over Cordova.

Her heart froze in her breast. Impossible to conceive that the child she was about to approach, attempt to abduct, was her own. Now that the yearning of thirteen years was within her grasp, some of her former urgency and need was lost. Where was satisfaction . . . the breathless expectancy? She suffered a compulsion to run, in fear of disillusionment. But if she departed now the yearning would quickly return to her, as future rationalizations convinced her she had been foolish.

Subduing apprehension, Jimena pounded the knocker hard against its metal resting place, listening to the sound echoing faintly within. Two dark eyes peered through the peephole, and a faint voice queried, "Yes?"

"I would see the Mother Superior," Jimena demanded, "as regards audience with Urracca Rodriguez."

"She will not see you; I am sorry."

Jimena controlled her temper. "I think," she began huskily, "that she will see me, since I have a letter for her from King Don Alphonso!"

"Oh," was the dull reply, "one moment, if you please."

The eyes vanished and the peephole closed. Jimena waited with toe-tapping impatience. Her eye cast back and over her shoulder. She smiled wanly at the two youthful Mozarabs faithfully at her heel. Estiano was at his station, she noted soberly, the others lying in wait as casually as their quaking hearts allowed. Estiano had known all along that she had no intention of merely looking upon her child. Take such risks for just a glimpse? But Hasan had not guessed, or had he? Pray God, let the fruit of circumstance be ripe for this play of destinies, or the

380

fate of that long dead Arab under her acacia tree would be her own.

The iron-faced door opened wide, and the persimmon grimace of the Mother Superior was before Jimena, the old woman's puckered mouth indicating annoyance and exasperation. "A letter from the king, eh—eh?" she rasped. "Give it to me, then—though I cannot see . . ."

"Here you are, Mother," Jimena interrupted civilly. She waited, giving the old woman time to read the message, then added sweetly, "Now, may I visit with Doña Urracca? Will you bring her out to me, please?"

"Certainly *not*! She is not allowed in this section of the convent. Harummmmf," she grunted, "even a king cannot interfere with the laws of the Church, with God's will." But she knew Alphonso well, by reputation if not personally, so she demurred. "You may see her for a few moments. She is a devoted child with many duties to perform and cannot dillydally conversing with relatives."

"Of course," Jimena agreed, worriedly considering how she was to get the child out of this door and into freedom.

"Follow me."

With amazing agility for her age, the Mother Superior huffed off down the dark corridor with a rustle of skirts and veils, Jimena and the two knights skipping to keep pace with her. They passed through a door that opened into a court. It was a bare, unplanted square of sand, furnished with hard wooden benches. A few novices sat quietly here and there, fingers busily working their beads, or sitting eyes closed, heads bowed, a broiling sun bearing down upon their black enshrouded heads. Then through the court, past the church, to a row of shabby stone hovels with numbers upon each door. The Mother Superior halted before hovel number nineteen, pointing haughtily. "She is within," she muttered, and stalked away mumbling something about the wrath of God and sin.

Jimena hesitated again. She stared at the cold numbers that represented her daughter here. Gingerly she moved up the two steps and placed suddenly cold fingers upon the latch, slowly opening the door. She threw her shoulders back and entered the dark room.

The girl reared up, startled, and turned and looked into the eyes of her mother. Her blue eyes registered no curiosity or distrust. She said flatly in a thick voice, "I am sorry, but you have entered the wrong cell, my lady."

Jimena could only stare forlornly at the creature, unable to speak. A stranger's face, starkly framed by a black wimple, was turned to her; her flesh was grayish, pimpled, and sallow from lack of sunlight and proper nourishment. Jimena looked into the girl's empty eyes and for the first time fully realized how she had appeared to Hasan, Estiano and Acacia in those years long past. This pathetic young girl was more than an extension of her own flesh, but a continuation of a disease that had possessed her at the time of giving birth. She had given life to this child and at the same time—death. Tears came, tears of guilt, regret, and a new hopelessness. "I have come to see *you*, Urracca," she whispered.

"To see *me*?"

Oh, God, Jimena thought, how tragic that any child should be so bewildered by the fact that anyone might wish to see her. How long ago had she given way to despair? When her mother denied a bishop's offer of escape—that day? Or when her mother lay in the arms of a man, again refusing to come to her. That day?

"Indeed—yourself." She tried to smile, walking toward the child, stopping short as Urracca backed away a little. "I was a dear friend to your mother, child. I found myself passing this way and thought to visit with you. Your mother and I were cousins. We are related, you and I."

"My mother."

"Yes, dear."

"But I am allowed no visitors."

Jimena smiled as warmly as she could, trying to break down the barrier between them. "I know. Fortunately I am also a close friend of the king's, who penned a letter to the Mother Superior. A special dispensation was made in this case."

"Oh."

The child was satisfied but had nothing further to say. She sat back upon the hard mattress and stared at her hands, not even curious about the woman who wanted so much to see her that a letter from the king was obtained; the calm sea of her mind remained unruffled. Urracca's mind was fully guarded by a shield of indifference; she was saved from despair by her inability to ponder. Never a tear shed, never a regret, and no dreams, for those were the agonies suffered by the contemplative. No smiles, accomplishments, or love, for those were the treasures reaped by the ones who dared ponder life and its meanings, thus mastering it. She did not know that to question, to cry out against life is to live, that to succumb to circumstance, to deny the mind, was to cease to exist. Thus she

sat vacant and isolated, not caring if her visitor stayed or retreated. She coughed violently, and passed a hand across her
burning forehead, suddenly feeling ill again. Her strength often
left her like this, her body becoming so weak she would lay
prostrate for days on end, unable to eat or sleep.

Jimena lunged forward with a gasp as the child fell forward, nearly slumping to the floor. "Child! You are *ill!*" she
exclaimed. She gently moved Urracca over to lay her upon the
bed, and loosened the neck of the black gown from about her
throat. Dear God! She was only bones. And the filth on her.
Lice were all over her. Her illness was malnutrition, probably . . . pray not consumption. "Have you eaten this day, Urracca?"

"No," was the hoarse reply, "it is penance. I shall eat tomorrow, perhaps."

"How many meals a day is regular?"

"One."

"Consisting of?"

"Broth, ummm—bread," and on a sigh, "mutton once of
the week, cheese and wine," all in dead tones, as the child
floated in half-consciousness, her eyelids fluttering weakly, then
closing altogether.

Jimena glanced around the room. It was a cell in fact, not
only in name. Small barred windows warned against any attempt to escape. The air was thick and stale, a heavy stench of
bodily excrement stinging the nostrils. Full center of the dirt
floor was an unemptied chamber pot. The walls were moldy
and crawling with insects. Jimena shivered in revulsion. It was
no use. She would not be able to reach this child if she remained forever. And, God forgive her, she did not love Urracca. She had adored a laughing baby, a twenty-nine-inch infant with no teeth and very little golden hair, a memory. Love
simply could not be brought forth on demand out of responsibility; those one ought to love and those one does love, often
never coincide. Again she denied her own flesh!

Casually, so that the child would not notice, Jimena
brushed the tears from her eyes and impulsively forsook her
plan for abduction. What could she do for this strange young
girl?

"Seeing you has given me much pleasure, Urracca. Be
happy, my child." She painfully swallowed anguish. "Your
mother would have wanted that very much." Then with a cry
she whirled away from Urracca's still empty, unimpressed
countenance and rushed headlong out of that vile prison cell.

Jimena waved aside the worried exclamations of the two
knights awaiting her, dashing tear-blinded past them, not knowing in which direction she ran. But fate directed her, bringing
her to a halt before another cell. It was to be a day filled with
sadness and illumination.

Jimena faced a thick, iron door with a small window near
the top. Almost completely covering its outer facing was a confession, written in blood-red paint; the heart's blood of a woman.

> I, Urracca, a miserable sinner, do confess to all the
> sins I have committed through pride, in thought,
> deed, word—of incest, murder, perjury. . . .

"Ah, no!"

Jimena covered her eyes with protesting hands, denying
them any further view of those crude and pathetic declarations;
but she could feel them there, giant, vulgar letters pushing
through the curtain of flesh that attempted to block them out;
Urracca's degradation spelled out for all the world, and history,
to note.

Why? Jimena hysterically asked herself—why had she returned to this cruel land? Whatever blooms had remained upon
the tree of the past were now falling from decayed branches; she
wanted to reach out and fasten them secure again, or her *self*
would be severed and without connection, a woman with no
beginnings, born at the age of twenty-nine. It was unbearable
letting her mind rest like this upon multiple disillusionments.

Slowly she lowered her hands, but avoided that disgusting
post. Urracca was an anchoress. This cell was more elaborate
than young Urracca's, consisting of two or perhaps three
rooms, the building placed beside the chancel of the church so
that the one enclosed might, through a small slanting window
in the wall, hear Mass and pray before the blessed sacrament
which hung in its pyx above the altar. Inside, there would be
two other windows, one into the servant's cell for the passage
of food, and one, covered by a curtain with a large cross upon
it, for conversation with visitors. Urracca would not have
looked upon another living soul in more than nine years.

Involuntarily, Jimena moved to that sinister door and lifted
the heavy knocker. The curtain over the door window moved
aside. One nondescript eye peered into Jimena's. A rough voice,
quivering with age, said, "What do you want, eh?"

"I would speak with Doña Urracca, please."

"Go away—she sees no one."

"Unlatch this door." Jimena choked on unreasonable rage. "Immediately!"

The curtain dropped back into place and was still. Silence. Infuriated, Jimena wildly beat upon the door. Then she ran to the high, slanted window facing the church. Stumbling, sliding between the close-together stone walls, she climbed to the top of a small boulder just beneath the window, clutching at the jutting sill with breaking fingernails. She called out hysterically, "Urracca! Urracca? It is your friend. You must see me. I last saw you as I departed in a carriage for Gormaz, but I never arrived at that place. Urracca, I beg of— Oh!" The wooden sill was rotted and gave way. She fell backward, sliding down the church wall to the earth. The breath was knocked out of her, and tears were hot in her eyes and blinding. She felt the numb contact of hands pulling her to her feet, heard a knight's voice murmuring concernedly as if from far away. She followed his lead obediently, sicker at heart than she had been in a very long time.

"*Now* you depart! Raise a bedlam of confusion and racket, disturb her ladyship's rest—then leave as soon as she would have you enter. *Stupida!*"

At the sound of that harsh voice, Jimena lurched round to face the withered old woman standing shoulders bent in the open doorway. Behind the hag, darkness, save for a white cross illuminated by the reflected light entering through the door. Jimena moved forward against the objections of her protectors and entered into another cell, irresistibly drawn to new punishments, into hell.

She sat gingerly down upon the stool, the white cross upon the heavy curtain defiantly glowering at her. Her ears caught a faint, heavy breathing on the other side. Urracca was close enough to touch, Urracca, the confident and indestructible. Such faith she had had in her ability to survive against all odds, needing no God, no permission, no justifications for her acts, asking no mercy. That this cross could represent the daughter of Ferrando, this black and filthy hole be her abode, was inconceivable. "Urracca," she whispered, "it is me. Do you know my voice? I have come back. I—" her voice broke. It was like speaking to one's self, with no eyes to look into.

"Jimena?"

It was a rasp, weak and ill-sounding; not Urracca's voice as she recalled it. "All thought me dead, but I live—I am alive, Urracca." Jimena felt a compulsion to apologize, to say You are the one who died, Urracca, while *I* live—not the reverse as all would believe. I am so deeply sorry.

"Yes," came the soft reply, the apology having been sensed. Then the voice came more naturally, the timber of that remembered tone returning, "Where? Where did they take you?"

"Must this separation remain between us? It has been thirteen years, and I leave this place with the sunrise. Can you not compromise your vow of celibacy just this once? Please, Urracca!"

"God's eye is upon us."

Jimena flinched, biting down hard upon her lip to hold back a cry at the pitiable, childlike innocence of that statement—the awful caution. "I know," she soothed, "but He would forgive your seeing me. We were once close friends."

"No! He cannot forgive me. I am evil. Sinful! He despises me. Oh, yes, He does . . . He hates me. I see it in His eyes. I beg Him, even weep at times, but He relents not. Each night He stands by my bed and He looks at me—*looks* at me!"

Urracca's voice was rising in pitch and volume. Jimena realized that she was standing now, for the sound came from above where she sat. She winced against each new utterance, now fully aware of the condition of Urracca's mind.

"THE—KINGDOM—IS COMING!"

It was a nerve-shattering scream, icy, chilling, emphazied by tortured sobs.

"He descends from the heights! The end of the world in a blast of thunder and flames. All will rise up to Heaven save Urracca. All save Urracca! Tied to this earth she will watch the rest ascend that golden ladder—up, up, left behind amidst the cataclysm, the flames, the flames—ahhhhhgg."

A lurching body fell against the heavy curtain, nearly unseating Jimena. The cross writhed ominously for a few empty moments, and then there was total silence. Jimena held her breath, her mind in a state of turmoil. Then she could bear the division no longer. She leaped to her feet and yanked the curtain down with both hands.

"Jesus—God—in *heaven*!"

Jimena clapped a hand over her mouth in horror. At her feet lay a writhing monstrosity, doubled over, twisting, jerking spasmodically. It was a grotesque human being with gray, stringing, and infested hair, with a body of skin-covered bones; a breathing skeleton with violet eyes that arched up into her own, glazed, unrecognizing, pleading, *help me, help me, save*

*me—I am forsaken, alone, dying—I am lost, lonely and defenceless. I
am frightened, so terribly afraid of death; please, please save me.*

Moaning, Jimena kneeled down upon the filth on the floor
and rocked Urracca in her arms back and forth, murmuring
comforting words, her own tears mingling with her friend's.

"A worm—in my stomach."

"Yes. Sshhhh, now . . . do not think upon it. It will pass;
quiet now."

"God placed a worm in my stomach—He did. I can feel it
there—it pains me so—it moves. Aieee," she wrenched loose
from Jimena's hold, rising up only to fall forward again, her
agonized wails ripping the air, as she thrashed wildly, on the
floor.

Jimena tried to catch hold of her, but clawing fingernails
cut jagged, red lines down one arm and tore her dress. A foot
caught her in the abdomen, momentarily and blessedly blacken-
ing out all consciousness. But awareness only too quickly returned, and Jimena was again face to face with reality. "Servant
woman!" she cried out, near collapse. "Where in God's name
have you *gone* to? *Servant woman!*"

She ran and began beating upon the door of the servant's
room, her head twisting back again and again to look at Urracca's tortured body.

"*Now* what d'you want, eh?" the Devil's assistant asked.

Was she deaf? Even now her eyes could see that convulsed
apparition, but she would not look. "Help her! In God's name
do something!"

"Bah! She gives birth to her blasted worm again. Leave her
be and she will pass out of it. What would you have of me, eh?
Assist in the delivery of imaginary worms from the gut of an
insane *whore*?"

"Witch!" Jimena shrieked, "you loathsome pig!"

Her arm shot out to slam a hand across the side of the old
woman's head, sending her reeling back into the room, shocked
and cowed. "I would not allow such as you to touch her, contaminate her with your vileness!" She reached around and
slammed the door closed, lunging back to a calmer but
exhausted Urracca, who lay still, her face pressed against the
floor, her ragged clothing wet from perspiration and uncontrolled body excrements.

Jimena searched the room, finding a pitcher of stale drinking water and a cleaner gown. She tore up the curtain she had
pulled down, using the pieces as wash cloths and towels. Strip-
ping Urracca of her stained, reeking clothes, she bathed her as

best she could, dried her pathetic skeleton and redressed her. She managed somehow to drag the woman to the bed and lift her up upon it.

Jimena kneeled on the floor beside the bed, holding Urracca's skeletal hand in her own, gasping for breath. She was suddenly overwhelmed by grief and a raw guilt—guilt because she possessed such abundance, while another suffered so. Though all searched for the same rainbow, so few ever reached it. Why? What was it, who was it, that so cruelly distinguished between two persons, saying to one, "You shall have it all," and to the other, "You shall have naught but the least that there is"? How inexplicably mean, this death without release that had been sentenced upon Urracca. It would appear that God had taken his vengeance, but Jimena did not believe that. No, *man* was her tormentor and destroyer, not God, nor life; Urracca had been slain by strictures placed upon every aspect of her existence. They were called *God's laws* so that men would heed them more closely, for if conceived by mere men no one would give them credence. Christian society had denied Urracca everything, giving her nothing. Her every thought and deed had been a sin, which had driven her to murder, guilt, and death.

Jimena's churning thoughts wandered outside this cell, to the hovel of a child named for this once beloved woman, and she saw the perverted hand of Christian society, knife upheld, prepared to commit this indentical annihilation. No. It would not happen, not as long as she lived to prevent it. One did not have to love a stray pup, to catch it up from under threatening carriage wheels.

"Is it indeed yourself, hmmmm?"

Urracca's eyes were clear and at rest, her mind lucid once more.

Jimena smiled, reaching to brush Urracca's forehead with her fingertips. "Indeed, it is myself. Do you feel better?"

"I am so ashamed. Understandable, is it not, why I allow no one to look upon me? It is not only my vow of withdrawal from the world that keeps me behind curtains, but this forty-two-year-old skeleton of mine, the ravishing Doña Urracca— old, withered, and *insane!*"

Jimena made no reply, avoiding Urracca's eyes.

Sluggishly Urracca moved to a sitting position, leaning back against the black wall her bed rested against, her fingers fluttering, unable to maintain a poised attitude. "You . . . Did you have audience with Alphonso?" she asked, her sunken, dark-shadowed eyes hungrily searching Jimena's face. "Is he well?"

"He is well." Jimena whispered, "and your child is lovely, with all the beauty and grace of her mother shining about her like an aura. She has hair of deep brown, nearly black, long and waving, and deep violet eyes like your own. She walks and speaks, stands and primps, the essence of the queen she will one day be. Alphonso worships her."

"Ahhhh," Urracca sighed, smiling wistfully, "you are perceptive. Or did he actually speak of it?"

"I guessed. Because she resembles you so strongly."

Urracca's eyes filmed over and she spoke in a voice without intonation, "I discovered my condition three months following Alphonso's marriage to Constanza. My heart was already weighted down with despair; he would have his love and also satisfy the priest's demands for a marriage and a proper heir. I was relegated to the status of mistress, visited occasionally, clandestine meetings full of shame and fear of discovery."

"Urracca," Jimena pleaded, "please. You need not explain, I—"

"No, no, I want to tell you. We were dear friends, you and I—please hear me out. Where once he had defied the world, now he was whipped by it; it was not love any longer, but incest. But . . . but he would not let me go. Over and over again he professed undying love, his need of me. I was a drug to which he was addicted. He was drawn to me, despising, loving, wanting, and denying me all at once." She choked back tears and threw her eyes upward to the ceiling in an effort for control. "When I knew I was with child, at first I was appalled by the monstrous shadow that would follow and plague the unborn thing all its life, but then came a most astounding joy. I was to bear Alphonso's child, he and myself mingled together, forming a composite, a miniature human being, the perfect and natural result of our love. But when I spoke to him, I—" her words broke off again, "—I saw his eyes turn cold, a mirror of the frightened thoughts that tore at his soul. And once he had said to me, 'Have a child for me, Urracca. . .' Dear God, I wanted to die. He loved me no longer, this was clear before my bleeding mind. Where was I to go? Then, one night as I lay wakeful, *He* came to me, and He said, 'The time has come, Urracca, thy punishments begin for all those sins thou hast committed against me. Thou hadst thy brother slain; thou hast denied me, cursed me; thou hast lain with thy brother, the foul seed of that hateful union growing within thy womb. It begins. Hell begins for thee, Urracca, but only an infinitesimal taste of what is to come. Thou art evil . . . damned—damned—damned.' I pleaded with Him for mercy, cried out from my hands and knees for forgiveness, but He listened not to my pleas." Urracca was wringing her hands together, the monotonous tone of her voice giving way to rising crescendo and falling whispers. "Thus I took myself to this cell where I could devote the remainder of my days to Him, in hope that He would one day forgive my forming child for her mother's sins. The sins of the fathers shall be. . . . And one dark night she came forth from me, but I never held her, nor kissed her, nor looked upon her face. She was snatched from me and named the child of Constanza, who had been in retirement for the required time. But, do you know, after all these years He still cannot forgive? But the night just passed, He said to me, 'The sins of the mother shall be . . .' Is she happy? Does He truly intend to torture her?"

"Urracca, I beg of you, calm yourself," Jimena cried, reaching out to catch hold of her arm, which was frantically slashing the air. Jimena recognized the glaze of insanity that was swiftly returning to drive out all intelligence and reason.

". . . He said unto me, 'I replace that foul seed that is now born with a devouring worm that shall eat away at thy vitals, ever reminding thee of thy degree of vileness, reminding thee of that unlawful part thou didst allow to penetrate into thee, the snake of lust, of sin, of incest; not until thou art *dead* shall it pass away.' "

"Oh, Urracca," Jimena cried out, weeping, "how terrible your guilt is, how ghastly the tortures you inflict upon yourself! You have created your own hell, believing it to be your just reward. There *is* no hell! God loves you and pities you. You are His own. He judges not!"

Urracca lurched forward drunkenly, her eyes blazing and filled with shock, "Heretic!" she screeched. "Come not to this cell where God dwells, and speak blasphemy to me in His presence! I pay now for such sins. Beware you do not bring a like reward upon yourself! He heard you—there, see?—just behind you . . . see? He heard what you said to me, and his eye is rageful!"

Jimena rose to her feet, allowing one hand to rest lightly for a moment on Urracca's hot forehead. "I leave you now, dear friend," she said tightly. Looking upon Urracca's sharp, skeletal face that pulsated and writhed in agony, useless, wasted humanity, she could not wring from her heart one more tear.

She could not help Urracca, could not alter a single tragic line in that face. All that she could do was step back into the world and be the living proof that life did not always destroy, but could plant a seed, nourish it, and send up a healthy shoot to a flourishing fulfillment. What use to mourn the dead; it was the living that mattered. "Farewell, Urracca. Pray God releases you soon from your torments."

"Doña Urracca Rodriguez! Wake yourself. On your feet now!"

The girl blinked at the woman bending over her bed, ran her tongue over dry, cracked lips, then slowly sat up, swinging her black skirts around to place her bare feet on the floor.

"Gather together any personal belongings you wish to keep, any clothing you have other than these black monstrosities, and bid farewell to this filthy hole you have for so long called home. I take you with me. It matters not to what place, sufficient to say that it is a far better place than this."

The child stared at Jimena blankly. Another place? It was beyond her conceptions. This monastery was the outline of her existence; the world was a church, a hovel, a dozen nuns, twenty priests, and surrounding walls. Her mother had known of an outside and perhaps different or better existence, but she did not. From whence her father had come on his three brief visits, she did not know, from Heaven, perhaps, or Hell—for these were the only other places.

"Urracca," Jimena said patiently. She sat down beside the child and took a limp, cold hand in her own. "Do not be afraid. I would not lead you into any circumstance that would bring harm to you. Come. Follow me, and I will take you to Paradise, mmm?"

Urracca obediently moved from her bed and walked slowly to the door. She took nothing, did not glance back, but departed from that cell which had been her entire life without the slightest regret or concern. She halted outside, shading her blue eyes from the harsh sunlight, waiting for the woman to lead the way. Jimena, shocked at the ease with which her will had been accomplished, shrugged and made straight for the main building, toward the gate that led to freedom. She moved through the court. She placed her hand upon the latch of the inner door, threw the door open, and crashed headlong into the bishop, Don Pedro, who was about to pass through from the other side.

Jimena's heart stopped, then flopped over in her chest.

Somewhere she had misplaced her veils. Ach, they were on the ground, where she had fallen from the boulder outside Urracca's cell.

Don Pedro stumbled backward, bewildered by the sudden obstruction. Then his tired eyes fixed themselves upon the four blurred figures before him. He squinted, peering, making out two knights and two women, one a nun, by the outline and darkness of her apparel. "What is this, eh? Eh?" he cackled. "Who goes there? What Sister is it before me, in this section where none is allowed? Speak up."

Jimena prayed the girl would not reply, and held a cautioning hand up to the bristling knights close beside her.

"Urracca Rodriguez, novitiate, Father," Jimena said curtly.

"Ahhhhh, my ward. Why did you not say so in the first place? Moody child," he complained, "always treats me like a stranger, when I have watched over her, been father to her all her days. Humffff." He hobbled up close to the woman beside his ward, blinking, wheezing, studying the fuzzy-edged outlines of her features. "And you? Who might *you* be?" Then his wizened mind was prodded, and he whirled back to his ward accusingly, "What do you think you are *doing*, wandering about like this? Get back to your cell, this instant. For shame, child!"

"Yes, Father." Like a string-controlled puppet, Urracca turned to automatically obey.

"No," Jimena said firmly, reaching out to stay the girl with a hand. "She remains with me, Bishop. I am removing her from this place, with the permission of the king."

"Eh? What is that? Who *are* you?"

"Doña Elvira Rodriguez, Father. You visited me a week past, at Garcia Castle."

"The name is new and of recent acquaintance, but the voice . . . strangely familiar." Don Pedro screwed up his wrinkled face, his hooked nose twitching, sniffing for a buried recollection. But one does not recognize what one does not expect to see, especially those things that are known to be impossible. Thus Don Pedro's efforts to remember were in vain. "No matter your identity. You will unhand this child. She is the daughter of El Cid, Rodrigo Diaz, and has been commended to this monastery by him, to me, and to God."

"Move aside, Bishop," Jimena said coldly. "I have no time to waste listening to empty words that cannot possibly dissuade me. The child is plainly ill, sir, and will perish if not cared for, nourished by sun and proper diet. You may send escort with us, Bishop, if it will relieve your mind. The Mother Superior has viewed my letter of permission from Don Alphonso, or how else might I have entered in for a visit with the child? I will take her to Gormaz castle, the house of her father, where she can recuperate."

"Aieee," Don Pedro shrieked, "brazen female, who do you think you are, to so order me about? You take her. . . "

Jimena brushed past him roughly, her breathing increased to near panting, perspiration wet upon her face. "Pen your complaints to her father, sir, and pester me no more. I intend to communicate with him, myself, this very day. You will find us at Gormaz castle. Out of my way, sir!"

Don Pedro was a man who could not so easily be set aside. "Halt!" he raged to the dim shadows falling away from his limited vision. "Guards! Call out the guard!" And the monastery bells began to clang in exclamatory warning.

Jimena reached the main entrance unmolested, and was just dragging her stumbling child through the gate when Christian knights thundered clumsily down the corridor.

"Estiano!" she wailed. He was beside her with horses before his name had left her lips. "Take the child," she gasped, as she lunged up to straddle the horse, kicking the animal soundly in the sides with her heels. They raced to Garcia Castle, where Jimena locked the doors against Don Pedro's army of a dozen knights until the bishop had calmed himself sufficiently to have the clearances from Alphonso read to him. Then he doubtfully consigned a chalk-faced priest to her party and retreated.

"Why did you *run*?" Estiano raged when the storm had broken. "For God! That was a fool's maneuver. You should have settled with the bishop at the convent."

"And if he had not relented? Then I might have had no further opportunity to get my hands upon her. Correct? Be quiet, man. I am still frightened to death. Now to the first leg of our journey, which will place us at the feet of the Guadarramas and success. Success, dear Estiano."

Chapter
✠ *FOUR* ✠

Winter was impatient, unwilling to wait out the finishing touches autumn was want to complete before moving on. It came in on icy explosions of rain and driving, screaming winds that ripped lingering leaves from not yet sleeping branches and drowned in crushes of water a bewildered butterfly, a quivering, delicate bird. In the mountains his angry, frigid breath roared over rocky crags and trails, spitting out avalanches of snow that mounted into drifts and froze into solid, impassable crags of ice.

A small party of nine knights, a lady, a child, and a distrusting priest, was encamped upon the plains of Castile, stalled by the torrential rains. They stood shivering and damp, staring toward the cloud-capped, whitening peaks. Toledo was across the mountains. Gormaz was forty miles to the north, there was no alternative but to turn and find shelter there.

Hasan, on the other side of the nountains, in a lavish room in a castle, stood gazing out his window to those same peaks, concerned for a woman he loved. The last message from her was dated more than three weeks past. He saw how the white robe of winter each day moved farther down the slopes. His single prayer was that she had not attempted those dangerous passes, was not trapped there, freezing to death in that distant, awful whiteness.

In the valley surrounded by the Pine Forest, a general stood high upon a boulder looking down upon an encampment of soldiers and knights gathered from all over the Christian world. With satisfaction he noted the ice in the air, the rain clouds thundering overhead, stabbing the earth with brilliant, fiery swords of lightning. Winter would last four months, then . . . *Toledo beware. I am the conqueror. I watch and I wait. My ambition is already attacking your ramparts with vaulting stones and*

*charging ramrods. My sword is already slicing through your heart.
Beware, Toledo.*

The wailing winds shrieked a futile warning to prepare . . . telling each that waited of the terrible events that lay
just ahead, when at last their wind-throats were closed by a
warmer sun and new and friendlier breezes.

Jimena hesitated in the tent opening, dejectedly peering out
into the gray light of midday. It had ceased raining, but the sky
was surly, warning of more to come. Her feet were wet and
cold as ice, her shoes sinking into mud to her ankles. She shivered, pulling her wind-whipped mantle tighter around her as
she sloshed out of the tent, splashing toward the tent directly
across the campsite from her own. She could hear the voice of
Don Pedro's watchful priest in murmuring conversation with
the child; the pompous—ah, but no matter. She was forced to
tolerate the man, for the present.

As she passed two knights who were vainly trying to keep
a fire burning in the center of camp, Jimena called out, "Patience, men," smiling broadly. What a pack of trouble she had
caused these friends of Hasan's and how joyful they would be
to have it done with—she, too, for that matter. A galling aggravation, this monstrous weather, rendering travel impossible,
the wagon and carriage bogged down in mud.

"Estiano?" Jimena pulled aside the tent flap, and ducked
down, glancing within. "May I enter?"

He leaned up on one elbow, looking at her from under
drooping eyelids. He had been trying to get some sleep for
hours. It was one cursed situation after another. Complaints
about the food supplies being damaged by the rains, wine bottles broken by ransacking winds, wet clothing, and colds in
their goddamned noses. A pack of whimpering bastards that
needed someone to blow their spewing nostrils for them! "And
what is *your* complaint?" he snapped, scowling viciously at
Jimena.

"For God!" Jimena gasped, slapping the tent flap closed
again. She stood poised outside for a moment with clenched
fists pushed against her hip bones, then she flounced away
completely infuriated. As if this day were not unpleasant
enough, without foul greetings from a friend. The devil take
him. She would return to her leaking, mud-floored tent, pout,
and cry out against cruel fate, which might relieve her temper.

"Here! Here, now. No need to act as though I slapped
your face," Estiano shouted after Jimena, as he splashed clum-

sily through the mud behind her, hurriedly pulling a mantle about his shoulders. "Raushana! For Christ, I . . ."

"Fool!" Jimena halted and whirled upon Estiano, so quickly and unexpectedly that he fell against her. "That *name*," she cried, waving an angry arm, "never, never speak it with the priest within earshot. What ails you, man?"

"The weather, that is what ails me. The blasted, calamitous weather! It freezes my mind, as well as my feet, hands, and all other extremities. I am up to here with rain, and adventurous, thick-skulled females who have not sense enough to stay in out of it!"

Estiano was yowling at the top of his lungs, shaking, as furious with Jimena as she was with him. He did not say that he was petrified with fear, that his heart was frozen with concern, not only for her, but for Hasan as well, who refused to leave Toledo even after being warned of the risks. Relentlessly they *both* pursued doom, as if it were a challenging adversary with which they could match wits and swords.

Jimena shouted back, "I will not stand here and be insulted! Take your foul disposition back to your tent, sir, and do not speak to me again until you can be civil!"

Estiano struggled for control. He bowed and said, "My apology, my lady. You are right. This winter will be endless enough without our biting at each other. I am tired. Forgive me, please."

"Well," Jimena pouted, fidgeting and refusing to meet his eyes.

"Please, my lady?" A little humor was in his tone now.

"I only wished to speak to you about . . ."

"Then let us talk. Come. Return with me to my tent. I will enter first, then you enter as before, and we will begin all over. And I will say to you . . . Ah, do enter, my lady; I am *so* pleased to see you. Can I be of service to you, this fine winter day?"

Jimena threw her head back and laughed, "Agreed, sir. A truce. Peace has returned to our humble camp." She took his arm and marched with him back to his tent, deliberately stomping her feet into puddles, splashing water and mud in every direction, upon her skirts and Estiano's tunic. "Best that we take all this cheerfully, sir, for no amount of weeping or grumbling is apt to render summer sunshine out of winter rain and snow."

"Cheerfully," Estiano echoed. "Indeed, we *must* be cheerful."

When Jimena was seated uncomfortably upon a rickety stool and Estiano had reestablished himself upon his cot, she said seriously, "Are you resigned to all this . . . as you put it at La Coruña, this insanity, Estiano? Truly, the child concerns me. She cannot endure this wet and cold much longer. She coughs and coughs until it breaks my heart to hear it."

"My honest opinion is that you have lost all your senses! What can you hope to accomplish?"

"Estiano," she interrupted, "you promised to be civil."

"But what about the great Cid, when he receives your unconvincing letter? A cousin to Jimena Gomez, indeed. You *are* mad. He will have you burned, or sliced into small pieces and served to his lions. It is not worth the risk. For God, woman, think upon it and you will see the . . ."

". . . The passes are closed now," she said patiently. "We cannot alter our course."

". . . But we might have chosen a better road in the first place!"

"And if I had left her ill upon her bed, then heard from Toledo that she had passed away? I owe her this much, Estiano."

"You owe no debt to Hasan, or to yourself?"

"Of course! But I must salve my guilt. I know we will reach Hasan in time. Ach! You worry needlessly. I know Rodrigo Diaz well. He will not thwart me. He is so occupied gathering his great army together that he will instantly accept the whole affair, considering Don Pedro's doddering complaints as the usual ravings of a fanatic who has temporarily lost control over a sheep. A courier sent to Gormaz for verification will inform him as to the truth in my communication, the child indeed ill, myself to all intents and purposes what I profess to be. Do not forget the priest who watches us like a hawk, prepared to strike the very instant all is not what it ought to be. I do not fear El Cid, Estiano, nor need you."

"Holy Jesus!" Estiano shouted. "Pray a little of your old self returns to you. Once you were protected by fears that forced you to tread life's road more cautiously. You can be overconfident, woman, too sure of yourself, too damned freewilled. Caution is a worthy virtue."

"For God, I would not be that simpering nonentity again for all the jewels in Damascus. I am caught in a web partly of my own creation, partly a trick of circumstance, and, as with all of life's complications, must ponder it, face it, and solve it to the best of my ability and ingenuity. If I quivered in dread, would that aid me? If I wept and bemoaned my fate, would that alter it?"

"I surrender! Decide upon the road, and I will follow— whether it leads to Heaven or Hell."

"Not Heaven *or* Hell, but Gormaz. It is only forty miles from this place. We will reside there warm and safe through the long winter. When the passes are open, we will fast-away to Toledo."

"Just like that, mmm?"

Jimena laughed, tossed up both hands and said, "Just like that, Estiano."

The carriage bogged down five miles from Gormaz and could not be rescued; so many times had it been extricated from the mire that two wheels fell into pieces as Estiano and the knights strained to heave it out. It was morning, but the rain was so torrential there was no more light than at dusk. The child's fever was rising and there was no way to keep the surging waters out of her tent. After examining the vehicle and accepting it as useless, Jimena wasted no time. She pressed through the driving rain to catch Estiano by the arm and pull him around to look at her.

Jimena shouted at Estiano, "Go to Gormaz immediately. And bring back help!"

Estiano shook his head, indicating by putting a hand to his ear that he had not heard what she said. She angrily repeated it. He whipped a hand up and swiped it over his face, to clear water from his astounded eyes. Rather than attempt argument against the odds of gale wind and rain, he jerked around and rushed off to the leader of his embattled guard. He ordered the man to ride to Gormaz and tell whoever was lord there that El Cid's daughter was mired here with the cousin of her dead mother. He returned to Jimena, faced her, and threw up his hands, making a face that said, That is the best I could do for you. He shouted, "A shame it is that *men* do not wear mourning veils. This face of mine will be my undoing, mark you."

Jimena impatiently shrugged and whirled around to rush to the child's tent. The priest was mumbling over the unconscious girl where she lay with only a glimpse of her face showing out of the folds of the sleep bag she was enclosed in. Jimena roughly brushed the priest aside, near unseating him from his stool. She took his seat when he had vacated it and leaned to feel Urracca's brow. At the intense heat she felt there, she bit hard at her lower lip. Dear God, the intention was to *rescue* her, not kill her. This devilish weather. Damn! Let it stop, at least until they reached Gormaz.

"I have bestowed the last rites upon her," the priest said comfortingly behind Jimena.

She whipped her head around and snapped, "*Have* you? Well, you wasted your breath, sir! I have no intention of allowing this child to die."

"That is in the hands of God, my lady."

"No, sir! Her life is in *my* hands. Get out of here. Go on, damn you, get out. I find you unbearably depressing."

"I . . . I beg your pardon?" he stuttered, eyes wide and showing lights of accusation.

"You heard me, Father. Out!" Then, uninterested in whether he obeyed her command or not, she leaned close over Urracca and whispered in her ear, "You are going to get well, my child, *believe* me. In the stars it is written you will live, so you *must* live; you cannot escape your destiny. You are on your way to Paradise, little one. Soon you will enter the Garden of Allah, I promise you. If you believe, so shall it come to pass. Hold on to your life—hold on to it, Urracca!"

Count Jaime Martinez hastily hid what he was reading. Someone had loudly knocked upon his door. "Enter," he said, making certain his face masked the pleasure of a moment ago.

"A knight begs audience with you, sire," his counsel said urgently, as he moved briskly to where Jaime sat relaxed in an elegantly leathered chair. "He is half dead, a victim of the storm. He says that the daughter of El Cid is ill and stalled about five miles to the south, with her guardian—a woman who is, I think he said, the sister, or the niece, of the child's mother."

Jaime bolted out of his chair as if struck by lightning. Before the stunned gaze of Don José, his young counsel, he thumped across his chamber and grabbed his mantle off the wall where it hung on a hook. As he swung out the door, he shouted over his shoulder, "I want a dozen armed men at the South Gate immediately, and a carriage, woolen coverlets, and a cook wagon, in case we, too, are stalled."

Don José Gustios stood immobilized for long moments. The count was a man of smooth disposition, a difficult person to rouse to any degree of excitement, whether anger or pleasure. At sixty years, Don Jaime was vigorously healthy in both mind and body, and the most influential man in Castile after the king and El Cid. It was rumored that his wealth exceeded that of both king and Cid put together, due to his unique position here at Gormaz. Shrugging off his bewilderment, Don José rushed out of the room and down the stairs, to see that the contingent was ready as ordered.

Enveloped in a hooded skin mantle, Jaime rode ahead of the contingent with a single knight as companion; the remaining men had been ordered to stay with the carriage and wagon, following as swiftly as possible. From the exhausted courier's description of the terrain, he knew exactly where the stranded party was located. It was all he could do to breathe, so intense was his excitement and uncertainty. Word had reached the bishop of Gormaz just yesterday, from Don Pedro at La Coruña, that Rodrigo's daughter had been abducted by a mysterious female bearing a letter of safe conduct from Alphonso — forged, of course. Ignoring the slanting rain that blinded him and the mire that stumbled his horse again and again, Jaime drove his mount at a full gallop.

Estiano was nodding, half-asleep under the outcropping of the tilted, mired wagon, when he heard the sound of galloping horses. "My lady," he shouted toward Jimena's tent, where she had gone to rest. "Horses! Put on your veils!"

Before he could get himself to a full stand, Don Jaime's mount was rearing to a halt before him. The count leaped to the mud, with amazing agility for a man of advanced years and only one leg. Jaime stood looking hard at Estiano, his eyebrows raised questioningly. "Where *is* she?" he barked. "And may I ask who *you* are? I have seen you before, somewhere."

Estiano's stomach sank. His mind's eye saw a stake; no, not one stake, but eleven, one each for Jimena, himself, and nine brave Mozarabs. Helplessly, Estiano half-turned and pointed to young Urracca's tent. "The man's daughter is there," he said, then had to repeat himself, because the wind carried his voice away.

"Not Urracca!" Jaime shouted. "The woman who *stole* her; where is *she*?" When the man only stared at him, apparently struck speechless, Jaime threw his head back in disgust and ran with a stilted gait toward the tent next to Urracca's. Finding it occupied by three mud-masked knights, he swore and stomped through the muck to the next tent.

When Jaime exploded into her tent, Jimena reared up on her cot in surprise, staring at him open-mouthed. She had not heard Estiano's warning and order to veil herself. He just stood there looking at her, his face expressionless. Still handsome, she thought irrelevantly—the lines of his face were deeper, his hair white now, but little else about him had altered. "Sir?" she said weakly.

"On your feet, woman!" Jaime ordered with a commanding swing of one arm. When she was promptly standing beside the cot, he strode over to her, severely examined her face, then ferociously barked, "Where in the name of Christ have you *been*, Jimenita? I expected you long before *this*!" He exploded into happy laughter and swung his arms around her, hugging her tight to his chest. "Dear God, woman," he said against her wet, filthy hair, "it warms my soul to see you and feel you close."

Stunned, Jimena pushed herself back to see his face. "You *knew*! But how, Jaime? How could you have even guessed it would be me?"

He put his hands one on each side of her face and kissed the end of her nose. "Because, my dear sister, I was the first to see the body, and it most certainly was not you. I said so. I swear to you I did. But Don Pedro insisted." He shrugged. "Who was I to argue with a bishop? At least I had the comfort of knowing that you were alive, and the hope that you were well."

"But the wounds. I was told that her face . . ."

"Yes, her face; but, whoever she was, she was definitely not seven months with child. I was, with your late aunt, aware of your condition, while the bishop and your husband were not. Don Pedro closed that coffin with a swiftness that caused me to wonder if he was party to a plot of some kind; he said it was to hide from the tender eyes of your loved ones the grossness of your body more than a week after your horrible death. I knew that if you lived, sooner or later you would return to Urracca, even if you had to make a pact with the Devil to do so."

Jimena laughed hoarsely and nodded. "She is desperately ill, Jaime. We must get her to a warm bed as quickly as possible."

"A carriage and wagon follow me," he assured her. "I could carry her on horse, but . . ."

"No. Oh, no, she would get too wet and chilled. We will wait for the carriage."

Silence fell between them as each studied the other questioningly. Jimena answered Jaime's unspoken question softly. "Yes, I have been happy; not at first, of course. I am Andalusian now, Jaime, and can never be anything less. And

you? You look well. I wouldn't have expected you to have survived the years so admirably. Time has, if anything, improved
upon what was already a very handsome figure of a man."

Jaime smiled his thank-you for the compliment. He
laughed, his face twisting into a playful grimace. "I hate to
admit it, Jimenita, but your father's decision, which I fought so
ignobly, as you well recall, was the best thing that ever happened to me, or to Gormaz. *Both* of us have thrived. As for me
personally, 'thrived' is a profound understatement!"

Jimena stepped back and fell to an exhausted sitting position on her cot. She reached and brushed a wet string of hair
from her face. "You accepted my statement that I was Andalusian as if you also knew that already. No surprise?"

He shook his head no. "Logically, if you were not dead at
the scene, and that was not you in the coffin, then you had to
have been taken captive. I chose to assume you survived."

"But I am *content* to be with them."

"Hmmmm," was his reply. With a raised eyebrow he added, "I will reserve comment on that point for the moment." He
paused, then said low, "Both your sisters have passed on,
Jimena. Leonora left me four years ago. Sol died in childbirth
soon after you disappeared. Only one of my sons still lives,
Francisco, and two of our four daughters. Your Aunt Galiana
lived, mean as ever, until less than a year ago." He hesitated
again, then asked, "You wish to spend the winter at Gormaz, I
assume? When you depart, to what place will you travel?"

"Cordova is my home, but I will first go to Toledo."

"Toledo! But it will be under attack. Rodrigo is there; do
you know that?"

She nodded, closing her eyes wearily. "But another man is
there, too, who must be retrieved before I go on . . ."

"I see— Well! I will leave you for a moment. The vehicles
should arrive any moment." Impulsively he stepped quickly to
her, leaning to kiss the top of her head where she sat. "No
words can express how good it is to see you, Jimenita," he
whispered roughly over her, than turned heel and left the tent.

Alfredo stumbled up the long flight of stairs, his permanently bent shoulders stooping so far over that his graying head
was on a level with his creaking backside. He had thought to
find some rest this winter, with the count's son, Francisco, at
camp with El Cid, his wife and children in retreat at the monastery of San Cugat de Valles. But now nine knights, each demanding a separate room, Doña Urracca, El Cid's eldest daugh-

ter, and the veiled woman who was cousin and dueña to her, and the ugly brute with the guilty eyes, all arriving today to prevent any relief, any mercy for a weary old man. A cousin, the woman called herself. Perhaps. But he had been in this castle since the age of ten and never had he heard of a family branch in Aragon; Castilians all and proud to be so-called. Truth, there was a family resemblance, especially favoring and bringing to mind the youngest Gomez, Jimena. Strange, uppity woman, flouncing into this castle as if she owned it, whipping the veils from her face, defying anybody to deny her right as kin. "Hot stones, to warm the child's bed," she had commanded, while the count stood aside and smiled. The Cook-room talk was that the woman was Count Martinez' next wife; it was well known that he still had an eye for a well-turned wench. He was not really alone all those hours spent behind the locked doors of his chamber.

Awkwardly switching the heavy box from one hand to the other, Alfredo knocked soundly upon the door, the room that long ago had belonged to Doña Jimena, God rest her soul. On hearing the word "enter" from within, he hobbled into the room, muttering complaints under his breath. This was an automatic reflex in his persistent effort to inform those upon whom he waited that he resented what was expected of him; he had never ceased hoping for one sign of sympathy or relief.

"Thank you. Your name *is* Alfredo, is it not?"

The man craned his neck and ceased his mumbling. He stared up into smiling, sympathetic eyes in amazement. Had he reached justice at long last?

"Is there no one else on the staff that can carry these stones?" her sweet, miraculous voice uttered. "You do seem too aged and weak for such an arduous task."

"No one, my lady," he replied respectfully, in a voice properly tremulous. "Fact is, nobody but me would be *expected* to . . ."

Jimena interrupted the man with, "Set your box down, Alfredo. One of my knights will perform the task hereafter. I will speak to the count, ask that you be relieved to kitchen work. Thank you for bringing them this once, sir."

Alfredo crouched before her, with soulful eyes, gaping up at his angel of deliverance. He could find no words as he reached up with a palsied hand to brush away a tear. His ear caught the sound of labored breathing and he turned his head to see a mound in the bed, a bit of yellow hair showing on the pillows. "Ah," he murmured sympathetically, moving purposefully toward the ill child. Quickly he began lifting the steaming stones from the box with his tongs, slipping them expertly in under the coverlets. "My lady," he said, "it is often good to place a stone in water beside the bed of the ill; the mist tends to clear the head."

Jimena smiled. She would have placed a hot stone in water as soon as he left the room. She nodded her approval and watched him perform the task with all the expertness of an Andalusian physican.

When the old servant had left the room, and Jimena was certain Urracca was comfortable and no worse, she sighed and began removing her soaked, mud-caked clothing. She would give her very soul for a bath. The water pitcher was full. A cloth dipped into it would make a fine substitute. Shivering, her teeth chattering, she splashed the water all over her naked body, rubbing her hair between two pieces of cloth, clots of mud and grains of sand raining around her. Then a clean chemise and tunic. But they were much *too* clean, she thought, looking down at herself. Angrily she wrenched herself out of the attire and threw the articles to the floor, stomping on them with bare feet until they had the proper lived-in-for-weeks appearance that was the "style" in Castile. Certainly every Christian woman had to wear a new gown at one time or another, but she did not wish to stand out as too fastidiously neat, to become suspect; she was already suspicious enough. She must attend Mass at dawn, make confession, take communion, be the epitomy of pious devotion.

Her toilet completed, Jimena at last let her eyes slide around the chamber. She suddenly shivered, as her mind slipped back to the day she had left this room to travel to Palencia; somehow she had known she would return someday far in the future and see it like this, as a place painfully familiar and at the same time unrelated to herself. Unaltered. The figure of the Virgin was still over the bed, but now a cobweb sparkled across the face, catching hold of the folded hands and fluttering loose from the carved skirts. The niche below was piled high with dust. The dim outline of a cross could be seen in the dust. Someone had lived in this room within recent years; she wondered who—Rodrigo's second Jimena perhaps? She moved to the window to watch the sky darken, the mountains turn to violet, the fields gashed by long, irregular shadows. She recalled another day, long past, when she had clutched the baby back to her breast. She remembered that strange, illuminated dream that had so enveloped her in joy, then depressed her with its falseness. How many years now, since she had had that dream? It was no longer required; she had moved out of the illusion into the reality. Once this room had been a prison. Now it was a haven, a sanctuary from which she would draw warmth and safety through a long winter.

Chapter
⚔ *FIVE* ⚔

In the bleak dawn light, Jimena made her way along the path from the courtyard to the church of Gormaz. The sky was crowded with threatening clouds, but the rain had ceased for the moment. She pulled her fur mantle tighter around her, yearning for the warmer climate to the south. The people she passed, or who saw her passing, inspected her curiously, and some whispered comments to a companion. She could not suppress a smile as she thought what their reaction would be if they knew exactly who she was . . . and that, under her wimple, over an inch of dark roots shouted the use of infidel cosmetics. Impulsively she turned right, where another path connected which would take her around and behind the church to the graveyard.

Jimena came to a halt before the headstone that bore her father's name upon it. Next to it was the grave of her mother. Leonora, too. Uncertainly she turned. Placing both hands upon a tall, granite stone with its back to her, she leaned over to see what was written on the other side. Her heart hesitated in her breast. She dropped one hand over and let trembling fingertips trace the rough-carved lettering.

> Here lies Jimena Diaz de Gomez, beloved wife of Ruy Diaz de Bivar, beloved daughter of Count Gomez de Gormaz, and beloved of the Lord in Heaven. Blessed are the pure in heart, for they shall see God.

She pulled her hand back and put it to her mouth, as if the gesture could somehow hold in the emotions she felt. Her eyes sought the sky and beyond it to where God dwelt. A profound sense of victory overwhelmed her; half her life had been a war and she had won the battles, every one. Thank God for the trick of circumstance that had set her feet upon the road to Cordova and her beloved Hasan. Estiano. Elvira. And the bishop. Without them she could not have become the person she was, at peace with herself.

Jimena moved around the stone and knelt before it. She placed a hand flat on the wet earth mound and whispered, "Rest in peace, Maria, in your mismarked grave, knowing that I am also at peace." She quickly rose and strode away to attend Mass. "Farewell, Jimena," she said to herself, "to the future, Raushana."

After Mass, Jimena deliberately took the path that would take her past the acacia tree. She stood before it, gazing up through its winter barren branches, searching for her childhood perch. When she found it, her calm was slightly disturbed by a faint screaming that emerged from memory. Hasan was at Toledo. Rodrigo Diaz waited like a hungry lion without. All the hell of war, fanaticism, and God-sanctioned burnings was in the hideous cries she heard from the past. She shivered, thinking of that young Arab that had died here, leaving his lovely little Koran behind him for a child to touch, wonder over, and imitate. Incredible. Today she could authentically copy that "Bible" in an elegant hand and do it guiltlessly. For the first time since her advanced education began, she half believed the Arab insistence that each man's fate was written in the stars; written and inescapable.

Immediately upon her return to the castle, Jimena set about establishing a schedule of daily routines. She would rise at dawn each day, attend Mass, then take her morning meal. She would nurse Urracca most of the day, but make certain she took a daily walk around the castle grounds for exercise. The midday meal would be taken in her room, but for the late meal she and Estiano would join Jaime in the dining room.

Estiano objected strongly to Jimena's decision to join Jaime at dinner, insisting that the count was going to remember where he had seen him before, which was, if she had forgotten, as her wagon driver to Zamora. Jimena laughed off his worries, informing him that Jaime was the last man on earth who would threaten them. He accepted her word for it, but entered the dining chamber that first night with extreme uneasiness.

Jaime was already at the table when Jimena and Estiano entered. He rose quickly, his face cracking into a broad smile. "Come, sit. I have invited no one else. It will be only the three of us tonight. We must bring each other up to date, Jimena.

And I have so many questions to ask; well, I shall likely keep you up half the night. Sit down, sir. Relax, please. Don Estiano, is it not?"

Estiano accepted Jaime's offered hand, making a noble effort to smile and appear relaxed. Searching for something to say, he cast his eyes over the table, then said, "You set a fine table, Count Martinez."

"I think you will be pleasantly surprised, sir, at just *how* fine it is."

Servants burst through the doors, carrying trays heaped with prepared, uncooked foods. The trays were placed in a neat row at the hearth of the blazing fireplace. A girl with a brooding face placed cooking utensils before Jaime where he sat, then curtsied and left the room. When all the servants had departed, Jaime got up and went to the door to lock it.

"There," Jaime said, grinning at the two who stared at him questioningly. He laughed, and stepped to the hearth to inspect the foods. "I have told them cooked foods are poison to my aged stomach," he said cheerfully. "They don't believe that, of course, and think me weak in the head, gone *squirrel* in my old age. Actually, I prefer my cooking to theirs."

Jimena laughed and walked over to the fire. She looked down at the paper-thin slices of kid and lamb, chopped vegetables and fruits, nuts and a bowl of raw rice. Her eyes darted up to Jaime. "It looks wonderful," she said doubtfully. "But what are you planning on doing with it all?"

Jaime told her to watch and wait, whereupon he began expertly preparing what he called "paella." When the aroma of what was cooking reached Estiano, he raised out of his chair and stepped over to look. into the huge cast-iron pot. It was *harísah*. He turned a grateful smile to Jaime and said admiringly, "Sir, you were right—I am indeed surprised. Basil. Where did you manage to get it? And saffron—?"

Jaime smiled, looking pleased with himself, but he offered no reply. He poked at the fire under the pot so that it blazed high, bringing the paella to a vigorous boil. "Count to two hundred for me, Jimenita, then I shall cover it, lower the flame, and leave it. We will drink some wine and talk while it cooks."

Over her wineglass, a few minutes later, Jimena eyed Jaime curiously. "I thought to be the one to amaze," she said, "but I find myself constantly surprised by you, Jaime. You have changed enormously."

"Yes," Jaime agreed, sipping his wine. He looked at Estiano and said, "Do not worry yourself, Don Estiano, as to my *mem-*

ory, eh? Wagon drivers all look alike to me."

"What did I tell you, Estiano?" Jimena said pointedly. Then, to Jaime, "We do not wish to endanger you, or place you in a position of having to protect us. If . . . your own. . . ."

"Jimena," Jaime interrupted enthusiastically, "there are things I had best explain to you. For one thing, I have not been in danger for fifteen years. There is not a man in this entire world as secure as I am. No man, no army, has threatened me since Rodrigo Diaz acquired the title of El Cid. I am showered with praise, gifts in gold—anything one man can give to another as a bribe. I am the single direct line to the eyes and ears of El Cid; it has not changed since Alphonso withdrew his exile. Rodrigo is constantly at battle, totally disinterested in Gormaz as long as my yearly payment to him is prompt. Introduce to me the man who is willing to challenge Count Jaime Martinez, knowing he must contend with El Cid afterward, eh?" He laughed delightedly. "Not even our bishop would consider arguing with me on the *smallest* issue. I am, quite literally, invulnerable."

Jimena smiled, nodding her appreciation of his position. "But there *are* limits," she said sweetly, "or you would not have gone to the trouble of locking that door before beginning to cook a foreign meal."

"Exactly," Jaime agreed, grinning at her. "I respect the limits, which creates no great difficulty for me. I still contend there is no freer man alive." With that he rose and moved across the room to a cabinet fixed against the wall. "Come here," he called to them. "I have something quite miraculous to show you."

Estiano and Jimena carried their wineglasses to where he stood, then watched him reach and trigger a hidden latch which swung the cabinet away from the wall. There, on a shelf, about a dozen books had been lovingly arranged, all recognizable as having originated at the library of Cordova. Estiano's face broke into a grin and he turned a quick, knowing glance to Jimena.

"Can you imagine," Jaime said with pride, "so many books in *one* collection? I have learned to read, Jimena, which is obvious, or why would I treasure so many books, eh? I had a cleric beside me constantly the first years, which became intolerable. I was forever telling him what to write to Rodrigo Diaz, or the king, and never certain he was writing exactly what I told him. He also had to read to me any communications that came to my office. Finally I told him to teach me to read, which he did. Then I promptly dismissed him. Here. This is a copy of the Ethics of Aristotle. Have you ever heard of the man? He . . ."

Jimena exploded into laughter, a hand reaching out to press Jaime's arm affectionately. "Oh, Jaime!" she exclaimed, trying to swallow amusement. His face had lost its glow, he was hurt by her laughter. "You just don't realize who Estiano *is*, dear Jaime. We most certainly do know Aristotle. I wager one of Estiano's copyists printed this very book. He is chief scribe of the library of Cordova. Estiano speaks seven languages, and writes them as well."

Jaime was gaping at Estiano in disbelief. "Seven? Are there that many languages in the world, sir? Truly?"

"Many more than seven," Estiano replied softly. He reached for the book and opened the velvet cover. "Yes, this is the work of Jiyád, who is one of my chief assistants today."

"An infidel . . ." Jaime exclaimed, scowling distrustfully, "printed this book in *my* language?"

Estiano smiled and said, "I print books in *their* language."

"I knew you were not a wagon driver but. . . . Well, I am dumbfounded." Jaime bit at his lower lip, then glanced to his treasured collection. Turning back to Estiano, he reached out and took back the Aristotle. "From this man," he began in an emotional voice, "I have learned to enjoy my own company. What I had once considered loneliness became time speeding too fast away from me. So many books on my shelf, and not enough time left to me to read them all. Sir, how many books have *you* collected at what you call your . . . library."

"One million two hundred thousand," Estiano replied matter-of-factly. "I have about five hundred at my home, all of which I treasure as much as you treasure these."

Jaime gaped at Estiano, speechless. "I'm sorry," he said at last, "but I am not well versed in numbers. Can you explain how many in words I can understand?"

"A million, Count Martinez, is one thousand thousands."

"Impossible! No building could house so many!"

"They reach from the floor to the vaulted ceilings, Count. The men reach them by use of ladders that are built on rollers; they scamper to the top and roll themselves along until they find the book they seek. All are what we call 'catalogued'— numbered. The building itself is as large as this castle and every chamber is filled with books from floor to rafters."

"Jesus Christ! I would give my very soul to see such a sight. Each one different; surely not. What could men find to say, to fill so many volumes?"

"It is not limited to *men*," Jimena informed him. "The poems of Sappho that have survived are there, and many other works by women from every civilized country of the world. Books to teach you the knowledge of numbers, Jaime, and about medicine, and languages—endless numbers of subjects. I myself have written three books of verse."

"No wonder you laughed," Jaime said wistfully. "My pitiful little collection must seem—" His words broke off and he shrugged, embarrassed.

"My dear sir," Estiano said, reaching to place a hand on the man's shoulder, "your collection has warmed me beyond my words to describe it. I had thought the priests here so omnipotent that no such cache of literature could possibly escape their eyes and punishments. How have you managed, may I ask?"

"I have an enterprising ensign, Estiano, who has nothing to do, since we fight no wars here. He finds them somehow. I ask no questions and pay him well." He laughed and added, "I shall have to scold him severely for bringing me so few over the years, when there are so many to be had, eh? Oh my God! My paella!" He suddenly whipped about and raced to the fireplace to inspect the somewhat overdone delicacy. "Damn," he swore. "I had so hoped to impress you with my culinary excellence."

"Don Jaime," Estiano assured him, "it has been so many weeks since we have eaten what we would call a good meal, that it will taste sublime, no matter what its condition."

Immediately upon settling Jimena and her party into the castle, Count Martinez sent a carefully constructed message to Rodrigo Diaz, informing him that his daughter was ill but quite safe; Doña Elvira Rodriguez, cousin to his dead wife, Jimena, was a middle-aged lady of quality with a deep concern for the welfare of the child. Don Pedro's alarm was totally unfounded. Within two weeks Don Jaime received a cordial reply from El Cid, asking that he thank Lady Rodriguez for him, for her magnanimous protection and nursing of his daughter. With the message Rodrigo sent gold, to be spent as the lady deemed necessary toward the quick recovery of the child. Jaime quickly carried the response to Jimena's quarters, a triumphant smile on his face. He found Estiano and Jimena sitting bolt upright on their chairs, across the table from each other, their faces blank of expression.

"Relax, for God's sake," Jaime laughed. "What have you hidden under the table *this* time, eh?"

Grinning, Estiano reached under the table and brought up

the backgammon board he had designed on wood for their secret entertainment. Jaime shook his head paternally, throwing Rodrigo's message onto the table for them to read. He said, "I wish you would believe me when I tell you that under my wing you are beyond reproach. Tell me, what game is this, mmm? I have only begun to understand chess, and you tease me with another?"

Estiano did not reply. He was engrossed in the reading of El Cid's amazingly trusting acceptance of Jaime's explanation. Jimena began describing the game to Jaime. "Incredible!" Estiano exclaimed, tossing the letter across the board to Jimena. She brushed the curled parchment aside, continuing with the rules of the game, as Jaime listened attentively. "For Christ's sake, woman, you must at least be curious!"

"Not even slightly," she replied absentmindedly. "I told you. I know him. I never doubted his acceptance, or his disinterest. . . . Do you want to try a game, Jaime? I warn you, I am seldom beat. And I never indulge beginners."

Estiano sighed and rose to his feet. He went to a window, where he leaned against the wall, gazing unseeing at the winter scene outstretched below and beyond the clouded glass. He was torn in half, wishing the winter to a hasty conclusion and at the same time praying it would never end. Since arriving at Gormaz he had begun cherishing the quiet hours spent with Jimena here in this room, holding each moment close. Soon she would return to Hasan, lost to him once again; lost, the miracle of this togetherness that shone in his heart. He tried to forget she belonged to Hasan, that she did not love him and would not whether there was a Hasan or not. Like a stricken schoolboy he fantasized her tight in his arms, her breath warm against his lips, body one with his own. But at night, when sleep would not come, all illusions vanished and he became cold, shivering against the truth and an awful sense of loss. Then reason would return and he would be grateful for the months that stretched ahead of them—in this hostile land they were friends and confidants, held fast by their mutual determination to survive. It was enough.

Pushing such longings from his mind, Estiano thought about the child that had brought them to this place and circumstance. "A weed" Jimena had called her, when putting her pleas before the king. Indeed an apt description; a more forlorn specimen of humanity he had not seen since looking into a mirror for the first time. Jimena had confessed to him that all love for the girl had been lost in time, but no one would suspect it by her actions; her dedication to the child was obsessive and tireless. Within two days of their arrival at the castle she had Urracca taking broth and sitting up, and, for a week now, walking the corridors for exercise. It was a constant struggle against the child's disinterest in food; Jimena coaxing, pleading, angrily insisting, until a flush of health had begun to glow and new strength rushed through young bones and muscles. But Urracca remained frozen and disconnected from her nurse and her surroundings. She blindly and automatically responded to orders given her. Attention, food and exercise could not cure the child's determination to remain withdrawn from the world.

Estiano turned and gazed across the shadowed room to where Jimena animatedly talked to Don Jaime over the board. She knew that it was now impossible to take the child back to Andalusia with them; she must be left behind, be returned to the monastery. The eye of Rodrigo Diaz was too clearly fixed upon them, the border too many days distant. The count's position here would be utterly destroyed, should she attempt such an abduction after having been under his protection so many months. He had not raised the subject, nor had she, but he was certain she understood what she would have to do—say goodbye to the girl, turn her back, walk away and never see her again. Jimena would carry it off bravely, without glancing back, but for the rest of her days she would be haunted by what might have been had she returned to the child sooner.

Jimena laughed, the sound slightly brittle and too high-pitched, as if she were reading Estiano's thoughts. He quickly stepped across the space between them, put a hand firmly on her shoulder and pressed reassuringly, leaning over the board to see where the game stood between the two.

Spring burst from its sleep, painting the plains pale shades of green, spreading blushes of color over the land. The acacia tree exploded into new bloom and the air was warmer, softer, the sky brilliant blue and cloudless. But the snows were reluctant to retreat from their mountain-peak resting places. The line of their retreat was depressingly slow, each day only a fraction of a degree. The passes remained choked with ice, defying travel. Jimena and Estiano were forced to be patient. Their eyes moved to the peaks more often now, however, seeing beyond to threatened Toledo.

Jimena awoke with a light heart, uplifted by the sounds and scents of spring on the morning air. Less than a month and they would start on the road to home. But even as her spirits lifted, she felt at the same time a pressing confinement. She rushed to the window and let her eyes stretch across the landscape, aching to set herself upon a horse and ride away from these restraining walls.

"Such deep sighs," Estiano said behind her, having entered the chamber without her realizing it. "Patience. The passes are clearing. We will soon enough be gone from here."

Jimena turned her head to study him. "You sound strangely sorrowful, sir. Surely you are not reluctant to leave this haven for lice and rats? With half a year's crust upon your once immaculate self?"

Estiano lurched away from her playfully. "Ach, my odor has offended you, my lady. I beg your forgiveness!"

"Not at all, sir. My own scent is so overpowering I can smell nothing else."

"Perhaps we can bottle it and sell it at home. . . ."

Jimena laughed delightedly and added, "We shall call it 'Goat.' I steal that idea from Acacia, who says that is what I smelled like—just like all Christians." She turned her eyes back to the window and her smile fell. "Oh, Estiano, let us mount horses today, seek out a sheltered nook near a stream . . . and enjoy a swim." As the idea grew in her mind she swelled with enthusiasm, whirling around to clutch him by the arms. "We will have Alfredo provide us with a basket of food. And take tents—spend a night, or perhaps two. I simply must get out of this castle or I shall go completely mad, Estiano."

Estiano eased away from her touch uncomfortably. "On what excuse, pray," he began in a rough voice, "do we depart on such an excursion?"

"Oh, anything," she shot back at him, annoyed. "A visit to some local shrine, or something. There must be one somewhere near; I will speak to Jaime about it. Please, Estiano . . . ?"

"You would have to leave Urracca. Do you think that wise?"

Jimena bit at her lower lip thoughtfully, frowning. "She is enormously improved." She looked hard at Estiano, urging him with her eyes to agree. When he nodded solemnly, she smiled and said animatedly, "Yesterday she *spoke* to me! Volunteered a comment. I make no joke, Estiano . . . when I sneezed, sitting there across from her in the silence as I do every day, she suddenly looked up and said, almost brightly, 'The Lord bless you, Doña Elvira.' Just like that." She laughed uneasily, aware that her voice was unsteady and revealed the stress she suffered. Af-

terward Urracca had instantly retreated again, not another word
uttered, not so much as a glance up from her steady, folded
hands. Pathetic, to brag of such an insignificant triumph. Tears
welled to her eyes. "Oh, Estiano, I need to get away, if only
for a few hours. What she seems to be telling me with her silence is that she hates me for removing her from that pesthole."

"It is the only home she has ever known," Estiano said,
putting a firm hand on Jimena's shoulder. "I think it unlikely
that her actions are intended to punish anyone but herself. She
simply does not trust you yet."

"In more than two *months?*" Jimena wailed, an unreasonable anger overtaking her.

"What price must she pay, mmmm? For the good things
you have done for her and given her? You promised her
Paradise, my dear, and she has been taught that you pay dearly
for a place in Heaven. She may be waiting for you to name
your price."

"Dear God!" Jimena spun around, putting her back to Estiano. "I recall her telling me that sometimes she was not allowed to eat for—; oh-my-dear-God."

"I think you are right. We should go on an excursion. In
fact, today. Within the hour, if you can ready yourself that
quickly. What do you say, mmm?"

"I am ready *now*," she whispered into the palms of her
hands. "By the time you have a wagon and horses waiting for
me in the courtyard, I will be there, wearing a smile. Damn
me, I will not allow that child to whip me with silence! Out of
here, sir. Get yourself busy preparing a wagon, for at least two
days' journey."

They rode all morning before reaching the wood, then
spent the remainder of the afternoon searching for a small river
or stream. There were many tiny rivulets hidden in among the
trees and underbrush, but they did not stop, for a better place
might lay just ahead. It was an excuse for riding on, drinking in
the quiet peace and sweet odors of a forest in springtime. The
sun filtered down in shimmering paths through the trees; wild
flowers turned dew-wet faces up to the light, pure beauty pushing up through tangles of vines and dead twigs. Birds were
busy building nests, twittering and squawking as they danced on
the soft breeze, undisturbed by the adventurous humans who
quietly passed their way.

"Here is the perfect place," Jimena exclaimed. There was a
swiftly moving stream, a grassy bank and a clearing where the

trees were separated sufficiently to allow in the warming sunlight. "It is ideal, Estiano, exactly what we have searched for.
And see there," she pointed, "a whole garden of flowers, so
perfectly arranged as to suppose an Arab gentleman lived here
long ago."

Immediately they set about the construction of a camp. The
sun was low, the wood falling into shadow. The stream was
held back by two mountainous boulders until the moving water
reached the crest of their gray bodies and then spilled over in a
miniature waterfall. They erected two tents side by side and set
a fire near the bank of the stream, laying out their coverlets.
Jimena brought a basket of food out of the pack and they sat
munching chunks of white, moldering cheese, washing it down
with vinegarish wine. There was hard-crusted bread and cold
mutton slices and sweet sugarcakes, and, of course, more wine.
They gazed into the crystal water, listening to the sighing,
murmuring sounds it made moving over the rocks and brushing
against the banks; hearing, too, the sounds of the forest coming
alive as the light faded. The crickets had awakened to sing,
night birds called out to one another, small animals played in
the underbrush, and the moon rose, shining its soft veil down
upon the sparkling water.

"Hear the moonlight," Jimena sighed. "It is like the lowest
note of the harp, or the resonant wail of a muted horn; the
music of love and of all that is soft and cool."

Estiano did not answer, only sat with arms hugging his
pulled-up knees, chewing methodically at a slice of mutton.

Jimena rose, tugging at the stubborn fastenings at the neck
of her dress. "I shall have that swim, or *bath*. I will not sleep
another night with these blasted lice crawling over me and biting at me. You did bring the soap I had hidden away in the
trunk, Estiano? Merely water would be grossly insufficient."

"I did," he replied self-consciously, his eyes avoiding her.
She was totally unconcerned with modesty and conducted herself as though he were her father or brother. Did she suppose
that he was inhuman? Or did she even think upon it? He went
to his tent, entered, and returned with the soap. He held it out
to her without a word, then stalked away to the tree-secluded
area behind the tents.

"Where are you going?"

"And where do you think?" he replied pointedly.

"Oh."

Jimena removed her remaining clothing and stood hesitating on the bank, reluctant to step into the sure-to-be freezing

water. The breeze was chill, but caressingly exciting. There was
not so free a sensation as that of total nakedness. How she had
grown to despise clothing, since knowing pride in her body.
But she had never felt so awesome an uplifting as she felt this
moment, standing fully nude in the center of a forest by the
side of a silver stream; God's creation unveiled, surrounded by
nature in all its perfection. She envisioned herself as if from a
distance—poised here as God had formed her, with the world as
he had first conceived it; Eve alone in the Garden of Eden. No.
Not alone. There was Estiano. Suddenly she was stabbed by a
heat in her groin, a reminder of a need that had been accumulat-
ing within her until it was a heavy weight almost too burden-
some to carry. She became self-conscious, realizing through her
awareness of him as a man, Estiano's knowledge of her as a
woman. Quickly she stepped into the water, gasping as the icy
shock of it slapped her warm skin. It was better to move
swiftly; the body adjusted more easily that way to the change in
outward temperature. She threw herself headlong into the
moon's path, coming up screeching, laughing, and shivering.
She swam in the pool, leaned her shoulders against a boulder
and kicked her feet playfully. She washed her hair with soap,
then lolled in the water on her back, gazing up at the stars. She
heard Estiano splash into the water, but he was avoiding the
pool. What a bother. It would ruin the whole excursion, this
consciousness of each other, this delicious and ignoble desire.
But it was the Garden of Eden. Ah, to run naked through this
wood, leaping, dancing—a fairy sprite falling easily and joyfully
into any or all of life's patterns. No social code existed here, no
false pretenses or modesty; no shame or repercussions could
possibly result from this glorious exhaltation that surged within
her now. The water caressed her limbs, kissing her breasts with
amorous lips, cool moist fingers moving up her spine and over
her shoulders.

When Jimena returned to the bank, Estiano, wrapped in a
robe of white linen, was sitting gloomily by the fire. On a
branch of a small tree that overhung the stream was a robe for
herself. A subtle hint that she was not to forget modesty again;
also, a loud pronouncement of his desires, his struggle against
the intoxication of this place. Jimena smiled and hid herself behind the heavy underbrush while reluctantly enshrouding her
body with the binding embellishments of civilization. The cloth
was soft enough, but felt foreign, unnatural.

"I feel marvelous," she exclaimed breathlessly as she flopped down beside Estiano, "alive for the first time in *months*. I

swear I shall spend the whole day in the water tomorrow; the whole day naked as a newborn babe." She hugged her knees close to her breasts, holding in the exploding energy that surged through every muscle and nerve, else she would surely go dashing about like a madwoman, thinking herself a cavorting moon-fairy.

"Mmm," Estiano hummed, keeping his gaze on the fire.

"Ah, now, Estiano," Jimena pouted, "do cheer up or you will ruin this heavenly night for me. Smile, do." She leaned close, placing a finger under his chin in an attempt to turn his eyes to her. "Can you not? Just a little smile?"

"Stop this!" It was a loud, emotion-filled cry. Estiano jerked his face away from Jimena's fingers. "Leave me be, for the love of God!"

Jimena recoiled as if burned, her face hot with humiliation, though she thought she understand his pain. He was as influenced by this night, this place, as she was, but was not so totally overwhelmed by the magic as to untether his conscience. Estiano was a man of principle, bound by ethics of his own creation that he thought to be most correct for himself.

Jimena was more than a little embarrassed, and the magic began diminishing for her. "Forgive me, Estiano," she whispered, her head turned away from him, her throat constricted by unexplainable emotions. She was keyed to a high pitch, so that she could either laugh hilariously, or weep unrestrained. "I will not touch you again. I understand."

"You understand! *Do* you now?" He whirled around and grabbed hold of Jimena's shoulders and shook her. "What do you understand of me, eh? What?"

Astonished, Jimena could only stare into his angry eyes.

"That I desire you; is *that* it? That when you touch me I become ill to my stomach with longing? Does it please you to torture me, flaunt yourself naked before me, insulting me with your brazen unconcern?"

"*Insult* you!"

"I am a man, ugly as I am! How *dare* you treat me as if I were not capable of desire, as if I were brother or father to you!"

Furious, Jimena wrenched her arm from his grasp. "Shut your stupid mouth!" she shouted back at him, leaping to her feet, her robe falling open to reveal her heaving breasts. With a vengeance, she caught at the edges of the robe and threw them back over herself, striding off toward the wood.

"Where in hell do you think you are going?"

"For a stroll. Do you mind terribly?"

"Get yourself back here and into your tent," Estiano commanded. When she ignored him it ignited an exploding rage in him that propelled him to his feet and sent him charging after her.

"Goddamn you, Raushana!" He caught her arm and jerked her to a halt, swinging her around so hard and swiftly that she lost her footing and was thrown backward against the rough, unresisting trunk of a tree and fell in a bruised heap into the underbrush. "Oh, Lord," he groaned, kneeling down beside her. "I am so *sorry*. Oh, *Raushana!*"

Jimena lay motionless, trying to catch her breath. The crash against the tree had been a lung-collapsing blow. She looked up into Estiano's anguished eyes so near her own and suddenly forgot the pain of superficial scratches and lost wind. The magic had returned. She lay below Estiano's crouched form, her gown a ruined blanket upon which she lay, her breasts upraised, her fully naked body laid out beneath him. Her eyes met his boldly, and in them was a silent question that he must answer.

Estiano reached out hesitantly and placed a hand upon her cheek, recalling a stormy night when she had been thus before him, when he had touched this same warm flesh, lightly kissed this same sweet mouth. When his fingers touched her face, they trembled and drew back quickly. "Raushana," he whispered huskily, "forgive me. I would not hurt you for—" His throat tightened and closed.

Her eyes were saying that she awaited his yes to her offer, that she regretted the removal of his hand from her cheek, that there was an ache within her that he could satisfy. He felt a terrible upsurging nausea that seemed to emanate from his groin; it was passion without love. Without *love*. What he wanted from Jimena was all there was to be experienced between a man and a woman, a return of what he would give to her. In weeks she would return to Hasan, the man she had given her soul to, and—. No, he could not do it, the little of her that would be given would only multiply his destitution. He slowly got up, turned and stood with his back to her. "Come. Let us return to our tents. We need rest after so long a day."

Jimena lay quiet a moment, then started to twist herself to her feet. A sharp pain caused her to cry out. She jerked her head around to see that a thorn, unnoticed in the brush, had torn her leg open in a jagged line. Her robe was caught in it. Tearfully, she tried to extract herself, and then felt Estiano's warm hands upon her. She was lifted out of the tangled robe and thorns, pulled tight against his breast, and silently carried to her tent.

Gently Estiano put Jimena down upon her sleep sack, then left the tent to return with a cloth wet with wine. He washed the wound, his fingers moving carefully, back and forth, his eyes filled with torment and indecision. When he had finished, he set aside the cloth and at last met Jimena's eyes. He then looked down to small, firm, pink-tipped breasts that were rising and falling, to her narrow waist, smooth abdomen, and slim, trembling legs, then back to her eyes. Breaths held, each waited for the other, suspended on the magic of a moonlit night in the Garden of Eden. In the same instant they exploded toward each other, clasping each other tightly. Estiano groaned, crushing her against him, feeling her breasts close against his own. Abruptly he pushed her away from him, so that he could remove the material that divided her bare flesh from his own, and then pulled her quickly back to him. His mouth searched hungrily for hers. All the years of longing, of withheld passion and love, were in the kisses pressed against Jimena's thirsting lips; she responded in kind, her mouth open, moist, pushing in gasping desperation against his, her body arched toward him, groans of desire equal to his own emerging from her throat.

"Raushana, beloved—God in Heaven," Estiano exclaimed against her ear, then let his face slide down to her throat that echoed his own need; he felt her racing pulse against his tongue. Then down to one pink tip that pulsated, hard against his searching mouth, then the other.

"No," Jimena protested urgently, breathing heavily. "Kiss me everywhere, *everywhere* first." She was unable to speak again, lost in a swirling, disconnected haze of light and darkness. She withheld nothing. There were no restrictions in this garden; any act that passion could conceive was God-intentioned and eagerly tested and savored. Their passion ended in a dark and flashing cataclysm of fulfillment. They lay still, exhausted and sighing in each other's arms. Estiano's lips resting against her cheek, his breath warm against her neck. They did not want to break the spell. They felt satiated, but the need for closeness remained, for flesh against flesh. They dozed off, sleeping folded together until the sun was up. The moonlight and the enchantment was gone. The night just passed must be reckoned with now in the clear light of day.

Estiano was the first to awake. For a moment he was stunned to find Jimena's head nuzzled into his shoulder. The realization of what had taken place between them came like a shock wave, then a softness, and tears welled into his eyes. He let his fingers move into her long hair, which fell in a disheveled veil over his chest. He kissed her forehead lightly, then eased himself from under her. He stood up and looked down upon her. She looked like a child, lay there with the composure of pure innocence, an attitude Jimena would maintain, he thought, if she lived to be one hundred. With a groan he swung around and stumbled out of the tent. Before his eyes unfolded a picture of their lovemaking, which, at this moment, he wanted desperately to repeat once more before the sameness, the lovelessness returned. He had never before known physical love combined with that more profound adoration, that of the soul. And it had vanished in a flash of spinning moments. "Dear God," Estiano whispered to the blazing sky, "what can I do? What?"

Estiano moved about the camp, bringing water from the spring that fed the mightier stream. He built a fire and prepared bread and fruit for Jimena's morning meal, dreading all the while that moment when she would emerge and their eyes meet. Would she hate him for taking advantage of her reckless mood? He imagined her harsh words of accusation as he sat by the fire and morbidly waited.

Jimena stepped out of the tent stretching and yawning deliciously, still as naked as when Estiano had left her side. She smiled and let her eyes slide up through the trees, then down to where Estiano sat staring glumly into the fire. "A good morning, sir," she chirped. "Is it not the most glorious day? I shall take a swim before the meal. And you . . . ? Estiano?"

Estiano was frozen where he sat, unable to find a single answer to the thousand riddles of her apparent unconcern. He glanced up at her with wounded eyes, his mind confused and limping. "No," he muttered, "I think not, Raushana." He watched her walk provocatively past him to the pool. His fingers knotted, aching with the need to touch her. Impossible. A relationship this impermanent was beyond his power to endure. The only tolerable consequence of his love for Jimena was forever.

After her swim Jimena went to her tent and dressed herself in a binding chemise and soiled pelisse. She tied back her wet hair with a length of ribbon, straightened her shoulders determinedly and moved out of the tent to confront Estiano, who was still sitting by the fire in a state of absolute desolation; obviously he was overcome by guilt. Sweet, foolish man. She sat down directly across the fire from Estiano and accepted the bread and fruit that he held out to her while avoiding her eyes.

"Estiano," she began around a mouthful of bread, "I can see you are considerably upset about last night. Clearly, I could have held you off with only a warning glance or one word of rebuff, but I did not. I cannot honestly say that I would have planned this, but I in no way regret it." She laughed softly, "Rest assured, my dear Estiano, you did not take advantage of me. Perhaps the reverse is more the truth, mmm?" She chewed at her meal, watching his face and waiting for some reply, but none came. "Sir, can we not *discuss* this intelligently? I am in no mood to make speeches. What are you brooding about, I ask you? It was a natural conclusion to a peculiar set of romantic circumstances—that and no more."

"Natural?" The question exploded from Estiano's throat as his head jerked around. His blazing eyes fixed upon her. "It happens that you belong to Hasan, that he is not a stranger to me, but a friend! Hasan, he—he is the one hurt most . . ." His words were choked off as he swallowed hard against the lump in his throat.

"Bother! Before *God* I am wed to Rodrigo Diaz. Before *Allah* I belong to Hasan. Adulteress . . . in any case. As for Hasan being hurt by this, I suggest that Nuzhab and Acacia are *my* dear friends, yet he regularly lays with them."

"That is irrelevant, damn it!"

"It is no such thing, sir!"

"He trusted me to protect you. To . . . "

"Ridiculous! You are insinuating sin, Estiano Antolinez, and I had my fill of sin as a girl . . . dirty connotations placed upon almost everything I did or dreamed of. We made *love* to each other."

"Love—" Estiano interrupted sharply. "Did my ears deceive me, or did I hear you say the word love? You surely mean passion. Hasan is the man you love. You will return to Hasan!"

"Oh, Estiano," she scolded, "how many women have you taken that you did not love? I wager you did not know some of them more than a moment before connection?"

His eyes reflected the wound her question had inflicted upon his spirit. Between clenched teeth he replied huskily, "Too many. . . ."

"Well, then. You do not love me, but, if I am any judge, you lost yourself totally on waves of rapture with me. I ask you, why do you consider a female to be a creature somehow foreign to you? I am as capable of rapture as you, and under the same circumstances."

Estiano was suddenly on his feet, overcome by conflicting emotions, barely conscious of what he was about to do or say. He was around the fire in an instant and dropped to his knees before Jimena. Clutching her shoulders in his two hands, and shaking her, he shouted at her, "Not *love* you! I do not love you? You fool! I have worshiped you as saner men worship gods and saints, for Christ's sake! Longed for you as others long for Heaven. For more than ten *years*! You can say such a thing to me, be so ridiculously *blind*?"

Stunned, Jimena let herself fall with Estiano's angry hands, back and forth violently, until his fury was spent and his arms swung around her, pulling her tight against his chest. "Oh God, Raushana, love me," he moaned in her ear, "Jesus God, love me if you can!"

"Oh . . . I do love you," Jimena whispered against his ear, as she wrapped her arms tightly around his waist. "Today I love you, no one but you. There is no day but today, no past, no future—just this moment. Beloved man, how could I *not* love you?"

Chapter
✠ *SIX* ✠

Jimena sat on the damp earth beneath the acacia tree, intently watching Urracca romp with the puppy she had given her. A half-starved, diseased pound or two of brown and black fur had managed to accomplish what months of human indulgence and attention could not; Urracca had emerged from her private world, to join her mother in her's. But it was not a complete surrender. Often the child, if vexed or disappointed, would sink back into the gloom, but at least she laughed now and was spirited enough to run with the pup around and around the tree in endless circles. Human, after all, with a short crop of yellow hair that curled upon cheeks now pink with health. Jimena thought that the child resembled herself quite strongly, except for her coloring; Urracca's hair was naturally platinum, her eyes the color of the sky. "*Chicita,*" Jimena called out to the girl, "come over here and sit by me. I want to talk to you."

Urracca came to an abrupt halt, breathing heavily and staring distrustfully at Jimena. She stood her ground a few feet away, watching and waiting. Doña Elvira was kind and she liked her very much, but the Mother had sometimes been kind, too, and then would suddenly strike with a terrible punishment for an offense she had not known she had committed. Her agile mind raced over her actions of the past few moments, when she had been running a race around the tree with Perito; perhaps she had laughed too loudly, or should not have tried to bark back at him. When her guardian again urged her to come and sit beside her, patting the ground with a hand in invitation, she dropped her chin and obeyed, moving to sit where she was asked to sit, eyes fixed upon her two felt-shod feet.

"Urracca," Jimena began, putting out a hand to lightly touch the girl's hair, "I must leave Gormaz within a few days.

424

You are well, now." She cleared her throat and glanced quickly to the sky. "It is time for you to return to the monastery, dear. I . . ."

"What did I do?" Urracca asked flatly, without looking up.

"Do! Absolutely nothing, child. It is just that you are well and . . ."

"How many days?"

"Until I leave?"

"Yes."

"Seven. A week, Urracca. One week."

"Why?"

Jimena flinched at the lack of emotion in the girl's voice; she was retreating from her quickly. "I have a home, *Chicita*, and a little son who misses me very much and needs me."

"In Heaven?"

"Yes, dear—my heaven."

"Do they have puppies in Heaven?"

"Yes."

"There are no puppies at the monastery. . . ."

"I know." Tears rushed into Jimena's eyes. She leaned over to take Urracca in her arms, but the child lurched away from her, turning her back on her completely. "Sweet one! I would take you with me if I could, but your father would not allow it. He is a very powerful man, a great man—"

"He has two other daughters, and a son."

"But we do not distinguish between our children. We love them all the same—"

Urracca turned slowly and for the first time met Jimena's eyes, coldly and accusingly. Her eyes said, You *lie*! I know and you know that no one on this earth loves me, not even you. Jimena's will dissolved, along with her good sense. She leaped to her feet, clutched up the girl's hand, and dragged her along on her race toward the castle and the search for a solution to her determination.

Within half an hour Urracca was in bed for an afternoon nap and Jimena was agitatedly pacing Don Jaime's audience chamber, spilling her frustrations before him with broad gestures and a confused tongue. She was so disturbed that she unconsciously jumped back and forth from Spanish, to Arabic, then to Spanish again, so that she made very little sense.

Don Jaime sat slumped in his chair, chin resting upon his balled fists, the boot heel of his good foot tapping rhythmically against his wooden peg. When Jimena hesitated to catch a breath, he said calmly, a slight smile turning up the corners of his mouth, "Are you trying to tell me you want to take Ur-racca *with* you, Jimena?"

Jimena gaped at him a moment, then exclaimed, "Well, yes! Yes, I *am.*"

"Why did you not just say so, instead of going on about injustice, the barbaric cruelties of monastic life, and the perverse nature of Rodrigo Diaz, all of which I consider so obvious as to avoid breath about them. If you want to take her, *do* so."

"*Do* so?" Jimena screeched, throwing her arms over her head in outrage. "It is impossible! If I thought it could be done, sir, I would not be—be babbling on this way. The accusation in her eyes, Jaime! It was devastating. When I promised her at the monastery that I would take her to Paradise with me I did not expect to take refuge here at—"

Jaime smiled and interrupted with, "How many books are there, did you say, at the library of Cordova?"

Jimena blinked, stared at him, and then asked him to repeat what he had said, certain she had heard him wrong. He lightly repeated himself. "Over a million," she replied sharply. "Why?"

"Astonishing!" he exclaimed softly, shaking his head in an expression of awe.

"If I believed you completely, Jaime," Jimena continued, annoyed by his apparent arbitrary change of the subject, "about your invulnerability here, I might risk a run with her to the border. But you could not possibly explain to Rodrigo your—"

"One million, you say."

"Jaime! Damn you, I am deeply—"

"Jimena, Jimena, calm yourself. Please." Jaime pushed himself to his feet and stepped close to her, taking her two hands in his own. He leaned forward and said in low tones to her, "The plans are all made. Every loose end of the wool of my life here has been tied. I knew from the beginning that you could not part with her. From the moment Estiano began to speak of his library, I determined that I would see such a sight. *I* will take Urracca to Cordova, Jimena—and there is not a man or priest in Castile, Leon, or Galicia that would dare to so much as ques-tion my motives."

Jimena burst into laughter, but her emotions were so high-keyed that laughing almost instantly turned to weeping. "Insane," she choked, squeezing Jaime's hands hard.

"I agree," he laughed, "completely mad. Come, see what your mad brother has done toward the success of the adventure we are about to embark upon."

Jaime led Jimena to his secret vault, opened it, and from

between two books removed several parchments. He put them in Jimena's hands for her to read. One was a blatantly forged letter from Rodrigo Diaz requesting that Count Martinez deliver his daughter, Urracca, to him at his earliest convenience, because Toledo lay before him and the battle would be long and hard; the Infidel would fall and so might he, therefore he would see his daughter once more before going into battle. Another parchment contained Jaime's disbursement of his properties should he fail to return from the field of battle. The last gave full authority in his absence to his ensign. Jimena read the documents in a state of numb disbelief. She looked up to Jaime at last and said huskily, "I cannot believe you would forsake . . ." She swept her hands in a gesture that took in the castle and all it represented in lands, power, and monies. "All this, Jaime? For a glimpse of the library?"

"Oh, no," he said emphatically, "for a glimpse of much more than *that*." He sobered and glanced away from her to the vaulted ceiling. "In Andalusia I hope to see what I might have been, Jimenita, had I been born but a few miles south of this place. A glimpse of what I still might become in the few years left to me."

"But you must *live*, Jaime! You are too old now to establish the kind of empire that you have here."

"Oh?" he said, grinning. Turning, he reached into his vault again and removed a small leather bag. "Hold out your hands, my dear sister," he said, and when she did so, he dumped into her hands a stream of jewels that would have dazzled the eye of any of the wealthiest Arabs in Andalus.

"My dear *God*," Jimena gasped, as rubies, pearls and sapphires ran through her fingers and over her palms to the floor.

"I told you. I am paid well by those who wish to bribe me. And I cannot spend such gifts in Castile, nor display them on my person. I presume these stones would bring sufficient monies in Andalusia to support me in comfort?"

"In luxury, Brother! You could buy a palace with this stone alone; it is the size of a bird's egg. Exquisite, Jaime!"

Jaime smiled, looking greatly satisfied with himself. "Well," he said on an outrush of breath. "It is decided, then. Let us both pray that *this* attempt of mine at abduction fares better than that attempted years ago, eh?" He winked at her, then leaned and kissed her soundly on the cheek. "Go to Urracca, Sister, and tell her she is going to Heaven after all."

Urracca's pup had been seized with a fit of barking, apparently at nothing, which added to what was already bedlam.

Wrapped in a fur-hooded mantle, the child clung to her struggling, yapping companion with a rib-crushing hold. She had
refused to get into the wagon until he was brought to her; if
Perito was not allowed in Doña Elvira's heaven, then she did
not want to go there either. The promise of a different puppy
when they got there had been a completely unsatisfactory compromise. She sat rigidly on the wagon bench, watching Doña
Elvira closely for any indication of another change of mind.
Horses, disturbed by Perito's persistent cries, reared and
shrieked in protest, straining against harnesses and reins It was
just past dawn and the courtyard was still in deep shadow, but
the entire population of the castle was crowded around the train
that was about to begin its journey to holy Toledo. Count Martinez was in full armor, a sight his people had not seen in many
years, which caused them to cheer him in rousing shouts of
admiration as he swung easily into the saddle of his black stallion and leaned over to pick up the staff that displayed his colors. Estiano took his place on the bench beside Urracca as the
wagon driver. He snapped the reins and shouted at the two
horses and the wagon jerked forward.

Urracca turned her head to be certain Doña Elvira was still
on the bench of the second wagon. The woman waved to her
and smiled. The priest from the monastery sat beside her guardian, his presence jabbing at the pit of Urracca's stomach with
needles of distrust. If they were not returning her to Don Pedro
at La Coruña, were actually going to see her father to ask him if
he would let her go to Heaven with Doña Elvira, then why was
the priest sitting there looking so pleased? She whipped her face
around and buried it in the puppy's shaggy body, sniffing in the
scent and warmth of him, feeling his tiny heart beating against
the end of her nose. Only the perfect could go to Heaven, and
she had not been allowed to attend Mass this morning. Tears
slid into Perito's fur and he stopped barking to furiously wag
his tail and lick Urracca's face. She began to giggle and pushed
him away a little. In his button eyes she saw love; Perito loved
her.

Jimena slumped deep into her fur cape, reaching up a
gloved hand to pull the hood well over her face. She had no
interest in the scenes passing by as they slowly moved under the
barbican tower and over the lowered bridge into the city of
Gormaz; excitement would come only when the first sight of
Cordova was about to appear on the horizon.

"The Cid will be very pleased, my lady," the priest said
beside Jimena. "God guided your hand as you nursed his
child."

Jimena turned to inspect the man's anemic countenance. He was sackclothed, and his hands were freezing because to wear gloves would have been a sign of spiritual weakness. "No doubt, Father," she murmured, smiling softly. "I pray He has not deserted me. In the next few days we are going to need some kind of unearthly assistance, that is for certain."

The priest lightly touched Jimena's fur-enshrouded arm comfortingly. "No need to be anxious, my lady. We carry the banner of El Cid."

"You say his name, Father, as you pronounce the name of God, as if that banner of his riding before us is the *cross*."

"Indeed," he replied emotionally, genuflecting, "Saint Lazarus came to him at Compostella, placing the blessing of God upon him and saying, 'Thou shalt be feared both by infidels and Christians, and thy enemies shall never prevail against thee, and thou shalt die an honorable death in thine own house in thy renown, for . . .' "

"Incredible!" Jimena exclaimed, laughing and pushing the fur away from her face so that she could see the man more clearly. "Do you honestly *believe* what you are saying? Saint Lazarus . . . ?"

"Can you *doubt* it, my lady?" he asked indignantly. "Surely he performs naught but good for the love of God and Saint Mary."

"Good?" she asked lightly, pulling the hood back to hide her contemptuous expression. "Well, I suppose the matter of El Cid's goodness is determined by whether one is facing the sharp edge of his blessed sword, or standing behind him."

"Toledo will fall to his sword; it is God's will."

"Yes," she whispered, shivering. She let her eyes lift and rest upon Estiano's broad back as he vigorously guided his horses through the narrow street toward the gate of Gormaz that led to the countryside.

"Complete love," that is what Estiano had said he wanted from her. When she had asked him to define the term, he had replied, "I offer you full ownership of me. For a thousand nights such as that just past, I would gladly forsake all other women; what use would they be to me, when I have the one my soul desires. Sexual connection is only release, without love, but it is soul-touching rapture when combined with the adoration I feel for you, Raushana. If you were completely mine, I would require no other woman, nor any other reward this life has to offer." She had not been able to promise him all of herself, and could only give him a genuine physical affection the past weeks. Amazingly, as their physical relationship progressed, she had begun to feel all the fervency and warmth she had thought she could give only to Hasan. In addition, there was an intellectual connection with Estiano never accomplished with Hasan, who was always divided from her mentally, his Arab mind remaining foreign and incomprehensible. Estiano had begun to seem like the other half of her soul, his mind often a mirror of her own thoughts, dreams, and beliefs, so that, at this moment, she knew a stronger adoration for him than she remembered feeling for Hasan. Dear God, she loved them both; one of them must end deeply hurt, but which? Perhaps fate would decide the matter, she thought, her gloved hands twisting tensely together in her lap, because she had missed her last period of confinement. Too early yet to be certain. She pushed down a surge of joy, refusing to allow such a hope to torment her. Urracca must be seen safely to Cordova. Hasan must be retrieved from Toledo. There was no time for thinking youthful dreams of many children. That was a fantasy put to rest long ago, and the better so.

Chapter
✠ *SEVEN* ✠

Ali Maymon, who had befriended King Don Alphonso when he was exiled in Toledo, was dead, and his son, Hicem, also. Yahia ruled Toledo and he was not a man who walked in the ways of his father; he was insolent toward his elders and cruel to his people. His yoke was so heavy that the leaders of the city had demanded that he stand up for them and for his country, or they would look elsewhere for a lord to defend them. Yahia had laughed and placed a heavy guard around his person and drunk himself into a stupor. Thus the sultan of Badajoz was invited to come and be the protector of Toledo; the people would deliver the city into his hands in spite of Yahia. But there were a few citizens within the walls of this city who saw the pages of history in advance; they sent word to Rodrigo Diaz, El Cid, of this Arab army already marching toward Toledo to save it, because they wished to be on the winning side.

Thus, as the train led by Count Jaime Martinez moved slowly through the rugged mountain passes, two armies, one from the south, one from the northeast, marched ever closer to the circle of destiny, Toledo. The sultan of Badajoz was Hasan's last hope for his beloved cause. Hasan stood on the gate tower watching the south, hearing in his heart rolling wagons and marching feet like a thunder, and the death groans of Andalus, too, wails against the inevitable. Was Andalus destined nevermore to smile, but just to linger on, wounded, diseased, dying a slow, agonizing, but certain death? Toledo was the heart of Andalusia—the very heart.

Count Jaime Martinez' party entered the city of Madrid for a day's rest, after the leader of Estiano's guard returned from the city with assurances that they would be welcome; they need

431

only leave their arms outside the gates, Allah, his Prophet, and the great Caliph Ghayur were merciful. The count, Estiano, Jimena, and the child were immediately escorted to the Caliph's chamber of audience, leaving the nervous soldiers of Gormaz and the priest to pace the courtyard under the glaring scrutiny of several hundred infidels. Within an hour Estiano ran from the palace, shouting and throwing his arms in the air. He ordered the soldiers and the priest to retreat in haste, for the Caliph had tricked the count and was holding him prisoner, along with Doña Elvira and the child. The Caliph had indicated no malice toward these men, because they were not as guilty as the count in their association with El Cid, but they must leave immediately before he changed his mind about them, or they would all be beheaded and fed to lions.

Estiano made no attempt to answer the confused questions bombarding him, and turned to run back into the palace. Over his shoulder he repeated the warning—they had best start riding northward while they could. Within moments he was again in the audience chamber, where the Caliph was in animated conversation with Don Jaime about the great library, which he had had the pleasure of visiting again quite recently.

"It is not gradiloquence," the young Caliph said, with elegant gestures of his jeweled hands, "to say that the library is the soul of Andalusia, the halo over the crown that is Cordova. A fitting tribute to the divine Aristotle, the first man to collect the thoughts of men in a library, the inventor of our means of cataloguing. To see this place is a fitting pursuit, Saíd, for a man of your wit and years. I bow to the wisdom that has brought you this far, and offer you my hope that it is written that no obstacle shall stand between you and your noble goal."

"I humbly apologize, Caliph," Jaime said, bowing to the handsome figure before him, "for the inadequacy of my tongue, that cannot find the proper words to thank you for your noble generosity and understanding."

"My good friend, Estiano," the Caliph said, moving smoothly to place a hand on Estiano's shoulder. "Such an artist as you should not be adventuring, eh? Take your rest, then speed yourself to Cordova. You and the library are one entity; while you are at risk, our soul is endangered. Allah be with thee."

Absentmindedly Estiano returned Ghayur's compliments, bowed, and, with Jaime, rushed out of the resplendent chamber. "I have found a companion for you," Estiano said aside to Jaime as they walked toward the baths awaiting them.

"On your journey to Cordova you will join the caravan of Ezra ben Gerson. He is a physician and philosopher known throughout Islam. Needless to say, he is an avid admirer of our library, as well as a noble contributor."

"Contributor? Of monies or books, Estiano?"

". . . Both. He travels with his son, Hasdai, and several grandchildren. One of his grandsons is about Urracca's age, a handsome boy with the seriousness of an aged rabbi."

Jaime came to an abrupt halt, catching Estiano's arm. "The man is a *Jew*?" he asked in astonishment.

"Yes. Does that bother you, Count?"

Jaime stared at Estiano, speechless. He let his gaze move around the brilliantly tiled walls surrounding them, the scent of unfamiliarity an overpowering perfume. "I don't know," he said at last. "I have never met a Jew."

"Then you have a treat coming," Estiano snapped, unable to subdue his annoyance at the man's blind prejudice. "No people are as intelligent or creative or wise. Come, we must bathe, then sleep, and be off before dawn."

From Madrid, where they had rid themselves of Christian grime and attire, traveling once again with the refinements of Arabs, Jimena and Estiano moved southeast to Talavera as a part of the Ben Gerson caravan. At the river Tagus, with Toledo rising in the distant haze, the two parties separated. The Ben Gersons, with Jaime and Urracca, continued directly south toward Cordova, while Jimena and Estiano crossed the river, then turned east toward that approach to the city where the river would stand between. In this way they could avoid the army of El Cid that would logically attack from the north, the single approach not barred to him by a mighty water and the natural ramparts of rocky cliffs. They planned to enter the city across the Bridge of San Martin. In Madrid they had heard that Alphonso had received word that El Cid was on the march, and the king himself would depart from Palencia within days to meet the army outside Toledo.

Encamped only hours from Toledo, Jimena found sleep impossible. She suffered from a gnawing impatience to have the night finished. She had wished to push forward without stopping, but Estiano would not hear of it. He wanted to know what lay ahead, he said, and be able to quickly reverse course if the Christians already had the city besieged. She gave herself up to wakefulness, dressed in blue trousers and a gold vest, and stepped out of the tent into a dark and moonless night. She wandered over to the mournfully smoldering campfire that gave off a halfhearted warmth against her legs. She thought of a house, a quiet sanctuary beside a green river. She saw a magnolia tree, an umbrella over a clear, flower-bedecked pool, and heard sweet music and soft voices in calm discussion—and words of love, whispered and tender.

"Worried?"

At the touch of a warm hand on her shoulder, Jimena started, turning to smile, "A bit, Estiano."

"But you must sleep. We have half a day's journey tomorrow, then the excitement of rejoining Hasan. Really, you must try to sleep." He turned her around to face him and looked deep into her eyes, silently speaking of the regret that had kept him awake.

"It is over," Jimena whispered.

"Yes, it is."

"I—I think that—"

"No." Estiano shook his head. "Do not wish for the impossible out of sympathy for me. It has been a rapturous forty days, a memory that I will treasure as a priceless jewel."

"Hasan is the kindest and gentlest of men."

"He is."

"We could never deliberately hurt him."

"No, we could not, Raushana. Anything is permissible in this life, if it harms no one but ourselves. When the sword of our actions slashes out to destroy the innocent, there lies *sin*."

"We will keep it from him, then."

"I could bear the deception more easily than Hasan's tears, the losing of a true friend."

"So be it, then, dear Estiano."

"*Kuzia-Fakan,* beloved." Estiano placed a hand against her cheek, leaning to kiss her lightly, his mouth clinging, fingers fluttering to her hair. "Now to bed. I insist that you get some sleep. And do not fret. We will have Hasan out of Toledo within one hour. Then on to Cordova. To bed, woman. Scat!" He slapped her playfully on the backside, laughing with difficulty.

Jimena could not smile. She started to enter her tent, then whirled around with a frown creasing her forehead. "But Estiano—. I would not hurt *you*, either! I think that Hasan's loss is insignificant when compared to your own, for without me he would possess four others who truly love him, but you will have no one. Would it not be best that—that I marry *you*? I would not have considered it possible to love two men at once, but I do, and I know that I would be happy with you. I could do this, dear man, but I must forsake that other love . . . which I find difficult to even contemplate. Oh, it's not physical things, for you please me as well as he, but his kindness, all the good qualities of character that a man can possess."

Estiano coughed to cover his intense emotion. "Be still, woman. I am not in the habit of entering the houses of my friends to steal their jewels. I might borrow, but my conscience will not stretch to theft. While Hasan lives and wants you, you are his and none of mine. So go to bed."

Estiano Antolinez left Jimena and the nine knights encamped on a hillside overlooking the city of Toledo, sheltered from easy view within a deserted orange grove whose floor was uncultivated, the branches of the trees all blackened from a past burning by Christian marauders. He rode down the low, rolling hill that was sketchily covered with scrub brush and small, spindly trees, his gaze resting upon the city shining bright and peaceful in the midday sunlight, the muddy river running around three sides. Not a single Christian soldier was in sight. He spurred his mount, following the road to the Bridge of San Martin, crossed it, halting at the gate tower to identify himself, and rode on into the winding, narrow streets. He was just one hour in advance of the sultan of Badajoz and his army, that was moving at full speed from the south.

Riding steadily uphill toward the castle of Yahia, Estiano noted the scars of years of tension upon the faces of the people. Market stalls were empty. A wagon of fruit was being mobbed by rioting, starving citizens. It was a hungry and frightened city, a rumbling volcano of human emotions. They were well aware of the impending attack, yet they clung to their homes and the pattern of their lives, hoping against all odds for personal survival, a bright hysteria in their eyes. He shivered, for the stench of death already hovered in the air; he felt depressed by the whole atmosphere of this city, by its depth of despair.

"*Auhashtani!*" Hasan exclaimed, rushing across the room to clutch Estiano's hand and pump it energetically. "By Allah, it is good to look upon your homely face. Where is she, my Raushana? She is well?" His eyes wavered to the open door in search of that loved and longed-for face. When Estiano hastily explained that he thought her safer outside the city, he said, "Of course! Come, sit down and tell me of your adventures. You cannot imagine how I have missed that woman. You are the single one to whom I would admit this, but her being so long divided from me has forced me to concede that Christian men might very well have a grand idea in the loving and cherishing of but one woman. Not once have I held a woman in my arms since she left me; not once have I given my wives a thought in all these months . . . only her, the Splendid One, have I yearned for. Is she well, happy? Was the sight of her child bearable? Tell me all, friend."

"How can I speak, when your own tongue keeps wagging?" Estiano tried to laugh, swallowing a painful guilt. Swiftly he summarized the entire venture, ending with, "It is a dangerous situation, Rodrigo Diaz about to descend upon this place, his abducted daughter well on her way to Cordova. We must leave immediately, must not run the risk of discovery."

"She took the child," Hasan said in amazement. "Miraculous! You actually made off with her. Raushana has strong innards, eh, Estiano? She has become quite the woman."

"Let us be off, Hasan. We can talk at another time. She is as eager to look upon you as you to see her."

Hasan grimaced, pulling at his beard thoughtfully, "Allah knows I am impatient to touch that sweet flesh of hers, but—I have just received word that the sultan of Badajoz approaches the city with his army. Estiano, it has been necessary for me to use every trick here; this Yahia is Allah's worst fool. If the sultan will take this town, his army, combined with this miserable excuse for fighting men in Toledo, might hold off the crusaders. Now why do you look at me like that?" he exclaimed, discomforted by Estiano's suddenly down-turned mouth and disapproving gaze. "I have spent half a year working for just such an event as this. Would you have me depart as soon as the sultan arrives, leaving him to Yahia's ignorant dissentments and the undermining influences of Mozarab Christian sympathizers?"

"She has not seen you in months, man! I cannot return to her and say that you are too occupied to come to her."

"But you do not understand," Hasan cried helplessly, throwing up his hands.

"Nor will *she*."

"You well know what it would mean to lose Toledo to Christendom. Toledo must not fall, Estiano!"

"Ach! For a man of intelligence," Estiano shouted, "you mouth strange words, words of childish, unreasoning delusion! Hasan, you see yourself as a crusading spirit that can save the world, your world, from destruction, but you are only a man—one man. Your true cause lies in the heart of that woman who awaits you so anxiously outside these walls. There is nothing here except defeat. You have bound yourself to the bright tail of a falling comet. The true measure of a man's intelligence lies in his ability to face reality, in his ability to separate hope from hopelessness and to go on living in spite of his disappointments. Toledo is lost; not tomorrow, nor a week hence, but this moment; and Andalus, and all else except the life that rushes through your veins . . . and love, that indestructible, realized hope, the best and all there is to this life."

Hasan shifted moodily away from Estiano's tirade. He sat down upon a mattress near a low, ivory table. He poured a glass of red wine, sipping it anxiously. "You have returned full of speeches, friend," he said flatly, "and once I thought to possess a friend who loved this land as deeply as I. What would you be without Andalus? A miserable Christian peasant herding swine, or shoveling dung. You should bend down and thank Allah for such a land, such splendid citizenship, yet you refuse to lift a finger or risk your already diminished future to preserve it for your children."

"I see the reality of hungry faces surrounding Andalus," Estiano argued heatedly, "a circle of jealousy and need. I see a paradise encircled by a hell. I see plenty surrounded by deprivation. I see joy being strangled by the python of misery. And I see the hatred of men for what has been denied them as individuals, the hatred of that soul who does not comprehend why you were born in Andalus to such abundance, while he was born to mere existence. I well know my good fortune, and thank Allah profusely, but I am not fool enough to waste those gifts upon a dream. That is all you harbor, Hasan, a fine, idealistic dream, a bit of fleeting, invisible stardust in your clenched fists. When you open those fists you will find them empty, and your soul equally as barren for having lost such a treasured illusion."

"Illusions," Hasan muttered, "all men live an illusory existence, seeing what they wish to see, knowing what they wish to know, denying what does not suit them. Must I deny myself such sanctuary?"

"Indeed! For you are above such self-deception . . . educated and introspective. This side of you leaves me baffled and amazed, Hasan. That you could place these trivial incidents of man's struggle for power and destruction above your personal commitments, that I cannot understand."

"Trivial incidents!"

"More than that! Imbecilic nonsense! Two groups of adult humans choosing sides like children at play, happily creating clever strategies for the death of thousands, the annihilation of an entire city. How can you stoop to it, I ask you? How can you play their pitiful games?"

"Yet you agreed," Hasan argued weakly, "when speaking to Omar Khayyámi, that one must have a cause worth dying for in order to call oneself, with any justification, a man."

Estiano shrugged. "Yes, but I have better causes. Causes that are more worth the sacrifice of my insignificant life."

"Such as?"

"A woman, perhaps. Those simpler, less spectacular things, but those with true meaning. For them I would lay down my life so that they might live. Tangible are these causes of mine in whom rest all my hopes, purposes and efforts. I went into Castile willing to give my life for your Raushana."

"And if Andalus vanishes? The base of all those things you spoke of is the country in which they bloom, the system under which they are governed and protected."

"No. The base of it all is love. If I gathered together all my humble treasures and a beloved woman, taking my mind and free soul with me to any land on this earth, it would not alter a particle of it. Sift your causes, Hasan. Weed the chaff from the wheat of your existence and know that it is only those things so worth living for that one gladly dies for. Do you live only for Andalus? No. Be exiled from this land and you would look about you for what you would take, and your arms would reach out for Raushana, a treasure of flesh, and you would exist even as before, fulfilled by love and tenderness."

"I will finish what I have begun," Hasan said, swirling the wine around in his glass, watching the flickering movement with intense concentration.

"Jesus!"

Estiano paced, as he always did when thwarted. "When? When can you manage to wrench yourself from these intrigues to visit her? Even now she must be concerned at our delay. Two hours since I left her, vowing quick return with you. If you do not go to her, there will be no keeping her outside these walls. Would you have her within the cataclysm; would you? For Christ's sake come to Raushana, to Cordova, and let these fools wallow in their madness and foul amusements!"

"Tomorrow!" Hasan shouted, slamming his glass down on the table. "By Allah, Estiano, I am full to *here*"—he sliced a finger across his throat—"with your virtuous speechmaking. I will go to Raushana at dawn—*tomorrow*. I make no promises regarding my return to Cordova. She might well be forced to return alone. Now," he rose up angrily, brushing the wrinkles in his tunic, " . . . now I must leave you, and go to greet the sultan at the gate. Go to her, Estiano and explain my dealy. I—"

"Damned if I will! Explain it to her *yourself*!"

"Estiano," Hasan pleaded, " . . . what is it with us? Is not friendship one of those worthy causes you spoke of? So easily lost in a mere difference of opinion?"

"It is that friendship that so disturbs me. I would have you live, not die!" Estiano strode to where Hasan stood near the door and took him by the hand. "Tomorrow, then," he conceded, sighing, "but I will accompany you now and see for myself the intricacies of the game of war, defense and offense. I would see this sultan's face when he looks upon the crumbling walls, the ramparts that already are half-fallen, see his fright when he contemplates the depth of this pit he has stepped into, the proportion of that vast army that marches toward us. This I must see!"

Hasan laughed, relieved to have Estiano's lectures hushed, for they poked and jabbed at open sores within his soul, and caused a bleeding and a pain that he wished to ignore and refused to succumb to. There was still hope. The sultan had come with his twenty thousand. There surely was hope.

Ten thousand citizens jammed the plaza, flaming and smoking torches held in their upraised hands, shouting and cheering the savior who now entered through the gate of the San Martin Bridge. The sultan, attired in his royal purple robes of office, a violet turban wrapped around his graying head, bejeweled, splendid, sat tall in the ornate saddle that rested upon the back of a slim-ankled white stallion. He smiled benevolently, bowing his head from one side to the other, graciously ignoring the rough shoving and pushing of the crowd that kissed the turned-up toe of his slipper, screaming out their gratitude, renewed hope as bright in their eyes as the flaming torches they wielded. One hundred and fifty officers of the sultan's elite guard followed close behind the sultan. Artistically designed and colorful breastplates were worn over their linen garments. They carried short reed lances and basketwork shields, and wore white turbans wound around steel helmets with pikes at the top. The ends of the turbans floated over their long hair. Their swords were inlaid in gold with sentences from the Koran, and daggers were thrust inside their sashes. When this proud sultan had reached the center of the plaza, he reined in his mount before the platform where the leading citizens of Toledo waited to greet him. There were twenty elders in that beaming group, Abu l Hasan full center, Estiano Antolinez glumly at his right.

"Welcome, oh beloved of Allah, Father of deliverance," Hasan called out, bowing deeply to the man just below him. "The citizens of Toledo render up their city into thy merciful, redeeming hands, and bow down to thee and name thee lord over us and all our lands, and full joyfully will live within the circle of thy compassionate protection. Allah's blessings on thee, oh savior of our destinies."

"And what of Yahia?" the sultan demanded. "Does he also name me savior, or are there hidden swords behind each shadow to cut out this compassionate heart?"

"As long as you are within this city you will be protected, Saíd, by all the people, for it is they who called you, they whom you rescue from infidels. Yahia sits alone in his castle, without army or sword at his command."

"Then lead me to this castle that I might rest and where my guards may keep watchful eyes upon this deposed monarch. Know that the sultan of Badajoz will do well by all your citizens, for I am not as depraved as your former lord, nor do I seek more riches for myself—only the saving of our land from Christian vermin." He smiled again as shouts of approval exploded a booming barrage from the crowd. "At dawn, Saíd, you will escort me around this city so that I may study the defenses, and I would see the army. I have been informed that Rodrigo Diaz leads not less than fifty thousand to this place. Not easily can such a horde be held off. Fully armed and defensible battlements are required."

Hasan's fingers fluttered nervously, and his eyes shot around to meet Estiano's now alert and withering gaze. "At dawn," he muttered. "At dawn, oh savior," he shouted. "You there! Soldiers of Toledo! Escort your lord to the castle." He watched silently until all were gone from sight, the clacking of hooves upon cobblestones, the groaning noise of human voices fading into silence. He and Estiano were left standing alone on the now deserted platform, the dark night close around them.

"Well," Estiano began sarcastically, "that quite takes care of *that*. At dawn you were going to Raushana. But, of course, there are more impor—"

"Enough!" Hasan whirled on Estiano. "Enough of this backbiting!"

Estiano flinched. "Jesus God, Hasan forgive me! The strain

and exhaustion of the past months has made me intolerant to a
fault. The descending doom here frightens and depresses me. I
am anxious to leave this place and all its defenseless agony."

"I know, friend, I know. So it is with all these citizens. My
heart goes out to them, bleeds with their's. I see on the faces of
the very young children that same sweetness and innocence, as
might have shone on the face of my own son. If I could only
blow out the spark that could light the fire of that mountainous
funeral pyre that presses. Even if Alphonso wanted to have this
city intact, the people spared, the legions of Italy, Germany,
and the Franks would laugh at him, for they do not seek land, a
city, or gold; they want blood, the death of every infidel within
reach of their animal paws. *Alhomdalillah* . . . I recall Barbastro!
Fifty thousand perished in one day. Allah spare this town such
wholesale slaughter!"

"What of Raushana?" Estiano asked gently, pity for Hasan
moist in his eyes.

Hasan glanced over Estiano's shoulder and out through the
still-open city gate into the blackness where she waited and
where the sultan's army noisily made camp. His forehead was
creased by a painful frown as he ran thin fingers through newly
graying hair. "I will go to her now," he said mournfully, "for
half of an hour. I must be here at dawn to escort the sultan . . . to salve his uneasiness at our weak defenses, with a
prayer on my lips that he will not run back from whence he
came. Fetch horses, Estiano, and we will go to Raushana. What
is sleep? It would not come this night at any rate."

"Raushana . . . ?" Hasan whispered, kneeling beside Jimena
as she slowly returned to consciousness from out of a fitful
sleep. He brushed his lips against her ear, "Raushana, wake
yourself and give me proper greeting after so long a desolation."

"Mmm," she moaned, stretching. Her eyelids were weighted down and she still floated in a mist. "Hasan? Oh Hasan, I
thought you . . . " She threw her arms around his neck and
pulled him close to her breast, holding on with strangling intensity. "I love you—I truly do!"

"Do not weep. Smile, beloved. We are together again.
Bright angel of my heart, please do not weep." He held her
close and brushed the tears from her cheeks with tender, shaking fingers, his own eyes moist. Estiano's words sounded clear
to him, ". . . love, that indestructible, realized hope, the best
and all there is to this life."

Jimena backed away, searching his weary face by tracing the outline of his features with her fingertips. "It has been a difficult time for you," she said, letting her forefinger touch the corner of his mouth. "I see new lines here, more gray amid the blackness of your hair. But it is ended for each of us. Now we can walk through our gardens again and live out our lives in peace. Home. Cordova. Oh, how I long to stand within the blessed walls of that house, to . . . What is wrong, Hasan? You cannot mean—"

He stopped her words with two fingers over her lips. "Ssssh," he whispered. "Do not plead with me, or torment me with protests, rend my heart with angry disapproval. I do what I must, Raushana."

"How long? How much time do you need to complete your mission here? When can we begin the journey home?"

"One week, perhaps two. But you must go on without me."

"No. I cannot. I am in danger here, and this knowledge within your heart is my single power over you, the only urgency sufficient to bring you forth from the city in time. I remain here, Hasan, until you are prepared to travel."

"But," he began to object, then shrugged in defeat. His head was splitting open, a slicing pain over his eyes. "You think me the fool, I know, but you cannot imagine—"

"No, not a fool, my Hasan, merely gentle to a fault, more so than myself. I loudly protest, but find so little pity within for strange peoples that I am unable to reach out the hand of help to them. You live outside of self, absorbing all the agonies and injustices of this world into your own soul, whereas I but consider Raushana and her petty little world, the rest go hang . . . their pain is nothing to me. Return to Toledo. Do all you can, but do not murder. Plot, struggle, connive—anything except draw your sword. The masses of men who come from my land to destroy Arab Toledo are only human and misguided. Forgive them, for they know not what they do?"

"I cannot that easily forgive and excuse," Hasan murmured, eyes cast down and away. "If a venomous snake strikes, intent upon sinking its fangs into one's flesh, one does not stand meekly by, but quickly takes a stick to pound and cut it into a hundred pieces. Not enough its unawareness, its incomprehension of the magnitude of its crime. So impractical, the gentle Jesus, Allah bless him, and all who purely follow his undistorted path to become equal victims nailed to crosses of equal mortification and martyrdom, ravished by beasts who know not what they do. And thus must be forgiven? I think not. I hold each man responsible for his acts. Bread cast upon the water, brutality returned a thousandfold for every act of savagery. One does not turn the other cheek to an enraged lion, but swiftly and with calm intent sends a lance straight through its heart."

"Indeed," Jimena said softly, and pulled his bowed head to her breast. She let her fingers gently stroke his hair, as she tried to hold back tears. "Let us not speak further of these matters, only of the rewards that will come afterward. A thousand kisses returned for one lovingly given, a thousand smiles, a wealth of love given and taken . . . for it is not all vileness and savagery, is it, Hasan?"

Hasan answered with an urgent embrace, telling himself over and over that this was all, the best, only love. But his mind stealthily crept away from that embrace and sped on stubborn wings back to Toledo; he saw the night blackness fading into gray, the sun hesitating but soon to creep over the horizen. He was cut in two, that part of himself that was fulfilled, sensible and content, clinging to Jimena, to the vision of his home, while that other part, so plagued by idealism and contrived utopia, deluded and dream-born, floated away and out of reach of logic. Thus he rose from Jimena's arms and walked out of the tent in search of that wandering ghost, that he might be whole once more, undivided and questionless. Within the walls of Toledo he would find himself, his conflict inevitably and pitilessly resolved.

Jimena stood beneath the blackened branches of a dead orange tree, leaning against its charcoal trunk, her eyes straining into the gray dawn that was dotted with campfires along the slowly developing outlines of the river. The towers gradually took form against a brightening sky, the sun turning dismal clouds into golden chariots and red tongues of flame. Hasan rode through the encampment of the sultan's soldiers, turned right, and then vanished from view, a tiny doll riding across a toy bridge, into a make-believe city.

By the time the sun was in full sight, Jimena had conquered despair. Hasan was not dead; he lived. It was more than ignorance to presume a gloomy future when a bright one was equally as probable. She whirled about, rushing to Estiano's tent. Prodding and pleading with him, she convinced him to follow Hasan into the city, to protect him and bring him forth in time. But he would not go unless she promised to immediately depart for Cordova. Jimena made the promise with no intention of complying. When Estiano was gone, leaving her alone in the quiet morning she whispered, "God go with you both." Then she closed her mind to all other possibilities except the one closest to her desire. She moved briskly about the campsite, her glance resting only upon what was near and needing attention, and not upon the far horizon.

It appeared a dark speck, without substance or significance. Then like a slithering, twisting reptile, it lengthened out and writhed its way down the landscape, pouring up from out of the horizon like a fiery rivulet, burning, scorching, following its predestined course, moving ever southward. The Alcantara Bridge was reached and passed by, a segment of the line remaining behind. The main body continued on, following the river Tagus, turning west as the waters turned. A fraction of El Cid's army had divided itself from the bulk, led by the famous captain of Castile, Alvar Fañez, and would close all routes of escape to the east, south, and west, leaving the north, the single approach that could be attacked without fording a river, to the main force.

Toledo, the indestructible city that harbored a not-so endowed people, lay calmly awaiting her destiny, unperturbed by the fears, ambitions, and barbarities of men. Out of the mists of antiquity she had arisen, a legend, said to have been founded by descendants of Noah about two thousand years before Christ. Of what possible concern to her, this petty struggle for ownership, of what possible consequence that Christians were returning after three hundred and seventy-two years, the Muslims retreating. Toledo's destiny was immortality, to live forever upon a hilltop, the scars of each battle weaving a bright pattern for her banner of glory. Toledo waited disinterested, while those within her timeworn walls sucked in their breaths and put unsteady hands over pounding hearts. It was a day still connected to that vanished three hundred and seventy-two years; the people were bewildered by the times they lived in, by the history they must be a part of. An end? Or a beginning? It depended upon whether you were within the walls of Toledo, or without.

The sultan of Badajoz was within, but his mind toyed seriously with plans for quickly placing himself without; he had seen ramparts decaying with age and neglect, and a large segment of the population that was unsympathetic to his cause. He had seen empty market stalls and knew that, even with the wagons of foodstuffs brought from Badajoz, he could comfortably hold against a siege no longer than two weeks. He weighed the odds and found them favorable only to the Christians. He listened not to the pleas of Abu l Hasan, only to his own good sense. Twice again he passed around the city, his frown deepening. Better to depart, alive to fight another day, than to die here playing hero to a pack of doomed citizens. Doomed in any case, if he fought or retreated.

Abu l Hasan clearly saw the curtain draw over the sultan's eyes, and knew the pain of speaking and not being heard. Then he discarded dreams and set his mind upon fact. It would be difficult, but he would attempt to keep up the spirit of the people by assuring them that when word reached the republics of Granada, Seville, and Cordova, the whole of Islam would rise to their cause and come en masse to deliver them from the barbarians. He would tell them that they must fight—death would be the result in any event if help did not come in time. Better to die with a sword in hand, than to walk like herded swine into the funeral pyres. Thus Hasan was too occupied with these tasks to watch the sultan of Badajoz ride back over the Bridge of San Martin. The sultan's twenty thousand hastily struck camp to follow him back to Badajoz. Yahia had regained his power and was determined to make a bargain with the Christians for his own life. But Yahia would have to contend with the citizenry that stood guard one hundred deep at each gate, before the streets of Toledo would be opened to infidels. Hasan unsheathed his sword, testing its sharpness with the flat of his thumb, as he contemplated the transition from teacher to soldier, from speechmaker and dreamer to man of action. Then he roughly sheathed his sword and went to his bed, sleeping with his hand upon the hilt.

Estiano entered the city just as the sultan was departing. He climbed to a high rock overlooking the bridge, querulously watching the sultan and his guard ride away from Toledo. Then his eye turned eastward, noticing a cloud of dust rising beyond the hills. He knew a sudden, compelling urge to run back over this last escape route . . . to Raushana, but was held back by a promise, a need to make one last effort to save Hasan from himself. He stood and observed the inevitable collision of forces. The Christian captain, riding tall upon his heavy warhorse, pulled in on the reins sharply, surprised at what his eye beheld—a scurrying, unprepared, retreating army. With gleeful shouts he waved his knights forward, sending them charging into the midst of the confused Arabs.

Thus did Alvar Fañez chase the sultan of Badajoz clear out

of sight, his foot soldiers slaughtering all those dragging behind. The San Martin Bridge was closed off. Estiano's eyes rose up from his rock tower to the distant hills where there was a blackened orange grove, and he whispered, "Run, Beloved—run." Then he turned to the task of finding Hasan and somehow escaping with the man.

Jimena had heard the noise of battle, and she rushed out of her tent to look down upon a churning cloud of smoke, dust, and confusion. But she could not bring herself to depart. Her eyes fastened upon the towers of Toledo; her heart and soul was within those walls. Thus, when Alvar Fañez rode back toward the town and cut away from the road over the hills, he rode straight into that little charred orchard and Jimena's camp.

The captain reined in, holding up an arm to halt his men. His brown eyes were startled and amused. "What is this, eh? What have we here?" He laughed at an indignant Jimena who stood surrounded by nine bristling young Mozarabs. "Did the sultan leave behind a wife? How careless of him. Who are you?" he demanded, pointing a finger at Jimena's wide-eyed face, his handsome features twisted into angry and suspicious lines.

"Raushana, my lord," Jimena said in carefully accented Spanish, "wife to Abu l Hasan ibn Al Hamman of Cordova, who is within the city. He would not allow my entrance into the town because of the danger. We await his return, my lord." Jimena held on to her leaping nerves as best she could, hoping to somehow confuse the issue and extricate herself from this monstrous turn of events. "My lord is a peaceful man, a teacher, and we are a peaceful party. Pray leave us be, oh good captain—as few as we are, we could be of no menace to so great a band."

Alvar Fañez sniffed vulgarly, then unsheathed his sword, leaning forward to place the point of the blade against Jimena's breast. "I suspect you are a Christian," he accused. "There is something here that stirs my suspicion, though what it could be evades me totally at the moment."

"We are of your race, and of your faith, my lord, but we are Mozarabs, born within the walls of Cordova and our father's before us."

Alvar Fañez had met Jimena Gomez once long ago, when his father, El Cid's brother, took him to Gormaz to meet his famous uncle. He was then about fourteen years old. It was her features that stirred the suspicion in him, though there was no actual recognition. Jimena, of course, could not have recognized the boy in the man of thirty. If he had spoken his name, she would have been far more in dread of him.

"Hoh—you there! Take them all. We will carry them to El Cid's camp, where we will have more time for investigation of my suspicions."

Jimena kept silent, allowing her wrists to be bound behind her. She was thrown on a horse before a sweating knight, who was sharply told by his captain to keep his vile hands off of her. Her mind was numb at first . . . unable to believe what was happening to her. Then she felt the scratch of parchment between her breasts. The letter of safe conduct from Alphonso. Dear God, she had forgotten it. What a fool she had been not to whip it out before this brutish captain. As soon as possible she would give it over to him. Alphonso would not allow her to be slain.

Her mind struggled with the contemplation of Rodrigo discovering who she was and eliminating her before Alphonso knew she had been apprehended. No. He would not *dare*. Never. Not Rodrigo.

Thus, as Estiano Antolinez searched futilely for Hasan, and as Hasan fitfully slept in the dark room of a wine merchant's house, Jimena was carried past the San Martin Bridge to a hastily fabricated barge and taken across the river. Bound and gagged, she was confined in a tent guarded by two Christian knights, and left without food or water. The night was filled with the sounds of hooves and creaking wagons and shouting voices, as the armies of Christendom arrived and made camp all around.

Estiano ducked quickly away from a whistling arrow and rolled over and over to the cover of an overturned wagon. He lay there on the cold cobblestones of the street, breathing heavily, his mind pressed by weariness and frustration. For two days he had walked uphill and through alleys, his eyes ever alert for that certain face in the crowds of strangers, but Hasan was everywhere that he was not. Twice he had missed him by no more than a few moments. And in the last six hours no one had seen the man; it was rumored he had been taken by Yahia's group to silence his encouragement of the resistance. He sighed, relaxing back against the stones. What use, this frantic search, even if successful? Hasan obviously meant to remain and fight, to play the role of martyr. By Jesus, it was time to call a halt, to take himself out of this holocaust while he still could. He glanced out from beneath the wagon into the empty street. The women and children had all been crowded into the houses and mosques in the center of the city, well away from falling stones and arrows. Every man and boy over ten was stationed either guarding the gates from Yahia's zealous surrender groups or manning the ramparts, pouring flaming oil down upon the Christians who attempted to ramrod the gates, or snapping futile sticks down upon the sea of humans below them. There was no panic. The fear of the last few years was blessedly relieved by action. The awful waiting was at an end. Now they could move against the menace, pour flames upon it, lash out against a seen and mortal enemy.

"Damn!"

Estiano careened backward as a boulder sailed over the wall and landed plumb center of the wagon, sending splinters and nails flying like arrows up, down, and around his head. "Blast you, Hasan!" he cursed out loud, his eyes flashing from right to left. "I have had enough, friend. I search no more; may Allah walk beside thee and protect thee."

He ran swiftly into a narrow alley and followed the twisting lanes and streets whose two-story houses protected him from the rain of flaming torches and arrows. When he entered a plaza, he saw a crowd of shuffling Arabs nervously pacing. He quickly moved among them, searching their weary faces. But all were strangers and none had seen Abu l Hasan this day. So he left them and moved east along the rocky cliffs overlooking the Tagus. He walked more than an hour before he found a spot where the cliff did not cut downward too sharply, but sloped at an angle to the river's edge, with precarious but possible footing down. But what was the difference—to be burned alive, have an arrow pierce his brain, or fall from this blasted cliff?

Christian troops were heavily emplaced at the bridge approaches, fanning out half a mile in each direction. Estiano observed for hours and found that two men rode sentry along the riverbank at approximate hour intervals, passing each other at just this point where he must cross. One hour to swim the river. He must wait until dark to be hidden from their eyes. He sat under a giant oak and eyed the hills in the distance, ignoring the sounds of battle emerging from behind him, his conscience jabbing him on occasion for deserting Hasan. Truth was, he simply was not the hero type, nor was he adventurous, or daring, or without fear. He had never been so totally frightened in all his life. If he did not move soon, his stomach would dissolve and his knees would become incapable of effort. Thank Allah he had never been forced to fight as a soldier; at the first sight of blood he would have crumbled into whimpering jelly. He pondered it, then conceded he was unusual for his time; he was forty-one years old and he had never killed a man. But now it appeared that this record would be broken. If Raushana had not escaped, Lord forbid, he would slay a hundred men if need be to save her. All a matter of values, it seemed, each man deciding for himself what was worth murdering for. Still, it was not a pleasant contemplation, that first thrust of a sword into the heart of a man.

It was an endless afternoon, but darkness came at last and all battle sounds ceased. Estiano painstakingly worked his way down the rocky cliff. His bare feet searched for a footing. Slipping he caught himself . . . swearing, sweating, and determined, he finally placed his feet solidly on the riverbank. Then, standing knee-deep in the icy, spring-swollen waters, he removed all his clothing except the linen undergarment that hung loosely about his groin and slid soundlessly into the river. He swam easily, careful not to tax his strength at the beginning, allowing the current to carry him, but steadily making progress forward. When he reached the bank, he laughed out loud in amazement at how very simple it had been. One by one, every citizen of Toledo might do the same, but then there were few as cowardly as himself, he mused. He shivered, his teeth clattering together; the sound of that chattering was loud enough, he thought, to wake the whole Christian army. He solved the problem of chilled bones and flesh by running, slapping his arms back and forth across his chest. He quickly made his way across the road and into the hills to where he had left Jimena.

Estiano stood in the center of the deserted campsite, his eyes moving from tent to tent. She had not left—she had been apprehended! He felt numb. At first his thoughts were cold, matter-of-fact, and bitter. She was captured. She was dead.

"Raushana!" he screamed. He shouted her name over and over again. "No! Not Raushana!" Estiano choked on a painful bulge that closed his throat and threw himself to the earth, digging his fingers into the soft, spring grass to weep unrestrained. Amidst the hell of this earth he had found two worthy things, a country and a woman. The one was doomed and he could bear that; the other was wrenched from his grasp, but he could not live without the woman. He cursed God, and he cried out against fate, even as he had as a boy when he could find no understanding of life, no purpose and no hope. He felt thrown back into the pit of misery he had so despised, the poison of his past was spreading within him and around him to devour all his precious illusions. Where were those treasured hours with paints and brushes, where the soft lips of a beloved woman against his own, where the peace of a quiet garden? "Raushana—you cannot be gone from me!" Finally he fell into an exhausted sleep, his body, mind, and soul gathering new strength through rest. The next day he would begin a search for her.

Chapter
✠ *EIGHT* ✠

For five days the battle had been pressed and still the men of Toledo held against the Christian horde. Wounded Christians were laid out in the north fields by the thousands, their unending moaning and screaming tearing at the nerves of all within earshot. Monks, their gray robes splattered with blood, wandered among them, mumbling over the dying, pointing out the dead to burial parties that followed them, encouraging others that were only slightly disabled to rise and return to the fight. Men screeched like wounded beasts as their shattered limbs were chopped off with axes and flaming torches touched to quivering, gushing stumps. The sun blazed down upon them, burning into their terrified eyes, aiding the progress of festering infections, adding madness to the total agony. A writhing ocean of suffering humanity, the stench of which defied the taking of another breath.

Estiano could bear it no longer. He stumbled over bodies, lurching away from clutching, skeletal hands, from tortured, unreal voices that pleaded for help that he could not give. He leaned against the trunk of a small tree just outside the area for the wounded and vomited up his abhorrence, his abdomen jerking spasmodically until nothing but air come up.

Estiano had easily slipped into the Christian camp. He stole clothing from a dead soldier whose body was as yet undiscovered; an arrow had pierced the soldier's fair head. A boy, not more than fourteen. Estiano had quickly fallen into the routines of the camp, moving from group to group, always avoiding too close contact with any knight or count. First he had joined in with the makers of bows and arrows at the west perimeter, then he had worked his way into the center of camp. He asked questions, but no one knew about a woman captive. Then he was herded in with a group at the labor of manufacturing boulders of mountainous piles of dry grass, twigs, and pitch, and was thus brought within close range of the tents of knights and counts; El Cid's tent was full center and much larger than the others. His banner, blown up to four times normal proportions, flew from a pole tied to the tent post. All that day as Estiano's fingers worked with the cutting brambles and burning pitch, he had kept his eyes fixed upon that single tent. Not once did El Cid emerge, nor did any woman enter, nor did he hear a single word to encourage his hope. Someone *had* to know what had happend in the hills. There had been marks of hundreds of horses moving into the campsite, pausing, then departing.

Then, as he was being led to the field of wounded, he had come upon a small tent that was set apart from all the rest, with no banner flying and two guards set at the entrance. He had heard Jimena's voice begging her guards for water. His heart had raced; all his efforts had been repaid; she lived. As he passed close to the canvas that separated him from her, he had deliberately stumbled, falling sideways so that his shoulder plunged against the tent. The two knights jumped around from the entrance. "Fool!" one shouted, "pick up your feet! Move, ugly one, or you will *have* no feet!"

"Forgive me, sire—I am indeed clumsy," he had shouted, thinking she would hear his voice and know that he was close. "What do you guard so carefully, eh?" he had shouted amiably, backing away. "Gold? What treasure is hidden by El Cid within this little tent?"

One knight leaped forward threateningly, "Scat. Flea! Louse! Get out of my hair!" He had laughed when Estiano turned and ran in pretended terror.

A full day had passed since he had located her. Outstretched before him was a maze of impenetrable barriers. Jimena's tent was in the center of the encampment. If this were a tale of fancy, penned by a romantic Arab, he, as the hero, would storm that prison tent and singlehandedly slay all who thwarted his purpose of rescuing the fair damsel in distress; he would, through wit and extraordinary luck, find that one path through fifty thousand enemies, and make a spectacular and dashing escape. But this was reality. The woman was assuredly in distress, but the hero was helpless to rescue her. If he made known even the slightest interest in her, his head would be neatly severed from his shoulders. If he managed to slice open the back of the tent at night, they would be forced to walk through and among Christians for more than two hours before reaching the river, which would have to be crossed some way, and when they did reach the other side, without food, horse, or strength, it was another sixty miles to the nearest city.

Estiano let himself slide down the trunk of the tree until he fell with a dejected thud upon the rocky ground. He placed his chin into cupped palms and stared straight ahead, dismally contemplating his predicament. He alone was safe, free to preserve his existence. He could leave this place just as he had come. He had had his fill of death, of digging mass burial pits. Dear God, the terrible price of war, spelled out in all those bloody trenches stuffed with bodies, and that incessant hurricane of hissing last breaths! Not one more day would he work the burial party or scrape the stinking pus from another purple face, arm, or thigh. Either he could rescue her, or he could not. It was time to decide once and for all. If not, then the only reasonable thing to do was withdraw from this Satan's funfest and leave these pitiful caricatures of human beings to their pleasures.

"Hell!" he wailed, jumping to his feet, "I *cannot* leave her!" He walked swiftly away from the tree and, skirting the edges of the field of wounded, made straight for the tent where Jimena was imprisoned. He had no plan, only followed a desperate need to watch over her. The afternoon attack had ceased, the new wounded were being brought back from the walls, soldiers trudging exhaustedly into camp, dropping maces, pikes, and axes upon steadily rising heaps, then falling into dugout earth hovels, too weary to even eat. The knights sat around campfires, laughing, rested, their armor laid neatly aside, for there would be no need of them until the city was penetrated by the foot soldiers and the gates were opened to them and their horses. Then they would ride in fully armored, with banners flying, to meet and do battle with the troops of Toledo. It was the lull before the next storm of attack, one hour before sunset.

Estiano was walking fast, his eyes cast down so that he did not see the knight moving with equal speed toward him. When he lurched sideways to avoid a fly-infested pile of human dung, he crashed headlong into a solid, iron breastplate. Stumbling back, he looked up into the face of the knight who was furiously glaring at him. "Good Christ!" he gasped. One hand flew to his heart, that threatened to burst out of his chest.

"In the name of" the knight spluttered, equally stunned. Then one powerful arm reached out and grabbed Estiano by the shoulder, yanking him nearly off his feet and dragging him forward for closer inspection. "It—*is*! The lost one! My ugly little brother. I will be goddamned to hell!"

Martin Antolinez stared into his brother's colorless eyes, his expression switching in turn from surprise to amusement, to bewilderment, then to fury. "And have you nothing to say in greeting to your elder brother, ugly one?" he spat out nastily, "after such a *long* time? . . . Christ, but you do turn up in the damndest places. Fortunate for me that El Cid has an understanding heart, or your escapade years ago might have been my death warrant. You have changed sides once more, eh? Have you forsaken the murder of Christian wives, coward? Or do you still receive the pay of infidels for Christian blood? Ugly pig! Have you no tongue? Speak up, or—"

"And, pray, which question would you have me reply to first?"

Estiano stood cool and resigned, giving himself up to the fact that now all three of them were caught in the same web; there were no more decisions to be made. He smiled, meeting the glaring eyes of his childhood torturer.

"Insolent you are . . . cool and confident!" Martin's scar turned a brighter purple and his mouth pulled down into vicious lines. His fingers dug into the flesh of Estiano's shoulder, watching for a light of pain to flame in his arrogant eyes. "I know someone who will be greatly pleased to have your answers, Brother. Come, allow me to introduce you to the husband of your victim, who at this moment craves some beast to vent his rage upon. The battle does not go well. You, ugly one, shall be a happy diversion for him."

Estiano was dragged to the enormous tent of the Lord of Castile.

"Cid!" Don Martin shouted, half-entering the tent, holding on to Estiano's hair, "I have a grand amusement for you. Look what I have found skulking among the foot soldiers." With a swift jerk of his powerful arm, Martin sent Estiano sprawling into the tent so that he fell flat on his face on the hardpacked earth.

When Estiano caught his breath and could focus his eyes, he saw a pair of mud-caked boots. He let his eye slide up, then gasped. He leaped up and backward; he had squarely met the yellow eyes of a full-grown male lion.

"Hah!" It was a booming laugh. "What is it, Martin, that so cowers at the sight of my kitten?"

Rodrigo leaned forward, his blue eyes, one half closed by an old wound, flashing down at Estiano. He reached out a hand and stroked the lion's mane affectionately. "Pretty kitten," he purred, grinning. "Inform this ugly fool that you are a cat of high tastes and would not degrade yourself with flesh as tough and distasteful as his. What is it, Martin, eh? Not a spy, surely. What possible danger could this loutish little runt be against my might?"

"No, not a spy, Cid—but a murderer, the associate of assassins and infidels. This,"—he pointed down to Estiano in disgust—"is my brother, Estiano. The ugly one, the lost one. The murderer, or accomplice to the slaying of your wife, Cid."

Rodrigo sucked in his breath and held it, his hand stiffening and drawing away from the lion's head. He moved backward and emptied out his lungs with a loud, hissing exhalation.

It was an ominous sight to the wide-eyed gaze of Estiano Antolinez; two lions sitting side by side, the mane of one no more full or yellow than that of the other. A giant he was, with arm muscles so protuberant as to defy credibility. His beard was braided into two plaits that fell to his waist. His granite features were pocked by hundreds of small scars, some thin and red, others twisting and of intricate design. He sat upon a white marble bench . . . a battle-scarred God, covered with filth and dripping with sweat, his attire of fantastic richness. Upon his bulging legs was hose of fine silk, and his boots were of the finest leather, richly worked. He wore a shirt of ranzal which had originally been the whitest white; all the fastenings were wrought with gold and silver. Over all this he wore a tunic of gold tissue, and a mantle of red skin with points of gold. On his head, nearly hiding his long and matted yellow hair, was a scarf of scarlet satin, also wrought with gold. All the outer refinements of an Arab had been thrown over the filthy carcass of a wild beast, the clothing wearing the man rather than the reverse. It was a ridiculous sight, such a man in such apparel, with such dirt upon his visible, sun-blackened flesh. Incautiously Estiano laughed out loud as he rose to his feet. He stood before the Lion of Castile, knowing himself to be a better man, and waited for the sentence to be pronounced against him.

"Just what do you find so amusing?" Rodrigo growled, glaring across the space that divided him from Martin's discovery, his mind struggling with an almost forgotten memory and pain. Jimena Gomez; he could not recall her face, though it was that very image that had ridden beside him for so many years. Since he had married again, the vision of her had faded; he had not thought upon that brief marriage in many years. He could muster no fury at having her abductor before him at last; his initial shock at being reminded of her was calmed already.

"That I was so frightened before such an obviously tame beast," Estiano answered smoothly.

"Hah! Following a week of fasting, my kitten would prove just how docile he is by tearing your frail self into proper portions for his devouring."

"Indeed," Estiano muttered, uncomfortably eyeing the lazy, paw-licking creature.

"So what punishment would you suggest, Martin, for this—"

"A tussle with the lion might well amuse the men, Cid."

"Hmmmm . . ."

Estiano's mind was a whirlpool of swiftly churning thoughts. He said innocently with mock bewilderment, "For *what crime* am I to be so tortured?"

"For the murder of El Cid's wife, lout! Play no word games with us." Don Martin slashed out with an arm against the side of Estiano's face; it was a jarring blow.

Estiano recoiled, his cheek hot and stinging. He looked from one man to the other, his eyes narrowed to thin slits, his long arms swinging tensely at his sides. "Ah Cid, you have nabbed me sure enough. But before I die I would look upon my *woman* just once more."

Rodrigo leaned forward, his mouth twisted to one side, spitting a spraying mess of saliva at Estiano's feet. "What manner of jibbering idiocy is this? I have a war to win, a thousand matters to be attended to. Must I be forced to look upon such as you, listen to such maniacal blatherings? Get him from my sight, Don Martin, and do not pester me with the details of his death; just make it sure and as painful as possible."

At Martin's immediate and gleeful response as he roughly yanked him from the tent, Estiano's stomach heaved over, threatening to toss up again. What manner of man was it who could so torture the child and so malevolently slay the man, a man more closely blood-connected to him than any other. Martin was more savage than a jungle animal; he would kill for pleasure alone, without personal need or terrible provocation.

"Remove your hands from me, swine! Swine!" Estiano wrenched his arm away from that detestable grip, looking into eyes first seen from a cradle. "Is it not enough that I am forced to admit that such as you shares my blood? Must I also be defiled by the touch of your hands! Handle me just once more, malignant abscess that you are, and I will beat you senseless, into pulp, and throw you on a dung heap with the waste and trash, where even the *maggots* would avoid your putridity, your—stench!" Shaking, Estiano whirled upon the now amused Cid, whose eyes brightly watched Martin's reddening face.

"Cid!" he bellowed for attention, in a desperate move to save himself and Raushana. "My woman is captive in this camp not fifty yards from this tent. She is the servant wench, Maria, who was captured when your wife met her death. Pray let me see her—I beg of you!"

"Do not feed your kitten, Cid," Don Martin raged, stepping between Rodrigo and Estiano, "and what a grand fiesta it will be, watching this one wrestle for his life."

"Close your mouth, Don Martin," Rodrigo said, waving the knight aside. He scowled upon Estiano, a foreign coldness growing in the center of his innards. "The servant girl you say, eh? When the woman was brought in, my nephew spoke of the richness of her dress, and that she had said she was the wife of a teacher or some such. Captured when my wife was slain? Then why did she not fall upon Alvar in relief, seeking his protection?"

Estiano's mind raced to keep pace with his increasing dilemma. If the man could be persuaded to see Jimena, he would never admit who she was, would either slay her or send her like the wind back to Cordova and out of his ordered life. Indeed El Cid was no slayer of women and children. He was a fanatically religious man according to his own interpretations of Christianity; he had a moral code all his own, invented by his reason for personal justification, and within the range of this code only certain kinds of murder were permissible. It was unlikely that he would slay the woman bound to him by the sanctity of the Church and still wife to him according to that sanction. Following this weak hope, Estiano frowned painfully and replied, "Ah, Cid—she has never been right in the head since that ghastly night for which I feel deeply responsible; with her own eyes she saw your wife slain. I beg you to believe that I had no hand in that foul murder, but accepted a fee for delivery of a letter and certain information as to her whereabouts. I was as revolted as yourself when I heard of the brutal killing. My wife thinks herself, and I most humbly beg your pardon—as I said she is ill of the head—she thinks herself to *be* your dead wife. She thinks that the servant, who is in truth herself, was slain and buried as your Jimena, for they were very similar in appearance, and, poor sick thing, she has become confused. A pity. I have cared for her all these years, and have grown fond of her. Thus I beg you, if you cannot release us, to allow us a tender kiss before death. . . . Pray send my brother from this enclosure, remove his stench from my offended nostrils, and I will fully explain my position now, and in the past."

"Aieee" Don Martin screeched, as if mortally wounded. In an instant he was upon Estiano, his huge, iron hands around the throat that had flung such insults at him, squeezing, his own throat croaking out guttural, animal noises.

But Rodrigo had decided to hear Estiano out. With one whispered word to his kitten, the efforts of Don Martin to strangle his brother were abruptly halted. Two giant paws reached out and up to rest upon Martin's back, and a hot, blowing breath bristled the hair at the back of the knight's neck. Don Martin instantly loosened his grip and crouched there terrorized and immobile, waiting for El Cid to order his lion back. But the order did not come, and the animal opened wide its fang-armed jaws to take a firm hold of Martin's right shoulder. "D-d-dear God," Martin moaned, sweat dripping from his trembling chin.

"Back, kitty!" Rodrigo exploded into violent hee-hawing. "Don Martin, for shame. After all these years you still panic when my kitten plays with you. Shameful, for such a brave knight to so quake in terror."

"Goddamn it, Rodrigo," Martin whimpered, still shaken by anger and fear, "that was not funny. One day that beast will become confused and tear to pieces someone who is a friend to you, whom you have chosen to tease in such a cruel manner."

"Ah, Martin, go rest yourself. You have overexcited your nerves. I will waste little time with your brother. Go and contemplate all the delicious torments your foul mind can conceive for this flesh that is of your flesh, for the murder of your brother."

"Now that was totally uncalled for, Cid. I—"

"Go! Damn me, Martin, I do not want to argue with you. Get out! . . . Out!"

Rodrigo closed his eyes to slits and stared down into the ugly brute's bland eyes, searching for some truth hidden behind the man's studiously guarded expression. "She thinks herself my wife, eh?" he said icily.

"Indeed. Quite sad."

"And who purchased the rich dress, hmmm?"

"I, Cid. I saw her out of Toledo, but was delayed myself, and alas, your soldiers . . ."

"In rags you stand before me and speak of personal wealth sufficient to maintain nine knights!"

"Ah. I worked with Yahia for surrender of the city, my lord, and was well paid, but seeing a battle to the death was inevitable, I, admittedly a coward, escaped by swimming the river."

Rodrigo sucked in another breath, unable to comprehend his patience with this runt. But there shimmered at the back of his mind a suspicion so incredible that he could not acknowledge it with conscious thought. Servant and mistress. Suddenly his cold eyes widened and he roared, "Alvar!" Almost immediately his nephew shoved through the tent opening, swiftly striding to a stand before his uncle. "The woman you took across the river, describe her to me!"

"But you said that—"

"Blast what I said! Describe your coming upon her, and her appearance."

Alvar quickly noted his uncle's black mood and shifted from nephew to businesslike captain. "I came upon her ten days past upon a rise south of the city. She is taller than average, well-proportioned, age about thirty, perhaps thirty-five. Handsome brown eyes. She is obviously of Spanish descent, with white-gold hair that falls to her waist. The knights with her were Mozarabs who when put to the torture proclaimed allegiance to Muhammed. They were, several at a time, burned by the monks on successive nights." At Estiano's sudden outcry of horror, he turned to curiously frown upon the odd brute. Continuing his description, Alvar said, "The woman is being guarded in a tent according to your command, until you have the time to give ear to her case, but I tell you the truth, Uncle, she appears suspicious. Damn me! I know that I have seen her before, or someone very like her. I did not believe her story for a second. She put into my hand a forged letter from the king, in which she was named Elvira Rodriguez—yet she had said herself that she was the wife of—"

"*Elvira Rodriguez?* Of Aragon?"

"Uh, yes, Uncle, but, as I said, I did not believe—"

"Fetch her! Bring her to me this instant, damn you to hell! Alvar, you *fool!*"

Alvar's thin lips twitched in bewilderment. Then he turned smartly, moving to do as he was told. He was horrified by the possibility that the letter from Alphonso was authentic. For Christ . . . and he had seriously considered taking it upon himself to allow his knights their pleasure with her, unbeknownst to his uncle. What had he picked up beyond the river—a witch? a spy? What?

When Alvar Fañez had dispatched the woman, with her two guards, to the tent of his uncle, he took horse and rode around the city, giving the embattlements a cursory examination. Further attack had been postponed by King Alphonso, who was encamped five miles to the rear with the infidel plaything he presumed to call wife. Apparently he had received information that Yahia would deliver word of surrender before dawn. It was nearly dark. The city arched upward before him, a mountain of towers and housetops, hesitant fires smoldering like the pox over the entire face of the town. Just as he began to depart from the compound of knights and men at the Alcantara Bridge, a shout halted him and he reined in to see a man scampering like a mole out of a hole at the base of the wall several yards beyond the river. Arrows were slicing down at him from the rampart above.

Alvar spurred his mount and raced toward the messenger. He scooped up the frail creature under one powerful arm to carry him to safety. From a leather pouch inside his shirt, the one-eyed traitor of Toledo put into Alvar's hands the open message from Yahia.

> Soldiers of Christendom! Know that Yahia will at last prevail over the fools who resist your crusade. When the sun sets and the sky is dark—look to the rampart o'er your field of the wounded, before the tent of Al Saíd, Lord of Castile, El Cid—and you and all the citizens of Toledo will observe a death, a death which will so shatter the passion for battle in the hearts of the citizenry as to cause them to open the gates to you. Their leader, their insighter, their strength, will be burned before their eyes. By dawn the city of Toledo will be returned to your god, and may your Jehovah be eternally grateful to Yahia who made it possible without further bloodshed.

"Ah, haw!" Alvar exclaimed triumphantly, "it is done, by Jesus! Knights! Arm yourselves. Take swords in hand; the blood of the Infidel will brighten your iron within hours!"

With hair caked with mud and falling in broken strands upon her bruised arms and back, her trousers stained and torn, Jimena once again, after sixteen years, walked unsteadily, with heart in her throat, toward a meeting with Rodrigo Diaz; today he would be no less detesting or horrified at the sight of her.

This time no sense of impending doom froze Jimena's mind. Fear was sharp, but did not subdue her, rather she challenged it with a firm control. Rodrigo could do no more than slay her. If not, she would continue to live. There were only two possibilities, and no amount of emotional gyrations would have any effect one way or the other. It was best to keep her wits about her. Urracca was safe, freed from an existence worse than death; perhaps she would have to pay with her life for that dream fulfilled. Dear God, if only Hasan could have *his* dream, but Toledo was dying, her wails and moans defying sleep or calm these ten nights and days since her capture. Every scream was uttered by Hasan, each moan was his last, each sigh was his despair.

She hesitated before Rodrigo's tent and turned her eyes to the mountainous, smoking city silhouetted against a blood-red sky. Then she gathered herself to her full height, sucked in a breath, and stepped into the enclosure. She proudly approached the grim giant scowling at her from his marble throne. The flickering light of an oil lamp shadowed his face with blackness and stark, contrasting whites. Jimena gasped at the sight of him; he was so monstrously scarred she would not have recognized him.

Rodrigo remained motionless, bent forward intently, eyes fixed upon the face of the woman moving arrogantly toward him. He heard her whispered cry when she laid eyes upon the ugly one, and saw their hands meet in quick and urgent greeting, but only her features concerned him; he studied them with cold determined dissection. The brown eyes were identical, no . . . larger than he recalled. The nose . . . not pronounced enough, but near enough to remembered image. The mouth— ah, there lay the dissimilarity; the lips did not fall downward at the corners, nor was the lower one folded over in perpetual pout; he could now vividly bring to mind his dead wife's countenance. Her hair was white, but there was an inch of darkness about her face that spoke of the Arab art of cosmetics. Her height . . . accurate. Her form was more full-bosomed and wider at the buttocks.

Rodrigo's heart suddenly collapsed in his chest. "Come, woman," he commanded, beckoning her with a viciously arched forefinger, " . . . so I can study you more closely." When she was less than two feet from him, he shouted, "Who ARE you?" in desperate tones. "Your eye is sane enough, but you are *mad*, eh?"

Jimena desperately looked to Estiano, whose expression was frantic, but otherwise uncommunicative. Instantly she let her expression fall apart into smiles and winces, "I am what you see, sir," she tremulously chirped in a high-pitched voice.

"The name—the name," he yelped, leaning forward to

thrash an arm close to her monstrously familiar face.

"Raushana, my lord," she quickly answered, cowering in exaggerated fear.

Rodrigo released a rasping breath of exasperation and threw his harried eyes to the tent roof.

Estiano seized the opportunity to cry out, "Maria! Beloved, I have told him who you *think* you are—"

"Silence!" Rodrigo roared. The lion at his side emitted a low rumbling growl from deep in its throat. It rose awkwardly to its feet, then sat back on its haunches and eyed Jimena and Estiano testily.

Jimena's knees were weakened by excitement, her ragged clothes were wet with perspiration, and her hands trembled as if they were palsied. But she had heard enough. Her eyes spoke to Estiano in gratitude. She proceeded from his hint. "And what is *your* name, my lord?" she said simplemindedly to Rodrigo, "you do appear so—so familiar somehow?"

"I *knew* the servant girl, Maria, you fools!" he raged unreasonably. It *was* Jimena, but she was not going to admit it. She was probably hoping he would seize the opportunity not to admit it either, and so clear her path toward freedom. She wanted him to know the truth so he would not slay her, but she sought escape from the vows that bound her to him. He was witlessly insulted by her refusal to acknowledge him, while at the same time he writhed in the shock of the possibility of six years of adultery with his second wife. No, damn him, he had allowed these two to fog his wits—it was not and could not be Jimena Gomez. Wildly his mind sought questions that only that wife long dead could answer, but all that came forth from his lips was, "What is your age, woman?"

"Thirty-three, my lord. Yes, I am quite certain of that—thirty-three the August last."

"August! The twentieth day?"

"Indeed! How did you guess?"

"If you are Maria, servant to my wife at Palencia, then you remember *me* very well!"

"If you say so, my lord, I do."

If *I* say so! Do you . . . or *not*? Damn me, what is this? You prance into my tent with that face, those . . . those eyes that spell—"

"I am familiar to you?" Jimena asked in guileful amazement, ". . . indeed, so are you to me. How strange."

"The name Elvira Rodriguez, do you know it, eh? My daughter was taken from La Coruña by this person. How did you get your hands upon the letter from Don Alphonso? Speak, damn you, or I will have both your heads!"

"Elvira Rodriguez? Your daughter? Do you have a daughter, sir? Ah, I had a child once, with golden hair and eyes as blue as your own. But we were attacked, I was carried off, and I never saw her again. You have many scars upon your face, my lord, but I think to see thin lines where tearing fingernails marked you in violent protest long ago. Your daughter? Ah, what would I know of your child, sir—I am only a captive servant with no purpose in life save one, that of swift return from whence I came. Obscurity, my lord. Please return me to my grave. I think at times that I am dead, you see . . . that there is a gravestone marking my resting place. If you release me, I will be dead again, and no one will ever know."

"Release you!"

Rodrigo lunged to his feet and paced furiously before the woman. It was Jimena, true enough—God burn her vile soul in hell. Did she come to him now like an accusing finger from God, to punish him further for that past fraternization with infidels? Would God never feel rewarded sufficiently to forget that sinful act? He saw a vision of his son, Diego, a worthy cub and predestined for greatness. A bastard. Illegitimate. He whirled upon Jimena, his volcanic gaze slicing first from her eyes to Estiano's. "Give back the child you stole," he hissed, afraid someone outside his tent would hear, "and I will release you. But if I see your face again, I will kill you before a word escapes your lips!"

"Child?" Jimena persisted, hope leaping in her breast, her hand reaching out to clutch at Estiano's arm.

"God damn you to hell! Would you *die?*"

"Ah, no, my lord, but what can I *do?* It was not I who stole her. She is not in my pocket, sir, nor at that camp where I was apprehended, nor where I was held prisoner. I cannot imagine what could have befallen her. Returned to La Coruña, perhaps."

"Ach," he fairly screamed, "if you did not have her, then I think a greater pain would fill your eyes, eh? Hell! Keep her, then—what do I care! But wherever you have sent her, to whatever place on this peninsula that you take yourself, I will be behind you. Very soon every swine who pollutes this land will be expelled, and Spain will be mine by right of conquest. I will come and take her from *you,* eh?"

Jimena fought against a fury of words that screamed in her head, insults and condemnations that she would give a king's ransom to spit at this man. An odious barbarian without a single saving grace, grunting and snorting before her, truly the most abhorrent of beasts, a man-killer. That such as he could call by foul name such as her Hasan was unjustifiable pridefulness. A man who screamed obscenities against better men than himself out of the terror of his own unacknowledged inferiority was pathetic. Indeed, this brute was to be pitied.

"Ah, thank you, oh gracious Lord of Castile, for your benevolence," Jimena purred easily. "Estiano and I will depart, and you will never see us again. I shall no longer exist—quite dead, hmmmmm?"

Alvar Fañez swept into the tent and rudely shoved Estiano aside to give the message from Yahia to El Cid. He watched his uncle's face, his eye fluttering again and again to that strange, damnably familiar woman.

When Rodrigo had finished reading the proclamation, he exclaimed, "You know, of *course*, who Yahia refers to. The man who called the sultan of Badajoz to the town, the one that your spies have sought these ten days without success, his foul tongue seemingly impossible to silence. But *he* will be our entertainment tonight!"

"Come. See for yourself, Cid," Alvar said eagerly. "Torches light the rampart now, and a rumbling thunder of protests can be heard like a mighty belch erupting from the guts of the town!"

"Oh, dear God . . . No!"

It had taken long moments before Jimena realized the meaning of the words spoken. Her eyes flew to Estiano's stricken face, then she lunged for the tent opening. Alvar Fañez leaped aside in surprise and caught her roughly around the waist; she fought hysterically to get free.

"Let her go," Rodrigo shouted, frowning viciously as a new and monstrous possibility entered his head. "She would see the sight, Alvar. Look to the ramparts, woman—look high and well, and know that what you see is prologue. Prologue!"

Estiano raced behind Jimena as she lunged from the tent, screaming "Hasan!" over and over again.

It was a moonless night, the sky blanketed from view by heavy clouds, but it was not dark. Ten thousand torches were lit and held in Christian hands. A breathless hush was upon the crowd, and all eyes were turned up to the city wall. Jimena stood outside the tent, hands over her mouth in revulsion and dread. Then upon the wall more torches appeared in a twisting, moving line until they spread forty feet to each side of a dark center. "Hasan," she whispered. "Dear God, not he—not my beloved infidel." A roar of cheers split the silence as a figure was raised to fill the dark gap at the center of the line of torches.

Rodrigo hesitated behind Jimena for a long, tormented moment as he eyed the toy figure being tied to the cross about two hundred and fifty yards distant. He looked at her quaking back, and he was suddenly overcome with rage. Abu l Hasan! A name as common to Arabs as Garcia was to Castilians. He had not once suspected that this inciter at Toledo was the same man. She, his wife, was weeping for that. Holy Jesus, she *wept* for him, preferred the man to him, just as Sabíhah had. "*Hasan*—is it!" he exploded, reaching to clutch Jimena up under one arm. He ran with her, shouting for Bavieca, the white horse awaiting him before he reached the edge of the field of wounded. Effortlessly he leaped into the saddle and threw Jimena across the stallion's neck. Rodrigo raced toward the city wall with her. When directly under the pyre just being fired, he reined in sharply and grabbed Jimena around the waist to hold her upright before the sight of her lover. "Swine! Wife-murdering swine," he yowled in a voice that echoed and si-lenced all other voices.

From fifty feet above, Hasan dropped his head to see Jimena below him, writhing in the hands of Rodrigo Diaz. He stared down horrified, thinking to see Allah below him with all humanity in his hands, holding the race of man up to face the hell of earthly existence. "Raushana," he whispered, then arched his head back to hold it rigid, as if nailed to the planking, his dark eyes raised to the black sky.

"Hasan!" Jimena screamed. Her hands raised to her face in horror as burning oil was tossed up from behind him to cling in droplets of flame upon his legs, his arms and thighs. He did not cry out; she cried *for* him. It was as if she was being held up from within a dark pit, staring up out of its mouth into hell. Rodrigo's arms never once wavered with her weight. Over and over again he shouted curses at the burning infidel.

Jimena saw an acacia tree that formed an umbrella over Ha-san's head, yellow pollen dust falling upon his sweet face and tender hands, hands now being splashed with flaming oil and turning black before her eyes. Suddenly she wailed, just as she had so long ago, "He is burning up—how can you *do* such a thing to him—burning to death . . . Dear God, *save* him!"

Jimena heard a scream of agony emerging from below and behind her. She twisted around in Rodrigo's grip to see her own grief and abhorrence reflected on the face of Estiano, as he clenched a bow in his hands, drew back, and released with deadly aim.

The splinter of wood sliced through the air, whirring a mournful dirge, and then stilled the beating heart of a beloved man.

From the conquered ramparts they were tossed, dark specks plunging downward into the devouring flames. Hell it was, heat so intense that half a mile away its touch could be felt against the flesh. Like demons, helpmates to Lucifer, were the Christian soldiers. The ramparts and walls became rocky cavern ledges, and the fires below them the blazing inferno for the torture of the damned. The battle was won, glory be to Jehovah, now the celebration. The echoing, overlapping screams, filled the night with music, the throbbing, pulsating melody of human agony. The screams melted in awful clamor with all those gone before and with all those yet to come, until the earth shook and the mountains fell and there was nothing left to believe in except the madness, the uselessness, and the pain.

Jimena swallowed hard against the hot, bitter sickness that spewed up from her convulsed and objecting stomach. She spurred her mount to faster pace. She could not breathe, her lungs were so choked by smoke, death, and grief; she could not see for all the tears that poured up from her broken heart. Heat and acrid soot seared her eyes. Estiano was directly before her, his own mount breaking a path though the clamor of drunkenness and death. Jimena felt a desperate reluctance to depart from this nightmare, for within it dwelt the soul of her savior, her beloved, an infinitesimal speck of dust amidst the holocaust.

The clamor of death slowly faded until life could be heard once more, in the soft chirping of night birds, in the whispering movements of swaying trees, in the quiet sighs of the river sliding over an obstructing boulder. They reined in their mounts, each turning around to look back at the red glow in the distance.

"Oh, Estiano, what pain was within him, what wounds were upon his soul at this terrible defeat and all the hideous implications for the future that he could not protect. His visions have all been burned with his friends; his own people burned him, his dearest friend put an arrow through his heart. What a tragic, ignoble end for so noble a man! Why do we struggle so . . . for what? When we finally touch a bit of gold, it is snatched from our grasp!"

"Not everything is snatched away. Some residue remains

forever, Raushana, once the contact with life's gold has been made. A house and beloved land awaits you, and a child whom you owe affection and years of effort. All is not lost. As long as one person remains in the world to love and to love you, all cannot be lost."

"Love," Jimena whispered and automatically placed a trembling hand upon her abdomen where a new life was forming.

". . . It is all there is."

"Yes. Let us go home, dear Estiano—let us go home."

They turned their eyes away from Toledo, to the south, riding close beside each other, and with them rode an unconquerable companion . . . Hope, which was the healer of shattered souls, the creator of future fulfillments, the foundation of life. Without Hope riding beside them they could not have continued to exist.

Jimena and Estiano caught up with the Ben Gerson caravan at the walled city of Andójar and from there traveled with Jaime and Urracca to Cordova. The golden weed had been successfully transplanted to new and more fertile soil. Jimena had suffered a great loss and a triumphant gain almost simultaneously. She would not waste the precious moments of the future with regret. As it was decreed, so had it come to pass. There was today to live well, and many, many tomorrows; she saw only good fortune ahead of her. She passed through the gates of Cordova and was home again, at last.

Jimena was indeed blessed with good fortune for the rest of her days, which were many, but Andalus was not so blessed. After Toledo, Madrid fell, and then Valencia, but Muslim Cordova lived on for another three centuries, to give abundance to those children and grandchildren emerging from the loins of love, to those who were willing to compromise ever so slightly with the African Moor who came to rule them.

When Muslim Andalusia passed away, the last of her citizens were herded together by the descendants of King Alphonso and Rodrigo Diaz, whose blood, through his daughters, ran in the veins of kings. All Andalusians who were not Christians were shepherded into the holds of ships and sent sailing into oblivion across the same straits from whence their conquering ancestors had come. The year of that final catastrophe was fourteen hundred and ninety-two. A new land was discovered across the great waters, a new civilization was born—the very instant Andalusia sighed her last sigh.

Historical
Note

The Infidel was originally going to be the story of El Cid, but early in the research I became fascinated with a mystery that surrounded the existence of Jimena Gomez. Because El Cid married a woman named Jimena *Diaz* ten years after his marriage to Jimena Gomez and because there was no mention of the fate of his first wife in any of the accounts of the exploits of Rodrigo Diaz, some scholars of Spanish history argued that the story of his marriage at the age of nineteen was a myth and that Jimena Gomez was merely a part of the romance that surrounded the hero. But other students of the history vehemently disagreed, insisting that El Cid had married twice; historians had simply failed to note what had happened to Jimena Gomez.

The historians who argued for a second marriage were the most convincing, so I included Jimena Gomez in the rough outlines of the story. But it was impossible to accept that a man of El Cid's importance and almost limitless power could have had a wife that his contemporary chroniclers had considered so insignificant that they had failed to mention her fate; the second Jimena had received an enormous amount of attention from them. For some reason Jimena Gomez had vanished from the pages of history, or she had been erased from them. What might have happened to her became my obsession.

Then, on a dusty stack in a used bookstore, I came upon a copy of Robert Southey's *Chronicle of The Cid*, copyright 1887, originally published in 1808, wherein the duel between Count Gomez and Rodrigo Diaz was related. Directly following the duel, the author gave this curious and intriguing account:

> There came before (King Don Ferrando) Jimena Gomez, the daughter of the Count, who fell on her knees before him and said, Sir, I am the daughter of

Count Don Gomez of Gormaz, and Rodrigo of Bivar
has slain the Count my father, and of three daughters
whom he has left I am the youngest. And, Sir, I come
to crave of you a boon, that you will give me Rodrigo of Bivar to be my husband, with whom I shall
hold myself well married, and greatly honoured. —
Certes, Sir, it behooves you to do this, because it is
for God's service, and because I may pardon Rodrigo
with a good will.

Not only had Jimena Gomez vanished from history, or
been erased from it, but she had gone alone to the King of Castile to ask that she be given in marriage to the man who had
just killed her father! It became a story that had to be written.

The Infidel, then, is a fictional account of the life of Jimena
Gomez as it very well could have been. Because of her hus-
band's close association with the family of King Ferrando,
Jimena could not have failed to get to know Doña Urracca and
her brothers, whose lives have all been thoroughly documented.
I have portrayed the brothers and their tragic sister, Urracca, as
I imagined they were, within the framework of actual historical
events. Urracca died in an anchorite cell, and, before he died,
King Alphonso had married six times. Alphonso's daughter Ur-
racca was, briefly, queen of Castile.

As it is related in the *Chronicle*, "the gates of Toledo were
opened to the King on Thursday the twenty-fifth of May, in the
year of Christ 1085. The first Christian banner which entered
the city was the banner of my Cid."

Georgia Elizabeth Taylor